"Now what, Samantha Forrester?" he whispered, his voice rough—and so close to her ear, it sent a chill down her spine.

She loved the way he said her name—with such intensity and gruffness. A spear of heat tingled her throat and plunged to the depths of her. He kissed her like a man accustomed to taking charge, a passionate, demanding man, who would have whatever he wanted.

His rough hands gripped her shoulders, and he held her away from him. "What are you trying to do, woman?" he panted, his voice gruff with desire.

"I'm . . . I'm trying to keep you here so you'll build my house," she said, knowing that she was lying.

"I'm not a house cat, Samantha Forrester."

He just looked at her for a moment. "Well, don't give up so easy," he whispered, pulling her back into his arms.

S0-AQI-838

Also by Joyce Brandon
Published by Ballantine Books:

THE LADY AND THE OUTLAW
THE LADY AND THE LAWMAN
AFTER EDEN

ADOBE PALACE

Joyce Brandon

BALLANTINE BOOKS • NEW YORK

Sale of this book without a front cover may be unauthorized. If this book is coverless, it may have been reported to the publisher as "unsold or destroyed" and neither the author nor the publisher may have received payment for it.

Copyright © 1993 by Joyce Brandon

All rights reserved under International and Pan-American Copyright Conventions. Published in the United States of America by Ballantine Books, a division of Random House, Inc., New York, and simultaneously in Canada by Random House of Canada Limited, Toronto.

Library of Congress Catalog Card Number: 93-90175

ISBN 0-345-36096-6

Manufactured in the United States of America

First Edition: August 1993

Dedicated to Aunt Mary with love

Nonfiction writers acknowledge their research sources, so it seems entirely appropriate for novelists, who write about relationships, to acknowledge the people in their lives who provide the warmth, richness, and variety of experience to keep the stories flowing. My thanks go to:

John C. Brandon, my much loved, though often neglected husband.
Our children and their children:
Robert, Su, Matt, and Brandi Firestine
Danny, Suzanne, Thomas, Brittany, and Rebecka Davis
John Lee Brandon
Brian Mark Brandon
Kristina, James, and Jeffery Wilson

CHAPTER ONE

February 10, 1889

Knock, knock, knock.

Startled, realizing she had probably been asleep, Samantha struggled to her feet, stumbled to the front door, and opened it.

Lance Kincaid, hat in hand, lifted one black eyebrow—and all her sleepiness left her. Seeing him there, so close, Samantha's throat went dry. Mute, she stepped back to let him into the room. A lamp burned low beside the chair she'd fallen asleep in. It must be the middle of the night.

"Sam . . ." Lance had always called her Sam. Never Samantha. His strong, brick-brown hands kept turning his white felt hat around and around by its brim. His eyes, the bluest and most affecting she'd ever seen, blazed with a look she'd longed to see since she'd first fallen in love with him as a five-year-old child. A need that had continued to grow after he had proposed marriage to her on June 4, 1880, only weeks before he had broken her heart by marrying her schoolfriend, Angie Logan.

"Sam . . ." The sound of his raspy, whiskey tenor filled an empty place in her heart. She had hungered so long for his love, his presence, even the sound of his voice. Her heart felt as though it would burst. She had a dozen questions to ask him, but was still unable to speak.

"Sam . . . I . . ." The burning, intent gaze he fixed on her ignited a shiver of excitement in her belly that grew until she was trembling uncontrollably. Usually, even when he was alone with her, he kept his demeanor neutral, his expression brotherly. But this time, something had changed.

"I was wrong, Sam." His voice was like smoke, tingling through her. "I don't love my wife. I love you."

"Please . . . don't say that unless you mean it."

"I have no right coming here. I'm sorry, Sam . . . I didn't realize until I had lost you, lost all hope of ever having you . . ." He tossed his hat aside, his hand reaching up, up, as if to touch her. But then it fell to his side and worried the seam of his black serge pants.

"I'm lower than a snake coming here and telling you this, but

1

I can't sit through one more family get-together pretending you're my sister." Lance's voice, a mere rasp of sound, reflected his misery.

"Oh, Lance . . ." Samantha whispered. She had waited so long for him to come to her, to say these exact words. She vibrated with joy.

"Send me away, Sam," he whispered, his lips twisting into a grimace that told her how difficult this was for him.

Samantha reached up and ran her fingers lightly across his warm lips. Lance could express more emotion with the lift of one corner of his mouth than any other man could with his entire face.

"I love you, Lance. You know that. I've always loved you. I'll be anything you want me to be—your mistress, your wife. I'll bear your children. Anything to be near you."

Lance pulled her into his arms and held her so tightly she could barely breathe. She surged against him, not minding the damp sweatiness of his back under his thin blue shirt and vest. He must have ridden all the way from Durango without stopping.

"I want you as my wife!" he whispered urgently, his warm breath like a feather against her throat. Tears of love and gratitude blinded her. "I want to walk down the street with you at my side. I'm sick of hiding how I feel, of pretending you're nothing to me, of knowing I don't even have the right to touch you . . ."

Samantha's body was flooded with joy—and a hunger for him so urgent it startled her. "But you do have the right, Lance. I give you the right."

"God, Sam, I tried not to come here, tried not to tell you this." He leaned away from her to look deeply into her eyes. "But I did, and it changes everything. There's no way I can go back to Angie. I can't pretend anymore."

"No." She lifted up on tiptoe, searching for his mouth.

Lance groaned her name, "Sam, love." He ground his mouth into hers with such aching need a flame ignited in her belly and roared into hungry life. He showered kisses on her mouth and throat and breasts until her knees buckled. Then he swept her up into his powerful arms and carried her into the bedroom.

As he lowered her onto the bed, his hands groped for a way through the many layers of her garments. She clutched at his damp shirt and slid her hands under it to caress the firm, sleek muscles of his back. She felt she would die if he didn't free her, so she could feel his naked body against hers. She wanted him to hold her tighter, to grind his flesh into hers. The need was so desperate . . .

As if maddened with desire, Lance ripped her blouse away. Samantha shivered with anticipation. She had been waiting for this moment for so long—

Knock, knock. knock. "*Señora* Forrester!"

The loud knocking on the door startled Samantha.

"*Señora!* Are you in there?"

Samantha turned away from the intruding sound. "Lance, darling . . ." Reaching for him, her hand groped an empty bed.

"*Señora!*" Recognizing Ramon's voice, Samantha groaned and opened her eyes. At the sight of the wooden parquet ceiling, she realized she wasn't in bed with Lance. She was alone in the sleeping compartment of her palace car, aboard her private train, and Ramon had just interrupted the best dream of her life. She groaned, turned over, and buried her face in the pillow. If Ramon would just go away she could recapture the dream. If she didn't reply, maybe he would leave. As if in answer to her prayer, she heard Ramon's footsteps receding.

Samantha lay perfectly still, willing her way back into the dream. But it receded swiftly into nothingness. Closing her eyes tightly, she tried to recover the blissful sensation of Lance's body against hers, his lips devouring her own. But even that was lost. She could no longer see him or feel him. He was gone. She wanted to weep with frustration.

"*Señora* . . ." Ramon was back, and he sounded desperate. Sighing, Samantha sat up in bed. "Yes, Ramon, what is it?"

"The engineer. He needs to talk to you."

"What about?"

"We're out of water, *señora*." Ramon Rodriguez was her youngest employee, barely sixteen. He had come along on this trip as porter, so he could visit his family in Phoenix.

Samantha pulled the window shade aside and saw the water tank looming up ahead. "We're at a water tank, Ramon."

"It is empty, *señora*."

"Empty!" she cried, sitting up. They'd left Phoenix at six o'clock this morning, and she'd been up since four getting everything ready and packed. Tired, she had lain down to rest fully clothed. Once the train had started to roll, the monotonous *chunka, chunka, chunka* of the wheels against the tracks must have lulled her into sleep.

"I'll be right out," she said, feeling on the floor for her shoes.

She buttoned them as quickly as she could and hurried through the palace car, careful not to wake her little son, Nicholas, sleeping in his own compartment. He needed his sleep.

Even this early in the day, the heat weighed her down. She clambered down the steps and headed toward the locomotive, chuffing noisily up ahead. Loose sand dragged at her shoes and burned the bottoms of her feet. By the time she reached the water tank, sweat was rolling down her temples.

"What is it, Lars?" she asked, stopping beside her portly engineer, who stared at the underside of the water tank.

"Twenty-seven bullet holes," he said, his Swedish accent strong.

"Twenty-seven?" She couldn't believe he'd stood here in the hot sun counting bullet holes. She glanced south. The railroad ran parallel to the Gila River, but it had been dry for weeks. The Arizona Territory was in the grip of drought.

"Unless I mist vun," Lars said, nodding with satisfaction.

"Mama!"

Samantha looked back toward her palace car. Nicholas stepped out the back door of her Pullman coach onto the small observation deck. Rubbing one eye with his left hand, he waved with the other, motioning her back to him. Six years old now, and he still hated waking up alone.

In the bright sunlight, he looked pale and confused. The sight of his thinness brought a rush of mingled emotions—part overwhelming love, part rage at the unfairness of the consumption eating away at his life, and part fear that something terrible might be about to happen to him, to all of them. Samantha hung on pretty well most of the time, but it took all her wits to do it. When something extra came up, like this bullet-riddled water tank, she felt nearly overwhelmed.

Despite the seriousness of the problem she needed to discuss with Lars, she wanted to run to her son, sweep him into her arms, and hold him tight. She never forgot, even for a second, that Nicholas could die at any moment, that without warning he might start coughing and not be able to stop.

Consumption terrified her. Articles in newspapers and magazines did little to allay her fears, calling it "the wasting disease," and with good reason. Since Nicholas had been diagnosed, his legs and arms had become as reedy as sticks. His skin was stretched so thin over his bony little frame that it barely covered his veins. Samantha had heard of grown men who had wasted down to ninety pounds while coughing their lungs out in pinto bean–sized chunks. Consumption was the most feared disease in America. The *New York Times* claimed that if scientists didn't find a cure soon everyone would die of it.

Instinctively she wanted to do anything Nicholas asked of her. But she tried, for his own good, not to overdo that.

"Be right there," she called out to him, reluctantly turning back to her engineer and the problem of the empty water tank.

"Can we make it home with the water in the icebox and gravity feed toilet if we put it all into the boiler?" she asked, glancing from Lars to Nicholas and edging closer to the Pullman coach where her son waited.

"No, ma'am," said Lars, mopping his forehead with his engineer's bandanna.

Ramon stepped out onto the observation deck and distracted Nicholas. Relieved, Samantha stepped back into the shade of the water tank and let her gaze sweep her short train, which consisted of a locomotive, a tender, her Pullman coach, and a caboose. A few yards away, a thirty-foot saguaro cactus lifted its round, blunt arms toward the turquoise sky dominated by a blazing sun. It couldn't be more than ten A.M. and already the temperature was close to a hundred, even though it was only mid February.

She should never have left Phoenix. But once her beloved Lance had left for Durango, neither the town nor her friends held any attraction for her.

She and Nicholas had gone to Phoenix to celebrate little Chane's sixth birthday. Little Chane was Nicholas's cousin, the son of Chantry III and Jennifer Van Vleet Kincaid. Nearly the entire Kincaid clan had been in Phoenix for the celebration.

Black smoke and cinders spewed out of the stack of the stalled locomotive. Steam escaped from behind the wheels. When a locomotive worked, Samantha didn't mind the noise or even the cinders, but now that it didn't, she wanted to kick it off the tracks. Usually it would have delivered her and her son to their own front door via the spur line she'd had built. But not today— unless a miracle happened.

"Mama!" The emotional pull became too much for Samantha. She turned and walked toward her son to allay his waking fears of abandonment. Family and friends urged her not to spoil him, but they had no idea how fragile he was.

She walked through the sand with the exaggerated steps of one slogging through shallow tar. Beads of perspiration rolled into her eyes. She brushed them away, but her sensitive skin smarted from the saltiness. Sweat trickled between her breasts.

Seven miles of desert lay between them and Camp Picket Post to the north. Seventeen miles of desert separated them from her home ten miles east of town.

If her fears were correct, and the holes had been purposely shot into the bottom of the tank by bandits, she and her son and crew could be in great danger. At any moment a band of violent men could ride down on them.

"Did you sleep well?" she called, nearing the observation deck where her son waited.

"Where were you?" he asked, whining.

Samantha climbed the steps quickly and felt Nicholas's warm forehead. She couldn't tell if it was warm from fever, which always scared her, or if it was from the heat of the desert. Fear made her heart skip a beat.

"We stopped for water."

As Nicholas opened his mouth to speak, the wooden wall of the Pullman coach above his head splintered; slivers of wood exploded in all directions.

Samantha screamed in terror and covered her son's body with her own. "Get down!" she yelled, unnecessarily, since she had already pulled him to the floor of the car.

Behind her, one of the crew yelped in fright. Lars ran for the locomotive, where he kept his rifle. Otto, the brakeman, dived under the Pullman coach. Then she heard him on the other side of the car, climbing onto the roof to get the rifle he kept up there.

Samantha picked up Nicholas, dashed inside the car, and slammed the door. Ramon ran to the back of the Pullman coach to get his rifle.

"Here they come!" someone outside yelled.

Ramon hurried back into the room carrying his rifle in his right hand. He wiped the stub of his withered left arm across his narrow, perspiring brow, and knelt at one of the windows.

Nicholas squirmed out of her arms and raised up to press his nose against the glass. Samantha yanked him back down. The thought of his being shot made her tremble so violently her hands were almost useless.

Nicholas squirmed to free himself again. "Nicholas! Keep down! They're shooting at us!"

"I want to see—"

"No! Follow me. Crawl. And keep your head down!" With

Nicholas beside her, Samantha inched toward her rolltop desk, unlocked it, lifted her revolver out of the top drawer, and rolled the cylinder to count the bullets. From the box in the drawer, she added a shell under the hammer, stuffed the others in her pocket, and crawled back to the window.

Holding Nicholas below the sill, Samantha peered out the window and wished she had a longer range weapon, like a .30-.30. Her little .32 pistol was deadly only at close range, and she didn't want their attackers to get that close.

She'd been raised since the age of four by the Kincaids. They spent half of their time in New York or traveling, and half on the Kincaid ranch near Austin, Texas, where every man and many of the women carried weapons. She knew how to handle a gun, but in all these years, Samantha had never personally been shot at.

She raised her head again. Half a dozen masked men were riding toward her, yelling and firing rifles as they came. The thud of Otto's boots running along the roof ended in a terrible cry. Otto toppled past Samantha's window and landed in the sand on his back, his eyes open. Blood darkened his shirt on the left side.

Nicholas eased up toward the glass.

"Stay down!"

"Mama! I want to see!"

"You keep down!" Nicholas's face flashed outrage at Samantha, but he obeyed.

Her anger at the men who'd killed Otto steadied Samantha's hands enough to lift the window and aim the gun at the men riding toward her car. But they were still too far away. With Otto dead, Samantha feared she and three men were no match for six bandits. Concern for her son filled her with rage.

The approaching bandits fired steadily. Bullets zinged over her head, breaking windows on both sides of the palace car. Broken glass rained down on them. Samantha covered Nicholas with her body until every window in their end of the car was on the floor.

The bandits' willingness to shoot in such a random fashion, not caring about anyone inside, even Nicholas, horrified her. She had not battled her son's ravaging illness these three years since her husband's death to lose him to a handful of bandits. She would personally kill every one of them first.

Samantha held her fire until they were close enough, so she

wouldn't miss. Ramon fired but hit nothing. Cursing, he stopped to reload.

A man with a red bandanna covering the bottom half of his face, his big belly bouncing over his belt, rode up to the observation platform of the Pullman coach, leapt off his pony with surprising agility, and landed on the deck. Heart pounding, Samantha raised her gun and tightened her finger on the trigger. But before her own gun fired, a dark hole appeared in the man's soft belly and his blood spattered the window-glass panels of the platform door. Another bandit rode up, fought his horse for a moment, then eased out of the saddle onto the platform. Again Samantha raised her gun, and again, before she could fire, a hole appeared in the man's chest, reddening his shirt as he, too, slammed into the platform door.

She looked down at her unfired weapon, then behind her to see if Ramon had fired, but he was facing in the opposite direction, firing at other bandits and missing. The shots, which had come from the southeast, puzzled her. Lars or Silas must have left the train. Samantha couldn't imagine why they would have done that when it would have been safer to huddle in the locomotive. Lars was too heavy to run far, and Silas looked too scared to try. But she knew that men under pressure did amazing things.

At the sight of their dead comrades, the remaining bandits reined their horses and turned tail. Another bullet struck one of the fleeing bandits. He fell off his horse and struggled to his feet, yelling, "Get my damn horse!"

One man caught at the reins of a riderless horse and led it over to him. Two comrades helped the wounded man onto his horse again, then all four of them flogged their lathered mounts into a wild retreat. Samantha stood up. Two of the bandits lay dead beside her brakeman.

In the sudden silence a cactus wren warbled a few tentative notes. A triumphant cry from Silas startled the bird into silence again. "Yahoo! We whipped 'em!"

Samantha let Nicholas stand up to peer out the window. She walked to the open door and stepped outside. The railroad had certainly gotten a bargain in Lars and Silas. She would make certain Chane learned how valuable they were. As majority owner of the Texas and Pacific Railroad, her adopted brother, Chantry Kincaid III, had the authority to reward their actions.

Relief made her knees feel wobbly. Samantha gripped the railing to steady herself.

"Ma'am, if you know anything about doctoring, you might want to take a look at Lars . . ."

Hearing Silas's voice coming from the direction of the locomotive puzzled her. The bullets that killed the two bandits hadn't come from that direction. She wanted to ask Silas about that, but the look on his face made her clamber quickly down the steps and follow him. As she passed Otto she checked for signs of life but found none. The sun was so hot, blood had already dried on the corner of Otto's mouth. Flies buzzed loudly over his blood, which smelled warm and sweet. She wanted to cover him, but there was no time. Feeling sick, Samantha fanned the flies away as if that might help, then stepped around the two dead bandits and hurried to the locomotive.

Lars lay on the floor of the cab, bleeding from a bullet wound in his side. His paunch rose and fell with his labored breathing. Blood soaked his canvas engineer's apron. Samantha eased his shirt aside. The bullet had entered just below his last rib. They'd have to get him to a doctor soon.

They had drinking water, but nothing to carry it in for any distance. She didn't trust Silas to walk to Camp Picket Post; he might get lost, or the remaining bandits might intercept and kill him. She knew the way, but she couldn't leave Nicholas. And she couldn't take him with her. Even a mile hike was too long for a small sickly boy in this heat.

"Let's wait here," she said. "I'm sure someone will miss us. They'll have half the territory out looking for us by morning."

"Ya, if da Apache devils don't kotch us first," Lars said, grimacing at the pain it caused him to speak.

Three years ago, in 1886, Geronimo had surrendered and been sent to Florida. In reality, few Apache warriors remained in Arizona, but people still talked as if every Indian were an Apache.

Samantha stood up. "I'll get the medicine box." She prayed it would have something in it to relieve Lars's pain. Samantha ran back to the coach.

She found the medicine box in the kitchen and was hurrying back through the palace car when a man's voice startled her.

"Hello! Anybody in there?"

Samantha pulled one of the bullet-tattered draperies aside and peered out the window.

The man straddled a big gray calico horse splotched with red, orange, and black. Behind him, astride a spotted pinto, was a young Indian woman, wearing a fancy white-feathered headdress and a white ceremonial buckskin dress that reached to midcalf. Her cheekbones were high and sweetly curved. Something about the girl caused an uneasy feeling in Samantha, though she was certain she'd never seen her before. Both horses pulled cottonwood branches behind them.

Gripping the smooth handle of the pistol in the deep pocket of her morning gown, Samantha walked to the front of the car. Nicholas peered out over a jagged piece of broken glass.

The man was dressed like an easterner in a dark frock coat, white shirt, and dark pants, their true color obscured by a film of yellowish dust. His knee-high boots looked new.

"Hello! Anybody in there?" he called again, his voice clear and commanding.

Samantha tightened her grip on the revolver in her pocket, opened the door, and stepped outside. At the sight of her, the man doffed his wide-brimmed hat. In spite of his dusty clothes, he had the sleek look of an otter, dark and lithe and smooth.

His horse pranced sideways. He controlled it with a sturdy wrist.

"What can I do for you?" Samantha asked, her voice more strident than she would have liked. She realized it was not a proper greeting, but this hadn't exactly been a proper day.

The man gave her a slow smile that called attention to the curve of his lips, the refined silkiness of his features, and the sparkle of amusement in his dark eyes, which were rimmed by long black lashes.

"I thought I might do something for you," he said. "Congress cut the Indians' rations again, and a half-dozen hungry Papago are on the prowl. I reckon by now they've heard the gunfire," he said, gesturing at the dead bandits. "They may be headed this way." At first she thought she detected an Eastern accent, but by the time he'd finished, he sounded like the drawling Texans she'd admired as a girl.

"I've lived next to the Papago for years now. They've always been good neighbors . . ."

"Maybe when they're not mad and hungry," he said, the smile in his eyes creeping into his deep voice, which was as deep and resonant as a bronze gong.

"What do you suggest then?

"Camp Picket Post is a few miles north of here."

"We can't leave. We have an injured man. Another train will come along by tomorrow. And the Indians might not find us anyway."

The man shook his head and looked up. Samantha's gaze followed his. Three buzzards soared overhead, their black shapes circling ever lower. His profile, made more distinctive by a slightly hooked nose, was clean and sharp against the blue sky. Navy blue-black hair curled around the white collar of his shirt.

To the south, a flock of crows let out faint cries. A lone crow perched on a nearby cholla cactus cawed in answer and lifted into the air. The locomotive wheezed like an asthmatic, sent up a last cloud of smelly black coal smoke, and fell silent, another sign that their resources were just about used up.

"How many in your party?" he asked.

"Four besides me. Our brakeman was killed."

"I can pack double and so can she," he said, pointing to the Indian girl. "The men'll have to walk alongside." He took off his hat and wiped an arm across his forehead. His smooth, ruddy cheeks were dark with the shadow of beard stubble. "My name's Sheridan," he said quietly. "Steve Sheridan. I know you don't have any reason to trust me, but I'm not going to do you any harm. After all, there's only one of me and five of you."

He turned in his saddle, his eyes narrowing as he scanned the horizon. "We could just settle in and let 'em come. We might be able to parlay with them. But maybe not. They're young and wild. And I don't care much for shooting hungry men."

"Is that a buffalo gun in your sheath?" asked Samantha.

Surprise flickered in Sheridan's eyes. "Yes."

"So it was you who shot these men," she said, gesturing toward the two bodies on the observation platform. "You saved us, didn't you?"

Sheridan shrugged.

"Thank you, Mr. Sheridan."

"My pleasure, ma'am."

Samantha relaxed a little. He looked more than competent. He had broad shoulders and one of those lean, whipcord bodies. It'd probably take a cannon to kill him. But the girl was Indian. And that confused Samantha.

Sheridan saw her look and shook his head. "No danger from her. Elunami's a Hopi. The Hopi are peaceful. Only bear arms in self-defense."

"She's a long way from home," Samantha said.

"She and her people were ambushed by some soldiers this morning. She's the only survivor."

"Oh, no. Do you have any idea why?"

"Nope."

"Where did this happen?"

"North of Pichaco Peak. They'd stopped at one of the few places on the river where there was still puddled water to let their horses drink." He looked west. "They were unarmed, except for a carbine that hadn't been fired. And they were old."

"Oh, my God," Samantha whispered, glancing with sympathy toward the girl, who sat her horse in silence, her only visible reaction a thinning of her pretty lips.

"I'm sorry and ashamed that something like that can still happen," Samantha said, shaking her head.

The girl nodded, her eyes reflecting her gratitude and her misery. Then she lowered her gaze again.

Still unsatisfied, Samantha looked back at the man. "She isn't dressed like a Hopi."

"I asked her about that. She said these togs were given to her people by a great white chief. I guess he didn't know the difference between Plains Indians and Hopi Indians."

"What do you do, Mr. Sheridan?"

"I'm a builder of houses, ma'am. Helping beautiful women fight their battles is not something I normally do. So I'd appreciate it if we could get moving before our situation becomes even more precarious." Amusement flickered in his khaki-colored eyes. Samantha had never seen anyone with eyes that color.

"I can't believe the army can justify killing old men," she said.

Samantha had heard of atrocities in Texas that were just as incomprehensible. Talk of them always saddened her and brought up an awful feeling of helplessness and shame.

"I'll take a look at your wounded man," Sheridan said, his tone kinder.

"He's in the cab."

Sheridan dismounted and strode toward the locomotive. Samantha turned to Nicholas. "You stay here," she whispered.

"Awww, Mama . . ."

"Keep Nicholas here, Ramon," Samantha said, giving him a warning look as she ran down the steps.

Sheridan was only a few inches taller than she, but his long legs carried him much faster through the dragging sand. He strode to the cab, climbed up, and reached down to help her up. His big, warm hands around hers were deeply callused. Rough and strong, they didn't seem to match the fineness of his clothes, which were too rich for a common carpenter.

Sheridan pulled her past him into the engine cab. Samantha caught the scent of dust, leather, sweat, and horses before her senses were overwhelmed by the oily cab smells of grease and kerosene. As her left shoulder brushed his chest, a tiny, brief flame ignited in the center of his pupils. It was a look she'd seen in her husband Jared's eyes—when he'd wanted her. Suddenly she felt breathless, a feeling she hadn't experienced since Jared died, almost four years ago.

Then Sheridan released her, turned away, and knelt beside Lars, who grunted an acknowledgment. Sheridan lifted aside Lars's shirt, looked at the wound, and nodded. "You look like you'll keep," he told the engineer. "We're going to move you into Picket Post."

Lars smiled. "Must 'ave been your gun I hurtd, yah?" His Swedish accent was more pronounced with the wheeze in his breathing.

Sheridan nodded. "A .57 Sharps."

Lars chuckled, then grimaced with pain. "I'd recognize a buffalo gun anyvhere. How far avay vas you?"

"About six hundred yards."

"Goodt shoodink."

Samantha offered Sheridan the medicine box. He placed a pad over Lars's wound, wrapped it tight enough to stop the bleeding, tied it securely, and squeezed Lars's hand. "You'll hold until we reach a doctor."

"Yah."

"What time's the next train come through here?" Sheridan asked.

"Tomorrow mornink."

He stood up, took Samantha's arm, and helped her down onto the sand.

"Elunami can rig a travois for your injured man." At Sheridan's words, the girl slid off the side of her pony.

Samantha flashed him a look that clearly labeled him a thoughtless brute. "Mr. Sheridan," she said, her pale porcelain cheeks flashing with attractive color, "the girl has just witnessed a terrible murderous attack and lost people who were undoubtedly dear to her. I hardly think she should be ordered around like a chambermaid."

"Sorry," Steve mumbled, thoroughly chastened.

Samantha motioned Silas to her. "Silas, please build a travois."

Steve could tell by looking at the man he had no idea what a travois was, much less how to build one. So he walked over to the water tank and kicked loose two two-by-fours and carried them into the shade of the train. There he slipped off his coat, turned up his sleeves, cut off a length of his reata, and began to unbraid it.

Samantha couldn't seem to stop staring at Sheridan. It was hard to tell how old he was, maybe late twenties. His arms were dark, his forearms and wrists muscular and strong. Against her will, she admired the manly swell of his shoulders and arms.

"Do you have a blanket or sheet we could use for the travois?" he asked, glancing up and catching her look.

Samantha took Elunami's hand and led her toward the Pullman coach. "I'll get one," she said, leading the reluctant girl up the steps.

"Where are you taking her?" Sheridan asked, frowning.

"To find her something else to wear. If soldiers are looking for her, we need to change her appearance."

"You didn't tell me your name."

"It's Samantha Forrester," she said, watching to see if her name caused any reaction in him. She decided he probably wasn't from around here, or he hadn't heard about her buying the old Spanish land grant. She'd been written up a number of times, once in the *Phoenix Gazette*.

Sheridan turned back to the task of unbraiding his reata. She led Elunami past Nicholas into the parlor car.

"Be very careful here," she said, looking down at the girl's moccasins. With glass crunching under her own shoes, she kicked a path for the girl. In her own compartment she pulled down a heavy blanket from the cabinet over her bed and carried it outside and gave it to Sheridan. He looked up at her with a quizzical look in his eyes, as if he were judging her and enjoying it. His interest caused an odd sensation in her belly. Samantha shrugged self-consciously and climbed back into the Pullman coach.

Elunami looked quite young, maybe sixteen or seventeen. Her lovely dark eyes were soft, the irises streaked with silver—unusual compared with the dense black of most Indians' eyes.

Looking into the girl's eyes alarmed Samantha. If eyes were truly windows to the soul, Elunami's were wide open, and her soul was in agony. Samantha's heart ached for the girl. Violent death was a terrible thing to see, even more so of family and friends.

"I guess you don't speak English," Samantha said, softly.

"I do," the girl replied. Her voice was an octave lower than Samantha's and husky as a boy's.

Samantha opened her armoire and searched through her things. "The problem is you're so slender . . . and much shorter than me." Finally she found the new white peasant blouse and black skirt she'd bought for Juana, her housekeeper, who was short and chubby. The blouse was too big, but the skirt appeared to be the right length. She could cinch it with a belt.

"I think these will change your appearance the most. Try them on. I'll look for a belt."

"May I wash first?" asked Elunami.

"In there," Samantha said, pointing to the lavatory.

By the time Samantha talked Ramon into taking a belt from one of the dead men, Elunami was washed and dressed in the new garments. Samantha secured the skirt around Elunami's tiny waist and stepped back. "How pretty you look! And how different!" Elunami's hair was deep auburn with red highlights.

"You can't be Hopi," Samantha said, shaking her head.

"Half Hopi, half Irish."

Still, the girl looked Spanish, at least enough to pass.

Samantha went back outside to check on the travois. Steve Sheridan was unbraiding the strands of the reata and didn't look up. Silas was spreading the blanket across the two-by-fours.

"Are you from around here?" she asked Sheridan.

"Nope."

Glancing around for the dead men who had been there a few moments ago, she asked, "What did you do with those men?"

"Put 'em in shallow graves."

"Thank you for doing that," she said. "I'll get some water to fortify us for the trip."

A smile brightened his eyes for a moment, then he looked down at the leather cords in his strong hands. "Thank you, ma'am. A drink sounds fine." He tied a knot, tested its strength, and stood. "If you don't mind I'd like to take a look inside."

At Samantha's nod, Sheridan gave the leather thongs and a knife to Silas, showed him how to punch holes and tie knots. Then he strode to the steps of the Pullman car, stopping to let her precede him. On the platform, she reached for the door, but he leaned around her and opened it. Inside, he stopped and let out a low whistle. "Looks like something out of the *Arabian Nights*," he said, with a boyish grin.

"Do you like it?"

"It's a mite fluffy for my tastes, but it suits you."

Samantha laughed. The darker blue of her gown did comple-
ment the lighter blue of the car's draperies and upholstery fab-
rics, though she hadn't chosen her outfit for that reason. Her
guardians, Elizabeth and Chantry Kincaid II, had given her the
Pullman coach as her wedding present seven years ago. Aunt
Elizabeth had chosen the decor well and spared no expense.
Satinwood paneling on the walls and ceiling complemented the
intricate marquetry of the built-in cabinets.

In New York, where the Kincaids maintained a part-time residence, many wealthy people, especially holders of railroad
stock, owned their own Pullman coaches. The Kincaid children
had each been presented with their own palace car if they showed
any interest in railroad travel at all.

Chantry III, the oldest Kincaid child, had gotten his when he
graduated from Harvard. Lance had declined in advance, saying
he had no need for anything bigger than a horse.

Nicholas turned from the broken window as they entered.
Samantha motioned him over. "This is my son, Nicholas."

Glass crunching underfoot, Nicholas stepped forward and
looked up at Sheridan calmly. Nicholas met all people as equals.
He had no awareness of himself as a child, and in many ways
he wasn't and never had been. From birth he had demonstrated
amazing dignity and presence. Samantha had known instantly
how special he was and treated him accordingly. Some claimed
she was spoiling him and would live to regret it, but she paid
them no mind.

Sheridan nodded at Nicholas's grave, assessing look, but neither spoke. Seeing her son through the stranger's eyes, Samantha
realized Nicholas was more beautiful than handsome. Dressed
in a white shirt and knee-length knickers, with a bow at his
throat, he looked every inch the rich woman's pampered son.
His straight black hair was cut short and combed straight down
from the crown of his head in bangs that curled under slightly
at midforehead. Juana cooked her fingers raw trying to tempt
him with special dishes, and still he stayed painfully thin. Since
his father's death it had been a struggle just to keep Nicholas
alive.

The doctor in Boston, supposedly the best in the United States,
had said that consumptive children rarely survived, that Nicholas would probably die before the age of ten. Samantha had been
so filled with rage at the prospect that she'd moved West that
very week. Her son was going to live, no matter what she had
to do to save him. *I've heard it helps to move to a dry, bracing*

climate, but I wouldn't count on it, the doctor had told her, shrugging.

And yet, Nicholas had improved. His fevers did not burn as high now, but the weakness lingered. He still coughed when he exerted himself, but she hoped, with time, even that would go away. Samantha took heart from the fact there were two types of consumption. Galloping consumption was almost instantly fatal; victims died within weeks of contracting the disease. Chronic consumptives, on the other hand, occasionally survived. Nicholas had been sick for almost three years now—longer, if she counted the time before he'd been diagnosed.

Nicholas straightened, as if sensing in Steve Sheridan a power to be respected. Apparently Sheridan saw this, too, for a spark of amusement twinkled in his eyes.

Elunami walked out of the lavatory carrying her clothes in a bundle. She had unbraided and finger combed her amazing auburn hair, and with her peasant blouse slipping off one slender shoulder she looked entirely different.

"Well, you were right," Sheridan said, nodding his satisfaction at Samantha. "Bury your other clothes in the sand," he told Elunami.

"Have Ramon do that for you," Samantha said, countering his commands. Elunami nodded, and Sheridan shrugged.

Elunami slipped past them, stepped outside, and spoke to Ramon, who jumped up and took the clothes.

"Didn't take her long to figure out who's boss here," Sheridan said dryly, grinning and kicking glass aside to reach the built-in bar. He ran his hand over the smooth satinwood top, the Carrara marble fixtures, the silk brocade portieres, and the heavy satin brocade draperies separating the dining area from the sleeping compartments. Samantha expected him to say something complimentary. Instead he shook his head. "I 'spect this'll burn like dry straw."

"The Papago wouldn't burn this, would they?"

"With you in it, if they can arrange it."

"Please, Mr. Sheridan, you're frightening Nicholas." Nicholas looked askance at her, but he did not correct her.

Samantha picked up a valise and began stuffing clothes into it. She moved with grace and competence—a woman who apparently had no trouble making decisions. She wasted few motions, and soon the bag was filled. Steve decided he liked what he saw. And heard. The calm, rich timbre of her voice reminded him of a Philadelphia society matron for whom he'd built a house two years ago. Except he was certain the woman back East wouldn't sound calm in these circumstances. Samantha Forrester was certainly unusual. And she had the appearance of a woman who'd just been made love to—a flushed and slightly disoriented look he particularly liked on a woman, especially one with such a lush figure and soft blond hair.

She stepped close to slip into the corridor that led to the back of the coach, and his body reacted strongly to her.

To hide his momentary agitation, Steve touched his hat and squinted through the gaping hole in the window on the north side of the coach as if scanning the desert.

Samantha walked to the small kitchen in the back of the car, opened the icebox, and poured the water.

She picked her way back through the glass and stopped before Sheridan, deliberately holding his gaze. Before she left the apparent safety and comfort of her parlor car, she needed to know if she could trust this man. In the intense light streaming in the broken windows, his eyes were clear and frank in the way they watched her. She saw a spark of admiration or amusement, but nothing alarming. He took the glass she offered and raised it in a small salute. Then he downed the cool liquid in a series of long swallows and set the glass back on the tray.

Samantha served Nicholas, the others, and herself. Elunami took a cautious sip, held the liquid in her mouth for a second, and finally swallowed.

Sheridan skimmed down the steps and checked the knots holding the blanket in place. Then he and Silas carried Lars from the locomotive and laid him gently on the travois, its leading ends tied to the back of Sheridan's saddle.

Steve lifted the boy, whose bones felt delicate, his weight light, onto the pony in front of Elunami. Astride the front of the saddle, Nicholas looked warily at his mother, who smiled her approval and reassurance. Steve liked the way her eyes softened when she looked at her son, the warmth in her voice as she leaned forward to say, "Race you to Picket Post."

Steve mounted Calico, kicked his foot out of the stirrup, and waited until Samantha had wedged her slender, high-topped, patent leather shoe into it. He reached down for her hand and pulled her up behind him. She was lighter than he had expected. She bumped his shoulder and withdrew as quickly as she could. He heard her arranging her skirts and could almost feel her resistance. She wasn't about to touch him.

Steve kicked his horse's sides; the big horse stepped forward smartly. To keep from falling off, Samantha Forrester grabbed him with her right arm. Smiling, Steve pretended not to notice her warm hand on his stomach.

Samantha wasn't accustomed to riding astride or bareback. Heat radiated from the horse's flanks. And she had forgotten how magnetic a man's flesh could feel. Steve Sheridan's flat stomach was warm and damp beneath her fingers. They twitched as she thought of Lance seeing her like this.

Samantha could remember everything about Lance, even the day she fell in love with him two years after her parents abandoned her.

She didn't want to think about it, but now that the memories had started to unroll, she couldn't stop them. She closed her eyes and remembered the last time she'd seen her parents. She'd been lying on a small cot in their stateroom, as her mother and father cuddled on their own bed, talking quietly. She was four then, and they were on their way to England. She remembered the way her parents lay with her father's back against the cabin wall, knees bent so her mother could lie with her legs over his. They looked happy.

The sound of their voices and the waves slapping against the side of the ship made her feel content and sleepy. She may have slept. She opened her eyes and looked over at their empty bed. Then a voice she didn't recognize said, *She's awake, Cap'n.*

The captain, a big man with curly white hair and beard, stomped across the room and peered over his big belly at her.

I want my mommy.

Your mother and father won't be back, child. His voice rumbled out of his chest. *They went for a walk on the deck, and your mother was knocked overboard by a swinging boom. Your father tried to catch her, and . . .* His voice thickened. He swallowed. *Your father . . . jumped after her, child. We put down a boat and searched for an hour or more but couldn't find either one of them.*

I want my mommy and my daddy. The captain shook his head. *Please,* she begged. The captain had tried to soothe her, but she cried more violently. Her parents did not come back.

Days later the ship docked in a strange town. Samantha listened to the voices coming from the wharf and decided she must be in England. The captain questioned her, rifled through the papers in her parents' trunks, and finally called the authorities and turned her over to them.

They said they could find no living relatives in England. She learned later she had been declared a temporary ward of the court and placed with a family. She would never forget the cold lump in her stomach when she first saw the pitiful, sparsely furnished, rough stone house. Nor was there any welcome from the cold-eyed woman, or the crowd of thin, silent children dressed in tattered clothing not nearly warm enough for the chill house.

Samantha was given a cot in a closet under the stairs. She had no clear remembrance of how long she remained in that house. The only thing she knew was that every night she cried, and every night the woman beat her for it.

During the day Samantha could contain herself, because the woman kept them all busy. Every morning when the older children went to school, the younger children, Samantha included, were taken out to the financial district to beg. In the afternoon they cleaned the house and the crude wooden furniture, which left Samantha's hands full of splinters.

But at night, even though she held the rough ticking of her smelly chicken-feather pillow over her face and prayed for sleep, the tears would come. At first they streamed silently down her temples and into her ears. But before long she would gulp or sob, and the woman would yell as if she had sensed a terrible crime in progress, stomp into the closet, jerk Samantha off the cot, and whip her with a wide belt until her legs were covered with welts.

Samantha screamed and screamed, but her parents did not come for her. After a while she realized they were never coming. They had abandoned her to this nightmare.

She learned later that six months had gone by before Chantry Kincaid II and his wife, Elizabeth—in America—learned that her parents had drowned at sea. Although Samantha called Elizabeth and Chantry Two aunt and uncle out of respect, in fact they were not related to her.

Chantry Two was fond of saying that he had hired one of the best firms in England to track her down. They came as soon as they received word Samantha was alive. According to Chantry's detective, a mix-up had occurred between placing Samantha in the home and notifying the remaining family, a lone Regier cousin. Somehow, and it was never clear how, her mother's cousin was told that all three had died at sea. It was only by happenstance that one of the detectives found paperwork showing that a Regier child had been made a ward of the court.

The Kincaids said that when they came to the house to get Samantha, they barely recognized her. *You looked like a little guttersnipe—dirty, ragged, and thin, with great staring eyes filled with fear and distrust.*

To her, the Kincaids in their rich clothes had looked like the ones she had come to hate—wealthy, thoughtless people who resented the sight of her intruding into their busy, happy, pampered lives.

Samantha! Child! My God, what have they done to you? Elizabeth had cried.

Done to 'er? Wal, my fine lady, I'll tell yew what I done to 'er. Kept 'er alive, I 'ave. Which is a far sight more than some would a done, what with 'er bloody screaming and carrying on all the time.

The Kincaids paid the woman for her "care" and took Samantha back to their hotel, where she was bathed and fed and clothed. Buffy, the youngest Kincaid daughter, had been less than pleased about her parents taking in a new child, especially one almost the same age as her. *Can't we get rid of her?* Buffy had insisted angrily.

Samantha had heard her through the thin wall of the hotel, while Mrs. Lillian, the Kincaids' housekeeper, was dressing her in the clothes Elizabeth had just bought. With tears of rage stinging her eyes, she wriggled away from Mrs. Lillian, grabbed her old clothes, and started for the door.

Elizabeth walked in at that moment.

Where are you going, child?

Away!

Mrs. Lillian flashed Elizabeth a look and whispered, *She heard Buffy. She's a proud one, she is.*

Samantha wanted to run, but something in their eyes held her there, perhaps the confusion and sympathy. She clamped her jaws, fighting back tears. Elizabeth looked frantically at Mrs. Lillian.

I could spank Buffy, Elizabeth whispered back.

Mrs. Lillian caught Samantha by the wrist and pulled her gently into her arms. *Come here, child. There are some things you need to understand.*

Mrs. Lillian smelled of lavender. Samantha felt paralyzed by the heady smell, which reminded her of her mother.

Now, this may not make a great deal of sense to you, but Buffy is still smarting from the last child we brought into this family. Until her baby brother Stuart came along she was queen of the walk. But, in her mind, when he appeared, she disappeared. No one else saw it quite that way, but she took it hard. It's not surprising she would be upset at the thought of another new youngster in the family.

I won't stay! said Samantha, through gritted teeth.

Well, of course, we can't make you.

That's when Lance Kincaid, a boy of fourteen but already a strapping youth, walked into the room. *What's wrong?* he asked.

She got her feelings injured and wants to leave, Elizabeth said.

Lance grinned. *In this family, someone is always getting their feelings injured. But if I were you I wouldn't want to go back where you were, no matter how bad this seems.*

Elizabeth smiled at her son with love and admiration. Seeing that look, Samantha hated Lance. He belonged. His parents hadn't abandoned him. She wished the Kincaids would die—and all the children would be driven naked through the streets to that witch's house—where they could cry in their beds and be beaten every night.

Did you see the look she just gave me? If looks could kill . . . Lance reached out to touch her. Her hand flashed out of its own accord and scratched him. Blood welled up on the back of his hand. *Ow! Dammit!*

Young man! Watch your language!

Sorry.

Samantha was elated. She had hurt him and gotten him into trouble. That was almost as good as driving him out into the cold.

She stayed with the Kincaids after all. But she spent the next year being more trouble than anyone could have imagined. She caused fights between the Kincaid children. She stole from them. She hid or broke their treasured toys.

But no one whipped her when she cried at night. The day before Buffy's sixth birthday, Samantha picked a fight with her and blacked both her eyes. Mrs. Lillian pulled Samantha off the bruised child and sent her to her room, where she listened to the family argue about what they were going to do with her. Samantha went to bed satisfied that even if they threw her out, she had given one of them what they deserved.

That night, while she was lying in bed with tears streaming into her ears, Lance stepped into her bedroom. *Hey . . . there, Sam.*

Shut up! Get out of here!

Happy to, but first I think you need to hear something.

Get out of my room!

We didn't kill your parents. They died at sea. It wasn't our fault.

So?

So, if you keep this up you're just going to make yourself more miserable than you already are.

So? Who cares?

I do. My folks love you. They loved your parents. They'd do anything for them or you, but you're making it almost impossible for them, and for yourself.

What do you know about anything?

Maybe nothing, but I hate seeing you turn yourself inside out.

So whip me!

No one in this house will ever raise a hand to you, Sam, Lance said softly. Then he shook his head and turned to leave. For the first time in a year, Samantha was feeling something for another human being besides herself. A new emotion trembled within her.

Wait.

Lance stopped.

Samantha didn't know why she had stopped him. Tears flooded her mouth and eyes.

Jesus, Lance said, *you've got to be the most miserable little creature I've ever seen.* She cried so hard her ribs ached, but she couldn't stop. He scooped her into his arms and carried her to the rocking chair, where he held her and whispered to her— and rocked her until she had cried out her bitterness and rage.

The next morning she apologized to Buffy without being asked. From that day forward she made a real effort to fit into the Kincaid family. Lance became her protector, her confidant, her beloved. She would do anything for him.

The horse stopped abruptly—and Samantha slammed forward into Steve Sheridan's broad back. "What is it?" she asked.

"Shhh. I want to listen."

They sat still for a moment, then he urged the horse forward again. Samantha lapsed back into her memories.

The Kincaids had tried to raise her as one of their own children, but she'd never accepted Elizabeth and Chantry Two as her parents, or Lance as a brother. She had eventually accepted Chane, Stuart, Maggie, and even Buffy as her siblings—but not

Lance. She loved him wildly and desperately, as only a heartsick child could, but he hadn't noticed her as anything but a sisterly nuisance . . . until . . .

Nine years ago, on March 11, 1880, Lance had been shot in a fight with a desperado, and Chantry Two had taken Samantha with him on a trip to the Arizona Territory to try to lure the headstrong Lance back into the family railroad business. He hated it that his middle son was risking his life as an Arizona Ranger.

Uncle Chantry finally gave up, but Sam had stayed in Phoenix trying to win Lance. In spite of her efforts he had fallen in love with Angie Logan, a girl Samantha had gone to school with. Samantha had almost died. But in the end she had forgiven him, because she couldn't help herself. She loved him more than life itself.

Brokenhearted, Samantha returned to New York and allowed Elizabeth to send her to Europe for her grand tour. Every Regier had taken one, and every Kincaid as well. It had been unthinkable to Elizabeth and Chantry that Samantha, the last of the Regier line, would not go.

Samantha had upheld tradition, but she was certain her grand tour had been the most miserable in history. She'd tried to keep up appearances, but she had almost no memory of the more than a dozen European cities she and her companions had "seen." She'd alternated between crying and trying desperately to forget that Lance had betrayed her by marrying another.

She had returned home just days before Lance brought his wife East to meet the family. Seeing them together, so obviously in love, Samantha had been driven half out of her mind with grief. Her first reaction was to look around for a man to make Lance jealous, as if that were possible.

About that time, Lance's cousin, Jared Forrester, fresh from ten years in North Carolina, arrived for a visit. With his shiny black hair falling across his handsome face, he'd looked like a younger version of Lance, which by itself intrigued Samantha. When Lance expressed disapproval about the focus of her attention, Jared became irresistible.

Unfortunately Jared wasn't Lance, and when Lance and his wife returned to Arizona, she was left married to the wrong man. Jared was tender and sensual, but almost completely worthless in every other way. He'd been raised a gentleman farmer, but he no longer had a farm to keep him busy, so he entertained himself by spending her generous inheritance. He probably would have bankrupted her if he hadn't died in a yachting accident when Nicholas was three.

Still, Jared's champagne tastes had been infectious and fun. He'd taught her that money was to be enjoyed. Without him she'd probably have turned into a tightwad stay-at-home. With him she'd traveled extensively and cultivated an interesting set of eccentric friends with whom she still corresponded regularly.

Once she'd gotten over her grief, she'd seen Jared's dying as a reprieve—and a sign from God that she was supposed to be with Lance. Before her western experience, that love had been like a flame at the very core of her that shimmered and danced within, tantalizing her until her desire for him had become like a consuming fever.

Now, after more than three years in Arizona Territory, Lance was no longer her whole life. She had gotten so busy managing a huge ranch, trying to save her son, dealing with a thousand and one problems—everything from drought and cattle rustlers to mundane household chores and serious injuries and illnesses among her hired help—that her dream of one day having Lance for her own became something she only thought about in the privacy of her bedroom at night. There, unbidden, the dreams came to haunt her, stirring emotions and needs she tried to deny. This morning's dream had told her that she still longed for Lance with the same passion and intensity as before his marriage to Angie.

Lance had looked wonderful in Phoenix. It was always a shock to see him in the flesh. Part of her dreaded it, and part trembled at the thought of it. He had beautiful eyes, and his finely chiseled features were so expressive that all he had to do was look at her . . . and she could feel herself falling apart inside.

Lance, more than anyone else, knew what was in her heart. Perhaps he had sent the dream because he wanted her. Lately he seemed to look at her longer and more frequently than ever before. Had she imagined it? Or had he looked lonely?

"How far do you live from Camp Picket Post?" Steve Sheridan's voice, so close to her face, jolted her back to the desert heat.

"How far?" she repeated, disoriented for a moment. "Uh . . . about ten miles east."

The horse paused, then lunged forward, climbing up the side of a sand dune. Stifling a cry, Samantha grabbed Sheridan and held on tight.

At the top of the dune, Sheridan reined in the horse. As he turned in the saddle to look back over the desert, his shoulder brushed her breast. A warm, excited tingle reached down into her belly and burned there. She became aware of her thighs, opened by the width of the horse's broad flanks.

To distract herself, she turned to look at Lars, who appeared to be asleep on the travois. "Is anyone following us?" she asked. Sheridan turned his head. Samantha could feel the pressure of his gaze on her, but she resisted looking into his eyes.

"Not yet." He turned his attention back to the horse. Samantha rubbed her hands against her skirt, trying to get the feel of him off her flesh.

It didn't seem right that she could love and long for Lance and still respond in this fashion to a stranger.

On Elunami's pony, slightly ahead of them now, Nicholas laughed. "Isn't this exciting, Mama?" he called out, his gaze on Steve Sheridan. Starved for male companionship, Nicholas was nevertheless picky about the men he admired and trusted. So it surprised her that he seemed so willing and ready to like this man whom he barely knew.

Sheridan smiled back at Nicholas. Samantha noticed that his dark brows were finely drawn, except for the left one, which had a cowlick at midbrow. There, the silky black hairs fanned upward into a spiky point.

"Yes, Nicholas," Samantha said, "This is . . . much better than walking."

Grinning, Sheridan urged the horse over a small sand dune, forcing Samantha to grab hold of him again. And again she felt the heat radiating into her hand from his hard, flat belly.

Off in the distance a coyote barked—a short yip, yip, followed by a long wail. Samantha prayed they reached Picket Post before Nicholas started to cough or Lars awoke—or the Papago caught up to them.

"Captain."

Rathwick turned at the sound of General Ashland's voice. "Sir!" He saluted with the ease acquired in West Point and practiced daily for the last twenty years. The commanding officer of Fort Thomas had returned from Washington, D.C., that morning, several days ahead of schedule. Rathwick wondered why.

"May I have a moment with you, Captain?"

"Of course, sir."

Ashland's smooth voice sounded polite, but Rathwick distrusted his politeness. Ashland was dishonest in small ways that made him undependable. The general assumed that all men had larceny in their hearts and justified his own as if it were an asset in dealing with other crooks.

Every officer under Ashland's command knew that if the general got in a bad spot, someone other than Ashland would be sacrificed. They all resented him for it, Rathwick more than most. He felt distaste for any man who couldn't accept the consequences of his actions. But Rathwick didn't let his feelings show. He needed Ashland's recommendation to be promoted to major.

Rathwick followed the general into his office. Ashland closed the door and seated himself on the chair behind the walnut desk. Rathwick took the chair facing him.

"Would you like a drink, Captain?"

"No, sir."

"Down to business, then. What I'm about to tell you is confidential. Top secret. For your ears only, Captain."

"Understood, sir."

"A most regrettable incident has taken place. Captain Lawson bungled an assignment this morning. An Indian woman escaped. She is armed and dangerous. Your job is to find and kill her."

Rathwick frowned. He was a captain in the United States Cavalry, not a hired assassin. "If I may ask, sir, what did she do?"

"You may not ask. I've told you all I can at this time. Suffice it to say that the secretary will be very grateful to the man who corrects Lawson's mistake." Ashland emphasized the words, "the secretary." He liked to give the impression he had a close relationship with the Secretary of the War Department.

Ashland scowled at Rathwick. "You've killed your share of Indians, Captain. Are you going soft on me?"

"The Indians are at peace now, sir. They're living on the reservations."

Ashland's lips thinned and his jaw seemed clenched, as if he resented every word he had to utter in this regard. "This woman was at least a hundred miles from the nearest reservation, Captain."

Rathwick stared down at the polished perfection of his boots. There was no law against an Indian being off the reservation, and Ashland knew that. Rathwick tried not to seem resistant, but he was having difficulty seeing why he should ride out and kill an Indian woman. A brave was one thing; they occasionally left the reservation to steal cattle and horses, and some would not be taken alive. But a woman . . .

"I'm not trying to be difficult, sir."

"Good, because your future depends upon your doing this job. Take as many scouts as you need to track her. Lawson will tell you where he saw her last. Report to me as soon as you've completed your assignment." Ashland stood up in dismissal.

Rathwick wanted to ask for more clarification, but he realized that whatever the Indian woman had done had rattled cages all the way to Washington. Even the secretary of war wanted her dead.

Rathwick saluted and walked out. Either he was getting too finicky for the army, or this assignment was not the sort he expected in a properly run military organization. He'd give a lot to know exactly what the woman had done to deserve all this high-level attention. Maybe he could find out from Lawson.

Rathwick found him in the officers' mess. Lawson was out of uniform, his boots were dusty, and he looked drunk. No wonder Ashland was testy.

Rathwick scanned the room, empty except for an enlisted man wielding a mop in the far corner of the bar. "You're supposed to tell me where you saw the Indian woman last," he said low enough so the man swabbing the floor couldn't hear him.

Lawson looked up and sneered. He had a perpetually cocky look on his thin face that seemed uncalled for.

"I wondered which son of a bitch Ashland would send." Lawson's words slurred. Rathwick glanced at the clock on the wall to confirm what he already knew. Lawson was drunk on duty; probably the result of failing on an important mission.

"Bucking for a promotion, huh, Rathwick?"

"No more than you're bucking for a court-martial."

"Did he tell you it was hush-hush?" Lawson leaned back to peer owlishly into Rathwick's face.

"As a matter of fact, he did."

Lawson made an exaggerated movement with his right hand, pointing his finger and shaking it close to Rathwick's face. "Well, you do a good job now! I'm just glad to see he found a man who can handle the job. Damned shame about Lawson. Fine young man, but he just didn't have it."

"If you're through feeling sorry for yourself, you might tell me where you saw her last . . . and what she looks like."

Lawson snorted. "Last? I think she was leaning over her dead grandfather's body," he said, frowning. "No, maybe that was her great-grandfather. They were all so damned old and so full of carbine holes . . . I purely don't know how the hell you expect me to tell one old man from another."

Rathwick scowled. "I meant the location."

"Ohhhh, the location. Sorry, old man. Location. Yes, I think they were in the riverbed due north of Pichaco Mountain."

"What did the girl look like?" Rathwick asked, suddenly feeling sorry for Lawson and wishing he didn't.

"Look like?" Lawson scratched his head and frowned. "All scared women look alike, don't they?"

"A description, *please*, Captain."

"Description. Yes, sir!" Lawson fell half off the stool, grabbed the bar, saluted, and did a caricature of a soldier standing at attention. He and Rathwick were of equal rank. The "sir" and the salute dripped with sarcasm.

"Scared as a deer staked out in the middle of a train track with the locomotive bearing down on it, sir."

"Description, Captain," Rathwick repeated.

"Yes, sir!" Lawson said. "Looked like an Indian." Once started, he just wanted to get it over with and be rid of Rathwick, so he could go back to his drinking. "Eyes . . . black. Height . . . short. Weight . . . a little on the thin side, sir!"

"Wearing?"

"Wearing . . . white. A white buckskin outfit with beads and fringe. White moccasins. A white headdress with lots of white feathers and streamers with beads on them. Fancy . . . real fancy. And not from around here. Maybe a Plains Indian, from the getup."

"Thank you, Captain," Rathwick said gently.

"Welcome, sir!" Lawson said, bringing his hand up to his chin in a sloppy salute.

Rathwick ignored the drunken attempt and strode out of the bar.

Lawson turned back to his drink. "Earn yourself a big fat promotion, Rathwick, old man. I couldn't do it, but maybe you can." He took a big gulp of his whiskey, put the glass down, and banged it on the bar three times. "Gimme another. And make it a double. I'm not nearly drunk enough for military matters." He groaned and lowered his face to the cool marble-topped bar. "I can still remember the look on her face. God forgive me."

CHAPTER TWO

Lance Kincaid dismounted and yelled for the stable boy, who came running and took the reins of his horse.

"Evening, Mr. Kincaid."

"Evening, Josiah."

The boy led the horse toward the stables. Lance glanced up at the house he shared with his wife, Angie, and their housekeeper, Yoshio. Angie's plank sign announcing, ANGELA LOGAN, PHOTOGRAPHER, still irritated him. He'd told her a number of times that they could easily afford to have another sign lettered. She'd only laughed and said, "Why bother? Men don't change the names of their businesses when they marry."

He hadn't pushed it, but it still rankled.

Lance opened the front door and stepped into the house. He had important and possibly disturbing news to share. Mentally girding himself, he sniffed, hoping to discern what Yoshio was cooking for dinner, as if that might tell him what kind of mood Angie would be in. But the sharp odor of developing fluid masked whatever it was.

The hallway was lined with negatives hanging like small, dark diapers on a wire Angie had stretched there "temporarily" six years ago, just after they had built this house. It was big and imposing, and Angie's studio and darkroom were spacious, but somehow she always managed to overflow into the rest of the house.

"Angie! Are you home?"

"In here," his wife called from the library.

Lance tossed his dusty tan hat at the mahogany hat tree beside the stairs. It sailed up and arced just enough to drop into place on the top center post, a good omen, he decided as he strode toward the library.

The enormous mahogany book-lined room was lit by an electric overhead chandelier and two lamps beside two massive leather chairs.

Durango was a hundred miles south of Phoenix. Even in February there was no need for a fire in the stone fireplace.

30

Angie was seated at a rolltop oak desk, her wheat-colored hair pulled off her oval face and tied with a red ribbon. He walked to her side, leaned down, and kissed the top of her head. It, too, smelled of developing fluid.

A photographer of growing reputation, she had probably spent the entire day in the darkroom. Her picture books featuring different frontier towns were reprinted year after year. She made as much money as he did—and she didn't have to swing a pickax.

She frowned up at him. Her intelligent, mobile face and large golden brown eyes were snappingly alert and almost too sensitive. "You're early," she said, with no hint of a smile.

"Ran into a problem too big to tackle tonight. What's wrong?" he asked.

"Nothing's wrong. Who said anything was wrong?"

"I did."

"Well, you're wrong."

"At least now we know it was me," he said, grinning at the incongruity she didn't seem to notice. "What's going on?"

"Just opening the mail."

That had an ominous sound to it. "Anything interesting?" he asked.

"Yes, but I don't read my husband's love letters." Angie handed him a letter from Samantha and watched as he opened and read it.

"It's not a love letter."

"We just saw her in Phoenix," Angie said, her tone accusatory.

Lance turned the letter over and looked at the postmark. "Must have gotten stuck in the mail sack. It's three weeks old."

Lance knew Angie hated his getting letters from Sam. The letters were nothing in themselves. Just expressions of Sam's loneliness and fears about Nicholas. They shouldn't have bothered Angie, but once she had realized they couldn't have babies, she had become jealous of Sam. Over the years, that jealousy had grown. Now, just the mention of Sam's name was enough to send Angie into a rage.

"Nicholas looked a little stronger this trip, don't you think?" he asked, hoping to change the subject. "I don't believe I could stand it if anything happened to that kid."

"You don't worry so about little Chane or Amy."

"I love my brother's children, too, but they have their health and a father," he reminded her.

Angie didn't answer, but the look on her face clearly revealed her misery.

"Don't worry," he said. "I'll just write her a short letter to cheer her up."

"I thought the mine kept you busy from night until morning."

"That's you," he corrected, grinning. "The mine keeps me busy from morning until night." Angie didn't smile at his attempt to lighten her mood. "Well," he said, shrugging, "it won't take me long to write a letter."

"Then she'll find something else for you to do—"

Lance laughed.

"It isn't funny," Angie insisted, her face suddenly clouded with frustration. "You always have time to do the things she wants you to do."

"I make time to do the things you want me to do, too," he reminded her gently.

"You're supposed to. I'm your wife. But you still don't do the important things."

"I do so!"

"You won't go to Mexico City with me." Angie had accepted an assignment to do a picture book of Mexico City. Ever since she'd signed the contract, she'd been trying to talk him into going with her. The trip was set for November through January, and she didn't want to be separated from him at Christmas.

"That's for three months, for Christ's sake."

"See?" she said, as if that proved her point.

"That's hardly the same thing," he said, protesting. "I have a business to run, too, you know."

"If what Sam wanted took six months, you'd do it."

"I would not."

"Yes, you would."

"I can't believe we're arguing about something as insignificant as my writing a letter to my sister."

"If she really were your sister, we wouldn't be having this conversation."

Lance sighed. Angie still looked like the beautiful young woman he had married. She had the same vital, healthy flush to her smooth cheeks, the same precise pattern of apricot-colored freckles across the bridge of her pretty nose. But her eyes, though still beautiful and dark and flashing with inner fire on occasion, were haunted now.

The third year they were married, she had gotten pregnant.

She had been sick from the day she conceived until she miscarried three months later. She'd almost died during the miscarriage, and the doctor had not known why. She no longer admitted any desire for a child and discouraged him from talking about it. However, he believed in spite of her silence and withdrawal that she still wanted a baby, but he was no longer willing to let her carry one for fear of losing her.

The doctor had told Angie that he didn't think she could conceive again. The infection from the resulting miscarriage had done permanent damage. Angie had never been able to hide things from him. Her eyes were so clear and expressive he could see all the way to her soul. The day the doctor told her, he had seen such grief and loss that he'd been devastated as well. Even now, remembering the look in her eyes, his guts twisted with pain.

"Well, how am I going to get you into a good mood so I don't have to eat dinner with a grouch?" he asked, raising an eyebrow at her.

Angie scowled. Lance's tone was humorous and mocking, calculated to remind her that he loved her and just wanted her to be happy. But it just made her feel like a bitch. He was patient and thoughtful—a far better husband than she deserved. And he had matured into an even handsomer man than the one she'd married. More solid, more confident. He exuded masculine authority. It was no wonder Samantha had never gotten over him.

"I don't know," Angie admitted reluctantly.

"Maybe I could kiss you. That used to work."

The attractive raspiness of his voice softened her, quickened her pulse. She drew in a long breath and forced a smile. "I guess we could try," she said, standing and slipping into his arms.

Lance pulled her close and breathed in the warmth and softness he loved. "So what naughty things have you been doing today that made you want to pick on me?"

"Me?" Angie asked, shaking her head and smiling in spite of herself. Lance had a way of getting her out of her bad moods. Now he lowered his mouth to hers and nibbled her lips.

"You're the one who's always just a heartbeat away from going over the line," she said accusingly.

"You've got me confused with someone else," he whispered, capturing her lips. He kissed her and felt her slowly relaxing in his arms. Kissing her, all their differences dissolved. She was still the saucy, unmanageable female who had captured his heart seven years ago.

He could have kissed her for hours, but she ended the kiss, sighed, and smiled up at him. "Welcome home," she whispered.

The impulse to tell her how much he loved her was strong in him, but words like that came hard lately. "I don't know where I got this terrible weakness for skinny girls with bad tempers," he said huskily. Angie reached up and kissed him again, this time with more passion. It was the sort of kiss that led to the bedroom, not the dining room. He felt no drawing back, no withholding. Hope leapt alive in him again.

This time he ended the kiss. It was that or pick her up and carry her upstairs, and Yoshio would not appreciate that after all the work he had probably put into cooking dinner.

Angie sighed, completely relaxed and compliant in his arms now. "I don't know where I got this terrible weakness for wandering men, either," she said, the expression in her dark eyes serious as she leaned back in his arms.

"Does anyone else know you lie like this?" he growled, with just the right note of mock authority.

"No, and it's a good thing for you," she said teasingly.

"So what did you torture poor Yoshio into cooking for us tonight?" he asked, taking her hand and leading her toward the dining room.

Angie laughed and swung his hand between them. "All you ever think about is your stomach. If I ate half as much as you, I'd have to roll to the table."

"See these calluses," he said, raising his deeply tanned right hand. It was strong and square. "I work hard—"

"Ha! Men always think they work hard."

They ate in companionable silence. Yoshio cleared the table and brought custard and coffee. "Great dinner," Lance said, leaning back.

"Thank you, sir. I thought it up myself."

During dessert, Lance told Angie about something funny that had happened at the mine. When he felt certain she was in a good mood, he broached the subject that had been on his mind most of the day.

"Oh," he said, as if he'd just remembered, "I brought you a letter from Sarah." Sarah Logan, Angie's best friend and sister-in-law, was married to Angie's brother, Laramee. Lance and Laramee were partners in the silver mine Lance ran. Laramee put his considerable energies into running the Boxer Brand Cattle Ranch, and Sarah into raising their two children. The ranch was so named because it boxed in a good part of the Santa Cruz River. If anyone had water, Logan had water.

Angie smiled and took the letter. "Well, it's about time. I haven't seen her in days!" She unfolded the letter and read.

Dear Angie,
   The worst possible news. Mary Beth died in childbirth this morning.

"Oh, no," Angie whispered, flashing Lance a look of horror. Then she glanced back at the letter.

   I wasn't there, but Doc stopped by on his way home. He was worn out. He brought the baby here for me to take care of. The other children are old enough to fend for themselves for a few days. I've written to the baby's grandparents in Prescott. Doc posted the letter for me, or he was supposed to. But he mentioned that the kids had told him their grandparents were too old and poorly to take on a baby. Hopefully they will answer.
   I wondered if you might want to consider adopting this baby. It is very sweet, and a boy. It looks a lot like Mary Beth, which would be an asset for a male. At the very least, you might want to come out and see it. I hope I'm not meddling.

                                     Love, Sarah

Angie let the letter slip from her fingers. She suddenly felt suffocated. Just the thought of adopting a baby awakened the ever-present hunger in her that had started practically the day she'd married Lance and hadn't let up once.

  Part of her desperately wanted a baby. And part of her just as desperately didn't want anything to do with a baby. Just the thought of having one increased the feeling of suffocation. And then there was Lance, whom she loved more than life itself. She was so aware of his desire for a child that her heart ached every time she thought about him. He, too, had become a constant reminder of her inability to have children. She felt bombarded from within and without.

It seemed to her that once a body could no longer have children, it should at least have the good sense to stop yearning for them. But that hadn't happened in her case. The older she got, and she was twenty-nine now, the more conflicted and confused she became.

Tears of frustration formed a hard knot in her throat. She turned away from her husband and tried to hold back the tears, but they flooded her mouth and eyes. All attempts to control herself failed, and she curled forward in deep pain, gritting her teeth to keep the howls and sobs from escaping.

"Hey, hey," Lance crooned, moving around the table to kneel beside her chair and take her into his arms.

Angie tried to turn away from him, but he pulled her into his arms and held her. She felt even more suffocated and jerked away from him. "I'm sorry," she said, at the hurt look on his face. "I don't know why I'm taking this so hard."

Lance didn't, either. Any death was an occasion for sadness, but this seemed to go deeper than that. Angie didn't really know Mary Beth, except as a neighbor Sarah talked about occasionally. The woman had lived seven miles away and only got into town occasionally. Angie's interchanges with her were limited to the weather and other small talk.

"I'm sorry," Angie repeated, wiping her eyes with trembling hands and trying to get control of herself. "At least the poor little thing's in good hands," she said shakily.

"I thought maybe," Lance said, shrugging, "that you'd want to go over there and see if there's anything you can do to help Sarah. She's already got her hands full, with two children of her own and another on the way."

His expression, the care he took trying not to upset her, the deep hurt she knew he tried so hard to hide from her evoked the full force of despair she had tried so long to ignore. With a shaking hand, Angie swiped at her eyes with her napkin.

"Don't you realize I have better things to do with my time than take care of a baby who'll probably just . . ." Her voice trailed off. A look of horror crossed her face; she threw down her napkin and ran from the room.

Lance scowled after her slender form. Well, so much for hoping she'd see the baby and get attached to it. She wasn't even willing to go out there. He knew he should give up, but he followed Angie up the stairs and stopped at their closed bedroom door. Through the solid oak he could hear her soft, heartbroken crying.

He waited until the sobs subsided, then tapped lightly on the door, opened it, and walked in. She was huddled on the bed with her knees drawn up to her chest. Even though the room felt warm to him, she had pulled the covers over her.

He sat down on the bed beside her and stroked her back. When they were first married, Angie had talked and acted like she wanted a baby. That first year she had cooed over babies and looked at baby furniture in the catalog. After the miscarriage she had stopped talking about babies. Now apparently she had moved on to not even permitting the subject to be discussed in the house. But he still couldn't believe she didn't want a baby as much as he did, that somewhere beneath that beautiful, hardening shell of hers, the hunger lived on.

"You know," he said softly, cautiously, "Yoshio could hire a nanny to take care of that baby. You wouldn't have to do anything you didn't want to do."

Angie rolled over and sat up, flinging the covers aside. "No!"

"Why not?"

"No!" she yelled, springing to her feet. "If you want a baby so bad, go to Samantha. She can give you one!"

"I want us to have a baby," Lance said carefully. "But I don't want you to give birth to it. You're too precious—"

"I don't want a baby in this house!" Angie shouted, trembling visibly.

"You don't mean that. Why don't you just go over to Sarah's and take a look at it?" he persisted.

"Ohhhh!" Angie sat up and looked at him with horror and outrage, as if he had suggested something so awful there could be no recovery from it.

"Why don't you just go over there," she shouted, "and get it and take it to Samantha!"

Lance put up a hand. "Leave Sam out of this."

"Look who's talking!"

Angie picked up her pillow and slammed it to the floor. Pain, despair, and frustration swirled through her so forcefully that she lost all reason. She looked around for something else to throw or kick or destroy. Finding nothing she yelled at her husband instead, "Get out!"

"Angie . . . I'm only trying—"

"I know what you're trying to do! Just get out!"

Lance scowled at her. "You don't mean that—"

"Yes, I do!" she shouted, her face twisting with pain and rage. "I really, really do! It's probably the first thing I've meant in years! Just go and get it over with! I'm sick of hearing about how much you want a baby. Go get yourself a baby! Now!"

Lance looked like a man turned to stone. Enraged at her inability to move him, she ran to the armoire, flung the doors open, and began tossing gowns at the bed.

"What are you doing?" he asked.

"You aren't leaving, so I'm leaving!" she shouted, panting. "I'm going to San Francisco tomorrow."

"When did this come up?"

"A week ago. I forgot to mention it."

"So you mention it now? In the middle of a fight?"

Angie grabbed another gown and tossed it at the valise, throwing clothes about in a frenzy.

"For how long?" he finally asked.

"I don't know," she said, turning away from the pain and confusion in his eyes. Her own pain was too great.

Lance walked over to her, turned her, and peered into her eyes. She flinched at his touch, and started to jerk away from him but stopped herself. Lance would put up with a great deal from her, and had, but even in her current state of pain and rage, she knew better than to push him too far. Apparently what he saw in her eyes told him this fight was different from the others. He let go of her rigid shoulders and stepped away from her.

"Are you coming back?" he asked.

"I don't know."

Lance was stunned. He had no idea what had gone so wrong. He looked at her for a long moment. Angry words seethed within, but he swallowed them and turned away.

"Where are you going?" she asked, her voice trembling.

"Out," he growled.

"Tell Samantha you have my blessing," she called after him.

"I'm not going to Sam."

"You will."

The door slammed hard. Blinded and furious, Angie stuffed carefully ironed gowns into her overpacked valises as if they were rags. When she had packed everything she could find, she ordered Yoshio to have the carriage hitched up. Then she sat down on the edge of the bed and folded forward, crying. She had lost him to Samantha, and it was her own fault.

They had been climbing uphill for a long time. Sand and cactus had given way to low growing mesquite bushes, bur sage, and brittlebush. Samantha wiped perspiration off her face and leaned around Steve Sheridan's broad shoulder to see how much farther they had to go. Only a few hundred yards away, on a level place on the side of the low scrub-covered mountain, Picket Post's faded gray buildings gleamed like silver in the sunlight. It had a small business section arranged around a quad. Miners lived north of the town in rundown shacks and pale canvas tents. Business owners lived east of town in whitewashed houses. From a distance, the white of the canvas and houses looked like lace trim around the town.

She had never been so happy to see anyplace in her life. Camp Picket Post was the only settlement of any size between Phoenix and Globe. Every Saturday, miners, cowboys, and farmers came from miles around. Today would be no exception.

With its squat, weathered buildings arranged in a square, Picket Post reminded Samantha of the settlement near the Kincaid ranch in Texas. Lance had said most Texas towns had been built around squares to make them easier to protect from attacking Comanche. But even after the Comanche were no longer a problem, people kept building Texas towns that way. Maybe this camp had been started by a Texan. They were everywhere.

"Are you from Texas, Mr. Sheridan?"

"I don't think so."

She had never known a man who wasn't sure where he was from. She wanted to ask him about it, but a dog ran out and barked so loudly Sheridan wouldn't have heard her anyway.

Up close, Picket Post looked like it was only weeks away from being a ghost town. The buildings couldn't be more than ten years old, but they already leaned slightly from the fairly constant northeastern winds whipping around the mountain.

Inside the square, horses stood in the hot sun and switched their tails at flies buzzing around them. Sounds of fiddle music came from one of the saloons, tinny piano music from another. A group of men standing in front of the tobacco store laughed and talked. Two old men with white beards sat on the steps of the general store and whittled.

The barber shop, where the town's closest thing to a doctor resided, was at the easternmost edge of town, so they didn't have far to go.

Usually Seth Boswell, skilled at picking bullets out of wounds, walked out smiling his good-natured smile and helped Samantha down from her horse. Today he appeared not to see them.

"This is the place," Samantha said, glancing around at the town, which looked smaller, meaner, and more run down than she remembered it.

Sheridan dismounted. He and Silas carried Lars toward the barber shop. Boswell stepped into the doorway, blocking it.

Samantha frowned. "Something wrong?"

"Gunshot wound?" Seth asked gruffly, looking at Sheridan.

"Yes," Sheridan said.

Boswell lifted Lars's shirt and frowned at the wound. "Should have taken him to the fort."

Sheridan looked irritated. Samantha felt a sinking in her chest. Seth Boswell had never shown any hesitancy about treating any type of wound. Usually, whether he was acting as barber to cut Nicholas's hair or as doctor to check his health, he always smiled at her and gave Nicholas a gumdrop. Today he looked like he wished she hadn't stopped here.

"There's a band of renegade Indians between here and the fort," Sheridan said. "I thought it best to bring everyone here."

Boswell still blocked the doorway to his shop. People had stepped out onto the sidewalk to watch. Samantha felt his desire to turn them away.

"Something's wrong, Mr. Boswell. I'd appreciate it if you would tell me what it is."

Boswell's gaze met hers for the first time. He shrugged and shook his head. "Ain't nothing, really. Bring him in."

Relieved, Samantha motioned Steve and Silas into the shop. They carried Lars through to a small examining room in the back and lifted him onto the table. Samantha patted Lars's warm hand. "I'll get Nicholas settled at the hotel and be right back."

"Nah, I'll be fine," Lars said, waving her away. "You take care of the lad."

"Thank you, Mr. Boswell," Samantha said, stopping deliberately in front of him.

"Welcome," he said, without looking up at her.

Samantha opened her reticule, fumbled through her bills a moment, then took out a twenty. "I'll pay the rest of his bill before I leave town."

At that Boswell looked up at her, his eyes miserable with shame or embarrassment, she couldn't tell which.

"That won't be necessary. The railroad will pay," he said gruffly.

"Well, that may take awhile. I don't want you to be out anything on my behalf."

He sighed heavily and took the money. "Thanks."

She sent Silas to the telegraph office to wire the Texas and

Pacific that there was a crippled train on the tracks, then walked to the door and stepped outside. Sheridan followed her.

Smiling, Chila Elaine Dart walked to the window of her suite at the Rawson Hotel. She pulled aside the sun-streaked maroon velvet drapery and looked down at the wide rutted road baking under the hot sun.

She felt good today. She and her son, Joe, had come into town to make the last payment on her ranch. Twenty years of paying off the bank and she finally owned the land she'd bought so long ago. If Chila were still speaking to her mother, which she wasn't, she'd enjoy letting her know that she had succeeded, against all her dire predictions.

Chila sneezed. Just touching the fabric had freed enough dust to irritate her nostrils. "I wouldn't give two shakes for the hotel's housekeeper."

Joe grunted to let her know he'd heard her, but he didn't look up from the newspaper he was reading.

"Must be a bear and bull fight, darlin'. That would account for all the commotion coming from behind Owen Parker's hotel. Ah wonder if he keeps his draperies any cleaner?"

"Unnnnnn."

A few people not at the bear and bull fight appeared to be looking out the doors and windows of the stores across the street. What had attracted them was not immediately apparent. Then Samantha Forrester stepped out of Seth Boswell's barber shop and paused on the sidewalk.

The sight of Samantha made Chila want to lean out of the window and wave and yell hello. But then she remembered about the article Claire Colson, Picket Post's official busybody, was showing around town, and that stopped Chila cold. She hadn't meant anything ugly by reading the article Claire had shown her, but she felt guilty nevertheless. And of course Claire had gotten on her high horse and told everyone in town who'd listen that Samantha Forrester was trying to give all of 'em the consumption, which apparently, if the article could be believed, was as contagious as typhoid.

Chila considered Samantha Forrester a friend. Yet she had to admit that the article, written by a real doctor, proved almost without a doubt that consumption was contagious. For years Chila had been reading articles that hinted at it. This was the first time she'd ever read something that actually convinced her. Unfortunately it had convinced others as well.

Samantha might be angry at her for reading it, but according to Claire Colson, it was the townspeople who had a right to be angry at Samantha, who exposed them all to the danger of contagion every time she brought that boy into town. Horrid disease and an absolutely horrid fate for a small child. Chila shuddered to think of it. She couldn't think about children dying, especially Nicholas, with his big solemn eyes and his earnest way of saying whatever was on his sweet little mind.

Consumption was such a touchy issue with Samantha. She wouldn't be pleased. Unfortunately Samantha was the only truly interesting woman in Picket Post. Chila enjoyed Samantha's friendship. The other women in town were mostly European peasants who cared only about their menfolk and their young'uns—and their endless chores. Wherever you looked you could see them waddling on their swollen stump legs, their faces grim with the struggle to survive. They lived in rude shacks with only the crudest tools, cooking utensils, and farm implements. Some lived worse than the poor white trash who used to sharecrop on her father's cotton plantation after the war and before her family disowned her. Her father was one of the few men in Georgia who had survived the Civil War without going broke, which just proved the devil looked out for his own.

Samantha was different. She read Eastern magazines and could speak interestingly about any number of subjects. She left the housework to her hired help and didn't apologize to anyone for doing so. Chila admired a woman who didn't let others decide how she would live.

Samantha always stayed in Owen Parker's hotel. She said she liked Mary Francis's cooking better, but Chila suspected it was because she didn't want to frequent the Rawson like Chila and be seen as a copycat. A leader herself, Chila respected that.

Chila's eyes strayed back to the street below. On the road in front of the barber shop, Nicholas Forrester straddled a pinto pony in front of a red-haired girl, probably a new employee to help Juana with the endless job of dusting that impossible house. Thinking of Samantha Forrester's misbegotten house caused Chila to smile. Her own house wasn't beautiful, but at least it suited the climate.

Samantha stepped out of the barber shop, followed by a man. He spoke to her, leaning a little closer than was absolutely necessary and touching her arm.

"Well, Ah'll be!" Chila grinned. "Samantha has a beau! And a good-looking one at that!"

Chila glanced over at the mirror to reassure herself. She was fifty-two years old to Samantha's twenty-seven, but she didn't look her age. Most women out here were dead by forty-three. Chila was proud of the fact that she didn't have to do anything special to stay young-looking. She was just lucky, even though she occasionally caught a glimpse of herself in the mirror that startled her. But usually she looked good. Her skin had dried up a little, but her body was slim and strong. Her gowns had to be made bigger now. She had no idea why. Usually the scale would testify that she hadn't gained an ounce, unless she got on Seth Boswell's contraption when it was acting up, which it did almost every time.

She turned back to the window in time to see Samantha Forrester look up at the man, who was a good head taller than she with stocky shoulders and a strong neck. Suddenly Chila caught sight of his face. Although she couldn't see it in any detail, the shape of it sent a jolt through her body. The feeling quivered within her for a moment, and her lips tingled with sudden dryness. She licked them, but even her tongue had gone dry.

By now the man had turned and was walking to a calico horse standing in the street. The way he moved, even the way he carried his arms and shoulders, seemed to increase the feeling of anxiety growing in her.

Chila got a tickle in her throat and started to cough. The man turned his horse to follow Samantha toward Owen Parker's hotel, which was across the street and west of the Rawson. As Samantha walked toward a store, people inside stepped away from the windows and turned their backs on her, pretending not to see her. Compassion for Samantha twisted Chila's insides and made her forget her coughing spell.

Chila's attention came back to the man. And suddenly she knew why he was so upsetting to her. It was Denny. She could never mistake that profile. No man had the same shaped head and shoulders.

A red veil misted the scene down on the street. At first Chila couldn't see through it. Part of her felt strangely blinded, as if her real eyes were no longer working and other eyes were seeing things they usually couldn't. Then, poking through the redness she saw the face of a devil—a horrible ravaged face with two terrible red eyes glowing with madness.

Chila thought he was about the ugliest thing she'd ever seen. As if he could read her mind, the devil glared at her for a moment, and something writhed within her, something that felt like a snake deep down in her belly. Heat loosened by the writhing inflamed her loins. Then the devil faded back into the redness and Chila couldn't see him any longer, couldn't see anything but the scarlet veil. But the memory of having seen him frightened her so badly that her hands started to shake.

Ah cain't go through this again, a voice within her whispered. Her body flushed with despair; her legs almost buckled. She sat down in the straight-backed chair beside the bureau and tried not to pant out loud, though she had no idea on Earth why she was being so considerate. She had been to hell and back, and Joe's towhead was still bent over his newspaper.

For a moment she sat in dumb silence. Then, as if her mind had started to work again, she realized that devil she'd seen was Denny. The thought so startled her that her heart skipped a beat. She hiccupped. *Denny is the devil.*

Terrified and curious in spite of it, Chila stood and looked out the window. Down on the street Denny rode toward her on a gray-and-calico horse. Despite herself she remembered things she'd never wanted to think about again.

Chila had gone West when Joe was still in swaddling. She'd told everyone that Joe's father had sold their original home and spent every cent on a ranch east of Picket Post. Then he'd died on the trip out, leaving her and her baby to survive as best they could in the desert.

She had never admitted the truth to anyone—that Denny had betrayed her, drowned her baby, and left her in an insane asylum in Dallas. The only way she could have survived all that was to put him out of her mind and go forward. She'd done that, but it hadn't been easy.

Ever since her baby drowned, she'd been given to blue spells, where she had no more energy than a dishrag and cried over just about everything. There were days when she could barely lift one foot in front of the other, and yet she'd forced herself to go on, even after being cast out by her own folks because they didn't want their neighbors to find out their daughter had spent a year in an insane asylum and come out of it with a baby of unknown parentage.

And now Denny was back. Chila had never dreamed that anyone would ever find her here in the high desert, especially not Denny, who should have been dead by now. It didn't make a bit of sense. No more sense than her first baby being drowned by him.

She closed her eyes and saw her baby's body, swollen and gray. His little wrinkled hand reached out to her, as if she should have done something to save him. The pain came up so hard she doubled over, panting.

"You okay, Ma?" Joe asked, still without looking up from his paper. Chila felt it was a sad commentary on their life together that she could be practically dying in front of him and he saw nothing unusual about it.

"Fine, darlin'. Just fine," she said, opening her eyes and wiping at the tears streaming steadily down her cheeks. She tried to stop the shaking inside her, but she kept seeing the face of the man who had ridden back into her life as if he had every right in the world to be alive and breathing when her baby wasn't.

Chila sank down onto the chenille counterpane. Oh, God! Oh, God! He's come back. The horrible sense of panic grew worse. Denny's come back. I told him never to make that mistake. I warned him I'd kill him. I warned him . . .

The pressure within became so intense she had to do something. With shaking hands, she wiped tears off her face and stepped to the window, where she saw that Denny was almost directly beneath her on the road. He was riding through town in broad daylight—as if he had every right in the world.

Rage flushed up from her newly awakened insides. With lightning speed, Chila leaned over and slipped Joe's pistol out of his holster.

"Hey, what are you doing with my gun?"

Chila pushed aside the dusty drapery, aimed the gun at the back of the man who'd ruined her life, and fired three quick shots. To her great disappointment, Denny didn't appear to be hit. But he was so busy fighting his animal he didn't have time to turn or shoot back.

Joe scrambled out of his chair, grabbed the gun out of her hand, and wrestled her down to the floor. "What the hell are you doing?" he hissed from atop her.

"Give that back to me!" Chila demanded, panting at the effort to get the gun out of his hands, which were a lot stronger than hers. "Let me up from here! I'm your mother!"

"Hush! You don't act like a mother," he whispered. "Never have, for that matter. Now you quiet down and be still! Who the hell were you shooting at?"

"None of your business!"

"Ma, I ought a take a strap to you. Hush! Listen."

"It's scandalous the way you talk to your own mother thataway. You've been back talking me since you were knee high to a—"

"Hush, Ma! You want them to hear you?"

Down on the road men were yelling and cursing.

"Did you see where those shots came from?" yelled a man who sounded like Marshal Daley.

"No, I didn't get to the window in time."

Joe let out his breath in relief. "They didn't see you," he whispered.

"Serves 'em right. They were all busy hiding their faces from Samantha Forrester."

"Who'd you shoot at?"

"You don't know him." She'd never told her son about the bastard who had betrayed her and robbed her of the one thing she held dear in life, her baby. There was no need for Joe to know.

"Ma! You shot at a stranger!"

"Ah know him, darlin'," she whispered fiercely.

Joe stood up, pushed the curtain aside, and looked down at the street. A crowd had gathered, and they were all facing his direction.

"Hey, Joe! See anything! A gunman took a few shots at this man," Daley yelled, pointing at a man on a calico horse.

"No. I was reading the paper."

Odd, thought Chila, watching him, how he could be her son and carry almost none of her good sense or her Southern accent. He had adopted the slang of the cocky cowhands who worked on their ranch.

Joe waved to the others and turned back to his mother. "You don't know him," he whispered. "I been everywhere you've been, and I never seen him before."

"You weren't born yet, that's why."

"He ain't much older than me from what I could see. How can you be that mad at a man who was just a kid the last time you saw him?"

Chila blinked. Joe was twenty-three years old. Denny would be in his fifties by now.

Chila shuddered. Her hands would not stop shaking. The heat was trying to suffocate her in spite of the fact that she was about to shake apart.

"Help me up from here, darlin'. Ah need to lie down for a spell," she said.

Joe gave her his hand. "You want me to get Seth Boswell?"

"No. No. Just leave me be awhile."

"I'm not leaving here till you promise me you'll behave yourself."

Chila scowled. Joe had been bossy as a child, and he hadn't changed much once he'd gotten his height. When he was twelve and one of her blue spells had gone on too long, he'd taken her to Doc Thomas at the fort against her will. The doc had asked her a lot of questions and recommended a rest at an asylum in Prescott. She hadn't gone and she had gotten over her spell. But ever since, Joe had been leery of her, his own ma.

"Are you going to behave?" he repeated.

"You'd steal flies from a blind spider, wouldn't you?" she asked, stalling for time to think. That devil needed killing, but not in front of Joe. Now that she'd had time to think it over, she realized it wouldn't have worked very well if she'd killed him in broad daylight.

"Ma . . ."

"All right."

"You're not lying to me, are you, Ma?"

"Ah don't lie."

Joe shook his head sadly.

"At least not much," she rushed to reassure him. "Not about important things. Well, sometimes Ah have to lie, darlin'."

"Ma . . ." Joe sighed, then stuffed his gun back into his holster. "Then get yourself a nap."

"You tell anyone about this and Ah'll take a whip to you, you heah me?" she called after him.

"I'm not stupid enough to turn my own mother over to the law, and that's what I'd be doing. It's against the law to shoot at people. In case you forgot."

"And . . . we got our pride to worry about."

"Pride," he snorted. "That's about all we do worry about is our damned pride."

Joe scowled at her again, and for just a second she thought she might know who his father was, but the look passed . . . and so did her near revelation. He stomped out of the room and closed the door.

She might never know who his pa was, she thought sadly. She had pitched one of her fits when they'd found the baby drowned. She'd tried to kill Denny. Apparently he'd used that to get them to take her to an insane asylum. She hadn't even known she was in one for over a year. And somehow, without her even being aware of it, she'd gotten pregnant while she was there and carried Joe to full term.

Her hands shook so hard she clasped them together and hid them in the folds of her brown skirt. She started to feel dizzy and realized she was rocking back and forth. She forced herself to stop. Her mind seemed to remember that Joe had said something important about the man, about his not being Denny because of some discrepancy. Whatever it was had slipped away.

It amazed Samantha that someone had shot at Steve Sheridan, who swore he'd never been in the small settlement before. Marshal Daley, groggy from his siesta, his hair standing up in back, asked questions and dispatched men to search the two-story buildings across the street. They looked everywhere for a lone gunman, but no one seemed to know where the shots had come from. It had all happened too fast.

"Well, stay out of trouble," Daley said to Sheridan, as if it had somehow been his fault.

"Good idea," Steve said, a sardonic gleam of amusement in his hazel eyes. Samantha smiled, and Steve saw it and winked at her. A warm feeling spread out from her middle. She felt young and pretty for the first time in ages.

In front of Owen Parker's hotel, Samantha stopped and turned to Ramon.

"Would you go to the general store and see if the supplies I ordered before we left came in?" she asked.

"Can I go with him, Mama?" Nicholas begged.

"*May* I go with him. No. You stay with me. Elunami can go with Ramon. She needs to buy some personal things," she said, reaching into her reticule and pulling out a twenty-dollar bill. She slipped it into Elunami's hand. "That's for letting Nicholas ride on your horse."

"I cannot take money for that."

"Then take it as a gift. You'll need it to start a new wardrobe, since I had Ramon bury yours."

Elunami nodded. "Thank you."

"You're welcome. If the supplies are in," she told Ramon, "ask him to put them on my account—if I still have one."

Steve helped Nicholas down, and Elunami rode on toward the general store. Ramon walked along beside her.

A hundred or so yards beyond Elunami and Ramon, a group of fast-riding horsemen galloped into the town from the east. Samantha recognized Ham Russell at the head of the half dozen ex-soldiers and Indian scouts hired supposedly to protect Chila Dart's stock from rustlers and hungry Apache sneaking off the reservation at San Carlos. Samantha hadn't approved of the men, and she'd voiced her opinion, but Chila was adamant. She feared the rustlers and Indians more. Samantha personally thought Russell and his companions were worse, but without proof she'd had to hold her tongue.

Sheridan's lips twitched as if the very sight of the men riding toward him was distasteful. He stepped back into the shade, hooked his thumbs into his gun belt, and leaned against the hotel wall. Nicholas pressed against Samantha, his eyes pleading with her to let him stay near her.

Fifty feet away, Elunami stopped her pinto in front of the general store. Ramon turned to watch the approaching men.

When he was about ten feet from Elunami, Ham Russell suddenly reined his horse; his companions slowed and came to a stop. Samantha would have been frightened if she were suddenly confronted by them, but Elunami held her pinto steady. Russell spoke to his men and urged his horse forward, to within touching distance of the young Indian woman.

Ham Russell was a big man with red hair and a red beard that had been parted at midchin and worked into two six-inch braids reaching to his chest. He had a mean temper, which had gotten him into trouble a number of times in Picket Post. Last year he'd killed a man over a woman. There had been a trial, but somehow Russell had gotten off.

Samantha eased her hand into her pocket to feel for her revolver.

Russell spoke to Elunami in a low tone that did not carry to Samantha. She saw Elunami shake her head no. Russell spoke again, eliciting another no. The girl's resistance was apparent and would have been sufficient to stop a normal man.

Samantha had never seen a man accost a woman in Picket Post, unless she was one of the prostitutes who worked at the saloons. Even then the men were friendly, since they wanted to stay on the good side of the working girls.

Russell reached for Elunami's reins. She tried to back her horse away, but Russell was quick and strong. Laughing, he turned and started to lead her and her horse away.

Steve Sheridan still leaned against the hotel. His relationship with Elunami was supposedly of short duration, but Samantha couldn't imagine his just standing there and letting a man like Ham Russell lead the girl away. Before she could protest, however, Ramon yelled, "Hold it, *Señor*." On foot and at a serious disadvantage, he lunged forward and tried to grab Elunami's reins.

Russell lifted the reins over his head and out of Ramon's reach. "Well, if it ain't the sheepherder."

"Leave her alone!"

"This ain't your girl, sheepherder."

Ramon swung his fist and missed. "I said leave her alone!" he yelled.

Russell laughed. "Who the hell's gonna make me? It sure ain't you, sheepherder."

Ramon lunged at Ham Russell, trying to grab his leg and unseat him. Letting go of the girl's reins, Russell kicked Ramon's arm and reined his horse to the side. He backed the horse out of Ramon's reach, then jerked the coiled reata off the side of his saddle and swung the loop over his head.

Ramon staggered back, bellowing his rage as the loop settled over his head and shoulders. Before he could throw the rope off, Russell jerked it taut, wrapped the end of it around his saddle horn, turned his horse, and spurred him hard. The horse screamed and plunged forward.

Ramon tried to run, but his legs couldn't stay under him; his body was moving too fast. He fell, and Russell dragged him through the loose, powdery dirt, which rose in a cloud behind him.

"Mama!" Nicholas yelped in outrage.

It had all happened too fast for Samantha. Glaring at Sheridan, she shoved Nicholas into the hotel, shut the door, reached into her pocket, and pulled out her revolver. Sheridan stepped close to her and clamped his hand over it.

"Let go! Ramon works for me. I'm not going to stand by and see him killed!"

"You want to be killed instead?"

"I'm not afraid, like some people!"

"I'll take care of it," he growled, his eyes blazing at her rebuke. Samantha let him pry the gun out of her hand. He stuck it in his belt and strode toward his own horse. He took the reata off the side of the saddle, shook it out, and twirled it over his head. As Russell and his pounding horse neared, Sheridan threw out his reata. It soared up slowly, almost too slowly, and fell abruptly, then settled over Russell's head and shoulders. Steve anchored his end of the reata around the nearest support post and held tight.

As Russell rode past he was jerked out of the saddle, but his right foot caught in the stirrup. Rather than see the man's leg torn off, Steve let him go. His reata snaked fast around the post and jerked free. Ramon and Russell skidded past behind the running horse. At least Ramon, farther back, was safer. Russell was so close to the horse's flashing hooves that he was in danger every time the horse's legs flew back.

Before Steve could reach his horse, Elunami galloped past on her pony. Riding alongside the runaway horse, she edged her pony close, caught the flying reins, and hauled up short on them.

About a hundred feet from where Samantha watched, the horse finally stopped. Dust settled and Samantha saw that Ramon lay motionless on the rutted road. Russell untangled his foot from the stirrup, stood up, and walked over to Elunami's pinto.

"Dang it, I knew when the chips were down, a fellow redhead would pitch in," he said, wiping dust off his face with both hands. Russell had a loud voice when he wanted to use it. Now it was clearly audible to Samantha.

"You'da been any quicker, sunshine, I wouldn't even a got dirty." People standing in the doorways laughed.

"If not for Ramon dragging behind your horse, I'd have used my quirt on it," Elunami declared hotly.

"What's yore name, purty thang?"

Elunami ignored Russell and walked her horse back to where Ramon lay motionless on the ground.

"That reminds me," Russell growled. He strode past Elunami and kicked Ramon in the side. Ramon coiled forward in pain. Russell drew back to kick again.

Elunami yelled, kneed her horse around Ramon, right at Russell, who yelped in surprise and stepped quickly out of her way. She sped past him, turned her horse, and, when she reached Russell's side again, launched herself onto his back.

Steve shook his head in disgust and started forward. He'd hoped he wouldn't have to get any more involved than he already was in the business of this town and this woman.

Ham felt the girl land on him, scratching and biting and screaming. At first he was too tickled to protect himself from her. He laughed and tried to throw her off, but, like a small maddened animal, the little wench hung on to his neck with one arm and punched him with the other. She was mad, but she wasn't hurting him. He kind of enjoyed having her all over him this a-way. She felt as alive and exciting as anything he'd ever touched.

Then she punched him in the eye, and that did hurt. Smarting with the sting of it, he jerked her off him, grabbed her arms, and pinned her to the ground.

"Let me go!" she yelled.

She was about the prettiest girl he'd ever seen—fiery and lithe as a kitten. "Letting you get away unkissed would be a crime, sunshine." She struggled wildly, but Russell pinned her hands over her head and her body to the ground and kissed her.

The girl bucked and kicked, but he kissed her until he was through kissing her. Finally he raised his head. The girl spat in his face.

Ham Russell laughed, sat up, wiped her spittle off his face, and licked every drop of it off his hand. The girl stopped struggling to watch him. When he was finished, he leapt to his feet and raised his arms over his head in the fashion of a prizefighter. His men hooted and hollered at his victory.

Ham strutted over to his horse, untied the rope that still held the little one-armed Mexican, mounted, and turned the horse as if he meant to ride right over the kid. Ham hadn't intended to, but his move scared the hell out of the girl and caused the Mexican kid to scramble up and run like a pig afire.

The girl cursed him in Spanish, and Ham grinned. Coming from her sweet lips, it sounded like love words. He would run this little turd down and then come back for her.

Steve drew his revolver and stepped into the deeply rutted road. He would have stepped in sooner, but it had been apparent to him that Russell was no match for Elunami. She was a feisty little thing; she had been all over Russell. Steve had been more concerned about Russell's companions, but they'd been content to shout encouragement to their comrade.

Unexpectedly Russell changed direction slightly, riding right at Steve as if he weren't going to stop for anything.

Steve lifted his pistol and aimed it at the big man's head. "Hold it!" Steve shouted.

His stern command so thrilled Samantha she held her breath. To her immense relief, Russell reined his horse.

"Mr. Sheridan—" Samantha started.

Steve raised his left hand—and she stopped.

"Got myself a challenge here," Russell said to no one in particular. "Hey, stranger, you know the definition of stupid?"

"Yeah, it's a cowardly cuss like you picking on women and children."

"No," Russell growled, "it's pointing a gun you ain't got the guts to use!"

Steve's gun flashed; Russell's hat flew off his head. "No," Steve drawled, "it's talking when you should be listening."

Before Russell could react, one of his men growled, "Hey, Dart's coming!"

Out of the corner of his eye, Steve saw a man step out of the doorway of the Rawson Hotel and walk across the road toward them. Russell let his hand relax and fall to his side.

Samantha let out her breath. She'd never been so happy to see Joe Dart in her life. The shy towhead was a capable overseer, even though at times he acted as if he had the weight of the world on his shoulders.

"What's going on here, boys?" Joe asked, glancing from Sheridan, gun in hand, to Ham Russell.

A small group of riders appeared at the east end of town, raising a dust cloud. "Cavalry's coming," one of Russell's men said to no one in particular.

Ham spat in irritation. Roy Bowles had a tendency to say things that were perfectly clear to anyone with eyes or ears, but Ham had never been able to get him to stop. He and Roy had been scouts for the army until Ham got tired of stacking dead Indians in wagons. He didn't mind tracking 'em or killing 'em, but he got real tired of picking 'em up after they'd been dead for a day or so.

"Those scouts look hot as I feel," Ham said, wiping his wet face and picking up his hat to examine the hole in it.

Steve glanced at Elunami to see if these might be the men who'd killed the old men in her party, but her back was to him. The leader of the group wore full uniform and captain's bars. The army scouts behind him wore civilian clothes. If these were the ones tracking her down, they might recognize her in spite of her changed appearance. And if they did, he might not be able to save her this time.

Samantha was glad to see the cavalry patrol. As the soldiers rode toward her party, Marshal Daley stepped out of the jail and headed toward them. The soldiers started past the hotel, but Rathwick, the officer in charge, recognized her and threw up his gauntleted hand.

"What's going on here?" he demanded of Sheridan, who still pointed his revolver at Russell.

Russell rubbed his head and gestured at Sheridan. "That man tried to kill me, Captain Rathwick."

Rathwick turned toward Sheridan. "That true?"

"Not yet," Sheridan said mildly, amusement twinkling in his eyes.

Daley stopped beside Samantha. "Reckon this is my baili-wick, Captain," he said grumpily.

"Daley," the captain said, nodding to him, "did you see what happened here?"

Daley frowned and turned to Steve. "Is this a new ruckus or more of the first one?"

Steve pointed to Russell. "He roped Ramon and dragged him behind his horse. I stopped him."

"Ramon, are you causing trouble again?" Daley demanded, scowling angrily at the dirty, bruised youngster.

Ramon uttered a string of Mexican oaths. Furious and not trying to hide it, he looked like he might pounce on Daley and throttle him with his one good hand.

"Ham Russell started the trouble, Marshal," Samantha interjected firmly.

A murmur of agreement went up from the crowd that had drifted over from the bear and bull fights. Daley scowled at Sheridan. "Well, Mr. Sheridan, I'm not surprised. I knew you'd be a constant source of trouble for me."

Captain Rathwick rode forward until he was about two yards away. "What are you doing in these parts, Mr. Sheridan?"

"I didn't realize you had a dog in this fight," Sheridan said, bristling.

"It may or may not be my fight, but I have a right to know what you're doing here."

"Is that a formal inquiry, Captain?"

"I can make it so," Rathwick said, pulling in his chin.

Sheridan raised the eyebrow with the cowlick. "Fine. Why don't you submit it in writing, then?" He sheathed the gun, turned his broad back, and walked into the hotel.

Rathwick dismounted and started after Sheridan. Samantha stepped in front of him. "Captain."

Rathwick removed his hat. Silver hairs gleamed among the dark brown hair, flattened under the sweaty hatband. "Mrs. Forrester . . ." The pinpoint pupils of his angry blue eyes widened slightly as he focused on her.

"Mr. Sheridan saved the lives of my party and myself. I'm extremely grateful to him," she said, loud enough for all to hear.

"In that case, Mrs. Forrester, so am I. I guess a man with credentials like that doesn't have to be civil. But I wouldn't advise him to make a habit of being insolent," he growled at Sheridan's receding back.

"What brings you to Picket Post, Captain?"

"Looking for an Indian woman wanted by the military—Who's the girl?" Rathwick asked, nodding at Elunami a few feet away. Sheridan stopped at the hotel door and leaned against it. Samantha hesitated, remembering what Steve had said about Elunami being attacked by soldiers.

"Her name is . . . Tristera Rodriguez," she said. "She's Ramon's sister."

"She looks Indian to me."

"You've seen a number of redheaded Indians, I suppose?" she asked, raising a skeptical eyebrow.

Rathwick felt his face grow hot. Samantha Forrester was a woman he admired. It stung to have her speak to him in that way. The girl he'd thought an Indian looked up at him, stared unabashedly into his eyes. She seemed to take him in, to see him completely and thoroughly, all the way down to his soul. Deep in his chest, something quivered. In spite of his discomfort, his gaze riveted on her. Finally she released him and turned back to her brother. Unencumbered by her disconcerting gaze, he saw a wild mane of shiny, auburn hair and a slim waist. Most Indian women were thick around the middle. Mrs. Forrester was no doubt right about her.

Reluctantly Rathwick turned back to Samantha.

"We rode past your house yesterday, Mrs. Forrester," he said, his tone softening. "I . . . was sorry to find you gone."

"I was in Phoenix to see my brothers. On the way home we were attacked by bandits. Mr. Sheridan ran them off and helped us get my wounded engineer into town."

"Were any of the bandits Indians?"

"I don't know. They wore masks," Samantha said.

"Perhaps we'd better take a look. Maybe we'll run into Wovoka."

Samantha knew he was being facetious. Some laughed about Wovoka, an Indian prophet in Nevada, but his Ghost Dances had upset a lot of people. Wovoka had sent messengers to all the tribes telling them that if they danced the Ghost Dances every night, everything they had lost to the white man would be returned to them, including the buffalo and their dead loved ones, in all their former youth, strength, and glory. The tribes had taken up the Ghost Dances as if they were a panacea. On the reservations, Indians danced all night. Many whites interpreted these as war dances and became uneasy. Samantha did not. She thought them harmless, but it saddened her that the Indians needed those empty rituals so desperately.

"I'd appreciate it if you could save my palace car."

He frowned. "Did you notify the railroad?"

"Yes."

"Where's it stranded?"

"At the water tank south of here."

Rathwick knew the place. He'd been chasing Indians around this desert for almost twenty years. He had helped Cook run the Apache to ground in 1886.

Rathwick frowned. He hated to leave town with Samantha here. He admired her and had been trying to court her, but his work kept him constantly on patrol. He and two hundred soldiers were responsible for this entire southeast corner of the territory.

Reluctantly he mounted and kicked his horse into a gallop. His thirsty scouts gazed longingly at the saloons as they rode past.

Samantha prayed they reached her train before the bandits came back.

Crows Walking heard the Indian agent's voice asking for him. His sister, Uncheedah, explained that Crows Walking sat with the Great Mystery, but Chandler, the agent for the Papago Indian Reservation, did not seem impressed.

"When can I speak to him?" he asked.

Crows Walking visualized his sister's noncommittal shrug. "When he is finished," she murmured in her soft voice.

Crows Walking had long ago learned that white men did not care about the Great Mystery. They trampled his creation into dust. They killed his birds, animals, and men with equal disinterest. They would not be impressed that an old Indian shaman sat each morning and night to open his head, so the Great Mystery could speak to him.

His concentration broken, Crows Walking struggled to stand. Holding on to the wall until he felt strength return to his numb feet, he called through the canvas curtain that divided the small adobe house. "I will see him."

Most nights he walked into the desert to sit with the Great Mystery. But last night he had fallen asleep. He'd had to ask the

Great Mystery to forgive him for his lapse. *I promise I will sit with Thee all night when darkness falls.*

Chandler looked robust and sturdy. Crows Walking did not begrudge Chandler the good food that had contributed to the paunch around the man's waist, but he did not like him. He knew Chandler did not like Crows Walking, either. At the sight of him, Chandler's eyes narrowed with suspicion. White men all looked a great deal alike to Crows Walking. They had hard eyes and thin, hairy faces. He did not trust them.

Crows Walking stepped outside. "Arden," he said.

Arden Chandler had to fight his body, which wanted to shrink away from the smelly old shaman. He clamped his jaws together and refused to step back. Chandler knew Crows Walking used his given name purposefully out of disrespect. The Indians knew he wanted to be called Mr. Chandler, so they always called him Arden. He refused to give them the satisfaction of complaining, but he didn't like it.

"Crows Walking," he said, nodding.

"What brings the Great White Father's Indian agent to this humble adobe house?"

"A favor I would ask of you."

"A favor?"

Chandler could practically feel the vibration of the old man's distrust as he fingered the wisps of hair at the end of his long white braids. Crows Walking's skin looked like leather that had wrinkled in spite of being stretched over a skull too large for it. His deep-set eyes, opaque as tar, hid whatever went on behind that wide Indian face.

"I sent for your adopted son, but he has not come."

"Ahhhh."

Chandler frowned. "Is he here? I would speak to him."

"He is gone."

"He left without seeing me?"

Chandler felt such frustration he could hardly contain it. He worked hard trying to make their lot more bearable, and they hated him for it.

"Will he be back?"

Although Steve had visited Crows Walking just the day before, the old man shrugged and said, "It has been five years since the last visit. As children get older . . ."

He did not say that since the white Indian agent had asked for him, he might never come back. Indians "invited" to appear before the Indian agent were frequently turned over to the military. Such men disappeared or were imprisoned or killed. Indians summoned by the Indian agent often slipped away into the desert to take their chances there. His adopted son, Steve Sheridan, had refused to do that. He had wanted to call on the Indian agent, but Crows Walking had prevailed upon him to leave. His staying could have brought trouble down on all their heads. The military looked for reasons to kill them.

"Do you know where I might find him? Where he lives?"

Crows Walking shook his head. Chandler knew it was a wasted effort. Even if the old fool knew, he'd never tell. Indians prided themselves on what they didn't say.

Back at the cottage, Chandler tramped across the porch and slammed the door. Selena was at her examining table, wrapping a bandage around an Indian boy's injured foot. She looked up from her work. "I suppose we can always get another door."

"Sorry," he muttered.

She finished with the boy. His mother stepped forward to take him. "*Muchas gracias, Señora* Chandler."

"You're very welcome, Brown Deer. Keep the foot dry. If he gets it wet, bring him back and I'll rewrap it."

"*Sí.*"

The woman carried the boy away. Selena walked inside and stopped near her husband. "Well, did you find him?"

"He's gone. I scared him away by sending for him."

Relief flooded through her. Selena bit back the words that formed in her mind and fairly ached to come out her mouth.

Why don't you give up? You promised me you would give up!

She knew he wouldn't, though. He was obsessed. Because of a remark about a cowlick in an eyebrow, he thought Sheridan was the one he wanted. He probably wasn't, but that wouldn't stop Arden. He had chased flimsier figments of his imagination through good weather and bad, a raging flood, even a blizzard one time. She prayed daily that he wouldn't find what he searched for. Maybe God had answered her prayers—

A knock at the front door startled them both. Chandler turned, saw it was a soldier, and motioned him inside.

"Message from the commandant," the young soldier said, offering a leather mail pouch with one hand and wiping sweat off his face with the other.

Selena prayed their urgent requests for more rations had been approved. The drought had severely affected the amount of food the Indians could grow. "I'll get you a drink," she said, going outside for the clay water *bolo*, kept cool by the desert breezes.

Chandler unsnapped the flap of the pouch proffered by the soldier, opened it, and took out an envelope sealed with wax bearing the general's stamp. He opened the envelope and pulled out a letter written in General Ashland's hand.

Chandler
Be on the lookout for a Hopi Indian woman named Elunami who escaped from custody this morning. She is armed, dangerous, and wanted by the government dead or alive. She is dressed in white ceremonial buckskins, white head-dress, and is young and attractive—for an Indian. This is classified information, for your eyes alone. If you find her, secure her by whatever means necessary and send word immediately. Destroy this transmittal at once.

General R.J. Ashland, Commandant,
Fort Thomas, Arizona Territory

Selena Chandler watched her husband's expression change as he read the letter.

"What is it?" she asked. "Are they sending more food?"

"No," he said tiredly. "Just a letter from General Ashland." Chandler held the letter over the table, struck a match, and set fire to it. When it had burned, he scooped the ashes into the pouch, closed it, and gave it back to the hot-faced young soldier to return to the general.

A girl dressed that distinctively should be easy to spot. Ashland's men had probably found her by now.

CHAPTER THREE

Elunami, Samantha, and Ramon, scraped raw on his chin and left cheek, followed Sheridan into the hotel. The dimly lit lobby appeared deserted. Outside, Samantha could see Owen Parker, the hotel owner, talking to a group of men.

"Did you recognize any of those soldiers?" Sheridan asked Elunami.

"They wore soldier boots, but they were not the ones."

"I thought not." Sheridan nodded his satisfaction. The girl walked to the window; Ramon followed her.

On impulse, Samantha asked the question that had been on her mind since Sheridan had ridden up to her palace car.

"Is Elunami your woman?"

Steve looked at Samantha in surprise. He was not accustomed to such bluntness in a white woman. "I found her a few miles before I found you. She was alone and needed help."

"Because of helping us, you've made an enemy of Ham Russell and Captain Rathwick," Samantha pointed out.

"Don't feel bad about it," Steve drawled. "I've been making friends and enemies for years without your help."

"Would you accompany us to my home? I'll pay you well." Sheridan frowned. "Where do you live?"

"Ten miles east of here."

"Mr. Forrester might want to send someone out for you."

"Mr. Forrester died three years ago."

Steve wished he could see Samantha Forrester with more clarity. Her personality dazzled him; it kept him from seeing her clearly, or from recognizing what he did see. He had the feeling that her every emotion, even the slightest flicker, showed in her eyes and in her mobile face, if only he could see it through the shimmer she caused in his brain. She had the kind of beauty that made men blind and foolish. He'd seen Dart, Rathwick, and even Ham Russell responding to her. They all wanted to look good in her eyes. But he had enough worries as it was. He didn't need another.

"I'd like to help you, but I'm not going in that direction."

Disappointment showed clearly on Samantha's face. Steve took some pleasure from that, even if it didn't mean what he might prefer it meant.

She turned toward the hotel. "Well . . . thank you again for saving us from those bandits."

"My pleasure, ma'am." Steve touched the brim of his dusty hat and strode purposefully away from her. Only a few steps past the bank, Marshal Daley pried himself loose from the side of the building and fell into step with him.

"I didn't want to make a fuss back there, but you look to me like a man riding away from something."

"That's quite an observation, Marshal. Do you mind if I ask how you came to that conclusion?"

"I don't mind a bit if you're testy," he said jovially. "I'm used to irritating folks. That's what this town pays me for."

Steve grinned and shook his head. He untied his horse's reins from the post and turned to Daley, waiting.

Daley took a piece of paper out of his pocket and waved it at Steve. "I just got a wire from the fort asking me to keep a lookout for an Indian woman, probably the one Rathwick was asking about."

"Did the wire say what they want her for?"

"I haven't seen that girl who rode in with Mrs. Forrester before today."

"Shouldn't be too hard for a cavalry patrol to spot an Indian woman riding around alone," Steve said. Something odd was definitely going on around the girl, and it looked bigger than the random killing of a few Indians.

"What are your plans, Sheridan?"

"Headed for Waco. I've been hired to build a house there."

"That sounds like a straight answer for a change, so I guess I can give one, too. They didn't say what they wanted her for, just told me to detain her and send them a wire." Daley touched his hat and sauntered back toward the jail. Steve mounted and headed toward the livery stable. He would feed his mare and then himself, and be on his way.

With Steve Sheridan gone about his own business, Samantha let Owen Parker know she was waiting to register. He left the group of men he'd been talking to and walked inside.

Parker had a large bulbous nose and sagging jowls. His chin was weak and disappeared too quickly into his neck, which was dominated by a large Adam's apple. Another man with his features might be ugly, but Owen was blessed with the warmth and vitality of his Greek ancestors on his mother's side of the family. His many kindnesses to Samantha and Nicholas had started the first day she'd ridden into town and had not stopped yet. This would be the test, though.

"I hate to put you on the spot, Owen, but I need two rooms for the night."

"I guess you've noticed the town is not exactly on its best behavior," Owen said, rubbing his hand from his forehead to the crown of his bald head.

"I wouldn't ask, except Nicholas is tired . . ." Samantha had held up through everything else that had happened, but if he refused her request for rooms, she might humiliate herself by dissolving into tears.

"Your two usual rooms be all right, my dear, or do you need more?"

"Is this going to cause you trouble?"

Owen looked up from where he was already writing her name into the register. "I may be an old man, but I still decide who I rent my rooms to."

The tension that had been building in her relaxed a little. "Thank you, Owen," she said gratefully. "I won't forget your help."

He passed her the keys. "I'll carry the boy."

"You don't have to do that," she said.

"I know." He looked willing to do whatever he could to make up to her for the rest of the town, and she was touched by his concern.

"Thank you, Owen."

"I'm stronger than I look."

Samantha laughed. "And stubborner. I'm not ready to go upstairs yet."

She walked back to where she had left Nicholas asleep on the sofa, out of the sun. His usually pale cheeks were pink with sunburn. She bent down and kissed his forehead, which was warm enough to cause her stomach to knot with fear.

On impulse, she walked out the door and over to where Elunami stood on the sidewalk outside the hotel. The girl was not her problem, but perhaps . . .

The still, humid air felt hot and muggy, the way it did before a storm. White-topped, gray-bottomed clouds had piled in, cutting off the sun.

"Where will you go now?" Samantha asked her.

Elunami shrugged. She looked tired and hungry, but whatever her pain, she seemed determined to endure it in silence.

"I've already told everyone you're Ramon's sister. It would look odd if you just rode away. Would you like to stop with us for a while? I need help with Nicholas. You wouldn't have to do much. And I'd like another woman around."

Elunami stared at Samantha for a moment, sifting through her words to confirm their sincerity. The kind words weakened her, seemed to remove the barrier that kept her apart from her pain. Now her soul felt weary. So much sadness waited within for her attention. It pressed down on her.

"I . . . know not."

"Then come home with me. You'll be safe there. I need your help, Elu—Tristera. You don't have to stay long, if you don't want to. But if you ride into the desert alone, the cavalry patrol might suspect you're the girl they're looking for."

Elunami nodded. She had no place to go back to.

"Good. It is important now that we call you Tristera. We mustn't forget."

"I will remember," she said, thinking that perhaps a new name would give her a new beginning.

"Ramon, please take Tristera's horse to the livery stable and have them care for it. Then you get some rest."

"Sí, señora." Ramon stood up, took the pony's reins, and limped away.

"Come, I'll take you up to your room," Samantha said, feeling more hopeful than she had in weeks.

"They will let me stay here?" Elunami asked, frowning.

"Owen has never questioned who I bring with me."

Inside the hotel, Samantha picked up the small bag she had packed, and Owen Parker carried Nicholas upstairs.

In their bedroom, Samantha undressed Nicholas and covered him with a thin sheet. Then she turned to Elunami. "You can take the next room." She walked to the connecting door and unlocked it. "Nicholas will sleep for a while. Would you like to go downstairs and have dinner with me?"

"No . . . thank you."

Samantha leaned down to kiss her son's sleeping face. Dirt smudged his cheek, which was hot to the touch. Sand from his dark hair fell onto the clean bed sheet. Except for his thinness, he looked so much like Lance her heart constricted.

"I'll get us some clean clothes and send supper up for you and Nicholas."

Elunami nodded. Apparently it was important for the *señora* to distribute food. It would do no harm. Perhaps the boy would eat it.

Chila got off the bed and walked to the mirror. She scrutinized herself carefully, patted her hair, lifted her shoulders, and tried to carry herself in such a way that the loose, sagging skin of her throat was minimized. The skin had wrinkled as if it had somehow come loose from whatever was underneath it. If not for that unfortunate condition, she might easily pass for thirty-five.

She had decided to buy a gun, so she wouldn't have to depend on Joe being around or not missing his.

Chila walked through the lobby, smiling and nodding to folks who spoke to her. She was proud of her ability to carry on as if nothing untoward had happened to her. Most women, if they'd seen the devil, would be laid up for a month. But not her. Still, just the thought of seeing that monster rattled her insides.

The sun hid behind thin clouds, but its brightness shone through with such intensity that her eyes hurt and her head ached dully. At the general store, clutching her reticule and fan in one hand, she pushed the door open and stepped inside.

"Chila!"

Chila recognized Samantha's voice and looked quickly around the dimly lit general store.

"Aftahnoon, darlin'," she called out to her. Samantha put down an undergarment she'd been examining and stepped around the display table to greet Chila.

"Afternoon. I'm glad I ran into you, Chila. I'm sure you weren't aware of this, but Ham Russell insulted Ramon's sister and almost killed Ramon."

"He did? Why, darlin', Ah didn't know that."

"I was hoping you might have a talk with him . . ."

"Well, of course. Mr. Russell knows better than that."

"Otherwise someone is going to get hurt."

"Ah don't know what could have gotten into him. Ah declare, there is so much meanness in the world," she said, fanning herself rapidly and looking out the window at the darkening sky. "Looks like one of them nasty old blue northers coming up, too," she said, fanning herself. "You've been away, haven't you, darlin'? Somewhere with better weather, Ah hope."

Samantha nodded, wondering why Chila looked a little distraught. "We just got back from Phoenix."

"And how is Nicholas? Ah hope the rigors of travel haven't aggravated his consumption."

"Nicholas is fine, thank you."

"Oh, Ah'm so very glad to hear it. Ah just hate to think of that poor sweet child suffering from the pestilence of that horrid disease."

"Chila, people are cutting us on the street. Someone even shot at us. Do you have any idea what started this?"

At that moment Claire Colson stepped into the store, closed the door behind her, and looked from Chila to Samantha. From the indignant look in her eyes, Samantha thought she had found the source of her trouble.

Ever since Claire had learned that Nicholas had consumption, she had been offering advice. Last month Claire had been convinced that consumption could be cured by purging all melancholy from the mind. She had assured Samantha that a happy frame of mind was the way to health. Now, however, she looked at Samantha as if she had brought a trainload of lepers into town.

"Afternoon, Claire. I wanted to thank you. I read the inspirational article you gave me a few weeks ago. It was quite refreshing. You do still have faith in it, don't you?"

Claire Colson cleared her throat. "If consumption is a mystic visitation from the Almighty, as I strongly suspect, then one should keep a jovial mood throughout. Anything the Lord visits upon us should be received with good grace. But that is not to say we should spread disease willy-nilly. I firmly believe that all consumptives should be isolated in sanitoriums to protect innocent citizens."

"I doubt you would think so if your son suffered from it."

"I should subscribe to that remedy no matter who had it," said Claire, huffily, "any right-thinking citizen would do no less. It is unconscionable to knowingly spread a fatal disease. I would seek out the most knowledgeable physicians in the country and follow their advice to the letter, which I am quite sure would include a lengthy stay in a sanitorium."

"I did—and discovered there aren't three knowledgeable physicians in the country who agree on any one regimen of treatment. There aren't even three who agree if the disease is contagious or not. My physician assured me that if we took certain precautions, there was no danger. And, as you can see, I have not been infected. And no one could be closer to Nicholas than I. If you'll excuse me, I have to get back to my son."

Samantha paid for her purchases and left. There was so much

she wanted to say to the woman, but she knew nothing would be gained by arguing. Too little was known about consumption. People believed whatever they chose.

Chila waited until the store was empty. Then she approached the gun counter.

"Decided on something?" the clerk asked.

"Ah'd like a .45, darlin'," she said.

"This for you, Chila?"

"Are you still bald, darlin'?" He laughed so hard he couldn't continue for a moment.

"Well, that's a pretty big gun for a little bitty woman like yourself. It might kick you back against the wall."

Chila smiled archly. "Ah'm not going to be shooting at mice, darlin'. Ah want to stop what Ah hit."

"Well, this .45'll do it," he said, taking a gun out of the case. "Make a hole big enough to walk a dog through."

"Ah'll need a box of bullets, too, darlin'."

Samantha stripped down to her undergarments and washed with a small bar of peppermint castile soap she took from her valise. She dressed her hair as best she could, given the heat, then put on the clean undergarments and gown she'd just bought.

Downstairs, she checked the register and saw that Steve Sheridan had not taken a room. She walked to the hotel dining room and looked in. He was seated at a table by the window.

Samantha was torn. She wanted to talk with Sheridan, but she had the feeling that if she sat down to eat Mary Francis would not have another customer until she left. The clock over the registration counter said it was only four-thirty—early enough that Mary Francis could recover with the late crowd.

Samantha walked into the dining room and angled toward Steve Sheridan's table. He looked sleek and clean and richly masculine in a black frock coat and faultlessly tailored trousers. His shirt and cravat were silk, she noticed. That must have been his satchel behind Tristera's horse.

He looked up, saw her, and for one instant a light she'd seen in the eyes of other men shone in his eyes. It was quickly masked, but she had seen it. Satisfaction quickened her heartbeat.

"Good evening."

He stood up and she caught the faint scent of bay rum. "Mrs. Forrester . . ."

"I was wondering if I might join you for dinner?" It was bold of her, she knew, but Samantha had no patience with rules that served only to place obstacles in her path.

His eyes gleamed with curiosity and amusement, but he pulled out a chair for her. "My pleasure, ma'am."

Samantha picked up the menu and glanced over it. She chose the fried chicken, potatoes, and gravy. Mary Francis raised her own chickens and browned her gravy perfectly.

"What are you doing in Arizona, Mr. Sheridan?"

"Leaving as fast as I can."

"You must be a very bad carpenter."

Sheridan chuckled. "You have an interesting mind, Mrs. Forrester."

"You must have come here for some reason."

"Passing through." Sheridan lifted his cup. Mary Francis walked over with the coffeepot.

"How's the coffee?" she asked.

"A mite puny," Sheridan said, grinning. "I like my coffee to kick up in the middle."

Mary Francis poured coffee into his cup. "A blamed Texan." She walked away shaking her head.

Sheridan's grin caused an odd sensation in Samantha's body. A sudden wave of heat warmed her belly, low down. Ignoring it as best she could, Samantha smiled and asked, "Headed for?"

Sheridan lifted an eyebrow at her persistence. "Waco."

Samantha was fascinated by the almost sinister masculinity she sensed in him. His forehead was broad and high, his hair so black it looked blue in the light. Even Lance's hair, which was considered black, had reddish highlights.

Except for Lance and Chane, her two favorites in the world, she'd never seen another man quite like Steve Sheridan, so contained and direct—and yet somehow mocking and amused—as if he didn't quite believe life was worth working up a sweat over. Yet when confronted he would engage and fight; he'd proven that this afternoon.

She'd never seen a man with a cowlick in an eyebrow before, either. The hair swirled in the middle as if a dust devil had set down there.

"Where did you come from?"

His eyes filled with that slightly mocking gleam of light, as if he might not answer. Again she felt that odd sensation in her stomach. "San Francisco originally. I took Calico—my horse— off the train in Phoenix a few days ago to visit . . . ah . . . someone."

"I was in Phoenix last week. We just came from there."

"It's a big town."

"What does Waco have that we don't?"

"Didn't make the decision to go there on quite that basis," he said, grinning and leaning back in his chair.

"You're a cynic, Mr. Sheridan."

"I allow myself that privilege. I've spent most of my twenty-eight years keeping myself safe from women and their intentions. I'm not willing to give up that habit."

"A bit melodramatic." Samantha's laughter turned to a frown. "Is this just to keep from answering my question?"

"I'm going to Waco to build a house for a man threatening to pay me a lot of money."

"You really are a builder?"

"You didn't believe me?"

"What kind of houses do you build?"

"Generally, expensive houses for men with no taste. The one in Waco is different. He wants a limestone castle."

"Italian?" Samantha asked, thinking of the beautiful Italian castles she'd seen on her grand tour.

Sheridan grinned; pure joy twinkled out of his silky khaki eyes. "German. A German Rhineland castle with a round turret." He began to describe the floor plan.

Samantha was thrilled by his enthusiasm. Speaking about the work he did, he became more animated. His ardor reminded her that it had been a long time since she'd had a conversation with a man excited by anything. Farmers and ranchers seemed to become one with the land they worked. They were more like stones than men. Steve Sheridan was dark and intense. She found him compelling . . . and a little frightening.

"How wonderful that you like your work."

"He let me design it. Gave me carte blanche."

"So where did you learn to be a house builder?"

"I served an apprenticeship with Frederick Allen Hughes."

"I'm impressed."

"You've heard of him?"

"Of course. Hughes designed some of the finest buildings in New York. We were introduced at a party at the Astor house. Why did you leave him?"

"I'd learned all I could there."

"I need a house built."

Steve grinned. "Sure you do."

"I do. You should see what I'm living in."

"Well, this should only take a year or two, five at the most. If you still need one built when I'm done . . ."

"So long?"

"It's a castle."

"I'm serious about hiring you." Suddenly her need to build was overwhelming. "I hate the house I live in. It's cold in the winter, hot in the summer, sand blows through the walls. Please reconsider?"

"What kind of house?"

"It needs to be cool in the summer."

"You'd need adobe. Thick adobe."

"And pretty on the inside . . ."

"Oak walls, floors, and ceilings."

"And open so I can see the beautiful desert . . ."

"With wide, deep-set windows."

"You'd do a wonderful job!"

"You have a house," he reminded her, grinning.

"A terrible house. Nothing like what I need."

Steve didn't think she was serious. She looked like a young woman flushed with the excitement of having someone to talk to. When the initial thrill wore off, she'd remember she couldn't afford it and didn't really need it.

"I'm curious, Mr. Sheridan. May I ask what you charge to build a house?"

"A thousand a month for me, plus a bonus on completion of ten percent of the cost of the building materials and laborers, which for a house like the Waco castle, if we take the limestone from the surrounding land, will come to between a quarter- and a half-million dollars."

"You're hired." Samantha said, decisively.

"Better be careful. I might take you seriously."

"You look like you know women better than that, Mr. Sheridan. Are you afraid of me?" she asked, with unnerving directness.

Her look sent a chill of foreboding down Steve's spine. He was more accustomed to young women who fluttered their lashes and looked away demurely. "I was given a rule book as a young man. Rule number seven says there're two things a man is supposed to be afraid of—a decent woman and being left afoot. I respect both."

Her dinner came. She ate slowly. Steve drank his coffee and toyed with the thought of wiring his partner in Waco and telling him to proceed without him. Then he dismissed it as fantasy. It felt good being pursued by a woman of Samantha Forrester's beauty and intelligence. Her eyes were the color of a clear mountain lake, the prettiest he'd ever seen. He couldn't imagine what had possessed her to honor him with her attention, but he couldn't accept her proposal, no matter how tempting.

"You've asked me questions. Now it's my turn," he said. "I'm surprised a respectable woman like yourself would be willing to protect an Indian girl wanted by the military. Why are you taking such a risk, a woman alone?"

Samantha put down her fork and dabbed her mouth with her napkin. "I feel sorry for her. And I need help raising my son. Nicholas and I like her. I have certain resources. I don't mind sharing them. And . . . I'm not exactly alone. I have a few employees."

"A few?"

"A hundred and three."

Steve laughed. "You must have quite a spread."

"Fifty thousand acres. Most of the men are housed some distance away, but two dozen or so are near the ranch house, which is impossible to keep clean."

She stopped. She had just realized that perhaps the house was contributing to her son's illness. Suddenly she felt certain that if they had a decent house, he'd get well.

"You run cattle?"

"Ten thousand head, most of them in the foothills. We've installed a few windmills, but if we're going to survive, we need canals. I'm building them now, while labor costs are so low. But I think this recession will end in a few months and labor prices will skyrocket."

"You're running it yourself?" he said, with obvious doubt in his expression.

"I try not to interfere with Mr. Bush when it comes to handling the livestock, but I make the other decisions."

"Were you trained to take this on?"

"I was raised in West Texas, but I went to school for three years in the East. I was lucky enough to have a teacher who realized that women might go West and that they needed to know more than how to embroider. I was a good student actually . . ." *Except for mooning over Lance, who had no idea how crazed I was for him, it had been one of the happiest times of my life, poised on the edge of maturity, and yet still safe.*

Sheridan seemed to sense she had withdrawn into her own

thoughts. He raised an eyebrow questioningly. Samantha noticed and smiled.

"I told you all this, Mr. Sheridan, to convince you I'm serious about wanting you to build my house. I really do need a new one. And, I can easily afford to pay you."

"I'm curious. How did you get a fifty-thousand-acre ranch, one hundred and three cowboys," he asked, his eyes lighting with amusement, "and the money for a new house—not just a house . . . a castle?"

"My parents left me a great deal of money, more than I can spend in two or three lifetimes, Mr. Sheridan."

"Your father was a pirate?" he asked teasingly.

His eyes seemed to caress her mouth. Samantha flushed. Heat stirred in her depths; it was a struggle to remember what he'd asked her. "My father," she repeated, praying his question would be evoked by repeating the only words she remembered, "was the only son of an English duke. Along with the title, he inherited an estate and a fancy brothel and gambling establishment that catered to the very rich. I believe my grandfather, who drank too much port, died of syphilis contracted from too many visits to the family business."

Samantha couldn't believe she was telling Steve these intimate family secrets, yet she couldn't seem to stop. She was aware that her voice seemed lower and huskier, and she hoped he didn't notice and think it had anything to do with him.

"Though there was a family rumor that he was pushed out of a window by a serving maid who was tired of his sneaking into her bed every night. Or perhaps by his wife, who was probably even more tired of it."

Steve laughed.

She asked questions about his childhood, and he found himself skirting the truth a little. He left out the part about being raised by Crows Walking and his sister, Uncheedah. Most white people, he'd discovered, feared and hated the Indians. They didn't trust anyone who was too friendly with them—certainly not anyone raised by them.

So where did you go to school?"

"San Francisco. I talked Hughes into taking me on as an apprentice. He didn't want to. He said young men were ingrates, but he made me a deal. He said if I would do everything he asked me to do without question or complaint for one year, he would teach me everything he could." Steve shook his head ruefully. "Those were some of the hardest months of my life. I swept miles of floors, washed toilets three times a day, and walked in the rain to pick up and deliver packets of things I'm sure he had no use for whatsoever.''

''A whole year he did this to you?''

''Well, no . . . . probably five months, but it seemed like a year. Once I convinced him that I meant business, he opened up to me and treated me like a son until he died.''

Samantha smiled frequently as she listened to him. Silken lines etched long vertical dimples into her lovely cheeks. Her eyes sparkled with interest and open curiosity. Speaking in a soft, quick, cultured voice, she interjected whatever occurred to her without the least hesitation. If he weren't already committed to building the house in Waco, Steve realized he would enjoy getting to know this woman. He might even give her many suitors a run for their money. Probably a good thing he couldn't stay.

They finished eating. Steve escorted her to the counter where Mary Francis waited, a smile on her face. Samantha opened her reticule.

''Dinner's on me,'' Steve said, grinning.

''No. You've done too much for us already.'' She hesitated. ''I'd love to take a walk, though. Would you walk with me?''

''Sure. Where do you want to walk?''

''It doesn't matter.''

''Okay.'' Steve nodded and stepped out into the lobby as Mary Francis figured out what Samantha owed for the meals. Samantha added an extra twenty-dollar bill.

''What's this for?'' Mary Francis asked, frowning.

''You didn't have another customer while I was here.''

''Business gets slow at times,'' Mary Francis said gruffly.

''Well, I've seen this place full at the dinner hour. I don't want you penalized for being my friend. Send up meals for Ramon, Nicholas, and Tristera, would you, please?''

''I don't feel right taking your money for something like that.''

''Please don't argue with me, Mary Francis. I'm a customer, remember?''

''And a good one,'' Mary Francis said, pocketing the twenty. ''I'm so ashamed of this town. It's a sorry thing when a sick young'un can't ride in without grown men and women acting like horses' behinds.''

Samantha felt so grateful for her support and friendship, she could hardly speak. ''Thank you so much, Mary Francis,'' she said softly.

Samantha walked outside and joined Steve Sheridan who, true to form, was leaning against the building. The topmost edge of the sun was all that showed over the row of hills to the west. ''I hope I didn't embarrass you, paying for your dinner like that.''

''I seemed to hold up under it.''

She laughed, then a trifle nervously set out at a leisurely pace down the plank sidewalk, Sheridan beside her. She realized that by walking around the town square, she was taking a chance of being further humiliated, but she didn't care. She would not hide in her room.

A warm breeze blew through town, carrying the smell of fresh, warm horse urine with it. Horses stamped and whinnied. The sound of a piano drifted over from the saloons on the south end of the town square. Samantha looked sharply at Sheridan.

''I hope I'm not keeping you from anything.'' She inclined her head at the row of saloons, billiard parlors, and brothels that serviced the town's miners.

''I'm not a drinking man.''

''Your vices run in different directions?''

''I've had no time to cultivate vices.''

They strolled to the end of the sidewalk. Sheridan put out his hand to help her down onto the dusty road. The warmth of his touch caused a rush of energy through her body. She laughed. He glanced at her, and she knew she was still young and pretty enough to make a man look at her in that special way.

Reaction sparked in the depths of his eyes. He narrowed them as if to hide it from her, but it was too late—she had seen it. Suddenly she felt as if she knew too much about him. She knew he wasn't a marrying man. But that was all right with her. She was already taken.

They crossed the deeply rutted road in silence. Steve stepped up onto the sidewalk on the north end of the town square and held out his hand to her; she took it again. His eyes watched hers as if to divine her thoughts, but of course he couldn't. She didn't even know them herself.

''How long have you been in Picket Post?'' he asked.

''Almost three years.''

''Did you come here alone?''

''With Nicholas.''

''Fine boy you have there.''

''Do you have children, Mr. Sheridan?''

''No.''

"Have you ever married?"

"No time for marriage," Steve said gruffly.

She felt good. Her shoes fairly skimmed over the sidewalk.

CHAPTER FOUR

From the hotel window, Elunami watched Sheridan and the *señora* as they stopped in front of the livery stable. He said something, and she laughed and followed him inside. Elunami sensed something between them, and this caused a heavy feeling in her stomach. Though her eyes were dry, she realized that deep inside she was crying. Seeing them together as man and woman reminded her of Yellow Fox. Until Yellow Fox, her problems had seemed manageable.

Elunami turned away from the window. Looking back on her life, she felt little joy . . . except for the brief time in her youth when she had been celebrated as a rainmaker. Her mother and grandmother had been very proud. Even her stepfather had stood in awe of her. They had not known it was nothing she could help.

It had started when she was almost five springs old. Her Hopi name, which she hardly remembered now, had been Tuvayesva, which meant Butterfly Resting. She had lived in Old Oraibi on Third Mesa, one of three high mesas that rose out of the desert like the long, ragged fingers of Black Mesa to the north. The high cliffs, six hundred feet or more above the floor of the desert, provided the Hopi with natural springs and protection from their enemies—the Navaho—whom they called *Tasavuh*, the "Ones Who Pound Heads." Away from the edge of the mesa, the pueblos rose up to five stories high. In front of every dwelling, against the high walls, tall ladders leaned, ready to be pulled inside if enemies attacked.

At night, Butterfly Resting would lie down next to her little sister on their rabbit-skin blankets in the corner of their small pueblo room and close her eyes. Within minutes a sound like that of running water would fill her head. It grew louder each night, until it was like the roar of a great river.

At some point the sound changed to that of holy men chanting and singing in the distance. Then it changed again to the clanging of heavy bells in the top of her head. As she strained into the darkness of her mind, searching for the source of the sound, her soul lifted out of her in a great rush of whirling energy, as if a dust devil had dipped down and scooped it up.

When the whirling stopped, she found herself perched somehow beneath the ceiling of an enormous round underground room. It was not one she recognized, so she believed it had to be the Flute kiva, where the holy men of her tribe carried out the many rituals of their spiritual life and in which the holy priests sat in meditation each night.

For a long time she seemed to float there, watching the old men meditate. After a time, Tuvi, the *pekwin*, an ancient holy man acknowledged by all as the most powerful priest of all the clans, a man who bore the responsibility for the spiritual welfare of the entire Hopi tribe, glanced up and stared directly at her. Her soul trembled at the contact. Then rushing feelings started again, and she found herself back in her bed, too stunned by what had happened even to cry out. Her mind swallowed the memory.

But the next morning in the square, Tuvi squatted against one of the pueblos facing the central plaza, peering at each person who walked past. At first he did not appear interested in Butterfly Resting. His gaze slid over her and onto the next person—then unexpectedly returned to her.

That evening, Tuvi came to speak to her stepfather, Gray Deer. Through his marriage to her mother, Gray Deer had become the son-in-law of Talasvenka and a member of the Bear clan of the Hopi tribe. This meant that although Gray Deer was a Sioux, he had been accepted in the village. He was very much aware of the high standing of his position, and, when sober, would not do anything to bring shame or dishonor to it. A visit by the *pekwin* could mean great honor or great dishonor, and this uncertainty flustered Gray Deer.

Butterfly Resting sensed her father's agitation and became afraid. Tuvi and Gray Deer spoke in low tones; she could not make out the words. After a moment Gray Deer frowned over his shoulder at her as if she had done something for which she would be punished. Fear tightened her body. Gray Deer was the only father in the pueblos who whipped his children. He whipped everyone, even their mother. Her grandmother claimed he had been raised by heathen whites, who were cruel to everyone, even their own young.

They stopped speaking; Gray Deer called her sternly to his side. As scared as she was, she did not hesitate for fear of increasing his wrath. He took her by the hand and followed the old priest to the Flute kiva. Tuvi sent runners to all the priests in Oraibi, a village of eight hundred people.

She sat on the ground where Gray Deer told her to sit, with her legs stretched out before her as all Hopi women did, and she stared around the inside of the holy Flute kiva with wonder. It was the same room she had seen last night. She had been in the other kivas several times for ceremonies, but this one was for priests only.

Within minutes, the enormous chamber was full of priests. With her father watching, Tuvi questioned her until he'd learned everything she knew about her night visit to the kiva. Tuvi was kind and gentle with her, but her voice and body trembled. She had no idea what Gray Deer might do to her for bringing herself to the attention of the priests in such a way.

The old men withdrew and spoke among themselves. Finally they approached Gray Deer and spoke to him in low tones, then more loudly, so she, sitting at a distance, could hear them. "She is young, but we will teach her." In the following weeks she learned that in her tribe, anyone with a spiritual gift was taken under the guidance of the priests, just as other children were taught sheepherding, farming, weaving, bowlmaking, or fighting. Children had many teachers. The whole tribe took responsibility for all children.

Word spread among the pueblos that Butterfly Resting was *kópavi*—that her head was open to the Great Mystery. She became the Hawk Maiden—the youngest child ever taken into the holy kiva. They taught her the Hopi way of meditation. Tuvi showed her how to sit, but he did not give her the holy words. She was too young.

The first evening she sat in meditation, her soul was pulled upward in a great rush just as it had been before. Afterward she opened her eyes; it was as if she had only just closed them, but it was morning. Streaks of sunlight filtered in through the holes in the roof of the kiva.

Tuvi seemed to know what had happened to her. He explained that in time she would remain conscious and would be able to remember what happened after her soul was pulled up to the level of the Great Mystery. His eyes smiled with joy when he looked at her. After a time she realized Tuvi could read the Great Mystery's soul tablets on which each person's history was stored. That was how he had recognized her soul.

A few weeks later, during the *Powámúya* ceremonies, the elder priests laid offerings of bean sprouts grown in the kiva as part of a ceremony to invoke rain. Days passed with no rain. People worried that the priests were not sufficiently pure of heart. The priests meditated all night every night.

Ten days after the ceremony, rain clouds darkened the sky, carried swiftly on a strong wind. People stopped work to watch them pass. The women sang a mournful prayer song as the clouds carried away the water so badly needed by their withering crops.

With the wind whipping her skirts about her calves, Butterfly Resting felt deep sadness. Her grandmother, Talasvenka, which meant Painted With Pollen, walked to her side and handed her a spruce limb. Talasvenka had told her that spruce was the most powerful of all the trees, with great magnetism to call down the rain. "Speak to them," she said. "Ask them to give us their water."

Butterfly Resting took the spruce limb and lifted it to the darkening sky. "You must not be selfish little rain clouds. Give us your water." She spoke as if cajoling one of her friends, and to her surprise, fat raindrops began to fall. Her grandmother called everyone around her and told them what she had done.

The wind changed direction, and it rained for three days, a steady soaking rain good for the crops. The grateful tribe made *pahos*, feathered prayer sticks, to give thanks to the Great Mystery. Tuvi smiled his approval. He called her to sit with him and told her she would become a priestess of the rain society. He would ask Gray Deer for permission.

Gray Deer readily agreed. The whole family was honored. The day of Butterfly Resting's initiation, her grandmother took her for a walk, just the two of them. At the cliff's edge they watched the sunset, as the all-covering Sky Father darkened around the Earth Mother. Talasvenka turned to her.

"I let you do this thing now even though I know it is dangerous. The post of priestess of the rain society is one of great responsibility. The welfare of the entire tribe rests in your hands. And you are only a child. There is always a possibility that you might make a mistake and be condemned as a sorceress. But I trust you will do nothing to bring dishonor on our clan.

"I will help you. I will teach you everything I know about the plants and herbs. It may not seem related, but everything helps. Everything works together—wind, trees, night clouds, houses, even the clothes on your back. They are all *hoi*, all living souls."

That evening Butterfly Resting became the *shiwanokia*, an important priestess. For a while her status upset the family routine. Her mother and grandmother spent more time teaching her than the other children, which angered Gray Deer, who resented anyone being more important than he. Behind Gray Deer's back, her grandmother sneered. "He is no Sioux. The Sioux would no more strike a child than I would. He is a white man in disguise."

Her grandmother could not stand his beating her daughter and grandchildren. She said it was not the Indian way, unless the man drank firewater, which was not allowed on the mesa. "The Sioux are good people, but he is not. They probably whipped him and drove him out of the village. Better a thieving Navaho," she grumbled when her son-in-law was not in hearing.

Her mother, Chu'mana, Snake Maiden, defended her husband, but it only caused more dissent. At the age of fifteen Chu'mana had been carried off by an Irish cattle rustler who kept her for six years, until he was hung for rustling. She came home to her mother's pueblo with two daughters, five-year-old Margarita and Butterfly Resting, then an unnamed infant. Both had red hair and fair skin. Chu'mana felt lucky to get any husband with such daughters.

Sioux were rare in Arizona. Only one driven away by the soldiers ever came this far south. Chu'mana had been fascinated by how different Gray Deer was from the Hopi men. Gray Deer, with his battle scars and bitterness, seemed manly and stern. And so she married him.

One day, in the year of Butterfly Resting's seventh spring, Gray Deer became angry with her and raised his quirt to strike her. Chu'mana, standing behind him, grabbed the quirt and would not let go. They fought, and Gray Deer slapped Chu'mana so hard that she flew against the adobe wall of the pueblo, slipped to the floor, and did not get up. She lay in a strange sleep for three days. Talasvenka tended her and flashed baleful looks at Gray Deer, who stayed drunk on *pulque* and cursed his wife for fighting back.

The afternoon of the third day, Chu'mana died. Gray Deer left the pueblo. Women came to sing prayer songs and prepare Chu'mana for burial in the Earth, which nourished all living Hopi and to which they returned. Butterfly Resting sat with the women until bedtime. Her grandmother put her gently to bed, saying she needed to visit the outhouse.

Pressed close to her sister, Margarita, Butterfly Resting cried herself to sleep on her blankets, the sound of the women's prayer songs in her ears. As she slept she saw, not a moving dream, as was customary, but a picture, for only a moment, of her grandmother at the edge of the mesa, her familiar silhouette outlined against the bright moon and twinkling stars, a heavy rock poised above her head.

When Butterfly Resting woke the next morning her mind had swallowed the picture. She did not even remember dreaming. Her father did not come home the next morning. One of the warriors found Gray Deer below the mesa, his head crushed. People said that perhaps the worn path had crumbled beneath him and sent him tumbling down. It was a path avoided by most, as the red rock broke loose at times. No one accused her grandmother. The Hopi did not kill their own people. When Butterfly Resting heard, she remembered the dream for a moment. She never spoke of it to anyone, but she no longer wished to be *kópavi*.

She and her sisters, Margarita and Little Bear, lived on the mesa with their grandmother in more peace and happiness than ever before. She missed her mother and Gray Deer, who had not always been mean to her. Sometimes when his temper was not bad, he had laughed and played with her and her sister.

They had plenty of food to eat. The crops of peaches, corn, melons, peppers, beans, and cucumbers were plentiful. They traded with clans who grew other crops or raised sheep or hunted. Life was good.

Until one day in her eighth spring. White government men came and walked through the plaza looking at the people. They talked for a long time with Lololma, chief of the "Friendly" faction of the Hopi. Lololma sent word to all the clans of Oraibi that he would come the next day to choose children to go to the white school in Flagstaff.

Before the appointed time, their grandmother buried them in the sand under a bush north of the pueblos. Only their faces showed, so they could breathe. It was a bad feeling, as if her body were suffocating. The sand was cool, but her face itched when insects crawled on it.

It did no good. The Indian police found them. They found all the children. Butterfly Resting learned later that Lololma had walked directly to their grandmother's pueblo and asked to speak to Butterfly Resting. Her grandmother pretended she did not know where her granddaughters were, but Lololma knew better. He sent the Indian police out to search the village.

The police dug them up and marched them to the plaza, where their parents stood in tense silence. Lololma ordered her and five other children to go with the white men. Her grandmother and the other mothers cried. The fathers were angry but silent. Lololma was the most high chief of the Hopi. He ruled the pueblos on all three mesas, over four thousand Hopi.

With fear so heavy in her she almost could not breathe, Butterfly Resting was lifted into the white men's box wagon with five other terrified children. No one told them what would happen to them. They rode for two days in the wagon, parched and scared and hungry, drinking and eating only when the white men stopped to feed themselves.

Finally they reached a building on the outskirts of a town where they were turned over to a stern-faced white woman with twenty or so other Indian children behind her and a heavy wooden ruler in her hand. She told them to call her Mrs. Addison. She would be their teacher. Mrs. Parker interpreted that first day. Butterfly Resting learned they had been taken to school, where they were expected to learn to be "civilized." Disobedience would not be allowed. If they were good, they would be allowed to go home in the summertime.

The stern white woman cut their hair, made them wear white clothes, and forbade them to speak their native language. Each child was given an English name. Butterfly Resting was named Elaine Norman. The girls wore high-necked, long-sleeved brown gowns with white pinafores. The boys wore black knickers, tall white socks, and high-collared white shirts with black cloths tied in a bow at their necks.

If anyone disobeyed the rules, the punishments were swift and hard—the heavy wooden ruler whacked across trembling palms or the sensitive backs of legs, a humiliating experience for children who had never been whipped.

The schedule was not too different from at home. The children rose at five o'clock in the morning to wash, dress, and do their morning chores, which consisted of sweeping and cleaning their dormitory. They ate at seven, washed their own dishes, and reported to their desks at eight, where they stayed until noon. They ate a meal of strange food, stood in line to wash their dishes in a pan of cold, dirty water, and filed outside, where they were free to run and play for an hour, after which they filed back to their desks, where the unlucky ones fell asleep and were whacked with the ruler.

Elaine had been fortunate. Each night her soul lifted out of her and flew back to the Flute kiva, where it hovered under the ceiling, watching Tuvi meditate. She had come to love Tuvi even more than her grandmother or sisters. He was sweet and beautiful and kind. Each night he looked up at her and smiled.

Her nightly trips made life bearable. And once she realized the white teachers did not intend to kill her, she learned quickly and even enjoyed her lessons. She liked Mrs. Parker, who had warm, smiling eyes, and with her help, Elaine soon discovered that the English language was an interesting and unpredictable challenge. She studied the dictionary in her spare time. Soon she used words even Mrs. Addison didn't know. Elaine was taken from class and paraded before inspecting dignitaries to convince them how readily the Indians could learn, if given the proper circumstances. Some discounted her, saying she was only part Indian. After this, Mrs. Addison had Elaine put her hair in a bun and wear a poke bonnet so they wouldn't see its striking redness. Then the school received proper credit and continued government funding.

Elaine pitied the children who had no way to go home. But after a while, even her soul trips were less frequent. By the time she was twelve they had stopped altogether. She didn't know if she had lost the ability or the desire. Perhaps as she grew older her body became stronger and her soul weaker. Her changing body stirred strongly at times, and she lost interest in meditating. The days in the kiva became dim memories.

Back at the mesa during the summers, her school name, Elaine Norman, was shortened to Elunami. The Hopi had no patience for queer white names.

It was the summer of her fifteenth year, when she returned to the pueblo at Oraibi, that she saw Yellow Fox for the first time. A Sioux, like Gray Deer, he was taller and straighter of limb than the Hopi. Young Hopi men, with their round bodies and moon faces beneath straight bangs, looked soft as women compared to him. Yellow Fox had broad shoulders and a deep chest. The sun gleamed on his strong, muscular arms.

Elunami noticed Yellow Fox the first day she arrived at Third Mesa. Though he showed no sign of noticing her, she knew he had. One evening when she went for water, she was not surprised to see him waiting at the well. She pretended to ignore him, but his bold gaze followed her. Unlike the white men who had looked too closely at her, Yellow Fox radiated dark power that spoke to her body. Her heart pounded as if she'd run up a steep hill.

"In my tribe you would be called White Buffalo Woman," he said, his deep voice teasing her.

"I know nothing of this Buffalo Woman. In my tribe, they are smart enough to call me by my name," she said.

Yellow Fox sneered. "Is this what happens when they let Hopi girls go to away school?"

Elunami's heart drummed, singing the song of dashed hopes. She was sorry she had antagonized Yellow Fox, but she had never heard of this Buffalo Woman and did not like being called by names she did not understand. She especially did not like being sneered at because she had been taken against her will to the white school.

Yellow Fox pushed her aside, lifted her full bucket out of the well for her, and turned toward her family's pueblo. At her door he handed the bucket to her. "Meet me at the well after dinner."

She barely touched her food. Her grandmother had seen her with Yellow Fox. She was angry and told her he was a dirty Sioux. Her face twitched when she spoke of him. Elunami helped with the dishes and then went outside with her sister, who told her that Yellow Fox was a member of the war society. He was the fastest runner, the best marksman, the most audacious leader. She said it was a great honor to be courted by Yellow Fox, who had bested every young man in the games. She admitted not everyone looked up to him, a Sioux, but she did. Elunami did, too. She valued the ability to fight and felt dizzy with the thought of being courted by him.

Surprisingly, Yellow Fox was waiting at the well. They walked away from the pueblos. Her cousin saw her with Yellow Fox and smiled. Elunami's lips trembled with the effort to keep her face from showing her great agitation. Her cousin would tell everyone that Yellow Fox courted her. Her grandmother would not be happy, but Elunami was a woman. She was old enough to make up her own mind. Many of her friends who had stayed at the pueblo had married and borne children already.

They walked to the rim of the mesa and looked south at the painted desert stretching to the horizon. Overhead, birds cried out. The evening wind cooled her face and arms. Beneath her plain cotton dress, her insides trembled with awareness of Yellow Fox.

"So you are the rainmaker?" he asked.

"I was, but no more."

"What did it feel like to have so much power?"

She did not think of it as power, but as a gift from the Great Mystery. When she lifted her arms to the sky, and the rain fell, she felt at one with the elements. It was not like power to her, but like surrender and belonging.

She could not find the words to explain this to Yellow Fox. His eyes intimidated her. "What does it feel like to be a powerful brave?" she countered.

Yellow Fox laughed, but she could see he much preferred the conversation to focus on him. The tension between them passed. He took her wrist and lifted her hand. "Did they tell you I am a fortune-teller?"

"No."

"Good. At least they do not lie about me."

They laughed, but he did not let go of her hand. They walked the rim of the mesa and watched the ever-changing colors of the sky until darkness fell.

It felt good to realize he, too, worried about how others perceived him. She felt closer to him.

Yellow Fox had come to live with his sister and her Hopi husband. These were hard times for the Sioux Nation. The horse soldiers harried them relentlessly.

He told her that the horse soldiers had killed his mother and younger sisters when he was eleven. They rode into the camp, left temporarily unprotected while the men hunted buffalo, killed the few old guards and all of the women and children. Big and smart for his age, he had been with the men.

He told her how much he missed the sweet, fat meat of the buffalo, the endless plains waving with yellow grass, and the vast sky overhead. His heart ached for his people, who had been herded onto terrible land by the soldiers. They spent most of their time trying to escape to find decent food, running from the soldiers, or fighting them. He alone had managed to get away.

She fell in love with Yellow Fox that evening. A part of her that had burned within, seeking expression, attached itself to Yellow Fox, and she looked with pride upon everything he did. When he kissed her, she felt weak with desire for more kisses.

The night of the full Cactus Moon, he lifted her skirt and touched her loins.

"No," she whispered, shoving his hand away.

"Are you afraid? Don't be afraid."

"It is not right."

Yellow Fox laughed. "Saying no is for old women with hanging skin." His hand found her again. This time it was harder to push his hand away.

"No . . ."

"You are young and beautiful. It will be all right."

She tried to say no, but her head was bad—weak from his kisses and the fire within. They became lovers. Elunami knew it was not right to do this before marriage. Hopi girls were strictly enjoined against lovemaking until after the marriage vows had been spoken. But her body was stronger than her soul.

He was so handsome, so strong. His arms around her promised that she would never be lonely again. Afterward she expected him to speak to her grandmother, but he simply left her at her front door. It was customary, when a couple made an impetuous mistake, to go immediately to the parents, who would scold them and make the marriage arrangements.

Instead, Yellow Fox came to her pueblo the next evening and said he was not going to call for her again. Her chest felt as though someone had filled it with cold spring water.

"But why?"

Yellow Fox looked angry. "I will marry Antelope Dancing."

Yellow Fox would not speak further about it, but Elunami got a flash of intuition. His brother-in-law wanted to be a chief. His good friend, the chief of Kykotsmovi, a village at the base of Third Mesa, had a marriageable daughter—Antelope Dancing. Yellow Fox was politically ambitious. He would rather be the husband of a chief's daughter. Yellow Fox did not call on her again. Soon he appeared in the plaza with Antelope Dancing, who smiled up at him with proud eyes. Elunami felt sick to her stomach whenever she saw them together.

In the fall, she returned to school as Elaine Norman and applied herself earnestly to her lessons. In the spring, because she was such a good student, she graduated and received a beautiful diploma printed in gold ink on parchment. Mrs. Addison wrote a letter to Lololma, telling him what an exemplary student she had been. She showed Elaine the letter before she mailed it and asked her to stay and work at the school. Elaine promised to consider it after her visit home.

The second week after her arrival at the pueblo, Lololma's daughter invited all the maidens of all the pueblos to take part in the spring plaza dances, all-day ceremonies customarily led by the chief's oldest unmarried daughter. The girls dressed as *kachinas*. During the ceremony it was customary for the watching people to concentrate their thoughts in a community prayer for the spirits to bring rain.

As the invited girls emerged from the kiva to dance in the

plaza, Yellow Fox stepped forward and pointed his finger at Elunami. The girls stopped dancing.

"She must not go. I lay with her in the sand."

Elunami's mouth felt suddenly as if the desert sun had sucked all the moisture out of it. Her heart hammered so loudly she could hear nothing else.

The chief's daughter gave Elunami a chance to repudiate Yellow Fox's claim, but she could not. Her lips felt frozen. She stumbled away from the kiva and ran to her family's house, where she lay on her blankets and refused to speak to anyone. From the plaza she could hear the dances until nightfall, but rain did not come.

Everyone knew and felt sorry for her, but their sympathy didn't help. She wanted to rip out Yellow Fox's heart and stuff it into his betraying mouth, but she was too filled with shame and guilt to leave the pueblo. If not for her little sister's kindness and persistence she might have starved.

Elunami lay on her bed of skins and tried to think why Yellow Fox would do such a thing. Her people had no ritual in which girls who had erred were humiliated. Why had he stepped forward with information that no one had asked for?

Two days later, Tuvi called on her. She walked to the door of the pueblo, saw him, and fought back tears. She could maintain her composure with anyone else, but she loved Tuvi so much that just to see him was to feel a great sense of love and an overwhelming sense of inadequacy.

His eyes were not like the eyes of anyone else in the world. When she looked into them she seemed to look beyond the physical eye to a tiny silver disk. Her mind had puzzled about this many times. Perhaps what she saw was the reflection of an image from below. It was only visible for a second, and from a certain angle.

The first time she noticed it, she made opportunities to look into the eyes of the other priests and found they were all different. Some had only one or two spots of silver with the rest of the disk covered by what looked like brown moss. Some were half silver and half mossy. Only Tuvi's whole disk was silver with no mossy spots.

Once, Tuvi had caught her peering into the eyes of the other priests and had smiled at her. He seemed to know everything and say nothing. She longed to ask him what her own eyes looked like inside, but she was too shy.

It was a great honor that Tuvi would come to her house. She

was so nervous and self-conscious she could hardly breathe. They walked to the southernmost tip of the mesa. It was good to feel the warm air on her face. She had felt suffocated in the small pueblo.

They sat on a boulder and watched the sunset. For more than an hour, Tuvi said nothing. Finally he looked at her.

"It did not rain."

Elunami realized that he connected her humiliation to the lack of rain. Her heart dropped. She wanted to beg his forgiveness, but words stuck in her throat. She wanted him to castigate her, punish her.

"It is time for you to have the holy words."

Elunami could not believe it. She had meditated for years with him and he had never offered her the holy words he shared only with his most trusted disciples.

"Now?" she croaked. "After what I have done?"

"The Great Mystery chooses the time. Who are we to question him?"

He told her the holy words and made her repeat them until he was sure she had memorized them. She felt dizzy with excitement and honor.

"Come to the kiva. Meditate. How can you make rain if your head is closed and your heart is not pure?"

That night Elunami tried to go to the kiva, but her feet would not climb down the ladder. Sweat broke out on her face, her hands shook, and her heart felt as if it would burst. She could not. She knew her soul disk must be covered with moss. Her heart felt like it would break. Tuvi had finally given her the holy names, but she could not use them. She was not pure.

The next morning she went to Flagstaff to live with her older sister, Margarita, and her Mexican husband, Luis. She learned Spanish and to love Mexican dances. Life would have been good, except that Luis tried to grab her every time she walked past him. No matter what he was doing—eating, drinking, even half-asleep—his hand would snake out, groping for her breasts or her loins. Margarita yelled at him, but he didn't stop. Finally she suggested that Elunami go back to the pueblo. *A year has gone by,* she said, *they will have forgotten.* Elunami resisted, but Margarita talked her into going for a short visit, just to see how things were.

Elunami arrived at Third Mesa in the month of the Water Moon. Icy winter winds blew across the high mesa, chilling her to the bone. She had forgotten how cold it could be this time of year. People seemed to have forgotten her shame, except for the mothers of eligible young men. They looked at her with suspicious eyes. Every time she saw one of them watching her it was like being exposed all over again.

Dancing Antelope no longer looked at Yellow Fox with proud eyes. She was married to him, but she did not look happy. She had no child in her cradle board, and her belly was still flat. Her eyes told Elunami that she already feared she would remain childless.

After Elunami had been home a week, Lololma sent for her. Lololma was relatively young for such a powerful chief. He was head of what the white people at the school had called the "Friendlies," a group who did not wish to resist the white invasion. He opposed the "Hostiles," or "Traditionalists," who wanted to guard their Hopi way of life against the attempts by the whites to change them into good Americans.

Lololma's house was clean and sparsely furnished. He led her to a feathered headdress hanging on one wall.

"See this feather headdress?"

Elunami nodded.

"Many years ago when I visited the Great White Leader, Chester Arthur, I was given this headdress. Now I give it to you." He bent to open a chest and took out an embroidered white deerskin dress. "This was given to me for my wife. Take it, too. On my journey I saw great cities with buildings as tall as these mesas. I saw white men who could build bridges across wide rivers, men who could build ships as big as villages."

Elunami had seen pictures of these things in her schoolbooks. She nodded.

"There are many wise men among us who have not seen these things. And because they have not, they do not know the true power of the white man. They think that all we have to do is kill a few of them and they will go away. But men who can build cities as tall as mountains will not be discouraged by a few arrows. I want to send these wise men to visit the new Great White Leader. Then they, too, will see these things and know that it is no longer good enough to live as we have. Our young people must be educated in the white fashion. I want you to go as their interpreter. And you must wear these ceremonial clothes," he said, lifting up a long, white, feathered headdress and the pure white beaded dress.

Confused, Elunami touched the finely worked leather, which was soft as silk. "These are not ours—"

"They were a gift from the white leader to all of us." He paused. "Do you know the school that has been opened for us in Keams Canyon?"

Elunami nodded.

"Five of our elders refuse to let the children of their clans attend. If they continue to refuse, the white soldiers will be called, and many will die." He paused. "Will you go?"

Elunami frowned. "I am not worthy."

A look of impatience crossed Lololma's broad face. "Even worth must be decided differently in this new world."

That evening she was presented to the elders. Two were her own great-uncles, chiefs of villages on Third Mesa. Two were chiefs from First and Second Mesa. Tuvi would accompany them. He smiled at her. She couldn't tell if he blamed her for running away. He would probably never say.

The great number of cities they passed during their long train journey caused the elders to mutter and shake their heads. Seeing the enormous numbers of white men wilted them. Elunami realized that the whites they saw from the train windows were merely little waves of an unstoppable ocean. Five thousand Hopi did not stand a chance against millions of white men. Tuvi watched everything with solemn eyes. The elders were less good at hiding their unhappiness. With each noisy, crowded town they sank deeper into their blankets.

In the bustling city of Washington, D.C., they were met by a crowd of white men, all intent on taking their pictures for newspapers or interviewing them. She was so busy that she did not have time to meditate. Her presence was needed from early in the morning until late at night. In honor of Tuvi's presence, each dawn she rose to meditate, but she kept falling asleep.

On the way back to the mesas, even though they did exactly as the government guide accompanying them directed, they got onto the wrong train and ended up in Tucson instead of Holbrook.

Riding their own horses, which they had transported both ways at government expense, they had left town early this morning, following the Salt River, which would lead to the Verde River that they would follow north. But Tuvi and the elders were ambushed at the confluence of the Verde and Salt rivers by an army patrol and killed. A captain, his bars gleaming in the sunlight, stood over her, holding the scouts back. She looked up at him and then, while she was waiting to die, looked at the soldier boots in the stirrups of the men behind him.

With Tuvi dead in her arms, she had wanted to die. Even now she was filled with rage at his loss. She could not believe that a holy man could be treated in this fashion. She had expected Tuvi to die of extreme old age and ascend to the heavens in a beam of light, carried by angels. That crude white men could shoot him down and leave his body to be eaten by vultures filled her with such frustration and rage, she wanted to tear her hair and scream.

She had not let *Señor* Sheridan lead her away until she'd dug a shallow grave for them all and piled rocks on it. To his credit, he'd used his rifle as a tool and helped her bury them.

Pain filled her body, but tears did not come. She tried to think of other things, but she kept wondering how they had become lost, ending up where the soldiers were.

It was possible their guide had led them the wrong way on purpose, but she could think of no reason why he would do that. She suspected him, but she would never know for certain.

A loud noise on the busy street below called her attention back to the present. Miners in dirty clothes yelled and laughed as they strode beneath her window.

The sun was setting. The *señora* was still in the livery stable with *Señor* Sheridan. In spite of her grief and rage about Tuvi and the elders, Elunami wished the *señora* had not gone into the barn with him.

Maybe wealthy white women did not have to worry so much about their reputations. She hoped not.

CHAPTER FIVE

Wrinkling her nose at the smells of hay, horses, and manure, Samantha followed Steve Sheridan into the dim livery stable. He walked slowly down the wide aisle separating the two rows of stalls until his horse stamped and snorted.

"Whoa, boy. Whoa," Sheridan said, caressing the beautiful animal's long nose. "Did you eat that grain?"

He picked up a brush lying on the ground beside the stall and opened the door, which creaked on rusty hinges. Samantha leaned against the stall and propped her chin on her hands, watching. As Sheridan brushed the horse's silky coat from neck to hind quarters, she imagined his back muscles rippling with each long stroke of the brush.

"Beautiful horse," she said. "What's his name?"

"Calico."

"Calico bugs have red, orange, and yellow dots on a black body. He's gray and orange and yellow and black."

"Named him after a cat I had as a boy. That cat would eat anything that wasn't nailed down."

"You should have named him Goat."

"I don't have such a good opinion of goats. I respected that cat, though." Steve straightened up. "You know some fairly precise things about animals and insects. Do you teach school?"

"Because I know the color of one bug and one type of cat?" she chided, enjoying the chagrined look that quirked his mouth at her teasing. She relented. "I teach Nicholas. There's no school in Picket Post. And . . . I sculpt animals."

"Sold anything?"

"Well, yes. I guess most of them have sold. I have an agent in New York who has an arrangement with a couple of art galleries."

"That's quite an accomplishment," he said seriously, his eyes filled with admiration.

"I do it for my own satisfaction. I'm glad they sell, though."

Steve turned back to his horse and brushed in silence.

"I asked Elu—Tristera to come to the ranch and work for me. I think she will," Samantha said.

"I'm glad to hear that." Steve smiled his approval.

After he had combed every inch of his horse, he walked out of the stall, closed the door, and turned to face Samantha.

Heart pounding suddenly, she almost backed away from him. In the dim light streaming in the far window, his narrowed eyes unexpectedly evoked that feeling of warmth in her belly again. "I've been asking myself what you're still doing here," he said, his voice so low she could barely make out the words. Before she could move away, he reached out and drew her slowly toward him.

She smelled faintly of peppermint—a fragrance he especially liked. In the dim light of the barn her skin seemed to pick up every particle of luminescence and transform it into star shine to dazzle him. Her slim, white stem of a neck balanced a well-shaped head adorned by golden hair cut in parted bangs that she was continually tossing back with a thoroughly feminine gesture.

He took her by the waist and pulled her nearer to him, but not quite touching. Beneath his hands, her slender waist felt warm and trembling. At his touch she seemed to stop breathing, to wait—like a caught bird.

Holding her, passion surged up in him, swift and searing. Yet still he waited, content simply to breathe in the sweet, peppermint fragrance of her, to savor this keen anticipation, this fierce desire—and equally fierce tenderness—welling up inside.

He could feel the throb of her pulse beneath his thumb, which was pressing lightly into her waist. Her lashes were dark and fine and sweetly curved. Her breath smelled sweet and warm against his face. Finally, his own heart pounding, he lifted her chin and lowered his mouth to hers.

Samantha closed her eyes. His kiss felt tentative at first, but as her mouth opened to the nibbling caress of his lips and tongue, his lips insinuated themselves into her mouth, opening it wider. His heat came as a surprise that caused a sudden weakness in her. She'd never felt such fire in a man's kiss before.

He kissed her until she couldn't think. By the time he finally raised his head, her arms were trembling around his neck. He led her backward until she found herself against the stall, sandwiched between the rough wood at her back and Steve Sheridan's body. He smoothed his hands up her arms and leaned down to kiss her again.

"Now what, Samantha Forrester?" he whispered, his voice rough—and so close to her ear, it sent a chill down her spine. She loved the way he said her name—with such intensity and gruffness. She felt more alive than she had in years.

She wanted to say something to show him that this wasn't the way it looked. She wasn't the least taken with him. It was just that her body, which longed almost constantly for Lance, was in a weakened condition today, suffering from passions awakened this morning in a dream she'd wanted desperately to finish.

She wanted to tell Steve Sheridan that her reaction had nothing to do with him, but his mouth brushed her lips lightly, slipped down to her throat, and a spear of heat plunged to the depths of her. Moaning, she groped until she found his lips with her own. He kissed her again, this time like a man accustomed to taking charge, a passionate, demanding man who would have whatever he wanted.

His lips evoked responses from every part of her body. Her head started to spin. She felt suddenly like a twig caught in a tornado. Although she knew it was only the closeness of the barn—and the extreme demands of a long and trying day—that made her feel so out of control, panic rose in her. Gasping for air, she broke free of his lips.

Rough hands gripped her shoulders; he held her away from him. "What are you trying to do, woman?" he said, panting, his voice gruff with desire.

"I'm—I'm"—Samantha blinked and opened her eyes with difficulty—"trying to keep you here so you'll build my house," she said, knowing that she was lying and exerting all of her strength to keep from moving back into his embrace.

"I'm not a house cat, Samantha Forrester."

"I can see that."

He just looked at her for a moment. "Well, don't give up so easy," he whispered, pulling her back into his arms.

Samantha laughed in spite of herself. "You could wire the man in Waco and tell him you've been detained . . ."

"Once I take a job, I do it."

"Too bad . . ." Samantha's heart pounded. "That was a good-bye kiss to remember, Steve Sheri—" Her voice broke and she gave up trying to appear nonchalant.

His eyes glittered with amusement or frustration, she couldn't be sure. Slowly his hands released her shoulders.

"Yes, it was, Samantha Forrester."

* * *

Samantha found Elunami sitting in a daze at the window, apparently too dispirited to move away. At her urging, the girl undressed and put on the extra nightgown she'd purchased that afternoon.

"I've told everyone your name is Tristera," Samantha warned her. "I think your safety depends on our not forgetting that."

"*Sí*, I am used to having many names."

Nicholas had napped, eaten, and gotten sleepy again. In his pajamas, lying on Samantha's bed, he looked too thin for the size of his handsome head. His face seemed to glow with spirit and self-possession, as if he'd been born knowing everything he needed to know. Samantha could see a little of herself in Nicholas. He had her hairline and chin, and some said her intelligence and determination. But she had the terrible feeling that of the two of them, he was the wiser, too smart to accept life on anyone else's terms.

Fear stirred in her at the thought; she swooped down to hug him fiercely. "Mama, you're hurting me," he whined.

"Sorry," she said, letting go. Tears blurred her vision and she turned away. "Good night, Nicholas."

"Good night, Mama."

Elunami followed Samantha into the other bedroom.

"He is very wise," Elunami said, with an odd, gentle smile that seemed too mature for such a young face.

Samantha wiped her eyes. One in seven people died of consumption. It was the most feared and dreaded disease in America. "You may be right. Good night . . . Tristera."

"Good night, *señora*."

Samantha closed the connecting door and stepped back into her room. She needed sleep, but intense fear welled up in her and she lay down beside Nicholas and felt his head. His fever seemed higher tonight.

Squeezing her eyes shut, she expelled a heavy breath, remembering how terrified she'd been when Nicholas had first been diagnosed. When Jared had died, she'd sensed her son's deep pain and bewilderment, his basic reluctance to live. This had persisted, until now she was afraid that if he did not acquire the determination to beat his disease—and soon—he would certainly die. What terrified her most was that none of it was conscious in him. It could not be fought directly.

Samantha pressed her face into the pillow to muffle her sobs. She aspired to faith, to believe that whatever happened to her son would be God's will and for the best, but in reality she loved

Nicholas too deeply. She was too attached to let go and trust anyone else to keep him safe, even God. And yet she knew there was no other way . . .

Please, God, she prayed, *if I'm supposed to let him go, then help me do it. Help me to trust that you really do love him even more than I do.* She repeated the words over and over, like a litany. *Please help me to trust . . .*

Suddenly Samantha's eyes flew open and she sat up. She must have fallen asleep. The room was dark, and in the distance she could hear the sounds of a tinny piano. She turned over and checked Nicholas. He felt cooler now. Relieved, she lay there a while but couldn't go back to sleep. She thought she heard Elunami moving around in the next room.

She slipped out of bed, walked to the door connecting her room to the girl's, and opened it. Elunami's room was quiet, but something alarmed her. Then she saw what it was: Elunami was sitting cross-legged on the floor in the light of the moon. The air around the girl seemed to shimmer, as if it had become visible. Then Elunami turned her head . . . and the sensation passed.

"What are you doing?" Samantha asked.

"You had a dream," Elunami said softly.

Image fragments returned briefly to shimmer on the edge of Samantha's mind. "It was about—about . . ." She struggled to remember. Saw herself kneeling inside a circle of entrapping swords, her hands up to fend off her doom. Outside the ring of swords and to her left stood a stern, angry man. To his right crouched three women, robed in black, with white, ugly faces, snake hair, and leathery bat wings. In the distance, menacing clouds hung over mountain peaks. One of the women beckoned her to slip through the ring of swords, but Samantha shook her head. The woman pushed aside the swords, so Samantha could leave without hurting herself, but Samantha motioned the woman away. The memory of it left her trembling.

"How did you know about my dream?" she asked.

"There is a power in me sometimes that knows things that I do not know. It is best not to question it."

"What do you know about my dream?"

"It is one you have had before."

Samantha nodded. It was one she'd had many times before. It glittered on the edge of her consciousness. Sometimes after this nightmare, she dreamed Lance came, saw her and her ranch in all its glory, and left his wife to be with her.

She stepped into the room and closed the door behind her. "Do you know what the dream means?"

Elunami felt despair suffocating her, dragging her down. If the *señora* knew that she, Elunami, had lost her own way, she would not ask for guidance.

"What should I do?" the *señora* asked again, softly. Elunami struggled up, out of herself. Outside the window, the eastern sky was gray. In a few hours the morning sun would eat the stars and stand up.

"It is not good to lose hope," she whispered, bowing her head.

Samantha felt tears well in her eyes. She yearned so for what she could not have—the health of her son, the warmth and closeness of a life with her beloved. Her soul ached for Lance in a way it never could for another man. Her love for him was nobler, truer, purer. What she could feel for a man like Steve Sheridan was nothing compared to that.

Elunami appeared to have psychic powers. If they became friends, perhaps the girl would bring Lance back to her.

Joy quickened in Samantha. *It is not good to lose hope. Someday, my beloved. Someday . . .*

When at last the kind *señora* went back to bed, Elunami closed her eyes to meditate once more. Her soul had not been pulled up for a very long time, and now she felt almost desperate for it to happen. She needed some sign that the Great Mystery had received Tuvi's soul, that it had not gone astray. . . .

Chila woke at midnight and dressed in the dark. Usually if she had to get up at this hour after falling asleep, she'd be groggy, but not tonight. Remembering that Denny was in town energized her, gave her the strength to do whatever needed doing.

She was a foot shorter than Joe; his pants were almost too tight for her. A roll of flesh spilled out over the waistline. But she got them buttoned.

Dressed, she carefully loaded the .45 and slipped it into her pocket. It would not be easy getting around without being seen, but with her hair up under a man's hat and her face half hidden by the shadows, she didn't expect to be recognized.

Feet up on the windowsill, Steve leaned back and listened to sounds of men reveling in the saloons below. The piano played for a while, then became silent. Frogs and crickets sounded an incessant harmony. Every now and then a bird sang.

Samantha Forrester's lovely face glowed on the surface of his mind, dazzling it the way her presence had earlier. As much as he might toy with the idea of staying, he knew he wouldn't. He couldn't. He was afraid. He knew from past experiences with women that Samantha Forrester had the power to entangle him in emotional bonds and present him with nothing but maddening choices.

He couldn't stay—no matter how lovely Samantha's face looked when she strained up to kiss him. She was a beautiful woman, and his heart beat with a heavy stroke at the memory of her—soft, sweet, and trembling in his arms—but such a woman would expect a man to marry and settle down and take care of her. There were things he couldn't do in a little backwater camp like Picket Post.

Still, his soul stirred, reached out to her. He could feel part of himself trying to encircle her, to bind her to him, to bind himself to her. It was a part of him that had caused trouble before, caught him for a time—but only for a time.

Maybe there was something wrong with him. Maybe being raised by the Papago had turned him into a misfit among normal white people. Part of him still sought the simplicity of that old, placid life.

He didn't remember his own parents. He remembered walking away from his home, knowing he didn't intend to go back. But he couldn't remember why. A time or two he'd tried to remember, but his mind always thwarted him. Whatever his secrets, they were well hidden.

He didn't need to delve into all that, whatever it was. He was considered successful now. He and his partners had a waiting list of people who wanted houses built. Some of their customers were among the wealthiest in America.

Success was nice, but he never forgot that he hadn't always been secure. At six, living among the desert Indians, contemptuously called the bean eaters by white men, he had already known he was unacceptable to most of the white people in the world, but he wasn't exactly sure why. Then one day Crows Walking had bought him a suit of clothes like the white boys wore. One of the women had washed his hair and scrubbed him until he felt raw.

They had gone to a white funeral, that of a man who had occasionally hired Crows Walking's brother. Afterward one of the white men gave Steve a penny. He ran to the general store. The owner's wife, who had never had a kind word for him when he was dressed in rags, practically fawned over him.

Well, what have we here? she'd asked, putting aside her magazine and heaving her fleshy body from her chair. She had actually smiled at him while he decided between the licorice stick and the candy cane. Usually she didn't get up until she had someone else to wait on. Then, grudgingly she would ask him what he wanted, reach into the big glass jar, and hold on to the candy until he gave her his penny.

The next month he had returned to the store in his rags, with his usual film of dirt and his friend, Speaking Water, and she'd been back to normal, hanging on to her candy and muttering under her breath, *Filthy Indian brats.*

He'd never forgotten the lesson he'd learned from that woman. So when he was old enough to make his own decisions, he washed carefully and dressed well.

Three days ago he had been on his way from San Francisco to Waco. He'd stopped at the Papago Indian Reservation to visit. Crows Walking had told him that Arden Chandler, the new Indian agent, had issued a summons "requesting the presence of Steve Sheridan, my white son."

Something about that message had set all Crows Walking's alarm bells ringing. He had ordered Steve to leave immediately. Steve had wanted to meet with Chandler, but Crows Walking warned him against it, insisting that Steve would have no defense if the agent meant him harm. An Indian agent had the power of life and death over his charges. At any excuse he could call in the soldiers, some of whom loved an opportunity to kill Indians—or a stray white man if he seemed too closely aligned with them.

Steve had felt a chill of apprehension knowing Arden Chandler was looking for him. That had never happened to him before. Even now, just thinking about it, his stomach felt heavy, as if he carried a rock there.

To please Crows Walking, Steve had cut his visit short and ridden away. That's when he'd come upon Elunami and her dead companions.

So now it seemed Chandler had two reasons to send the soldiers after him. But he had no intention of playing into their hands or of walking into a trap that might destroy him. Steve considered himself a pragmatist. In this world, he knew, there were winners and losers, and he knew which he'd rather be.

He admired Indians for their honesty, spirituality, courage, and ability to survive under circumstances that would break a cockroach. He knew few white men he looked up to in the same way. But he *was* white, and he had no intention of deliberately joining the losers. Money was power. And he wanted power for himself. He was a good builder. People wanted the houses he could build, and they were happy to pay his price. He was not about to jeopardize his future by meeting with Arden Chandler or by tying himself down with Samantha Forrester—or any woman. He'd made that mistake once.

Caroline Plummer, the daughter of wealthy financier Atchison Plummer, was beautiful and popular and busy. She had a wide, full-lipped mouth, slanted green eyes, and pretty little pink freckles scattered over her cheeks. Steve had fallen in love with her and she with him, apparently. He had intended to marry her. But one day at work, a man had fallen off a scaffold at quitting time and broken his leg. Steve had loaded him into a wagon and taken him to the hospital in the northern part of San Francisco. He'd stayed until the doctor had reported that all was well and the leg would probably mend just fine.

Then he'd taken the man home to his worried wife and gone home himself. Already late for his appointment with Caroline, he'd changed into his dinner clothes and rushed to her house. But instead of being glad to see him and listening to his explanation, she'd been furious. He endured her angry tirade for a while, then turned and walked out. She followed him outside, yelling something about his making her late to *the* social event of the season. He'd told his driver to take him home.

Caroline had screamed and run down the street after him, but he'd never looked back. He'd sat inside with sweat running down his forehead and into his eyes.

Until that night she had been his ideal woman—half courtesan, half playmate. A week later she'd come to his office and apologized, told him she loved him and wanted him back. He had been kind to her, but he had not called on her again. He'd missed her and been fairly miserable for two months before he left San Francisco, but he hadn't gone back to her.

He didn't know why he was so unforgiving. Other men he knew condoned a lot more. Some even forgave infidelity. But he couldn't, even when part of him wanted to. He didn't like knowing that, either, because it implied things were happening in him without his permission.

Leaving San Francisco hadn't changed that. At any given moment, he couldn't decide whether to worry about Chandler setting the soldiers on him, strangers shooting at him from ambush, Ham Russell threatening him, or Samantha Forrester disappearing from his life forever. The last seemed the most urgent and disconcerting, however.

An image of Samantha's face filled his mind and interrupted his thoughts. Her skin glowed with the softest, steadiest light. It seemed to gather light and reflect it back with more capacity to confuse the viewer than any face he'd ever seen. The slim, white stem of her lovely neck gleamed with the same soft light. Her light hair added to the illusion. She was a passionate, intense young woman and thoroughly accustomed to getting what she wanted.

He was still surprised she'd let him kiss her, though. He must have been at least half crazy to do it, but with all the opportunities he'd had today to get himself killed he must have felt he deserved a kiss or two.

He stood up abruptly. Fantasizing about Samantha would get him nowhere. He glanced at the sagging mattress on the bed across the room. His roommate, a tall, skinny whiskey drummer, had gone out for the evening, saying he'd be back later. Steve knew he should lie down and wrestle himself to sleep, but he didn't feel tired. He just felt restless.

At last he left the room and headed for the Red Rock Saloon, which seemed the liveliest. Inside, the smell of unwashed male bodies mingled with the acrid pungencies of beer, tobacco, whiskey, sawdust, and cheap perfume. Men played cards around rickety tables and danced with the girls who worked there. A lone man at a table by the window gave his whole attention to the beefsteak swimming in blood on his plate. One young woman served drinks and flirted with miners and cowboys. Steve chose a chair in the corner beside the swinging doors separating the saloon from the back. A man played the piano.

Steve ordered a beer, watching the men at the next table play poker. After a while, one of them, a sharp-eyed man in his fifties, with a week's stubble of gray beard on his face, turned around and looked at Steve pointedly.

"We're looking for a little new money for this here game."

"I don't mind making an occasional donation," Steve replied.

The man introduced himself as Eagle Thornton and the other three as Bill, Santa Fe, and Artemis. They, too, sported a week's growth of beard, dirty clothes, and a fragrant aroma.

After about an hour, Steve had a sizable pile of money in front of him. One of the men dropped out.

Eagle Thornton pushed a chip into the center of the table. "It was a mistake inviting Sheridan to sit in. He's about to take all our money."

Steve chuckled. "If you haven't got any more money than this little pile, you aren't going to miss it."

Thornton laughed. "I guess you got a point there."

The game broke up at midnight. Steve bought the players a round of drinks, relieved when it looked as if they were going to let him get away without gunplay. Some men took losing money a lot harder than these boys did. The other three wandered out of the Red Rock, but Thornton seemed inclined to talk. Steve still wasn't sleepy, so he listened.

A little later, a tall, thin, well-dressed man with shifty black eyes stopped at the bar. He downed a couple of drinks in quick succession and then hunched over the counter, glancing up now and then at the mirror to catch sight of the swinging doors behind him. He seemed to be waiting for someone.

"Who's that?"

"Grover Bush," Thornton told him. "He's ramrod at Mrs. Forrester's spread."

"He any good?"

"Depends on what you want done." Thornton turned a piercing glance on Steve. "For some things, I guess he'd be handy as molasses to have around."

Ham Russell and the men who'd ridden into town with him entered the bar. Engrossed in their conversation, they walked through the room without looking either way and disappeared into the back. A girl followed them and came out shortly with orders, which she relayed to the bartender. She carried a tray of drinks to the back room and came back smiling and counting money. A moment later Grover Bush walked through the swinging doors into the back.

Steve had an irresistible urge to see if Bush and Russell were together. He hefted his beer bottle and groaned. "I think I'm overdue to read a catalog," he said, referring to the paper used in many frontier toilets.

"You'll smell it before you see it. Just bear to your left."

Steve walked through the swinging doors into the shadowy hallway and glanced back at the room he'd left. No one seemed to pay any attention to him. He eased past a closed door, through which he heard men talking, and stepped into the room next to it, an empty office. He walked quietly over to the wall and pressed his ear against the pine.

"... Mrs. Forrester ..."

One of the men laughed. "Kind of a shame in a way. A pretty lady comes out West to lose that much money."

"Hell, any woman who'd buy a bunch of cows and expect them to just sit there until it was time to pluck money out of their ears don't deserve to have money." The voice was Ham Russell's.

Steve found a crack wide enough to see through. Six men sat around a poker table, each with a pile of bills in front of him. They were easy with their conversation. Steve picked up other comments that told him they were rustlers living off Forrester beef. Bush and Russell sat side by side, engaging in low-voiced conversation; money exchanged hands. Grover Bush stuffed the money in his pocket, nodded at the men, and walked out.

A surprising anger swelled in Steve. Samantha Forrester didn't stand a chance. Her own foreman was taking money from the men rustling her cattle.

He gave Bush time to get out of sight, eased himself past the private room, and walked back into the noisy barroom. Thornton nodded at him, tossed down a drink, wiped his mouth, and set the glass back on the table.

"Well, I can see you ain't taking it all that well. The way I look at it, they're probably doing her a favor. Without their help it would take her years to go broke. She might as well get it over with while she's young and beautiful and can make a fresh start."

Steve grimaced. He wondered if everyone in the saloon knew what he had just learned. "That's about the crookedest piece of logic I've ever heard."

"Stinks, don't it?" Thornton said, grinning. "Well, I have to admit, you're right. But since there ain't a damned thing I can do about it, I guess I'm entitled to my own way of thinking. 'Least I don't have any trouble sleeping nights."

At the hotel, Steve found a crowd of people in the hallway blocking the door to his room.

"What happened?" he asked, elbowing his way through.

Daley glanced up and saw him. "What the hell are you doing here?"

"This is my room."

"Well, I might of known," he said, gesturing to the twin bed on the left side of the room.

Steve glanced at the bed and saw that a man still lay on it. Blood splattered the wall in front of the man and covered the back of the man's head.

"Dead," Daley growled. "Looks like an execution. Someone slipped in here and put a gun against the back of his head." He shook his own head in disbelief. "He was a whiskey drummer with no known enemies as far as anyone knows. Only been in town two days. So, maybe you'd like to explain this."

"I don't know him. We're sharing a room because we had no choice."

Daley and the crowd finally left. Steve was given another room, this time with two men who snored loudly. But it didn't matter. He didn't feel sleepy. The thought that someone wanted to kill him badly enough to fire at him in broad daylight and then sneak into his room in the middle of the night, was unsettling. He sat by the window, waiting for the sun to come up. Gradually, however, he relaxed. A knock on his door startled him. One of the men bolted forward, looked around, and then settled back into sleep.

"Who's there?" Steve yelled through the door.

"Samantha Forrester."

"Just a minute." Light streaming in through the window and the noise of traffic in the road downstairs told Steve he had slept, and later than he'd meant to. He rummaged through his satchel, found a bottle of bay rum, and splashed it on his face and chest and under his arms. He waved the bottle at the snoring men, then pulled on his pants, ran his hands through his hair, and walked to the door.

Samantha gave him a hesitant smile. "Mr. Sheridan . . ."

From what he could see of her through the mist she created between his usually keen eyes and his dazzled brain, her skin looked clear and silvery, her eyes the color of turquoise.

Samantha stopped. Her gaze lowered to his bare chest, lean and hard and covered with wet black hair, then returned to his face. He smelled strongly of bay rum. "Excuse me . . . I didn't think you'd still be asleep at this hour." She particularly hadn't expected him to come to the door shirtless and with his pants only half buttoned up. His smooth arms gleamed in the morning light, looking amazingly touchable; for a second she forgot what she'd come here to say.

"Good morning," he said, watching her intently.

"I—I just wanted to get my gun back . . ." Her words trailed off. The look in his eyes caused odd things to happen in her body. "Is your shirt torn?" she asked.

"I don't have on a shirt."

"I . . . know that . . . I was just wondering if it was because it was torn," she said, flushing.

In a black riding outfit and black-and-white hat, she looked dressed for traveling. A strand of her hair had escaped from its pins. He reached out to push it back, but the look in her eyes stopped him.

"Sorry," he muttered, putting his hand in his pocket, where it wouldn't get into any more trouble. Beads of perspiration formed on his forehead.

"I . . . can't believe I forgot my gun . . . So much excitement, yesterday . . ."

"S'all right," he said gruffly.

"And I wanted to thank you again for saving our lives yesterday, both times, and to see if there was any way you might reconsider. I'm willing to pay more than the man in Waco," she ended breathlessly.

"I'm . . . deeply honored, but I already have men on the site, preparing the limestone bricks." He walked to his cot. From under his pillow he picked up her .32 revolver, a small Hopkins and Allen Ranger, hefted it a moment in his hand, then walked back to the door and presented the handle to her.

Samantha Forrester slipped the pistol into her pocket and started to turn away. "I don't suppose you're going to church this morning, Mr. Sheridan?"

"No, ma'am. I don't believe in hell, so I don't have to go."

Samantha's laughter was so rich and spontaneous, it made him feel good all over. "I'd be willing to see you to your ranch, though."

For one moment, Samantha wondered if there was any way she could get rid of Grover Bush without Steve's finding out he was in town. "Thank you, but my foreman is in town and will escort us. You're welcome to ride along with us, though."

"Wrong direction." Mention of her foreman made him want to tell her that Bush was stealing from her, but since he would not be around to protect her from Bush, that could be dangerous information for her to have. He didn't like the idea of her at the mercy of every crooked man in the country, but unless he was willing to stay around himself, he might as well get used to it.

"There may be half a dozen trains piled up down there by

now,'' she said, smiling a wan little smile that tugged at his heart.

"I guess I'll just have to take my chances. Good-bye, Samantha Forrester.'' It was a wrenching experience to watch hope fade from her wide eyes.

"If you change your mind, just take the Boston House Road northeast. The first valley belongs to the Darts. The second is mine. You can't miss my house. It's so out of place the natives renamed a mountain and a road for it.''

"I'll do that.''

Regretfully she turned and left. The sound of her footsteps died away. Steve closed the door and leaned against it. He should have confronted that foreman of hers and showed the man up in front of the town. But that wouldn't stop the rustlers, who at least were robbing her in an orderly manner and not hurting anybody.

Again he reminded himself it was none of his business. He'd saved her life—that was enough of a service. She was happy for it. He just needed to let it go now.

On the sidewalk Samantha executed the plan she'd made during breakfast. She started with the shop next to the hotel and worked her way around the entire quad, buying some trinket in each one, chatting with the reluctant shopkeeper until he or she had remembered who she was and how long they had known each other, and then moving on. By the time she had made the circle, she had her arms full of packages—and people were no longer avoiding her.

At the hotel she put away her packages and came back down to the lobby to find Grover Bush looking for her.

"Morning, ma'am,'' he said, taking off his hat.

"Good morning, Mr. Bush.''

"We've had a streak of good luck,'' he said, watching her carefully.

"Well, please tell me about it. I could use some.''

"An Indian by the name of Silver Fish wants to sell us his herd of sheep.''

Samantha frowned. "I thought you were opposed to running sheep on our range.''

"Ordinarily I would be, but this is too good a deal to pass up.''

"What makes it so good?''

"The price, and I've looked at the sheep. They're worth a lot more on the market than he's asking for them."

"How much does he want for the herd?" Samantha asked. Bush had hit a sore spot. She had wanted to run sheep and cattle on her ranch from the beginning, but he had objected.

"Five hundred dollars."

"For how many sheep?"

"Two hundred or more. I saw the herd."

That *was* a good price. Sheep were selling for eight fifty now. Wool was going for about seventy-five cents a pound, and it was almost time to shear. There didn't appear to be any way she could lose money on the deal.

"Is there something wrong with the herd?" she asked.

"I didn't see a thing wrong with any of 'em."

"All right. Tell him to meet me at the bank."

Twenty minutes later she and Bush waited for Silver Fish inside the bank. Even though Samantha had a large account there, Eugene England, the banker, a small man with a big mustache, could not hide his discomfort at seeing her. He was not a man she particularly liked, however, so she didn't mind when he pretended to be too busy for their usual chat.

"That's him," Bush said, pointing.

Samantha glanced out the window at a tall, slightly bow-legged Indian dressed in a black frock coat and black trousers. He wore shiny knee-high black army boots and a black top hat. He could have passed for a businessman, except for a dozen or so necklaces of beads, claws, and animal teeth around his strong neck. The redness of his face appeared to come from an excess of alcohol rather than heritage. She had come to recognize that unnatural flush. The man staggered through the door and approached them, weaving slightly from side to side.

"This is Mrs. Forrester," Bush said when Silver Fish stopped in front of her.

Silver Fish nodded. He had such opaque black eyes that she had no way of knowing if they even registered her presence. Looking into them, she felt as if she disappeared entirely.

Mr. England rushed over with the bill of sale form and filled it out. Silver Fish made his mark, and England witnessed it. Samantha signed, then England processed her withdrawal. Samantha passed the money to Silver Fish. Through the entire proceeding, he hadn't said one word.

Samantha watched him lurch away. "I hope you know what to do with a herd of sheep."

Bush grunted. "We've got Ramon. He was a sheepherder before he was a *vaquero*."

At ten o'clock, Samantha saw Steve ride east out of Picket Post, probably to intercept the noon train at Camp Pinal. The knowledge that he had not, in the end, changed his mind disturbed her more than she would admit.

She strolled over to Seth and Lydia Boswell's to check on Lars, who was resting comfortably in a feather bed in the extra bedroom. His color and his spirits were good. Samantha said good-bye, confident he'd be well taken care of. Lydia Boswell was a good cook.

Outside again, Samantha walked quickly toward the general store. The sky had darkened with thunderheads, and a cold breeze whipped through the town, lifting the dust and swirling it around.

It felt good to get out of the cold wind. The general store smelled of garlic, dill pickles, new fabric, and bakery goods. Samantha bought a riding skirt for herself, coats for Elunami, herself, and Nicholas. She couldn't find a warm enough coat to fit Elunami and finally settled for a blanket she could wear over the lightweight coat. Samantha considered buying an entire wardrobe for the girl but feared that might alert someone to the fact that her new governess had arrived without clothing of her own.

At the hotel, Bush waited for her, looking irritable. "You're late," he said impatiently. "Ramon has the herd of sheep on the move. I got six riders waiting."

"We'll be ready in a few moments," she said.

"You're not bringing that Mexican girl, are you?"

"I beg your pardon?"

The pink in his face darkened to red at her tone. "I hired a cook," he said, unwilling to back down. "We don't need another Mexican cook."

"She's not a cook, Mr. Bush. She's a governess."

He snorted his dislike.

Samantha decided to give him the benefit of the doubt. Bush was originally from Illinois. Perhaps Mexican cooking didn't agree with his Illinois, corn-fed stomach.

Two miles out of town they were stopped by the largest herd of antelope Samantha had ever seen—a tawny, white-tailed flood of them, galloping flank-to-flank. As the antelope pounded straight toward them, Samantha took the reins to Nicholas's horse and held tight. Bush pulled his gun and aimed it at one of the leaders.

"Don't shoot them," Samantha cried.

"You want to be trampled into dust or have your brand-new herd of sheep scattered from here to Nogales?"

Miraculously, even as Bush spoke the leaders turned and the entire herd changed direction as one. One moment they were aimed at Samantha's small party, the next they swerved to the left. As they clattered past, about fifty yards away, hundreds of white cottony rumps caught the sunlight; sharp little hooves cut the grass into dust.

"Damned nuisances!" Bush cursed, coughing.

"They're beautiful," Samantha said. She had never seen so many antelope in one herd before.

"They may be beautiful, but they eat the grass your cattle and sheep need."

Samantha laughed. "Well, it's good of you to be concerned about my interests, but I don't begrudge them food to live."

"Well, you will, if the rains don't come this year. They'll be drinking the water you'll want for your own cattle."

Samantha wasn't that worried. She had formed a canal company and hired an overseer, an engineer, and a full company of laborers to dig canals from the Salt River to the ranch, where a natural basin waited for water.

"That reminds me," she said, turning to face Bush. "We need to round up a herd to sell."

"Now?"

"As soon as possible."

Bush scowled. "I thought I was the ramrod of this outfit."

"I can't see how my needing to sell stock can be construed as undermining your authority, Mr. Bush. If I go broke, there won't be any need for your services . . . or anyone else's."

"You just bought stock."

"A tiny herd of sheep? I have thousands of cattle, and they sell for a great deal more."

He backed down, but the look in his eyes told her he resented it—and probably her as well. "How many do you want to sell?" he asked, his tone gruff.

"A thousand head or so."

"That's a lot."

"I have a payroll to meet on the first." He didn't know that she could always transfer funds from her New York account, and she wasn't about to tell him.

Bush nodded his agreement and galloped ahead.

As they rode along, Elunami turned in her saddle occasionally to look back at the terrain behind them. The third time she did, Samantha rode close to her. "What are you looking for?" she asked.

"You are followed."

Samantha turned in her saddle. At first she didn't see anything, then she saw a group of riders in the distance, so tiny she was amazed Elunami had seen them at all.

"They're probably just men from one of the other ranches going home after the weekend."

Elunami shook her head. "I don't think so."

Samantha asked Bush to send a man back to check. He returned in a few minutes. "Well?" she asked.

"They're Indians, Papago, I think. Led by a big warrior by the name of Silver Fish." Bush's messenger squinted at the overhung sky as if embarrassed. "Says he sold you his herd and then was robbed of the money. Says he has been shamed, and the only way he can save face is if he comes and works for you until he earns that herd back. You want us to run them off?"

"Yep, they'll just be trouble," Bush interjected.

"No. Let him come," Samantha said firmly. "We may need their help with the herd. And, if he's working for me he might not steal it."

"I wouldn't count on that," Bush growled, obvious displeasure in his eyes.

A short time later, clouds covered the sun—and an unaccustomed chill added a sting to the wind now coming from the north. Within minutes the wind picked up speed and began lifting the sand and flinging it into their faces. Samantha stopped and unpacked the coats she'd bought. She tied Nicholas's cravat over his nose and mouth. Elunami draped the blanket around her shoulders. Bush's riders put on their jackets and pulled their bandannas up over their noses.

Steve Sheridan was somewhere to the east. At least she and Nicholas and her riders knew where they were going. Steve had probably never seen the railroad station at Camp Pinal. Even in good weather, it was hard to spot.

"Are we almost—" Nicholas broke off, coughing so hard he could not continue. Samantha looked anxiously at the darkening sky. A wind storm was especially bad for his lungs.

"Ride faster," she urged. She had to get her son out of this storm. That need drove everything else from her mind.

CHAPTER SIX

By noon Steve decided he was lost. Somehow, in the blowing sand, he had missed Camp Pinal, or else it was farther from Picket Post than he'd thought.

An hour later the wind stopped as abruptly as it had started. The sand sifted down, and the air became clear enough to see through. Steve found that he was in a shallow canyon at the juncture of two nearly dry creeks. High limestone cliffs soared upward in a smooth sweep. A grazing mule deer raised its head, looked at Steve, and bounded away, its big ears lifted high. If his memory served him right, he'd once traveled through here with a band of braves on a hunting expedition. This was one of the most beautiful places in the territory.

He stopped and dismounted to let Calico drink from the shallow creek. The sun was high overhead. He couldn't tell which direction he was going.

Calico raised his head and cocked his ears. Having learned to trust his horse's instincts, Steve listened intently, but all he heard was running water. He walked away from the stream and listened. Finally it came again—the distant sound of a horse whinnying. Unsheathing his gun, Steve walked toward the sound, rounded a boulder, and saw a dun gelding about a hundred dred yards away, its reins tied to a manzanita bush.

He squatted and watched the small clearing for a time. When he was sure the horse was alone, that no one shared the canyon with him, he walked forward. "Where's your rider?" he murmured, stroking the horse's nose.

The horse snickered and stamped as if happy to see him. On a chance, Steve untied the horse and let him go. The animal hesitated, looked back at Steve, then walked into the brush. Steve followed, wishing he'd taken the time to get Calico. Just when he felt sure the horse was going to run away, it stopped and hung its head. At first Steve didn't see anything. Then, walking over, he saw a hand protruding from beneath the thick brush of a recently fallen limb; he lifted the limb away. On the

111

ground lay a young man, no more than seventeen years old by the scant stubble on his face. His shirt was bloodied.

Steve knelt down and felt his neck for a pulse. The boy's skin was warm, his pulse a little thready. He'd been shot in the shoulder, high up enough, so it might have missed his lung.

"Reckon you're gonna live," he muttered.

Steve filled his canteen, mounted Calico at the creek, and returned to find the boy hadn't moved. He swabbed the boy's face with his wet bandanna. After a bit, the young man opened his eyes.

"Am I daid?"

"Does this look like hell?"

"I might a been going to heaven."

"Sorry. I thought you were a cowboy."

The boy tried to sit up, groaned, and eased himself back onto the ground. "Ow! That hurts like a two-forty trot."

"What happened?"

"You got any water? Mine ran out sometime last night, I think. I cain't remember when."

Steve held him while he drank a few swallows of water from the canteen.

"Thanks. Come onto a pack of running iron specialists Friday afternoon late. They shot me, but I managed to git outta sight before they came riding past. They never seen me or I'd be daider than I am. Name's Sender Thompson."

Steve had hoped to get clear of this country before he met everyone who lived here. "Steve Sheridan," he said finally.

Even wounded, Sender Thompson was quick. "Jones, huh? That's a good name. I've used it myself a few times."

Steve laughed. He couldn't imagine one so young having done much of anything for more than a few minutes. "Think you can make it home by yourself?"

"Always been able to before." He struggled to his feet and collapsed in a dead faint. Steve caught him in middrop, eased him down, and waited. When Thompson came to, Steve helped him onto his horse.

"Which way's home?"

Sender puzzled over this for a moment, then looked around to get his bearings. "Where the hell did that creek go?"

Steve pointed at the creek.

"Once we get back to the Gila you can see the Forrester spread—Boston House Mountain—from there," the boy told him.

A thrill of dread and anticipation shot through Steve. Samantha Forrester's house! So, he was fated to see her again.

Steve rode along in a daze, barely noticing the cactus-strewn country through which they passed. A small tingle of excitement had started in his belly at the mention of Samantha Forrester. A warning probably that he had no business running into her again. Something in him yearned for contact with her. He felt it now, straining toward her. He was no better than a schoolboy with his first crush. She seemed so determined to entice him into staying, what might she do if he showed up at her door?

The thought caused a heavy tingle of fear and excitement to course through him. At that moment, if he could have pointed the wounded boy at the Forrester spread and let him go, Steve would have taken off in the opposite direction at top speed. But Sender Thompson was too shaky to make it to the ranch alone. The sky was growing dark again, threatening another windstorm. The boy could get lost, fall off his horse, and die before anyone found him.

Samantha saw the white facade of her two-story house with relief. She moved aside the sheltering blanket and peered into its folds at her son, whom she had set on her own horse, so she could protect him from the desert winds. She'd traded her coat for Elunami's blanket.

"Hang on, sweetheart. We're almost there."

Nicholas coughed, then nodded to reassure her.

"We're almost there," she repeated, glancing up to gauge how much farther they had to go.

The two-story house, which sat on the north side of the mountain behind it, was about a quarter of a mile away. Although the frame house was totally out of place in the desert, it still called to her. She loved it as home even as she resented it as inadequate living quarters. Sand seeped through every crack. In the winter, wind whipped through the almost nonexistent walls.

As they rode up the long, gentle slope to the house, Juana ran out to greet them. Almost as broad as she was tall, the Mexican cook had a sweet round face and smiling eyes. She doted on Nicholas, whom she called by a hundred pet names.

"*Buenos días, niño mio! Buenos días, señora!* I'm so glad to see you, *pequeño!*" she said, lifting Nicholas down and hugging him against her ample bosom.

"Are you hungry, dumpling?"

"I ate a big breakfast," Nicholas said. Juana led Nicholas,

who was talking nonstop about the sheep and the storm, straight to the warm, fragrant kitchen. Samantha followed them. Elunami hung back.

"Juana, this is Tristera. I've hired her as a governess for Nicholas."

Juana smiled at the girl and put an arm around her shoulders. "Are you hungry? Come, eat something."

"Thank you, but I'm fine."

"Come sit with us anyway," said Samantha. "No one can resist Juana's chili. Eat just a bit. You're too thin."

The kitchen smelled of fresh-brewed coffee. Tristera ate a few bites of chili and drank two glasses of cool, sweet milk. Samantha ate a little of everything—chili, corn bread, apple pie, milk, coffee. Nicholas picked at his food, but Juana coaxed him into eating several spoonfuls of everything.

When he closed his mouth, refusing to take another bite, Samantha put him down for his nap. For once he didn't fight her, he just closed his eyes and fell asleep almost instantly. Samantha stood by his bed anxiously. It was always a little frightening when Nicholas went to sleep too easily.

"How is he?" Tristera asked as Samantha returned to the kitchen. She and Juana were already washing and drying the dishes; the room smelled faintly of Juana's strong lye soap.

"I think he'll be all right. Let me show you to your room."

"I can sleep outside."

"No. I'd prefer you to be in the house, if you don't mind." Tristera shrugged. "I don't mind."

The house had six bedrooms on the second story, three on each side of a long hall. Juana slept in the one nearest the stairs. Nicholas had the middle bedroom; the one next to his was empty. Samantha put Tristera in the one across from her own room. Both of them opened onto the sleeping porch, where everyone slept on really hot nights.

Tristera frowned at the sight of the room. "Is something wrong?" Samantha asked.

"Is this all for me?"

"Yes, it is."

"At the school, I slept in a dormitory with twenty other girls."

"Then I guess it's my job to spoil you. Once you adjust you'll never be able to share a room again. I couldn't survive without a room of my own." She glanced at the girl's borrowed clothes. "I have some clothes we can take in for you. Do you sew?"

"Yes. It was required."

"Your sheets are clean. We boiled them just before I left for Phoenix. But everything sifts into this house, so I'd check for spiders and maybe shake out the sheets before I got into bed. Rest for a while or do whatever you want. I'll look through my clothes."

Samantha went outside to check her greenhouse, which stood on the shady east side of the barn, so it would receive direct sun only in the morning. Twenty-by-ten feet, it sported a double roof and side walls—lattice on the outside to keep out some of the sun, glass on the inside to hold in moisture. With diligent care and persistent watering, Samantha had kept alive a number of flowers that wouldn't otherwise have lived in this climate—roses, mums, daisies, zinnias, a few houseplants, and some orchids she'd brought from the East.

She stepped inside and took a deep breath of the moist, woodsy air. It was like walking into a roomful of beloved friends. She needed flowers. To her, a house without plants was a house without life.

"Are you all okay?" she asked them. To her immense relief, she found Juana had done a good job of keeping everything watered. She walked down the aisle between the two rows of tiered wooden shelves, stopping to pinch a dead leaf or speak to a blossom.

"Good job, Juana," she whispered.

South of the greenhouse, on the same side of the barn, the workshop where she sculpted was open to the elements under a high shed. It had fared less well. The storm had blown sand onto her modeling tools, the canvas covering her wet clay—everything.

She lifted the canvas. The clay she'd brought down from the mountain last month was still damp and pliable beneath its soaked canvas cover. *I must be the only person in the world who has to water dirt*, Juana had grumbled good-naturedly. She didn't understand why a woman with money would take on a whole passel of chores where it wasn't necessary, but Samantha knew Juana took an odd, complaining sort of pride in her mistress's many interests and oddities.

In the barn, Samantha checked each of her horses, stopping longest beside Brickelbush, her favorite. "How are you, boy? Did you miss me?"

Brickelbush snorted and nuzzled her hand. She reached into her pocket for sugar, felt only the cold metal bullets she'd put there earlier and brought her hand out empty. "Sorry, boy. It was a rough trip home.'' She patted his head and stroked his long, silky neck. The smell of her barn reminded her of the livery stable at Picket Post . . . and Steve Sheridan.

On the porch she stopped and checked her bird feeder. It was quiet for the moment, unattended by the hundreds of birds who regularly stopped to eat the seed she ordered from a Chicago catalog company. The feeder, one of the few earthenware pieces she hadn't glazed, was half full.

The parlor smelled of sand and chili. From the kitchen, the clatter of dishes and the sounds of Juana and Tristera talking gave her a good feeling. She liked her house filled with the smells of good food and the sounds of happy people. She loved harmony, cleanliness, and order. Unfortunately it was rarely attained in this house. If only Steve Sheridan had agreed to stay and build her a real house. . . .

They had to travel slow. It took three hours to cover less than ten miles. Near sunset, Steve got his first glimpse of Samantha's house—a two-story, New England–style cottage set at the foot of an Arizona mountain.

He shook his head at the sight. Samantha Forrester had done all the wrong things. For starters, this desert fairly cried out for adobe at least two feet thick, and she'd built a toothpick house under a mountain that looked precarious as hell. And then . . .

And then nothing, he told himself abruptly. What Samantha Forrester did or did not do was none of his concern. He hoped he could remember that.

Next to the trickling creek, a family of Indians had erected tepees using government canvas instead of buffalo or antelope hides. This signified either a more civilized or a poorer Indian. They were dressed like Papago, who had adopted European-style shirts, pants, dresses, skirts, and blouses. Steve peered at the faces of the women and children who stepped outside to watch them ride slowly past.

Nearby, a dozen horses grazed. Two sheepdogs slept in the shade of a tree. *Ricos*, Steve thought. Rich Indians. Steve suddenly understood when he saw the tall warrior step out of the tepee to stand with one hand on each woman's shoulder. Steve recognized Silver Fish, whom he'd seen leaving the *papaguería*—the Papago Indian Reservation—the day he'd arrived. According to Crows Walking, Silver Fish was a hero to the reservation Indians. He stole horses and cattle from the whites, and they never caught him.

Steve nodded at Silver Fish, who showed by the slightest flicker of his narrowing eyes that he acknowledged the greeting. Steve led Sender up the long incline toward the house, which sat between an enormous barn and a locomotive turntable with its own train shed. Railroad tracks stretched to the south, gleaming in the sunlight. Apparently Samantha Forrester was better connected than he'd thought. She had a spur line practically to her front door. As they climbed the gentle hill and neared the house, he saw that the train shed was empty. At least her palace car hadn't beaten her home.

At the front porch, Steve hallooed the house. Nicholas's face appeared at the window, and he let out a yell.

"Hey, Mama, it's Mr. Sheridan and Sender!"

Footsteps sounded on the wood floors. Samantha Forrester opened the door and stepped out onto the porch.

"Mr. Sheridan . . ." Her cheeks flushed with rosy color. She looked from Steve to Sender, and her color quickly faded. "Bring him in, please."

Sender swayed in the saddle a bit melodramatically. Steve helped him down and supported him on one side. Samantha rushed down to support the other, and together they half carried Sender up the steps. Steve saw a Mexican woman poke her head out and rush back into the house. "Juana, get the medicine box," Samantha called after her. "And bring a clean sheet. We'll put him on the sofa."

The house was richly furnished, but what piqued Steve's interest was the lack of family pictures on the walls. Every house he'd been in since leaving the pueblos was cluttered with family photographs.

"Did your family's home burn down?"

"No. Why?"

"You don't have any photographs."

"Oh." Samantha avoided his eyes. "Not everyone worships at the hearth of a family tree."

"I suppose not."

Samantha turned away. She didn't know Steve Sheridan well enough to tell him she had no photographs of her parents, because she hated them.

Juana waddled back into the room and spread a quilt over the sofa's heavy leather cushions. Unlike the dainty Louis XIV sofas that were all the rage back East, and about as useful to a tired or wounded man as tickets to the opera, this one looked comfortable. Steve eased Sender onto it; the young man closed his eyes in gratitude.

"What happened to him?" Samantha asked, straightening to face Steve.

He took her by the elbow and led her out of Sender's hearing. "He happened onto rustlers. One of them took a shot at him and left him for dead."

Rage flared in her lovely eyes. "Those rotten . . . I don't mind about the cattle, but why do they have to shoot my people? This is twice now. Last time the young man died. He was only twenty-three years old." Emotion thickened her voice, and she turned away. "I shouldn't be standing here. He needs help." Samantha walked out of the room, returning a few minutes later with a pitcher of water, a bowl, a towel, and a box of medical supplies. Steve pulled up a chair for her. She nodded her thanks and sat down beside Sender.

"Juana sent a man for the doctor," she said quietly to Sender. "He'll be here soon, but in the meantime . . ." She gently cleaned around the wound, then wrapped it with clean, boiled cotton strips. "You look awfully peaked, Sender."

"I'd give my saddle for a biscuit."

"How long has it been since you've eaten?"

Sender looked puzzled. "Pretty sure I ate on Friday before I was shot."

Distressed, Samantha rushed from the room.

Sender motioned Steve closer. "What day is this?"

"Sunday."

"No wonder I'm a bit puny. Mighty fine woman, Mrs. Forrester," he said, shaking his head. "I didn't want to upset her. They coulda just run me off, but they wanted me daid. On Friday I happened onto our ramrod with two of those rustling scalawags who work for the Dart spread. In case Bush kills me, I wanted someone to know."

Samantha walked back into the room with a bowl of soup. She sat down beside Sender, scooped up a spoonful of the warm liquid, and offered it to him. Sender was so embarrassed at having a beautiful woman hand-feed him that he choked up and wouldn't open his mouth. Steve had to take the bowl from her and lead her aside.

"What?"

"He's just a boy. His nervous system isn't set up to accommodate such intimate attention from a beautiful woman."

Her eyes twinkled. "Would you like some soup, Mr. Sheridan?"

"I wasn't blessed with Sender's good sense."

"I'm glad to hear that. I suppose you're going to get back on your horse and leave again?" Steve watched the smile fade from her pretty blue eyes. He got the feeling that if he stayed around a little longer, he might figure out what she really looked like behind the dazzle.

"As much as I hate it, I guess I do have to be going."

"Hallo the house!"

Steve glanced outside. Ham Russell and five of his henchmen sat a few feet from the porch.

"I can't believe he would have the gall to come here after what he did in town," Samantha said, stalking to the front door. Tristera rushed from the kitchen, flashed Steve an alarmed look, and followed Samantha outside. Steve decided to remain out of sight, just in case he was needed. From outside, he heard Samantha's voice, cool and haughty and completely in control.

"What can I do for you, Mr. Russell?"

"We were just riding by and wondered if you might need some help clearing the trash off your creek banks."

"Trash?"

"Seen about a dozen Indians camping down there."

"Silver Fish and his family work for me, Mr. Russell."

"Work for you? What the blazes you doing here—starting a new reservation?"

"I hire whom I please, Mr. Russell." Samantha let her gaze flit over the scruffy lot riding with him. "I see you do, too."

Russell's face reflected sudden anger. "Us being neighbors and all, I thought we was friends, but you ain't treatin' me like a friend, Mrs. Forrester."

"Anyone who'd rope one of my hands and drag him behind a horse doesn't deserve to be treated as a friend, Mr. Russell."

"Now, that was a little fracas between Ramon and me. Wouldn't expect that to affect us."

"You would be wrong, then, Mr. Russell."

Russell scowled. "Temper is a downfall with me, Mrs. Forrester. I have to admit that."

"Good day, Mr. Russell."

But Ham wasn't ready to leave. He had come miles out of his way to get a glimpse of that little redheaded gal. He wanted to spend time with her, to somehow get her to stop looking at him as if he were a tomato worm.

Grover Bush walked around the side of the house, saw them, and turned to leave.

"Mr. Bush," Samantha called after him.

"I need to be getting back to my . . ." He headed back around the side of the house.

"Mr. Bush!"

He stopped. "Yeah?"

"Please escort these gentlemen to our property line. They have concluded their business here."

Bush looked from Ham Russell to her. "Excuse me, ma'am, but I didn't sign on as a gunfighter. And I ain't being paid a fighting wage."

Samantha flushed with embarrassment. He was right, of course, but it seemed a cowardly excuse.

Ham Russell snickered as Bush walked away, then he slid out of his saddle and started up the steps. To Samantha's immense relief, Steve Sheridan opened the door and stepped outside, her shotgun in the crook of his right arm.

"You boys don't look bulletproof to me," he said.

"Son of a bi—"

"Would you mind spelling that for the lady?" Steve interrupted, lifting the shotgun slightly, so it pointed straight at Russell's chest. "Why don't you boys just climb back aboard and see how fast you can hightail it on home?"

"Well," Russell said, looking angrily from Samantha to Steve, "what do we have here?"

The implication was obvious in the tone of his voice. Steve pumped the shotgun. "Unless you want to look like you've been catching cannonballs with your midsection, you'd better mount up, turn that horse, and move it."

"Hell, we can take him," said Roy Bowles, spitting tobacco into the dust.

Halfway up the steps, Ham Russell looked as though he just might call Steve's bluff. At that moment Ramon stepped around the side of the house and leveled his shotgun at Bowles.

"Reckon I shoulda killed you when I had the chance," Bowles growled.

Ramon pumped his shotgun. "Maybe I should take that as advice myself, *señor*."

Russell turned to Sheridan. "You planning on staying in these parts?"

"I'll stay as long as I want to."

"Uh-huh. In that case, maybe you better remember that you

ain't bulletproof, neither.'' Russell turned and mounted. Their horses kicked up a dust cloud as they galloped away.

Steve glanced at the house and saw Sender's pale face behind the window glass. He walked to the door and opened it. "Were they the ones who shot you?"

"Nope."

Steve searched the young man's face, decided he was either telling the truth or the best liar he'd ever met. "You don't look strong enough to be standing up," he said.

Sender nodded. Steve closed the door and walked over to Ramon, who had sagged against the side of the house in immense relief.

"Guess you've earned your pay for this month," Steve said, grinning at the look on the young man's face. Ramon was probably the feistiest scared man he'd ever seen.

"Maybe I've just repaid the help you gave me in town, *señor*."

"Fair enough," Steve said. A smart man knew when to be afraid. A courageous man didn't let that stop him from doing what needed to be done. Ramon's willingness to step forward meant a lot to Steve.

Suddenly Samantha sat down on the top step. Steve walked over and sat down beside her. "You lead an exciting life for a widow woman."

Samantha flinched—she hated the term "widow woman"— and then smiled. "You don't do too badly yourself."

"Just since I met you. I used to lead the quiet life of a gentleman builder."

"I can't believe Mr. Bush just ignored my request to see them off my property. I should have fired him on the spot. But then who would ramrod my ranch? It isn't that easy to find a good man."

Steve had an opinion about that, and now that he believed Sender Thompson was going to tell her that he'd seen Bush with the rustlers, he no longer had a reason not to give it to her.

"Sender thinks he was shot because he saw Bush with two men driving a small herd of your cattle."

Samantha paled. Her wide blue eyes searched his. "Why didn't *he* tell me this?"

"Maybe for the same reason he couldn't eat soup out of your spoon." Steve smiled at her, and for a moment Samantha lost herself in those wonderfully expressive eyes. Of its own accord, her hand reached up to his face. At the touch of his warm, slightly moist skin, she realized what she was doing and how it must look.

"I . . . thought you had . . . a . . ." She lapsed into silence, flushing at how easily she could get herself into trouble with this man whose skin she longed to touch . . . again and again . . .

"Get it off then," he said, assuming it was a bug.

"It's . . ." Her heart pounded at the obvious lie.

"Go ahead. Hit it if you have to. I'll be still."

Suddenly the thought of pretending to slap a nonexistent bug off him caused her to feel foolish. But, even though she felt ridiculous, she knew she was going to go along with it.

"Go ahead, before it bites me."

"It's gone," she fibbed.

"What was it?"

Samantha was saved by Grover Bush, who came tramping around the side of the house leading a gray mare. A dozen riders followed him, stopping a few feet from the house to watch.

"I took that as a firing," Bush said simply.

"If I were a man, I'd horsewhip you until your hide wouldn't hold water," she said. "Sender Thompson saw you with the men who're rustling my cattle. I guess I shouldn't have been surprised, but I was. Where I come from men don't ride both sides of the fence and get away with it."

Bush's face turned red. "You go telling lies like that about me and your being a woman won't save you. I won't stand for it!"

Steve rose beside her. "Keep a civil tongue in your mouth, Bush, or I'll shoot it off and shove it down your lying throat."

Bush turned white around the mouth. He looked at the men who had followed him around the side of the house. "This is a frame!"

Steve counted it as significant that the men stayed silent and watchful, none of them murmuring their support.

The front door opened, and Sender Thompson, white-faced and shaking from the effort to stand, groped his way outside and leaned against the doorjamb. "You're a lying coyote, Bush. I seen you with them rustlers. That's why they tried to kill me. So's I wouldn't come back here and tell the truth about what you and them're doing to a fine widow woman."

Samantha cringed. She had thought that once her husband had been dead a year, she could revert to being a single woman without having to marry another man just to get rid of the title.

An angry murmur interrupted her thoughts. The other riders

were beginning to turn against Bush. His face flushed red; he looked like a man about to burst a blood vessel.

"If I were you, Bush," Steve said, loud enough for all to hear, "I'd beat it out of Arizona Territory, because the next time Mrs. Forrester goes into town she's going to talk to the marshal. I reckon there'll be a warrant out for your arrest shortly—and for the men who shot Sender Thompson."

Bush gave up the charade, turned his horse, and dug his spurs into its flanks. "Damned liars!" he yelled over his shoulder.

Steve watched until Bush was out of sight, then looked quickly at Samantha. She was so angry her face was pink. An ache of compassion started low in his spine. It shouldn't be so hard for a woman. If he were free, he'd stay on until she could find an honest man to help her. But under the circumstances he might just bring more trouble down on her.

"I'm curious," he said. "What are those Indians doing at the foot of the hill?"

Samantha briefly told him. "The whole family followed us home. Apparently I bought their livelihood as well as their sheep. I didn't mean to. I knew he was drunk. I suppose I should give back the sheep."

"If I know Indians, Silver Fish is too proud to take charity. He knows he did wrong, and he's lost face. The only thing he can do now is work off his shame." Steve had known other men like Silver Fish, who possessed a strong mixture of pride and cunning. He would wager that the Indian would steal from anyone except the person who employed him.

"I've decided to hire Silver Fish." Bush's duplicity had confused her, made her question her own judgment. If she could hire a man like Bush, what else might she be doing wrong?

"May I ask you a question?" she asked, hardly knowing what was about to come out of her mouth.

"Anything."

"I've long thought it might be a good idea to sell all of my stock," she said hesitantly. "I'm basing my opinion on the fact that we're still being targeted by rustlers. But I'm also afraid that this drought is going to get worse." She paused and glanced quickly at him. "You may already know this, but we haven't discussed it. El—Tristera told me she was her tribe's rainmaker. She says it may not rain at all this year. I don't really believe in people being able to predict the future or make rain, but just in case, I wanted to know what you think about selling the cattle."

Her nearness mesmerized Steve. "I'm not a cattleman, but I

think you're right. If I were you I would sell as many cattle as I could. In a drought you could lose every head you keep."

Samantha nodded and turned to look at the dust Bush was kicking up as he rode away, presenting Steve with her lovely profile. "Thank you," she said. "I can't tell you how grateful I am for your advice. I've thought that was the right thing all along, but Mr. Bush said the drought didn't matter. He advised me to buy cattle to hedge against losses. I thought that was wrong. It felt wrong, but I dared not go against him. He had prickly pride."

"Bush was a crook. He was helping steal your cattle."

Samantha thrilled at the anger she sensed in him when he mentioned Bush's stealing from her. Knowing Steve agreed with her, relieved the anxiety.

She smiled at him. "Will you stay for dinner?"

He hesitated. He should be on his way, but he'd long ago missed the noon train at Camp Pinal. Besides, he wanted to stay, and there would be another train . . .

"Yes, thank you." He had the urge to tell her he'd like that very much, but part of him wasn't willing to admit that out loud. "I might have a better chance of catching a train here anyway," he said ruefully, his eyes intent on her face.

Samantha laughed, pleased and suddenly breathless. "I'll tell the plate, so she can set another Juana."

Steve frowned. "You'll what?"

"I'll tell . . ." Samantha realized her misstatement and stopped. "I'll tell Juana," she said, flushing but unable to look away. She was supposed to leave, but her feet didn't respond. The way his eyes softened when he smiled held her there. It was a look she'd longed to see in Lance's eyes. It reminded her of the dream—and evoked an odd little tingle of excitement and fear and longing.

"I'll take care of Calico . . ."

"Yes . . ."

Steve turned and sauntered toward the barn. Samantha's feet barely touched the floor on the way to the kitchen. She told herself it was because she loved entertaining. This amazing new energy and aliveness she felt was normal for her at the prospect of a dinner guest. She loved company. It was nothing more than that.

While the women in the house prepared the evening meal, Steve walked up the mountainside toward an overhanging rock he wanted to inspect. The climb was steeper and rougher than he'd expected. By the time he reached the plateau, he was panting and glad of an opportunity to rest and admire the view—desert blending into hills and rough, wooded country.

At close range, the rock that jutted out over the ranch house was higher and more precarious than he'd thought. It was taller than it was deep, and it sat on a collection of other big rocks. It probably wasn't going anywhere. Still, it wouldn't take much to send it rolling down the mountain. And Samantha's house sat smack in its path.

Fortunately the rock was stable—as long as nothing happened to shake the mountain. The Arizona Territory had experienced a few earthquakes, but they generally weren't much. Samantha Forrester's Boston House might last as long as she did.

He walked down the mountain to wash up.

Samantha met Seth Boswell as he rode up to the house.

"Thank you for coming, Seth. I can have Sender carried outside if you don't want to come into the house."

"Naw, that's nonsense. I've been in this house too many times to start worrying about it now."

"He's in here," she said, leading the way to the parlor.

Boswell checked Sender's wound and smiled. "I couldn't have done better myself. The bullet went clean through. The only thing to do now is keep him down until he gets his strength back. It'll heal or not, depending on him."

Boswell left some of Lydia's gunshot tonic with Samantha. "Give him this morning, noon, and night. It'll perk him up."

When Boswell left, Samantha had two men move Sender into the bedroom across from Juana's.

Samantha bathed, and for the first time in months, she put on a formal evening gown for dinner at home. She had bought it in Paris on her honeymoon—a royal blue velvet with a lace collar at its jewel neckline. She enjoyed dressing up when there was someone around to appreciate her efforts. An expensive, pretty gown made her feel pampered and young and pretty. And it might make Steve Sheridan squirm. She hoped so. Teach him a lesson for kissing her and riding away.

Samantha asked Tristera to join them, but she declined. The girl was deeply grieving. Samantha wanted to comfort her, but she knew from her own experiences that only time would heal grief.

Juana set the table in the dining room for three. Nicholas appeared, freshly washed and eager for company. He had awakened from his nap rested, his cough gone. Samantha felt such pride and love at the sight of him. He didn't chatter like other children she had known. Being with him was almost like being with another adult. Although he lacked experience and education, his mind was as good or better than hers.

Steve walked in from the front porch and smiled at them. He had shaved; a fresh cut adorned his strong chin. His hair was wet, recently combed. The look in his dark, silky eyes told her he always cleaned himself up for dinner, that she wasn't to make more of it than it deserved.

"Would you like a tour of the house?" she asked lightly. "So you can see the grinding poverty to which you are about to abandon us?"

Steve smiled. "Sure."

The house was big and rectangular. Sand sifted into it at will. "I can't believe a reputable carpenter built this here," Steve said, gazing around him. "It would have been just a little harder to go up onto the mountain, but there you'd have had the benefit of tall trees and cooler weather."

"It was my fault. I brought my builder with me from New York, because I didn't know if I'd be able to find someone here who knew how to build a house. He didn't know anything about this land. He advised against going up on the mountain. Said we wouldn't be able to find water."

"Or he didn't want to go to the extra trouble. He was going to get paid no matter where he built."

"Maybe. That's the outhouse," she said, pointing out the back door at a structure a hundred yards from the house.

"You should have asked him to build you a brothel."

Samantha was surprised and delighted at his boldness. "Why?"

"Because I built one not too long ago in San Francisco. They insisted on a bathroom for every bedroom, with nothing but the most deluxe accommodations."

Samantha laughed. "I guess I should have."

"What's that?" Steve asked, pointing to the shed.

"That's where I work with clay. I'll show it to you after dinner if you like." .

"Thanks. I'd like that."

Steve sat at the head of the table. Samantha had expected him to be embarrassed or discomfited. Most single Western men would have been. They'd had little contact with what they called "drawing room ladies," but Steve seemed at peace with himself and with her. He began the dinner conversation with questions about Nicholas and his schooling.

Tonight Nicholas was in an observant mood. Samantha realized it was just as well Steve Sheridan wouldn't be staying. The boy wanted a father. Steve looked like a man who kept moving.

As Juana served dessert, Nicholas opened up to Steve. "I found a prairie falcon," he said. "Mama needs models to sculpt, but she's not as good at finding them as I am."

"Near here?"

"On the mountainside."

Steve sipped his coffee.

"We've been watching it for a month now. Since we've been watching, the parents have brought in two mourning doves, eight burrowing owls, three horned larks, nine jays, fifteen . . . or maybe it was fourteen meadowlarks," he said, glancing at his fingers, where he was keeping track. "Three blackbirds, two shrikes, one rock wren, one chicken, one pocket gopher." He ran out of fingers and started over, "And eight ground squirrels."

"That's a lot. How many in the brood?"

"Four."

"How old are the falconets?"

"About four weeks."

"Around five weeks they'll leave the nest."

Nicholas frowned. "They might fall or something. They're about fifty yards up on the side of the mountain."

"How'd you find it?"

"Easy to spot a prairie falcon nest once you know what to look for," Samantha said, "isn't it, Nicholas?"

"Bones," Nicholas said, grinning at Steve.

"Bones?"

Samantha smiled at Nicholas. "Of mourning doves, owls, larks, jays, meadowlarks, wrens, chickens—"

"Pocket gophers," Nicholas interjected. Then he seemed to remember something unpleasant. "Have you ever seen a prairie falcon spit up bones?" he asked.

"No, I don't believe I have."

"I did," Nicholas said proudly. "I thought there was something wrong with that bird. It drew its feathers down flat, stood up as tall as it could, then started sticking its neck out funny. Then it kinda squatted down, stretched up, and bobbed its neck up and down until a lump slid up its throat and plopped out its mouth. Yuck.''

"I wouldn't want to be a mama or papa falcon," Samantha said. "Feeding time gets a little frantic. A couple of times one of the falconets took a bite out of the parent feeding it.''

Steve rose and smiled at the boy. "I'll say good-bye now, because I plan to leave early in the morning.''

Nicholas scowled. "Will you ever be back?''

"Maybe, in a year or so.''

"Will you stop by to see us?''

"Sure, if your mother doesn't mind.''

Juana led Nicholas away, and Samantha turned to Steve. "Well, it looks like you've made a conquest there.''

"He's a fine boy.''

"Yes, he is.''

"Does he look like his father?''

She hesitated briefly. "Yes.''

"Any chance you might leave Arizona, go back to wherever you came from?'' he asked.

Samantha thought about that. She loved Arizona. Lance was less than a hundred miles away. The climate agreed with Nicholas, who was better now than he had been in years.

"No. No, I guess not.'' *If you stayed* . . . she thought, looking into his eyes. Samantha realized that despite her deep love and unwavering loyalty to Lance, she felt an undeniable attraction to Steve Sheridan.

"Well, it's my bedtime," he said abruptly.

She averted her gaze, nodding. "I'll show you to your bedroom.''

"No, thank you. I prefer to sleep out on the desert.''

"On the desert?'' she repeated in disbelief. "There are scorpions, tarantulas, fleas, Gila monsters . . .''

Steve laughed. "Rattlesnakes, coral snakes, centipedes, ticks, chinch bugs . . .''

"Then why?'' she asked.

"I was raised by a Papago Indian woman named Uncheedah, who told me that nothing will ever happen to me unless the Great Mystery permits it for my spiritual growth. You wouldn't want me to avoid my destiny, would you? There may be a chinch bug out there who's been waiting for me all week.'' His eyes sparkled with amusement.

"You grew up near here?''

"About fifteen or twenty miles away, yeah.''

"I never saw you . . ."

"I've been gone from here since I was sixteen."

"And do you really believe that philosophy?" she asked.

Steve thought about it for a moment. "Pretty much."

"Is that because you haven't been bit much?"

"Probably," he conceded.

"Well, if you change your mind . . ."

Steve grinned. "Thanks."

The gold filling in his right canine tooth gleamed. Samantha suddenly recalled the sensation of his kiss. How his mouth had tasted like sweet figs and the stubble on his chin had felt like sandpaper. "Well," she said, turning away in confusion, "I guess you'll need a blanket."

"Thanks, but I have blankets."

"You're very self-reliant, Mr. Sheridan."

"I've had to be. Now, if you wouldn't mind telling me how to get to the nearest train station . . ."

"Just follow the tracks south. They'll bring you to a water tank. The passenger train stops there at eight in the morning."

"Thanks for a wonderful dinner and charming company."

Samantha laughed. "Not taking any chances on missing that train, are you?"

"A man can't be too careful." Smiling, he turned toward the door.

"Good-bye," she said softly.

"Good-bye." He closed the door behind him.

Disappointed, Samantha turned out all the lamps except one, which she carried up the stairs to her room. She wrote a letter to Lance, asking him to help her find a buyer for her cattle, then undressed, put on her nightgown, and climbed into her feather bed.

Usually going to bed triggered thoughts of her beloved. This was the time of day when she imagined herself on the porch swing with his arm around her shoulders, feeling loved and protected and treasured. She tried to summon up the image, but it didn't come.

Instead she heard Steve Sheridan's voice, asking about family pictures. That innocent question had reopened an old wound. And reminded her Steve was not alone in his puzzlement. Everyone in the Kincaid family—except Lance—thought it odd that Samantha didn't revere her parents. But they hadn't been the ones abandoned.

Anger and sorrow battled just below the surface as Samantha

firmly closed the door on those memories and turned her attention outward.

Her room was cool and dark. Night winds sighed around the eaves of her second-story bedroom. Something tickled her face. She reached up and felt sand on her cheek. Sighing in frustration, she sat up and brushed off her pillow, which was already gritty with it. Then she shook off her counterpane. How she hated this house!

Steve Sheridan wouldn't stay, but she could hire someone else to build her another house. She should have thought of that sooner.

Relieved, she settled down to sleep. It was the right thing to do, but somehow it didn't please her as much.

CHAPTER SEVEN

Steve walked out about two hundred feet from the house, spread his blanket, and sat on it. He loved the desert at night. Some people thought it frightening, but he never had.

The stars were big and bright, the sky gray at the horizon, darker overhead. A dog barked. Horses whinnied, and crickets made their ceaseless *creee, creee, creee* sounds.

Minutes passed. He thought about lying down, but then he caught sight of a female form walking toward him. His body reacted as if it were Samantha Forrester coming to him, but he saw it was only Elunami—Tristera, he corrected himself.

Steve waited in silence, torn between a desire to let her know he was there and the desire to let her pass by without seeing him.

She walked right up to his blanket and stopped. "I'm sorry," she said softly, "I did not see you come out here."

"S'all right," Steve assured her.

Tristera had left the house to escape people and the necessity to speak with them. Finding Steve Sheridan here confused her, because she had a need to thank him for his many kindnesses, but she had no energy for words. They felt stuck inside her, unmovable. She would have to force them out, as she had done at the school so many times.

"Thank you for your help yesterday."

"I was glad to do it." Steve scooted to the far end of the blanket and gestured with his hand toward the other end.

Tristera sat down, not touching him. She listened to the sounds of crickets and an occasional barking dog. Then, in the distance came the sweet sound of Samantha Forrester's voice lifting above the other noises. Tristera didn't recognize the song, but it sounded joyful and lilting. She imagined the boy cuddled against the woman's side; the distrust she usually felt for white women softened.

"*Señora* Forrester is young and beautiful. She needs a new house. Why do you refuse to build it for her?"

"You don't miss much, do you? Well, you've pretty well

131

summed it up. She's young and beautiful and determined to have her own way," he said, remembering the aplomb with which Samantha had invited herself to dinner *and* paid for it. "I'm a lonely man who'd just fall in love with her. I've got buildings to build, a reputation to make for myself. If I stay here, a determined woman like her would either make me miserable by ignoring me, or more miserable by paying attention to me and turning me into her lap pet. Then none of my buildings would get built, and it would be your fault for talking me into it."

Tristera laughed. She had not expected to enjoy herself. A moment passed in silence.

"You make magic, El—Tristera?"

"No longer. Once I could make small magic. At times."

"If I stayed, could you promise me my poor heart would not pound with love for the beautiful widow?"

Tristera saw beneath Steve Sheridan's teasing and smiled gently. "No man stays free forever," she said.

"You know anything about failure?"

Tristera nodded. She had failed her duty and her people, by losing her purity. This afternoon she had awakened to the realization that her people were kind and well intentioned, but they deluded themselves. They could not stand against the greater strength and numbers of the white soldiers. Even their Great Mystery had failed to protect Tuvi, or He no longer loved the Hopi. Since she could not believe that, she was faced with accepting the fact that even He had lost His powers to protect them.

Her mind had finally put words to what she had struggled with for days. Now she knew—the Indians were doomed. The old ways were doomed as well. Her tongue tingled as if it had tasted metal.

With the sage-scented darkness pressing around her, bitterness burned in her heart. She would reject the ways of her people. She would do as they had urged her to do at the school. She would live her life as a modern woman and never go back to her village. She would work and live in the white man's world. She would sleep with men if she wanted to, risk anything that attracted her. She would no longer be limited by the simplistic traditions of a dying race or their powerless god. She would not be like Steve Sheridan, either, so ruled by his fear of Samantha Forrester that he rode away.

Steve sighed. "I don't want to be a failure. I need to make

something of myself. I can't do that perched on the arm of a rich woman.''

Tristera closed her eyes and saw Steve Sheridan holding Nicholas in his arms, cradled like a baby. The *señora* stood at his side, her eyes shining with tears of love and gratitude. Tristera's heart felt full and warm with her vision, but it seemed Sheridan was determined to leave. There was nothing more to be said. She stood up.

"Thank you again," she said, and walked away.

Steve watched until she was out of sight, then lay back on his bedroll. The sound of Indian drums and chanting drifted up from the river. In his mind he saw Silver Fish and his family dancing the Ghost Dances to bring back their dead loved ones and their lost lands.

The chanting—*"Aiyee, ha, aiyee!"*—called out to something in Steve. He listened with dreamy contentment, halfway wishing himself down there among them, dancing mindlessly. Part of him would probably always respond in that way.

He had declined the offer of a bed in the house because he needed the healing touch of the Earth under his back. He was like the antelope Crows Walking had told him about who, when wounded, pressed the injured part to the Earth and waited.

Steve thought it odd he should think such a thing about himself. He wasn't wounded. He had suffered a little when he broke off with Caroline, but it was over. He needn't think of himself as wounded.

Steve wanted to go directly to sleep and usually did, but tonight, with the new moon high in the western sky and the sweet lilt of Samantha Forrester's voice lifted in joyful song, her image eased into his mind and stayed. He could almost feel her softness, waiting for him, calling out to him.

In spite of the reality of her marriage and her motherhood, there was something innocent and vague about Samantha Forrester. Part of her knew about men, and part of her did not. Even when he had kissed her and she had responded with passion, she didn't appear to comprehend fully what was happening between them.

The night grew relatively quiet. Samantha was probably in bed. The house was quiet now. An occasional mockingbird trilled a variety of melodies, sounding now like a lark, then like a thrush. The wind came up, making him glad he had taken his heavy blankets with him. Stars overhead twinkled. He closed his eyes, but it was no good. The Earth beneath his back did not soothe him. Something kept him from sleep, something besides the woman tugged at his spirit and would not let him rest. Steve tried to ignore it.

He'd had this feeling the first time he'd gone into a cave filled with bats. Then the feeling had urged him to get out of there. Now the impulse seemed to urge him to go north. Steve fought it. He sensed that whatever he found there would embroil him more deeply in Samantha Forrester's business, and he didn't want to get any more involved than he was. The pressure of her appeal and her beauty was more than he wanted already.

But the feeling grew stronger. Finally, it could not be denied. Steve threw off his blankets, loped to the barn, and tossed his saddle onto a startled, sleepy Calico. The horse took the quick cinching in stride and allowed himself to be led outside.

Steve rode north awhile, stopped and listened, then rode some more. He didn't know what he was riding toward, but he knew he had no choice.

The wind was cold and sharp. He dismounted and put his ear to the Earth. Finally he heard the rumble of hoofbeats and the bleating sounds of sheep in distress. When he'd lived with the tribe, he'd been around sheep enough to recognize their fear and terror. A sound like gunfire caused him to straighten. It came again—not the sound of a night hunter—more erratic.

Calico reared and pawed the air. Steve pulled him down and mounted. In the starlight bathing the rolling hills, he saw the silhouettes of half a dozen men riding away from the stampeding herd. These had to be Samantha Forrester's sheep, Silver Fox's herd. And this had to be her land. Yet he couldn't believe these were her hands. Without Bush, her crew had no direction. No doubt they were in their beds sleeping, waiting for a new boss to tell them what to do.

Steve unsheathed the Sharps, sighted on the ground in front of the foremost rider, and pulled the trigger.

A moment of panic followed his firing. Men yelled and fought their frightened horses. Someone fired an answering shot. It missed so completely, Steve decided they had no idea where he was. He sighted again, this time aiming to hit something. One man cried out. Steve fired again and again. The men turned their horses and fled.

The bleating sheep reached Steve and spilled around Calico, who stood his ground, trembling at the smell and feel of the milling bodies. Steve waited until most of them had passed, then urged Calico through a small herd straggling at the rear. His presence spooked them at first, then they calmed down.

A mile farther on, beside a bed of glowing coals, Steve found Ramon, lying face down. He lit a match, turned the boy over, and held a hand to his throat. A light pulse throbbed beneath his warm, damp skin. Steve lit another match and examined him more closely. A bullet had dug a groove across his scalp. Blood soaked the sand under his head.

Ramon opened his eyes. "*Compadre* . . ." he whispered.

"Did you get a look at the men who did this?"

"They wore bandannas."

Steve found Ramon's horse and tied him onto it. An hour later they reached the house. Samantha Forrester answered the door. In her nightgown and robe, she looked soft and sleepy, still closed in on herself.

"I'll send a man for Seth Boswell again," she said, pulling her robe around her.

"May not be necessary." The wound looked less serious in the light. There was some blood loss, but the bullet had only nicked the skull. Ramon would have a headache and a bald spot, but he wouldn't die. There was nothing much the doctor could do for him that she couldn't do. They put him to bed in the room with Sender Thompson.

Samantha cleaned the wound, dabbed it with kerosene to prevent infection, and bandaged it. Ramon slipped into sleep; Samantha left Juana with him and took Steve into the kitchen.

"Who did this?"

"He didn't see their faces, but I reckon you can thank Bush for this. He probably had the rustlers lined up before he talked you into buying the herd."

She looked puzzled. "I thought maybe Silver Fish."

Steve shook his head. "These were not Indians."

"How did you know about it?"

"I couldn't sleep." He did not question the power in him that had gotten him out of his warm blankets and made him ride through the cold night to an unknown camp.

"You seem determined to be our savior."

"In spite of myself," he said ruefully, rubbing his strong hand through his sleek black hair.

Samantha walked to the kitchen window. "I thought it would be easier than this," she said softly.

Steve followed her. "Ranching?"

"Life."

She looked so forlorn, so slender and soft and delicate, that Steve felt a rush of compassion and desire. He remained still. If he moved now . . .

"Steve . . ."

Like the echoes of a gong, her voice created a heavy pulse in his loins and temples.

Samantha saw the desire in his eyes. "Steve, I know you're supposed to go to Waco, but I wish you'd reconsider."

"You've got more problems than I can solve," he said huskily, his voice as difficult to keep control of as the rest of him. "I'm just a house builder."

"Then build me a house."

"You think I can stay here and just build you a house, with nothing else ever coming of it?"

Amusement sparkled in the depths of her lovely blue eyes. "What are you afraid of, Steve?" She lifted her chin, as if daring him to lean down and taste those sweetly curved lips.

Steve chuckled. "So Tristera squealed on me."

"Some things women just know."

Steve pulled Samantha close to him. The teasing laughter in her eyes gave way to momentary panic, and he knew she felt it, too, this strong attraction between them.

"I'm not a marrying man," he said, his voice gruffer than he would have liked. "I can stay here, build your house, make love to you, if I should be so lucky, and still ride away."

"Can you?" she asked, her voice appealingly breathless.

"I think so," he said. "I've done it before, and I need to do it again."

"Why?"

"Because I'm a builder. I have to go where the houses are being built. I can't stay in one spot."

"I accept your conditions," she said firmly, her gaze clear and earnest—and oddly disconcerting to him.

Steve hesitated. His partner was already at the Waco site overseeing the preliminary phase of cutting the limestone from the mountain. That would take a while. "What kind of house do you want?"

"I want the castle you told me about."

"Wait here." Steve released her and walked to the barn, where he reached into his satchel and pulled out the plans for the house in Waco.

In the kitchen, Samantha poured two cups of coffee and set them on the table. Steve smoothed and spread out his plans.

The line drawing showed a three-story stone castle framed by two wide gateposts. The structure's focal point was a round turreted tower between two square, protruding porches supported by arched stone columns. French doors on the upper story opened onto the top of the porch, which served as a veranda off the master bedroom.

"Ohhhh! It's perfect!" Samantha said, leaning closer.

Steve envisioned her standing on the porch or walking out the French doors onto the veranda. "It would look right at home on the side of your mountain."

"I can see it there, too."

"I'd have to do some testing. See what that mountain's made of . . ."

"Could we build it with adobe?"

"Have to. Unless you wanted to import stone from somewhere else. That would be expensive."

"I don't care about the expense. What you told me in town, is that really what you charge?"

"Yes, ma'am. A thousand a month, plus expenses—and ten percent of the finished cost of the house."

"So if it costs half a million dollars to build, you get a fifty-thousand-dollar bonus."

Steve nodded. "It could run over that."

"You're hired. How long will it take?"

"Depends on how many men I hire."

"How many would it take?"

"Depends on when you want to finish."

"Soon!"

"Six, eight months, a couple hundred men."

"What is that total?"

Steve barely paused. "One hundred twenty thousand for workmen, eight to ten thousand for me, plus building materials. Depends how fancy you want to go. My guess, three, four hundred thousand dollars."

Samantha knew where the money would come from. She would sell her house in Manhattan. Jared had bought it with her money. She'd only kept it because she wasn't sure she'd stay in Arizona. With this house, she would stay. Tomorrow she would send word to her attorney in New York, have him transfer a sum of money into her Phoenix account and sell the house to replace the funds. She had enough in her accounts in Picket Post and Phoenix to handle the start-up costs.

"You can't afford this," he said in one last attempt to stop her and save them both.

"My parents did one thing right. They left me almost a million English pounds, which my guardian invested for me. He is a shrewd businessman. My money doubled twice while I was growing up," she said firmly. "Will you build it for me?"

With her cheeks glowing with excitement, she was incredibly appealing to him. "You realize we're getting off the mark. You need a man to ramrod your cattle, not a builder."

"I know, but with you here, advising me, I won't pick another Grover Bush. Please say you'll do it."

Steve knew he needed to say no, but under the power of Samantha's beautiful shining eyes, he nodded. "Suppose I build you a smaller house from adobe instead of a palace? It wouldn't be so expensive or take so long to build, but it would have most of the features you want."

"No. I'm attached to the Waco castle."

Steve laughed. "All right. I'll take a look at your mountain and see if I can find an appropriate site."

Samantha extended her hand. "We have an agreement, Mr. Sheridan."

Solemnly Steve shook her hand. "Yes, we do, Mrs. Forrester."

Too excited now to sleep, Samantha pored over the plans for an hour, asking questions and finding out exactly what their agreement entitled her to. She had certain minimum requirements—a trunk room next to the laundry room in the basement, a dumbwaiter between the kitchen and dining room, and inside toilets on every floor.

Samantha gazed at the plans. "How big is this round room?"

"Fifteen foot across."

"Oh! How wonderful!" The round tower room would be hers and Lance's private hideaway. She smiled, envisioning Lance and herself snuggled together on the window seat. "Can you build a seven-foot-long window seat under each of these windows?"

"Sure." Steve made quick notes. Samantha was like a child in a candy store, and that enchanted and excited him.

Finally, near dawn, Steve went back to his blankets. Samantha checked on Ramon and Sender, both sleeping quietly, and then went to her own room. She undressed and slipped under the covers. Shivering at the coldness of the sheets, she called up an image of Lance and herself swinging on the swing on the porch of the Kincaid house near Austin. She pressed against his warm side. *Darling, I'm so happy. Steve has agreed to stay and build us a new house.*

Steve? he asked, scowling down at her.

Mr. Sheridan. I've hated this house for so long. It'll be our house. And when it's finished—

Who the hell is Steve?

Samantha laughed. She loved it when Lance was possessive. *Just a builder.*

Smiling, Samantha fell asleep with Lance's face warming her heart, his wonderful presence filling the room.

The next morning Steve spread the plans on the dining room table and worked steadily for hours. When he'd made as many of the changes as he could without the proper tools, he walked into the parlor where Samantha sat at her desk, writing.

"Finished?" she asked, looking up.

"Barely started. I'll have one of my partners send a draftsman to make a clean set of plans to work from, but these will get us started. Thought you might take a look at what I've done and see if it suits you."

Samantha leaned over the plans and studied them. "What's this?"

"That's the basement door."

"What's wrong with it?"

"Nothing. It's just a standard basement door."

"It looks like it's lying down."

"It is. Basements are generally underground."

"I don't want it that way."

Steve frowned. "How do you want it?"

"I want to walk out of the basement standing up."

"If you build it above ground it's not a basement."

"Well, couldn't we build it the usual way and then dig a trench around the basement to accommodate a standard doorway?"

"What about drainage when it rains?"

"You're the builder. Isn't there any way you can provide for drainage?"

Steve frowned. He didn't mind making a few changes, but he didn't like it when a client tried to change basics.

"What's this?" she asked, turning back to the plans.

"Bedroom."

"Where's the bathroom?"

"Down the hall, here," he said, leaning around her to point with his pencil. The silky dark skin of his forearm gleamed with the lightest mist of perspiration. He smelled wonderful—the perfect scent for a warm, living, breathing male. It made her dizzy.

"Only one?" It came out as a near croak.

"How many do you want?"

"I want one for every bedroom and one on every floor for guests." Her face felt hot. His nearness, even though he wasn't actually touching her, played havoc with her ability to concentrate.

Steve laughed. "You want that bawdy house I told you about, don't you?"

"Yes."

"The plans don't call for all that plumbing, but there's no reason why we can't do it. At this stage, you can have anything you want to pay for."

"Wonderful!"

His eyes gleamed with admiration. Samantha exulted in the glow for a moment, before he turned back to his plans. She glanced lingeringly at his broad, tapering back and then wandered to the window. Halfway between the house and the creek, near where the Indians camped, she saw Nicholas squatting in the grass.

"Come here," she said to Steve. "What is he doing? Spying on those Indians?"

Steve walked to the window and pulled back the curtain. "I'm surprised at you, Samantha Forrester. Any kid worth his salt knows what he's doing."

"What?"

Steve laughed. "Didn't you ever try to weasel your way into playing with a kid you didn't know? The first thing the outsider has to do is show interest. He does that by squatting in the grass and watching. Pretty soon, if I know anything about kids, a boy will run out and pick a fight with Nicholas."

"He does, and I'll—"

"Whoa!" Steve said, holding up a hand.

"I won't have them come here and fight with my son."

"How else is he going to learn how to get along with people?" Steve knew this was none of his business, but she was wrong to coddle the boy so. "May I ask you a hypothetical question?"

"I guess," she said grudgingly.

"What are you doing with Nicholas?"

"I'm raising him."

"With what goal in mind?"

"To be sure he survives."

His face said, *No wonder you're doing it wrong.*

Anger flashed in her. "He's alive, isn't he? He's been a very sickly little boy. All his life I've had to fight just to keep him alive."

"According to the Indians, the Great Mystery decides when people live and die. As a parent all you have to do is be sure what you raise turns into a man."

"I don't think it's that simple, and even if I did, I don't know how to do that," she admitted.

"That's why most kids have two parents, one male and one female. The woman can show the girls how to be women, and the man can show the boys how to be men."

"Even if I believed what you say, which I don't, I still say women are perfectly capable of doing anything they set out to do. All I need to teach him is how to be a person. And I can do that."

"Does he have a grandfather or an uncle nearby?"

"No."

"Too bad."

"My son is fine!" she snapped. This felt too much like an attack on her for not remarrying. She'd heard that too many times already. At one time or another, every member of the Kincaid family had urged her to marry again, to provide Nicholas with a father.

Steve shrugged. "Sorry."

"This happens to be a touchy subject with me," she admitted grudgingly.

"No!" he said, grinning.

A sound halfway between laughter and a sob escaped from Samantha just as Juana walked into the room.

"The trays are ready, *señora.*"

Samantha followed Juana back to the kitchen, glad of an excuse to escape for a moment. She took a tray for Sender; Tristera took the one for Ramon.

Samantha kept busy all day, but Steve's comment about Nicholas nagged at her, made her feel so cranky she couldn't concentrate on what she was supposed to be doing. Finally she walked back into the dining room. Steve wasn't there, so she studied the building plans until he returned.

"I think I want two more doors from the basement," she announced casually.

"Two more?" He looked startled.

"I see no reason why I should have a basement with only one door. The basement is as big as the rest of the house. Why shouldn't it have as many doors?"

"The idea of a basement . . . in the past," he said, "was as a safe place, accessible only from inside the house. Standing the door upright was a big enough change, I thought."

"Well, I like the idea of several doors. Unless you have a better reason than that, I don't see why I should be constricted within my own house. Will you please make the changes?"

"Yes, ma'am." For once his usual sense of humor seemed to have deserted him.

Samantha turned away, smiling. If he could tell her how to raise her son, she could tell him how to build a house.

At dinnertime, Juana stood by the back door and called Nicholas, who returned looking flushed and hot. "Wash your face and hands, *mono. Dese prisa! Mama es espera!*"

"Don't call me a monkey," Nicholas said, protesting.

Juana laughed and reached under his arm to tickle him. "You are a *mono*. Why shouldn't I call you one?"

Laughing, Nicholas ran down the hall. Samantha and Steve seated themselves at the table and waited until Nicholas joined them. "Did you get to play with the Indian boy?" she asked as she passed the platter of chicken to Steve Sheridan.

"Dumb Indian! Who'd want to play with him?" Nicholas said, flashing her an angry look.

Samantha lifted her eyebrows at Steve. *See, he isn't interested in playing with the Indian boy.*

"I even took my ball, but he didn't care. He was hunting *rabbits*," he said, sneering, then frowning in frustration at his plate. "It wouldn't have killed him to let me help."

Steve winked at her. Samantha felt her face grow hot and averted her eyes, concentrating on the food in front of her.

After dinner they moved into the parlor, which was well lit by kerosene lamps. Samantha picked up her knitting and settled on the sofa. Nicholas sat beside her, reading a storybook. Steve sat in Jared's big leather chair and studied the house plans. No one spoke, but it was a companionable silence. Samantha felt strangely content.

As the grandfather clock next to the front door struck seven o'clock, someone knocked on the front door.

Samantha set aside her knitting and walked to answer it. Charlie Turner, the rider she'd sent to find and report on Ramon's lost flock, tipped his hat to her.

"Evening, ma'am."

"Evening, Charlie. Did you find the sheep?"

"Mr. Sheridan was right about them rascals. They didn't stop running until they reached the heavy brush in them canyons. It'll take an act of Congress to get 'em outta there."

"Thanks. You've missed dinner, but Juana will have something around back for you."

"Thank you, ma'am."

Samantha closed the door and turned back to the parlor. Steve had put aside the plans.

"What are you going to do?" he asked.

"I'm going to get them back." She picked up her shawl and headed for the door. "I shouldn't have bought that herd, but I did, and I'm not going to lose it."

"Where are you going?"

"I'm going to hire Silver Fish."

"I'll go with you."

"Me, too, Mama."

Samantha wanted to tell him no, but it wouldn't hurt to let him come. His bedtime wasn't for another hour yet.

Steve got a lantern, and, with that little bit of light, they walked through the darkness toward the Indian camp, where the family danced around a smoky fire. The men moved with exaggerated, energetic steps, prancing like peacocks. The women danced with little outward movement, but the dance quivered through their bodies. The children copied the parent of the same sex.

Suddenly all eyes turned their way; the dancing stopped. Silver Fish's two male companions edged toward their rifles, leaning against the tepee. The children moved nearer their mothers. Silver Fish stepped forward, looked at Steve and Samantha, and waited. It appeared he held her no rancor, even though she had bought his herd while he was drunk—and he had ended up with nothing.

"I have come to ask Silver Fish for his help to find a runaway herd of sheep," Samantha said firmly.

"The white woman, she has lost the sheep?" he asked, looking at Steve instead of her. Steve remained quiet.

"I'm afraid I have," she said loudly.

Silver Fish grunted. "You pay wage?"

"Forty dollars a month per man."

"We four go," Silver Fish said, pointing at two men and a

boy. He waited a moment. When she said nothing, he nodded at his wives in farewell, pulled his blanket around him, and led the way toward the horses tethered in a grassy spot beside the river. The youngest boy's eyes pleaded with him to let him go also, but Silver Fish shook his head.

"You stay here. Keep the fire."

The men saddled their horses. Silver Fish slipped onto the back of his and kicked him into a gallop. The oldest boy and the two men followed, two sheepdogs running behind them, barking their excitement.

At breakfast the next morning Samantha asked Steve to ride with her to her favorite spot on the mountain. "I want to show you where to build the house."

"Don't get too attached to any one site. We have to let the test results tell us where to build."

"I thought you could build it anywhere I want."

"If I was fast enough," he drawled, "I suppose I could even build it on quicksand."

"I might not choose a site with quicksand on it."

Steve grinned. "Just giving that as an example."

He saddled two horses for them, and they rode in silence for a while. As they started up the side of the mountain, Samantha leaned forward in the saddle to help her horse with her body. The trail grew steep, the trees taller. A mountain laurel sang in the high branches overhead.

"What has to happen first?" she asked, looking for the briefest of moments at his lithe, smooth-muscled body as he, too, bent and swayed to ease Calico up the hill.

"Find a solid granite base for the house, find drinking water and soil with good percolation for the sewer system. We have to build a road to the site. Order supplies. Hire men. Have my building tools delivered. Level the site and clear it of underbrush, trees, rocks. Dig a basement. Build forms for bricks. Lay pipes . . ."

"Heavens!"

". . . build a toolshed and shelters for workmen and stock. Order Portland cement, lime, lumber. Hire blacksmiths to forge nails and other things we'll need. Maybe build a reservoir or a water tower, or hire a well driller. And not necessarily in this order."

"How do you decide where to site the house?"

"Based on a number of things—the land's ability to support

the structure we want to build, availability of water, and the type of soil we need for a cesspool. Also how you want it to look on the outside and what you want to be able to see from the inside. Do you want it to face south, north, east, or west? Do you want to be able to see a moonrise from your veranda? Or a sunrise from your dining room? Or the reverse?"

"What do you mean, how I want it to look on the outside?"

"I can explain that more easily when we get to the site you've picked."

"All I need now is a good ramrod. Maybe I could hire one from among the men who already work for me."

Steve shook his head. He'd walked through the bunkhouse earlier, checking to see if he'd find a man to depend on. There wasn't a-one he'd want in charge of his cattle. "They're no doubt fine men, but all of them are young and inexperienced with gunplay," he said.

Her lovely eyes flashed in frustration. Steve didn't tell her that the men who worked for her had probably been chosen by Bush for their inexperience, so they wouldn't interfere with his plans.

"Next time I go into town I'll see if I can find a man," he said.

"Why not wait until we all go into town? Why make a special trip?"

"I'm a fairly patient man, but I do like to make a few of my own decisions."

Samantha recognized the note of restlessness in his voice. He didn't like being questioned this way, but she couldn't help herself. "Ham Russell might kill you."

Steve laughed. "I guess if I rode in unarmed and blindfolded he might."

"No, really. Ham Russell is a vicious killer who might shoot you from ambush."

"He might, but I expect him to get busy doing other things. Let's hope Chila Dart has work for him to do."

The climb grew steeper. They dismounted to lighten the horses' loads, and climbing left little breath for discussion.

About noon they reached the place Samantha had picked from her own trips up the mountainside. Steve walked the site for ten minutes before he came back to where she sat under one of the towering pines. A cool, resiny breeze whispered through the pine needles, sounding like the patter of rain. Birds screeched overhead. Their horses munched ferns growing up through the pine needles.

"It's a beautiful site. Might work, but you won't be able to see the moon at all. It's mostly in the southern sky."

He liked her site; she was pleased. "How long will it take to test the site for all the things you mentioned?"

"A week or so."

"Why so long?"

"There's only one of me and a lot of testing to do. It's much easier to move a house or a wall with an eraser than it is to move a building put in the wrong place."

Steve walked over to where the horses grazed and mounted Calico. "Are we going back?" Samantha asked, disappointed. It was so beautiful up here.

"No. I want to see another face of this mountain."

The afternoon sun grew warmer as they rode south. Steve led the way around the mountain and stopped where one of the contours of the mountain provided an almost level shelf about halfway up. The desert spread out all the way to the southern horizon. The vista of pale sand and distant mountains, bluish and ghostly, was framed by a rugged growth of trees and bushes.

"Wouldn't this be hard to reach?" Samantha asked.

"We'd have to build a road to either site."

"But it's farther away."

"Not from anything important. Once you move the house up here and build a road, it's only another hour to the old house and your spur line. You'll be able to see the moonrise from your bedroom."

"It's wonderful!" she said, knowing she had already fallen in love with it.

Steve helped her dismount and led her to a spot in the middle of the plateau. Behind them on the mountainside, trees soared fifty feet high.

"This is your bedroom," he said, "and this is your front door, framed between these oaks." He led her to the southernmost edge of the plateau and turned her around, so she could look at the spot where she'd just been. Her waist tingled beneath his warm hands; she felt conscious of every breath.

"Now imagine the house soaring up two and a half stories above the ground. The basement will be half buried in the mountainside," he said, framing the center of the plateau with his two hands. "Arriving carriages will see the gateposts framed between those two giant oaks. With the house gleaming pink, and the green pines towering in the background . . ."

The image he painted was so beautiful she felt speechless. It would be worth whatever she had to pay. "I want it here," she whispered.

"Don't decide yet. I still have to do some drilling, check the base, the soil, and find water."

"Find it all here."

Steve chuckled with pleasure. Samantha liked the way he laughed . . . and the way sunlight glinted off that tiny gold filling in his canine tooth. Darkly masculine, he looked as strong and sure of himself as a healthy male panther.

He must have sensed her thoughts. "You look beautiful with your eyes shining like that," he whispered.

"So do you." She hadn't meant to say that.

Steve leaned down and brushed her lips lightly. Her hand slipped up his vest to touch the short hairs on the nape of his neck.

"You know if I kiss you, I might not stop," she said, using a line one of the Kincaid girls had used to shock one of her beaus.

Steve laughed. "I guess I can complain to the builder's union if I need help. Should only take them about six months to get here."

Steve reached out to pull her into his arms. His eyes flashed with desire, and she felt her body respond with a hunger that surprised and frustrated her. It wasn't fair that she could experience such intense feeling for a man she didn't even love, and yet her body burned and her head spun.

With deliberate slowness, Steve lowered his mouth to hers. His lips, so warm and smooth, melted something inside her. She recognized her own voice moaning low and pitifully in her throat, but he gave her no quarter. His kiss deepened—and his arms pulled her so close she could feel the outline of his manhood against her belly. His lips burned into her, igniting fires on the inside, and she went weak all over.

Steve must have felt her collapse. He picked her up in his arms and carried her toward a grassy spot. Sheer panic gave Samantha the strength to resist. "We'd better . . . get back," she said, her voice hoarse.

Steve searched her eyes a moment and nodded. He put her down and steadied her.

"You okay?"

"I shouldn't have left Nicholas alone so long . . ."

Steve narrowed his eyes but didn't respond. He helped her mount and led her down the mountain.

It was hotter this time. Sweat streamed down her temples and between her breasts. Confused, she concentrated on controlling her horse. The old house appeared much sooner than she had expected. Despite all that traveling they were only about an hour from the ranch house. She felt disoriented somehow. Could it be Steve's presence confusing her so?

At the barn, Steve helped her dismount. Again her body tingled at the touch of his hands on her waist. Samantha thanked him and moved quickly out of his grasp.

He turned abruptly and led the horses into the barn.

"You'll join us for dinner, won't you?"

Steve stopped and looked over his shoulder. Narrowed hazel eyes told her very little, except that he wasn't pleased.

"I've got at least a week's work up there. Might as well get started."

Samantha wanted to call him back, to explain why she had seemed to lead him into kissing her and then backed out; but she wasn't sure she knew herself. Before she could think what to say, he turned and walked away.

Steve gathered his things from the barn, found a shovel and a few tools he could use, caught a mule from the corral, and put a pack on its back. Once he had everything in readiness, he walked to the house.

Juana gave him a big glass of lemonade, which tasted wonderful to his parched throat. Samantha was nowhere in sight. He was glad—and miserable—about that.

In the dining room, at the end of the table not yet set for dinner, he wrote out two wires, one to his San Francisco office, telling them to send Ian Macready, one of the best building superintendents in the country, and enough tools to build an adobe palace bigger than the limestone castle in Waco. The other wire went to his partner in Waco, telling him that he had taken another job and to carry on without him.

As he straightened, Samantha walked into the room. She'd changed into a white gown of some light fabric that made her look cool and sweet, as much like an angel as he was ever likely to see on this Earth.

"Send a man into town with these wires," he said, handing them to her. "I may be some time getting back."

Samantha frowned at the prospect of his going off without her. "I don't wait well, you know."

Steve laughed. "No."

That lightened the mood. Samantha relaxed slightly. "Are you taking enough food?"

"Juana's packing at least a month's supply."

"Well, if you run out, send up a smoke signal."

"No one knows where I'll be except you."

His statement implied . . . what? That she wouldn't come even if he sent up a distress call? "I may look useless, but I've been known to accomplish quite a lot."

"I'm sure of that," he said, stalking toward the door.

She followed him out onto the porch. Steve clumped down the steps, stepped into the stirrup, and swung into the saddle with ease. *"Adios,"* he said.

"Hurry back."

"If I were you, I'd set my men to riding the boundaries and mending any breaks in the fences."

"Thanks, I'll do that," she said, and smiled sweetly.

That stumped him. Just when it seemed she'd do anything except what he wanted, she became tractable. Confused, Steve touched the brim of his hat and kicked the borrowed horse into a gallop. The pack mule, its reins tied to Steve's saddle, brayed loudly, but it followed.

What Samantha had told Steve was true—she did not wait well. She hated uncertainty. She especially hated not knowing what was happening.

The days passed so slowly, she lost all hope. She was convinced that he had found no granite, no water, and no place on which to build a cesspool. They would not be able to build the house on the site she wanted, or on any other.

Nicholas sensed something was wrong. When she tucked him into bed, he asked solemnly, "Did Steve get killed like Daddy did?"

"Heavens, no! Now you go to sleep."

Angie Kincaid stepped off the train in San Francisco to a gust of cold, damp air. She grabbed her hat and inhaled deeply, glad for a town that had something that passed for seasons. In Durango, every day was a different sort of summer.

She hailed a conveyance and gave the driver the address of her publisher, Rutherford and Marks, on Market Street.

She kept so busy the first three days she didn't allow herself time to think about Lance or what she had just done to her marriage. But after the initial meetings with her publisher and her editor, and a few authors she knew from past visits to the city, she found herself with an hour to kill and no camera in her hand.

Her hotel room, while quite opulent in the style of better hotels, did not afford her any activity other than reading the newspaper or looking out the window.

So she stood by the window, drapery in hand, glancing down at the passersby on the street three floors down. A man, tall and broad of shoulder, stepped out of a store on the ground level, and Angie gasped. For just a second she was stunned by the thought that Lance might have followed her here. As the man walked into the wind, pulling his greatcoat around him, even the way he held his shoulders reminded her of the husband she'd left behind.

The image of Lance's face, confused and hurt and angry, filled her mind. She remembered the first photographs she had taken of him. She had been amused at first by his expressions and how easily and effortlessly he projected his emotions—in one picture he'd looked tired, in another curious, in yet another cranky. But in all of them he'd exuded that smoldering energy and intense concentration that had eventually been her downfall.

Lance Kincaid had been an Arizona Ranger when she met him. Mrs. Lillian, the Kincaid family nanny, had fondly told her he was strong and intuitive—and almost as blind as a stick when it came to seeing anything he didn't want to see.

Usually Angie loved remembering those old days, but so much had gone wrong since then they seemed a hundred years ago.

She had met Lance in Nogales when she was on her way back to Durango after being at school in the East for three years. He'd ridden into town with an exhausted posse and eighteen dead bodies draped over tired horses. He'd barely dismounted before he'd been challenged to a gunfight in which he'd been shot. She'd taken pictures of it all.

They had gone their separate ways that day, and she had never expected to see him again. But she remembered mooning over those photographs of him time after time, wondering if he'd lived or died.

It hadn't occurred to her at the time, but later she'd realized that the tiredness she saw in those first photographs must have been bone deep. Because he wasn't a man who believed in killing. There had been rage underlying his words when he'd told the townspeople: *I had to see them die. You can see them dead. Maybe folks'll finally understand that the law isn't going to put up with all this rustling of cattle and fleeing across the border.*

Lance had been a magnificent specimen of manhood. Still was. He had matured into an even more attractive man than he had been at twenty-eight. Seven years of operating the mine—and occasionally swinging a pickax alongside his men—had hardened him into such virile manhood that it almost hurt her to look at him. Especially lately, because it reminded her that he was being wasted on a woman who couldn't give him the family he needed and wanted and deserved.

Of course, darling, Lance does have that smile. He could sell dead horses to the cavalry. Virginia Trumbull's voice reminded Angie that before he'd married her and been so disappointed by her inability to give him the children he wanted, he had smiled more than he had scowled.

The second time Angie saw Kincaid, she and Virginia and Tennessee had been riding in a cart like witches to the woodpile. They'd been arrested for inciting a riot on the mayor's lawn in Phoenix after he had made the comment that, *Women, with their limited mentality, need to be protected from the rigors of the voting process.*

Virginia and Tennessee were cousins and best friends—as well as being two of the leading militant feminists in America. Their dry wit and provocative remarks about Lance Kincaid as they clung to the sides of the wobbly cart had only increased her fascination with him. And remembering the sardonic smiles between her friends, she was sure now that that was exactly what they had been intended to do. Both women loved a good scrape and a good romance. They flaunted their many love affairs in print, which had made them unacceptable even to many feminists who should have been their allies.

Angie's throat tightened. Rather than stay in her room and cry, which was what she was about to do, she grabbed her coat and rushed out the door, almost colliding with an elderly couple coming out of the door across the hall.

"Sorry!" she called, not slowing as she ran past the lift. Elevators were too slow for the demons chasing her.

She was more circumspect in the lobby, forcing herself to walk and nod and smile at all the right times until she was through it. Then out on the street, she ran toward the cable car tracks. That was one of the reasons she loved San Francisco. It was acceptable, even for a woman, to run in the streets.

She caught the cable car just in time and clambered aboard, accepting a man's hand to steady her as the conveyance clanged forward and up the hill.

The car took on so many people as it headed for the Embarcadero that Angie was almost crushed in the crowd. But it felt good to be outside and to have other things to look at and think about. She didn't want to think about her handsome husband falling into the clutches of a woman who had loved him since childhood.

The cable car clanged to a stop and people were streaming off. Angie stepped down and walked toward the ocean. On the pier, she walked out and leaned against the waist-high fence that kept pedestrians from falling off into the murky, choppy water below.

Lance's face floated between her and the water. The image that tormented her now was another of those early photographs she'd taken of him. In it his narrowed eyes had looked directly into her camera. The deep smile lines on either side of his sensuous mouth looked sardonic. He looked like a man capable of anything. Of tenderness, or violence, or strength. A man who could kill a man in a dusty road or take a bullet in the side and joke with his men, even while he winked at her to allay her fears for his safety.

Her throat constricted. Love and pain were so mixed up in her she bent nearly double. She wanted to let the angry tears out, but she was too aware of the presence of others promenading on the wharf. She prayed for the strength to do what she had to do to put Lance out of her mind.

A woman walked by with two children—a girl seven or eight, the other no more than two. The girl held the toddler's hand. They both wore dresses under their open coats, but the toddler might be a boy. All toddlers wore dresses, regardless of sex. The girl smiled down at the child with open adoration.

A terrible feeling welled up in Angie. She wanted to tell the girl not to do that. Let his mother take care of him. Don't get involved. Don't start to love him, because—

Her mind refused to finish that thought, but tears filled her mouth and eyes. *Oh, God.* She prayed for the strength to hold them back, but they spilled down her cheeks and into her mouth.

Four days had passed, then five, without Steve's coming back. On the sixth night, Samantha woke to the sound of the barn door creaking on its rusty hinges.

Heart pounding, she threw off the covers, picked up her robe, and ran to the window. In the moonlight silvering the chill landscape, a man walked from the barn toward the desert. She recognized Steve Sheridan's sturdy form and opened her window.

"Steve!" she called.

At the sound, he changed direction. Barefoot, she skimmed down the stairs and through the silent, darkened house. Steve waited on the porch. A cold wind whipped her gown and robe around her feet and chilled her legs. The dry air smelled of sage. Bright stars twinkled overhead.

"I thought you'd been killed," she said.

He gave a soft laugh. "I thought *you'd* be sleeping."

"I heard the barn door creak."

She looked pale and slim in her nightclothes. He'd thought he was tired, but the image his mind made—of her warm and naked under her bedclothes—tingled through his loins. All tiredness left him.

"You shouldn't be out here like this," he said. His words came out huskier and more revealing than he'd have liked.

"What happened up there?"

"I found everything we need."

"At the site I wanted?"

"At both sites. So, you'll have to choose."

"I want the second site. The one you found," she said, without hesitation.

He was so pleased, he wanted to pick her up and swing her around. At the very least he wanted to touch her, to get close enough to smell the warm, peppermint fragrance he knew surrounded her. He was only inches from her sweet, upturned face.

"You must be hungry," she said, watching him.

He hadn't eaten since breakfast. At the mention of food his stomach growled. "I'm okay. You need to get back to bed."

"We still have some of the peaches Juana put up last summer. There's cold milk in the springhouse. And I can slice some of the leftover chicken and put it between a couple of biscuits . . ."

Steve's stomach growled again. Samantha laughed. "Come along. It's been taken out of your hands."

Steve had six biscuits with chicken, a quart of peaches, and two glasses of milk. Then he leaned back with a sigh and held his stomach. "I think I overdid it," he groaned.

"Nonsense. Any man who finds everything we need to build my house is entitled to eat anything he wants. What will you do tomorrow?"

"I'm going into town to start hiring men to build your house and ramrod your stock. Did Silver Fish come back?"

"He sent word that they'd found the sheep. They're holding them in a canyon with a small creek and good graze."

"How're Ramon and Sender?"

"Ramon's long gone from our hospital ward. Sender is healing very fast. He'll be well in no time."

"Pays to be young."

"So what happens next?" Samantha asked.

"When I come back from town, I'll take you up, so you can christen the site."

"Let's go now," she said, eagerly.

"You mean tomorrow?"

"Please?"

She looked so lovely that Steve relented. "Okay. You need to make some decisions before I go into town. They might be easier if you're at the house site."

"I'll have Juana pack us a lunch."

Steve laughed.

Samantha went back to bed, but she couldn't sleep. She kept seeing how handsome Steve Sheridan was when he laughed, the way his khaki eyes narrowed, the manly shape of his strong chin. He was more appealing than she'd thought when they'd first met.

Annoyed at herself, she decided to put thoughts of Steve Sheridan out of her head. He was building a house for her. For her and Lance, if her dream came true. She needed to sleep now, so she would be fresh tomorrow.

Samantha punched up her pillow and closed her eyes. Her mind conjured up another picture of Steve Sheridan smiling at her. She tried to change it into one of her beloved, but the image stayed steady. The tiny gleam of gold on his canine tooth would not go away. She noticed how neatly his features fit his oval face. Some men's features seemed to be crowded too closely around their noses or spread out too far.

Irritated, she tried to clear his face out of her head, but she couldn't. Then his smile changed, and a heated look came into his thickly lashed eyes. He reached out and pulled her into his arms.

"No!" Heart pounding, Samantha sat up in bed. Maybe it hadn't been such a good idea to talk Steve into taking her back up to the house site.

Slowly she lay back down. No, this was just because she

was tired and lonely. She'd be fine by tomorrow. She had nothing to fear from Steve Sheridan. He worked for her. He'd behave himself because he had to. And she would behave, too.

CHAPTER EIGHT

Late February was beautiful in the low mountains. The long, high sweet warble of an oriole sounded in the trees overhead. The weather was warm and pleasant. Riding beside Steve made Samantha feel carefree and excited, and only a little guilty. Nicholas had wanted to come with them, but she'd refused because they might not get back before the afternoon winds came up.

They reached the south plateau in less than an hour. It was cooler up here, and the wind made a wonderful soothing sound in the treetops high overhead.

They walked the plateau for an hour, then Steve sat her down where the house would be, got out his tablet and pencil, and asked her a thousand questions. She had to decide what kind of wood she wanted for the interior walls, floors, windows, doors, ceilings of each room. She had to decide between marble and hardwood, between light and dark oak, cherry wood and mahogany, between plain or fancy ceramic toilets and washbasins, between six-foot or eight-foot bathtubs, between thirty-inch and twenty-four-inch adobe walls for the basement. Steve patiently explained the meaning of each choice in terms of benefits, dollars, labor, and length of building time.

By the time he was satisfied, she was dizzy.

"You've earned your lunch," he said.

"So you've decided exactly where you'll put the house?" she asked.

Steve laughed. "I wish I were that fast. While the men are building the road, I'll spend another week or so up here siting the house on the lot."

"Why so long?"

"Tests take time."

"Well, why didn't you just say so," she said, laughing.

They ate Juana's cold chicken and biscuits in silence. When they finished, Steve lay down on the pallet and closed his eyes. Samantha watched his even breathing for several minutes, but it did not make her sleepy. The sight of him, stretched out so

156

relaxed and unself-conscious, stirred the part of her that had missed having a man in her life. She could not imagine any of the men who had courted her stretching out like that without half a dozen apologies. Every one of them would fear that action would be misunderstood.

Steve just seemed to take it for granted she would understand him and his intentions. His taking a nap was fine, though. She didn't see it as an affront, the way some women might.

She stood, stretched, and walked the site over again, looking at it from every direction. It was so perfect that it reminded her of a Japanese garden she'd seen in Tokyo the year of her grief-stricken grand tour following her beloved's marriage to another woman.

Samantha closed her eyes and leaned against a tree. She shouldn't have remembered that. When Lance married Angie Logan, the grass turned brown, the skies black. Remembering that terrible time was almost as bad as living it originally.

Tears slipped down her cheeks. Glancing at Steve, she wiped her eyes and stepped behind the tree trunk. She didn't want him to see her crying like a schoolgirl, but once started, tears were not that easy to stop. Thinking about losing Lance filled her with such grief, tears were not enough to relieve it. She cried silently, harder than she had in years. She could not imagine why she was reacting this way today of all days. Today she should be happy; she was starting a new and better phase of her life.

"Hey," Steve whispered, so near she jumped. "Sorry."

"It's all right. I just . . ."

"I doubt this is any of my business, but if you want to talk about what's bothering you, I'd be honored to listen."

"I get so confused sometimes." She knew she shouldn't tell him, but she wanted to talk about it. She needed to talk about it. "I know you probably think I'm insane . . . It's just"—she inhaled a deep breath—"I'm in love with another man."

"Ahhh." His first thought was that now he didn't have to worry about getting involved with her. But strangely the realization did not bring relief or ease his mind.

"Where is he?"

"Durango, Arizona."

"Why isn't he with you?"

Stunned, childlike misery darkened her lovely eyes. "He's married. He's with her."

"He had any sense, he'd be here with you," Steve said, his voice gruff with emotions set in turmoil by her misery.

"I know . . . it," she said, ending on a sob. She couldn't continue. She didn't want Steve to know how stupid she was. When Lance had told her he was in love with Angie and was going to see if she'd marry him, Samantha had stopped listening to his words. Actually her mind had no longer been able to heed them. It was showing her a picture of what looked like an over-ripe piece of fruit nestled within her where her womb was supposed to be. As Lance spoke those dreadful words, she saw his hand reaching out and pressing a finger into the too soft flesh of that imaginary fruit. At his touch, the whole piece of fruit turned black; blood seeped slowly out of the bruised place.

Are you going to be okay? Lance had asked.

What? She was so engrossed in watching the image within that she only vaguely remembered his question.

Are you going to be okay?

Yes, of course.

Good girl! I love you, Sam, but it's not the kind of love you want. I'm your brother. You'll do better with another man who loves you the way you deserve and need to be loved.

The next morning she woke up sick and could not get out of bed. Her insides felt so badly bruised she could barely walk. The doctor in Phoenix had diagnosed sciatica. She'd been sure she had cancer or some massive infection.

She went back East and pretended to be okay, went on her grand tour, and struggled daily with the pain. She was bedridden for three weeks in a hotel in a city whose name she could not even remember. During that terrible time she wrote lies to Mrs. Lillian and Aunt Elizabeth, telling them what a wonderful trip she was having. She'd limped on the left side for almost a year.

"Here, lie down," Steve said, startling her back to the present. "You're shaking all over."

Her legs did feel shaky. She allowed him to lead her back to the quilt Juana had sent.

"So tell me about this wonderful man," he said, settling down next to her.

"Are you laughing at me?"

Steve shook his head. "I'm assuming you have good judgment in men."

"I do."

"So what's he like?"

"He's wonderful. After my parents died, he would let me

sneak into his bed.'' She stopped at the look on Steve's face. "I was only a child then. And so was he. My parents abandoned me, and I cried a lot as a child.'' She brushed tears off her cheeks. "This isn't like me. I never cry anymore.''

Steve pulled out his handkerchief and gave it to her. "It was fresh this morning. Abandoned you?''

"Yes.''

"How old were you?''

"I was four when they drowned at sea.''

"Wait a minute. Did they drown or abandon you?''

"Both.''

"If they drowned . . .''

"They abandoned me when they drowned,'' she said, as if that made perfect sense. "Anyway''—Samantha dabbed at her cheeks—"when I cried, Lance would hold me until I fell asleep. When kids at school or in the family hurt my feelings, he whipped them. Once, I took one of Uncle Chantry's guns out of his gun cabinet. Lance told his father he did it. I probably could have gotten away with it, because I was younger and a girl, but Uncle Chantry whipped Lance hard, because he expected him to know better.''

"How old were you when he did all these things?''

"From four to seventeen.''

Steve looked confused. "And you're still in love with him? Your cousin?''

"He's not my cousin.''

Steve laughed. "He's your uncle's son but not your cousin?''

"Uncle Chantry is my guardian. We're not related.''

"So this Lance, what has he done for you recently?''

"Recently?'' Samantha asked, frowning.

"Yeah, recently.''

"He doesn't have to *do* anything for me. When I love a man I love him unconditionally, whether he does anything or not.''

"I'm sure that's a wonderful quality, but it's impractical.''

"You don't understand, do you?''

"I understand he didn't marry you.'' Steve felt like a heel the minute the words left his mouth.

Samantha inhaled a long, shaky breath. "I think he married someone else to avoid a deeper soul connection with me. I'm not saying this out of pride. It's not that I think I'm so wonderful, but he was badly hurt in love. The first woman he loved—before I grew up—was brutally murdered. He never got over it. Losing her was very painful for him. I think he wanted not to have to go through that again. It was awful for him.''

"I'm sure it was, but life is too short to settle for the safest way out, especially in something as important as marriage.''

"Well, that just tells me you've never really loved anyone or lost anyone you loved. Love is a terrible thing. It makes you horribly vulnerable.''

"I guess it does.'' He didn't sound convinced.

They sat together without speaking until Samantha could bear the silence no longer. "I'm sorry,'' she said miserably.

"Don't apologize for things you can't help,'' Steve said. "I learned a long time ago that feelings are whatever they are. We can't help them, so we shouldn't be ashamed of them.''

"Sounds like justification for chaos,'' she said, sniffing.

"I didn't say you have to act on them. Just that you have to know what they are and respect yourself. If you don't do that, you'll lose sight of who you are.''

"Maybe I should,'' she said darkly.

"When I was seven, Crows Walking used his shamanic powers to save my life during an illness that should have killed me.''

"What does that mean, shamanic powers?''

"He was the medicine man, the keeper of the Medicine Basket. Anyway, within days of my getting well, Crows Walking's natural son died in a freak accident. The traditional Papago are mostly fatalists, believing that whatever happens is what the Great Mystery wanted to happen.''

"Some aren't?'' she asked.

"Some are Christians, and they believe differently. Crows Walking seemed to accept his son's death, but occasionally he'd get angry at me for no reason, so I began to believe that if he hadn't saved me, his own son would have lived.''

"How awful for you,'' she whispered.

"His sister, Uncheedah, made up for everything, real or imagined. As far back as I can remember, she never used the word *love*, but I remember her eyes, shining with love for me.''

Samantha seemed to have drifted off into her own thoughts. "Where are you from?'' he asked her.

"I was born in Old Bolingbroke, Lincolnshire, in a castle owned by my grandfather. But I spent most of my childhood on a ranch near Austin, Texas.''

"I'm glad you added that last. You've no English accent.''

"I can fake it, though. Where are you from? I can't believe you don't know.''

"You'd be wrong. Never had a chance to ask my folks where home was."

"They're dead?"

"I don't know."

"How sad."

He shook his head. "I was too busy surviving to be sad. I suspect sadness is for old folks who have plenty of time to think about things."

"Where did you go to school?"

"At the Carlisle Indian School in Carlisle, Pennsylvania. We called It 'away school.' Then I was apprenticed to a builder who taught me everything I know about working with brick."

"Why did you go to an Indian school?"

"Every now and then, the federal government picked up a handful of Indian kids and sent them to school away from the tribe."

"But you're not Indian. And I'm surprised the authorities didn't take you away from your Indian family as soon as they realized you were white."

"They did, when I was almost sixteen. Since I had no other family they sent me to away school anyway, to try to undo the damage the Indians had done to me, they said. Then they wouldn't let me go back to the tribe. When I finished school, I started my apprenticeship. Now I go back to visit whenever I can."

"So you didn't know Elu—Tristera before?"

"No, the Hopi reservation is hundreds of miles north of the Papago Reservation where I grew up."

"Were you kidnapped by the Indians?"

"I ran away from home. The Indians saved my life."

"What was it like being raised by Indians?"

"Indians, at least the ones I was with, spend all their time teaching their youngsters how to do things. They work and play with them all day. Kids belong to the whole tribe, not just to their parents. Everyone takes responsibility for the kids' education. Depending upon their interests and talents, the children are taught woodworking, basketmaking, jewelrymaking, painting, house building, farming, animal tending, fighting, or riding. If they're going to be warriors, young Indian boys Nicholas's age have almost no duties except to play competitive games to build strength and the ability to run, climb, ride, and shoot arrows. I had no inclination to be a warrior, but by the time I was twelve I could work all day beside the men building houses."

"Houses?" she asked.

"Well, they were dome-shaped brush houses, but a man's got to start somewhere. I'd rather have been a Hopi and lived up on the mesa with Tristera's people. Some of the Hopi pueblos are rumored to be almost a thousand years old." Steve sighed. "That would be a good feeling, looking at something you've built and thinking it could still be there in a thousand years."

"Nothing I've ever done will last even a hundred years. I graduated with high hopes from the Mount Holyoke Seminary for Young Ladies of Talent, but nothing has come of it except a few sculptures that will be thrown away someday."

"Yeah," he said drily, "I've been lucky all my life."

Samantha laughed. "What happened to your parents?"

"I don't know. I remember following a band of Indians who kept trying to drive me away. They were probably afraid someone would come looking for me, think they had taken me, and kill them. I remember being cold and digging in the snow looking for nuts or berries to eat. Crows Walking saw me doing that, thought I belonged to the Indians trying to drive me away, and traded a blanket for me. He took me a long way to his home in Arizona and gave me to his sister, who couldn't have any children. From then on life was pretty sweet."

"I can't believe the whites just let them keep you."

"They didn't know. The Papago are nomads. We kept moving most of the time. Looking for food mostly. I was so dirty most of the time no one could tell me from them."

Samantha tried to imagine what it would be like, living among Indians. "I'd like to meet Uncheedah. No one has ever loved me like that," she said wistfully.

"I find that impossible to believe."

"It's true. Even Lance abandoned me."

Sunlight glinted off the golden crown of her hair. Bangs fell over her eyes; she tossed them back, only to have them fall over again. The rest of her hair was twisted into some sort of braid. Her sweetly curved cheeks were pale, her lips pinched. "It isn't like you think," she whispered.

She told Steve about being on the ship with her parents, waking up alone, and being taken to that terrible woman's house. She told him about begging in the streets and hating her parents for abandoning her. About the Kincaids finally coming to get her and taking her home with them, only to find that she hated them instead of being grateful. She even told him how Lance had finally broken through her rage and brought her into the family.

"How old were you?"

"Four when they left. I'll never forgive them for it, either."

"That's a little harsh for what appears to have been a tragic, unavoidable accident," Steve said softly.

Samantha sucked in a shaky breath. "Lance tried to make up for it, though. He'd hold me at night, rocking me in the rocking chair, stroking my hair, and letting me cry. He probably saved my life."

"How old was Lance then?"

"Ten years older than I. Most boys his age would have been mean to a little pest like me, but he never was. He was my protector. Until . . . the day he told me he was going to propose to another woman." Samantha shuddered. "The world ended for me then." For a moment she could not continue. "When you love someone, the worst thing in the world is for them to leave you."

"You hate your parents for dying, but you've somehow forgiven Lance for marrying another woman."

"He made a mistake. Anyone can make a mistake."

"It may have seemed a mistake to you, but what if he's in love with his wife?"

"He isn't," she said, suddenly weary. The conversation had started a heavy hum that swelled dark and ugly inside her. "We'd better be heading home," she said, standing up. "Nicholas will be waiting for me."

"One more thing for you to see, then we'll go."

Steve led her up the mountainside; they climbed for five minutes. The activity helped. At last Steve called a halt. Hot and panting, Samantha stopped at the crest of a small box canyon with a shallow stream cutting through the middle of it. She stood on a narrow shelf overlooking the ravine.

"I have a few more tests to make, but see this natural basin?" Steve said, pointing. "If I'm right and the tests confirm it, we can dam it here and create a reservoir. You'll have all the water you'll need."

He placed his hands on her waist and faced her back down the hill, so she could view the site she'd chosen. "The bunkhouses will be over there . . . about two hundred feet from the main house and separated from it by that line of trees for privacy," he said. "The toolsheds and barn will be there, so you don't have to smell the horses unless you want to or unless the wind changes. The road will wind from there . . . to there . . . to there . . . to the old house.''

She laughed. They were already calling it "the old house." His warm breath near her cheek seemed to interfere with her ability to follow everything he said.

"The sewer lines will go off in that direction, downhill to the septic tank," he told her. "We'll store your new furniture in the barn under canvas until the house is finished. Smokehouse over there. Women's quarters over there. The outbuildings will rise faster than the main house, or they'll seem to because they're simpler. After we finish the house, if we have enough steam left in us, and you want us to, we'll put adobe around the outbuildings, so they'll be more comfortable. You've picked a good site. It couldn't be any better."

Steve felt the tug of her nearness. Her cheeks were pink from the climb, polished with a light film of perspiration. Her lips were partly opened, as if waiting.

"Is there anything I should be doing?" she asked, watching him with wide, dark eyes.

You should be kissing me, Steve thought. The urge to pull her into his arms was overwhelming. He cleared his throat. "You could be ordering your furnishings. You'll probably want a couple of crystal chandeliers, some hand-blocked wallpapers. What do you think?"

Samantha had been watching the way the light changed the color of his eyes from khaki to hazel. She felt sweat beads forming on her forehead. Her mind was entirely blank. In a panic, she said the first thing that came into her head. "New gowns, shoes . . .''

"New gowns?" he asked, frowning.

"I'll want to have a party when it's done, won't I?" she asked, covering her blunder.

"And fancy mirrors to hang on the walls," he said. "New furniture, area rugs, carpets, and draperies."

"All that?"

"It's a bigger house than the one you have. Should be plenty to keep you busy, just selecting, ordering, and unpacking everything."

Samantha felt dizzy at the thought of trainloads of furniture arriving. "I'll make a list," she said halfheartedly.

"I just wanted you to see this. We can go now."

Steve's voice was gruff. He turned abruptly and started down the hill. Samantha followed, panting to keep up with him. She was so aware of his body beside hers, and she wanted . . . she wanted. She didn't even know what she wanted, just that his easy acceptance of her love for another man disappointed her, made her unsure of herself in a way that disturbed her more than she cared to admit.

The next day Steve woke up cranky. He didn't realize it himself exactly, but Juana did. She greeted him with a smile and shook her head at his surliness as if she had expected it.

"What?" he growled. "What's the matter?"

"Nothing, *señor*, nothing." Juana's eyes sparkled with mischief. "Did thees old woman say somezhing?"

Steve scowled and poured himself a cup of coffee. "God sends meat, and the devil sends cooks," he said, scowling and pouring himself a cup of coffee. "Maybe I woke up cranky," he said. "But if I'm left alone, I'll be fine by the time I finish this. If not . . ."

Juana giggled, not overly upset at the threat, and turned back to the stove. She served up tortillas, *refritos* and a pan of fried eggs. Steve ate, finished his coffee, and walked outside.

Samantha Forrester was in her work area, her round, slender white arms bare as she worked clay on a pottery wheel with wet, clay-covered hands. At the sight of him, she called out a cheerful, "Good morning! Where are you going?"

"Town." Steve sensed she wanted to chat, but he kept walking toward the barn. He saddled Calico and rode into town.

The ride took some of the edge off his mood. At the general store in Picket Post, he wrote out and nailed up signs asking for carpenters, woodworkers, bricklayers, hod carriers, laborers, ditch diggers, blacksmiths, brick molders, loggers, cooks, harnessmakers, and a ramrod for a cattle operation.

That done, he sent a wire to his office in San Francisco. Then he settled down at a table in Mary Francis's dining room and wrote out a detailed order to his office in San Francisco requesting everything he was going to need to build an adobe palace for a beautiful, unavailable woman—the finest hardwoods obtainable, the stoutest wrought-iron window sashes, the most elegantly engraved ceramic toilet bowls, the smoothest marble for the entry hall, the richest stained glass for the fanlights over the doors. He ordered miles of pipe for plumbing and tons of Portland cement, quicklime, and mortar.

As he calculated all this, men wandered in to stand before him, introduce themselves, and state their craft if they had one.

By noon he had twenty men signed on. The ad was working well. By the end of the week, he expected to have a hundred men. Many were tired of working cattle in desert country, and he was offering a decent wage. Word would spread. When men found they could earn the same money or better for making adobe bricks, they'd ride out to the Forrester ranch looking to hire on.

As he finished his list, a boy ran up with a telegram from San Francisco. Ian Macready would be arriving in a week with everything he needed to start building.

Steve stopped at the general store and bought most of the staples on hand—sugar, flour, beans, lard, eggs, sides of beef and pork, potatoes, rice, and canned goods. Feeding an army of workmen was expensive. He also bought almost every weapon and all the ammunition the store had. He signed a chit, asked the man to bill it to Mrs. Forrester, and got no argument. Word had spread that the Forrester woman was hiring everyone in town to build her a new house.

Steve caravanned to the ranch in rented buckboards driven by newly hired hands, others rode in the back. At the ranch, Steve found Eagle Thornton waiting in the shade beside Samantha's house.

"Eagle!" Steve said, pleased.

"Heard you were looking for a ramrod for some cows."

Steve dismounted and strode forward to shake the older man's rough hand. "I thought you weren't interested in taking on trouble?"

"Changed my mind. I figure if you can stand up to Russell and his thieving band, I reckon I can, too."

"Well, you'll have to talk to Mrs. Forrester, but I think with my recommendation, you'll be hired."

"That easy, huh?"

Steve glanced up and saw Samantha Forrester waiting on the porch of her Boston House. In a white gown, with her hair pulled away from her face and tied with a red ribbon, she looked fifteen years old. Steve realized he'd been avoiding seeing her. Part of him dreaded contact. Part of him strained toward her.

"Afternoon." His gruff tone caused her eyes to widen, making her look even younger to him.

Steve introduce Eagle Thornton.

"Mr. Thornton, do you know how to gather a herd to sell?"

"Yes, ma'am."

"Do you think you can do so without word getting around? I

want to sell my entire herd, but I'd prefer we don't announce that to the rustlers who are preying on my cattle. They might just double their own efforts.''

"Good idea. I don't see any problem with it. We just won't tell the youngsters, so they won't blab it around.''

"You're hired.''

"Thank you, ma'am.''

Steve took Thornton to the corral and introduced him to a group of men breaking horses. Most of them already knew Thornton. They hit it off at once, which relieved Steve's mind.

He walked back to where Samantha waited.

"I see you hired some men,'' she said.

"Within a week I expect we'll have as many as we can use. Word spreads fast in this country.''

"Any problems?''

"No.''

"Dinner will be ready soon. Are we supposed to feed the men you hired?''

"I hired a cook who'll take care of them. Bought supplies in town.''

"Good.'' That relieved her considerably. Juana would not take kindly to having another twenty or thirty men to feed.

"I thought I'd just lead the men and supplies up to the work site, so they can get settled.''

"It's too late now. They won't get fed until bedtime. Let your cook prepare the meal here. I want to hear about everything that happened in town.''

Steve hesitated, then nodded. "I have to get the men settled then.''

He should have been hungry, but he wasn't. Just looking at Samantha made his blood pound. Wearing a simple high-necked blue gown that molded itself to her round breasts, slender rib cage, and waist, she was hopelessly alluring.

"Hi, Mr. Sheridan.'' Nicholas sidled up to him and gave him a tentative smile. Steve smiled back at him. The boy was hungry for contact with a man. Samantha shouldn't be holding him in a manless prison on the Arizona desert. If she was going to take him away from the rest of his family, at least she could marry and provide him with a father. Still, it was none of his business. If she wanted to perch here—within range of her married lover— there was nothing he could do about it.

Samantha worried all through dinner. Steve seemed withdrawn, almost resentful at having to go over everything for her. But she was anxious to see progress, even to hear about progress. Now that she was committed to building, she wanted the house to spring out of the ground.

Feeling cross, Steve gave a sketchy report of his activities in town and excused himself right after dessert. The disappointment on her face gave him some small measure of satisfaction, but it didn't last long. Once he was alone, he became furious at himself for being rude to her. He stalked across the yard to the barn, got his bedroll, and climbed the side of the mountain. He felt too restless to sleep. It wasn't high enough up to be cool, but when he needed to look at his own life, he climbed a mountain if there was one around. Being able to see for miles helped put his life into perspective.

The climb took a little of the edge off his feelings. He spread his blankets and lay down. At first he just lay there looking at the desert, the sky, and the emerging stars, feeling hot and angry inside. Then slowly his mind settled into it—and he realized what he was so disappointed and mad about. Samantha Forrester was in love with another man. Of course that was no surprise—she was beautiful enough to have any number of men in love with her. But part of him still wanted to try for her anyway, even though another part knew it was useless to chase after a woman in love with someone else. It was like trying to fill a full cup.

Besides, he had things to do with his life. Things he couldn't do married and rooted in one place. Samantha Forrester had done him a favor by being unavailable. But the thought gave him no comfort. It just left him feeling restless and disturbed and not knowing why.

For the last ten years he had traveled over most of the continent free as the wind. He'd enjoyed himself, and, except for Caroline, never once looked back with regret. Staying safe had been his first priority. But now that he was assured of safety, he wasn't all that happy about it.

Samantha Forrester must never know how affected he was by her. He needed to find a tactic, a way to keep relations friendly between them while maintaining enough distance, so he could build this house. He'd learned long ago that the most dangerous woman was the one who felt spurned. So he reasoned the best strategy would be to pursue her gently, so she wouldn't feel unattractive but would still continue to resist him. It didn't please him to deceive anyone, let alone Samantha, but at least it salvaged his pride to be the one deciding how their relationship, such as it was, would progress.

Finally he slept.

Steve rose early the next morning. His midnight vigil had strengthened him. He had a job to do. And he felt he'd decided on a course to follow with his enchanting and disturbing employer that would at least keep him sane.

From the crew who'd just finished digging the canal from the Gila River to the house site, Steve selected a handful of men to build a road up to the site. After the way was cleared, widened, and leveled, they would dam the new reservoir and dig trenches for the water and septic systems.

From the men hired in town, Steve chose two to act as foremen for the building project. He put one in charge of excavating the basement for the new house and the other in charge of building the forms and molding adobe bricks.

Adobe was made very cheaply, using straw, water, and clay. He had increased the expense by deciding to fortify the bricks with Portland cement and quicklime. It would cost more, and technically it wouldn't be pure adobe, but the house wouldn't come down in the first gulley washer, either.

Men piled into wagons heading for the mountain as Steve mounted Calico and prepared to follow them. Samantha stepped outside. He touched his hat and kicked Calico into a walk; she called after him. "When will I see you again?"

"I don't know," he said, without turning to look over his shoulder.

"But how will I know what's happening?"

Sighing with resignation, he reined his horse and turned. Samantha was clear-eyed and sweet-tempered, smiling at him with a serenity that bespoke no unmet needs. Feeling far too aware of his own, Steve forgot the strategy he'd worked out the night before. The wagons rolled past him. Dust and noise and the knowledge that the men were watching added to his sudden confusion. "Maybe you could just trust me to build the house."

Samantha frowned. "I do."

"Good." Steve kicked Calico's haunches and cantered away.

When they reached the place where the road led up the mountainside, the buckboards slowed to a crawl. In places the men had to climb down and move boulders or cut brush, so the wagons could pass.

Even so, Steve was glad to be on the mountain. Work would

even him out. It would remind him he could do anything he had
to do, even ride away when he was finished, no matter how
beautiful or appealing his employer might be.

They reached the work site at sunset.

Every day for the next week men showed up looking for work.
By the end of the week, a hundred men were laboring on the
road; another hundred were building forms for bricks. Until the
heavy equipment arrived, they had to pour and mix cement in
the forms. A steady stream of hands worked on the road, widening and grading it.

By the end of the second week, two dozen carpenters had
built bunkhouses for themselves, the laborers, and their cooks,
as well as a small wooden cottage for Steve. By the end of the
third week, they'd built a row of bunkhouses for two hundred
men and had started to lower the mountaintop where the house
would sit. Dynamite speeded the work of digging the basement.
Row upon row of bricks baked in the hot Arizona sun. Men
built wooden forms for the foundation. The site now looked like
a small town, bustling with constant activity. Lusty male curses
rang out through the clearing. Even the birds had adjusted to the
constant activity, singing out as the men worked.

Soon they would begin receiving three-by-sixes from the lumber mill and have stockpiled enough bricks to begin raising walls.

Samantha kept busy with all the details of running the ranch.
She met with Eagle Thornton, paid bills, ordered supplies, and
supervised the household help.

As often as she could, she and Nicholas rode into the desert
to see if they could spot a prairie dog family. They didn't find
one, but the ride relaxed Samantha and gave Nicholas something
to do.

One afternoon, on their way back, she saw the Indians camped
beside her creek. The women walked out to meet them, as if
they were their guests. This irritated Samantha; she didn't appreciate feeling like a guest on her own land. In the past, she
had enjoyed looking out her front window and being able to see
great distances without human beings to mar the landscape.

"Can we stop, Mama?"

Samantha didn't want to, but to do otherwise would have been
rude. The Indian women smiled at her with openness and
warmth, motioning her to get down. Reluctantly Samantha dismounted. The Indian boy, probably nine or so, took their reins

and held the horses for them. The women motioned her to the small fire they'd built, where they had been cooking. A rock in the fire glowed with heat. Gesturing at Samantha to come close, one of the women knelt, poured a thin batter over the rock, let it sizzle and bubble up slightly, then peeled it off. With a shy smile, she offered it to Samantha.

"What is it?"

The woman mimicked a chewing motion and nodded. Then while Samantha hesitated, the woman made another one and gave it to Nicholas. He popped it into his mouth and chewed as if he knew it would be tasty. Whatever it was crunched loudly.

"It's good," Nicholas said.

Tentatively Samantha took a bite. It tasted like sweet corn, only crunchy. "It is good," she said, surprised.

The boy, called Young Hawk, spoke English fluently. He introduced himself and the women. Their English was not good, but Samantha found they could communicate. The younger woman, Little Dove, had a sweet, round face. Red Star was older, taller, and the more dominant of the two. She must have been Silver Fish's first wife. When Red Star spoke, Little Dove obeyed. They seemed as comfortable with each other as sisters.

Nicholas and Young Hawk looked at each other frequently, but they didn't speak directly. It occurred to Samantha that little boys were as wary of one another as wild animals. Even so, she enjoyed her visit. Although Nicholas didn't want to go, after about an hour she said good-bye. The Indians waved and smiled.

The next day Samantha packed a basket to take to them. Juana helped her choose things the women could use—beef from the smokehouse, corn from the corncrib in the barn, salt, molasses, flour from town, and a bolt of calico. She wanted to take more, but Juana convinced her they wouldn't know what to do with much else.

The women received the gifts with amazement and gratitude. They gave Samantha a soft rabbit-fur blanket. She demurred at first, because they had so little, but they insisted. Nicholas loved the blanket, so she let him keep it in his room.

Each day, after their forays into the desert, Samantha and Nicholas stopped to visit. The women were soft-spoken and charming. The Indian children were polite and serious near the adults, but out of sight they were as rowdy and boisterous as white children. Nicholas loved playing with them.

Samantha relaxed and began to enjoy the company of the Indian women with their soft, smiling eyes. The baby girl, a round-faced, cooing infant with bright eyes and a sweet smile, enchanted her. Smelling a baby brought back memories of Nicholas when he was first born. Little Dove did not know the date of her birth, but according to Young Hawk it was in the month of the Dangerous Moon, November, which would make her three or four months old.

Holding the baby, crooning to it, Samantha felt a surge of hope. For the first time in years, life was good. Steve Sheridan was building her a new house. Tristera seemed to have a steadying, calming influence on her son, who looked healthier and seemed happier than he had in a long while. And her new ramrod, Eagle Thornton, had inspired her men with new confidence and esprit de corps. The herd in the holding pens was growing daily. Cattle bawled as they were roped and branded and added to the herd. Her world was whole and peaceful. All this freed her to look forward, to dare to believe that her future in this beautiful territory was going to be much brighter than her past.

Joe Dart rode in at the end of the day and found his mother sitting on the porch in the rocking chair. He dismounted, tossed his reins to Piney, his mother's farmhand, and tramped up the steps, two at a time.

"You been sitting here all day?" he asked.

His mother didn't answer. Her eyes had not registered his presence. Joe yelled after Piney, "She been sitting here all day?"

Piney turned and smiled at him, the vacant, aimless smile of a man who had no worries because he didn't have the sense for them. "Beg pardon?"

"I said, has she been sitting here all day?"

"Seems like, Mr. Joe."

"Thanks." Joe was gentle with Piney, because he was good-natured and as polite as a well-trained schoolgirl.

Joe sat down beside his mother. She had been a little moody ever since their trip into town. "Chased a dozen cows half the dern day trying to save their lives, and they acted like I was going to shoot 'em if they came outta that chaparral."

"Cows aren't smart, Joe," Chila said. "That's why we have to take care of them."

Ham Russell walked up from the barn, knocking dust out of his dirty trousers with his gauntlets. At the foot of the steps he stopped and looked up at her. His face and hands were covered with pink, white, and brown freckles. Chila shuddered at the thought of his hands on her body. What a gross invasion that would be. Yet ever since seeing Denny in town, her body hungered to be touched.

Ham slapped his gloves against his thigh again. "That bastard Sheridan hired a new ramrod for the Forrester spread."

The name jolted Chila. Sheridan was the name Denny was going by now. Joe had told her that in town. Sheridan . . . The red haze got between her and the pastureland.

"Who'd he hire?" Joe asked.

"Eagle Thornton."

Chila's lungs quivered. "Ah thought he rode off."

"Well, I did, too, but when I was in town yesterday I learned that he hired on to build the Forrester woman a house."

Chila knew that was not why he had stayed. Denny had stayed because Samantha Forrester was a beautiful woman, and devils preyed on helpless, unsuspecting women with sons to drown. And Denny would keep on doing that until he was stopped.

For the first time since she'd killed the wrong man she felt energized again. Denny was still alive, and he hadn't ridden off like he should have. She vowed he'd be sorry about that.

CHAPTER NINE

Samantha and Nicholas took their morning ride as usual, but this time they rode along the railroad tracks.

"Mama, what are you smiling about?"

"Nothing, Nicholas."

"You keep doing it, though."

"It's nothing. Really."

They rode back to the ranch a little early, and she sent Nicholas to the kitchen for a bite to eat, washed her face and arms to cool them, splashed peppermint water over them to refresh herself, then walked into the parlor to look at what her son had written about the marmot they'd found on the desert. Tristera sat on the sofa, reading *David Copperfield*.

Samantha sat down at the desk. Juana padded into the parlor, her sandals making a shuffle-slap sound on the bare wood floor, then a softer sound on the carpet. "Cavalry's coming! I see from kitchen window."

The muffled clatter of horses' hooves sounded on the slope leading up to the house. Tristera put aside her book and ran to the mirror on the parlor wall to push tendrils of her long auburn hair away from her face. Samantha had suggested she continue to wear it loose to emphasize the difference between herself and Hopi Indian girls, who wore their hair in maiden whorls over their ears. It worked. Tristera looked more Mexican than Indian. And she acted more Mexican.

Seeing Tristera at the mirror, her cheeks flushed with new color, her hands fluttering over her hair, Samantha realized she might not have to worry about Rathwick any longer.

"Tristera, could you greet them? I need to finish reading Nicholas's school work."

Tristera let out a soft, excited groan. *"Sí, señora."*

Rathwick halted his ragged column of men and waited for someone to invite him down. Tristera Rodriguez stepped out of the open door. Her sweet face satisfied something in him.

"Good day, Miss Tristera."

"Good day, *Capitán* Rathwick," she replied, affecting Juana's accented English. Tristera had a natural ability with languages. She spoke English, Spanish, and her native Hopi language. She could mimic almost any accent.

"I'm surprised to see you, *Capitán*. It is a long ride from the fort." The sight of him caused a slight sinking feeling around her heart. He wasn't here to see her but to court the *señora*. That thought made her more irritable than she'd felt canning tomatoes at the school—and she hated canning tomatoes.

"Chasing a band of renegades who left the reservation without permission," he said gruffly. "Thought for a minute we'd caught them when I spotted that band camped by the creek."

"Renegades?" Tristera hooted softly. "Or starving *Indios*, *Capitán*?" It pleased her to irritate the handsome captain, to see the pained expression on his ruddy face. "That particular family of renegades works for *Señora* Forrester," she continued. "You harry them, she'll not take it kindly."

He spread his hands in surrender and smiled, revealing deep dimples on either side of his mouth and good teeth beneath a neatly trimmed mustache.

"Well, maybe you could put in a good word for me, Miss Tristera," he said. "I'm just a poor, tired old soldier, trying to do my job."

"I would invite you in, *Capitán*, but *Señora* Forrester allows nothing in her house that is not useful or beautiful."

Rathwick laughed. "I've been in there before."

"It's a new rule." Tristera tossed her hair. Sunlight glinted off the shining auburn mass. Her dark, challenging eyes sparkled with amusement.

Rathwick laughed again. Tristera's heckling invigorated him, dispelled his tiredness. "If you're not careful, Miss Tristera, I'm going to hire you away from Mrs. Forrester and take you home with me, so you'll have to keep a civil tongue in your head."

"Don't waste your money," she said, snorting. She looked haughty and untouchable, but her cheeks took on color.

"I lie wounded at your pretty feet, Miss Tristera."

Tristera rolled her eyes. "Another mess to clean," she said, flashing him an arch smile. "I'll get a broom and tell the *señora* you're here."

Samantha took that as her cue to appear at the door.

Rathwick bowed low, sweeping the porch with his black felt campaign hat. "I hope I did not catch you at an inopportune time, Mrs. Forrester.'' His voice, which had been playful with Tristera, sounded formal now.

"Good afternoon, Captain. Please get down and come in."

Rathwick complied. His men dismounted with much creaking of saddles. They walked toward the barn to water their horses from the trough.

"What brings you here so early in the day?"

"Chasing renegade Indians who left the *papagueria* last night, probably drunk on mescal. I thought I'd found them when I saw the Indians camped by your creek. Miss Tristera tells me they work for you . . . ?"

"Yes, they do."

"That's too bad." Rathwick scowled. "The only safe place for an Indian is on the reservations they agreed to stay on. According to my orders, if a full-blooded Indian is on the reservation, he's a friendly Indian. If he's off the reservation, he's hostile."

Tristera made a small strangled sound.

"Are you all right, Miss Tristera?"

Tristera lifted her chin. Her brown eyes flashed with fire. Rathwick thought it a shame for the girl to side with the Indians. She was blessed with the prettiness of a young Spanish *aristocrata*. Any Indian blood in her had not hurt her. Her brother, Ramon, was a different story. Rathwick had arrested Ramon once for fighting with three drunken soldiers. He was so difficult and stubborn he might not be a full-blooded brother to Tristera. Rathwick wouldn't be surprised to learn the boy was part Apache.

Rathwick's response thrilled Samantha. She saw his attraction to the girl and felt a rush of warmth for him.

"We'd love to have you stay for dinner, Captain."

"I wish I could, but General Ashland is waiting for my report. I only stopped to pay my respects and to tell you that we secured your palace car and train before any hostiles found it. A Texas and Pacific crew took it back to Phoenix."

"Oh! Thank you so much."

Rathwick glanced from Samantha to Tristera. "There'll be games and dancing at the Picket Post camp a week from next Saturday. I was wondering if I might be so fortunate as to escort you ladies and your party into town?"

"Thank you for asking us, Captain. The last time I was in town I got the distinct impression they didn't want us there anymore."

Rathwick nodded. "I heard about that. Perhaps that's all the more reason you shouldn't let them keep you away."

Samantha frowned. "I've toyed with that approach."

"It's a sound one. I hope you can both go," he said, glancing quickly at Tristera. "Every man will be the loser if the two loveliest women in the territory don't attend."

Samantha had not missed a single dance since she'd come to Picket Post. Social events were infrequent and looked forward to with anticipation. Everyone who could go did so. Men outnumbered the women three to one, so any woman who attended would dance until her feet were sore, and generally with a different man each time. So it wouldn't matter who she officially went with, but he had caught her off-guard. She liked Rathwick, and she realized it would be awkward for him to take Tristera alone. Also Samantha knew it would be good for her to continue being seen with him. It might forestall any gossip about herself and Steve Sheridan.

Samantha glanced quickly at Tristera. "Why, yes, Captain. We'd be happy to accompany you."

Rathwick bent forward in a slight bow. "I'll be here Saturday morning about nine o'clock to escort you ladies into town."

"This coming Saturday . . . ?"

"No, Saturday next."

Rathwick turned smartly on his heel and clumped down the steps. He mounted his horse with a dashing clank of saber and creak of saddle and raised his black felt hat to them. The soldiers led their horses toward his and mounted.

A frown darkened Rathwick's face. "Oh, by the way . . ."

"Yes?"

"I'm still looking for that Indian woman. You haven't seen her by any chance?"

"Why, no. Is she still supposed to be wandering around in the desert alone? I can't imagine such a thing."

"Could be."

"You didn't say in town. What did she do?"

Rathwick hesitated. He wasn't sure he was supposed to be sharing information he'd been told so grudgingly by Ashland. But he liked Samantha Forrester, and it would be unfortunate if anything happened to her because she didn't realize how dangerous the Indian woman was. "She killed five men," Rathwick said, repeating what he'd finally been told.

"Heavens! Are you sure?"

"Yes. And from what the general's investigators found, it was an act of coldly calculated murder."

"If I see her I will definitely send for you."

"Thank you. Don't leave yourselves unguarded. Keep men around at all times. The woman is extremely dangerous." He placed his hat on his head. "Good day."

Rathwick motioned to his lieutenant, who yelled, "Company ho!"

The column snaked back on itself and turned north. Samantha knew they would follow her valley north, then cut east toward Camp San Carlos.

Tristera looked stunned. "I killed no one!" she whispered. "*Señor* Steve knows!"

"There must be a horrible mistake. We'll send for Steve. He'll know what to do."

Abruptly Tristera turned, jerked open the door, and stalked through the house. Seconds later, the back door slammed.

Samantha started after her. Nicholas came out of the kitchen. "Mama, can I go out and play?"

"No. It's your nap time."

"Mama! I'm not sleepy."

"You haven't even tried to sleep."

"I can tell!"

"You know what the doctor said. Lie on your bed for however long it takes. Sleep will come, young man."

Groaning, he turned toward his bedroom.

Samantha hurried to find Tristera. The back screen door hung half off its hinges. Tristera sat on the ground, her back against the house, her face buried in her hands.

Samantha sat down beside her and waited.

Finally the young woman uncovered her pale face. "I did not mean to break the back door," she said, her words choked with fury. "But I am so angry."

"You have every right to be angry. Steve will know what to do. If they catch you, he will testify on your behalf. Surely, once they know the truth . . ."

"With white justice, nothing is sure."

Samantha had no answer. Her own life had never depended on the mercy of the government. She'd always had money, prestige, and the protection those afforded. It was hard to imagine being alone in the world, poor, and dependent upon the questionable justice of a race who had, according to its own newspaper accounts, taken everything from her people.

"Do you have family somewhere, E—Tristera?"

"I can't go back there," she whispered.

"May I ask why?"

Tristera looked like a child, her face pinched with outrage and bitter fury. "Tuvi trusted me. He chose me to go with the delegation to Washington, and they were all killed."

"But you couldn't have saved them. Surely your people could not expect you to save the delegation from armed men?"

"They wouldn't have died if I had been good enough. If I hadn't let Yellow Fox shame me," she whispered.

"That doesn't make sense."

Reluctantly, Tristera told Samantha about falling in love with Yellow Fox, his betrayal, and the attack on the delegation. The betrayal seemed insignificant now, in light of Tuvi's death.

"Tuvi is dead," she ended bitterly, "and my people are doomed. Without Tuvi to protect them, the whites will take away their land—and they will starve. I am labeled as a murderer and a loose woman. So I can't even help them. They wouldn't listen to me now." Her voice failed her. She covered her face and gritted her teeth so hard her cheeks ached.

They sat in silence for a moment. Samantha's heart went out to her. She wanted to pull Tristera into her arms and hold her, but the young woman looked rigid with grief.

"Now it will never rain again," Tristera whispered.

"Rain?" Samantha thought she'd heard wrong. "What has rain to do with it?"

Tristera's eyes filled with shame and guilt. "I was the rainmaker for my village. It has not rained since I lay with Yellow Fox. If it doesn't rain, they will all die."

"But it wasn't deliberate."

"It matters not. Only purity matters."

"I don't know anything about your Indian way of life or your religion, but Steve said that nothing can happen without the Great Mystery's approval or permission. Is it possible the Great Mystery wanted you to experience this for some reason?"

Tristera rolled her eyes. "What reason? If so, then I hate Him, too. Even more than Yellow Fox! What kind of God is He, to let Tuvi die?" Her voice was choked with fury. "What kind of God would let the soldiers shoot a holy man down like a dog?"

Samantha turned away from the harsh, angry light in the younger woman's eyes. She could not defend God. He had taken her parents. He had let Angie Logan steal her beloved away from her. Painful emotion quivered within.

"If you were an outcast, what were you doing with the Indians who were killed?"

"I think they were trying to bring me back into the circle of the tribe. It had not rained in a long time."

"I've never believed in rainmakers," Samantha whispered. "I guess I have a very limited view of the world."

"One day when I was five, my grandmother saw me watching the clouds and she asked me to make them give up their rain because we had been in a drought for so long. To please my grandmother I held up my arms. My grandmother tells people I said, 'It is time to stop being bad little clouds. Give me your rain.' Within seconds the first raindrops fell. It rained for three days."

Samantha didn't know what to say. Obviously Tristera believed she had caused the rain. "I'll send for Steve. Maybe he'll know what to do."

A column of black smoke moved steadily along the southern horizon, creeping north toward Samantha Forrester's house. Steve watched until he confirmed that the train carried freight. This could be Ian. If so, he was right on time. Steve ordered men to hitch horses to the buckboards.

Men tired of the hard work of leveling the roadbed without proper tools, rushed to comply. Steve saddled Calico. Every available buckboard rapidly filled with the men needed to unload the supplies, and they followed him down the hill.

About halfway, Steve saw Ramon coming up.

"Looking for you, *señor*," he said, lifting his floppy brimmed hat and wiping the sweat off his face with his sleeve. His wet thatch of hair was plastered to his head.

"We saw the train," Steve explained.

"Don't know anything about a train. The *señora* asked me to fetch you back pronto."

That had an ominous sound to it. Steve kicked his horse into a gallop.

Jennifer Kincaid looked up from the limp, feverish form of her daughter and out the window, trying to gauge by the cactus formations how far they still were from Phoenix. They had just come from Los Angeles yesterday and should reach Phoenix by noon—if they were on schedule.

Amy was asleep now, but if she woke and they were still on the train she might start vomiting again.

Jennifer glanced from the window to her husband's tall form, sprawled comfortably in one of the Pullman coach's upholstered chairs. His eyes were closed, but under her scrutiny, he opened them and caught her glance.

"How is she?" he asked.

"Not good. The fever seems to be rising."

"It's probably measles," he said quietly.

"Oh, God, I hope not." Every year children died from measles. Little Chane hadn't had them, either. Jennifer glanced at her sleeping son. He wasn't sick yet, but . . .

"Hey, don't cry," Chane said, getting up to come feel his daughter's forehead. "We'll get them through this. We all got through it."

"I was just thinking how awful it must be for Samantha, with no husband to support her through these crises."

"Yeah, it's rough on her."

Jennifer took Chane's hand and squeezed it. "It's a lot easier when you have someone to be scared with."

They pulled into the Texas and Pacific Railroad Company's Phoenix station at 11:55 A.M., right on schedule. Even worried about his daughter, Chane looked at his watch and said, "More of my trains arrive on schedule than any other company's."

Jennifer smiled. Her husband took a great deal of pride in his work. Chane carried his sleeping son, and Jennifer carried Amy, who was awake now and groggy and fretful. Jennifer covered Amy's head with a light blanket, but the girl pushed it aside and cried. "Shhhh," Jennifer whispered, "you need to keep this over your head."

As they stepped out onto the platform, Bill Penney, the stationmaster, hurried toward them. Penney was a tall, thin man who looked more like a town doctor. His hair had all been worn off, probably from worrying over schedules and wearing a green eyeshade eighteen hours a day. He lived alone and rarely went home except to change clothes and eat.

"Got some news for you, Mr. Kincaid," Penney said, pushing his eyeshade up on his forehead.

"Oh?"

"It's about your sister, Mrs. Forrester."

Chane led the group into the shade of the covered platform. "What about her?"

"We got her palace car back a week or so ago all shot up. The brakeman had been killed and Lars was shot bad. He's still laid up in Camp Picket Post."

"Oh, no!" Jennifer whispered.

"What's wrong, Mommy?" Amy whined.

"Nothing, sweet," she murmured. "We're just worried about Samantha."

"Have you heard any word from her?" Chane asked Bill Penney.

"Well, no, not directly. But we got a wire that there's a crazy Indian woman killing folks all over that area. And we got a bunch of workmen and a big shipment of building materials for Mrs. Forrester. Looks like she may have been burned out or something. There're enough men and enough stuff on those flatcars down there to build a couple of houses."

Chane scowled. Amy whined, and Jennifer bounced her to quiet her. "You'd better go see about Samantha," she said.

"I can't leave you now."

"You'll be back by tomorrow, latest, won't you?"

"I suppose so." He turned to Bill Penney. "Put together a train for me with my palace car and the flatcars of building materials. I'll take Mrs. Kincaid home and be right back."

"Oh, I forgot to tell you," Penney said, following them toward the Kincaid's heavily sprung brougham carriage that had just rolled up to the station platform. "Mr. Lance Kincaid has requested a special train to take him to Mrs. Forrester's house, too. I just got the request this morning and was going to act on it favorably, but I realized you'd be here by the time I could anyway . . ."

"Thanks, Bill, you did well. Route my train through Durango and I'll pick Lance up. Wire him and tell him what time to expect me."

Bill Penney grinned. "It's as good as done, sir." There was only a narrow gauge track to Durango, installed to service Lance's mine and the copper mine, but Penney knew how to handle the transfers.

Two hours later, Chane knocked on the open door of the L & K Silver Mine in Durango. Logan was a silent partner. Lance made all the daily operating decisions. The part of the building visible to Chane was empty, and no one answered. Chane glanced around the deserted work site.

A man strolled up the slope from town, saw him, and angled over to greet him. "Looking for Mr. Kincaid?" he asked, pulling a toothpick out from between his front teeth.

"Yes."

"He's in the mine. We sprung a leak this morning, and he's working with the engineers to try to stop it before it puts us out of business."

"Can you show me where I might find him?"

Just as he asked the question Lance strode out of the mine shaft with three other men.

Chane waved, saw Lance wave back, then walked over to meet him. Lance didn't look happy, but that was to be expected. No man wanted water instead of silver.

Lance wiped heavy beads of sweat off his forehead. His shirt was sweated through, his face streaked and dirty. "I guess Yoshio couldn't keep his mouth shut," he growled.

"I don't know anything about that," Chane said, surprised at his brother's truculent mood. "You requested a special train to Samantha's house. Since I'm going that way, too, I decided, if you don't object," he said, squinting at his brother's obvious hostility, "that we could share the same train."

Lance turned to the men who had followed him out of the mine. "You know what to do. I'll be back in a couple of days."

Without another word to Chane, Lance strode down the slight incline toward town. Chane scowled and followed. Something was amiss.

"How's Angie?" he asked of his brother's broad back.

"How the hell should I know!"

That answer explained a lot. "Something happened?"

"She moved to San Francisco and filed for divorce."

"Why?"

"I guess she found someone else."

Chane lengthened his stride to walk beside Lance. "I'm not the smartest man in the world when it comes to women, but I'd have bet all my stock in the Texas and Pacific that Angie was and still is deeply in love with you."

"Well, you'd be looking for work now, wouldn't you?" The bitterness in Lance's husky voice evoked an ache of compassion in Chane.

"So, what now?" he asked.

"Now?" Lance repeated, squinting through narrowed eyes. "Now I guess I just pick up the pieces and go on. Unless I've missed something . . ."

"You're bitter now . . ."

"No!" said Lance, his tone sardonic.

"Angie loves you, and you love her. I expect this'll work out, if you give it a chance."

"Talking to Angie lately has been about as easy as kicking a mule up a ladder." Lance stopped abruptly. "If you didn't know, what brought you to Durango?"

Chane told him about Samantha's train and the crazy Indian woman who was killing people. "You want to go with me? If not I'll wire Bill Penney to send another train whenever you say."

"I don't mind going with you, but I have to change first. You can wait at the train if you want."

"I'll walk with you. It'll do me good. I've been cooped up on trains for the last two days."

They skirted the small town's main street in favor of one less traveled. The houses looked deserted. Sleepy dogs lay on porches or under trees. Occasionally one got up enough energy to bark at them.

Walking beside his brother, matching his long strides in silence, Chane realized he had felt uncomfortable ever since he'd seen his brother coming toward him earlier. Now his mind was giving form to that feeling. He realized Lance looked exactly the way he'd looked and sounded after Lucinda died—like a wounded animal gathering its energy to do destruction.

Chane did a quick calculation. Lance was thirty-five now. He had fallen in love with Lucinda when he was seventeen. Lucinda had been twenty, three years older than Lance, and that had been enough of a difference to incur the Kincaid family disapproval. In spite of that, Lance and Lucinda had planned to marry when he graduated from Harvard Law School. Three weeks after his graduation, she'd been murdered.

Lance had tracked down two of the three men who'd done it and had killed them with his bare hands. Afterward, he'd been so horrified at what he'd done that he hadn't pursued the third. At their father's suggestion, Chane had taken his brother off to France for a holiday. Unfortunately Lance had done anything but rest. He had broken hearts and savaged women's lives all over Paris. It had taken the experience with Colette, Chane's fiancée, to finally stop him.

Chane had heard the truth about what had happened between Lance and Colette only after it was over. Colette was tawny skinned, tawny haired, and lithe as a young kitten, and Chane had loved her. Lance and Colette had known each other without his knowledge. Apparently she had flirted with Lance every day as he walked by the small dress shop where she worked. Lance had warned her that she couldn't get away with that forever, but she had only smiled her seductive smile at him and continued to tease him.

Finally Lance had kidnapped her and kept her for three days, making love to her repeatedly, even though he would not tell her his name or allow her to tell him hers. He told her he didn't want to know anything about her except the smell of her flesh as he made love to her. When the three days were over he took her back to her shop and did not ask her to keep the secret, even from the police. But of course she did. By then she was madly in love with him and would have done anything for him.

A month went by, and Lance did not come back for her. She almost died of a broken heart. Then he showed up at the shop and spirited her off for another three days. Same rules. Same disappointment when he returned her.

Finally Colette came to Chane and told him she needed to break their engagement to marry. She admitted she was in love with a mystery man whose name she did not even know.

Shortly after that Chane started following Colette and saw the mystery man who had enchanted his fiancée. Then he confronted his brother. Lance was devastated to learn that Colette was Chane's fiancée and that he had ruined Chane's relationship. Lance had gotten staggering drunk that night and sailed for America on the next available ship.

In New York he had quit his job at his father's firm and taken a train to the Arizona Territory. When their mother had asked why he was leaving, he'd said, *Maybe if I stay away from civilized people I won't do any more damage than absolutely necessary.*

Then, much to his family's chagrin, Lance had taken one of the most dangerous jobs on the frontier—Arizona Ranger. Their father, Chantry Two, had been furious but impotent to do anything about it.

And now that same bitterness and hardness were back in Lance's blue eyes. It did not bode well for any woman he singled out.

Lance changed clothes at the house. They walked back to the mine and boarded the narrow gauge train that had brought Chane on this leg of his journey. When they had transferred to the palace car and were finally headed toward Samantha's ranch, Chane broached the subject again.

"So what now?" he asked cautiously.

Lance shrugged. "Maybe I'll court Samantha."

Chane scowled his displeasure.

Lance quirked an eyebrow. "You have some objection to that?"

"I guess not. As long as you remember your manners."

"And what if I don't?" he asked grimly.

"If you hurt her the way you hurt Colette . . ."

"Is that a threat?" Lance asked, his eyes narrowed.

"A concern."

"Sam's a big girl now."

"You're my brother, and I don't intend to meddle in your affairs, but I feel the need to speak my mind." He paused. "Where you're concerned," he said carefully, "Samantha is completely vulnerable. You have the ability to deal her a killing blow."

"Or to make all her dreams about me come true."

"If I trusted that—"

"So why the hell don't you?" Lance snapped.

"When you're in your right mind, you wouldn't hurt anyone, especially not Samantha. But you're . . . confused right now. You might do something in bitterness that you'll regret."

"And I might not."

"So, big brother," Chane said, "butt out."

"Good advice," Lance growled.

An hour after Samantha had sent Ramon to fetch Steve, a train pushed its load up the last grade to the house and chuffed to a stop. Recognizing Chane through an open window of the palace car, she picked up her skirts and ran down the porch steps and across the yard.

"Chane!" she cried.

His black hair rumpled by the wind, Chane skimmed down the steps of the observation deck, caught her in midflight, and spun her around. "We thought you'd been killed," he growled. "We came back from a trip to Los Angeles today and found out from Bill Penney your palace car had been all shot up. If Amy hadn't been sick, Jennie would have come with me."

"I'm sorry. I . . ."

"Are you all right? Jennie was worried sick."

"I meant to send a wire, but—How is Amy?"

"Running a fever. Measles are going around. You're all right? And Nicholas?"

"Yes. Yes, we're fine."

Lance stepped out onto the observation platform, leapt down, and strode toward them.

"Lance!" Samantha cried, her heart flipping over at the sight of his grim, handsome face relaxing into a smile at the sight of her.

Chane scrutinized his brother carefully. The smile was a good sign. Maybe, just maybe, Lance would behave himself.

As Chane watched, men swarmed out of the lead boxcar and walked past them toward Samantha's water trough. "What the hell are you doing to need all this?" he asked.

Samantha laughed. "Building a house. Thanks for bringing them. Can you stay for a while?"

Chane's green eyes narrowed against the sun. "Who's building it for you?"

"I hired a man by the name of Steve Sheridan."

"Never heard of him."

Samantha glanced from Lance to Chane. Lance shrugged. Chane's wide jaws clamped in consternation. He pinned her with a look that clearly said that his never hearing of Steve was final condemnation. Every year, Chane looked more like Uncle Chantry, one of the handsomest older men she'd ever seen.

"Well, I think he's very good," she said defensively.

Lance scowled, too, and it was clear he also didn't think she should be making decisions like that all by herself.

"I'm a big girl now," she said.

Chane gave a condescending grin and walked back to the train to tell the engineer to shut down the engine and relax while the men unloaded the freight cars. Samantha led Lance into the house.

"Can you stay awhile?" she asked hopefully. "Come say hello to Nicholas. He'll be upset if you don't."

"It's up to Chane."

They found Nicholas asleep on his bed. Lance leaned down and kissed his forehead.

"I'd better wake him," Samantha whispered.

"No."

Chane joined them. He, too, bent to kiss Nicholas's forehead. Lance led them out of Nicholas's room.

"Jennie wants you to come back to Phoenix with me," Chane said, glancing around the parlor.

"Why?" Samantha asked, puzzled.

"In addition to getting your palace car back with bullet holes in it, and one dead and one wounded employee, we heard there's a crazed Indian woman murdering people. Jennie wants you to stay with us until they catch her."

"That is such a lie!" Samantha said indignantly. Glad that Tristera was outside, she told Chane and Lance what Steve and Tristera had told her. "The cavalry made up the story," she said, ending.

Chane asked a few questions, then nodded his understanding. "Well, that should relieve Jennie's mind. But I'm still worried about your building another house."

"You're probably still upset about this one."

Chane nodded.

"The new house will be nothing like this." Samantha showed Chane a line drawing of the house Steve was building.

"Pretty fancy," Chane said. "Are you sure he can actually build this? It would take quite a builder to make a project like this come out right."

"He's built them before."

Chane shook his head. "I'll do some checking. If he's any good at all, someone will have heard of him."

"I don't think that's necessary."

"I know you don't, but humor me, okay?"

Samantha sighed. "Okay."

Juana waddled into the room. "*Señor* Steve is here."

"Here?" Samantha asked, horrified.

"*Sí, señora.*"

Samantha couldn't imagine worse timing. Chane was in a perfect mood to take Steve on. And for some reason she couldn't articulate, she didn't want Lance and Chane picking on Steve.

"I'll be right out." Samantha turned to Lance and Chane, who were both looking at her.

"You wait here," she ordered firmly.

Steve rode up just as Samantha stepped out onto the porch. With an odd sinking feeling around his heart, he realized that his time away from her had not dimmed his attraction to her one iota.

"Afternoon," he said glumly.

She looked up at him, and he knew she had a serious problem of some sort, but a smile started in her beautiful blue eyes and spread over her face until it completely erased the tension he'd seen there. In that moment, with her happiness to see him radiating out of her lovely face, he forgave her anything and everything she might ever do to him. An answering smile took over his own face. They just stood there, smiling at each other.

Finally Steve said, "You sent for me, remember?"

"Oh, I forgot! I had something else on my mind."

"So do I," he said, smiling so widely he exposed the gleam of gold in his canine tooth.

Even confused as she was, Samantha was inordinately pleased by Steve's teasing, but before she could think of a witty rejoinder, a short white-haired man strode around the corner of the house, stopped at the sight of her, and lifted his battered black derby.

"Call me a bloody Jacobite!" he murmured. His Scottish burr and the tartan of his vest labeled him a Scot. Merry blue gnome's eyes looked out of a round, smiling face framed by frizzy sideburns that grew in wispy white arcs from his ears to the corners of his mouth. His chin and the rest of his face were clean-shaven.

"Would you look at the lass!" he growled. " 'Tis no wonder we're riding trains through a Godforsaken desert to build a house not even on the schedule."

Steve grinned. "I see your sight hasn't failed you."

"A beautay!" Macready said loudly, waving at Samantha. "Why, son, she's a miracle, that she is. A lass with eyes the color of a Highland lake . . . set in one of the sweetest faces on God's green Earth."

"She is indeed," Steve said, smiling at Samantha. "Macready has been in America for twenty years, but he drops into an impressive Scottish burr at will. I think he heard from someone that women find it exotic."

Samantha laughed, and Steve felt her laughter all the way to his toes. "Actually my partner, Frank Jakovich, says Ian's half Scot, half Irish, and all son of a gun when crossed."

"Don't you go believin' a smidgen o' that," Macready said, protesting. "Me beautiful bride's a bit o' a nag, so I spend me time at one work site or anither. Thanks to me careful planning, lass, we've been 'appily married now for nigh onto twenty-seven years." Ian Macready slapped his thigh with a meaty hand. "Leastways now," he said to Steve, "I dinna nee' to check if ye've lost yer senses, lad."

"Samantha Forrester, Ian Macready. Ian's one of the best building supers on either coast."

"You must be hot and thirsty, Mr. Macready."

"Aye, and she's as smart as a whip, too!" Macready said, smiling at Steve. "How air ye, lad?"

"Couldn't be better now that you're here. We've been working with hoes and scraper boards."

"Well, lad, yer days of hardship air over, or they're just beginning, one or t'other. We've brought tools enough for every man in the county."

Ian Macready turned away to answer a question from one of the men he'd brought with him. Samantha wanted to warn Steve before he was confronted by Chane and Lance.

"I need to talk to you," she said.

"Give me a minute with Ian."

Steve spoke briefly with Macready, who then left to oversee the unloading of the equipment and supplies into the wagons Steve had led down the mountainside. Steve took Samantha by the elbow and steered her toward the barn.

"Where are you taking me?" she asked, laughing even as she checked to be sure Lance and Chane were not watching.

"Privacy." When they were deep in the barn and well away from prying eyes, he stopped and faced her. "What's up?"

Dust motes gleamed in the sunlight slanting in the window near the stall where he'd stopped. Steve had sprouted a growth of beard on his usually smooth-shaven cheeks. Somehow that changed him, made her even more aware of his masculinity and the way his eyes softened when he looked at her.

"Rathwick was here," she said. "He claimed the Indian girl he's looking for is wanted for murder. He says she killed a whole party of Indians. And Chane and Lance are here."

"Lance? The one you're—"

"Yes. They came because Chane got my palace car back all shot up. He said they'd heard in Phoenix about a crazy Indian woman murdering people all over this area. Tristera was furious at that—and I haven't even told her all of it."

"Don't blame her."

"What should we do?"

"I know Tristera didn't kill anyone, but if the army is determined to say she did, it'll be her word against theirs. I know she wants her name cleared, but I got there after the men were dead. I'm a fugitive of sorts myself. I lived with the Indians long enough to know better than to advise her to turn herself in, even with my testimony. I'm sure Tristera's learned that lesson, too. She won't volunteer for trouble."

"So we just continue to hide her here?"

"Unless you're no longer willing."

Samantha looked startled. "Why wouldn't I be willing? You mean, do I think she killed them? Of course not."

Steve peered into her eyes, searching for she knew not what.

His gaze seemed to see inside her, as if this had taken on some special significance for him. Finally he nodded.

"Then I'll talk to her."

"Thank you, Steve. She respects you so much."

He grinned. "And what about you? Do you respect me?"

Samantha smiled. "Of course."

Steve learned close to her; his nearness ignited such warmth in her belly she felt the smile on her face wavering. Steve closed his eyes and touched his warm lips to hers. A spear of heat impaled her; a tiny moan escaped.

Steve took that as encouragement. His tongue teased her sensitive lips, seeking entry into her mouth, and his arms came around her, pulling her closer against him. His kiss turned devouring, and much to her surprise and chagrin, Samantha realized she was as hungry for his touch as he seemed for hers.

Her mind still struggled for some way to explain this amazing behavior of hers, with Lance in the house waiting for her. But she could not will her arms to push Steve away. To her further astonishment, they twined themselves around Steve's warm neck and pulled him closer. Her mouth, her traitorous mouth, opened to his devouring kiss, and the weakness grew more debilitating and intense.

Long before she wanted him to, Steve relinquished her lips and buried his face in her throat. "Samantha," he groaned huskily.

The main barn door creaked, and a man yelled, "Samantha!"

Despite her bedazzled state, Samantha recognized Lance's voice and flinched. Fortunately Lance could not see them from there, but ever mindful of her reputation, Steve groaned softly and stepped away from her. Luckily she was still leaning against the stall, so her feeble legs didn't actually collapse as she feared they might.

"Yes?" Samantha called out.

"Where are you?" Lance demanded, irritated.

"Get rid of him," Steve whispered.

"I can't," she whispered. "Be right there," she yelled, rushing forward with pounding heart. Steve followed. She looked back at him, willing him to stop or disappear, but he just kept coming.

"Wait here," she whispered loudly over her shoulder.

Something about her expression must have alerted him.

"Why? Who is it?" he asked.

Too late. Lance was upon them. She almost bumped into his broad chest. "Sam!" he said, steadying her.

"Lance!" she gasped, as breathless as if she'd run a mile.

"What's going on?" Lance asked.

"On?" Samantha repeated, stalling for time. "Nothing. Steve was just . . ."

"Is this Sheridan?" Lance asked, his eyes meeting Steve's.

Steve knew instantly this was going to end badly. The man was at least two inches taller than he was. His finely chiseled features fit together into a thoroughly masculine face dominated by heavy black brows and piercing blue eyes. His smile was one women would like—it could mask anything or promise the world. Steve would have preferred that Kincaid be more obviously flawed. Like maybe an extra hand coming out of his forehead.

With a sinking heart Steve stuck out his right hand. "Yes, it is, and you must be . . ."

"Kincaid, Lance Kincaid," the man said, slowly extending his right hand.

Steve shook his hand, a little more forcefully than he needed to. Then both of them turned in unison to look at Samantha, whose cheeks flushed becomingly.

"Let's get out of this barn. It's hot in here," she said, leading them toward the barn door.

Just as they reached the door, Chane opened it and peered inside.

"Chane!" Samantha said, again showing a little too much excitement.

"What's everyone doing in the barn?" he asked, glancing from Samantha, to Steve, to Lance.

"I just needed to ask Steve a question," she began lamely.

"In the barn?" Chane asked, looking at her, then at Steve.

"It was a structural question," Steve explained smoothly.

A milk cow walked toward Chane as if to step around him and go outside. "I hear you're a builder, Mr. Sheridan," Chane said pointedly as he pulled the barn door closed behind him to thwart the escape. He elbowed the cow aside and pushed her back toward the stall she had somehow escaped.

Chane Kincaid was an inch taller than his tall brother. He was also broader of shoulder and with an even more commanding presence, if that were possible. He looked like a captain of industry. Steve could imagine him at the helm of a large corporation. Lance was impressive as well, but he looked like a loner. However, side by side, the brothers were undeniably a formidable team.

"Yes," Steve drawled. "I guess Sa—Mrs. Forrester told you I'm building her a new house."

"We brought a lot of men and building materials with us, but I failed to see any activity to justify it," Chane said, scowling. Lance watched Steve as if he expected him to crumble under the pressure of two Kincaid males glowering at him.

"I'd have to be a fool to recommend that Mrs. Forrester build near here. This is hardly an appropriate site for anything, much less a private residence."

"So, you're recommending another site?"

"I consider that one of the least of my responsibilities," Steve said curtly.

"I see," Chane said, squinting suspiciously.

Samantha couldn't believe Chane was acting so pompous and brotherly. "Steve picked a beautiful site, actually."

"Mind if I ask where?" Chane asked, still pinning Steve with his most penetrating look.

"About a mile from here, on the side of the mountain," Steve said. "I'll be happy to take you up there to see it, if you like."

Chane nodded. "Thanks. That'll do for starters."

Samantha realized that Chane, who was also a builder of some repute, fully intended to inspect every inch of the work site and second-guess every decision Steve had made. If Chane found any flaws at all, he might just insist that she turn the project over to someone else. The thought of his humiliating Steve in that fashion frustrated and irritated her. Suddenly she felt sixteen years old.

Before she could think of any way to stop Chane, he took Steve by the arm and led him outside. Samantha started to follow them, but Lance caught her arm and held her back. "What is this?" she demanded, suddenly angry.

"For your own good," Lance rasped. "If he's a shyster, better you find out now, before you've dumped any more money into this—" He paused.

"Boondoggle?" she demanded. "Is that what you were going to say?"

Lance shrugged.

"You think I'm not perfectly capable of choosing a builder and . . ."

Lance pointed at her house, visible through the barn window, as if that were all the proof he needed.

Samantha frowned. "That's not a fair comparison. This house was built by an Eastern builder before I got here. He had no idea what he was doing."

Lance laughed. "I rest my case," he said, grinning. Samantha expelled a frustrated breath.

"Relax," he said. "If this guy's any good, Chane will know that, too."

"I just don't like the idea of my brother storming in and taking over. As if—"

"As if you don't have perfectly good sense yourself," he finished for her.

"Right."

"Is this builder someone special to you?"

"No." Her quick response didn't ring quite true, but fortunately Lance didn't seem to notice. "Chane could have checked up on me by himself. What brings you here?" she asked, hoping to change the subject.

Lance shrugged. "I just wanted to see you."

"You did?" she asked, surprised.

"Yeah. Something wrong with that?"

"Not wrong. But unusual. Is everything okay?"

"No," he rasped, scowling suddenly. "Angie left me. She's filed for divorce."

"Oh, no!"

Pain clouded his usually clear blue eyes. "Yeah."

"Why?"

"Hell . . . I don't know."

Samantha wanted to press for information, but it was apparent he wasn't ready to talk about it yet."

Steve's men loaded the supplies onto wagons. Steve introduced Chane Kincaid to Ian Macready, dealt with Ian's questions, and then excused himself. While Kincaid was grilling Ian, Steve tracked Tristera to the kitchen. He found her talking to Juana, who was stirring a pot on the stove and nodding occasionally in sympathy as she listened.

"*Señor* Steve!" Tristera cried out at the sight of him.

"Rathwick made you mad, huh?"

Tristera told Steve the same story he'd already heard from Samantha. "What can I do?" she ended.

"Stay here. Apparently you're safe here." Steve thought of a question he'd wanted to ask before but hadn't. "Where were you coming from when they attacked your party?"

"We left the train at Globe and were going home."

"Why were you on the Globe train?"

"We had been to see the Great White Leader of the American people. We got on the wrong train somewhere."

"You saw President Cleveland? Why?"

"He wanted to give us a new treaty that would guarantee each person in our tribe forty acres of land. But I explained that this would not work for the Hopi. I told him that we must live on the mesa—where it is safe—and only go down on the plain to farm in the daytime when the men can protect one another from the Navaho."

"And that was all right with him?"

"*Sí.*"

"Do you think the old men were killed on purpose?"

"I don't know. Why would they be?"

"Was anyone else with you?"

"The Indian agent went to Washington with us, but he didn't come back with us. He entrusted us to a guide."

"Was this guide killed?"

"No."

"What happened to him?"

"I had forgotten that. He said he was going ahead to scout."

"He was in on it then. You were set up." Steve pondered for a moment. "I'm not doubting what you say, but it's a little hard to believe that the Hopi elders would take along a female to an important meeting like that," he said, frowning.

"They didn't want to take me, but Tuvi convinced them to do it."

"Why?"

"I don't know why, but I know how."

"How?"

"He asked them to search their hearts for reasons why I should not go, and they went inside and then came out and they were silent."

Steve frowned his puzzlement. "I don't get it."

"Disputes," Tristera explained, "among the Hopi elders, are settled by the priest with the highest spiritual attainments."

"So, Tuvi won on that score, and they invited you, in spite of . . ." Steve stopped.

But Tristera finished it for him. "Yes, even in spite of being a female who had been publicly shamed. The Hopi care less about those things than they do about the Great Mystery."

Steve remained silent, remembering.

"Someday," Tristera said softly, "the *capitán* will figure out that I'm the girl he's looking for."

"Not as long as you keep making eyes at him. You'll keep him so off-balance, he'll be lucky to walk upright."

"Thank you, *Señor* Steve."

"Be careful, little one."

Steve went back outside to supervise the unloading of the train and the loading of the wagons. In less than two hours, the men had filled the wagons and were ready to head up the hill. Unfortunately Chane Kincaid was still determined to go with them.

Steve looked for a chance to say good-bye to Samantha in private, but it didn't come. Her lover had spirited her to the far corner of the porch and was keeping her to himself. Steve had never felt lower in his life. He was going to be chaperoned by the big brother while Samantha was courted by a man who looked like nothing but trouble to Steve.

As they set off for the work site Chane and Ian were talking like old friends. And Samantha was standing on the porch beside her lover looking sweetly confused by the attention he was showering on her. It was a dark moment for Steve.

Lance remained quiet through dinner and putting Nicholas to bed. Then, instead of the usual awkwardness between them, he took her hand and asked her to walk with him out on the desert.

Samantha was so aware of his warm hand on hers that she felt jumpy all over. They walked out a-ways and stopped by the rock-strewn creek bed south of the Indian camp. Lance let go of her hand and leaned against one of the boulders. She leaned on the other side of it.

"I've decided to sell my cattle. My herds are being ravaged by the drought and rustlers. Steve and Eagle Thornton, my ramrod, are urging me in that direction."

"Sounds like good advice to me. If you're going to do that you might want to do it soon and get a jump on the market. Prices are still good right now."

"I have five hundred head of my special breeding stock and I thought I had ten thousand head of range cattle, but my foreman says I'll be lucky if they find three thousand head."

"You're missing seven thousand head of stock?"

"I guess so."

"That's highly unusual, even if you lost them over the entire three years you've been here. I've chased a lot of rustlers in my day. They were small operations, though."

"I've decided to sell the rest, before they all starve to death or get stolen."

"You know . . . we did have a large-scale rustling operation near Phoenix in '88. Peter was instrumental in breaking up that gang."

Peter was Jennie's brother, who had been missing for seven years. He had turned up in Phoenix last year alive and well, long after Jennifer had given him up for dead. She learned he had been forced into outlawry following the murder of his wife and unborn child. Only last year, with Chane and Jennie's help, he had finally cleared his name and paid his debt to society by breaking up Dallas Younger's rustling operation, one of the biggest in the territory. This had earned him a pardon and the right to re-enter society as a respected citizen.

Peter was currently working for the Texas and Pacific as head of their security network. His reputation alone was almost enough to assure the safety of the railroad's cargoes.

Lance scowled and narrowed his eyes in chagrin. "But some of them may have resettled here. I'll talk to Peter about that possibility, and I'll start looking for a buyer for you as soon as I get back to Durango."

"Thanks." They stood in silence a moment, then Samantha ventured gently, "It might help to talk about what's bothering you."

"I was just wondering why no one ever mentions that loving someone isn't enough to make a marriage work?" he asked, shaking his dark head and looking past her toward the horizon, where the luminous gray of the sky was turning purple.

"What happened?" she prompted, studying his face in the moonlight. She remembered how he had looked at every age. Even as a youth he had been tall and beautifully proportioned. He had never gone through a gangly, awkward stage. Most boys grew in spurts, with one feature leading the way. But Lance had grown with steady grace, elegance, and masculine proportion. Now he had matured into an even handsomer man than he'd been at twenty-eight when he'd married Angie. At thirty-five, he seemed to have become even more solid, more confident, more magnetic. Tonight he looked like a man in torment. Compassion twisted her insides.

"We had a fight. Angie walked out."

"But why?"

"It doesn't make any sense, so quit asking me that."

"What did you fight about?" Samantha persisted.

"Damned if I know," he growled. "A friend of Sarah's died in childbirth, leaving a baby boy behind. I suggested Angie go help with the baby . . ." Muscles in his square jaw bunched beneath his smooth skin. His eyes were bleak and filled with despair, but no tears came. Some men could cry, but Lance wasn't one of them. He cried on the inside, where it hurt more. Samantha ached for him.

After a moment, he continued. "I . . . uh . . . mentioned . . ." he said, his husky voice a low rasp of suppressed pain. "The woman's husband had died a few months ago, after a fall from a horse. I suggested to Angie . . . that maybe we could adopt the baby. Angie got so furious with me that she packed and left. I got a letter a few days ago from San Francisco saying she wouldn't be coming back. That she's filing for divorce."

Samantha was confused. "I thought she wanted a baby."

"It's not the baby she doesn't want. It's me."

"I don't believe that for a second. Angie loves you."

"I always knew she'd leave. Maybe she used this thing to get done what she wanted to do all along."

"No, I've seen the way she looks at you. I know her better than that."

"She's changed, Sam. Something in her has hardened against me. Everything I do is wrong now."

"Maybe you just don't understand her."

"Well, you've got me there," he growled. "I sure as hell don't."

"I can't believe it," Samantha whispered.

"Then you weren't married long enough before Jared died. You probably didn't have time to fight. I don't think we fought much either in the first three years."

Samantha laughed softly. "You're wrong. We had our things to fight about."

Lance scowled. "Like what?"

"Jared was happy-go-lucky with everything, especially money, most of which was mine. We argued a lot actually."

"It never showed."

"I was too proud to let anyone suspect I'd made a bad bargain."

"Did you?"

"It seemed so at times, but Jared taught me a lot of things I'm glad I know. And he gave me Nicholas. I'll always be grateful for that."

Lance's eyes narrowed; she guessed what he was thinking.

"Yes," she whispered, "Even though Nicholas has been sick, I've loved having him. Even if he dies, which is unthinkable and will break my heart and probably kill me, I'll never regret having him and loving him."

Tears flooded her eyes. Lance pulled her into his arms. "You're a brave little punchkin, Sam."

"I'm no longer a punchkin," she said, protesting his use of a pet name he'd made up years ago after taking her to a Punch-and-Judy show.

"You'll always be a punchkin to me." He kissed her temple and sighed. His warm breath on the side of her face filled her with happiness. She felt safe and secure for the first time in years.

"I don't want to be a punchkin to you. I want . . ."

"What do you want, Sam?"

"I want you. I know it's too soon and I have no right. But I want . . . to be anything you want me to be." She felt odd, as if she were parroting words she'd heard in her own dream.

Before she could say anything more, he lowered his head and kissed her, and it was like the dream, only more unsettling. His touch disoriented her, made her want to cry. She couldn't comprehend if it was love or relief or sadness—for what she didn't know.

Sam's lips were soft. Her mouth opened under his probing, and he felt her tremble and move herself to accommodate him—whatever he wanted. Once she had adjusted to his kissing her, he slid his hands up her sides and cupped her full breasts. She trembled again, and he had the awful feeling he could read her mind, just as he had when she was little. He felt her struggle to accept his more intimate touching.

He knew he was pushing her too fast. But, driven by his own demons, he slid his hand down and stroked her belly and thighs; she trembled violently, as if she could barely keep herself still under his touch.

She was like a child, trusting him, forcing herself further and further to please him. Her acceptance and acquiescence inflamed him, filled him with lust and exultation. He wanted to take her there. To lift her skirts and . . .

His mind flashed him a vision of himself driving into her, not caring who she was or what she meant to him. The image so horrified him that he dispelled it. He knew Chane had been right to warn him. This wasn't love he felt. It welled up from the depths of him, and once loosed, would be no more controllable now than it had been with Colette.

He ended the kiss and hugged Sam. Her cheeks were wet with tears that scourged him. He knew Sam loved him, and that he had trampled on that love. He knew that when she gave herself to him, everything needed to be right between them. And . . . dammit . . . it wasn't.

But his impulses were strong. Even her tears fed his lust. He wanted her on the ground, naked and crying, to receive his rage and lust and despair. But he still had control enough to realize that if he took her now, in the mood he was in, it would be an act of violation, not love.

But the demons urged him to ignore that. They urged him to take her, to make it right later. All he had to do was give in to them and pretend he didn't know what was coming. Pretend that he fully expected himself to court and marry Sam. But in all honesty, he didn't know what he might do. And until he did— if he were going to face himself in the mornings and shave without taking the blade to his own throat—he had to wait.

He took Sam by the shoulders and held her at arm's length. "It's late. We need to get some rest."

"Why?" she whispered, searching his face, no doubt wondering if she'd done something wrong.

"Because if I don't, I'll do something unforgivable."

"You can't. Nothing you can do will be unforgivable."

Lance gripped her shoulders and scowled down into her lovely face. "Then you don't know me, Sam!" he growled in anger and despair. "I've done things . . . even I can't live with."

His fierceness sent a thrill of excitement and fear up her spine. "I know it's too soon to say this, but I love you, Lance. I belong to you," she whispered. "I've always belonged to you."

Lance knew Sam was right about that. She had always belonged to him. She wanted him, but whether she realized it or not, everything had to happen in a certain order. Even for her.

With a supreme effort, he turned her with firm hands and walked her back to the house. At the front door of her ridiculous house he stopped her and turned her to face him. She tried to put her arms around him, but he took them and put them at her sides.

"Go upstairs and lock your bedroom door," he growled.

"Lance, I trust you."

"Don't!" he said through clenched teeth. "Haven't you heard

a word I've said? Don't trust me! And don't let me into your room.''

Samantha stepped close to him and tried to put her arm around his neck. "Lance . . ."

She pressed against him, and lust was so strong in him he felt crazed by it. A voice within urged him to take her anyway. He took her hands and forced them down—and her away from him. "Dammit! I'm not fit to be trusted!" He turned and tramped down the steps.

"Lance, where are you going?"

"For a walk."

Samantha ran after him. "Are you coming back?"

"I hope not." Lance stalked across the yard and strode down the railroad tracks, walking fast. "If I do, shoot me."

She wanted to follow him, but she stopped. She knew Lance well enough to know that once he made up his mind, only a loaded shotgun would stop him. And only then if she used it.

Samantha lay awake half the night, burning from the first real kiss he'd ever given her, tinglingly alive with emotions and dreams.

Lance wanted her. His kiss had shown her how much, though he was too honorable to take her until after his divorce from Angie. But he had told her, or at least implied, that he might not be able to wait. She knew, with a certainty that amazed her, that he would be back. Probably unannounced and unexpected, but he wouldn't be able to wait any more than she would. Next time things would be right between them. And then they would be married. She'd be safely home again, where she belonged. After long years of insecurity and struggle all her dreams were about to come true.

She slept lightly and heard him come in just as the sky was turning pink. The hostess in her felt a strong need to rush downstairs to see that he found his room and everything he needed to be comfortable. But she had grown up with him and knew that he was perfectly capable of making himself comfortable. She might love him to distraction, but she had lived with him in the same house long enough to know that men, at least Kincaid men, could take care of themselves when they had to. And Lance had ordered her to stay away from him.

That thought caused her to smile. Lance wanted her. He wanted her so much that he had to walk the desert all night just to behave himself. A sense of power and euphoria fused into something very near ecstasy within her.

She burrowed down under the covers and smiled into her pillow. Then her mind flashed on a picture of Steve, his expression grim, his eyes flashing with anger. Her smile turned into a grimace. Chane may have made Steve so angry he'd quit. When he got into his protective-brother mood, he could be very annoying.

She might get up to find Steve on her doorstep, resignation in hand. That thought caused a sinking feeling somewhere deep inside.

Usually, if she awakened before her alarm clock went off, she savored the warmth of her bed and the early dawn sounds of birds chirping, roosters crowing, hens clucking, and horses neighing.

As a rule she could easily and deliciously slip back into sleep, but this morning slumber evaded her. The longer she lay there, the more tense she became. Finally she threw off her covers and sat up.

CHAPTER TEN

Samantha found Lance asleep on the sofa, fully clothed even to his brown leather boots, which looked white with fresh scuff marks and sand. She was standing over him, trying to decide if he'd want to be awakened for breakfast, when he opened one eye and caught her.

"Good morning," she said.

"That's one woman's opinion," he rasped.

"Are you going to be this cranky all day?" she said teasingly.

"Hope not." He groaned and sat up.

"Breakfast is ready," she said, turning away to give him some privacy. She hated waking up with anyone watching her.

Nicholas met them in the hall. He attached himself to his uncle Lance, which precluded any chance of her getting to speak privately with him again.

Chane returned from the work site in time for lunch. Samantha recognized Steve's horse beneath Chane's tall form and rushed down the steps to greet him, her heart beating faster in anxiety and dread.

"So did you kill and skin him, or did he loan you his horse willingly?" she asked, trying for a humorous note.

"It was like taking candy from a baby," Chane said, grinning.

"Lunch is ready," she said, ignoring the bait he was dangling before her.

"I checked the foundation they've poured and it seems to be in order, in case you were worried."

Samantha expelled the breath she'd been holding. "So they've got that much done?"

"Moving right along. The foundation is well placed," he said grudgingly.

"How did Steve take it? Your going up there to check on him?" she asked cautiously.

Chane grinned. "Took it like a man. Hardly showed his dander once. But I gigged him a little, just for good measure."

"What did you do?"

"Oh, nothing you need to worry about."

"Chane! What did you do to my builder?"

"Is that all he is?" he asked, quirking his eyebrows. "Your builder?"

Samantha flushed.

" 'My builder,' " Chane said, mimicking the tone the Kincaid males had used to tease the Kincaid females about their beaus fifteen years ago.

Samantha took a swing at Chane. Laughing, he blocked her swing, caught her arms, and twirled her around so that she couldn't hit him again.

"What did you do to him?" Samantha whispered fiercely.

Chane shrugged. "Just pointed out a thing or two that he could have done better."

"Like what?"

"Oh, nothing you'd understand. It was just builder talk," he said, grinning his enigmatic grin. She knew he wasn't going to be pinned down, and it frustrated her enormously.

Fortunately for Chane, Lance stepped out on the porch. Chane released Samantha's arms, hugged her, and steadied her before letting go and focusing his attention on his brother.

"You look like hell," he said to Lance.

"Not my fault. Sam made me sleep on the sofa. Remember that next time she comes to visit you."

"I did no such thing!"

They both laughed. Chane took Samantha by the waist and guided her through the front door. "And now she won't feed us, and we're about to starve," he growled.

"You two are incorrigible," she protested, laughing.

Chane and Lance left shortly after lunch. Samantha stood on the porch beside Tristera and Nicholas and watched them board the palace car. She had wanted them to stay for dinner, but Chane was eager to get back to Jennie and Amy.

The train left, and Samantha's disappointment was sharp. She and Lance hadn't had another chance to talk; Nicholas had stuck to his uncles like flypaper.

She felt cranky about Steve, too. She worried about how Chane had affected him, and how he would respond when she told him that Lance was free now and threatening to court her. Not that it was any of Steve's business . . . but they had kissed. And maybe those few kisses entitled Steve to expect certain things from her, like fidelity or something. But they'd made no commitment to one another.

The train receded until it was the size of a toy. Regretfully she turned away and ran into the screen door, which someone had left open at an odd angle. "Damn!" she said, letting out an unaccustomed curse word.

Tristera frowned her sympathy and concern. "Did I . . . ?"

"It doesn't matter," Samantha said, forcing an even tone and turning away. Somehow everything was wrong. Finally Lance had come to her and let her know he wanted her, but her traitorous mind was busy worrying about Steve Sheridan.

Purposefully and carefully she opened the door, walked through the house, and bolted up the stairs. Safely in her room at last, she lay down on her bed and let the tears come.

All her life she had wanted only to have Lance's love. Now, at last, she was within hope of reaching that goal. Lance had as good as told her he wanted her and would be back for her. So why was she crying?

No answer was forthcoming. The tears continued flowing until Nicholas knocked on her door and demanded she come out and read his lessons.

That evening after dinner, Tristera talked Samantha into playing the piano and singing duets with some of the songs she'd learned in "away" school.

Shortly after sunset they were interrupted by one of Samantha's riders coming back from town with the mail. Samantha thanked the rider and carried the single item of mail—a small, cheap envelope—to the table. There was no return address.

Nicholas followed the rider outside.

"Excuse me," Samantha said to Tristera, as she tore off the end of the envelope. The letter was printed on cheap tablet paper in large, childlike letters.

Mrs. Forrester,
Steve Sheridan is a devil. Keep him away from your son. He will kill him and break your heart.

                                   A friend.

"Someone's idea of a bad joke," Samantha said quietly. "Read this." She handed the letter to Tristera.

The girl read in silence. "Who sent this?" she asked, turning the letter and envelope over.

"Sounds like a woman, doesn't it?" Samantha asked, taking the note back and rereading it. "It has to be a woman." That gave Samantha an odd feeling. She had never thought of Steve as having women in his past. But of course every man did. It was an unsettling thought, though. She tried, unsuccessfully, to fit what she knew about Steve to the message in the letter.

"Do you suppose there could be any truth in this?"

Tristera shook her head. "No. Do you?"

"I don't think so, but I wish Steve hadn't just left. I want to show it to him. What do you think?"

Tristera closed her eyes and fingered the letter. A vision came to her, but it was of Steve, his head bowed and bloody. He appeared in great pain. "I know not. But he is a great warrior, a good man."

While Samantha trusted her instincts about Steve, the note had hit her weakest spot. "Do you think I have anything to fear from Steve? Where Nicholas is concerned?"

"I have seen *Señor* Steve with Nicholas many times. I do not pretend to be an expert on white men, but I would swear that he would never hurt a child."

"Damn!" Samantha whispered. "Why couldn't I have just married the man I loved years ago and been safe by now? All my friends from college did that. I'm the only one still hanging by a thread."

"You went to college? I thought only men did that."

Samantha shrugged. "I was fortunate. My guardian believes in educating women as well as men."

Samantha pondered the problem in silence. She wanted to show Steve the letter. It didn't really alarm her, because she trusted her own and Tristera's instincts about him. But if he didn't ride down in a few days, she would ride up to the work site or send a man to fetch Steve.

Ian Macready took over much of the supervision of the workmen, which left Steve free to concentrate on the coordinating and planning. Work went well. Only days after Ian's arrival his bricklayers laid the first course of adobe around the basement perimeter.

One afternoon a rider came with a note from Samantha Forrester. With quickened heartbeat, Steve opened the envelope and read the beautiful script. She needed to see him. Excitement vied with frustration.

Every night since he'd ridden away and left her at the mercy of Lance Kincaid, Steve had agonized over just how far that relationship had progressed. Then he'd realized, after much more agonizing, that it was none of his business. But that didn't stop the empty feeling around his heart.

Steve had tried, unsuccessfully, to put Samantha out of his thoughts. Yet every night when he lay down, her face filled his mind. He saw her smiling down at Nicholas as she sang to him. He saw her lovely face gleaming softly after he'd kissed her, and then there would be no sleep for him. Just the thought of her set his blood beating with a stronger stroke.

Excited by the prospect of seeing her again, and terrified that she would tell him she was about to be married or something equally terminal to all his own hopes and dreams, Steve crumpled the note, finished what he was doing, packed a change of clothes, and rode down the mountain.

He arrived at sundown. The whole western sky was red and gold and purple. As if she'd been watching for him, Samantha stepped out onto the porch. He rode up to the steps and dismounted, glad to get out of the saddle. He limped up the steps, feeling as melodramatic as Sender Thompson.

Samantha greeted him with a smile. "You look all in."

In spite of all his resolve, an answering smile took over his face, and they just stood there smiling at each other. Finally he remembered himself and said, "These kinks'll work themselves out in a minute."

Samantha walked to the end of the porch, Steve followed. She wore a white gown that made her pale face glow in the fading light. "I don't know how to start," she said, her melodious voice more hesitant than usual, softer. "I guess you should read this." She proferred a wrinkled sheet of paper.

Steve read it, glanced up at her, and the fleeting bleak look in his eyes told her that he did have something to hide. Then his barriers came up; his mouth tightened into a thin line. "Where did you get this?" he asked, his voice tight.

"It came in the mail. Here's the envelope."

Steve took it and held it up to read the postmark. "Might be Ham Russell trying to stir up more trouble. How far is the Dart spread from here?"

"No," Samantha said, shaking her head. "I won't have you going over there to fight with him. If you say you know of nothing that would precipitate such a letter, I'll accept that," she said, giving him a chance to repudiate her hasty impression.

"I swear to you, Samantha Forrester . . ." His voice broke.

He appeared to struggle with strong emotions, not the least of which was rage at being so accused, ". . . that you can. I have never in my life deliberately hurt a child." His voice was hoarse with feeling. His eyes seemed to glow with the intensity of his denial.

"I think I knew that," she said, touched in spite of her former perception. Maybe she'd been wrong.

"You trust me then?"

"Yes, I . . ."

"Can I keep this?" he asked.

"Of course." She turned away and faced west. The sky flamed above the brilliant desert sunset. The red and gold of the clouds had now turned coral, floating above them like a fleet of galleons.

Samantha glanced back at Steve. Even tired and dusty, he looked intense and appealing. His khaki eyes had softened at her avowal of trust. It pleased her tremendously that she was able to give it wholeheartedly. Something in her strained toward him. And something in him appeared to respond.

"Well, if you have no more questions about the letter, I guess I'll go take care of Calico. Thanks for sending him back up the mountain." His voice was husky, dry. "He's had a hard day."

"Has he?" she asked, her voice oddly breathless.

A breeze blew a tendril of her hair across her lips. Of its own accord, Steve's hand reached out to brush it off her warm, magnetic skin. "No," he said ruefully. "My horse spent most of the day eating grass at the house site. I'm the one who's had the rough day, and it's getting rougher by the minute." He needed to walk away, but with Samantha gazing up at him so intently, it was impossible.

"Have one of my men tend your horse," she whispered. "Dinner will be ready in a few minutes. You could at least stay for dinner and catch me up on what's been happening up there."

"We're building a house," he said gruffly.

"Stay," she said, her voice softer. "Stay and tell me about the house. Let someone else tend your horse."

"I like to tend my own horse. I can catch a bite in the kitchen."

"Would you rather do that?"

With anyone else he could have lied. But in spite of how confusing she was, she had believed in him when it mattered. And she was vulnerable and lonely. She wanted him to eat dinner with her. And even if it was just her loneliness and had nothing to do with him as a man, he couldn't deny her. He seemed to need to be in her company, too.

"So, what did you and Lando do?"

Samantha flushed. "Lance," she said, stalling for time. "His name is Lance."

"Oh, yeah, I forgot," he said, lying.

"We didn't do much."

"A smooth-talking, fast draw like him? You don't have to lie to me, you know."

"No, it wasn't like that," she insisted. "Steve . . . I hope Chane didn't upset you too much."

"Lando upset me more."

"Did he?" she asked, foolishly.

"You know damned good and well he did. So," he asked, "what did you two do?"

Samantha had hoped he would take another tack. "We just walked on the desert."

"And he kissed you."

"How did you . . . ?" She stopped, realizing he'd tricked her.

"And you kissed him back," he whispered. "And if this were a penny novel, we could change scenes now."

"No, he didn't make love to me, if that's what you're thinking."

"I'm a big boy now. I can take the truth."

"I'm happy for you. But he didn't make love to me."

Steve's heart was joyful, but part of him didn't believe her. "You don't have to lie to me," he growled.

"I'm not lying."

"Look, I don't need this aggravation. I hired on as your builder, and I'll build your damned house in spite of your brother's second-guessing my every decision, and in spite of your carrying on in front of me with your lover. So don't think you have to justify yourself to me." He turned and stalked down the steps.

Samantha ran after him. "Steve, wait! It isn't— I didn't— Oh, damn!" She stopped. It was and she had. She may not have been made love to, but if he had tried instead of running away, she would have. But somehow it didn't matter faced with Steve's disappointment and upset. She just wanted to see him smile again.

She ran after Steve again and caught him at the barn door. "I want you to stay for dinner."

''Why the hell should I?''

He looked furious. His rage alternately enervated and energized her. ''Because,'' she whispered.

''It doesn't make any sense for me to be chasing after a woman who's already in love with another man.''

''Even if she's confused?'' she asked, biting her lip. She was betraying Lance now, but she couldn't stop herself.

''What are you confused about?''

''Everything.''

''I'm within seconds of falling in love with you, Samantha. You already mean more to me than any other woman I've known. Don't lead me on if there's no hope.''

''Have dinner with us,'' she said softly.

''And then what?''

''I don't know.'' She held her breath waiting for his answer.

Steve searched her face and realized that she might be telling the truth. Lando may have tried to make love to her, but it might not have happened.

''All right,'' he growled. ''I'll probably regret it.''

Samantha smiled—and Steve felt the beauty of her smile resonate the length and breadth of his body.

''We'll wait for you,'' she said.

He nodded and opened the barn door. She watched him disappear into the depths of the barn. His limp was gone now. Slim-hipped and lithe, he had a strong, quick stride. She was confused about everything else, but pleased with his answers about the letter. He had been sincere, concerned, and intensely grateful to her for believing in him.

Samantha went to tell Juana to set another plate at the table. Half an hour later, Steve appeared at the front door, clean-shaven, his wet hair slicked back from his strong face. He wore a clean shirt and pants. He was still wary and cautious with her, but at least he was there.

Nicholas was so pleased to see Steve that he wanted all his attention. Samantha was mortified to notice that she wasn't much better. She kept flirting with him.

When she passed him the mashed potatoes, she touched his warm hand. When she poured his coffee, she brushed his arm. It was probably apparent to him as well. His eyes told her she was disturbing him—and she would not get away with it forever. She wasn't sure that was the message he intended to send her, but it was the one she received.

Dinner was over too soon. Before she could forestall him, Steve stood up and excused himself.

"You don't have to go to bed so soon, do you?" she asked, fighting her disappointment and the urge to ask him to stay for a while longer.

"Yeah," Nicholas piped in.

"Four o'clock comes early." His eyes were hooded against her. "Good night, Nicholas."

Tristera sidetracked Nicholas. Samantha flashed her a smile of gratitude, then followed Steve out onto the porch. They stood at the top step in awkward silence. Darkness was closing down fast. Crickets chirred. In the dim light streaming out the window, Steve looked dark and mysterious. She didn't know why she had followed him out here or what to say. But she luxuriated in his closeness—the already familiar aroma of his bay rum aftershave lotion, the sturdiness of his manly frame.

She felt torn between her torment at not being true to Lance and her inability to resist contact with Steve. But torment wasn't enough to stop her. She heard herself saying, "I don't see why you have to run away. It's hardly dark . . ."

Steve grabbed her firmly by the waist and pulled her into his arms. "You don't, huh?" he asked, feigning surprise.

"Nuh—no." Sudden breathlessness overwhelmed her.

"What if I told you I don't want to talk about cattle or houses when I'm with you?"

"What do you want to talk about?" she whispered, her heart pounding. She knew where this was leading, but she had no strength to resist him or herself. Part of her clamored for his touch. Her hands tingled to feel the warm skin of his neck. Her lips ached to feel his strong mouth.

"Us," he said firmly.

"I can't believe I'm hearing this from a man who hasn't even sent me one note in all the ti—"

Steve cut her off by lowering his mouth to hers and wrapping his long arms around her. His mouth was hot and demanding. She was surrounded by him, engulfed by him. He kissed her until dizziness overcame her and she felt the unmistakable rising of his desire for her.

"I can't do this," she said, pushing with trembling hands against his chest.

"In case you haven't noticed, *you* didn't do anything," he said, lifting his unruly eyebrow at her.

Samantha couldn't breathe or think. Her head spun. "I can't . . . I mean . . . I can't. I'm sorry," she ended miserably.

Steve laughed softly. "Okay, okay. You belong to someone else." His words were correct, but his tone mocked her. "So tell me. Did he propose? Or did he just come for more free milk?"

Of its own volition, her hand arced up and slapped him on the cheek. It wasn't a hard slap, but it embarrassed her, and his expression changed, hardened. The look caused a sinking feeling in her stomach.

"I don't care what you think!" she lied, panting with sudden emotion. "I haven't slept with him, but I can't sleep with you, either. Not until I decide what I'm going to do."

Steve parted his hands in a helpless gesture. "But he's married," he said.

"Not much longer. Angie left him. They're getting a divorce."

"So, he did propose."

"No, he didn't."

"But he let you know that he's free now."

"Well, I guess so."

Steve's eyes flashed with some emotion she could not fathom. Then, without another word, he turned and stalked into the desert.

Samantha wanted to call after him, to say she was sorry, that she hadn't meant to strike him, but she couldn't. Confusion overwhelmed her.

Frustrated, she sought out Tristera, who had already gone to her room. The girl looked up from her book and smiled. "Has your *carpintero* slipped into the desert so soon?"

"I'm afraid so."

"He is a fish, caught but still struggling against the hook, no?"

"I don't think so."

Tristera's laugh was one of the most mischievous Samantha had ever heard. Once she had gotten to know the girl, she realized Indian maidens were as playful as girls anywhere.

"Have you been spying on me, Tristera?"

"*Sí.*" Her pretty eyes flashed with merriment. Since Rathwick's visit, Tristera had gotten over her initial anger. Life had slipped into a comfortable, lazy pattern. She still grieved, but she was even-tempered and thoughtful. Samantha liked the girl far more than she had expected to.

"At least you're not shy about your sins. Tell me, Tristera, what does an Indian maid do if she finds herself infatuated with two men at the same time?"

"She picks the one with the most possessions."

Samantha laughed. "But seriously, if I gave you something that belonged to one of them, could you answer a question for me?" In New York City, Mrs. Lillian had taken Samantha to a psychic who could discern things by merely holding a piece of clothing belonging to the person about whom she wanted to ask questions.

Tristera shook her head. "Sometimes in the past I could see things, but no more."

"Please! Just try."

Interpreting the look on Tristera's face as false modesty, Samantha ran into her bedroom and rummaged through her bottom drawer. She uncovered her picture album, carried it into the parlor, sat down beside Tristera, and opened it to a picture of Lance.

He did not like having his picture taken. In this one, he scowled directly into the camera. Samantha had gone with him for the mandatory class photograph. When the photographer told him to smile, she'd said, "Say money," which worked better than cheese with the Kincaid children. Lance had quirked up one corner of his mouth and narrowed his eyes at her. The brown-tone print did not do justice to his brick-brown skin and his cathedral blue eyes. She called them that because they looked lighted from behind, the way the stained-glass windows did on church murals.

Staring at the picture, Samantha felt a rush of love and longing. It was unfair that all she had to do was see him, even a picture of him, to feel intense emotion.

Next to the picture lay the cravat Lance had worn the day he graduated from Harvard Law School. Samantha picked it up and handed it to Tristera.

Resigned, Tristera studied the picture of the man, closed her eyes, and sat in silence for a moment, holding the fabric. To her amazement, she did see a vision.

"I see the man in this picture coming to the new house and discovering that a miracle has happened in his life."

Samantha's heart turned over. "This miracle . . ." She stopped, afraid to ask the question. "What is it?"

Tristera closed her eyes, but nothing came, only a vague feeling. "I know not. It is something someone has wished for for a long time. I know not . . ."

Samantha wondered if it had already happened.

"Tristera, do you think it's possible to be in love with one man and attracted to another?"

"*Sí*, why not? We are only human."

Samantha groaned. "Then I don't want to be human anymore. I need to keep my life simple."

"In my village, the elders say that challenges are good and not to be avoided."

Samantha turned away. She didn't want to hurt Tristera's feelings, but life was not so simple here. Steve Sheridan wasn't a challenge, he was an opportunity to make a fool of herself, to be unfaithful to Lance, and to ruin any possibility of developing the kind of relationship she had always wanted with Lance.

"Thank you, Tristera." Turning away, Samantha vowed to avoid Steve Sheridan and the trouble he could cause between herself and Lance. She vowed to behave herself tonight, to be grateful when Steve rode away tomorrow, and to ignore the empty feeling around her heart. It had nothing whatsoever to do with Steve Sheridan.

Before dawn, while the sky was its darkest, Steve rose from his bed on the side of the mountain and walked through the morning chill to the house. A lone light burned in the kitchen. Juana had coffee perking and bacon frying.

"Don't you ever sleep, Juana?" he said, sticking his head in the outside back door.

"Morning, *señor*."

Steve helped himself to coffee. Juana finished frying the thick bacon, and scrambled a pan of eggs. Then she took biscuits, hot and fresh from the oven, and gave him some of everything.

Steve ate slowly, enjoying the food and Juana's undemanding presence. He hadn't slept well last night. He had been puzzling over the note Samantha had received. His mind had kept playing with it, searching for a reason, or a person, or anything else that would explain such a note.

He drank another cup of coffee and watched the sky outside the kitchen window turn blue. Finally he stood up.

"Good breakfast, Juana. If your old man doesn't come back soon, I'll marry you myself."

Juana giggled.

Smiling, Steve stepped outside and walked toward the barn.

Halfway there, a sting like a hornet's hit his arm. Then he heard the distant *crack* of a rifle echoing between the house and mountain. Dropping onto the ground, Steve rolled sideways until he reached the water trough near the barn. The rifle kept firing. A woman screamed repeatedly, probably Juana.

Bullets spanged up puffs of dirt all around him. Keeping the water trough between him and his assailant, Steve crawled into the barn. At Calico's stall, he jerked Eagle Thornton's .30-.30 out of his saddle sheath and crawled to the window. Bullets peppered the barn. Whoever was up there was enjoying himself . . . or themselves. It was hard to tell how many men were firing.

Steve found a knothole to look through. Nothing moved on the mountainside. His first wish was that he hadn't loaned his Sharps to Eagle Thornton, but he had wanted Eagle to have every possible advantage against any would-be rustlers.

Steve untied his bandanna, draped it over the end of the rifle, and slowly lifted it into sight. A flash of gunfire up on the mountain gave away the hiding place of one of his assailants. He was south, quite a distance from where Steve had slept. He must have been up there all night waiting for daylight. Steve assumed there was more than one. He felt lucky he hadn't been killed in his sleep. Either the gunmen had arrived after Steve had climbed the mountain and hadn't seen him in the dark, or they had arrived after Steve was asleep. If he'd been awake, he'd have heard them. Sound traveled at night.

Steve propped the barrel on his knee and sighted through the knothole, adjusted slightly for shooting uphill, and waited for the man to show himself. Finally a head appeared. Steve squeezed the trigger.

The recoil slammed his shoulder. The acrid smell of gunpowder filled his nostrils. Slowly the air cleared. Bushes on the left of the assailant's hiding place moved as if someone were scampering through them. Steve fired a few shots into the brush, but he didn't think he'd hit anything. He waited a few minutes, took off one of his boots, and tossed it out the barn door. No shot came in response. Either the sharpshooters had hightailed it for home or they were waiting for something better than a boot.

Steve waited a few more minutes and then decided to test it. No gunfire marred the silence. He stood, made sure he had a shell under the firing pin, and walked to the barn door. Tensed and ready to fire, he stuck his head out and pulled it back in. Still no gunfire.

Steve heard the front door open. He looked out in time to see Nicholas run down the steps.

"Stay inside!" Steve yelled.

Nicholas didn't appear to hear him. Tears streaming down his cheeks, he ran toward the north side of the barn. Fortunately no shots rang out. Steve took that as a sign that his attackers had fled. To test his theory, he stepped squarely into the doorway. Still no shots.

Relieved and curious, Steve followed the boy around the barn. Nicholas stopped beside a young steer that must have been hit during that first burst of gunfire. Nicholas hugged the dead steer and cried as if his heart were broken.

Steve knelt beside the boy, stroked his head, and let him cry for a while. At first he couldn't think of what to say, but then an idea came to him.

"Do you have a reata?"

Confused, Nicholas looked up at him. "What?"

"Do you have a reata, a lariat?"

"No, sir."

"Since you love this steer, it would be good if you kept part of him with you."

"How could I do that?" Nicholas wiped his eyes and sniffed back fresh tears.

"I could show you how to make a reata from his hide. You'll need one someday."

Nicholas sniffed and muttered, "Okay."

Other men ran out to see what had happened. The steer had been shot in the head. Steve asked Louis Bandini, the head horse wrangler, to have someone skin the steer for him. "Take care not to mar the hide. We're going to make a reata."

Steve knew he should be pursuing his attacker, but he took Nicholas's hand and led the boy up the steps to where his mother had just appeared, prettily disheveled in robe and slippers.

"What happened? Was Nicholas hurt?" she asked, alarmed at the sight of blood on both of them.

"Nicholas is fine."

"Then you've been hurt."

"It's only a scratch if I have."

She knelt beside Nicholas and peered into his face. "Why are you crying?"

Nicholas's chin puckered with his attempt to keep his mouth from contorting into a wailing display of grief. "Dakota . . . got . . . killed."

"Oh, no! Your steer . . . Oh, poor baby." She pulled him into her arms. A fresh burst of tears wet her nightgown. Samantha picked him up to carry him inside. She turned to Sheridan, who had stopped on the porch and looked as if he were leaving.

"Come inside. Let me get the medicine box."

"It's only a scratch," Steve said, protesting.

"Only a wonderful place to get an infection and lose your arm if you take care of it the way most men do. Come inside. That's an order."

Grinning, Steve winked at Nicholas and followed her inside. Nicholas slipped away to his room. Usually he would want to watch his mother, who could pore endlessly over a cut or a scratch, putting iodine on it and tearing and wrapping bandages, but today he just wanted to be alone. Dakota had been his best friend among the barn animals.

In the kitchen, Samantha found the medicine box. "I can't believe I slept through gunfire," she said to Steve, who had followed her. "But I was dreaming that someone was shooting at me. What happened?"

Steve explained about the sniper.

"I feel terrible about this, and about last night. I shouldn't have hit you. I'm sorry."

Steve's khaki eyes held hers for a moment, then he nodded his acceptance.

"If I hadn't asked you to stay . . ."

"Maybe he was trying to rid you of a devil."

"You think it was the same person?"

"Could be."

"Be still," Samantha said, rolling Steve's sleeve up. But his arm was so big the sleeve wouldn't go past his elbow. Glancing quickly at his amused eyes and then away, she unbuttoned his shirt and slipped it down to expose his left shoulder and upper arm. Blood oozed out of a long open gouge just above his elbow. She caught the flow before it reached her doily, but she couldn't stop it from getting on her fingers, where it felt warm and sticky. She wiped her hands, unscrewed the lamp shade holder from the base of an unlit kerosene lamp, dipped a clean cloth into the smelly liquid, and pressed it over the gashed skin.

Just touching such tender redness made her stomach twist with empathy. It must feel like a thousand ants biting him at once, but he didn't move away. He just sucked in his breath and held it, blinking against the stinging pain.

"Most of the men I grew up with were like you," she said to

break the silence, "so stubborn you could cut off one of their legs and they wouldn't mention it until years later."

Steve laughed. "You may have me overrated. Them, too, if those two bruisers who came the other day were any example."

She ignored the jab at Lance and Chane. "So what will you do now?" she asked, wrapping the gash with clean cloth. Steve eased his shirt back on and buttoned it.

"Oh, maybe lie down for a little while."

Samantha was relieved. Steve headed for the barn, and she cleaned up the mess she'd made. When he didn't come back with his things, she went looking for him and learned he had ridden away on Calico.

Fear formed a hard knot in her chest. He was going after the sniper. He would probably confront Russell and get himself killed.

Steve felt light-headed after the climb up the side of the hill. After resting for a few minutes, he checked the mountainside for signs and saw where a horse had been tethered a half mile from where the man must have hidden in the rocks. Steve followed the trail northwest. At a dry riverbed, he found tracks where a horse had walked into the gravel-covered river bottom. He followed it for a mile or so north until the faint trail was obliterated by tracks of a cattle herd crossing it.

He could follow the cattle or the creek bed, or he could turn back. Even if he found the trail, he couldn't prove his suspicion that the attack had come from Ham Russell. He was pretty sure it had—and also pretty sure that wasn't worth much in a court of law.

From the parlor window, Samantha saw Steve ride into the barn. She ran out and found him dumping grain on the ground of Calico's stall.

"Did you find anything?"

"Nope."

He looked pale. "How's your arm?"

"Arm's fine."

"You shouldn't have gone. You belong in bed, and I want you to stay there tomorrow and the next day. After that, we'll see how you are."

Steve started to protest, but he'd lost enough blood to feel the difference. And at this stage of construction, Ian Macready didn't

need much in the way of supervision. If he did, he'd come looking for him.

That night Samantha tossed so much her bottom sheet worked
itself into a tangle. Lying amid the rumpled mess, she listened
to night sounds and puzzled about the odd way her fingers tingled. At first she couldn't think why, but then her mind flashed
a picture of her hand, covered with Steve's blood.

She rubbed her hand and felt again the odd feeling that his
blood had stirred in her. It had been so warm . . . and so red!
Nothing pale or thin about his blood. Or about his stamina.
Some men looked like they were working at the outer limits of
their endurance. Steve Sheridan looked like he was holding back.
Every time she saw him, whether he was with other men or
alone, she had the sense that he worked effortlessly. Even
wounded, he had ridden half the day.

Maybe someone's trying to help rid the territory of a devil.
She could hear the bronze undertones in his husky voice.

She needed to sleep. Morning would come early, and with it
many chores. Nicholas was an early riser. But she didn't feel
like sleep. She felt like . . .

Maybe his blood had bewitched her. She wasn't supposed to
be thinking about him. But she felt as though she would suffocate if she stayed inside another second.

She flung aside the thin sheet, put on her robe and slippers,
and walked quietly down the stairs and through the dark house.
Out on the front porch, she breathed deeply of the crisp desert
air. The night was beautiful. Bright stars filled a cloudless sky.
The air smelled so strongly of sage she could almost taste it.

She pulled her wrap close around her. Alone here, with the
cold, dry northwest wind on her face, she felt the magnificence
of the desert and the joy of owning this piece of it. Ever since
she'd seen the Arizona Territory from the window of her Pullman coach, she'd wanted to own every acre of it. Odd, since
she'd never seen a desert until this one. She'd never expected to
love it so.

Samantha closed the door behind her. She would walk. She
liked to walk at night. She realized there were creepy crawly
things on the desert, but she always stayed on beaten paths and
had never had any problems.

Tonight she felt a pull from the south. She walked toward the
bend in the creek, enjoying everything; the sand under her light
slippers, the wind at her back, even the coolness.

She felt freer, lighter, more joyful. She liked knowing she was the only one awake. She especially liked knowing that she didn't have to worry about running into anyone. She had such a compulsion about her land. She was like her uncle Chantry in that. Having to share it irritated her. Even having to worry about running into someone irritated her. And yet, she needed people, occasionally.

A hundred yards from the house she stopped. As if driven by some need she could neither understand nor resist, she knelt down and dug her hands into the sand. Sometimes she had such a need to do that. And tonight the need was stronger than usual. She wanted to reach all the way to the center of the Earth, to feel the—

"I knew the minute I saw you step out onto the porch that you'd come this way." The weighty bronze timbre of Steve Sheridan's voice startled her, sounding just the way it had a few minutes ago in her mind.

Heart pounding suddenly, she knew now what had drawn her here, straight as an arrow. She recognized the pull. It was the same one she'd felt that day she'd followed him into the livery stable in town.

Steve stepped forward, knelt behind her, and reached around her to slide his hands down her arms to where her wrists disappeared into the sand.

"You are a devil, aren't you?" she whispered.

"Not toward children . . . I've never seen anyone else do that," he said, his voice low and gruff against her cheek. "Reach down to feel the Earth's heartbeat."

She had never articulated it before, but he was right. That was what she wanted—to feel the heartbeat of the Earth. The same compulsion that drove her to touch the Earth, also drove her to want to own it and hold it and somehow keep it.

"I own this land all the way to the center of the Earth," she said.

Steve chuckled. "You had that written into the deed, did you?" His breath was warm and soft against her cheek.

"As close as they'd come to actually saying it. Deeding is so ritualized. I thought everyone was in bed," she said. "Especially you . . ."

"I don't like beds, remember?"

"You're not very obedient, either."

"No."

"At least you don't try to defend your disobedience."

"No."

He seemed strangely quiet and fatalistic. His touching her settled her down in one way and agitated her in others. At least she no longer felt tired or restless or suffocated.

"So you couldn't sleep, either?" She wanted to apologize again for slapping him, but she couldn't think of how to begin or even how to sit in silence in the circle of his disturbing arms. Perhaps too much time had gone by.

"I'm like the Indians," he said gruffly. "A brush with death makes me feel more alive, not less."

Steve moved slightly, and his warm lips touched her neck and clung for a moment. Heat pooled in her belly and sent tingling spears of warmth into all her secret places.

"This can't be comfortable for you," he whispered, rising and lifting her with him. Samantha started to resist, but she needed his touch now almost as badly as she had needed to touch the Earth.

Slowly she allowed him to turn her in his arms, to pull her close against his sturdy, warm body. Part of her watched, and another part felt oddly resigned to whatever would happen between them. His hand caught in her hair and pulled, tilting her lips up to meet his. Her heart's sudden racing made her dizzy. She wanted to pull away from Steve Sheridan, to revoke whatever license he thought she'd given him, but words didn't come. Her body didn't respond to mere willed commands.

Steve looked into her eyes for a moment and then kissed her. The sensation she'd felt earlier, of being caught up and whirled around, overwhelmed her with simultaneous urges to surrender and fight. He was a man of passion. She wanted peace and tranquility, not this madness, certainly not the searing need his kiss evoked in her.

His tongue forced its way into her mouth—and her body reacted as if he'd entered her in a deeper way. Heat flushed upward, scalding her.

His hands slipped down to her hips and held her against him. She could feel his heartbeat against her belly. The vibrations from him, pressed so hard against her, rattled her, caused her to cling more tightly. The Earth no longer felt solid under her feet.

Suddenly she realized just what it was that frightened her about him. Steve Sheridan represented the reality of a living, breathing man with whom she could actually build a life. He wasn't a ne'er-do-well, flighty boy-man as Jared had been. He wasn't someone else's husband. Steve wanted all of her. And while she knew she was supposed to want that level of maturity and commitment, part of her still wanted Lance, whether he could commit to her or not.

That knowledge gave her the strength to end the kiss. But not the strength to extract herself from his arms. Panting, she clung to him, still unwilling to relinquish the feel of his body pressed against hers. His heart drummed like a powerful engine, faster than her own, if that were possible.

She knew Steve Sheridan wanted her passionately. She could feel his desire for her. And that healed something in her she hadn't even known needed to be healed. As paradoxical as it seemed, his wanting her gave her the strength to signal to him. She moved slightly, and he released her.

The world felt different outside his arms—more awkward. She hadn't felt awkward since she was a teenager.

"I guess I'd better get back before someone misses me."

"Juana does bed checks?" Laughter warmed his rich voice.

"She'll probably be looking for her patient," she said pointedly.

"Well, she's too smart to expect me to behave myself, don't you think?"

"Yes, she's probably known other men."

Steve walked her to the front porch. "You're not coming in?" she asked softly.

"No. I'm even less sleepy now than I was."

She felt the need to explain to him, to tell him that she wanted a man—at times. But she was too selfish to want him to have his own personality and needs and ideas. And now that she was waiting for Lance these kisses, however sweet and heady, could have no permanent meaning in her life. But words didn't come, and he didn't seem to need an explanation.

"Good night then."

Steve's chuckle was low and sardonic, reminding her that she'd probably wrecked all hope of his sleeping. Strangely pleased, she slipped inside and back to her bed. If he were a devil, as the note had said, he was more fun than she'd ever expected one to be.

She fell asleep almost instantly.

The next afternoon, a rider came from town with a letter from Lance.

Dear Sam,

I'm still looking for a buyer for your cattle. It has proven harder than I thought, probably due to the drought and the recession, but I expect a positive answer from the last man I spoke with. In the meantime, have your riders gather the herd and brand them so that when I get word, we will be able to move quickly.

Perhaps you can come into town with the cattle. A holiday would do you good.

Love,
Lance

With pounding heart, Samantha smoothed the letter and re-read it. Lance had actually used the word "love."

Her heart felt full. She read the letter again. He had invited her to Durango. Since his visit to the ranch—and his admission that he wanted her and could barely restrain himself from taking her—her mind had given free rein to her daydreams about him. She had imagined him making love to her a number of times, and it had always been vaguer and more fantastic than her experiences with Jared.

She was not a virgin. She knew the mechanics of love, but somehow this invitation agitated her. She wondered if going to see him would imply a willingness to sleep with him. With Steve she knew how to set limits. But with Lance it was more difficult. She'd already told him she belonged to him. And it was true. Part of her would always belong to him. But in her heart she was beginning to realize that she wanted to belong to him the way she had in childhood—to be taken care of. Lance had represented safety and a place where she could hide from responsibility.

And part of her was used to mooning over Lance and never expecting to have him. Now, with the prospect of marrying him, she realized that part of her was happier with the fantasies in her head than the reality of actually having him. There was a certain security in living a fantasy life. And she'd been married long enough to know that real men made a lot of demands. If a woman stayed with one long enough he would step blindly and uncaringly on every sacred cow she might harbor. And she knew Lance and Chane well enough to know they were basically no different from other men. They expected the world to adjust to their needs and wants. She had grown accustomed to the freedom of her life. She now expected the world to adjust to *her* needs.

Tristera walked into the room and looked wistfully at the letter in Samantha's hand. "I always wanted to get a letter. In all the years I was at away school, I never did."

"Would you read this?" Samantha offered the letter to her. Tristera looked surprised, then read it.

"What do you think? He used the word love. He's never done that before."

Tristera shrugged. "It's not notarized."

Samantha laughed. Tristera occasionally used words and phrases that surprised Samantha. "But don't you see this as hopeful? He's never used the word love before."

"I know not. The only experience I had with soft words uttered by a man was a bad one."

"Putting that one aside, can't you see how hopeful this looks? He's getting a divorce now, and he's using the word love."

Tristera paused, shrugged, said, "He's a handsome man. He has money and position. But he doesn't love you the way *Señor* Steve does."

"Steve has never said that he loves me."

"Some men don't use words lightly. That is the Indian way." She handed back the letter. "And some men do. I'll go see if Nicholas has finished reading his assignment."

Steve walked around the house to check the rawhide strips they'd laid out two days ago. Nicholas was hunkered down with his back against a tree, watching the strips drying in the sun. That seemed pitiful to Steve. Either the boy was visiting his steer or waiting for his reata. Steve wasn't sure the boy knew which.

"What happened to Young Hawk?"

"He has to work. His ma wanted him to gather wood for the fire. His pa left him *in charge*." Nicholas sneered, but Steve heard the longing in that complaint. Nicholas would give a lot to have a pa ordering him around.

Steve checked the taut leather of Dakota's hide.

"Seems dry enough to me."

Nicholas grinned and jumped up. "What do we do now?"

"You're lucky it was my left arm that got shot and not my cutting arm. Watch close." Steve slipped his razor-sharp shaving knife from the hiding place in his boot and cut a hole in the center of the hide.

"The trick is not to cut it too wide or too narrow." Starting from the hole, Steve cut a strip around the hole, spiraling outward until he had cut one continuous strip sixty feet long. He'd lost enough blood to have to stop a couple of times to rest. Nicholas watched in awed silence.

"All right, young man, fetch me a bucket of water."

At the order, Nicholas's face reflected something akin to ecstasy. In minutes Nicholas came back with a bucket full of water thudding against his wet pants. Steve pushed the strip into the water, which spilled over the sides and soaked into the dirt.

"Now what?"

"When they get soft, we'll stretch 'em."

An hour later, with Nicholas on his heels, Steve walked back to check on the leather strip, which felt soft enough to work with. "Now I'm going to need your help."

Carrying the strip, they walked up the mountain until Steve found two trees the right distance apart. He tied one end of the strip to a strong, low limb of the tree. Then he gave the other end to Nicholas. Steve pulled a limb down and held it while Nicholas tied the other end to the limb. When he let it go, the limb snapped back into place, pulling the leather taut.

"How long do we have to wait?"

Steve eyed the sun, which got pretty warm in the afternoon. "Not long, I'd say. A couple of hours or so."

Two hours to the minute, Steve looked up from the newspaper he was reading on the porch and saw Nicholas coming for him. Together they walked up the slope and found the strips stretched out tight and dry. Steve realized they were rushing this reata, but apparently the boy needed it.

Steve untied the end on the low limb and pulled the other limb down low enough for Nicholas to untie the reata from it. They walked down to the corral, dragging the stiff strips of rawhide behind them.

Steve showed Nicholas how to scrape the hair off the hide with a sharp knife. "Keep the blade turned slightly, so you're not cutting, just scraping. If you cut it, you'll have the shortest reata on the place."

Nicholas worked slowly, painstakingly. They spent an hour scraping. The boy worked with silent determination.

When they had stripped it clean, Steve separated out three long strips, found the middle, and tied it tight around a corral post.

"How come you tied it in the middle?" Nicholas asked, frowning as if Steve meant to cheat him out of half his reata.

" 'Cause it's too long to braid otherwise. It'd take forever to get anything done. You ever tried to untangle thirty feet of rawhide everytime you do one braid? Fifteen feet is going to be bad enough. Fetch us another bucket of water."

Nicholas got the water. Steve wet the strips again, worked the first few braids, and passed the strips to Nicholas. "Braid and pull. Braid and pull. You have to keep it tight and wet. Think you can do that?"

Nicholas braided for a few minutes in silence. "Why do I have to keep it wet and pull it so tight? It hurts my hands."

"You want it smooth, don't you? You wouldn't want a lumpy reata. There's no rush. You can work on this for a week, a month, however long it takes."

Nicholas braided and Steve watched, correcting him when he let the strips get too loose or when he forgot to wet them.

"Nicholas!" Samantha called, peering into the dim recesses of the parlor. She didn't find him downstairs, so she checked upstairs, then went back to the kitchen a second time.

Juana stepped inside from the back door, carrying a pan of green beans from the garden.

"Have you seen Nicholas? I thought he'd be taking his nap."

"Maybe he's with *Señor* Steve."

"Where?"

"Up on the mountain I think."

"What would Nicholas and Steve go up on the mountain for?" Samantha tried to contain her growing alarm, but her mind flashed her the message in the note. *He'll kill your son and break your heart.* She realized that maybe Steve *had* lied to her about the note and his innocence. "Why would he take Nicholas up there?" she repeated, her voice rising.

Juana frowned. "Why do mens do anything?"

Samantha bit back her reply, picked up the skirt of her gown, and ran out the back door toward the mountain.

Steve looked up from watching Nicholas with his braiding to see Samantha Forrester running toward them. Steve walked forward to meet her. She stopped a few feet from him and peered around him at her son, who was concentrating on the task before him. In a pale yellow cotton gown, her damp skin gleamed silvery against her soft golden hair. Her cheeks were bright pink. Steve felt her prettiness down the entire length of his body.

"What're you doing, Nicholas?" she asked.

Engrossed, the boy didn't answer, so Steve answered for him. "Making a reata. Doing a first-rate job of it, too."

Samantha brushed a shaking hand across her eyes. "Where did he get the leather?"

"From Dakota," Nicholas said proudly.

Samantha blinked. The thought of her son making a reata from his dead pet revolted her. It seemed uncalled for. And diabolical . . .

"Nicholas, it's time to come in," she said sharply.

Steve couldn't believe she would call a halt so abruptly to something the boy was so absorbed in. But her mouth was tight with disapproval and her tone indicated she would brook no opposition. Steve realized that either he or Nicholas must have said or done something wrong, but he couldn't think what it might be.

"Did you hear me?" she asked grimly.

Nicholas looked up at his mother in dismay. "But, Mama, I want to finish this."

"I have something *else* for you to do."

"Mama, this is important!"

"Nicholas, do as I say!" Her voice shocked her, it was so strident. She lowered it. "Run along now. I'll be there in a moment."

Nicholas flashed a pleading look at Steve.

"You heard your mother."

Reluctantly Nicholas let go of the leather strips and turned toward the house.

Samantha watched her son drag his feet into the house and slam the back door. Then she faced Steve. "I know you mean well, but I do *not* want Nicholas playing with his dead pet."

That was an odd way to put it, Steve thought. But he ignored it to make his own point. "Before we started the reata, he was grieving about the loss of his steer. Since then, he's been fine."

"I'm his mother, and I know what's best for him. I know you don't understand, but I hope you will at least honor my request." Samantha pulled at the strips around the tree and tried to free them, but her hands were shaking so hard she couldn't.

"I'll do that," he said, moving her aside.

"Thank you."

Steve untied the reata. Samantha took it from him, wadded

up the strips, and strode angrily toward the house, leather strings dragging behind her.

"Am I fired, or should I just quit?" he called after her.

Samantha stopped. "No," she said, turning toward him.

"Well then what the hell does it mean?"

Samantha sighed. "It means—it means . . . that I don't want Nicholas playing with any part of his dead steer."

"Bull," he growled. "At least have the courage to say what's on your mind."

"I did," she said firmly, and turned and ran toward the house.

Confusion turned to anger in Steve. He stalked to the barn, saddled Calico, and galloped toward the work site. It was that or head for Waco.

CHAPTER ELEVEN

From the upstairs window, Samantha watched Steve ride away. Her chest felt cold and hollow, but she refused to stop him. Her son was more important to her than any man.

She found Nicholas at his window, crying. He, too, had probably witnessed Steve's leaving. She reached out a hand to comfort him, but he pushed it away. "I want my reata."

"No."

"Why not?"

"Because I said so." It was an inadequate excuse and Nicholas knew it. He was used to more logical reasons from her, but she couldn't articulate her sudden fears for his safety. She tried again to touch him, but he stepped out of reach and then threw himself on the bed, crying as if his heart were broken. He seemed more upset about losing the reata than he had been about Dakota's death. Samantha suddenly wanted to strangle Steve Sheridan.

She tried to ignore Nicholas's crying. It was difficult because emotional upsets were usually followed by higher fevers. But this time she couldn't give in. Better he should cry for a few minutes than have a living reminder of a dead pet forever.

That evening, she slipped outside and sat in the dark on the front porch. Stars flickered overhead. A few night-singing birds trilled their short songs. It was a good night for sitting on the porch swing with a man. The evening was beautiful but useless. Steve was furious with her. She probably wouldn't see him again until the house was finished. Lance might never be back. He may have made up with Angie by now or found someone else who knew how to respond to him and when. Frustrated with herself, she stood up and walked inside.

Tristera sat in the parlor reading a book. Samantha had been surprised to find that the girl was as polite and deferential as any white girl raised in a strict boarding school. She would do any task assigned to her—read to Nicholas, wash dishes, cook, or clean. In her spare time, she read.

"Is Nicholas asleep?" Samantha asked.

"*Sí*. After six stories."

"You read him six stories?"

Tristera laughed. "Well, I wanted to read them anyway. They were good."

Tristera was a paradox—one moment she was a child playing in the sand with Nicholas, making pretend houses and roads, and the next she was a young woman struggling to cope with her attraction for Captain Rathwick. Samantha felt closer to Tristera than she had to any woman since Mrs. Lillian.

In her bedroom, Samantha slipped into her gown and climbed into her cold bed. She wished she didn't care so much what Steve thought, but she did. Loving Lance as she did, she shouldn't even be affected by Steve Sheridan. It took a long time to get to sleep.

The following morning, Samantha had a sudden urge to ride up the mountain and apologize to Steve. But she realized she'd just look like a fool. He was the one who had interfered. But, of course, he'd meant well.

She fretted over this all day. And it was the last thing she thought about before falling asleep that night.

Tristera knew the *señora* was suffering, but she had her own problems. In her anger and unhappiness about Tuvi's death, she had vowed never to meditate again, but at night, the sounds came, and the light. She tried not to listen to the sounds or look at the light, but she lay there half the night at the mercy of her soul, which seemed to need it. Still, she refused to say the holy words. She would not give in.

Tuvi had told her that the ability to meditate was a gift from the Great Mystery. His grace alone made it possible. Now, even though she no longer wanted His grace, because she didn't want anything to do with a god who couldn't even protect Tuvi from the soldiers, she had it.

Thinking rude thoughts about the Great Mystery frightened her, but she would not relent.

The next day she worked harder.

The *señora* walked into the yard and caught her beating the rugs on the clothesline.

"I think Juana is working you too hard, Tristera."

"Juana didn't tell me to do this," she said, afraid the *señora* would say something to Juana.

"She didn't?"

"No, ma'am."

"Then why?"

"I felt like it. Rugs can always use cleaning."

The *señora* walked back to her work area, shaking her head.

The following morning a locomotive chuffed noisily up to the house. She had planned to sell the cattle, and she still thought it was the right thing to do, but the necessity of it rankled her. Selling off her cattle signaled a major setback in her hopes of building a burgeoning cattle empire. The taste of that defeat was sharp in her mouth as she walked forward to meet the train.

The engineer, sweat beaded on his high forehead, jumped down and walked over to meet her.

"Morning, ma'am. These are from Mr. Kincaid."

He handed her two envelopes. She thanked him, and he shuffled away a respectful distance and stood in the shade of his locomotive, waiting for her response.

One was a letter from Lance. She tore it open and read.

Dear Sam,

    I have found a buyer for a hundred head of your breeding stock at a hundred dollars a head, and four hundred head of range stock at twelve dollars a head. It is a little lower than I'd hoped, but I think you should take it. He is eager to get his hands on some more of your breed stock, but I told him only if he pays more for the next herd.

    If you agree to the sale, load and ship the five hundred head as soon as possible. Also, I've made arrangements with the owner of a feed lot in Phoenix, so you can ship your entire herd here for safekeeping until we are able to find buyers for them.

    If my calculations are correct, your men can load five hundred head for shipment by Sunday, the rest over the next few weeks. Unless I hear differently, I will expect you Sunday afternoon in Phoenix. We'll seal the deal and then celebrate.

                                          Love,
                                          Lance

Her mood lifted. Apparently the reward for failure was greater than for success.

She informed the engineer that he could leave the cattle cars and return for them Sunday morning. She asked him to bring her palace car if the repairs were completed.

She took her mail inside and sat down at her desk. The other letter was from Jerome Abbott, her attorney. Samantha opened it and slipped out the thick packet.

My Dear Mrs. Forrester,

It grieves me to be the bearer of bad news, but I must inform you that a suit has been filed in federal court claiming ownership of the parcel of land your late husband purchased. It is a complicated matter and one I would prefer to explain in person, but my business does not allow me freedom to travel at this time.

I must inform you, even though I do not consider it a serious claim, that a Papago Indian by the name of Crows Walking has produced papers indicating that he is the real owner of the land your husband bought from Frederick Beaumont.

I have examined the records carefully and checked the plat maps, and apparently there is some basis for this claim. The parchment Crows Walking put forward explains that a Papago woman—whose name translates to Sun In The Sky—saved the life of a Spanish conquistador who married her and left the land he had acquired by land grant from the king of Spain to Sun In The Sky in his will. The land granted to her and her descendants is quite extensive, including thousands of acres of land in addition to your parcel.

I will explain in more detail later if you like. I know you would prefer this not come up at this time, especially after all the improvements you have made on the land, but it must be defended in court.

Since it has to do with Indians, the case will be heard in federal court in Washington, D.C. I could hire a solicitor to represent us there, but my belief is that too many cooks spoil the stew. If you have a preference as to how you want this handled, any questions, or any information I would find useful in defending you against this claim, please let me know at once.

In the meantime, do not be alarmed. Our government is not about to start giving land back to the Indians, no matter how valid their claims. That is not our government's policy. But unfortunately, this suit does have to be defended. However, it would upset me greatly if I thought you were seriously discomfited by this pseudothreat. Please rest assured that our government is still run by sane men.

Remaining yours truly,
Jerome Abbott, Esquire
Attorney-at-Law

Samantha looked through the thick sheaf of legal papers and the handwritten copy of the document filed against her by Crows Walking's attorney.

Supporting documents proved that Crows Walking was the descendant of Sun In The Sky, who had married a Spaniard and inherited the Rio Conchos Land Grant upon his death. The suit included a copy of a codicil to the will that went into great length about how adamant the Spaniard was that his wife, who had taken care of him with great tenderness and borne him two sons, should be given the same respect in court that he would be entitled to if only he had lived.

Samantha walked to her desk and sat down. Apparently the Papago Indians inherited matrilineally. The suit laboriously traced Crows Walking's descent from Sun In The Sky to the present. Samantha could not believe the court had accepted his claim. Surely he had no formal birth certificates for all these intervening people. That alone should disqualify his presumptuous suit.

However, reading further she learned that apparently the Papago did have formal historians who had recorded births and deaths in verifiable ways. The most damning evidence seemed to be that Crows Walking had in his possession the original parchment land grant dated August 9, 1710.

A knot formed in Samantha's stomach. Of all the things she'd worried about, losing her land to the Indians had not been one of them.

In bitterness and silent rage she walked outside and looked around. The usual fragrance of the desert was obliterated by the stench of cattle being branded for sale—another sign of her failure to conquer this land.

She would have to tell Steve Sheridan. At the thought of seeing him, a thrill of pleasure momentarily lightened her savage mood. Would this calamity soften his granite heart?

She imagined herself confronting him. Would his sometimes hazel, sometimes khaki eyes reflect sympathy or derision?

The thought that he might be against her in this caused a heavy sinking in her middle. It would change nothing, though. She would have to stop construction immediately, send Steve away, and wait alone through the agony of a court trial to decide if she owned her own land—land she'd paid for.

If she won, she could ask him to come back and finish the house. But he might be committed elsewhere by then. And there probably wasn't even a house started yet. But thoughts of not building the new house increased her rage and grief. She was losing everything all over again.

As a child she had lost her parents. As a young woman she had lost her beloved to another woman. As a wife she had lost her husband to death. As a mother she was constantly threatened by the fear of losing her son to consumption. She tolerated all this, and had even learned to live with uncertainty, grief, loss, and fear.

Now she stood to lose fifty thousand acres of land and three years' work. Three years of her life wiped out as if it had never existed. This morning her life had seemed good, purposeful, useful. Now, with the specter of losing her land, losing her home, the world was suddenly a terrifying place again.

Overwhelmed by her feelings, she stood and walked quickly away from the house. After a time she stopped and looked around her. She'd walked south, to the bend in the creek, out of sight of the house and the cattle and the Indians' camp. She could still hear the raucous cries of the cowboys and the outraged bellows of the branded cattle, but she was glad for that racket.

Concealed from all prying eyes, she sat down by the tiny trickle of slimy water and let the tears come. Once started, the pain was terrible. She felt as if every disaster of her life had coalesced into one horrible grief-stricken moment. She cried hard and bitterly. She renounced life. It was too difficult, too unrewarding, too uncertain.

After a time, the tears stopped; she roused herself. Catastrophe had struck, but she had realized in the midst of all that crying that she still had something to be grateful for. This calamity wasn't the loss she feared most. Nicholas was safe and getting stronger each year. And she had enough money to buy another piece of land. The Arizona Territory was enormous.

And it was good she'd found out about the suit in time, before she'd put a great deal of money into the new house. She could still start over again.

She would have to tell Steve, send him away. She needed to do that immediately and get it over with, but her body felt like lead.

Finally she forced herself to get up and walk to the house. She changed into her most attractive riding habit—cerulean blue with black piping around the high neckline and at her wrists. She put her hair up and attached a high-topped, black riding hat.

Whenever she felt insecure, she dressed more carefully. Her reflection in the mirror pleased her. Her eyes appeared bigger, more luminous, with only slight puffiness. The hat attracted attention upward, gave her a haughty look, which was exactly what she needed now.

At last, she blew her nose again and went to tell Juana and Tristera where she was going.

Steve looked up from his work to see what the commotion was about. Men had stopped work to crane their necks. Steve rubbed his back, straightened, and saw Samantha Forrester riding up the hill. The sight of her—slim and proud astride a racy black mare—the two of them silhouetted against the light blue sky, jolted him, caused his heart to pound and his stomach to tighten. Her pale blue riding habit emphasized her tiny waist and the fullness of her breasts.

In spite of the control he exerted over himself, his heart expanded with joy at the sight of her. Then he remembered their disagreement, and his tongue tasted iron. She'd come to apologize or fire him, and he didn't care which. Maybe firing him would put him out of his misery.

Steve looked down at his sweat-soaked shirt and his callused hands. He wasn't a laborer, but he was as filthy as one. Whenever he was upset, he took refuge in physical labor. Wearing himself out was better than riding down the mountain, dragging her out of bed, and forcing himself on her.

Samantha dismounted in the shade of a pine tree, dropped her reins, and watched Steve walk slowly forward to greet her. She could almost see him tamping himself into containment. Anger in her felt like an overwhelming need to do something, even if it was wrong. Apparently in him it turned stubbornness to stone. By the time he reached her, he looked fully composed behind his sleek, unsmiling facade.

He looked browner and stronger, and even more resistent, if that were possible. Samantha knew he would kiss her if she fell into his arms, but he wouldn't put himself out to try to win her.

The sleeves of his shirt were rolled up. Except for the dirty bandage above his elbow, his arms were bare and gleaming with sweat.

"Are you supposed to be digging ditches?" she asked.

"As the boss I can do anything I want."

He was still furious with her. She girded herself against him, felt a tightening down the length of her body. Despite his anger and his dirty, sweaty clothes, he was virile and attractive. His heavy shoulders strained against the fabric of his once white shirt.

"I have bad news," she said, looking away to recover her train of thought. She was glad she had important business to discuss with him; she would have hated to confront so much masculine resistance otherwise. "I'm being sued. I may lose my land. Even the land under the new house."

"When did this happen?"

"I received this packet today."

Frowning, Steve wiped perspiration off his damp forehead, took the packet from her, eased the papers out, and read. Samantha leaned against the tree trunk and waited, tapping her riding crop against her skirt.

At the house site, men worked in unaccustomed silence. Sounds of tools striking and wheelbarrows rolling on makeshift wooden ramps competed with the calls of mockingbirds and sparrows. White puffs of clouds had formed near the horizon. The air was clear and warm. She could see almost to Tucson.

At last Steve folded the papers and passed them back to her. "I think you're being sued by the man who raised me."

"I wondered about that. Does that make you my enemy?"

"You mean more than I already am?" he asked, fixing her with a piercing look. "Shouldn't, I had nothing to do with it."

"Is it him?"

"I'd been visiting Crows Walking and Uncheedah just before I came upon you and your train. He didn't mention anything about this to me, but I was only there a couple of days."

"It's probably him," she whispered.

"Though, I do remember Crows Walking talking about a paper a few years ago that was supposed to undo the damage the whites had done to his people. I told him once if this paper was so powerful, he should use it. But he could never bring himself to do it. Indians are slow to act. They prefer to bide their time. And when they finally do act, it is a tribal decision, agreed to by all the elders. And it's damned hard to get all those old men to agree to anything. I don't know how Crows Walking did it."

"Well, apparently he did."

Samantha turned away. "It doesn't matter, really." She faced south and looked at the desert glistening silvery gray under the afternoon sun. "I've tried to do too much here. I wanted this land to flower. I hired men to survey and build canals, but canals only work if there's water. I'm selling my cattle because I have no choice. Now I'm in danger of losing everything, even my home, of being put off my own land. What an outrage!''

Fury sparkled in her lovely eyes. It was not surprising that she was taking it hard. She was a woman connected to the land. In his mind, he saw her the way she'd been the night he kissed her—kneeling, reaching down into the sand, at one and at peace with the Earth.

Steve couldn't imagine her actually losing her land. But if somehow she did, he could imagine her wreaking her vengeance on her betrayers, whoever she perceived them to be.

''My stock is being rounded up for sale. For all intents and purposes I'm no longer a rancher,'' she said angrily, ''The rains haven't come. I thought every problem could be solved. I've thrown money at them, but they may be bigger than my bankroll.'' Her voice was husky, slightly tremulous. He had never seen her so agitated or so vulnerable.

''What will you do if you lose?''

''I won't lose!''

''Pardon me, but you were the one who said you were going to stop building the house, so in case you lose . . .''

''Well, I won't lose. I can't lose. This is my land. I own it, and no one can take it from me. I'll fight him to the death. Attorneys cost money. How long can a poor Indian afford attorney's fees?''

''Maybe someone took the case on speculation.''

She blinked. ''You're not . . .'' Her voice faltered.

''Paying for this? No.''

''Even so, I don't expect to lose.'' She paused, waiting to see if she meant it. ''In case I do lose, do you think Crows Walking would sell me this mountain?''

''Indians don't sell land. And I can't imagine an Indian winning anything away from a white woman in court.''

In a sudden display of anger, Samantha thwacked her riding crop against the tree trunk. ''Damn! I don't want to throw good money after bad, but . . .''

Steve frowned. ''I feel like a traitor saying this, but I think your attorney is right. Every year the reservations grow smaller as the government opens more Indian land to settlement.''

That was what she wanted to hear, but it made her cautious. ''What if . . .'' She stopped, unable to find the words for her most deeply felt terrors.

"Anything *might* happen. My guess is you're safe, but it's your decision. If you want us to stop, there's nothing here that can't be stopped."

Samantha glanced at the building site. Three tiers of bricks rose along one side of the house. It was already started. Her heart felt crushed at the thought of stopping work. She didn't want to lose the wonderful house he could build her.

"I hesitate to tell you this, because it might be misunderstood," said Steve cautiously, "but building the house might even strengthen your case. I can't imagine any court giving away your land with improvements on it. They would have to reimburse you somehow."

"Why are you telling me this? Crows Walking raised you."

"I'm a pragmatist. In the long view, civilizations are always built on the bones of the past."

"My uncle Chantry talked once about how he'd deliberately built something that had to be torn down, just to increase the value of the property for a condemnation action."

She sensed Steve waiting for her decision. "No," she said, taking a deep breath, "continue. If I lose, I lose. I'll deal with it then."

"I hope I didn't talk you into anything."

"No, this is what I want to do."

"Good." His smile of approval warmed her. "How's Nicholas?" he asked.

"He—he's fine." She glanced at him warily. "I'm sorry about the reata," she said. "I didn't mean to be rude. I realize now that you were just trying to help him. I know you went to a lot of trouble for him. I didn't mean to . . . embarrass you . . . or hurt your feelings."

Steve nodded.

"Please forgive me."

She sounded so sweet and humble that he softened. "Nothing to forgive," he said huskily.

"Please?"

Steve spread his hands. "Yes. Whatever you want."

Her smile warmed him all the way to his toes. She surprised him further by reaching out and touching his arm above the bandage. "Thank you, Steve. Now, show me around the house. I want to see everything. I hate gambling worse than drinking quinine, especially where my land is involved. But if I'm going to roll the dice, I might as well enjoy the game."

The foundation had been poured and was still drying in the

forms. Steve showed her where men were building forms for the enormous one-by-two-foot adobe bricks. Along the perimeter of the house men were nailing up two-by-fours to frame the interior walls. In another area, men were breaking out the formed bricks and lifting them onto pallets. Others loaded them onto flat wheelbarrows and rolled them to where the bricklayers worked. Each one of the adobe bricks was so heavy it took two men to lift it. A dozen bricklayers worked at intervals around the basement walls.

"How wonderful," exclaimed Samantha. "So much has been done!"

Pleased with her excitement, Steve showed her everything. When she was ready to leave, he walked her back to her horse, who was munching ferns beneath the pine tree.

She picked up her horse's reins and turned to face him. "There's a social in Picket Post Saturday morning. I'd like you to come with us."

"Me? Why?"

"Do I have to have a reason?"

"I thought a visit from a lively fella like Lando would keep you breathless for at least a month." He looked like he could say more, but his lips tightened and his jaw clamped shut. She noticed that he sported what looked like a razor cut above his top lip. Her own lips tingled with the sudden memory of his mouth, which had tasted like warm, sweet sun-dried figs—a heady experience for her.

Samantha frowned. She had lost her train of thought. She decided to ignore this new opportunity to fight with him. "I want you to go with me," she said simply.

"Are you going alone?"

"Captain Rathwick is riding out to escort us," she said. "I think it's mostly for Tristera, though."

"My old friend Rathwick, huh?"

"He's much nicer than you might think. You don't have to spend time with him."

"Does Lando know you have all these other beaus?"

"No, because I don't. Please?" She could have cut her tongue out for pleading. Her face felt hot as fire. She had no idea why she was even asking him.

"I'll see how I feel on Saturday."

Perturbed that it was the only commitment she could get from him, she mounted and frowned down at him. "We can at least hope that you will feel up to it," she said stiffly.

The left corner of Steve's mouth quirked up, which infuriated her. She should fire him. He seemed bent on humiliating her, or else he was punishing her for the sacrilege of making him angry the other day. Either way he was entirely too prideful.

But he didn't relent. His eyes, hazel in the bright sunlight, sparkled with male purpose and indignation. Her gaze was the one to drop. Feeling suddenly as if she'd bitten into something bitter, she turned her horse and galloped down the hill, feeling like an out-of-control child—rushing around trying to get her needs satisfied and disgracing herself in the process.

Halfway down the hill, Samantha stopped her horse abruptly. She must be out of her mind to get upset over Steve Sheridan. Only this morning her beloved had invited her to meet him in Phoenix on Sunday. He'd never done anything like that before. And what was her response? She had immediately ridden up the hill and invited Steve Sheridan to go to a social with her on Saturday!

A month ago she would have put Lance's letter next to her heart and begun packing that moment. But, she thought, defending herself, it wasn't every day that someone filed suit against her. The suit had distressed her, that was all.

Yet, despite Steve's recalcitrance, she felt her trip had not been wasted. She'd decided to fight the suit in every way possible. And that felt more natural for her. This was her land, and no one was going to take it from her without a fight.

That decided, she proceeded down the hill.

CHAPTER TWELVE

Saturday morning, Camp Picket Post was noisy and crowded with people talking and laughing excitedly.

Just north of town Samantha spotted a tree near the creek bed that wasn't yet taken, and they spread their pallets under it. Steve hadn't shown up at the house, and she had been inordinately disappointed.

While Juana and Tristera unpacked the food, Samantha walked from tree to tree, visiting with the women who'd ridden in from the surrounding ranches and farms. She sensed no hostility from them. Either they hadn't been privy to the article that had upset the townspeople or they had less fear—or perhaps better sense. She hoped that the bad reception she'd gotten had been confined to Claire Colson's clique.

It felt good to talk to other women, but she found herself watching for Steve, which irritated her. Every time a man approached, she'd glance up and be disappointed when it wasn't him.

The youngsters tired of three-legged man and took turns racing horses and practicing their skills at picking a handkerchief off a bush at full gallop. The men did another version, trying to pick a handkerchief off the ground. One man slipped out of the saddle and took a tumble, but he leapt up unhurt. People cheered.

Samantha strolled back to her own picnic spot, where Juana was napping. Tristera had kicked off her sandals. Each time she moved, Rathwick sneaked a look at her slim ankles and dusty feet.

Later, just as Juana began serving the food, Sheridan cantered to within a few feet of them and lifted his black hat. He had shaved and slicked back his thick black hair. He had not been able to subdue the unruly eyebrow.

"Hey, Juana, did you save me something to eat?" Steve's hazy bronze voice was like no other man's. As quiet as it was, it jangled something inside Samantha. Her heart gave such a leap she felt it must have been visible for a hundred yards.

"I knew you wouldn't want any chicken," Samantha said, answering for Juana, who rolled her eyes and smiled happily.

Steve dismounted and lowered himself onto the edge of the quilted pallet, his strong back and shoulder muscles straining against his shirt. Samantha tried not to notice the way his broad shoulders tapered into slim hips.

Steve glanced at her and his eyes narrowed ruefully. "Hunger can make a man do terrible things."

Samantha had no idea what he meant, but heat flushed from her belly outward. Alone or in a crowd, Steve had the ability to establish a curious, taunting intimacy between himself and her. In spite of her desire to distance herself from him, she was captivated by his smiling eyes and the curve of his slightly mocking lips. And she felt sure that he knew it.

Fortunately no one seemed to notice her distress. Steve grinned at Tristera. "Hey, Tris. I'm even ready to tackle one of your cathead biscuits."

"Well then, good afternoon, Mr. Sheridan," said Samantha quite formally.

"Mrs. Forrester. Miss Tristera. Juana. Nicholas," Steve said, nodding at Rathwick.

"I'm glad you could summon the energy to join us," Samantha said.

"Are you?" he asked softly.

"Of course."

Frowning, Rathwick leaned forward and held out his right hand to Steve. "I wanted to apologize for being a little testy the other day. We'd been riding in the heat too long, I guess."

Steve gripped the extended hand and shook it. "I don't do well in the heat myself."

They ate Juana's excellent food in near silence, a tribute to their hunger and her cooking. Then Tristera, who could not seem to keep from picking on Rathwick, looked up with big, innocent eyes and asked, "*Capitán*, have you heard any more about that Indian woman you were chasing?"

"Why, yes," he said, wiping his mouth with his napkin. "A fourteen-year-old boy was kidnapped by her a few days ago."

"Really?" said Tristera, her eyes getting rounder. "They saw her?"

"Good description of her actually. The boy said she's close to six feet tall and strong as a man. She would have killed him, too, except he outsmarted her and got away."

Samantha thought it sounded like a story told by a boy needing a reason to be out too late. But she didn't want to question a rumor that removed suspicion from Tristera.

Silver Fish and his wives and children rode up. The girls doubled up on ponies behind the women. The boy, Young Hawk, proudly rode a pinto pony. Steve put his plate down and walked out to speak to them.

Samantha followed, smiling at Red Star, Little Dove, and the children. Nicholas ran out to stand and stare up at Young Hawk, who looked very regal on his mount.

Silver Fish and Steve spoke Papago. When they finished their conversation, Silver Fish turned his horse and led his family toward a group of Indians on the other side of the creek. Samantha waited until they had passed out of hearing.

"I'm still amazed that two women can share a husband."

Steve grinned. "Maybe it was that or no husband."

"Is he Papago?"

"Ute. He lives among the Papago, probably because he married Papago maidens. But, since he's also a Mormon, maybe he's more comfortable among the Papago, who don't draw any fine lines. They pretty much do as they please. Silver Fish is a fine example of a Ute warrior."

"In what way?"

"You saw his horses, sheep, women, and kids, all eating food and wearing clothes. By reservation Indian standards, he's a *rico*, one of the rich ones. Anyone who knows anything about this country's Indian policies knows that means he has to be one damn fine rustler, not to starve or get caught."

They walked back to the quilt under the tree in silence. Games went on all afternoon. The Indians across the creek played their own games and cooked over smoky fires.

Rathwick dozed against the tree trunk. Nicholas ran and played with children he hadn't seen since the last social. It was good to see him so well and happy, but Samantha worried that he was wearing himself out and would cough all night and run a fever. At last he ran panting up to the pallet and threw himself down.

"Water," he gasped.

Samantha gave him a drink and felt his forehead, which was warm and damp. "You sit down and rest," she said firmly.

"Mama!"

"I don't want you sick."

"I won't be . . . I promise!"

"Sit, young man."

Groaning, Nicholas sat down on the quilt. He squirmed for a few minutes, then turned to Samantha with a frown on his face. "How many kids die of consumption?" he asked.

"I . . . don't know," she answered, lying. She had recently read an article that claimed all of them did, but she didn't believe it. Everyone knew at least one man or woman who was supposed to be suffering from consumption and hadn't died. Robert Louis Stevenson was a good example.

"How many adults?"

"I don't know that, either."

"Indian boys get to shoot bows and arrows. How come I don't have a bow and arrows?"

"Because you don't have to kill for the food you eat."

"Do Indian boys kill people?"

"I don't think so."

"I need to know."

"Has an Indian boy tried to kill you?"

"Not yet. Do Indian boys get sick?"

"I suppose so. Of course."

Steve came over, took a piece of lemon meringue pie, and leaned against the tree. Nicholas watched him eating for a moment.

"Mr. Sheridan, do you know how many children die of consumption each year?"

Steve chewed the last bite of his pie and squatted down beside Nicholas. "You worried about getting consumption?"

"No, sir. I already have it."

"Then you're worried you might die of it," Steve said, glancing quickly at Samantha, who looked alarmed and leaned forward as if she wanted to constrain him. Her frown was fierce, intended to stop him before he said any more.

Steve continued as if he hadn't noticed her distress. The boy deserved an answer. "I knew this old woman in Galveston, Texas. I was building a house for her son. She told me she got consumption back in 1820. The doctor told her folks she'd be dead before she reached twelve. They didn't like hearing that, so they took her to another doctor. He told her consumption was nothing to worry about. He said all she needed to do was plant herself a garden and spend most of her time out in it, that the garden would cure her. Well, she told me this two years ago, and she was eighty years old at the time."

"Eighty years old!" Nicholas marveled, and immediately changed the subject. "Indian boys get to have their own bows and arrows. I'm almost seven years old—and I don't even have a slingshot—''

"Nicholas," Samantha cut in.

"I'm rested now, Mama. Look, I'm hardly breathing at all. Please?''

"All right," she said—to get rid of him before he asked any more unsettling questions. Nicholas ran down the hill toward the children playing near the shallow creek.

Steve gave her an odd look and strode off toward town. Frowning, Samantha turned away in frustration and began to help Juana clean up the mess of their picnic. Steve had responded well, but he might be upset with her for not telling him sooner.

Sounds of a Mexican band playing in the distance drifted to them. With a long look at Rathwick, Tristera waved at Samantha and headed toward the music.

Rathwick continued to sit under the tree in the oncoming dusk. He seemed to want Tristera, but he just closed his eyes, content to laze by the tree.

"I'm worried about Tristera," Samantha said to Rathwick. "Ham Russell was very rude to her the last time we were in town. Is there any chance you might be willing to keep an eye on her?''

Rathwick opened his left eye and scowled at her. "If we're going to be coconspirators, you should call me Matthew.''

Samantha smiled into his eyes as he slowly stood up. She watched him until he was out of sight, then strolled toward the creek, shallow at the best of times. Now it had narrowed to a slimy ooze of water trickling between green mossy rocks. The brush along the creek bed had turned yellow.

Eventually Samantha sat down in the shade of a scrawny tree and listened to the cries of children and babies, the laughter of men and women, the shouts of gamblers betting on the horse races. She watched giant mosquitoes squat on the water, heard finches sing and crickets chirp. Beneath a fiery red sky, the sun slipped beneath the horizon.

"I heard a saying," Steve said, his voice so near her ear that her heart skipped a beat. His sudden presence reminded her of the night he'd kissed her by that other creek. "Brigham Young said it's better to fight the Indians with biscuits than with bullets. Do you suppose that might be true of women as well?''

Samantha turned. Steve hunkered down beside her and proferred a biscuit, split, with bacon between the two halves. Smiling, she took half out of his hand.

"So, you're restless, and your beau's gone off," he said.

"Widow women aren't as exciting as virgins."

Without taking his warm khaki gaze off her, Steve grinned, took half his biscuit in one bite, chewed it awhile, swallowed, and grinned some more. He didn't need to say a word. He might not approve of her, or admire the way she protected Nicholas, but she knew Steve Sheridan much preferred a woman to a girl. Heat warmed her middle and spread out.

"Are you upset with me, for not telling you about Nicholas?"

The odd look she'd seen when Nicholas told him sparkled in his eyes again. "Yes and no. Yes: If I'd known, I might have understood why you're so careful with him. And I might not have trampled on your sacred cows. And no: I'm too humbled to be upset with you for anything right now."

"What do you mean?" Samantha asked, her heart beating faster.

This wasn't what he wanted to be discussing with her. Tristera had told him that she was going to Phoenix to meet her lover tomorrow. He wanted to ask her not to do that, but he couldn't. "When I first met you, I thought you were too young and beautiful to be wasted in a desert. Now, I understand what you're doing here, and I realize . . ." He paused, scowling at her. "I shouldn't be telling you this—you're already too difficult to handle."

Samantha smiled at the chagrined expression on his handsome face. "Telling me what?"

"Now," he whispered, "now I realize why you've always had such a strong appeal for me. A woman with a purpose and a mission is something more than just a woman. I'm not saying this very well, but you're special, and now I know why. And that I'm . . . doomed."

A pulse punched against her throat, making her self-conscious. "I don't understand."

"Being with you is like being base metal that has come into contact with a philosophers' stone," he said, his voice dropping down into huskiness. "I'm being changed against my will."

"Is that so bad? Turning into gold?"

"I'm comfortable being base metal. I might not know how to act if I suddenly turned into gold."

He was paying her a wonderful compliment. She felt honored and humbled by his sincerity, felt herself swaying toward him.

He leaned forward as if he were going to kiss her, but of course he couldn't. There was enough daylight left that nearly everyone at the picnic would see them.

But the urge was strong in her, too. Then, into the growing tension between them wafted the sweet strain of a fiddle responding expertly to the pull of a bow. Steve grinned ruefully. "You think you can dance with me without picking on me?" he asked.

"I don't know. Maybe."

His eyes sparkling with humor, Steve took her hand and pulled her up. For one moment he smiled into her eyes—and she thought he was going to kiss her, in spite of everything. But then he turned and started to walk toward the sound of the music.

Nibbling her biscuit, she walked beside him toward the clearing by the water tower where the fiddlers were warming up. People from all over town were heading in the same direction. Watched by their elders, the children continued to play their towsack games in the dying evening light. Samantha looked back at Juana, who nodded and waved. Samantha relaxed, sure in the knowledge that Juana would keep an eye on Nicholas and her own son, Eliptio.

Tristera danced the fandango, its music vibrant and pulsing like her blood. When she was at the school in Flagstaff, sometimes her sister and Luis would come and pick her up for a weekend. Luis's sisters had taught her to love the Mexican dances.

Clicking castanets tossed to her by a smiling musician, she felt totally alive for the first time in weeks. Eyes closed, her body twirling with the music, she pretended the *estúpido Capitán* Rathwick was watching her with great longing in his icy, military heart.

The dance ended. To her amazement, the first face she saw was Rathwick's. He looked pale, stiff, and out of place. He belonged with the white people, dancing their waltzes and polkas, and yet he looked only at her.

Before she could approach the *capitán*, Joe Dart caught her hand and pulled her away from the ring of clapping, yelling Mexicans.

"Hi, Tris."

"Hi, yourself," she said, tossing her hair and smiling for Rathwick's benefit.

"Hey, you're the prettiest girl I've ever seen! And the way you dance! You're enough to make a man crazy."

Joe Dart tried to pull her into his arms, but the heat of his body irritated her. Still hot from dancing, she didn't want to be held by a man. Besides, men leered at her. And she could no longer see Rathwick's pale face in the crowd. He must have left.

"Let me go," she said, twisting away from Joe.

"Hey, Tris, how we going to get married someday if you won't even talk to me?"

"Married?"

"Well, why not?"

"Because, little boy, you do what Mama tells you."

Joe flushed. "I do not."

Tristera laughed and walked away from the dancers. Joe followed. "Wait up, Tris."

"No."

Tristera let him catch her. Joe's mentioning marriage put him in a class by himself. No man of any kind had ever proposed to her. Indian men were respectful, but no Indian would risk losing status to marry a half-breed who no longer had her virginity. Being accused of murder had made her think about where she was going with her life. She still didn't know, but she didn't want to be an outcast ex-rainmaker to a clan of Indians who hated her. She wanted to have something, be somebody. She wanted Captain Rathwick to look up to her, to want to marry her . . .

Rathwick was still watching her. Joe leaned down and kissed her. He tasted of beer and smelled of horses and sweat. His tongue pressed into her mouth, and suddenly Tuvi's face appeared before her. She could see it as clearly as if he were with her. His image floated in space a foot from her head, startling her so badly she felt scalded by shame, as if Tuvi were actually there, seeing her with this man. Tuvi's likeness didn't say anything. He just looked at her the way he'd always done, with his heart so pure she could see it shining in his eyes.

She struggled out of Joe's arms and ran away. He tried to pull her back down. "Aw, Tris . . ."

"No! Stop it!"

"Aw, Tris, come back here!" Joe heard her footsteps running away from him into the darkness, just outside the lantern glow. He followed her and lost her. He ran smack into Roy Bowles and Ham Russell less than a hundred feet away. "Did you see which way she went?"

"You look madder'n a wet hen," Roy said, grinning.

"Jest answer my danged question."

Roy nudged Ham Russell. "That's what happens when the sassy little gal you're hankering after runs off from you."

Joe glared his displeasure at Roy. "You counted your teeth lately?"

"Hell, she ran past here like a scalded dog. Saw her go down that hill. You'll never find her in the dark. Come on, Joe. Let's get drunk," Roy said.

Joe expelled an angry breath. "I might as well, for all the good I'm doing myself sober."

Joe and Roy walked off toward town. Ham Russell leaned against the tree and took out his makings. Tristera's kissing Joe had upset him. She didn't have the time of day for him, but she could kiss Joe Dart because she thought he had money. If Joe kept chasing her, he'd probably catch her, and one day Ramon Rodriguez would be Ham's boss's brother-in-law.

Ham sure hated that thought. It wasn't fair that men with money and land got all the best women. And that a piece of offal like Ramon could move up in the world and Ham couldn't. He hadn't spent his life fighting Indians so little bastards like Ramon could strut around.

Ham pushed away from the tree and walked into the darkness. Maybe he'd find Tristera himself.

Walking felt better, anyway. He wasn't like them cowboys who wouldn't walk a foot farther than they had to. He'd been raised in Ohio, where it was good to walk.

He angled toward the creek.

Samantha danced the first dance with Steve. One of the men who occasionally courted her cut in. She saw glimpses of Steve, though, lively and smiling, twirling other women. She didn't like the feeling this gave her and tried not to watch, but her gaze kept following his lithe form.

Rathwick cut in. "Did you find Tristera?" she asked.

"I found her." His grim tone discouraged further questions.

The dance ended. Samantha waved away her suitors and walked to the table, where a tub of lemonade floated a big block of ice, brought in on the train from Phoenix, no doubt. She scooped a dipperful of the cool liquid. "Would you mind pouring me one of those?" Steve asked from behind her.

Smiling, Samantha gave him a lemonade. "Enjoying the dance?" she asked.

"Yes. It's been a long time since I've had this much fun," he said, his grin making him look younger and more boyish.

She finished her lemonade and put the cup down. "I need a breath of fresh air," she said, fanning herself with her hand.

Steve followed her away from the crowd. The ground where they had danced was packed down, but a gray cloud of dust hung over the revelers. Hanging lanterns ringed the noisy throng, casting little light into the middle of the horde. In the distance children yelled, probably playing blindman's buff.

"You could earn money building a dance hall," she said.

"I seem to have my hands full now."

"Yes, you do."

"What's that supposed to mean?" he asked softly.

"Nothing. Just agreeing with you."

"So," Steve said, pausing, "I hear you're going to see Lando tomorrow."

Samantha had hoped he wouldn't find out, but since he had . . . "Yes," she said firmly.

Steve scowled. "I know this is none of my business, but I have to tell you that I got some strong feelings from him when he was at the ranch."

"Such as?"

"He's like a wounded bear right now. He may love you, but even you might not be completely safe with him," Steve said cautiously.

"Lance would never hurt me," she said firmly.

"Not if he could help himself, maybe, but . . . uh . . . I've known and worked with men all my life. Men aren't like women. We've got some special problems."

Samantha laughed. "Like what?"

"We have needs that keep bothering us . . . whether we've got a woman or not. And sometimes, anger makes those needs more insistent."

"So. You think he might just whisk me off to his lair and . . ."

The thought of it made Steve angry. "It's not funny."

The look in his eyes challenged her to be as frank as he'd been. She wanted to say something outrageous, but her mind went blank. "It isn't like you think," she whispered.

Steve could see she was attached to her own reasons, so he backed off.

"I don't want to talk about it anymore," she said.

"Then we won't," he said, agreeing. He turned to leave.

"Steve, wait."

He stopped and faced her. "Why the hell should I?"

Light from the lanterns swaying in the breeze moved shadows over his face, so she couldn't see his expression. The shadows revealed a small vertical dent in front of his ear. The rest of his skin was smooth, probably slightly damp from the exertion of dancing. She wanted suddenly to touch it. It was very upsetting to want such a thing given her love for Lance, but her fingers tingled with the desire to stroke Steve's face. It felt awkward to be so aware of her love and longing for Lance and feel this attraction to Steve Sheridan. Maybe something *was* wrong with her.

"What do you want from me, Samantha Forrester?"

Steve's voice was husky. The sound caused a quickening in her belly. His hands reached out and caught her by the shoulders and shook her, gently, in contrast to the fierceness of his holding her and the fierceness she sensed in him. "What?" he demanded, shaking her again.

Mute, Samantha shook her head. The look in his eyes told her he wanted her.

"I guess I want to enjoy you while I wait for Lance," said Samantha, "but I don't want you to have any strings on me when he comes for me. It's callous of me, but knowing that doesn't stop me."

"You're honest like a man," he whispered.

"I've been lonely and miserable too long. You might want me for the moment, but I know you're a tumbleweed. When it's time for you to move on, you will say a graceful—possibly even a grateful—good-bye."

His hands tightened on her shoulders. "What if you're wrong about me?"

His face, half hidden in shadow, looked mysterious, handsome, and inaccessible. She could feel the power of her ill-fated attraction for him all the way to her toes. "I'm not. In the meantime, though, you might kiss me," she whispered.

"I could kiss you, but what if I fall hopelessly in love with you? What will happen to me if he doesn't let you come back tomorrow?"

"I don't know. I just want you to kiss me," she said, her face like a beautiful, sweet flower. The thought of kissing her caused his blood to burn through his veins.

"I'm a simple man, Samantha Forrester. I don't stir up a 'hornets' nest unless I've figured out how I'm going to survive the attack."

"I'm not a hornet's nest. I'm a woman," she whispered, her skin glowing in the moonlight. Her voice was sweet and tremulous, her eyes dark, haunting.

"There's a difference?" he asked. She laughed, and he realized how much he loved the rich, mocking sound of her laughter. It made him feel both better and worse.

"You've kissed me before. Were you so much braver then, or have I become less attractive?"

"Neither. In town I was leaving, never to see you again. I couldn't leave without that kiss."

"And down by the creek?"

"The moonlight got to me."

"Apparently the moon no longer works, so if I want to be kissed, I have to fire you?"

Steve laughed, and Samantha's expression changed from teasing to hurt. She turned away, but he had seen, and seeing that flash of emotion caused an answering ache in him. He knew she felt rejected, and he couldn't stand it. He reached out and grabbed her wrist. She jerked it away. He caught her by the waist and pulled her into his arms. She lifted her fist to hit him. He caught her arm and lowered his head to kiss her.

"No!"

Steve immobilized her and stopped her protests with his mouth. He kissed her until she stopped fighting, then raised his head. "Yes," he said, his voice harsh.

Samantha pressed her face against his chest. She felt weak and strong at the same time. Her body wanted to melt into his, to be swallowed up by him.

Steve lifted her chin, found her mouth again, and this time she surged up to hold him. His kiss opened something in her. She felt filled up with sweetness and melting and heat.

The music in the background stopped. Suddenly, over the heavy hum of her own body, she heard chanting.

"Lunger! Lunger! Hope you die of hunger!"

Samantha struggled out of Steve's arms. "Oh, no!" she gasped.

"What is it?"

"Nicholas!"

She broke free and ran. Steve ran after her.

Halfway to the creek, Ham saw a group of boys fighting and stopped to watch. It was Nicholas Forrester and a playmate, facing six bigger boys. Ham recognized the biggest one as Claire Colson's young'un.

"You play with him, you're gonna catch it!" Colson's boy yelled at Nicholas's friend. The youngster looked at Nicholas, then shrugged and ran away. Now it was just Nicholas against the six boys. The Colson boy picked up a stick.

"You better stay out of this town, if you know what's good for you," he said, walking forward and menacing the Forrester boy with the stick. To his credit, Nicholas stood his ground. Ham was just about to break it up when he saw Ramon Rodriguez come running from the creek.

"Hey, you boys quit that!" Ramon yelled.

Ham reached down and grasped the handle of his revolver. Footsteps sounded behind him, but it was only Piney, humming to himself. Piney stopped beside him.

"Them boys fighting?" Piney asked.

Ramon was exchanging taunts with the six boys. Ramon wore a gun, but that didn't seem to scare the boys. They knew he wouldn't use it on them.

An idea came to Ham. Piney had an advantage most folks didn't. Because he was a known fool, he could walk right up to just about anyone, and they wouldn't get down on him the way they might a man with all his faculties. Ham put his arm around Piney's bony shoulders.

"Hey, Piney, you remember the thump-thump game we played with those hollow cardboard tubes at the picnic today?"

Piney grinned. "Yes, sir, Mr. Ham."

"Well, I want you to play it again. All you have to do is thump Ramon a couple of times and you win the prize."

"What prize is it, Mr. Ham?"

Ham smiled and squeezed Piney's bony shoulder. "It's a pint of ice cream all to yourself."

Piney loved ice cream. He grinned and touched his hair, which smelled of the pomade his employer made him wear to town. "This won't make Miz Chila mad at me, will it?" He'd lived around pranksters all his life. He'd learned to be careful of anything another man told him to do.

"Naw!" Ham walked Piney back to where he'd seen a three-foot piece of two-by-four earlier today. It was still there. Ham picked up the club, hefted its weight a moment, and handed it to Piney.

"Ramon likes to play the thump-thump game." Ham could

hear the boys and Ramon yelling insults. "Let me show you where Ramon is," Ham said.

"You boys get back to your mamas!" Ramon bellowed, taking Nicholas by the arm to lead him away before one of the children lost his temper and hurt someone. As he turned, a dark figure of a man loomed up between him and the lighter sky. The man's arm raised and smashed down. A sharp pain jolted from his head to his knees, buckling them. He sank to his knees, stunned, momentarily blinded, and unable to rise. Dimly he heard Nicholas struggling with someone. He willed his legs to react, his arms to strike out, but they would not.

Nicholas yelled. Ramon's vision returned enough so he could see the man raise the club again. Ramon remembered the gun in his holster, clawed at it, and felt its reassuring coolness and heaviness in his hand. He lifted, aimed, and fired at point-blank range—and felt grateful for the small, sharp recoil against his palm. The intruder staggered and fell.

The boys stopped yelling and started running, scattering in all directions. Ramon struggled to his feet and tried to focus his blurring eyes on the man . . . lying so still on the ground. He could hear sounds of people running toward him. He tried to straighten, and finally his legs worked. Panting, he touched Nicholas's arm.

"Are you all right, *niño*?"

"Yeah."

"What's going on out there?" a man yelled.

"Those kids," Ramon said, pointing after the kids who had run away, "harassed Nicholas. Then a man attacked me from behind. I had to shoot him."

Cautiously men walked closer. "That you, Ramon?" The voice sounded like Marshal Daley.

"*Sí, señor.*"

Within seconds Ramon was surrounded by dozens of silent men. Ham Russell stepped out of the crowd, knelt beside the fallen man, and looked up at Marshal Daley. "Dead," he said flatly.

Ramon's heart sank. Daley turned him. "Why'd you kill him?"

"It was me or him, I tell you."

"I doubt that," Ham Russell said, elbowing his way through the crowd. "You know who this is?" he demanded furiously.

"No."

"It's Piney, you little bastard."

"Piney?" The blood drained from Ramon's heart. Piney was old, and harmless as spit. He turned to the marshal. "I tell you, *señor*, that he attacked me, hit me so hard my knees buckled."

Men muttered among themselves. Ramon explained to the marshal. Nicholas told what had happened as well, but the muttering grew louder.

"Piney didn't no more attack Ramon than I did. I say get a rope," a man in the back yelled.

Daley turned to the crowd. "There'll be no ropes."

Ham Russell waved his arms angrily. "Ramon shot and killed Piney. A rope is the least of what we should do to the little bastard." He turned and hit Ramon in the mouth.

The sudden blow jolted Ramon so bad he fell. He started to get up, but lying beside Piney made him realize what he'd done. He just lay there, feeling awful and waiting to see what they were going to do to him.

"I cain't abide a mean-tempered man like that," Ham yelled. "I say we hang the lying little bastard!"

Fear and rage brought Ramon to his feet. He launched himself into the air and landed on Russell, hitting him midchest and knocking him back against the man behind him.

"Hey!" Russell yelled, flying backward.

"Ramon's gone crazy!"

Men tackled Ramon and pulled him off Russell, who struggled to his feet, cursing. Blood poured from his mouth into his beard. Ramon struggled, but the men held him tight.

"That little son of a bitch tried to kill me! I say we put a stop to his damned temper fits once and for all!" Russell yelled.

Cries of "Yeah!" came from all around.

Held securely, Ramon looked from face to face. He couldn't believe this was happening.

"Steady, boy. I'm not going to let them hang you," Daley said. "Let 'im go!" he yelled at the men holding Ramon. "He's due a trial."

"Like hell he is!"

Daley could tell the crowd was close to turning into a killing mob. He lifted his gun and aimed it at one of the men holding Ramon. Cursing, the man let go. The other one did, too.

Ramon wanted to trust Daley, but he was only one man. Few of the men in the crowd carried guns at their hips, except Ham Russell. Ramon had dropped his gun after shooting Piney. It could be anywhere.

"You can't stop 'em," Ramon said, backing away from Daley.

Ramon saw the *señora* and Steve Sheridan run from the dance toward the back of the crowd.

"What's happened?" the *señora* asked, her sweet voice rising above the murmurings of the angry men.

The men turned toward her—and Ramon took that moment to push his way into the crowd, so Russell wouldn't be able to shoot him without shooting other men as well. Ramon saw a pistol in the holster of one of the few men packing guns. He grabbed it and aimed it at the horseman.

"Get off the horse, *señor*!"

"Now, don't go adding horse thievery to your other sin, Ramon," Daley cautioned.

"Get off!" Ramon shouted.

The man dismounted. Ramon sprang into the saddle, turned the horse east, and kicked him into a fast run.

"Doesn't anyone have a damned gun?" Ham yelled. He and Daley had guns, but they were in the middle of the crowd. They'd have to shoot ten men to clear a path.

Daley grinned in spite of himself. Twenty years ago, few men would have come to a dance without hardware. But this was 1889, and no one expected trouble, just an opportunity to dance and flirt a little.

"He's getting away!" Ham yelled in frustration, elbowing a path through the men around him.

"What the hell can we do?" one man bellowed back. "I ain't got wings or bullets."

At last, Ham broke clear of the crowd. He leveled his handgun at Ramon's fleeing back and pulled the trigger. Steve pushed the man next to him into Russell. Russell cursed and pushed the man aside and continued firing at Ramon until he emptied his gun.

CHAPTER THIRTEEN

"You're going to *what*?" Samantha demanded.

"Join the posse," Steve said, frowning. In the light of a hanging lantern, his face was in shadow, but his tone and stance were those of the stubborn, inexplicable male. His mind was made up. He would do as he pleased. A small fury rose in Samantha.

"And what about Nicholas's safety? What if those men come back and try to kill him again?"

"According to the report I heard they were only boys."

"Whose side are you on, anyway?"

Steve pondered his answer. Samantha was frightened and outraged on Nicholas's behalf and worried about Ramon. He didn't want her mad at him, but he didn't want Ramon to face that posse alone in the mood they were in.

"Rathwick will protect Nicholas. Most posses are like short dogs in high grass, but every now and then one gets lucky. If they find Ramon, would you rather someone was there who wanted to see him get a fair trial—or just twenty or so men who think a cottonwood tree needs another decoration?"

"What can one man do against twenty?" she demanded. "I know he didn't kill Piney, at least not like they say he did, in cold blood, for no reason . . ."

It would do no good to fight with her. Steve turned back to his horse, tightened Calico's cinch, and mounted. Steve turned Calico and kneed him into a gallop. Samantha watched until he was out of sight, lost in the milling posse.

Steve realized at once that the posse should have waited until morning. Daley fancied himself something of a tracker, though, so they'd set off in the dark as if it made sense.

Ramon had made the mistake of many panic-stricken men. He'd stayed off the roads and left a clear trail across the desert, where very few horses or anything else traveled.

Steve stayed close to Daley, who turned out to be a pretty fair tracker after all. He was a little slow and hampered by darkness, but he was almost as good as an Indian. Steve could have led the posse faster, but he kept quiet. They were already going faster than he wanted them to.

Something about the trail puzzled him. Slowly he dropped back and let the others go on ahead. When he'd put a little distance between himself and the rest of the posse, he dismounted, struck a match from the tin he carried in his pocket, and studied the trail. Then he saw it—a dark spot in the sand. He touched it with his finger, which came away wet with blood. Daley had to know, but he hadn't said anything to the others. Either Ramon or his stolen horse was bleeding.

Steve caught up with the posse. About two A.M. by the stars, the moon went down. Without that light Daley called a halt; men bedded down for the night. Steve lay on his saddle blanket until everyone was asleep, including the man who was supposed to stand the first guard.

Silently he stood up and walked away from the camp. When he was out of earshot, he cut a branch off a mesquite bush and tied it to the back of his belt with his handkerchief. Satisfied he would leave no trail, he settled into the long, ground-eating pace he'd learned from the Indians. Over time, a man in good shape could outrun a horse. Except for that scratch on his arm, almost healed now, he was in good shape. He would have preferred to be wearing moccasins, but his low-heeled shoes, chosen for dancing, would have to do.

About ten minutes from the posse, he thought he heard a horse. He stopped to listen. The sound came again, a whinny. Slowly he walked through a stand of cactus toward a riderless horse outlined against the lighter sky.

"Easy, boy," he said, stepping close and grasping the horse's reins. Heat radiated from the quivering animal, which smelled strongly of sweat. "Where's your rider?"

Steve reached into his vest pocket and found the sugar cubes he kept there for Calico. He let the horse have them, then lit a match. He checked for a bullet wound and the ground for signs. The horse's tracks led from the direction of the hills north of him. Leading the horse, Steve backtracked.

Seconds later he found Ramon, motionless on the ground. Steve knelt beside the boy, felt for a pulse, found one, and then struck another match. Ramon had been hit in the back, low down on the right side. Steve ripped Ramon's shirt into strips and used it to bind his wound. Then he unsaddled the horse, slipped the top saddle blanket out from under the saddle, and covered Ramon with it. The one next to the horse was sweated through, but this one was fairly dry. Steve draped Ramon over the saddle, tucked the blanket around him to keep him warm, and led the horse toward the mountain, looming black against the skyline.

Steve knew this part of Arizona. He had hunted in this area as a boy. At the base of the hill, Steve broke through a heavy thicket and found a cave he remembered. He searched his mind for a better place, but this cave narrowed into a natural tunnel that opened onto a hidden valley where Ramon would be safe from pursuit.

Steve checked Ramon, then led him and his horse into the back of the cave, where he was plunged into such dank coolness and impenetrable darkness he might as well have not had eyes. The cave smelled of bat droppings. It felt cold and still, and filled with unseen presences. But that was probably just his imagination, he hoped.

Steve stepped carefully and kept his right hand on the cold rock wall. The horse's shod hooves made sharp sounds on the rock. The walls echoed each step. About a hundred yards in, the cave narrowed to a tunnel barely wide enough and high enough for the horse to walk upright. The horse whinnied its displeasure, but it had no choice, either.

Steve stepped carefully, but soon lost track of time. So much darkness disoriented him. He needed to get back to the posse before they woke and missed him, but he could only go so fast.

At last the darkness was relieved by faint light. His hand became visible on the wall, then his feet and the floor of the cave. Finally he saw stars shining through a slit and realized that he'd somehow gotten through.

At the pivot rock, he wiped cold sweat off his forehead. Still holding the reins, he put his back against the rock and pushed. It turned slowly on its axis, letting in cool air. The night didn't seem so dark after the cave.

Steve led the horse out of the opening, lifted Ramon down, and checked his wound, which still seeped blood into the cloth around it. From the canteen he'd found on the stolen horse, he dribbled water into Ramon's mouth, then wet his own mouth with a swallow of the water. The saddlebags yielded dried fruit and jerky. Steve put the food and water near Ramon and led the horse back to the pivot rock.

"I'll be back as soon as I can," Steve said to the unconscious boy. He felt frustrated, but he'd done everything he could. Ramon was warm and alive. He was on his own now.

* * *

Chila woke to the sound of a wagon rattling up to the front porch. She put on her robe and walked out to see who would be arriving in the middle of the night.

As she stepped out onto the porch, Ham Russell and Roy Bowles got down from the buckboard and walked up the steps.

"What's going on?"

"Got Piney here. That little greaser killed him."

"Oh, no!" Piney had been with her since Joe was a little boy. "Put him in the parlor, Ham. I'll clean him up and . . . get him ready to bury." The thought of burying Piney brought a quiver to her insides.

She rushed to light a lamp. Grunting and complaining, Ham and Roy carried Piney up the steps like a sack of potatoes. They bumped him through the door and laid him on the floor beside the window.

"You need anything else?" Ham asked.

"Get me a bucket of water and put it on the stove. I don't like working with cold water." She knelt to be sure Piney's eyes were closed. She didn't like no dead man staring at her. His eyelids felt warm to her. She knelt and pressed her ear to his heart.

"Why, you fools," she said, standing up. "He's not dead."

Sunday morning dawned clear and bright. If not for her fury at the whole town, Samantha might have gone to prayer meeting. Any other Sunday, she, Tristera, and Nicholas would have dressed, eaten breakfast in the hotel dining room, and walked to Mary Francis's house for church services.

As it was, she and Nicholas ate in their room and then prepared to ride directly back to the ranch. As they left their room, Tristera, dispirited and pale, stepped into the hall.

"Good morning," Samantha said.

"*Buenos días, señora,*" Tristera mumbled.

A few paces further, Juana stepped into the hall.

"Morning, Juana."

"*Sí, señora,*" Juana murmured, not looking at her.

Samantha put her arm around Juana's shoulders. "Juana, please stop blaming yourself. There is nothing we can do for Piney, but Nicholas is safe, and Steve will save Ramon." Nicholas reached up and patted Juana's arm.

Juana wiped away tears. "It is easy for you to be forgiving of others, *señora, niño mío*," she said, giving Nicholas a squeeze, "but not for me. If I had not gone to sleep . . ."

"You work hard. You're entitled to sleep occasionally. I don't want to hear another word about it."

Samantha knew where the real fault lay. She had known about the mood of some people in the town. If she'd been watching Nicholas instead of mooning over Steve, Nicholas would not have been frightened and humiliated, and Ramon might not have shot Piney.

Piney was dead. Samantha had cried about that and written a note to Chila, telling her how very sorry she was, but she knew that wouldn't lessen Chila's pain.

Samantha had agonized half the night about going to Phoenix after all that had happened. She had finally decided it was still important to sell that herd.

In the hotel lobby, Rathwick put aside his newspaper and stood up.

"Good morning, ladies," he said stiffly, avoiding Tristera's gaze. "Are you ready to go back to the ranch?"

"Yes, we are."

At the creek below the house, Rathwick stopped his horse. The others continued on up the hill. Tristera felt the pull from Rathwick's body. In spite of her wishes to the contrary, she reined her horse and looked at him. She had stolen glances at his stony profile, but this was the first time she dared look into his eyes.

"I'm sorry about your brother," he said. "If there is anything I can do, please let me know."

Tristera nodded her thanks.

"Did Joe Dart hurt you?"

Surprised, Tristera blinked. "No."

"I saw you crying."

"I let him kiss me. I felt ashamed."

The look on Tristera's face caused his insides to twist with compassion. She was so young and so innocent. Even a kiss could torment her.

The sun was setting; dusk turned the desert and her lovely features gray. Rathwick was close enough to touch her. She looked into his eyes with that strange unabashed openness that told him nothing, yet made his heart pound in spite of his anger and jealousy. "I wish I had asked you to dance," he said.

"And risk your spotless reputation dancing with a . . . Mexican girl?'' she asked, her bitterness causing one corner of her mouth to pull down.

On impulse Rathwick dismounted, helped her down, and held out his arms to her.

"There's no music," she whispered.

"I could be killed by renegade Indians tonight. I don't want to die without ever once holding the prettiest girl in the world in my arms."

Tristera's face felt tight. If she had any tears, the muscles of her face would have squeezed them out of her. "You are *loco*," she whispered.

"You are obviously a princess," he said solemnly. "You can't risk your reputation dancing with a lowly infantry officer," he said with a smile, holding out his hands and crooking his fingers in a gesture that motioned her into his arms.

He was tall and solid; heat radiated from his body. Surprised at the strength she felt in him, Tristera realized that her tight face was relaxing into a smile. Suddenly she felt better than she had in days.

They waltzed in silence. Tristera felt dizzy, as if she might say or do anything. Too soon, Rathwick stopped dancing, took her by the elbow, and guided her toward an imaginary lemonade tub. "May I dip you a drink?"

"*Sí.*"

Her answer was so soft Rathwick almost didn't hear it. He pretended to dip two cups of punch. She pretended to drink hers slowly, watching him with dark, challenging eyes.

"Do you have family around here?" he asked.

"No."

"Anywhere?"

"No."

Rathwick scowled down at his boots. He would have rather heard that she was surrounded by people who loved her.

"What about Ramon?"

"I thought you meant my mother and father. They died when I was little."

Rathwick thought of her as a child. And himself bordering on lunacy. He had no business being out here with this girl, but he couldn't make himself lead her to the house. His body seemed out of his control.

"What do *you* want, Miss Tristera?" he asked, touching her arm. His hand tingled, felt more alive than any other part of his body. In the dying light, her cheeks were sweetly curved, her lips plump and smooth. The urge to kiss her made sweat bead on his forehead. He took out his handkerchief and dabbed at his face.

Tristera had the sudden impulse to see if kissing the *capitán* would elicit the image of Tuvi. "Why don't you just do it?" she asked softly.

"Pardon?"

"Kiss me. Why don't you just kiss me?"

Rathwick's stomach felt as if it had suddenly filled with hot water. Heat spread through him. He leaned down and tentatively touched his lips to hers. She didn't draw away. Her mouth opened, and it was the sweetest, warmest mouth he had ever tasted, as smooth as warm butter. Her arms curled around his neck. Her tongue licked the corner of his mouth, sending a heated thrill down his spine.

Rathwick pulled her into his arms and kissed her the way he'd wanted to since the first time he saw her.

Tristera received his kiss on two levels. Part of her responded wildly, with raw emotion, and she knew that she loved him and her life would never be the same again. Another part of her waited to see if Tuvi would appear.

The kiss ended. She sighed and tossed her hair. "I will put that in my scrapbook, *Capitán*." She had proven something to herself. He did want her, and he was man enough to do something about it if the circumstances were right. But he would never marry her or even think of her in that way. And she was not about to make the same mistake again. Tuvi must have known. He had not felt it necessary to show himself.

Before Tristera could finish that thought, Rathwick stepped away from her, turned jerkily, and mounted. He touched his hat, turned his horse, and galloped away. Tristera sank down on a rock. If she had any sense at all she would cry, but she couldn't make rain inside or out.

Samantha sent for Eagle Thornton. When he arrived, she stepped out on the porch to meet him. "How many head have you loaded into the cattle cars so far?"

"Five hundred, give or take a few."

The locomotive came just after lunch to claim the filled cattle cars. Samantha recognized her palace car, its brand-new windows gleaming in the sunlight. As the locomotive chuffed up to the house, there was still no sign of Steve. She packed an overnight bag while the crew coupled the cars. When everything was in readiness, to the lowing sounds of mournful steers and the yips and waves of tired cowhands, Samantha kissed Nicholas good-bye and carried her satchel aboard her newly refurbished palace car.

"Mama, take me with you."

"No, this is going to be a quick business strip. You'll be better off here."

"But I want to see Amy and Chane."

"Amy was sick last time I heard. By now little Chane may be sick with whatever she had. So, no."

"Please, Mama!"

"No, you'll be safer here with Tristera and Juana."

This was a business trip, but she had packed one of her prettiest gowns, just in case.

Samantha was grateful for the time it took to reach Phoenix. She used the time to try to figure out how she felt about being courted by Lance. She struggled with it for hours, but Steve's face kept coming between her and her beloved, irritating her. It seemed unfair that now, when she'd finally gotten something she had wanted all of her life, Steve could show up and make such a nuisance of himself.

Phoenix smelled of cattle dung. Although it was still April, and supposedly springtime, a blistering hot sun burned down at midday. Samantha felt a little disoriented as she stepped off the cool train and glanced up and down the station platform, looking for a familiar face.

"Over here!" Lance called out from a buggy parked beside the platform.

Samantha lifted her skirts and stepped down. "I wasn't sure you would meet me."

"Then you must have forgotten Chane's superior system of scheduling," Lance said, raising an eyebrow at her.

He took her elbow and led her toward a man who had been standing beside the buggy. "Samantha Forrester, Jed Sparks."

A typical cattleman, rawboned and tough as leather, Sparks's seamed face broke into a warm smile.

"How do, ma'am."

Samantha and Lance closed the deal with Sparks by three o'clock, then Lance drove her to Chane and Jennie's. In front of the enormous two-story house, Lance helped her out of the buggy; his warm hands lingered on her waist. At the stairs he turned her and looked into her eyes. "I forgot to mention that Chane and Jennie and the kids aren't here."

"Where are they?"

"San Francisco, for a week or so."

"But Amy was sick . . ."

"She's fine now."

Suddenly Samantha felt odd. If this were any other man but Lance, she would suspect his motives. He must have read it in her eyes.

"You can stay here. I'll stay at our—my house."

Lance still maintained a house in Phoenix. It was one he had owned before he married Angie.

"You don't mind if I eat dinner here with you, do you?" he asked, eyeing her carefully.

"Of course not," she said, a little too quickly.

"Yoshio's in Durango, and I'm not much of a cook."

Samantha tried to shrug off the feeling, but she was strangely uncomfortable. It was ridiculous. After all, she loved Lance. Whatever he wanted, she wanted, but . . . this just didn't feel quite right.

"Dinner at seven?" he asked.

"Yes, that will be fine, thank you."

Malcomb, the Kincaid's elderly butler, confirmed their dinner plans. Lance thanked him, scowled, and turned back toward his buggy. Malcomb led Samantha upstairs.

In the guest bedroom, she took off her clothes, washed in the basin, and then lay down to rest. The room was cool, despite the afternoon heat. Chane had built the house with two-foot-thick bricks. This was what her house would feel like, if Steve ever came back and finished it.

She wanted to think about Lance, but Steve's face, as she'd seen it that night when he was about to ride away with the posse, filled her mind. He seemed so open and friendly, but mystery surrounded him. Since she'd known him he'd been shot at twice and maligned in an anonymous letter.

Someone in Camp Picket Post obviously did not like him. But she and Tristera and Nicholas did. And she trusted their instincts before those of someone she didn't know.

Lance would be coming to dinner soon. And if the feelings she was getting from him were any indication, he was planning to seduce her. She needed to know how she felt about that. *I know men,* Steve had said. *He's nothing but trouble now. He'll hurt you.*

Would Steve care?

Suddenly irritated, Samantha sat up in bed. "Listen to me, Steve Sheridan," she said angrily, "I love Lance, and I'll go to bed with him if I want to."

A knock came on the door. Startled, she grabbed her robe and ran to answer it. Malcomb's quizzical face peered in the crack.

"I thought I heard madam calling."

"No," she said, flushing. "I was talking to myself."

Malcomb shuffled away. Samantha closed the door and leaned against it, hoping Steve hadn't been hurt by that posse or gotten lost or killed.

Lance couldn't rest. His muscles felt tight. Usually on a Sunday he'd lie around the house and start to feel sleepy. But not today—all he could think about was Angie.

He'd done a lot of thinking in the weeks since Angie had left him. And he'd realized that falling in love had never worked for him. He'd loved Lucinda, only to lose her. Then he'd loved Angie and lost her.

Well, he'd gotten over 'Cinda—he could get over Angie. He trusted that. But still, night after night he had worked himself to exhaustion, only to go home and be haunted by her. To save what little sanity he still had, he had decided that the solution was to marry Samantha. He would propose to her tonight and marry her as soon as his divorce was final.

He closed his eyes; Angie's face appeared before him, her porcelain-smooth skin glowing, her small coral freckles perfectly positioned to make his lips long to kiss them. The vision of her, so still and perfect, caused a pang around his heart. Love seared him. Scalded him.

Angie was an odd combination of toughness, sweetness, and fragility. She was soft as a kitten in some ways. Tough as catgut in others. And only she knew when she'd be which. He liked being kept a little off-balance by a woman. Part of him liked routine and knowing what to expect, but part of him liked her stubbornness and wildness and independence.

One night they had gone to a party. She'd danced with other men, so he had danced with other women. After a while, he had looked for her and been told she'd left. He had gone looking for her, only to find her at home, naked and furious with jealousy. When he opened the door, she'd thrown a perfume bottle at him, barely missing. He'd tackled her and they'd made love the rest of the night. She had just the right amount of wildness and passion.

Now the image he carried in his heart—of a fragile beauty with vivid, flashing dark eyes and shining, wheat-colored hair—tormented him nightly. She had slim fingers with perfect little oval fingerprints. Slim, golden, delicate feminine fingers. Hands so soft and fragile to the touch that he felt certain he could crush every bone in them with no trouble at all.

But those same hands got strong when she wanted to do something with them. He'd never understood how that happened. They could be so soft and delicate to touch, and yet so powerful when she was working. He'd seen her lift and position the heaviest camera effortlessly.

She could handle anything she wanted to handle. But she couldn't handle his wanting a baby. Even when she didn't have to do anything about it. Rage came up in him; he had the insane desire to throttle her.

Instead he stood and walked into his office to the telephone he rarely used. He gave the operator his brother's telephone number and waited until Malcomb answered.

"Malcomb, this is Mr. Kincaid—Lance," he said, clarifying.

"Yes, sir?"

"After you serve dinner tonight for Mrs. Forrester and myself, you and your staff may be excused."

"Why, thank you, sir," Malcomb said, his thin voice registering his surprise.

"You're welcome."

"Shall we stay to pick up the dishes, sir?"

"That won't be necessary. Does my brother happen to have a bottle of good wine in the cellar?"

"A very nice one, actually. Tastes like rum punch. I think you had a bit of it at Christmastime."

"We'll have that."

"This neckline is cut lower than I remembered," Samantha said to Jennie's maid, Amanda, who knelt beside her smoothing the blue silk princess gown that hugged Samantha's slender waist and fanned out in gores to her ankles. Long blue velvet ribbons streamed from the poufed blue lace sleeves to her hem. She touched her diamond-and-sapphire pendant. The jewels glittered, and her breasts looked full and rosy in the light of the electric lamps on either side of the vanity.

A knock at her door caused Samantha to turn from the mirror. "I'll get the door," she said, stepping around Amanda.

She opened it to find Lance there, looking extremely handsome in a dark blue serge suit that showed off his broad shoulders and slim hips. His white shirt and collar gleamed brightly against darkly tanned skin.

"I thought I'd save Malcomb a climb up the stairs," he said, smiling.

"Oh, well, thank you. I'm ready."

Lance held out his arm for her. "You look beautiful in blue . . . any color for that matter."

The look in his eyes caused heat to flush her cheeks. "Why, thank you," she said, her heart pounding against her suddenly dry throat.

He walked her downstairs with unaccustomed gravity and seated her at the head of the table with himself on her right. She felt very much a queen, looking down the long, highly polished mahogany table, bare except for two place settings.

Lance remained quiet while dinner was being served. Only after Malcomb and Amanda withdrew to the pantry did he speak.

"Sam," he began, a pained expression mottling his usually smooth brow, "I need to apologize to you for my behavior when I visited you."

"You don't," she whispered.

"Yes, I do. I acted like a damned fool—"

"Then I forgive you," she said interrupting him. "For anything and everything you think you did wrong."

They sat in silence for a moment. Then Lance looked at her closely. "If we marry, will you come and live with me in Durango, where I work?"

Caught off-guard by such bluntness, Samantha stammered. "Why . . . uh . . . yes, of course."

Lance digested that for a moment, then asked, "Do you think you might want to have another . . . uh . . . other children?"

Surprised, Samantha put down her fork. "Why, yes. I suppose so."

They ate in silence for a moment. Then Lance took a bite of his dessert and swallowed it without chewing. "Sam, have you ever, or maybe I should say, do you now harbor a burning desire to be a career woman?"

For the first time in his life, probably, he now sounded like an attorney. Samantha stifled the urge to smile. He was being so serious, uncharacteristically serious. "Why, no. I don't think so," she said carefully.

Malcomb stepped into the room. "If that will be all, sir . . . ?"

"Thank you, Malcomb. Good night," Lance said firmly.

Malcomb bowed stiffly and backed out of the room. Lance stood abruptly and offered Samantha his arm. She looked from Malcomb's retreating form to Lance's hand, feeling like a woman who had missed a beat on the dance floor and was now hopelessly out of step.

Confused, she stood, and Lance guided her to the veranda doors. He opened them and led her to the stone railing that enclosed the small patio, his hands firm and purposeful on her waist. Then he turned her; his eyes burned into hers.

"You look stunning in that gown," he said, his raspy voice barely more than a whisper.

"So do you," she said nonsensically.

Still gazing intently into her eyes, he leaned down and brought his lips to her forehead. Her own eyes closed; she waited with heart barely beating. He kissed her lightly, first on the forehead, then on the cheeks. Being in his arms felt like a homecoming, but something vague and disquieting niggled in her mind, causing her to pull back.

"Malcomb—" she began.

Lance raised an eyebrow at her. "Has gone to bed," he whispered, pulling her forcefully against the length of him.

Sam was so different from Angie, who would have been as wild and greedy as he. Sam was soft and richly endowed—and sweet as a child. He kissed her slowly, savoring the taste and texture of her mouth, the tremulousness of her body. He knew she was fighting the urge to stop him, to push his hands away from her breasts, praying they didn't slip even lower. But knowing all that only inflamed him the more. He teased her nipples and reveled in her struggle for perfect submission. Knowing how difficult this was for her fed his lust.

He remembered nights when she'd climbed into his bed for comfort. Long after he'd comforted her, he had lain awake, aching with the need to shove his young tool into something, anything, to cool the fires that her nearness had roused. He'd never touched Sam inappropriately then, because it had been unthinkable to him. She was a child then, even softer and needier than now.

But she wasn't a child now, for all the emotional similarities. She was a woman, opening her mouth and her legs to him. And he was the needy one now, too ravaged by Angie's leaving to stop himself from taking the comfort Sam offered.

Sam pushed against his chest. "What?" he asked.

"I can't do this," she whimpered.

"What's wrong?" he rasped.

"I don't know," she wailed. It didn't make sense, because this was exactly what she had always wanted. But a sense of panic almost overwhelmed her.

Knock, knock, knock.

The sound was coming from the front door. Lance frowned and released her. "Stay right here," he said. "I'll get it."

She barely had time to catch her breath before he was back. "It's a telegram. For you."

"Oh, no."

She ripped it open, saw the words, but at first her mind refused to read them. "It's Nicholas," she whispered.

Lance took it from her and read it aloud. " 'Nicholas taken sick. Come at once. Juana.' "

"Oh, God." Juana was not a sophisticated woman. She would not think of a telegram unless something awful had happened. Panic gripped her. Tears streamed down her cheeks. And she knew suddenly that this was the moment she had dreaded all her life. This was the moment she had come to Arizona Territory to avoid.

Lance insisted on going with her. They reached her house at midnight. Samantha could hear the wheezing from the front door.

"Oh, God!" She groaned, cursing herself for leaving him. She ran all the way to the bedroom.

"*Señora!* Thank the good Lord you've come," Juana cried, wiping tears from her eyes.

Lance stopped at the door of the sickroom. Samantha checked Nicholas and found his forehead hot to her touch. His fever was at least a hundred and four degrees. His nose ran. His eyes watered. He shook with chills. His breathing was labored.

"Oh, baby, I shouldn't have left you," she whispered.

Nicholas opened his eyes and then closed them again.

Lance sniffed the air of the sickroom. "Sam, come here a minute."

Frowning, she turned and walked toward him.

"Smell that?" he demanded. "He has measles. I can smell them."

"Measles!" Samantha said between ragged breaths.

"Yes, measles," he said, grinning. "They smell like red ants taste."

She turned to Juana. "Have you had measles?"

"*Sí.*"

Then to Tristera. "And you?"

"Yes, it was the worst two weeks of my life. Four children at the school died."

"He'll be fine. This isn't wonderful news, but it's better than I expected," Lance said, backing out of the room. Samantha followed him outside.

"Take care of my boy," he growled, pulling her into his arms for a quick hug.

"I will."

"I think he'll be all right now that his mother's home." Lance rubbed her cheek with his hand. "In case you didn't understand what was going on back there," he said, tilting his head toward Phoenix. "I . . . uh . . . think . . . hope . . . that I proposed to you."

"You did?"

"In my own clumsy way, yes."

Samantha frowned. "And what did I say?"

"I think you said yes."

That jolted Samantha. "It wasn't very romantic."

"I'm too old for romance, Sam. If there is one thing I've learned from my experiences in love, it is that life is too serious to take casually. I've tried romance. It doesn't work."

"But . . ."

"Trust me, Sam," he said firmly. "I can be romantic later, after we settle our differences, if there are any."

"This feels too much like the last time you proposed to me."

Lance sighed. "Sam . . ."

"Don't say it. I've gone along with everything, because I love you. Really love you. But I—I," she said, pausing to gather her courage, "I think you had better settle things with Angie before we consider ourselves engaged."

"I can't settle things with Angie. She's . . ." He stopped.

Samantha frowned, guessing what he'd been about to say. "She isn't dead, Lance. She's angry."

The stubborn look was back in his eyes. Muscles writhed beneath the smooth, darkly tanned skin of his jaw.

"She's dead as far as I'm concerned."

"Lucinda is dead. Angie is alive and well and probably suffering."

Raw pain flashed deep in Lance's eyes; she saw the reflection of it. Compassion for him ached through her. This was the Lance she loved. She longed to take him into her arms, but she resisted. "Lance, you need to talk this out with Angie. I won't promise to marry you until you do."

"All right, Sam, but it won't do any good. I don't give any woman two chances at me." Before she could reply, he turned and strode toward the waiting locomotive.

Steve hadn't returned. Samantha noted that fact with concern, but she was too busy taking care of Nicholas to think about anything the rest of that night. At first she had been as relieved as Lance, but as the disease progressed she worried anew. Measles often turned malignant, and after seeing how ill her son was, she realized they could be deadly to him, already weakened as he was by consumption.

She sent Juana to bed to keep her from collapsing with worry. Then she and Tristera sat with Nicholas through the night, applying hot bran poultices to his chest to ease the breathing.

The next afternoon, Samantha walked wearily to Nicholas's window and looked out. From the north she saw a man on horseback riding toward the house. It was too far away to be sure, but it looked like Steve. Her heart leapt and began to beat faster.

"Watch Nicholas for me," she said to Tristera.

"*Sí,*" she said, not looking up from the sleeping boy.

Samantha slipped out of the room and hurried down the stairs. She stopped on the landing to look into the mirror and groaned at the disheveled image that looked back at her. She looked wan and tired. Hair straggled from her bun, but there was nothing she could do about it now. She pinched her cheeks, wet her lips, and tried to push some of the wisps of stray hair back into place. She couldn't look worse!

Finally she continued on down the stairs and out onto the porch. Steve dismounted at the house and started up the steps. His cheeks were dark with beard stubble, his hat and clothes coated with sand. In spite of it, or perhaps because of it, he exuded male power.

"Better stop there," she said, stepping out onto the porch.

"That bad, huh?" he asked ruefully.

"Have you had the measles?" she asked.

"Years ago."

"Well then, I guess you'll be safe here. Nicholas has measles."

"I wouldn't go that far," he said dryly. "How's he doing?"

Samantha ignored his jab at her. "Not good. He's resting now, though." She paused. "We've been worried sick about you and Ramon. What happened? Did the posse find him?"

Steve's eyes, hazel in the sunlight, seemed to shine with reflected light. His gaze flitted over her, causing her chest to tighten. Her right hand stole up to rearrange her hair. She should have changed her gown. It was old and unattractive.

"The posse didn't find him, but I did. Ramon's been shot. One of those bullets we heard caught him in the back."

"Oh, no! How bad?"

"Bad enough. Fortunately for him, the bullet went all the way through. I took him to a safe place, then rejoined the posse. After they gave up, I bought supplies in town and took them back to Ramon. I stayed with him as long as I could. He's doing better, but I'll need to go back soon with more food."

"I thought you were wasting your time," she whispered, ashamed.

"I saved Ramon twice before. What made you think I couldn't do it again?"

"I don't know."

Steve had expected her to attribute the very finest motives to everything he did, but her eyes told him she'd had experiences with other men that had left her unsure of all men.

Steve started past her. She reached out and touched his arm. She wanted to let go of his arm, but once touched . . .

"Steve . . . I'm sorry."

He glanced down at her hand on his arm. It was slim and beautiful—and seemed to gleam with the same shimmer as her bewitching face. Her touching him triggered a sudden release of rage, like steam, into his blood.

"Do I look like a house cat to you?" he snarled.

"What do you mean?" Samantha asked, her lovely face flushing with embarrassment, her hand wavering, then dropping to her side.

Steve glanced quickly around to see if anyone was watching, then he grabbed her wrist, dragged her into the parlor, and kicked the door closed.

"Just what I said," he growled. "Do I look like a damned

pet, that you can flaunt your lover in front of me, spend the weekend with him, and then pet me a few times and I'll forget?''

The sharp light in his khaki eyes told her he was furious. His hands held her arms above the elbows, immobilizing them. Such heat had come up in him that she felt it arcing the short distance between his body and hers.

''I didn't mean . . .''

''Yes, you did,'' he growled. ''You aren't a child, Samantha Forrester. You know what you're doing to me. And to him. We're both dancing to your tune.''

''No, it isn't like that—''

He cut off the rest of her words with his mouth. Samantha tried to resist, but the heat and excitement of his kiss devastated her. She felt herself collapsing, even as his arms closed around her, pressing her weakened body against his angry one. His kiss was hard and demanding. She felt it the length of her body, as if all her most sensitive places had fused into one contact point that responded to his lips and tongue, invading even her soul.

He released her abruptly, leaving her gasping for breath and sanity. ''So, what did you two do in Phoenix?''

''Noth—nothing.''

''Did he make love to you?''

''That is none of your business,'' she said weakly.

''He did then,'' he said grimly. The anguish in his eyes caused her heart to constrict.

''No, he didn't.''

''You don't have to lie to me.''

''Thank you, Mr. Sheridan. I appreciate that concession.''

Defiance and anger sparkled in her lovely eyes. Steve could not believe that Lando would pass up an opportunity to get her into bed, but she looked so indignant, perhaps it was possible.

''His tough luck then.'' He released her abruptly and stalked past her toward Nicholas's room, leaving her still gasping for breath and wishing she could throttle him.

Samantha expected Steve to go on up to the work site, but he took one look at Nicholas, saw how sick he was, and stayed to help take care of him. The boy seemed to draw strength from his presence. That night, Steve sent Samantha, Juana, and Tristera to bed, insisting they needed the rest.

Samantha laid down to rest her eyes and opened them to bright sunlight streaming in her window. Amazed that she'd slept the whole night through, and remembering suddenly the note she'd gotten, she ran down the hall and slipped noiselessly into Nicholas's room.

She didn't know what she had expected, probably anything except the sight that greeted her: Steve asleep in the rocking chair, her son cradled in his arms. Nicholas's face was pressed to Steve's breast, his thin arm crooked around Steve's sturdy neck.

Emotion swept through her. Tears tingled in her throat, aching to be cried. Tristera tiptoed into the room and stopped beside her.

"Perhaps we should take a picture of this for the one who wrote the note."

"What?" Steve croaked, blinking groggily.

"We were just admiring your motherly ways," Samantha said softly.

"Nicholas was having trouble breathing," he rasped. "So we sat up."

Gratitude was so heavy in Samantha it felt like tears. She turned away, so he wouldn't see them.

"Hey, look at this," Steve whispered, lifting Nicholas's pajamas. His stomach was covered with tiny red points. "That's what I was waiting for," he said, smiling at Tristera, avoiding Samantha.

By midmorning the measles began to appear all over Nicholas's body, from his scalp to the bottoms of his feet. By noon, he was covered with tiny red points. As if that signaled the worst was over, even his breathing came more easily.

"This is great," Nicholas said, marveling at the density and redness. "Can I keep them?"

"I doubt you'll want them once they start to itch," Steve said, grinning.

"Tristera," Samantha said, "Would you ask Juana to find the calomel lotion."

Samantha turned to Steve, smiling. "Thank you for all your help."

"Welcome," he said gruffly.

"Are you still angry at me?"

Steve shrugged. "I decided maybe you were telling the truth."

"Oh, and why?"

"Because," Steve said, grinning, "if he'd made love to you, he wouldn't have let you come back. He'd keep you there with him. Probably forever."

The way he said it sounded like an admission of what he

would have done. And the look in his eyes was revealing and stunning at the same time. She felt humbled by so much honesty.

"Thank you."

"Welcome," he said, his voice gruff. "Well, I guess I have to check on this house I'm supposed to be building. I think I've still got a job."

At the house site, Steve found Ian Macready at the west end of the new basement, yelling at a man who had just spilled a load of adobe bricks off a gangplank laid over a small ditch.

"Air ye blind or drunk, laddie?" Macready bellowed.

"He was daydreaming about his ladylove," another hod carrier yelled.

Steve answered Ian's questions, ate the evening meal with him, then shaved, washed, and changed. Ian followed him to the barn, just finished that morning. Steve saddled and mounted Calico.

"I'll be back in a day or so. In the meantime, I know you'll make it come out right."

"Ho, laddie, that we will."

Steve reached the old house at sunset. Juana packed two saddlebags full of food for Ramon. Steve turned Calico out to pasture, saddled a fresh horse for himself and a mare for Tristera, and led them out of the barn. Samantha Forrester blocked his path.

"You're taking Tristera?"

"Ramon might need a nurse."

"I generally decide which of my employees does what."

"I guess I was thinking of her as a friend of Ramon's, not an employee of yours. I suppose I could take Juana," he said, grinning at the thought of Juana's bulk bobbing around on a horse.

"There are others on this ranch besides Tristera and Juana."

Steve frowned. "Like who?"

Samantha's lovely eyes reflected deep hurt. "I could nurse Ramon," she said, her voice husky.

"I thought of that, but I knew you wouldn't leave Nicholas here sick," he said.

"He's over the worst of it." She realized she had momentarily forgotten about Nicholas, but remembering didn't stop her from feeling rejected. "Fine," she said, turning away, "take anyone you want."

Steve expelled a heavy breath and shook his head. It was his curse to rub her the wrong way. He'd be lucky to stick here long enough to build another outhouse.

With Nicholas recovering, life began to return to normal. Samantha looked up from figuring a payroll to see a train inching across the desert. A spiral of black smoke lifted into the still air behind it.

The train arrived minutes later carrying the lumber Steve had ordered. The engineer gave her a letter with a Los Angeles postmark from her sister-in-law, Jennie, which was chatty and full of family gossip.

The train's crew unloaded stacks of yellow, gleaming oak, which smelled resiny and wonderful. She was pleased. She had been waiting for the lumber. Digging a basement might be necessary, but it didn't look much like progress. She wanted to see walls go up.

That afternoon Marshal Daley rode out with a small posse looking for Ramon. Samantha told them she hadn't seen Ramon since the night in town, but they searched the house and barn and all the outbuildings anyway.

That evening Steve and Tristera rode up to the barn and dismounted. Samantha waited on the porch swing.

Steve walked from the barn and sat down on the porch swing beside her. He stretched his legs out and sighed, and Samantha realized how tired he must be. He'd been riding since Sunday night. Ramon wasn't even Steve's problem.

"How was he?"

"I think he was still there, but he didn't show himself. We left supplies and blankets."

"He may be dead."

"Dead men don't walk away."

"Why would he hide?"

"He could have been off looking for food. I fired a couple of shots to bring him back and that might have scared him. I think he'll find the things we left. When did this come?" he asked, pointing to the lumber stacked beside the barn.

"This afternoon. There must be a reason why you didn't find him."

"It's a big valley. One man could easily conceal himself. I'm not as worried as I was. I'll go back in a week and see if he took the food. In the meantime, try not to worry. His not being there is a good sign. We could have found a body."

* * *

A week later Ed Stokes, one of the cowhands, approached
Tristera awkwardly, shyly, as if the act of stopping her were as
serious as proposing marriage.

"Miss Tristera, ma'am?"

"*Sí?*"

"That Silver Fish, he's lookin' to tawk to y'all."

"Did he say why?"

Stokes recovered somewhat. "Danged if I know."

Curious, Tristera caught one of the horses in the corral, slipped
onto its bare back, and rode to the Indian camp. The women
looked at her with curious eyes. She nodded to them and rode
to where Silver Fish worked with a hide. He was one of the
handsomest warriors she had ever seen. His fine black eyes
watched her closely. His body was tall and straight, his limbs
clean and well developed.

"You wish to speak with me?"

Silver Fish put down his skinning knife. "In town we met
with Indians who say you look like the Hopi Indian woman who
killed the five old men."

Fear ached dully around her heart, like an old wound. "Do
they look for her to kill her?"

Silver Fish shrugged. The soldiers wanted to kill her, and it
was probably the same with the Indian police.

Tristera was not surprised that her own people would send
out scouts to kill her. People harbored misconceptions about the
Hopi, thinking them peaceful, placid, and accepting, when in
fact Hopi warriors were as fierce as any.

She was filled with shame and despair. Part of her hoped they
did kill her. Then at least she would not have to suffer these
horrible pangs of guilt about Tuvi's death.

"They are right. I am the one they all look for," she said
defiantly.

"The rainmaker?"

"*Sí.*"

"Perhaps for us you could make small rain."

"I cannot."

"Too bad," he said. "My first wife, she has planted the seeds,
but seeds need rain to grow."

Tristera shook her head. "I cannot make rain."

"The Hopi would like to know where you are," Silver Fish
said, watching her closely.

She had to be careful. Whatever she said, Silver Fish would

carry these words to others, who would carry them to her people at Third Mesa. "I suppose you will tell them."

"No. Unless you wish me to."

"I do not wish it."

Silver Fish nodded. Relieved, Tristera mounted and rode back to the barn.

General Ashland waited impatiently. At last, footsteps sounded in the outer office. Captain Rathwick stopped in the doorway. "You wanted to see me, sir?"

"Sit down, Captain."

Rathwick crossed the office and sat down facing his commander. Ashland reached back, picked up a box, and dumped its contents on his desk. "Do you know what this is, Captain?"

"Looks like dirty white buckskin."

"It's a buckskin dress and a feather bonnet." Ashland raised his eyebrows. "You were supposed to bring this to me with the woman still in it."

Rathwick frowned. "Where was it found?"

"About six miles from Picket Post, beside the railroad tracks."

"Maybe that's why we didn't find her."

General Ashland slammed his fist down on the desk beside the dirty buckskin. "I don't want excuses. I want you to find her, dammit!"

"There are thousands of Indians in the Arizona Territory, sir. I don't even know what she looks like. It would make more sense for Lawson to look for her. At least he saw her."

"Lawson is insubordinate. Unless you want to be labeled the same, bring me this woman!" Ashland repeated grimly.

"Yes, sir." Rathwick stood up. He wadded up the dirty buckskin and carried it out of the room. At least he could take some measurements and figure out how big she really was. Rumors placed her size at close to six feet.

Back in his room, he spread the buckskins on his bed and went to find a tape measure. A few minutes later he was back. He found a pencil and paper, smoothed the garment out on his bed, and stretched the tape measure from neckline to hem.

Twenty minutes later he sat staring at the paper. According to his measurements, the woman was small. An image of Tristera Rodriguez flashed before his eyes.

"No," he said aloud. It couldn't be. Mrs. Forrester had vouched for her. But somewhere in Arizona Territory there was a woman he needed to find. And she wasn't six feet tall as the boy had said. She was closer to five feet tall. And she wasn't Hopi. This was a Plains Indian getup. No Hopi would have been wearing this.

A week dragged by. Then another. On Tuesday evening, after two weeks without a sight of Steve's sturdy form, Samantha stepped out of the bathtub in the kitchen and took the towel Juana held out to her. The room smelled of warm water and peppermint castile soap.

Samantha dried herself and spread peppermint-scented lotion on her skin from throat to toes. In the lamplight, her skin was soft and lovely. This should have made her feel good, but she realized time was passing, her beauty was fading, and even though men showed occasional interest in her, she was still alone, with no one to share herself or her life.

"The *señora* will go to the new house tomorrow?"

"No. No, I don't have to go every single week," she said irritably. "We'll can peaches tomorrow. The early peaches are ready. The trees are heavy with them."

"Sorry," Juana mumbled.

In her bed, Samantha tossed half the night. She kept seeing Steve's face when he told her that Lance wouldn't have let her leave if he'd made love to her.

She was suffering from badly mixed emotions. On the one hand she realized that by sending him back into the arms of his wife, she'd probably ruined any chance of having Lance.

And she hadn't heard a word from Lance. He must be in San Francisco by now. They'd probably made up. It would be just like him to forget to write and let her know.

On top of that she'd infuriated Steve, again. She closed her eyes, saw Steve's face and the momentary anguish in his eyes when he'd thought she had slept with Lance, and smiled into the darkness. She hated to think of herself as a mean woman, but she liked knowing how that had affected him.

There was the nicest curve in his neck, chin, and jaw, especially when he was frustrated and angry. Anger seemed to enhance the manly fierceness he exuded.

Then, unbidden, her mind recalled how his lips had felt, claiming hers. A warm, sweet, achy little itch started deep in her belly, and once started, it tormented her most of the night.

* * *

The next morning she washed in her basin, dressed carefully, choosing one of her most attractive riding habits.

"I thought you wanted to can peaches today," Juana said when she walked into the kitchen dressed for riding.

"I changed my mind. I don't feel like it." That admission made her feel weepy. No tears came, but Juana saw it in her eyes and turned away.

"Go see new house. That will make you feel less bad."

"I don't know," Samantha said, flushing that she would lie to sweet, loyal Juana. "Maybe I should. I'm feeling restless. A ride *might* help. Will you sit Nicholas down with his lessons? Tell him to read the novel and work on his book report."

"*Sí, señora.* Read nobbel, work on book report."

CHAPTER FOURTEEN

Near the work site Samantha stopped behind the last bush big enough to shelter her from view of the noisy workmen.

Shamefully aware of her shaking hands and pounding heart, she was glad for this moment of privacy before she faced Steve Sheridan. His piercing eyes would just have to glance at her to know she'd lain awake most of the night, rehearsing what to say to him.

The lusty cries of male voices mingled with the crack of hammers on nails. Every hammer crack was echoed back by the mountain, setting up a wild cacophony. Steve's deep bronze voice rang out above the others, sending a thrill down her spine and making her even more reluctant to ride out and let him see her. With trembling hand, she patted Brickelbush's damp neck.

As she watched, Steve stepped out of the barn and walked with springy step toward the basement walls, rising raggedly out of the Earth, ten courses high in one area, twenty or more in others. Steve stepped through the basement doorway and disappeared inside. Samantha urged her horse forward.

Out of the corner of her eye she saw a movement on the hill overlooking the house site. The movement was significant enough to make her look again—this time more carefully. Facing the house, with his profile to her, a man with a bandanna from nose to chin rested his hands on what looked like the T-shaped handle of a butter churn.

Samantha realized from the mask and the furtive way the man squatted over the handle that he probably did not work for Steve. Then she realized the butter churn might be a plunger.

In the basement, Steve stopped at the door. Eddy Nabosky was bent over—looking at something his broom had uncovered in a pile of sawdust and wooden blocks. "What'd you find?"

"I don't know," he said, trying to lift it. Steve stepped closer, saw the sticks of dynamite tied together with two leather strings, a wire leading away from it.

"Dynamite!" a voice yelled from outside.

* * *

"Dynamite!" Samantha yelled again, leaning over her horse's neck, urging him toward the masked man, now bending forward to lean on the plunger. It was probably too late to do anything for Steve or the men working below, but it was not too late to ride down their attacker.

The man pushed down the plunger and ran. Samantha kicked her horse's sides, her mind not fully accepting dynamite and all it would mean.

Steve looked over the shoulder-high brick wall and saw Samantha Forrester spurring her mount up the hill, a masked man running ahead of her. Steve reached for an ax someone had left standing beside the door.

"Get out!" he yelled at Eddy, and lifted the ax over his head, bringing it down into the new subflooring with a solid thwack. Ian wouldn't be pleased about that.

Steve checked to be sure he'd cut the wire in two, then turned to Nabosky.

"Are you all right?" It was a foolish question. Steve could see Eddy was fine, except for the fear that had rattled them both.

"Yes, sir."

"Good."

Samantha spurred her mount up the last steep embankment. The man reached his horse the same time Samantha's horse heaved over the top, too close for the saboteur to mount without her riding into him. He drew his pistol and fired. Samantha felt herself lose her seat, lift up, and soar over her horse's head, straight at the barrel of the gun.

As she flew through the air she had all the time she needed to think about her life, which might be over in a moment. It occurred to her that in spite of the mask, the man was too big-eyed and delicate-looking for a killer. She would have thought more about that, but her mind settled on the fact that she was going to die . . . and she hadn't even made love with Steve Sheridan.

Before she was entirely through regretting that, she heard the crash of gunfire and hit the ground. Aside from not being able to breathe, she was surprised that it didn't hurt and that she hadn't heard the explosion. Maybe it hadn't been dynamite at all. Or maybe she was dead and wouldn't hear anything . . . ever again.

* * *

The sound of gunfire brought Steve running. He saw men yelling and charging up the hill behind the house site.

"The bastard's shot Mrs. Forrester!" a man shouted.

A hundred men dropped their tools and swarmed up the slope. Steve put down the ax and ran up the hill, dreading to see what he might find when he reached her.

The crowd around Samantha parted for him. Steve knelt beside her, felt for the pulse in her throat, and found it, pumping nicely. He looked for bullet holes but didn't see any.

"She's . . . alive," he croaked, his voice breaking. "Best not to move her until she wakes up. She may have broken something," he said to the men standing around them, muttering their relief.

"Did anyone see who did this?"

"Damned right we did! But he got away on horseback."

Steve turned back to Samantha Forrester, who was stirring. "Is everyone all right?" she asked, looking around her at the silent, watching men.

"Everyone but you. How d'you feel?"

"What happened to the man with the . . . ?"

"He got away."

With Steve's help, Samantha sat up. "I thought you'd be killed," she whispered.

Steve told her how Eddy had uncovered the dynamite just as she'd yelled. When he finished, she tried to stand, only to discover her ankle had been sprained in the fall. Steve offered to carry her, but Samantha shook her head. She was shaky enough without being carried by Steve Sheridan.

"Just give me your arm."

She took a dozen steps on the painful ankle; her lips turned white. Steve scooped her up into his arms and carried her down the hill toward his cottage, one of the first buildings completed.

Once it was done and she was in his arms, she tried to relax, but every nerve in her body responded to him. It wasn't fair that she could love Lance and respond to Steve in this way.

"Isn't that better?" he asked.

"I thought . . . when I realized that was an apparatus for setting off an explosion, I thought you'd all be killed."

"Your warning probably delayed him just enough so I could cut the wire."

"Then I'm a heroine. How nice."

Steve laughed. Beneath his laughter, she sensed a hard edge

of masculine purpose. It was that hard edge that kept leading her on. She had realized at the beginning that she could say anything to him and be fully understood, but theirs was no benign friendship. He was male and she female. No matter what else conspired between them, she remained vibrantly aware of his implacable masculinity. He glanced down at her; a light deep in his eyes made her catch her breath.

"You're panting, Steve Sheridan," she said. "Better stop and rest. This wonderful frame of yours isn't as powerful as it looks, is it?"

Steve glowered down at her. His arms around her were too strong. His shirt against her face smelled of resin and his own male scent, which was salty and disturbing.

Still dazed by the fall, her mind drifted. She imagined Steve carrying her to his lair and ravishing her. She hoped he didn't feel her trembling, or if he did, that he attributed it to the fear of their near disaster.

The inside of his cottage smelled of new pine furniture. In his bedroom, he lowered her gently onto a feather bed. "You rest here. You've had a nasty spill."

"What will you do?"

"Go back to work," he said, his tone closing the subject. "I can't loaf with the boss up here."

Samantha laughed. "You must be the most diligent man I've ever known. Certainly the most diligent I've ever hired. To go back to work immediately after almost being blown up. Will you send a man to tell Juana I've been delayed?"

"Good idea."

Steve stalked outside and yelled for the men to get back to work. Samantha relaxed into the feather mattress. She lay there for a while, listening to the sound of men working.

It felt good to lie in Steve's bed, smelling his pillow, which still carried his scent. But something about the incident bothered her. Something didn't ring true. She had the feeling that she'd missed an important detail, although she couldn't think what it might be.

Samantha had no memory of falling asleep, but she woke in a dark room, her mouth dry, as if she'd been breathing through it. A sound in the other room told her she was not alone.

"Steve?"

Footsteps stopped at the bedroom door. "Aye, lass?"

"Where's Steve?"

"Went to call on a neighbor."

Ian Macready lit the lamp on the bureau, carried in a tray, and put it down on her lap.

"You're a good nurse, Ian."

"Aye, lass. And rainwater is dry, too."

"Which neighbor?"

"Now you'd already be knowing, lass, that I dinna have the least idea."

"We only have one neighbor on the north and one on the east. Joe Dart or—"

"Aye, lass. That's the name," he said, smiling.

Fear gripped her, but it was apparent Ian didn't know Steve had ridden into danger.

"Did he go alone?"

"Aye, that he did."

Samantha felt faint. Steve had gone to pick a fight with Ham Russell and his men. He would probably be killed. She calculated how long it would take him to get there and back.

"What time is it?"

Ian Macready pulled his gold watch out of his vest. "Seven o'clock, almost."

"He's been gone for hours!"

"Aye, mayhap they invited him to sup. He's a right charming lad when he puts his mind to it."

Samantha felt panic rising within her, but she controlled it. After all, Steve Sheridan was a grown man. He wouldn't deliberately go off to get killed.

She picked at the dinner Ian had brought her, brushed her teeth with a toothbrush and some tooth powder she found on the bureau beside the basin, undressed, put on one of Steve's nightshirts, and climbed back into bed. Her ankle was much better. She barely limped. Lying in Steve's bed reminded her of being with Jared, and there were many good memories from that time.

Ian knocked on the bedroom door.

"Come in."

He brought her a selection of books he'd found in the parlor and moved the lamp from the bureau to a table he pulled next to the bed. It was apparent Steve didn't read in bed.

"Sleep tight, lassie."

"Thanks, Ian."

Samantha picked through the magazines, chose a trade journal for builders, and leafed through it until she felt drowsy. She turned down the wick until the flame guttered out and closed her eyes. Except for the sound of crickets and men snoring, the work site was quiet. She pressed her face into the pillow. The smell—salty and slightly oily—reminded her of Steve, whetting some hungry part of her.

Steve should have been back by now. She refused to give way to her terror, but it was like tottering at the brink of a dreadful chasm, knowing what she would see if she dared look into it. Even so, she tossed and turned for what seemed most of the night.

Midnight. Steve still hadn't come. The nightshirt itched. She slipped out of it, tossed it to the foot of the bed. What a relief! She scratched herself all over in a virtual frenzy.

One o'clock. He still hadn't come. She may have drifted off. She woke suddenly, feeling startled, as if she'd had a bad dream she couldn't remember.

Outside, she heard the ring of a shod hoof on rock and jumped up. Grabbing the blanket off the bed, she wrapped it around her, and limped through the dark parlor.

She waited at the front door, her eyes scanning the darkness. Finally she saw a horse, walking slowly, as if trying not to awaken the sleeping camp. Samantha wished she had a gun.

At last the rider came close enough for her to see his silhouette against the lighter sky. "Steve?"

"Yeah, it's me," Steve said, his voice low.

Joy flooded her body. Tears of relief spilled over and ran down her cheeks. The dread chasm did not have to be faced. She had never been so relieved in her life.

Steve dismounted and walked toward her. Shivering, she met him halfway. "Hey," he whispered, "you shouldn't be out in the cold with bare feet."

"I thought they'd killed you."

"I'm fine."

"You liar," she said accusingly.

Steve chuckled. "That's a hard name for a man who's been riding most of the day. Just goes to show you don't have a real fine appreciation for how hard I work."

"You could have been killed!"

"I almost was."

Samantha pressed against him, so glad to see him—to smell his familiar fragrance—that she couldn't stop crying. She just stood there, huddled in the blanket, shivering and crying silent tears.

"Hey, what's wrong?" Her hair smelled faintly of peppermint. She seemed to be trembling and crying. Confused, he eased his finger under her chin and lifted it. Moonlight filtering through the pine trees reflected off tears. "Did someone hurt you?"

"I was scared for you."

"For me?" His own heart pounded hard. "I should think you'd be glad to be rid of me."

"Glad? Steve Sheridan!"

"Well, all you've done is fight with me. And tell me about your married lover."

She shook her head in frustration. She looked beautiful and sweet and miserable.

"You lied to me!"

"I did not," he said, pulling her into his arms. She surged against him strongly. The blanket dropped away. "Hey," he repeated, grabbing at it and missing, all his tiredness leaving him. Her body shimmered in the moonlight.

Steve didn't know whether to kiss her or grab her blanket, but his body seemed to know. He gathered her into his arms and kissed her.

Samantha moaned with pleasure. His arms around her, his mouth on hers, were the most necessary things she had ever felt. If she lived to be a thousand years old, she felt certain she would never need anything as much as she needed the feel of his mouth and body this moment.

Still kissing her, he picked her up, carried her into the house, and lowered her onto the bed. She opened her eyes to see him unbuttoning his shirt, his broad shoulders blocking out the window square of moonlight as he peeled it off and tossed it on the floor.

She closed her eyes, but not seeing didn't slow her trembling. Steve dropped his boots, his socks, and finally his pants on the floor. The bedsprings screeched as he lay down beside her. She didn't breathe. His hand touched her cheek, then slid down over her quivering flesh from throat to loins.

"I've been trying to avoid this ever since I met you, Samantha Forrester." His voice accused her.

"I know," she whispered, gripped by a strong sense of destiny. She, too, had been trying to avoid it. "At least we don't have to worry about it anymore."

"I hope that wasn't supposed to make sense," he whispered, pressing his face against her cheek. Samantha knew she was supposed to ask him something, but she felt mesmerized by the radiant warmth of his hands stroking her, holding her, guiding her. His rough cheek felt like sandpaper as his open mouth found hers . . . to kiss her long and deeply.

With Jared her body resisted the moment when he would enter her. But with Steve her body was aware only of the necessity of it, the wonder of him and how he could possibly know exactly what she wanted him to do and how to do it, even to the lightness or insistence of his touch.

At the very end, when she was so crazed by him she felt mindless, he finally slipped inside her. He hardly moved. She moaned and spasmed so hard her legs went straight, her hips arched, and her whole body pulsed with pleasure.

After a time he eased himself out of her and lay beside her, caressing her face. "You're wonderful," he whispered, sliding his warm hand over her breasts, her incurving waist, the slight rise of her mound.

The unfortunate thing was that the minute he said she was wonderful, it reminded her of why she wasn't. She had no business being in love with Lance and in bed with Steve. "No, I'm not. I feel terrible," she said, struggling into a sitting position. His strong hand pushed her back down, cuddled her close to him.

"I hate to argue with you at a time like this, but you feel wonderful—as smooth as a silky kitten."

"I didn't mean on the outside," she said darkly.

Steve grinned, resigned to his fate. "So, what is it you want to fight with me about now?"

"Nothing," she said grumpily. "I just can't imagine you thinking highly of me, in love with another man as I am—and in bed with you."

That sobered him. It took a minute to decide what he did think. "I fell in love with a girl once when I was seventeen or so. She was about as sweet as a girl can be. I'll probably always have a soft spot in my heart for the girl she was. But the woman she is now is married to someone else, the mother of six kids, and fat as a woman can get and still walk upright. I don't see why I should let my boyish love affair spoil the rest of my life."

"But I'm still in love with another man."

"Maybe you are and maybe you aren't."

"I am," she said stubbornly.

"Then how'd you get in my bed?" he asked.

"I don't know," she said, miserable.

Steve cupped her face in his warm hands. ''Look at me, Samantha.''

''Nooooo.''

Steve kissed her lips, gently at first and then more urgently. Samantha held out a moment, but her body started to tremble, and her hands slipped up to caress his neck.

Steve kissed her neck, her chin, and finally, long after she wanted him to, her mouth again. When the kiss ended, she pulled him over on top of her, partly to still the shaking in her body and partly because she wanted to feel the weight of him there. It had been a long time since she'd felt a man's weight on her. It was a feeling she particularly liked.

''I'm too heavy for you,'' he said, rolling onto his side. ''Turn over onto your tummy.''

''Why?''

''Don't be so suspicious. I'm going to rub your back.''

He gave a wonderful back rub. His hands were strong, and just rough enough to feel good on her skin. Her body seemed starved for his touch. She couldn't remember anything feeling so good.

''You remember what I told you about the Great Mystery?'' he whispered, his breath tickling her neck.

''Yes.''

''You know how powerful the Great Mystery is, don't you? He made this whole creation. Made pigs from scratch. Set everything you see here into motion without any help at all.''

''Yes,'' she said, smiling in spite of herself.

''Do you think you could end up in my bed without His permission?''

Samantha laughed. ''I knew your odd philosophy was going to come in handy someday.''

Steve kissed her ear. He nibbled at it with tiny little sucking nips that sent chills down her body all the way to her toes. She forgot to be upset. She turned her face, so he would kiss her mouth, but he didn't. He just kept rubbing her back. He massaged her hands, her arms, her feet, her legs, never touching the parts of her she'd been taught to guard from men. His hands on her back, legs, and thighs excited her so much that her breath came in short, self-conscious pants.

By the time he turned her over, slipped inside her, and cuddled her close to his heart, she was aware of nothing except the wonderful way he held her, rocked her, breathed her in with every breath, seemed to be inhaling her through his pores, his mouth, his body . . .

Afterward, as they lay together, Samantha's body glowed with contentment and bliss. She could have lain there all night, content just to feel his warm skin against her own. Steve finally broke the dreamy silence.

"Your body is smarter than your head," he whispered, his husky voice possessive.

"I think I've just been insulted," she whispered.

Steve chuckled. Samantha liked the sound of his laughter. She didn't feel insulted. She felt wonderful. Night-singing birds called out. She pressed against Steve, sighing, appreciating him. With Jared, once he finished, he was asleep. Steve Sheridan was awake, alert, and charming to her.

"At the picnic you didn't even want to kiss me. Have you figured out what happens next?" asked Samantha.

"No."

"Then why did you change your mind?"

"I didn't."

"But . . ."

"This wasn't my mind."

She couldn't imagine Steve Sheridan out of control enough to do something he didn't want to do. It pleased her tremendously that he had made love to her in spite of himself.

"What happened at the Darts'?"

"Not much, as it turned out."

"Tell me."

"I rode in to ask Ham Russell if he was the one who'd tried to dynamite the house. He wasn't there. Neither was Mrs. Dart. But young Joe came out of the barn and asked me what I wanted. I told him someone had tried to dynamite your new house, but he appeared not to know anything about it. He was pretty decent actually, invited me in to cool off and have a drink of water."

He stretched and slid a hand down her backside. "And we found out why the marshal hasn't come for Ramon."

"You did? Why?"

"Because the man Ramon was supposed to have killed was sitting on the porch in a rocking chair when I rode up."

"Piney?"

"I rode into town and asked Daley about it. He said Joe Dart had come in the following week and said that when they took Piney home to bury him, Chila discovered he wasn't dead."

"What a relief! I'm so pleased! But someone is determined to kill you."

"And whoever it is, is very smart," Steve said.

"What do you mean?"

"To plant that dynamite, he had to sneak up here in the middle of the night without rousing anyone, place it where I'd be likely to go, and then have the guts to wait in broad daylight, watching for me to step into that basement."

"Was that the first time you'd gone into the basement?"

"That day. Yes."

Samantha sighed. "That is pretty determined."

"Well, since I'm probably doomed anyway, maybe you should take pity on me and . . ."

"And what?" she asked, smiling as he nibbled her nose.

"Make love to me again."

"Well . . ."

But he was already moving to take her.

Samantha woke up alone. For one second she couldn't orient herself. Then she recognized the room as Steve's and remembered everything.

"Mrs. Forrester?" Steve's voice, coming from the next room, sounding so formal, made her heart sink.

"Yes?" she asked stiffly.

"May *we* come in?"

Samantha pulled the covers up under her chin.

"Yes, you may!"

"Give me the tray," he said to someone Samantha couldn't see. "I'll take it from here." Footsteps sounded; the front door closed. Samantha licked her lips, sat up in bed. Alone, Steve stopped in her doorway.

"Your breakfast, madame." The warm smile in his eyes answered her most urgent question. "Did you sleep well?"

"I don't know," she admitted ruefully.

Steve laughed. "Me, either."

"Why did you sneak away?"

"Oh, I just thought it might be nice to leave a little doubt in folks' minds," he said, raising an unruly eyebrow at her.

He was right, but she hadn't liked waking up alone.

She ate, washed, and dressed. Then Steve carried her to the buckboard and propped her foot up on the splashboard. She could have ridden home by herself—her ankle was better—but she liked letting him take care of her.

The air was clear. Mountains looked like paintings set at random on the desert. In fact, Mount Lemon to the south looked so close Samantha felt she could reach out and touch it. The desert was pocked with blackbrush and purple sage, pungent and bittersweet. Spring mornings were so beautiful it was easy to forget the afternoons might turn ugly.

Halfway down, Steve stopped the wagon, picked her up, and carried her to a rock with a vista he wanted her to share. She sat for a long time, his arm around her, lost in thought.

It was nice that he didn't try to kiss her or make love to her again, that he just held her and didn't feel the need to talk. The sun rose to the zenith. Regretfully he picked her up and carried her back to the wagon. By the time they reached the desert floor, the winds had risen to a howl, picking up dust and sand and turning the particles into hateful missiles that stung the skin and blinded the eyes. "We stayed too long," he said apologetically.

At the house, Lance stepped out onto the porch, grinned, skimmed down the steps, and reached up to help Samantha down.

"What are you doing here?" she asked as he swung her into his arms.

"What are you *not* doing here?" Lance countered, adjusting her weight in his arms.

Samantha felt her face getting hot. Lance looked from her to Steve and scowled as if he were going to ask a question. But his mouth closed purposefully—and Samantha knew that he suspected there was something going on between her and Steve. Instead of putting her down, he leaned against the banister and shifted her weight slightly.

"Is everyone okay?" she asked to cover her uneasiness.

"That's what I came to find out," he said. "When we didn't hear from you about Nicholas, we assumed everything was okay, but . . ."

"I've been so busy lately, what with building the house and life," she began weakly.

"Yeah," Lance said dryly, "I can see that."

"You can put me down now. I think I can walk."

"Hurt yourself, did you?"

She knew if he had been there long, Juana or Tristera or Nicholas would have told him about her injury. "Not badly."

He set her down and reached out a hand to Steve.

"Sheridan, good to see you again."

"Same here," Steve said, taking the proffered hand.

Samantha wanted an opportunity to say good-bye to Steve in

private, but Nicholas ran out to greet her. Lance surprised her by picking her up again, carrying her inside, and slamming the door against the wind.

"Why is he carrying you?" Nicholas asked, following.

"I sprained my ankle."

Lance set her down on the sofa. She showed Nicholas her foot, which was slightly swollen.

"There's no blood!"

Samantha laughed. Lance and Steve grinned. "No."

"May I have Young Hawk inside to play?"

"Doesn't Young Hawk have things he has to do?"

"In this wind, Mama?"

Samantha looked at Steve. "Don't ask me unless you want the truth," he said.

"Which is?"

"That Nicholas could have worse friends."

Lance nodded his assent.

"All right," Samantha said grudgingly.

"Yippee!" Nicholas bolted toward the door.

"Wait a minute, young man. You know you're not allowed outside in that wind. Have Juana send Eliptio for Young Hawk."

"Oh, Mama!"

"You heard me."

Samantha waited until her son was out of sight. "What are you going to do now?" she asked, turning back to Steve.

"Going to find Ramon and tell him he's not a murderer. If he's well enough to travel, I'll take him into town."

"Is that wise?"

"Unless he wants to stay an outlaw. They'll probably try him on a reduced charge, he'll get a tongue-lashing from the judge, and it'll be over. I'll talk Juana out of some food."

Steve wanted to say more, but he couldn't with her lover there. He, too, wanted to say good-bye to her alone, but he knew that wasn't possible now. He headed for the kitchen in search of food for the trip.

Instead of Juana, Steve found Tristera in the kitchen reading a newspaper one of the riders had brought back from town. She looked up from the paper.

"Lies," she whispered, her voice breaking, her cheeks flushed with rose spots. "All lies. I went with my people. I interpreted the words of the Great White Leader. I know what was said by each person around the council table."

"What are you talking about?" Steve asked.

Tristera folded the newspaper and slapped it against the table. "Now they say," she ground out, her husky, boyish voice rising, "that the Hopi Indians agreed to a new treaty that would give each person in the tribe forty acres of individually owned land. That is a lie!"

Samantha and Lance had apparently followed the sound of her angry words. They stepped into the kitchen as well. Steve took the newspaper and read the article.

"I explained to them," Tristera said forcefully, "that what they proposed was not the Hopi way, that the Hopi must live in their pueblos on the three mesas and walk each day to their farmlands below. Otherwise, unprotected on the plains, our people will be at the mercy of the Navaho, who pound our heads with rocks. Many will die.

"The Navaho raid as far north as Colorado, as far south as Mexico. They rustle cattle, steal baskets of food, drive off sheep, and smash the head of anyone who gets in their way. Nothing is safe from the Navaho," she ended bitterly.

"Well," Samantha said, "the other side of the coin is that the government could have given the Hopi nothing, as they have done with the Apache. Forty acres is a pretty big plot for one farmer who only needs to grow his own family's food."

Anger sparkled in Tristera's dark eyes. "Forty acres is nothing in the desert! The Hopi will think I betrayed them."

" 'If the Dawes Allotment Act passes,' " Steve read aloud from the newspaper, " 'excess Indian lands will be made available for homesteading.' " He dropped the paper onto the table. "That's the reason. They want to open the Hopi lands for homesteading. Settlers coming into an area held by Indians always cause a rash of broken treaties."

"There's no way to stop it then," Lance said. "Congress responds to voters, not to Indians who don't even have the vote."

Tristera looked so miserable, Steve tried to soften the truth for her. "It isn't final. It still has to go through both houses of Congress and be signed by the president."

"To my people—who will hear about this—it says that either I did not do a good job, or that I betrayed them."

Steve felt sorry for her, but he knew there was probably no way to help the Hopi. Once the government decided to open land to homesteading they did it, one way or another.

"Is there anything I can do?" Tristera asked Steve.

He pondered it for a moment. His sympathies were with the Hopi, but even so he couldn't think of anything that wouldn't put her life in danger. It infuriated him, but Kincaid was right. Congress responded to voters, and justice be damned.

"No. There're a lot of things you could do that would just get you killed. But that wouldn't help them." He paused. "I'm going after Ramon." Steve told her about Piney being alive. "Will you stay here until I get back?"

Reluctantly, Tristera nodded.

Nicholas tugged on Samantha's skirt. "Young Hawk can't play now. Let me go with Steve. Please?" he entreated.

"How far is this hidden valley?" she asked Steve.

"Not far, maybe eight miles north of here."

"Still on my land?"

"I think so."

Samantha glanced out the window. The winds had stopped. "Well," she said, relenting, "if you're sure there's no danger."

"Shouldn't be any," Steve said, glancing from her to Lance as if to say, *No more than you're in here.*

Steve and Nicholas packed and left. Lance carried Samantha up the stairs and into her bedroom.

He closed the window she'd left open, wiped the light film of sand off the quilted counterpane, and laid her gently on the bed. He looked like he might leave, but then he sat down on the edge of her bed.

"So, are you in love with Sheridan?"

"You're certainly not one to mince words," she said, frowning.

"Neither are you," he growled. "So, are you?"

"No, I'm not," she said firmly, lifting her gaze to his defiantly.

"You probably wonder what business this is of mine," he said, tracing a finger along the diamond pattern of the quilt.

Samantha denied that with a shake of her head.

"Well, I've been thinking a lot about what you said about my getting straight with Angie before I come to you, and I've decided you're right, as usual. I do need to settle that. I can see things could easily get out of hand, otherwise."

"So, did you go see Angie?"

"No. That is harder to do than you'd think." He scowled down at the quilt and expelled a breath. "I probably shouldn't admit this, but as long as I don't go, there's always the hope that she'll come back. Once I go and see her established in her new life, with no desire to come back . . ."

His words trailed off; Samantha felt the depth and breadth of his pain. It surprised her. It shattered her illusions about Lance loving her more than Angie, but somehow today she could hear that without anguish. She realized that he still loved Angie, and that she might really have left him with no intention of returning.

Muscles bunched in his wide Kincaid jaw, and Samantha could not resist reaching out to stroke his cheek. Lance closed his eyes, lay down beside her, and gathered her into his arms. He felt like a little boy seeking comfort, and Samantha freely gave it. They lay like that for a long time, with her holding him close and stroking his neck and back.

Finally she felt him relax. His arms were strong and warm and protecting. She felt safe and loved, just as she had growing up. She floated in warm bliss, remembering that being loved by him as a child had been like swimming in an ocean of love. And she could have it again.

Too soon her arm cramped and she stirred. Lance scooted down and kissed her breast through her gown. A bad feeling started in her middle.

"I can't, Lance," she said, tugging on his head.

Lance sighed and rolled onto his back.

"Because of Sheridan?"

"No," she said firmly, wondering if she was lying. "I think it's because you're married. I was so hurt last time, when you went back to Angie—I can't do that again. I have to know that it's really over between you and her."

"Do you love me?"

"Yes," she said truthfully.

"If I go to her and finalize the divorce, will you marry me . . . when the bookkeeping is in order?"

Samantha swallowed. Lance was watching her carefully, waiting for her response. "Yes," she said firmly.

"Are you sure, Sam?"

"Yes," she whispered, "I'm sure."

Marshal Daley was surprised to see Ramon Rodriguez and Steve Sheridan walking toward his office. A crowd had formed and followed from a safe distance.

This promised to be more exciting than shuffling through Wanted posters. Daley heaved himself into a standing position and walked out onto the sidewalk.

"*Buenos días, señor.*"

"Took you long enough to get here, Ramon."

"They start shooting at me again, I might not stay around this time, either."

"Well, at any rate, I'm glad you turned yourself in. Makes a lot more sense than running from the law."

"Especially since the man he was supposed to have killed is alive and well, and sitting on the porch of the Dart ranch house," Steve said for the crowd's benefit.

A murmur went up.

"Is that right, Marshal?" one of the men asked.

"Reckon so. Joe Dart confirmed it."

"You see a need for a trial?" Steve asked.

"Maybe not . . . if I knew what took Ramon so long."

Steve turned Ramon, lifted his shirt, and exposed the angry red scar on his back.

"Wal, seein' as how he's been indisposed . . ." Daley scratched his head and peered at the faces of the men standing around him. He had kept his job because he didn't forget he worked for the townspeople.

"Could wire the circuit judge, if I can catch him. He might be willing to set bail. Can't promise, though."

"I'll pay for the wire," Steve said.

Daley gauged the mood of the crowd, which did not seem violent. The sight of Ramon's wound had quieted them. They'd had time to remember that Ramon had lived peacefully among them for years and might have been telling the truth about Piney's attacking him.

Steve left Ramon at the jail and picked up Nicholas, whom he had left with Mary Francis. Together they walked to the general store, bought a few items he needed, and stepped out onto the sidewalk. He saw Daley angling across the wide rutted road toward him.

"Well," Daley said, stopping, "you're gonna get your way. The judge said that since Ramon came in on his own and had been wounded and all, and Piney wasn't dead, to let him go back to work. No sense having the county feed him if we don't have to."

Steve walked back to the jail with Daley.

"Keep a close eye on that kid," Daley said. "He's hot-tempered. It's gotten him into more than one scrape. And I might add, they're getting more serious each time."

"I'll keep him busy."

"You do that. I personally don't see any need for a trial. I think Piney did attack him. Probably someone put him up to it.''

"Thanks, Marshal."

Steve, Nicholas, and Ramon reached the house at sunset. Samantha limped out onto the porch and waited, looking pretty and fresh in a figure-hugging white cotton gown.

"What happened?" she asked, looking from face to face.

Nicholas dismounted and walked right past her—as if his being gone all day was not the least unusual. When he went inside, she heard him calling out to Juana.

Steve reported briefly about his meeting with Daley.

"Thank goodness! Oh, I'm so glad!"

"Silver Fish can handle the sheep," Steve said. "I'll take Ramon up to the work site and keep him busy."

"Good idea. Would you like some dinner?"

"We ate in town." Steve realized that had been a grave tactical error. But he'd done it purposely, in a fit of temper, knowing full well that he was destroying any chance to linger at the house. He was piqued that her lover had stayed with her while he'd had to go off again.

Juana and Tristera rushed out to greet Ramon and made a fuss over him. Steve leaned closer to Samantha, sniffing discreetly for the scent of her peppermint soap that he liked so much. "So, what did you and Lando do while I was riding in the heat?" he asked softly, so the others wouldn't hear him.

"Nothing."

"Why'd he come?"

"To talk to me."

"About what?"

"About . . . his situation. He's in a lot of pain."

"Does pain impress you? If so, I could show you a few of my scars."

"His wife didn't come back," Samantha said.

"I have one scar that might even be worth something," Steve said, stepping so close she could feel the heat of his body. He glanced over his shoulder at Ramon, who, in spite of all the attention he was getting, sagged in the saddle.

"Are you really . . . in pain?" Samantha asked weakly.

"Terrible pain," Steve said, his voice husky.

"Maybe you should stay and rest awhile—"

"Wrong kind of pain," he said, quirking his unruly eyebrow at her.

"Señor," Ramon whined.

"Just a second, boy," Steve said, glancing over his shoulder at the youngster. "I've got to go," he said to Samantha. "Maybe you'd better come up and be sure I'm doing it right. Never know when I might take a wrong turn in construction . . ."

"We wouldn't want that to happen," she whispered.

Steve inhaled a regretful breath, stepped back, and then plunged down the steps.

Steve's invitation haunted her. But her near promise to Lance kept her from riding up the hill to seek the solace she needed. In spite of her ambivalence, the days passed quickly for her, and even quicker for Nicholas, who seemed to be thriving in his new friendship.

He was learning a great deal from Young Hawk. Now he could kill a rabbit with a rock, find water in cactus, and make a blanket from rabbit hides. Samantha had drawn the line at letting him grow his hair long enough to braid.

Samantha was getting used to her son's going out in the morning and not coming home until Juana rang the dinner bell. They hadn't even needed the bell before.

That evening Nicholas ran to meet her, his suntanned face flushed with healthy color. "We caught *huge* crawdads."

"Well, where are they?"

"Young Hawk took them for his family. Ugh, huh?"

At the Kincaid ranch in Texas, crawdads would have been fed to the chickens. Here they would be the Indian family's main course. She was beginning to understand what Steve had meant about Indians having a hard life.

The next day, Nicholas came in before she called him.

"My goodness. To what do I owe the honor of your presence? And without even calling you."

Nicholas flung his slim body into one of the chairs and slumped down. "Young Hawk can't play."

"I should have known it wouldn't be because the *two* of you couldn't think of anything to do."

"I don't know why he had to get sick," he grumbled.

"I'm sure he didn't intend to."

"We were going to do something fun today."

"Well, maybe tomorrow."

"Yeah." Nicholas brightened.

Young Hawk couldn't come out to play the next day, either,

or the next. Samantha ordered Nicholas to stay away in case it was something contagious.

She took this opportunity to catch Nicholas up with his lessons. Since Young Hawk was being kept inside, Nicholas wanted more attention from her.

They ate lunch together, then Samantha put Nicholas down for a nap. She read to him for an hour, until his eyelids drooped and his breathing deepened. Then closing the book, she kissed her sleeping son and tiptoed out of the room.

In the parlor, she settled down to work on payroll. Juana waddled into the room.

"I think maybe you better come, *señora*."

"What is it?"

"My boy, Eliptio, went down by the Indian camp. He says them all seeck."

"Who?"

"Them *Indios*."

"All of them?"

"All that's there."

Samantha grabbed her medicine box and hurried out the door and down the hill.

CHAPTER FIFTEEN

At the Indian camp, she heard the coughing first, then the wail of a sick child. The tepee smelled like red ants. A chill started at her neck and raced the length of her spine. *Measles!*

Young Hawk was the sickest. His head was so hot it almost burned Samantha's hand. His sister and the infant had fevers, too. Little Dove and Red Star were sick but staggering around trying to nurse the children. Red Star's forehead was hot. Her hands shook.

Samantha sent a rider on a fast horse for the army doctor at San Carlos and a rider for Steve. Seth Boswell was good at cuts and bullets, but she doubted he knew anything about epidemics. She went back to the house, packed remedies she'd used on her son when he'd had the measles, and ordered Juana to keep Nicholas in the house.

Steve arrived first.

"Measles," he said, confirming her diagnosis.

"Thank God it isn't consumption."

"Don't thank him too soon."

Dr. Frank Easterby arrived late that evening, checked the sick Indians, and walked outside the tepee, waving the stench of their unwashed, feverish bodies out of his nostrils.

Steve stood off to one side, leaning against one of the old oak trees that lined the creek.

"Yup, measles," Easterby said. "Doesn't look good, either."

"I tried to keep Nicholas away from them—"

"They could have gotten it anywhere."

"Nicholas played with Young Hawk—"

"Dwelling on what might have started this is a waste of time. You didn't arrange it so they don't seem to have any immunity to our diseases."

"Nicholas will find out he gave it to them and he'll die. I know he will." She started to walk away, but the strength went out of her legs. Steve pulled her into his arms and led her to a rock to sit down.

"Nicholas will be fine," he said, his hand on her arm biting into her flesh as if he were trying to inject his belief into her. "Nicholas is a fine boy. He'll do what he has to do."

Samantha started to cry. She knew her son. He wasn't like other children, even other adults. Life wasn't that important to him. But his life *was* that important to her. If he died, her life would end.

"He mustn't find out," she whispered, her eyes pleading.

Easterby looked askance at Steve. "He's only six years old," Easterby said, protesting. He couldn't see why she was making such a fuss over a six-year-old boy giving measles to a bunch of filthy Indians. If she'd smelled them . . .

"He mustn't find out," Samantha said through clenched teeth, rage bringing strength into her legs. She pushed Steve's hand away.

"Promise me you won't tell anyone."

Easterby spread his hands. "Who'd care?"

Steve posted an around-the-clock guard to keep people from accidentally stumbling into a highly contagious situation. He didn't expect Silver Fish until Friday night, but he ordered Ed Stokes to keep everyone away, even Silver Fish and his brothers, until the crisis passed. He didn't want to risk giving this to anyone else.

"What's wrong with them?" Ed asked, his face pinched with worry about himself catching whatever it was.

"Measles."

"Oh, I had the measles."

"Good. Keep everyone away. No one comes near here."

Steve sent word to Juana that she, Nicholas, and the others were to move up to the new house site and that she wasn't to tell Nicholas any more than she had to.

After he saw them leave the house and head up the mountain, Steve went to the house for more supplies. He brought back washcloths, towels, and more supplies for poultices.

Samantha nursed them as diligently as she had nursed Nicholas, but the disease took a nasty turn. The skin eruptions came only in patches and then receded, which Easterby had warned her was a dangerous sign. She noticed it first on the little girl, whose upper arms broke out with black points that quickly receded. Then her neck and thighs, but not her trunk or lower legs. The points were purple and black instead of florid red.

All her patients had dry hacking coughs and breathed laboriously. She changed poultices hourly.

The second day, a dark brown fur formed inside the oldest girl's mouth and on her lips. Samantha applied garlic-and-mustard poultices more frequently and spooned herbal tea into the girl's mouth, but near dawn she lapsed into a coma and died.

Crying so hard she could hardly walk, Samantha tottered outside to tell Steve. As she cleared the flap of the tepee, the top of the sun rose over the eastern mountains.

Steve held Samantha until the worst of her crying had passed. Then he sat her down on a boulder beside the almost dry creek, walked into the tepee, and took the girl. Little Dove was asleep. Red Star was delirious and didn't notice, either.

Steve buried the girl. That night Young Hawk's fever rose to a hundred and six. Samantha immersed him in warm water and slowly cooled it by additions of cooler water until his fever went down. She had hoped the warmth would bring the disease out instead of driving it in, but his symptoms went the way of his sister's. He died two days later.

They buried Young Hawk, and Samantha prayed the dying was over. She turned her attention to saving the last three. Red Star seemed to be recovering. Her symptoms had not turned nasty the way the others had.

"You get some sleep," Steve said, leading her to a pallet he'd laid beside the creek. "I'll take over now."

Samantha dropped into sleep effortlessly and woke suddenly, filled with alarm.

"Are they all right?" she asked, stumbling into the tepee.

"Seem to be."

Near exhaustion, Samantha made another pot of beef tea, gave some to Steve, and drank a little herself. Slightly refreshed, but still feeling half dead herself, she carried a bowl of it to Red Star.

"Can you sit up a little? Here, let me help you," she said, putting the bowl down. Red Star didn't move. Samantha couldn't rouse her.

"Steve." He must have been right outside the door. He stepped inside, checked Red Star, and shook his head.

"She's dead."

Samantha hadn't thought she had another tear left in her, but she stumbled outside, crying.

Steve followed her. He held her until her sobs quieted. "I'm sending you up to the house," he said firmly.

"No."

"Yes."

"I won't go. I shouldn't have gone to sleep."

They argued, but she was adamant. Steve waited until Little Dove was asleep to carry Red Star outside for burial. Samantha felt it her duty to watch, but she couldn't. She'd seen too many people buried already.

Little Dove saved her from wallowing in guilt though. She woke up struggling for air. Samantha prepared a fresh poultice, which eased her breathing slightly.

That night Little Dove's baby went into convulsions. Samantha stripped the baby and bathed her with alcohol, stroked her hot skin with an alcohol-soaked rag, and sat on the dirt floor, eyes closed, rocking the baby.

Steve stepped inside the hot tepee. "How is she?"

"She's better now," Samantha whispered, touching the baby's face. It felt odd, as if the elasticity had gone out of it. Alarm quickened in Samantha. Steve picked up the lantern and held it near the baby's face. The infant's pupils were fully dilated. The baby felt heavy and still.

"Oh, no," Samantha moaned. Stricken, Samantha looked up at him, her eyes unguarded. For the first time since he'd known her, all her barriers were down. He could see her heart seared and perishing within her, as if struck by lightning. Part of him wanted to turn away from the sight, but he couldn't. She just sat there, looking up at him, tears streaming down her cheeks. Steve felt his own heart sear and shrivel within him.

Finally he walked over to her, lifted the baby out of her arms, and carried it to Little Dove, who took it and wouldn't let go of it. She just lay there, wheezing for air, stroking her baby, and crying weakly. Steve thought about taking it from her, but he couldn't.

Toward dawn, Little Dove died with the baby in her arms. Steve walked out to where Ed Stokes was standing guard. He stopped twenty feet away from the young rider. "Go up to the house and find a change of clothes for Mrs. Forrester and one for me. Bring washrags, towels, shoes, and a couple of strong bars of Juana's lye soap."

"You don't want me to stand guard anymore?"

"No. They're all dead now."

Steve dug another grave. When it was ready, he carried Little Dove and her baby outside and lowered them down with ropes. Steve knew this burial would not be seen as ceremonial enough to satisfy Silver Fish, if he were there, but it would have to do. Looking sick enough to die herself, Samantha walked to the grave, knelt down, and said a short shaky prayer asking God to look after these brave people.

Steve picked up the shovel. Samantha continued to kneel there and cry. When Steve pitched the last shovelful of dirt on the grave, he tossed aside the shovel and walked over to her. He believed a little crying was good for the soul, especially when it was so well justified, but too much might make her sick.

He lifted her up and into his arms. "Oh, Steve . . ."

"I know. I know. It hurts like hell."

Sobbing louder now, she clung to him. She smelled like the smoky fire he'd been tending to keep water hot, coffee made. He stroked her hair and her slim shoulders. Tenderness was so strong in him it felt like lust, centered in his heart instead of in his loins. He held her until he saw Ed Stokes ride up and stop a distance away. Steve steadied her.

"I've got to see Ed." Steve walked out, took a bundle from Ed Stokes, and walked back to Samantha.

"What's that?" she asked, her voice thin and shaky from so much crying.

"A change of clothes for both of us. I want you to take off your clothes. I'm going to burn them along with everything else you see here."

Samantha went into the bushes to undress. Steve walked back to the tepee, gathered cooking utensils, water jugs, soft rabbit skins, heavy buffalo hides, grinding stones, a tapestry of spun yucca fibers one of the women had been working on, a hoe made of bone, a string of chilis hanging from a nearby tree, everything in the camp, including Samantha's household items brought down for nursing, and tossed all of it into the opening of the tepee. When everything was inside, Steve unbuttoned his shirt and stripped it off.

To Samantha, shivering beside the tree, Steve was a blur. She saw a flash of a broad chest and his hands unbuttoning his trousers. She looked away.

"Take a bar of lye soap and scrub yourself until your skin feels raw," he directed.

Steve stepped out of his pants, gathered up their clothes, tossed them into the tepee, and threw matches on them until the flames caught. Naked, he walked to the creek. Samantha glanced up once, then quickly down.

His back to her, Steve picked up a bar of soap and began to scrub himself. Samantha felt no sexual stirrings, but it was nice to watch his strong back, his long, straight legs while she mindlessly scrubbed her own limbs.

Steve finished as she did. He dried himself with one towel while she used the other. They dressed in silence.

"Decent?" he asked as he buttoned clean trousers.

Samantha pulled her gown down over her breasts. "You'll have to button me."

Steve turned. Samantha's eyes looked big and serious in her pale face. She reminded him of Nicholas.

He buttoned her gown. "I'll take you to the new house now. You get into bed and don't get out until you feel too good to stay there any longer."

"I don't think I'll ever feel good again."

"Now you know why I don't believe in hell." His khaki eyes looked sadder than any eyes she had ever looked into. "After life, hell would be redundant."

Lance walked home from work to further tire himself out. At the front porch of the house he had built for and shared with Angie, he stopped and frowned, irritated that her sign still hung over the front door: ANGELA LOGAN, PHOTOGRAPHER.

He felt like ripping it down and breaking it into splinters. He settled for stalking past it and slamming the front door behind him.

He knew he was supposed to do something about the stalemate with Angie, but he had no energy for anything except going to work, coming home, and collapsing. The occasional rushes of energy he felt, the first of which had sent him to Samantha, had been labeled "unacceptable" behavior by his brother Chane.

He knew it was, but the energy was still there, waiting for an outlet. He channeled it into work as much as he could, but if Jennie's letters to him could be believed, that, too, was just another way of avoiding dealing with his problem. Jennie wanted him to go to San Francisco and talk to Angie. Jennie believed that Angie was pining away for him, that all she needed was the sight of him to bring her to her senses.

"That you, Mista Kincaid?" Yoshio called out from the kitchen.

"Yeah." Lance picked up the mail on the hall table and carried it into his office. He shuffled through the envelopes and stopped at one with a San Francisco postmark.

He tossed the others aside and reached for his letter opener, his heart suddenly pounding. His hand fumbled and missed it, so he ripped the end off the envelope instead and slipped the thick packet out. He flipped through the pages until he saw Angie's name signed neatly at the bottom of the page. He sagged into a nearby chair and read from the top.

Dear Lance,

I'm sorry that the first and only letter you get from me is all business, but I guess that's what our relationship has degenerated into.

I waited all this time to give you an opportunity to provide me with grounds for divorce. I don't mean to insult you, or the healthy male appetites I remember you having, by implying that it would take you this long, but I also didn't want to be disrespectful, either. It's a shaky business, trying to guess exactly how long it takes a man to go from feeling married to acting on impulse. I hope I have done you justice in every respect. Please know that no disrespect was intended . . .

The letter continued in that self-conscious vein, but Lance only scanned the rest, too furious suddenly to read any further. The papers accompanying her letter were from an attorney firm, Stern and Pentecost, naming him an adulterer and a wife-deserter.

He scanned the papers, then crumpled them in his fist. Yoshio walked into the room. "You 'leady eat now?"

"Pack my bags. I'm going away for a week or so."

"Away?" Yoshio repeated.

"Away," Lance said firmly.

At the new house, Samantha and Steve found Nicholas and Juana camping in the basement instead of in Steve's cottage. "It was almost feenish," Juana explained. "So *señor* Macready bring our beds from the old house. And, since we would be here for such a short time—"

"We're not going back down the mountain," Samantha said, interrupting her.

"Then, can Young Hawk come up here?" Nicholas asked.

"It's too hot down there, now that summer's coming. We'll stay in the basement here. It looks fine to me." The basement had no roof, but it had a subfloor and walls to shoulder height.

Samantha knelt down, pulled Nicholas into her arms, and hugged him.

"You smell like lye soap."

Samantha expelled a heavy breath and held him away from her, so she could see him. "Your friend Young Hawk and some of his family died."

The glad light that had shone in his eyes at the sight of her faded. He seemed to shrivel up before her eyes. It could have been her imagination, but he seemed to shrink, to turn inward on himself. He looked so miserable she ached.

Steve watched the boy, too. When the truth registered in him, he flashed Steve a look that caused deep uneasiness in him. It was the sort of look a man didn't want to see on a little boy's face. It was too complicated a look to interpret in a flash, and before Steve had, it was gone. Nicholas turned away and started to cry.

He asked several questions, but not the one Samantha had been afraid of. Nicholas cried long and hard, and that was good, but Steve couldn't shake the feeling that Samantha had been right about the boy.

Lance stepped off the train in San Francisco two days after he'd left Phoenix. The weather alone would have been worth coming for. A cold breeze whipped off the ocean.

Lance breathed deeply of the chill, salty air and then headed for the curb. He caught a cabriolet to a nearby hotel and then asked directions to the offices of Stern and Pentecost.

He spent ten minutes with Mr. Elroy Stern, a middle-aged man of medium height with a thin, arrogant face and the glinting eyes of a tent preacher.

"I realize my wife is hoping that I will provide her with grounds, but unfortunately, I'm not an adulterer, Mr. Stern. And I didn't desert her—she deserted me."

"Well, I don't handle complaints here, Mr. Kincaid," he said, with a facetious smile.

Lance pinned him with a hard stare. Stern reddened.

"I'll get in touch with Mrs. Kincaid," he said, clearly flustered, "and arrange a meeting, so we can discuss the matter."

"Thank you."

That very afternoon a messenger came to Lance's hotel with a note telling him that Mrs. Kincaid could meet with them at three o'clock on the following day.

At the appointed time, Lance was ushered into Stern's office, where Angie was already seated across from the attorney. She was dressed in what had to be the latest San Francisco fashion—

a lovely yellow velvet gown with matching hat and gloves. She looked paler and thinner—and even more beautiful than he remembered. The sight of her caused the blood to pound in his temples and loins.

"Mr. Kincaid," Stern said, rising to shake hands across the desk.

Angie glanced up and nodded at him. He took the seat beside her and rearranged it, so he could watch both of them.

Stern cleared his throat. "It seems we have a slight problem . . ."

"A bald-faced lie is hardly a slight problem," Lance said bluntly.

"I assure you, Mr. Kincaid, that no papers have been filed in court as yet. Our paperwork was preliminary in nature and based entirely on the testimony of your wife—"

Angie flashed him a look the likes of which he hadn't seen since the day he'd met her, brawling on the mayor's lawn in Phoenix.

"I signed an affidavit," she said through clenched teeth, "saying that I had personal proof of your infidelity and desertion."

Lance pinned Angie with a hard stare. "Oh, really. When and where did I . . . perform this dastardly deed? Before or after I deserted you?"

She shrugged and smiled her sardonic smile. "How was I to know that your healthy male drives would fail you?"

"Fail me? Did it ever occur to you that perhaps not every man on this continent is in rut?"

"Not once, unfortunately."

They sat in silence for a moment.

Stern cleared his throat and began carefully. "I was under the impression . . . ummm . . . based on my conversations with Mrs. Kincaid—"

"That," Angie said firmly, flashing Lance a clear warning, "this was going to be an amicable divorce."

"Amicable divorces do not start out with blatant lies and name-calling," Lance growled.

"I warned you that adultery was the least objectionable of all the choices."

"Then why the desertion?" he growled.

"Because unfortunately, adultery alone is not grounds for divorce against a man. Only women can be divorced for adultery," she ended acidly.

"Well, if you want this divorce so badly, why don't you provide the grounds?" he said angrily.

Stern rolled his eyes. "I warn you that I am an officer of the court; I cannot be a party to any attempt at collusion."

"Read the grounds to him," Angie insisted.

Stern picked up a book from his desk. " 'Inability to consummate the vows, insanity, conviction of a felony, cruelty, habitual drunkenness, desertion for one year, habitual drug addiction, neglect to provide—' "

"I know all that," Lance growled, waving the man into silence.

"Then why didn't you volunteer a basis?" Angie hissed.

"Why the hell didn't you pick something that you could confess to? Like desertion?"

"I didn't desert you," she said, protesting.

"What the hell do you call it? I'm cooking my own meals and sleeping by myself."

"Yoshio cooks your meals, and I don't believe the other, either."

"She's a lousy judge of character, too. Mark that down somewhere, Stern," Lance directed. "Mark it down," he growled, when the man hesitated.

"Yes, sir," Stern said, picking up a quill and making a few scratching sounds on a piece of paper.

"This is ludicrous," Angie said, glancing from her attorney to Lance.

"Well, it was your call. Why don't you tell us what your next brilliant move will be?"

Angie exhaled a frustrated breath. "Well, apparently we need to negotiate suitable grounds that don't upset your sensitive feelings."

"How the hell would you like being labeled an adulterer and deserter?"

"I thought you'd see it as a compliment—"

"Like hell you did."

Angie shrugged and crossed her arms. Stern glanced up from the paper he'd been writing on. "How about desertion?"

"He wasn't deserted!"

"Yes, I was."

"You were not! You practically ran me off."

"Liar!"

"Who left the conjugal home?" Stern interjected.

"She did. Months ago."

Stern cleared his throat. "Then it appears that Mr. Kincaid should be the one filing for divorce . . ."

"I've paid you all this money," she said to Stern. "I expect results."

"Well," Lance said, "since we're going to change the grounds for divorce, maybe I should take over paying the rest of the attorney's fees."

"You're trying to buy my attorney," Angie shouted.

"*Pay* our attorney," Lance corrected firmly.

"Ohhhh!" Angie stood up and flounced out of the room.

Lance peeled off two hundred-dollar bills and tossed them on Stern's desk. "Don't do anything until you hear from me."

Angie ran down the steps, not choosing to wait for the elevator. Lance caught her at the second landing. Angie had sagged against the wall and was panting for breath. She refused to look at him.

"Hey," he said softly, "I'm not your enemy."

"How can I remember that when you're buying off the only protection I have?"

"Protection? Do you really believe you need protection from me?"

Angie shrugged.

Lance put his finger under her chin and tilted it until she finally lifted defiant eyes and looked at him.

"Do you?" he asked again.

"Maybe not from you personally."

"Then what?"

"I don't know."

"Can we go somewhere and talk?"

"It won't do any good."

"Maybe not for you, but I need to know why you left me. Why you've stayed away."

"I've told you that already."

Lance took her arm and led her out of the stairwell and over to the elevator. "Well, I need to hear it again."

He took her to the hotel dining room in the next building and ordered from the dessert menu to satisfy the food requirement. After the waiter left, Lance asked. "How have you been?"

"Fine, thank you."

"What are you doing?"

"Same thing . . . just different location."

"Where are you living now?"

"In a brownstone on Davis Street, near the Columbo Market.'' She smiled. ''I can shop there as early as four in the morning.''

''Not like Durango,'' Lance agreed ruefully.

''No.'' Angie sighed.

''You look beautiful,'' he said, his voice husky. ''I guess being rid of me agrees with you.''

Angie felt perilously close to losing control. Lance looked wonderful to her, too. Handsome, virile, rugged. Her heart ached with all the things she didn't dare say to him.

''I guess I'd better go,'' she said softly.

''You haven't told me why you left.''

''I . . . had to. I can't give you what you need. Samantha can. No sense my being in the way.''

''Angie, dammit, did I ever once say you were in my way? Be truthful.''

''No,'' she said firmly, ''you never did. But some things can't be said. And you were always a gentleman.'' She stood up. ''I really have to go.''

''Let me walk you home.''

''It's a long walk,'' she protested.

''I may not be competent enough to commit adultery on cue, but I can walk.'' Lance tossed a bill on the table and followed her out the door. On the sidewalk, she headed toward the waterfront.

They followed Market Street to Davis, and then Davis to Pacific. In front of a discreet brownstone, she stopped and faced him, her cheeks flushed from the cold wind whipping off the ocean.

''Thank you,'' she said softly.

''Let me come up?'' His question surprised him as much as her apparently. But he clamped his jaws and didn't back down. Angie knew better, but she couldn't refuse him.

''It's probably a mess,'' she said weakly, turning to unlock the door before he could leave. The entry opened onto a parlor, filled with late afternoon sunlight from a row of tall windows.

''This isn't bad,'' he said.

''You haven't seen everything yet.''

''I don't need to see everything,'' he said, his voice a mere husk, a warning. He reached out and touched her arm, and his touch vibrated through her. She felt disoriented again, and it reminded her of a time long ago, before they'd been married, when they had walked together on the desert. He'd made love to her that day, with the wind blowing her hair and skirts around her and thunder rumbling in the distance.

"I've missed you, Angie," he rasped, the words coming of their own volition, despite his careful plans to remain as aloof as she.

"How's Samantha?" she asked pointedly.

"Don't know. I haven't seen her lately."

"How was she last time you did see her?"

"A little jangled. Nicholas got sick."

"How is he?" Angie asked, her dark eyes filled with real concern now.

"Fine. It turned out to be measles. I smelled them when I walked in the door."

"I remember you claiming to have that ability." She paused. "So why didn't you make love to Samantha?"

"Clumsiness on my part and wisdom on hers."

"So, you admit you tried."

"I was in so much pain, I would have tried anything." Lance hadn't meant to say that, either.

Angie frowned. "Just . . . how clumsy were you?"

"Incredibly clumsy."

"I can't imagine such a thing."

"Well, I guess you haven't seen me at my halfhearted best."

Angie looked into his eyes; something twisted in her belly, deep down. Anger? Jealousy? Relief? She couldn't tell, but she was suddenly glad he hadn't made love to Samantha. If he hadn't.

"Remember," she whispered, slightly dazed by the warm, masculine smell of him, so close and yet still so far away, "what you told me once? You said, 'I have no heart for marriage.' "

"I don't remember that."

"Well, you said it. And as it turned out, I'm the one who has no heart for marriage."

"Yes."

"That same day you asked me if I wanted romance. I do want romance, but apparently I'm the one who can't stand the responsibility of making someone else happy."

"I was happy," he growled. "I just wanted more than you could give."

"You'll always want more than I can give," she said, suddenly despairing.

"No. I've learned my lesson. I can be happy without anything, except you."

"I don't want to talk anymore."

His hand slipped down and tightened on her wrist; she turned blindly into his arms. Lance enfolded her and pulled her against the heat and hardness of his strong chest. She wanted him so badly her whole body burned and throbbed.

She was trembling so hard he could feel it beneath her long coat. He lifted her face and kissed her warm, hungry lips, and his own body began to shake. He tasted tears, and he didn't know whether they were his or hers. Groaning, he picked her up and carried her toward the sofa.

"No," she whispered. "The bed is in there." She pointed down a long hallway.

For Angie, it was like *déjà vu*. He lowered her onto her bed; with trembling hands she helped him lift her skirts and unbutton his pants. In a fever of wanting she guided him into her, kissing his face, his throat, his lips, stunned into blindness by the achingly familiar feel and taste and smell she had hungered for so long, cried herself to sleep remembering on so many lonely nights. She clung to him and allowed him to immerse her once again—perhaps for the last time—in the wild feverishness of their own special madness.

He stayed with her all that night, neither of them sleeping lest they miss one minute of their time together.

The next morning they ate breakfast in bed. Angie was about to prepare a bath for them when a knock came on the front door.

"Drat," she muttered, grabbing a bathrobe and hurrying to answer it.

She opened the door to Savannah, the seven-year-old daughter of her best friend and neighbor. "Hi, Savannah."

"Mrs. Kincaid. My mother wants to know if you'd like to come over for breakfast. It'll be ready in a few minutes."

Lance, who had somehow managed to dress himself, stopped behind her and touched her waist. She glanced over her shoulder in time to see his face soften at the sight of the girl.

Lance noticed her watching him and masked his reaction, but she'd seen enough. He wanted a child of his own, and he was entitled. His need triggered an answering need in her. It all came back to her. She ached for a baby to give him. It was an awful feeling—needy and hungry and despairing—and she hated it as much now as she had in Durango. And him for causing it.

She felt like a woman teetering on the brink of an emotional precipice, and she knew that to go over was to fall into some horrible gaping maw from which there would be no escape.

In the grip of that terror, she thanked Savannah and asked her to give her mother her regrets, explaining that she had company. Then she led Lance back to bed and made love to him one last time. This was different from the other times. More violent. More angry.

Even Lance noticed it. "You've become a predator, woman," he whispered, as they lay there panting.

"Have I?" she asked, forcing herself to laugh.

"I think I've just been ravished," he said, pulling her back into his arms.

She realized that she loved him enough to die for him. She loved the way he looked, the way he smelled, the way he felt under her hands. As long as she lived she would hunger for him. She knew that everywhere she went, she would search for the sight of his dear familiar face, the angle of his jaw, the way his hairline angled over his forehead that little bit. And knowing that, filled with the pain of that knowledge, she kissed him one last time, pressing her lips against his with such an aching need that she felt certain he would see her heart bleeding. But she allowed herself this luxury.

Then when she couldn't stand it any longer without bursting into tears, she relinquished his lips, turned away from him, and buried her face in the pillow until she had regained control. Then she stretched langorously against him, rubbing her breasts against his chest. "Well, darling, this has been wonderful, but if you don't get out of here soon, you're going to run into my fiancé."

"Fiancé?" Lance asked, looking stunned.

"Well, it isn't official yet, but you remember Hal Stockton, my editor and cowriter who sometimes accompanies me on field trips?"

"Yes."

"Well"—she shrugged and gestured prettily with her hands—"you know how things happen."

Lance stood up and began to pull on his pants. "Apparently not," he said grimly.

"Where are you going?" she asked, pretending not to know.

"Back to Durango."

"Well," she said, stretching luxuriously, hoping he would look at her body, not her face, "if you're ever in San Francisco, let me know. I don't mind cheating on Hal with you. 'Turnabout is fair play,' they say."

"Thanks," Lance said. "Your generosity sickens me."

Lance went directly to Stern's office. The male secretary tried to stop him, but Lance opened Stern's door and stalked into the room. Stern looked up, frowned.

"Don't bother to redo those papers," Lance growled.

"But you said—"

"Forget what I said."

"But we have to have proof of desertion and adultery—"

"You'll have it. As soon as I can get it for you."

Samantha got sick. She stayed in bed for two days with fever, chills, and headaches. Juana diagnosed it as influenza. At first every time Samantha woke up and remembered the Indians' dying, she cried, but after the second day she started to get control of herself, mostly because she didn't want to be a constant reminder to her son, who shouldn't be dwelling on death or dying.

The basement they had moved into was separated by canvas to give the illusion of privacy. At first Nicholas came periodically and slipped into bed with her. Juana would find him there, get him up, and give him something to keep him busy, so Samantha could have her privacy, but Nicholas peeked in at her every few hours. Finally the afternoon of the second day he caught her awake. She welcomed him into her bed and held him close.

"I was worried," he said, his slim body tense.

"I'm sorry. I didn't mean to upset you. I got sick."

Nicholas burrowed against her, pressing his face to her breasts the way he'd done as a baby. "I wanted to see Young Hawk before they buried him. I wanted to say good-bye."

"I know you did, but . . . we couldn't wait. We had to bury them right away."

"But I needed to say good-bye."

"There was no time, Nicholas."

"Why did they die?"

Samantha was ready for his question. "An Indian disease. I don't know the name of it."

Nicholas leaned away from her and looked into her eyes. "Did they cough a lot?" The question was phrased so innocently. As if he had no stake in the answer.

"No," she said firmly.

His blue eyes watched her with solemn regard, weighing whether she had just lied to him.

"Have you been reading your lessons?" She kept up a steady barrage of questions until he tired of trying to answer them and wandered outside.

The next morning Steve sent two dozen men, a dozen wagons, and Juana and Tristera down the mountain to supervise moving the furniture up to the new house. They managed it in one trip.

That night Nicholas couldn't get to sleep. She read him a story, which usually worked, but this time it didn't. He started to cry when she tried to leave him.

"Don't go," he pleaded.

Samantha sat down on the side of his bed. "I'm only a few steps away. What's wrong?"

"I'm afraid."

"Nightmares?"

"Yes."

"Did you forget how to chase off monsters?"

"It doesn't work anymore," he said accusingly.

"How come?"

"I don't know." He thought about it a moment. "The monsters are okay, but now I have wolfess."

"Wolfess? What are wolfess?"

Nicholas bared his teeth and made a mean dog face.

"Wolves?"

"Yes, wolfess."

"Tell me about these wolves. What do they do?"

"They ate Young Hawk and his family, and now they're going to eat me."

That chilled Samantha. They were only dreams, but panic seized her. "That's nonsense," she said.

Nicholas waited for her to show him what to do about his nightmare *wolfess*, but her mind refused to function. She couldn't think of anything to do. "I'll read you another story," she said.

Steve hired Nicholas to sweep up after the carpenters and pick vegetables from the cook's garden. The boy was such an enthusiastic worker, Steve had to give him additional assignments to keep him busy. When Nicholas ran out of other work, he pulled nails out of the scrap lumber, his thin arms straining against the big hammer to get the square iron nails out of the boards. When he had a bagful, he delivered them to the blacksmith to have them weighed and tallied on his worksheet. When he didn't have anything else to do, he watched the blacksmith melt and repour the nails.

To keep him motivated, Steve paid the boy at the end of every day. Each night Nicholas brought his coins to Samantha; she watched him proudly count them and write the amount in a logbook Steve had given him.

"A dollar twenty-seven. Steve says if I save my money I'll be richer than Midas," he said proudly.

"I wouldn't doubt it. That's as much as my cowhands make in a day."

"It is?" Nicholas's eyes were round. "Wow."

Whenever Nicholas had spare time, he followed Steve around. Steve showed him how to drive a nail, saw a board, use a level, and finally how to inventory building supplies, a daily chore to make certain the workmen didn't run out of some critical piece of building material.

It gave Samantha enormous pleasure to look out the window and see Steve and her son sitting on a stack of adobe bricks, ledgers in hand, Nicholas so slender and serious, Steve so sturdy and patient.

Between following Steve, harvesting vegetables and nails, and sweeping, Nicholas was so busy he stopped asking about his dead friend.

It became clear to Steve that something had changed between Samantha and himself. He waited to give her time to recover from her ordeal and then he caught her alone on the hillside behind the house.

"Wait up," he called after her.

Samantha turned, surprised.

Steve climbed the remaining distance between them. "You've been avoiding me lately," he said.

"Have I?" she asked, stalling for time.

"So, what happened between you and Lando?"

Samantha had dreaded this moment. Her heart started to pound, but she would not lie to him. "Lance proposed to me."

"And?"

"And I accepted, conditionally."

"What condition?"

"That he get over Angie or go back to her."

"Well, I guess that'll be no problem for him. Thanks for being honest with me." Steve turned and climbed back down the hill. Samantha sat down, suddenly too weak to continue her climb.

Samantha waited for word from Lance, but it didn't come. And without it, all she could do was struggle with her attraction

to Steve. She knew it wasn't fair to lead Steve on. There could
be no future in it, but the more she denied the attraction, the
stronger it seemed to become. It grew increasingly difficult to
work in such close proximity with him and not be constantly
aware of how deeply he affected her.

Steve dominated the entire mountainside. Morning, afternoon, and evening, she could hear his voice ring out, catch the
sound of his laughter, the sight of his broad shoulders that
seemed to taper into an ever leaner waist and hips. Her hands
remembered the feel of him, her lips the taste. She felt certain
he was going to drive her crazy.

At such times she stopped what she was doing and listened.
Wishing for . . . she knew not what. She had promised Lance.
But she hadn't expected it to be this hard. She loved Lance. She
wanted to marry him and have his children, but . . . somehow,
trying to deny her feelings for Steve seemed to make them grow.
Now she was thinking about Steve all the time.

When she could stand it no longer, she finally set aside whatever she was doing and searched him out on some pretext. Today
she found him giving instructions to the carpenters building the
dumbwaiter between the basement kitchen and the first-floor
dining room.

"How's it going?" she asked, stopping beside him. He looked
at her; she felt the tingle of his glance all the way to her toes.

"Depends on how much frustration you like in your life,"
Steve said, tilting his head toward the dumbwaiter. "Let me
show you how it works, or better yet, how it was supposed to
have worked, if they'd sent all the parts, which they didn't." He
explained in such detail, the cooks clanged their dinner bells
before he finished. Men put down their tools, looked askance at
him, and headed for the eating area behind the house.

"Can I be doing anything for ye before I go, lad?" Ian Macready asked, stopping beside them.

"See you in the morning, Ian."

"If I be living that long, the way this madman be pushing
us," Ian said, doffing his hat at Samantha.

Mumbling to himself, Ian walked out the front door. Gradually the incessant hammering and banging and rolling of heavily
laden wheelbarrows up the wooden planks ceased. Smells of
chili and corn bread mingled with the aroma of beef cooking
over an open fire. The house grew quiet.

Samantha felt suddenly self-conscious about being alone with
Steve. Her heart pounded. She walked to one of the window

openings and looked out across the desert. "It's so beautiful from here . . ."

Steve walked over to stand behind her. Beneath the lace of her white blouse, her skin looked warm and inviting, her breasts rising and falling with her breathing.

"What does the second floor look like?' she asked.

He cleared his throat. "Maybe we'd better take a look," he said, his voice still husky. He followed her up the stairs on the west side of the house to the second-floor bedrooms and bathrooms.

Samantha stepped over nails and hammers and piles of lumber. Resiny smells of pitch pine stung her nostrils. Three walls of windows encircled the sun room. Looking south, she could see for miles. "I can't believe I own this," she whispered.

"Indians don't believe anyone owns anything. They say the land belongs to the one it wants to belong to."

"How quaint."

"Quaint?" he asked. "To me the land looks powerful enough to do anything it wants."

Samantha laughed. "Maybe you haven't seen my deed."

"Men have fought and died to own land. But we come into this world with empty hands, and we leave the same way."

"I don't understand."

"Well, if you own the land, command it to do something."

Samantha laughed. "That's ridiculous."

"No, when you really own something, you can make it do things."

Samantha frowned, then a thought came to her. "Okay," she said, facing the window. "Remain as you are," she commanded.

Steve walked to the window and stood beside her. As they watched, a dead tree chose that moment to fall with a loud crash and send a boulder bouncing down the mountainside.

"The Great Spirit has spoken," Steve whispered.

"Bull! That was sheer luck on your part." She decided to take the offensive. "You believe in this Great Spirit?"

"Don't you believe in God?"

"Yes, of course."

"What difference does it make if we call the Creator 'God' or the 'Great Spirit'?"

"Oh. When you put it that way . . ."

She'd been avoiding looking directly at Steve, feeling safer gazing out at the mountainside. Now she turned to look at him.

Thumbs hooked in his belt, he looked every inch the man who had carried her to his bed those long weeks ago. Her blood punched against her throat.

"How's your arm?"

"My . . . arm?"

Her body burned. She knew better than to touch him, but her hand reached out and stroked his left arm. "You were shot here, don't you remember?" She was glad his intent gaze stayed on her face. He didn't see her hand tremble.

His brows knit. When he scowled like that it made her heart flutter. "I may lose my ranch." She had no idea what made her say that. Perhaps a plea for mercy from this man who didn't look like he had any.

"I can't believe that'll ever happen."

"I received a letter from my attorney. He's delayed the court hearing a number of times, but it can't be delayed again. He's going to Washington next month."

Steve moved to stand behind her. The heat of his body roused an answering heat in her. He didn't touch her, but he might as well have, considering the effect his nearness had on her heart.

"Have you heard from your . . . fiancé?"

"No, but he's never been much of a writer." She had no idea why she hadn't heard from Lance. Maybe he had made up with Angie. Any number of things might have happened.

Steve could see nothing had changed there. Samantha would defend Lando with her dying breath. Unexplained rage flushed through him. He either had to walk away or do something he would regret. "Well," he said gruffly, "my dinner is waiting."

Samantha watched his broad back as he strode across the cluttered floor and skimmed down the stairs. Frustration almost overwhelmed her. Her heart ached dully. If she didn't hear from Lance soon, she would die trying to be true to a promise he might now have forgotten.

Chila couldn't sleep. She got up and looked at the clock. Only two o'clock. She'd awakened at midnight, at one o'clock, and now.

She threw the sheet aside and stood up. She checked on Piney, sleeping in the spare bedroom. She had nursed him for weeks, but he didn't seem to get any better. He would wake up every now and then and be in a lot of pain. A time or two she had helped him out of bed; he had sat on the porch in the evening cool, but if he was actually recovering, it was the slowest recovery she'd ever seen.

She was wide-awake, and there wasn't a blamed thing to do in the middle of the night except eat, and she wasn't hungry. She lit a lamp and looked around for a book to read. But she knew there wasn't a book in the house she hadn't read. Then she remembered her sister had sent her a box of their grandmother's things a few years ago. She'd never gone through the box because it made her feel sad. But she couldn't feel any sadder than she did now, so she might as well open it.

The box was in the spare bedroom under the bed. Chila carried it into the parlor. Under the first layer of newspaper she found a porcelain doll her grandmother had treasured. Ever since Chila had been old enough to understand words her grandmother had told her that doll would be hers someday. But she hadn't wanted it. She called it the choky doll, because when she spent the night at her grandmother's house its white face seemed to glow in the dark. She was sure it was going to wait until she was asleep, fly across the room at her, and choke her to death.

Chila carefully set the doll aside. Its face still seemed to glow. She turned it over, so she couldn't see its face. The next level was a set of saucers and teacups, all broken from their ride across the country. Chila set the broken pieces aside to take out to the garbage dump behind the house.

"Too bad your face didn't break," she said to the doll. The third level was all books. Chila grinned. Just what she needed. She picked one up and found it wasn't a novel at all. They were her grandmother's diaries.

Chila opened one.

The best remedy I've found for stammering is to have the child read aloud very slowly.

Chila smiled. Her grandmother was a great one for remedies. She must have had a remedy for just about everything. That gave her hope. Maybe there was a remedy for Piney's gunshot wound.

At first Chila felt odd reading her grandmother's diaries, but once started she couldn't seem to stop herself. She picked through them and found the ones for the years after she was born. She would start with those. Maybe her grandmother was the sort who got smarter every year of her life.

Chila read until dawn. The kerosene lamp started to flicker, or she would have probably kept reading. The diaries would have been fairly dull to anyone else. Her grandmother had kept them instead of gossiping with her neighbors, who lived too far away.

Chila moved to the window to see if there was enough light yet to read by. There wasn't really, but she could make out the words. She started to close the book, but she just had to turn one more page.

"How to kill a devil."

Chila blinked. "Well, Ah'll be . . ." She read the page with growing excitement. *A devil is impervious to bullets. That's one way you can tell he isn't a human being,* it said.

Chila realized the truth of that immediately. Bullets had never touched Denny. They seemed to just slip around his body. She'd sort of suspected it, though. That's why she'd walked right into his room and held the gun against his head. But being a devil, he'd probably known she was coming and had placed a decoy in his bed.

Chila read the remedy for killing a devil; it made sense to her. She marked the page, but she knew she wouldn't forget what to do. Carefully she put the book away, comforted by the knowledge that the Lord had led her to the diaries just exactly when she needed them.

CHAPTER SIXTEEN

According to the Phoenix Gazette, that summer was the warmest and driest on record. Steve worked the men from dawn until the heat of the day; then they took a siesta and worked from sunset until dark. Samantha couldn't tell if he did it because he was anxious to leave, or if it was only because he knew she was tired of living in chaos and wanted the house finished.

The longer she stayed away from Steve, the more she missed him and the harder it became to play the role of aloof employer. The need to do so was real. She was engaged to Lance, and she had to live in this territory after Steve left. Besides, everyone at the work site, including her own closest allies, kept watching for any sign of a romance between them.

Samantha tried to put Steve out of her mind, but every time she saw him, even from a distance, her mouth got dry and her heart stopped and then started again with awful suddenness. Even when it was only a man whose shoulders squared in the same way, or whose hair shone blue black in the sunlight . . .

She'd never felt this sexual pull with Lance, so she had been unprepared for the way it threw her into turmoil. But the day dragged unless she could find some excuse to at least exchange a few words with him—always in plain sight of others and usually only for a moment. Each time, her heart pounded and her palms sweated, but she had to do it.

Steve was grim lipped and formal with her, not helping in the least. She knew just by looking into his eyes that he was deeply hurt by her sudden, and to him unexplainable, engagement. But in her own mind she was committed to Lance. It seemed crazy, even to her, when she lay in bed and trembled from wanting Steve. But she couldn't give Lance up. She'd waited too long for him to finally want her.

Long after the workmen had lined up for chow, Ian Macready walked over to where Steve was pounding an unfortunate nail into wood. "Hey, laddie . . . hey!"

Steve straightened and let the hammer hang down by his side.

"Laddie, laddie. It's only a house we're building here."

"No, it isn't!"

"It isn't?" Ian asked, frowning. "Then mayhap ye could be telling me just what the hell it is we're doing here?"

"We're . . . never mind," Steve growled.

To Ian, Steve had the alert, worried look of a man in love. Ian would have said more, but one of the cooks came by and stopped to ask a question.

Steve fled. At first he didn't know where to go. Out of sight of the men, he changed direction and climbed the mountain. At the top, panting and exhausted, he sank down on a mat of pine needles. Dusk had dimmed the desert. Glorious red and purple clouds hung above the horizon, casting a warm glow on the glistening treetops. To the south of Samantha's adobe palace the desert shimmered like a vast ocean.

He was losing his mind. He'd almost told Ian . . .

Only a fool would have gotten that involved. He lay there until the sky darkened and filled with stars. He wanted her so badly he ached all over.

His mind flashed an image of Samantha holding the dying Indian baby, crying silently and with fierce hurt, then to another image of her holding Nicholas on her lap. She loved deeply—from a compassionate heart—and she evoked fierce tenderness in him.

Steve had had relationships with women, but he'd never fallen in love. And it was a good thing. When Samantha Forrester withdrew, he ached like a bad tooth. What if he'd fallen in love with her?

He was grateful he hadn't. She was a woman tied to the land. She wouldn't leave, and he couldn't stay. There was no future for them together. Even so, he yearned for her, saw her face in every window, smelled her peppermint scent in his dreams, worried about her problems, and her son.

He and Samantha had been estranged ever since he'd made love to her. And it had felt perversely good to deny himself the luxury of pursuing her. He had remained aloof because he knew he didn't love her. He wanted her, but he fully intended to ride away when this house was finished. With that as his goal, it would have been wrong to pursue her. Wrong to continue something he had no intention of staying around to finish.

Someone below called his name. He heard it faintly but didn't respond. He couldn't go back to the work site until he knew what to do. He realized he might starve to death or freeze before he figured it out, but it didn't matter.

He stared at the stars. He didn't remember the sun setting. The moon rose, and still he lay there, slightly chilled, paralyzed into immobility.

Finally the answer came to him. The last of the human freedoms was the ability to choose one's attitude in any given circumstance. He had to remain aloof, polite, deferential. He would not fall in love with her, and he would not allow her to make a public fool of him.

In August a letter finally arrived from Jennie Kincaid announcing that Leslie Van Vleet, Peter's wife and Jennie's sister-in-law, had given birth to a boy. ''Why don't you give a party to show all of us your new house?'' Jennie suggested. ''I'm sure by the time it's done, the baby will be old enough to travel.

''We don't see much of Lance anymore. He went to San Francisco for a few days and then had an accident stepping off the train. He tripped over a trunk and broke his left arm. He's been laid up for weeks. Chane saw him last week, and he's finally out of the cast and beginning to be his old self again. I would have written immediately, but he asked me not to. You know how he is with his stubborn pride.''

Samantha sagged into a chair. Lance had been injured and hadn't even bothered to write to her. Add to that the birth of a new baby in the family. She knew he had to be miserable.

Samantha considered going to see him, but now her pride wouldn't let her. She'd rushed West years ago when he was injured, and all it had gotten her was a broken heart. If he wanted her, he would have to send for her.

But the party was a good idea. Samantha set a date for the first weekend in November, a belated Halloween party. She would invite Rathwick for Tristera. And she would invite Joe and Chila Dart, but she didn't expect them to come. All the Kincaids—Jennie, Chane, and their children; Uncle Chantry, Aunt Elizabeth, and Mrs. Lillian; Peter, Leslie, and the new baby; Lance; Stuart, Maggie, and Buffy. All her neighbors.

The next morning she wrote out the invitations and sent a man into town with them. Samantha suddenly felt as if she were hitched to a team of horses, being pulled toward an unknown fate. She tingled, energized by impending disaster. She had a great deal to do to get ready. In only a few weeks, Lance would come to see her new house. And she would know what his miracle was, and if she was really going to marry him. She trusted that it would all come clear to her—that even her confused feelings for Steve would finally make sense.

The second Sunday in September, Nicholas talked Tristera into going with him up the mountainside. When he didn't have anything else to do, he liked to hide and watch the pine squirrels.

As they neared his hiding place, Nicholas shushed Tristera. "Now sit real quiet. I want you to see this."

Smiling, Tristera sat where he pointed. Nicholas was much better at keeping himself busy now. Steve Sheridan had had a good effect on the boy. She hoped Samantha realized that.

"See up there?" Nicholas whispered.

High up in the top of the pine tree, a squirrel bit off a pinecone and dropped it. The squirrel watched until the pinecone hit the ground.

As Nicholas and Tristera watched, the squirrel on the ground ran over to the pinecone, barked, picked it up, and ran off with it. "See?" Nicholas whispered, "They're partners."

Another pinecone dropped; a blue jay from a nearby tree swooped down, picked up the cone, and flew off with it. In a few seconds he flew back, looked around to be sure the squirrel was nowhere in sight, and swooped down to get another.

As he picked it up and flew off with it, the squirrel ran into the clearing and saw the blue jay flying away, pinecone in its beak. The squirrel turned around and ran behind a bush and waited. Soon the blue jay came back for another of the cones that were dropping every few seconds from the top of the tree. While the squirrel chattered incessantly, the jay took a cone and flew away with it. This time the squirrel on the ground followed him to his cache—a hollow stump of a tree, not far from Nicholas and Tristera's hiding place.

The blue jay dropped the cone into the stump and went back for another one. But the squirrel climbed into the stump, picked up one of the cones, and carried it away.

From that time on, the blue jay took the dropped cones, flew them to the stump, and the squirrel on the ground took them out and carried them away.

"Isn't that something?" Nicholas asked, his voice filled with wonder. "They're about the smartest animals I've ever seen," he said.

"All animals are that smart. Otherwise they'd be dead," Tristera said.

"Are they?"

"Sure."

That pleased Nicholas. "You think they're as smart as us?"

"Maybe smarter."

On Monday Nicholas finished his chores early. Tristera was busy with his mother, so he climbed up the mountain alone to watch the squirrels again.

As he sat in his favorite place, one of the pine squirrels ran down the tree trunk and into the clearing. It picked up one of the pinecones and began to tear into it with its sharp teeth. As the squirrel sat there, biting at the cone, a coyote ran in from the side of the clearing opposite Nicholas, right toward the small unsuspecting squirrel's back.

"Run!" Nicholas yelled, jumping up to scare the coyote away. All his yelling did was confuse the squirrel, who dropped his pinecone, barked at Nicholas, and turned to run the wrong way.

"No! No!"

The squirrel ran right into the mouth of the coyote, who grabbed it by the neck and shook it hard. The squirrel screamed; other squirrels joined in with their frightened cries. Nicholas ran at the coyote, who dropped the squirrel and loped away.

Nicholas knelt beside the squirrel. He picked it up; its head fell limply to the side. Crying, Nicholas carried the squirrel down the mountain.

Steve heard the sound of Nicholas's wails and started up the mountain. "Hey, what's wrong?"

Tears streaming down his cheeks, Nicholas held out the dead squirrel. "I tr—tried to save it," he said, sobbing.

Steve took the squirrel in one hand and lifted Nicholas into his arms with the other. "What happened?"

"A coy—coy—coyote . . ." His sobs overwhelmed him.

From inside the house, Samantha heard Nicholas howling. She dropped the broom and ran outside, her heart constricted with fear. Following the sound of his sobs, she ran around the side of the house and froze in place.

Steve was holding a limp, bloody squirrel in one hand and Nicholas in the other. Nicholas's arms were around Steve's neck. Her son's loud sobs were filled with heat and anguish. She wanted to rush forward, but something held her there, unnoticed by either of them.

Gently, without disturbing Nicholas, Steve lay the squirrel on the waist-high porch rail and cradled Nicholas with both arms, rocking him from side to side. Nicholas's arms were tight around Steve's neck, his legs hung limply. The two seemed welded together in shared sentiment. Steve's eyes were closed, but emotion radiated from him. Samantha had never seen such communion between a man and a boy. Her lungs quivered with her own emotion. Finally Nicholas's howls subsided into quiet sobs.

"I sh—should have saved him," Nicholas wailed.

"You did the best you could, son. That's all any man can do."

Nicholas sucked in a shaky breath. Deeply touched, Samantha turned and slipped back into the house.

"What happened?" Tristera asked.

"I don't know, but a squirrel is dead—and Nicholas feels terrible."

"Ohhhh," Tristera said, her eyes filled with sadness. "Nicholas loves the squirrels so much."

Later, when Nicholas came in and told Samantha about the incident he was calm and amazingly composed. That night Samantha couldn't sleep. She kept seeing Steve holding Nicholas, rocking him from side to side, eyes closed.

She had no idea why, but she felt four years old and abandoned by parents, who had only pretended to love her. She felt sick and awful, as if she were back in that smelly orphanage with the icy English winds blowing through it.

Samantha sat up in bed, too agitated to lie still any longer. She slipped into her robe and slippers and walked to the outside door. Steve would probably be asleep. She had no business seeking him out at this time of night, but she had to thank him for his kindness to Nicholas.

The compound was silent. Even the birds were asleep. Stars in the crisp, cold night air were as bright as candles on a chocolate cake. She hurried across the yard to Steve's cottage, knocked lightly on his door, and waited.

Finally, running one sturdy hand through dark, tousled hair, Steve opened the door.

"I'm sorry," she said. "I didn't mean to wake you."

Steve looked groggy. "What's wrong?"

He smelled like soap. A pulse started in her throat. She could suddenly feel the way his skin would taste to her lips. "I needed to thank you . . . for being so kind to Nicholas today . . . when the squirrel was killed." Her throat was so tight the words squeezed out husky and constricted.

That cleared his sleep-dazed mind. "I'm no Lando, but I'm

not such an animal that I can't extend a little human kindness to a boy in need.'' Furious, he started to close the door.

Instinctively Samantha stepped into the opening. ''Steve, please don't be angry—''

''If you want to maintain a professional relationship with your builder, don't come to his house in your nightclothes.''

Samantha swallowed. ''I only wanted—''

''I don't want your gratitude,'' he said, interrupting her. ''I don't want anything from you.''

''I'm sorry,'' she whispered, her face crumbling. A low moan in her throat echoed in his loins.

She looked so miserable, he jerked her inside and closed the door. ''Are you trying to drive me crazy?'' he demanded.

''N-no.''

''What the hell are you doing here then?''

Samantha couldn't answer.

''Don't you know what animals men are? You can't come to my house in the middle of the night in your goddamn nightclothes.''

''I'm sorry,'' she repeated miserably.

''Dammit, Samantha, I have good intentions, but they only work if you help them. I can't do it all,'' he said gruffly.

''I'm so . . . sorry—'' She started to cry.

''Samantha,'' Steve whispered, groaning and pulling her into his arms. ''Don't cry. For God's sake, don't cry.''

Her muffled sobs shook her whole body. Steve leaned against the wall and cradled her wet face with his hands. ''Oh, God, Samantha. Don't you know how weak I am?''

With a groan he lifted her face and set his mouth over hers, tasting her tears and the sweetness of her wet cool trembling mouth. It slowly warmed under his kiss; he knew he had to stop, but he couldn't. The part of him that was still furious with her for becoming engaged to another man wanted to fling her away from him, but the silkiness of her hair, the warm, woodsy fragrance of her peppermint perfume, the magnetic attraction of her skin, all worked to undo him.

Samantha was barely aware that he picked her up and carried her to his bed. She was too caught up in the whirlwind of her own emotions. Her head spun. Her body responded to his every touch. She wanted everything, even his fury. And he seemed as out of control as she. As caught up in the madness and hunger and pain as she.

He claimed her roughly; too soon she groaned and felt her

insides spasming in the first waves of ecstasy. She tried to hold back, to prolong the rapture, but her body felt like a bellows pumping out warm, hot liquid to match his own.

"Oh, God, Samantha," Steve moaned, going limp. He pulled her close to him, kissed her mouth, then fell back on the bed, groaning. "I spend half my life trying not to let you seduce me."

"And the other half?" she asked, panting.

"This changes nothing," he said wearily. "You still have Lando, and I'm still unemployed when I finish this house."

"What are we going to do?" she asked, choked with sudden grief. Tears filled her eyes and wouldn't be gulped back.

Steve groaned. "Don't cry," he whispered. "I can't stand to see you unhappy."

"But . . . I . . . am." She had never been more unhappy in her life. "I shouldn't have come here . . ."

Steve wanted to kill that bastard Lando. "You're engaged to a damned phantom," he growled.

"It's my fault, though. Everything is," she wailed.

She cried, and Steve held her. Finally her sobs subsided; she pressed her wet face against his chest. "What are we going to do?"

"I guess you'll marry Lando, and I'll ride away cursing you both," he whispered, his lips finding hers.

The image his words had painted caused a sharp spear of pain that started at her heart and moved slowly downward, engulfing her. Samantha sobbed and returned his kiss.

"Make love to me, Steve."

"I'm not going to fall in love with you," he whispered, kissing her cheeks, her eyes, her chin.

"I'll stay away from you," she vowed. "I promise." She knew she was babbling, but it didn't matter. Nothing mattered except being in his arms.

"Samantha, dammit, I can't keep making love to you. I'm getting in over my head here." But he knew it would have been easier to leap off the mountain than to let her go.

"Damn me," she whispered. "Do whatever you want, but hold me," she begged, tears streaming out of her eyes.

"Damn, damn, damn," he groaned, smoothing back her damp hair with a trembling hand. He needed to send her back to her own bed, her own fiancé, but he couldn't let go of her, either. In despair, Steve kissed her.

He was more tender this time, but his tenderness hurt her

more than his rage had. Samantha took his kisses and gave back her soul. Nothing mattered except this giving, this man whose mouth teased and tortured her with soft, sweet, provocative kisses. And finally, with his weight pressing her into the mattress and his mouth caressing hers, he entered her, and, for the second time in months, her body no longer felt deprived.

Samantha's intentions were good, but she couldn't stay away from Steve. And he seemed to have forgotten his vows to avoid her, too.

The last two weeks of September were hot, but it was one of the happiest times of Samantha's life. Two or three times a week Steve left Ian in charge and they sneaked away separately and met on the mountain to talk, kiss, and sometimes, when they felt secure enough, to make love.

Samantha took an avid interest in the building. Every day she went to Steve with another small change she wanted. When he glanced up and saw her he smiled—and she felt young and pretty again. The world was a brighter place. Even Nicholas looked healthier than he had in years.

Steve smiled a lot in spite of her ''help'' on the house, the heat, coping with cranky workmen, and the party that was hanging over all their heads, threatening to be the culmination to everything—the housebuilding, their affair, even the land dispute.

The second-story brick walls were in place; two porches had been added on the ground floor. The house looked almost finished on the outside. Inside, carpenters pounded oak boards into place. The house smelled of new wood, glue, and varnish.

On the following Monday a letter came from Lance. Surprised, Samantha tore it open and rushed inside to read it in privacy.

Dear Sam,

Thanks for the party invitation. I'll be there, but I need to talk to you sooner than that. So, unless I hear from you otherwise, I'm coming to see you on Wednesday. I have a great deal to tell you and share with you, but the important thing is that you were right to send me to see Angie.

I went to San Francisco and found her. It was painful and worse than my worst nightmares, but it's over now, and I'm free at last. And in getting free I realized something very important and miraculous about you that I think it best to tell you in person. Until I see you, please know that you are always in my heart.

Lance

Samantha read the letter three times. That night she dreamed that the main house Steve had built for her had somehow moved on its foundation and now sat next to Steve's cottage. The two were so close together she couldn't tell where one started and the other left off. The wood appeared to have merged with the adobe.

It was such an upsetting dream she woke in the middle of the night crying, and she hadn't done that in years.

Tuesday was hot. Tristera felt tired and restless at the same time. Something tugged at her, made her irritable. Finally, to stop the tugging, she took one of the horses and rode down the hill.

At first she didn't know where she was going, but she knew she had no choice. If she was to have any rest at all, she had to do this thing that seemed to have something to do with the old house.

She followed her instincts. An hour later the mare stopped beside the graves of Silver Fish's family. Tristera slipped off and knelt to pay her respects. Then she followed the pull within her and walked to the place where the tepee had been. As she neared it, a cold chill crept into her and caused her to stop. Now she knew why she'd been summoned. The spirits of Young Hawk and his family were still here.

Tristera backed away from the place where their tepee had stood. The day was hot, but gooseflesh pimpled her arms. Turning, she ran back to her horse.

The next day, she approached Samantha. "Will you ride with me today?"

Tristera rarely asked anything of Samantha. It took her by surprise. "Where?"

"To the place where the Indians camped."

Samantha shook her head. "That place has bad memories for me. I'd rather not."

"It is important."

"Why?"

"I have to show you something."

"What?"

"I think the spirits of the dead Indians are still there."

Samantha searched Tristera's pretty face, saw the fear and certainty there. Tristera had somehow frightened herself. Samantha was expecting Lance today, but perhaps it would be good to ride down and meet his train. That way she wouldn't have to worry about his finding the trail up to the new house.

"All right, I'll go with you . . . to show you they aren't there."

Tristera nodded. She didn't care why.

After breakfast, she and Tristera rode down the mountainside. As they approached the old house and creek, Samantha grew reluctant. Just seeing that spot from a distance called up all those painful memories. She could almost feel the Indian baby in her arms.

Tristera dismounted and knelt beside the graves. Reluctantly, Samantha knelt beside her. Tristera said a short prayer and walked to where the tepee had been. Samantha expected to feel nothing, but as she neared the place where the tepee had been, a chill tingled her skin, growing colder and more intense until she could not force herself any nearer.

"You feel it too, don't you?" Tristera whispered.

"No . . . no. I don't feel anything."

Tristera reacted to the answer she saw in Samantha's eyes, not to her words. She breathed a sigh of relief. "It's them."

Samantha didn't want to agree, but in her soul, she knew. "Let's get away from here."

They mounted and rode toward the old house. Samantha saw the feathery plume of smoke from a distant train also headed toward the house. Apparently Lance was right on time.

The locomotive reached the house at the same time as Samantha and Tristera. Lance leaped down and walked toward them, smiling. He looked thinner and handsomer than she remembered. Samantha dismounted and ran into his arms.

Lance held her tight for a long time. Then he stepped back a little. "You look so good to me," he said, his eyes telling her he didn't lie. He looked wonderful to her, too.

"Come in out of the heat," she said, tugging on his brick-brown hand.

They tramped through the sand and onto the porch to get out of the sun. "Don't you want to go up to the house?" she asked.

"I can see the house when it's finished."

"I'll wait for you in the shade behind the house," Tristera said softly.

Samantha flashed the girl a look of gratitude and led Lance toward the swing that still hung on the porch.

"I got a letter from Jennie," she said, sweeping aside spider webs and sitting down.

Lance scowled. "I asked her not to tell you that I'd been hurt. I know I shouldn't have done that, but I was in such a rotten state when I came home from San Francisco that I didn't want to see anyone."

"What happened?"

Lance inhaled a heavy breath. "Angie's having an affair with her editor."

"I don't believe it," she said firmly.

"Well, it's true. She was quite blatant about it."

Samantha swatted at a fly that had settled on her arm. "Angie isn't the type. Are you sure she wasn't lying to you?"

"Why the hell would she lie to me?"

"I don't know, but I just can't believe it."

Pain clouded Lance's fine blue eyes. Samantha got a glimpse of something raw and aching. Then he shrugged, and the image was gone.

"Believe it, Sam. I do, and it has freed me." He paused. They sat in silence a moment. Then he turned to her. His eyes searched hers. "Have I waited too long?"

"No. No, of course not," she whispered. He sighed, pulled her into his arms, and cradled her close to him. She could feel the heavy beating of his heart, and she realized that she was in love with both of them. She had denied her love for Steve, but it was as real as this.

"Come with me, Sam."

"Where?" she asked, drawing back, frowning up at his troubled, handsome face.

"I have to go back to San Francisco soon, and that's going to be a nightmare. I need you now. I need to spend time with you."

"Where would we go?" she asked, stalling.

"Denver, Los Angeles, wherever you want to go."

"But the house—"

"It'll still be here when we get back."

"What will we do?" she asked.

"Have you forgotten that people go places just to enjoy themselves and relax?"

"But . . ."

"No buts. Tell Tristera you'll be back in a week or so."

"But, I have nothing to wear," she protested.

"I have money. Last time I checked, far more than I'll ever need. And so do you."

"But . . ."

"Tell her," Lance urged, burying his face against her throat. Slowly, as he held her, the feeling of being safe returned, and Samantha relaxed.

"Tell her, Sam," he urged

"Okay," she said. "It'll take a moment."

Lance grinned. "Stop frowning. This isn't the end of the world. It's the beginning."

CHAPTER SEVENTEEN

March Newman grimaced and yelled at her daughter, "Savannah Newman, stop that!"

Savannah appeared not to hear her mother. Angie Kincaid looked over at her friend. March's soft, round, pretty face clearly reflected irritation that Savannah continued to fill her bucket with sand and pour it on her little brother's head.

"I'm sure this new ritual must have some special significance," March said, grinning ruefully with the good humor Angie was accustomed to seeing in the woman who had, in a very short time, become her best friend. They were at a public beach watching March's children play. The weather was unseasonably warm for early October. So half the city had turned out to enjoy it. The beach was crowded with families and couples.

March's little girl, Savannah, was seven. Her son, Jeffrey, was two. Jeffrey whimpered and tried to cover his head to block his sister's actions. "Savannah!" March said a little louder. "Stop that!"

A wave of nausea almost overwhelmed Angie. She stood up and walked blindly away from the pallet they had shared.

"Hey, where are you going?" March called after her.

Angie couldn't answer. She waved her hand in desperation, but March jumped up and followed her anyway.

"Is it time to go home?" March asked. "Hey, are you sick again? You poor thing. I've never seen anyone with such persistent morning sickness. It seems to last the whole day," she said, her pretty green eyes shining with sympathy. "Hey, you're crying," she said, catching up with her. "What's wrong?"

"I'm just tired of being sick, I guess," Angie said, lying and sniffing back tears. She hated seeing anyone be mean to a young child. It just killed her.

"Well, I understand completely. I was only sick for the first few months each time I was expecting. And that was way too much. Do you want to go home?"

"It won't be any different at home," Angie said, groping for a handkerchief in the pocket of her coat. "I'll just be throwing up in more familiar surroundings."

"Well, honey," March said, hugging her, "you've been through hell in the last few weeks. You have every right to cry or be sick. Crying might even be good for you."

That night Angie couldn't sleep. She felt sick at heart. The trial date was set. Now she had two weeks in which to worry about facing her husband in court and going through a rotten, demeaning ritual. She didn't mind for herself, but it had been clear to her that despite Lance's stoicism, he was taking this hard. Remembering his face when she told him she was having an affair with Hal Stockton made her stomach hurt.

She punched up a pillow and rested her left leg over it, taking some of the pressure off her back, which was more prone to ache now if she stayed in one position too long. She still felt sick, but she couldn't tell if vomiting would help. Periodically, almost like clockwork, she'd throw up and then be ravaged by hunger almost instantly. She'd eat something then feel sick again. Sometimes she could slip by without vomiting. But not usually. This went on all day. Fortunately March seemed to understand how she could throw up and then be immediately hungry. Lance had been aghast by her doing that during her last pregnancy.

Angie closed her eyes and saw again the image of her husband scowling at her in consternation—because that's what he did when he felt helpless to relieve her suffering. His face seemed so real and so dear that she felt as if she could reach into her mind and touch it, feel his warm skin and the way it smelled when she woke up next to him in bed in the morning.

Her soon to be ex-husband. Unexpectedly she started to cry and couldn't seem to stop. She cried until her eyes hurt, and still she couldn't sleep.

She felt hungry, but she didn't feel like throwing up again, so she decided not to eat anything else. She tossed and turned until her clock chimed three A.M. Aching from head to toe, she struggled out of bed, stood up, and waddled to the window. She was beginning to feel like a belly with legs. The night was still and cold. The smell of smoke tingled her nostrils. She looked back at her room and saw that the top one-third of it was filling with a gray mist.

Alarmed, she ran from room to room, checking for any sign of fire. Then she saw smoke pouring under the door that connected her half of the brownstone to March's. "Oh, no!" she screamed, rushing forward to pound on the door. "March! March! Fire! Fire!" she screamed.

Smoke pouring from under the door burned her eyes. She picked up a heavy chair and used it as a battering ram on the door. Then she heard March's voice, and the door swung open.

"What?" March asked, dazed with sleep.

"Fire!" Angie said, ignoring her friend and surveying the apartment behind her. A reddish glow flickered in March's kitchen. "It's in the kitchen," Angie yelled. "Help me get the kids out."

Still stunned and half-asleep, March followed Angie into the children's bedroom. Angie took Jeffrey, and March took Savannah. The children's room was closer to the kitchen and already filled with smoke. Jeffrey was coughing in his sleep. Savannah woke instantly and was terrified. Together, Angie and March made their way to the front door and into the cold, clear air. March left the children with Angie and ran to wake up their neighbors.

Fire trucks arrived too late to save the brownstone. Four families, two upstairs and two downstairs, lost all of their possessions. The fire had started in an upstairs heater and burned through into March's kitchen. Fortunately Angie had gotten into the habit of leaving her camera equipment at her studio, which was provided now by her publisher. All she lost were her personal articles. She'd rented the apartment furnished.

Angie and March moved into a nearby hotel. A local newspaper ran a story about the fire, and gifts poured in. By the end of the second day, March and the children had coats and shoes and clothes. Angie declined donations for herself. She had money and enjoyed shopping, which was unlike her. Usually she kept so busy shopping was a nuisance. But since leaving Lance, she seemed to have less energy for work and more time.

She hadn't been hurt, but the fire had left her strangely shaken. Two days after the move to the hotel, Angie was still upset, with no idea why. She cried easily and often. She decided to talk to March. She waited until tea time. She and March and the children had tea together on Sundays, if neither of them had other plans.

Angie ordered tea and cakes from room service and invited March over. She waited until the children had finished their tea and cakes and gone into the bedroom to play.

They ate their cake in companionable silence. Then Angie put down her fork. "March . . ."

"Yes, sweetie."

"You've been a good friend to me. Can I ask you a deeply personal question?"

"Of course." March squared her shoulders in preparation.

"I've been crying ever since the fire, and I don't know why."

"You don't know why?" March asked in amazement. "Well, how about getting a divorce from a man you obviously still love, being alone through a pregnancy that should be a time of joy and closeness in your life, and being burned out of your apartment by a careless neighbor? How's that for starters?"

"I don't think it's that simple," Angie said, shaking her head. "Those things don't make me cry. This feels like a bigger wound, a deeper wound. One I don't even seem to know about. Maybe one I don't *want* to know about."

"Well, what could it be?"

"I don't know." But Angie's mind flashed an image in response to March's question, and hot tears flooded her eyes.

"Ohhhh," March breathed. "You do know," she said, leaning forward to hug her.

Angie did know. Images came as if in a kaleidoscope, searing her with grief. She cried freely for a moment, and then struggled for control. "Maybe," she admitted shakily.

"Can you tell me?"

Angie dragged in a ragged breath. "When I was little, I think I was probably seven like Savannah . . . my little brother died. I loved him so much . . . and his dying hurt me so deeply. He was like my own little child. I was totally engrossed with him. My mother was a wonderful mother, but she was overwhelmed with Laramee and me and my father and cooking and cleaning and trying to grow enough food to keep us all alive. I didn't have anything else to do, there was no school in our little town, so I took care of the baby. He was sickly and needed a lot of attention. He had croup. Anyway, he became my entire life. I slept with him and carried him into my mother's bed for his nighttime feedings. She didn't even have to wake up. Then one night there was a fire in the kitchen. We put it out without anyone getting burned, but when I went to check on the baby, he wouldn't wake up. The doctor said he died of smoke inhalation. Probably because his lungs were weak anyway—"

Her face crumpled, and she couldn't continue for a moment. "Anyway," she said, wiping tears aside with an impatient hand.

"I had a miscarriage a few years ago . . . and it hurt so bad to lose that unborn child. . . . I remember thinking that I hoped I never got pregnant again." Angie's voice broke, and she covered her face with her hands. The pain was hot and awful, and she wished she hadn't remembered.

"Poor baby," March said, stroking Angie's hand.

"It hurt so bad when he died," Angie whispered. "Do you think it's possible that maybe . . . I kept myself from getting pregnant all these years because I didn't want to risk losing another baby?"

"To anyone but me that would probably sound odd, but I have no problem believing it," March said firmly. "I could tell you stories about women who've done more bizarre things than that. And honey, you love so deeply, even now. And love and everything else is stronger when we're children. I watch my children, and they feel everything with so much power and passion. All their emotions are so much stronger."

"I remember looking for him and asking my mother when he was going to come back. She said, *He's dead, Angie. He isn't coming back.* But I just couldn't seem to remember that. I kept expecting him to be where he was supposed to be. And the look in her eyes when she had to tell me just killed me. I've never felt anything so awful. . . ."

"Oh, sweet heaven, you poor little creature."

"Maybe I'm just a coward. I forgot my brother, and I didn't remember him until this week."

"We forget those things that are too painful to remember."

Angie gulped back a sob. Hot tears welled up and spilled over. Her body shook with silent sobs. March held her and crooned. Angie realized this was the gaping maw she'd tried to avoid all those years with Lance. This was what she hadn't wanted to be reminded of. She cried for her little brother, for herself, and for what she'd done to her husband.

Finally her tears subsided; she felt better, cleansed somehow. "Thank you . . . for listening to me," she said shakily.

"Does it change anything? Now I mean?"

Angie knew her friend was asking her, does it change anything in relation to the husband you've rejected. "No. I think too much water has gone under that particular bridge."

Steve saw Tristera coming back from the old house leading Samantha's horse. He put down his notes and walked to meet her.

"Where's Samantha?"

Tristera's eyes filled with misery. He could tell she didn't want to answer him. "She went with *Señor* Kincaid."

"Where?"

"Denver, I think."

"For how long?"

Tristera shrugged miserably. "A few days."

Steve felt as if a hole had opened in his chest and someone had filled it with snow. The following week was the most miserable of his life. He felt like a man waiting to hear if a loved one had died in a terrible accident. He longed to see her, and at the same time, he dreaded it, because he feared that it would be blatantly apparent that he was a thing of the past and Lando was her true love.

Steve watched the horizon. Barely five minutes went by without his looking up to scan for the sight of a locomotive chugging up the grade toward the old house. Seven days went by. On the eighth, he finally saw a feathery plume of coal smoke inching northward.

His heart lurched suddenly, as if it would stop under the weight of the load he carried. He wanted to drop everything and gallop down the hill to meet her, but he forced himself to remain busy. Fortunately, with two hundred men swarming over a nearly completed house, that was not a problem.

Two hours later, Samantha rode up to the front door on one of the horses they'd left at the old house for the cowhands to use. A packhorse carried boxes and bundles and hatboxes. Steve took one look at her and knew that his fears had been justified. He put down his clipboard and plunged up the mountainside as if he were walking on level ground.

He hoped Samantha would follow. When it became clear that she wasn't going to, he knew his worst fears were confirmed.

Samantha had not seen the new house from a distance in a long time. Riding toward it on the locomotive, she was stunned by its beauty. The hexagonal tower room surrounded by the two balconies was regal and distinctive. The house fit perfectly on its site, dominating it and complementing it. Steve had chosen well, in all respects.

She refused to think about Steve, though. She had made her choice, and now there could be no looking back. She arrived in a daze and worked in a daze, because she knew there was nothing she could say to Steve that would lessen the impact of what she'd done to him.

She saw him only from a distance, but she could feel his pain evoking an answering response in her. He had vowed not to love her, but she knew now that he had, at least a little. She felt terrible for him, and for that part of herself that had fallen in love with him, but she couldn't think of anything to say to him that wouldn't make it harder. On both of them.

One night after she put Nicholas to bed Tristera asked her what had happened.

"Tristera, you are like a sister to me. I love you and I would trust you with my life, but . . . I just don't want to talk about this yet," she whispered.

"I thought it might help to talk about it."

"No, it won't. Nothing will help. I've dealt Steve a terrible blow. I can see it from a hundred yards away."

"*Sí*, that is true," Tristera said, sympathy for Steve making her eyes soft.

"Take care of him for me, will you?"

"When a man is in love, only one person can take care of his heart, and that is the woman he loves."

"Oh, God," Samantha said, groaning, her own heart aching.

"You do not look happy, *señora*. Are you sure this is the right path for you?"

A stubborn light flashed in Samantha's blue eyes; Tristera knew the answer even before she heard the words. "How could I hurt Steve and feel good about it? But I've waited for Lance all these years. I love him. We'll be very happy together."

Steve and his crews finished the house a week before the date of the party. There was still a month's work to finish the rest of the house site, but that could go on while they moved furniture into the house.

With the interior complete at last, Samantha worked harder than ever, supervising the men who had been assigned to uncrating and carrying in her new furniture, and staying out of the way of the women Juana had hired to help with the cooking and cleaning and furniture arranging. Samantha stayed busy from dawn until dark every day.

Finally everything was in readiness. And not a minute too soon. She looked up from admiring the perfect shine on the mahogany bed frame in the last guest bedroom and saw train smoke etching a line toward the old house. That was either the musical group she'd hired from Phoenix or the family—or perhaps both. Jennie had written that the family would gather in Phoenix and take one train.

Samantha sent a guide down to lead them up the mountain. At three o'clock, she saw sunlight glint off the polished paneling of a carriage—Chane, Lance, or Uncle Chantry's, no doubt. Few carriages gleamed with such richness. Not one to trust to fate, Uncle Chantry and his sons generally brought their own carriages. That was another benefit of owning railroads. Nothing was too much trouble or expense. *That way my old butt doesn't end up bouncing on a bare board,* Uncle Chantry had growled.

Another carriage followed far enough behind to escape the dust cloud raised by the first.

Samantha looked in the hall mirror to check her hair and saw that she was still wearing her afternoon gown. She squealed in horror.

Tristera ran out of the next room. "What?"

"My gown! I have to change! It might be him!"

Tristera rolled her eyes and followed her fleeing mistress up the stairs.

The first carriage rolled to a stop in front of the porch. Samantha glanced at herself one last time in the mirror and ran down the stairs.

A tall, broad-shouldered man had already stepped out and was leaning into the carriage. From the back it was almost impossible to tell Chane from Lance. Let it be Lance, please . . .

At the sound of her step on the porch, the man turned. For one second Samantha thought her heart would stop. Chane! Disappointment was rapidly followed by joy at the sight of the second-most loved man in her life. Third-most, a small voice said, reminding her of Steve.

Chane turned, held out his arms to her, and she flew into them. "Chane! How wonderful you look!"

He leaned down and hugged her, then held her at arm's length. His warm green eyes smiled into hers. "Hello, Samantha."

From behind Chane came Jennifer's familiar voice. "Look at you! You're absolutely glowing," she said, pausing on the carriage step.

"Jennie!" Samantha laughed and held out her hand to her

sister-in-law. Dressed in a purple faille traveling gown, Jennifer looked a little wan from the long, hot trip, but her violet eyes flashed with warmth and humor as she took Samantha's hand and stepped down to hug her.

"You look so beautiful, Sam! I can't imagine why you want to hide yourself in this desert."

Samantha felt lucky to have a family in which everyone liked everyone else. Lance, Chane, Stuart, Maggie, Buffy, and herself had all fought as children. But Aunt Elizabeth and Mrs. Lillian had handled their rivalries in such a way that they didn't escalate into real hatred.

Samantha hugged Jennie. A boy and girl followed her out of the carriage. "Where's Nicholas?" the boy asked.

"My, how you've grown! I can't call you little Chane any longer," Samantha said.

At six and a half years old, Chantry Kincaid IV, looked like a smaller version of his father. Amy did not look like either of her parents. She had a sweet, shy expression, and her body was soft and round. Her toes pointed inward.

Nicholas came around the side of the house. Chane and Amy ran toward him, then stopped short in sudden shyness. Samantha turned back to Chane and Jennie.

"Come in out of this heat," Samantha said, steeling herself to incorporate the right amount of sisterly interest in her next question. "I thought Lance might ride with you."

"Too smart," Chane said. "My brother isn't going to spend an hour cooped up with squirming children if he can help it."

That told her nothing. Either Chane didn't know that Lance had gone to San Francisco, or he was afraid she didn't know and he didn't want to be the one to tell her.

On their way back from Denver Lance had told her that he was going to San Francisco to testify against himself in the divorce action, assuring her he would return the minute he was finished there. He would be a free man at last, and nothing would stand in the way of their marriage.

Samantha had no idea how long this might take. She still hoped he might be back by now, though. It would be just like him to surprise her.

Another carriage appeared on the trail, heading toward her *porte cochere*—Chantry Two's. His matched team of six big-footed black shires with white leggings and white manes braided into jaunty upright pompoms were instantly recognizable, even from a distance. Lance might be with them.

Samantha's heart almost stopped.

CHAPTER EIGHTEEN

The second carriage raised a dust cloud as it swayed around the last corner before it reached the carriage entry. Samantha felt like a woman with few chances left. The carriage finally rocked to a stop in front of the porch.

"Samantha!" A woman's face, vibrant with color, appeared at the window.

"Leslie! You look wonderful!" Samantha said, trying to ignore the knot of disappointment in her throat.

Peter flashed Samantha a look of proud agreement, opened the door, and turned to help his wife and baby out of the carriage.

"So do you," Leslie said, passing the baby to her husband and turning to hug Samantha.

Peter Van Vleet was Jennie's brother. Samantha had met him once or twice before. His story intrigued her. According to what Chane had told her last year, Peter had once been an outlaw named Ward Cantrell. Only months ago Leslie, Peter, Chane, and Jennie had returned to Dodge City, Kansas, where Peter had stood trial on the old charges that had originally sent him into the wilds. He'd been cleared of all counts of murder, and the men who'd killed his first wife had been identified. Most of them were dead, but the blame had been placed where it belonged at last.

With a heavy dose of masculine energy, tawny blond hair, challenging eyes, and a sensual mouth, Peter was one of the most attractive men Samantha had ever seen, except for Lance of course. And, a small voice added, *Steve*. Life had matured Peter into glistening, steely control, evident even with a child on his arm.

The boy's blue eyes were softer and more childlike, but his features already showed signs of being duplicates of his father's. The boy scowled intently at Samantha.

"I've never seen a baby scowl before," Samantha cried.

Peter grinned proudly. Leslie smiled. "Yes, our son is quite remarkable," she said. "Oh, what a marvelous house! I want a house like this," she whispered to Peter.

"It's a lot of work getting to this point," Samantha said, smiling with pride. "Please, come in out of the sun. You must be hot."

"This little guy's hot," Peter said, calling attention to his son, whose cheeks were flushed.

"Poor baby."

"Easy there," Peter growled. "He's already three months old."

Samantha laughed. "He's still a baby."

"Girls may be babies, but this little tyke's a young man."

Samantha laughed. "Here, give him to me." As she held out her hands for the baby, she glanced over Peter's broad shoulder at the carriage they'd come in.

Leslie saw her. "Lance isn't back from San Francisco yet. He . . . was . . . supposed to be home by now."

"That's what I expected. Really."

Leslie felt torn between her love and loyalty to Angie and her compassion for Samantha, whom she also loved and admired. She knew it wasn't wise to encourage Samantha's passion for Lance, but she couldn't condemn her for it. She trusted Samantha to do the right thing, whatever that might be. "Maybe he'll be along later," she said, squeezing Samantha's arm.

The baby started to cry. "It was so hot in that carriage! Poor baby!" Leslie said, taking him back.

Peter scowled his displeasure at his son's being called a baby yet again. Leslie glanced up at her husband; her eyes softened. "Isn't Peter something? A few months ago he had no use at all for babies. Now you'd think the sun rose and set in this one."

"This one's mine."

"You certainly couldn't tell it by looking at him," Jennie said, stepping out onto the porch and slipping her arm around Peter's waist as everyone laughed at the obvious joke.

Elizabeth and Chantry arrived last. The other guests were upstairs changing or resting after the long ride. Samantha met them alone at the front door and hugged them.

"How was your trip?"

"Not as bad as we expected," Chantry Two said jovially.

"We've brought you a housewarming gift," Elizabeth said, motioning the driver to unload a big box. The driver struggled with the heavy box until he and Chantry got it onto the porch.

"Shall I open it here?" Samantha asked, pulling at the lid, which was firmly nailed down.

"If you like. I've had these paintings all these years, but they really belong to you."

"Paintings?"

"Family portraits, a few photographs. I thought since you've built this grand house it was time to bring them to you."

Samantha's hand dropped away from the box. She had no desire to open a box of family portraits, not now, and probably never.

Watching her, Elizabeth realized she may have made a mistake. Samantha did not have a good relationship with family photographs. After Samantha had been with them a few weeks, Elizabeth had placed one of her favorite photographs of Samantha's parents, Regina and Jonathan Regier, on the bedside table near Samantha's bed. It had disappeared shortly after that. Mrs. Lillian missed it and asked Elizabeth if she'd taken it back. When asked, Samantha would not say what had happened to it. During spring cleaning, the maid found it at the bottom of Samantha's dresser drawer. The faces had been scratched off, all the way to the back of the stiff cardboard.

Elizabeth had had no idea why Samantha would do such a thing, but she hadn't risked any more treasured photographs.

Jennie and Chane stepped out the door.

"Mom! Dad! How was your trip?"

The men put the box down to wait for directions.

"Bring it inside, please," Samantha said. "We can put it in the pantry for now. I'll unpack it later."

Chantry tried to shush Elizabeth with his fiercest Kincaid scowl, but she wouldn't be stopped. "Your mother was my dearest friend in the world," she said. "She loved you more than life itself. So I have to speak my piece. You are the spitting image of your mother, Samantha. I realized that with a start as you walked out the door. And I've never thought that before . . ."

"My mother abandoned me!"

"*Abandoned* you?" Elizabeth cried, shocked. "What a thing to say! Your mother drowned!"

"She didn't come back for me! They took me to a terrible place . . ." Samantha couldn't continue.

Elizabeth remembered the dirty little street urchin Samantha had been when they'd come for her. Struggling to control sudden tears that burned behind her eyes, she said, "*We* failed you then, not your mother. We didn't hear about their drowning until six months after it happened. Then we found out what had happened to you through a solicitor. It was unthinkable that a child with so much family, here and in England, would end up begging in the streets. I still shudder to think what you went through.''

Elizabeth dabbed her handkerchief at her damp face. She knew she was hot and tired from the trip and probably about to say something she shouldn't, but the words fairly ached to get out. ''I probably shouldn't say any of this, but I won't let you malign Reggie for drowning. No matter how hard you had it.''

''You don't understand,'' Samantha whispered.

''Yes, I do! I haven't even been inside your new home, but I'd wager my life that there isn't a portrait or a daguerrotype of your mother or your father in that house,'' Elizabeth said angrily. ''Not one! And they loved you so much. They idolized you. I have your mother's diary, which she left in New York before their last trip. Sometime when you're in New York, I'll let you read it. Every entry mentions you. The words you spoke, the things you did, your every look, were lovingly and painstakingly recorded. I dare you to read that book and tell anyone that she didn't love you.''

Samantha trembled with emotion. ''I . . .''

Chantry glowered at Elizabeth. She remembered what he'd told her as they were packing them. *Don't worry if she doesn't want the portraits now. At some point in the future, she will, and they'll be there.* So she shut her mouth.

Elizabeth was happy to see everyone, but she was sixty-three years old now, and with age had come change. She no longer enjoyed socializing. Even family members she loved stressed her after a few minutes, but she enjoyed the children—when they were away from their parents. Even the best parents spent a great deal of time doing and saying things to their children that irritated Elizabeth. If left to their own devices, children were naturally wonderful.

As soon as she could, Elizabeth excused herself and followed the youngsters outside. When Amy and Chane left to climb the hill behind the house, Nicholas came and sat beside her. Elizabeth noticed he looked sturdier than last year. Something about the way he carried himself and the expression in his eyes.

In February, when she had last seen Nicholas, he'd had the fragile look of a boy groping his way toward manhood—with no idea how he was going to get there. Now, less than a year

later, he had the sturdy look of a healthy boy. Somehow he had
found that solid masculine base that every man had to find one
way or another. Little Chane had always had it. Now Nicholas
had it, too.

Thank God. The overwhelming relief she felt took her by
surprise. She needed to search out whoever had brought about
this change and thank him.

Elizabeth realized with consternation that she seemed to love
her grandchildren more than she had her children. Or at least
she was more aware of loving them. She couldn't be sure which.

She had blithely thought herself a good mother at the time.
But the older she became, the more she realized she'd been
anything but. With her busy social calendar of afternoon teas
and evening parties, she'd seen very little of them. If it hadn't
been for Mrs. Lillian, her children would have been strangers
to her.

Chantry had tried to assuage her guilt a number of times over
the years. *All women in your social set hire other women to raise
their children. That's what servants are for*, he'd told her. But
now, seeing how little satisfaction she'd derived from her social
life and how much she enjoyed the company of her grandchildren, she rejected his easy salve.

"How do you like the new house?" Elizabeth asked.

"It's great," Nicholas said softly. "I helped build it."

"You did?"

"Yeah, Steve showed me how to do things."

"Who's Steve?"

"He's the builder. You want to meet him?"

"Of course I do."

Exhilarated, Nicholas leapt to his feet. "I'll go find him. You
wait here."

A moment later Nicholas returned, followed by a man who
was not as tall as her sons, but the way he carried himself, the
level gaze of his hazel eyes, brought Elizabeth to her feet in
admiration.

"Please, don't get up on my account," he said, his deep
bronze voice sending a chill of recognition down her spine. This
was the man for Samantha. Broad, powerful shoulders tapered
to a lean waist and straight, manly legs. When he smiled down
at Nicholas, his eyes twinkled with warmth. If Samantha didn't
have the good sense to fall in love with this man, there was no
hope at all for her.

"You're very kind, but I've been sitting in that coach for an hour. It feels good to stand."

"This is Mr. Sheridan, Grandmother. We call him Steve."

"As I shall. Tell me, Steve. Where did you learn your craft so thoroughly to build such a magnificent house?"

Steve chuckled. "I'm not sure I did."

"Well, it certainly looks like you did. And what will you be doing now that you're almost finished here?"

"My partner is in Waco building a limestone castle. That'll probably take a few years. The limestone has to be cut from the hills around the house. I'll probably join him."

"Well, that's a shame."

If she was not mistaken, he seemed to think so, too. A flicker of something very close to despair flashed in his handsome eyes, and then he excused himself, saying, "I think I hear Ian calling me. It was nice meeting you, ma'am."

"I'm sure we'll run into each other again before we leave."

" 'Bye, Steve." Nicholas watched him walk away, then took his seat beside his grandmother again.

"You still miss your dad, don't you?" she asked.

Nicholas looked into her eyes. He had the wisest eyes she had ever seen on a child. She loved Chane and Amy, but Nicholas was the one whose pain and joy she felt most keenly.

"Yeah. But not so bad anymore."

"Your dad was a nice man."

They sat in silence. Amy and Chane laughed and yelled and charged up the hill.

"You may play with your cousins if you like."

Moments passed. "If Grandfather died, would you feel bad for a long time?"

"Yes, I would."

"If a whole lot of people you knew died, would you feel bad forever?"

"I guess that depends on who they were, but probably not. We grieve for a while and somehow get over it. Why, did someone die?"

"A whole family."

He didn't expand on that. From the house, Elizabeth heard laughter and voices she recognized. She felt tired from the long train and coach ride, but it felt good to sit under the trees, listening to the whispering wind, watching her grandchildren play. The wind in the leaves sounded like rain on a wooden roof.

Nicholas stood up and scratched a piece of bark off the tree.

He picked a small bug out of it and put it on the ground. He started breaking little pieces off the sides of the bark until it was all crumbled. Then he broke off another piece. His hands were strong, but he was too thin. Elizabeth knew it was uncharitable of her, but she blamed Samantha. If she'd get over her foolishness about Lance and provide the boy with a father . . .

"Tell me about this builder."

"He's nice. But Mom's always making him mad."

"Too bad."

"Yeah. He showed me how to make a reata, and grow a garden, and drive nails, and saw boards." His face was filled with wonder at the male world he had glimpsed.

"Any chance your mom might marry him?"

"I don't know. Maybe . . ."

Elizabeth doubted it. From what she'd seen, Samantha was as determined as ever to have Lance. She'd have him if she had to destroy Angie, Lance, and herself. *Why, Elizabeth Kincaid, you are bitter! Well, why not? What is so unreasonable about expecting a beautiful young woman to do anything as sane as provide her son with a decent father?*

While the others dressed for dinner, Elizabeth lay on the bed in the room they'd been given and wished she could skip dinner. Talking to Nicholas had left a bad feeling in her chest.

Chantry sat down on the side of the bed. "You going to wear that down to dinner?"

Elizabeth sighed. "I suppose that would be too much to ask, that I should wear something halfway comfortable."

Chantry scowled down at her. She had that look on her face, the one she got when she was champing at the bit to tell him about something that was none of their business.

"What's wrong now?" he asked, resigned.

"Nicholas."

"He looked fine to me."

"Well, if I'd seen him from fifty yards away, I'm sure he would have looked fine to me, too. There's something wrong with that boy," she said, stalking to the armoire and yanking it open. She jerked the gowns as if they were wood instead of silk.

"You want a new gown, go buy one," Chantry drawled.

Elizabeth expelled a frustrated breath. "Did you see the way Samantha greeted me? She can be perfectly natural with Leslie, Jennie, and you, but with me she becomes stiff and formal, as if I'm a stranger."

Chantry frowned. Before he figured out what she was talking about, she changed the subject. Or else he really was getting senile. Elizabeth slammed the armoire door and faced him, hands on hips. Riled up like that, she was as pretty as she'd ever been.

"She's never really loved me or needed me—or even accepted my love. When I look at her, I want to reach out and slap her till she's empty . . ." Surprise stopped her. "That's it! She's like a full cup. And I feel like I've stood at attention all her growing years, waiting with pitcher in hand for that one moment when she'll need what I have to offer her." Tears gave her eyes a glazed sheen.

"But she never wanted anything from me. All her life with us, I was the one trapped by her need, which I felt as painfully as I would have felt the need of any one of my own children, maybe more so because of my love for her mother. But I couldn't fill her need no matter how hard I tried, because she didn't need me. She was filled up with grief."

Chantry didn't know what to say. His wife was clearly agitated, but the situation was just as clearly out of his control. "Is this going somewhere?" he asked.

"God made idiots for practice, then he made husbands," she snapped.

Relieved, Chantry threw back his head and laughed.

Despite his almost seventy years, her husband was a fine-looking man. His green eyes still snapped with humor or menace, depending upon the situation. Elizabeth picked up her hairbrush and threw it at him. He caught it in midflight, strode toward her, and pulled her into his arms. "You want me to use this on your pretty little bottom?"

"Any man who still thinks my bottom is either pretty or little is undoubtedly too senile to do it."

"Is that right?" he asked, grinning with such good humor that Elizabeth put her arms around him and hugged him.

"I'm sorry," she whispered. "I just get so mad at Samantha. I know she can't help it, but . . ."

"I know, I know," he said soothingly, kissing her forehead. "You can walk away from anything except a child in need. You've always felt you didn't do enough for these kids, but you've done far more than any woman I've ever known. You've managed to let every one of them know you love them, and that's the most important gift you can give a child."

"The tyranny of need." Elizabeth sighed, touched by his

loyalty. "I'm still waiting to be a mother to that girl, and she isn't even a girl any longer."

"Maybe it's time to give up."

"No!" That renewed her anger. "She's held me at arm's length all these years. We opened our house to her. We opened our hearts to her. She lived in both like a stranger trying not to get contaminated by us. She poured all her love and hunger into Lance—at my expense and her own. I know she couldn't help it then, but she's a grown woman now. It's time for her to let Lance be."

"Is this all because that handsome young carpenter made eyes at you?" Chantry demanded. "I saw how he smiled at you. Not bad for a carpenter . . ."

Elizabeth doubled her fist and hit him in the shoulder.

"Ow! Dammit. I've got lumbago in that shoulder."

"It's breaking my heart," said Elizabeth, with a heavy sigh. "Samantha looks so much like her mother now, she's like another Reggie!"

Samantha dressed for the party. She'd thought her heart wouldn't be in it because Lance hadn't come. Everyone maintained he had meant to come—but he hadn't. She'd finally given up hope. Even so, she felt excited and energized.

She dressed carefully, taking special pains with her hair and perfuming every part of her body before she slipped into the gown she'd had made for this night. The gown was red, to match the red-and-black mask that would cover her eyes and forehead and extend its white plume upward to sweep back over her golden hair.

Dressed, she gave herself one last look in the mirror and went to meet her fate, whatever it might be. In the second-floor parlor, she stopped by the door. Leslie and Jennie sat beside the window, dressed for dinner. Leslie wore a green silk gown that exposed a goodly portion of her milk-white breasts, enlarged now from nursing her son. Jennifer wore royal blue, which brought out the purple in her lovely eyes.

Leslie waved to Samantha and walked to the window. "I hate to be a tattletale, but the children are squatted down, digging in the dirt in their clean clothes."

"Nicholas, too?" Samantha asked.

"At least that'll make someone happy—Elizabeth," Leslie said, smiling.

Jennie and Leslie laughed. Samantha scowled. The two women stopped laughing at the look on her face.

"What's wrong, Samantha?" Jennie asked.

"I don't think we should make fun of Aunt Elizabeth," she said, unable to help herself, the words just spilled out.

Jennie looked quickly at Leslie, whose mouth had dropped open. "I would never make fun of her. I love Elizabeth," Leslie said, protesting.

Jennifer's eyes widened, but she remained silent. Embarrassment almost overwhelmed Samantha. "I'm sorry," she said, flushing. "I know you do. I don't know why I said that."

In the hall, Elizabeth stepped back from the door and prayed they hadn't heard the taffeta swish of her gown. She had almost followed Samantha into the room. Unfortunately, or fortunately, she'd heard every word. She had no idea why, but what Samantha had said caused an odd sensation within. As if . . .

Elizabeth shook her head. She was getting too sensitive. Now it even irritated her that Samantha defended her.

A knock sounded on the door. Steve yelled, "Come in."

Tristera opened the door and stuck her head in. "It is me, *señor.*"

Steve stood up. "Sorry, I thought it would be Ian."

"The *señora* sent this for you," she said, walking into the room and unfolding a bundle.

"What is it?"

"The costume the *señora* bought for you."

The shirt, frock coat, and trousers were black worsted—expensive and soft and finely made. The mask, which would cover his entire face, was baked red ceramic with short, spiked horns curving out of the sides of the mask's glossy forehead. The wide mouth was represented by a jagged white line that stretched like rickrack all the way across the mask. The eyes were painted on—round black circles surrounding the openings where he could look out. Diagonal black lines slashed in from both sides and down from the top.

Steve took the ceramic mask and held it away from him. It was a work of art—skillfully painted in red, black, and white.

"What is this?"

"A *kachina hu* mask."

"Do you know where she copied it?"

"I know not. I have a *kachina* doll in my room, but it is not an ogre doll."

"Well, you can take it back to her. I'm not going."

"You are afraid?"

The implication irritated Steve. Samantha Forrester demanded too much of a man she only intended to abuse. "I'm too smart to go to a party so I can make a public fool of myself."

"She will be there, wearing a very beautiful gown that she made especially for you."

"What a little liar you are."

Tristera shrugged. "She may not even know herself. In my vision, the gown was made and worn for you."

Sweat broke out on Steve's forehead. His whole body ached for the opportunity to be near Samantha. "You've got to be the most heartless little wench I've ever known."

"Her heart will be broken if you do not come."

"You should be ashamed of yourself, Tris."

"It was a vision. How could I ignore it?"

Steve fingered the glossy mask and the fine worsted material of the costume. There was probably a message in it for him, if only he could figure out what it was. "Are you sure she meant this for me?" he asked.

"Yes. And in case you are not familiar with Hopi tradition, there is great power in a *kachina hu* mask. It is a chief mask."

"If I show up in this and she throws me out because I'm wearing his costume, I'm going to look you up."

"It is for you! She borrowed one of your suits to have it made to your measurements."

He knew that Samantha would be wearing something sensational. He wouldn't stay long, though, just long enough to torment himself with what he couldn't have. In front of the bastard who could.

After dinner Samantha's houseguests went upstairs to freshen themselves. As other guests arrived for the party, Samantha greeted them. Chila Dart arrived with Joe and Ham Russell. Chila wore an elaborate bell-shaped, ground-sweeping dress left over from the sixties. She carried a tiny matching parasol and an ornate ivory-handled fan, and she'd pulled her graying hair up onto her head in a spill of ringlets. Ham Russell looked out of character in a black serge suit and shiny black shoes. He had combed and freshly braided his red beard for the occasion.

"Good to see you here, Chila," Samantha said.

"Your house is smashing, darlin'. Ah wouldn't have missed it for the world."

When the ballroom was filled with jubilant, milling people, Samantha slipped away, leaving Juana and Tristera to supervise the young women hired to keep the champagne glasses filled.

Samantha rushed up to her room and brought out the box of masks she'd made as gifts for her guests. She found the family in the ballroom a few paces from the stairway.

"What's this?" Elizabeth asked, spying the box in Samantha's arms.

"I made masks for everyone. They aren't much, but I thought you might not have the time or opportunity to get any yourselves."

For Jennie, who had been a ballerina before she married Chane, Samantha had crafted a mask painted to resemble the perfectly made-up face of a beautiful ballerina, with classic round eyes, rouged cheeks, and pouty mouth.

For Leslie, an artist, she had created a Madonna mask. "It's exquisite!" Leslie said breathlessly, looking at Samantha with new respect.

Samantha lifted out Peter's mask—fierce eyes above a bandanna painted over the bottom half.

Everyone laughed, including Peter, and Samantha relaxed. That had been her biggest risk. For Elizabeth and Chantry Two she had made Queen Guinevere and King Arthur masks and crowns.

"Why, they're beautiful," Elizabeth said in amazement.

For Chane she had made a simple half mask, because she knew he wouldn't wear anything else.

Only Steve's mask had gotten out of control. She'd known exactly what she was going to make for each of the others. But Steve's mask had designed itself. She could not explain it. She dreaded to think what Steve's reaction might be.

"I didn't know you were so gifted," Jennie exclaimed. The others echoed her. "I love it! You should have let us know you had such talent."

"Dance with me, someone," Samantha cried, her cheeks burning.

Chane held out his arms; Samantha smiled her gratitude as he whirled her toward the center of the enormous ballroom, where other couples already danced.

"Your party is already a big success," Chane said, grinning down at her, twirling her to the waltz being played by the band from Chicago that had arrived barely an hour before the party was supposed to start.

Chane wore a black frock coat, black trousers, and a white linen shirt. The black half mask covered his face from nose to forehead. But no one could mistake his wide, angular jaw, or determined mouth.

Mrs. Lillian always said that Chane would be a hard man to change. *Wherever he sits, that* is *the head of the table.* Chane wasn't belligerent the way some stubborn men were, but he was quietly and guilelessly immovable. He did not adjust to the family. The family adjusted to him.

Relaxing in his arms, Samantha scanned the ballroom for Steve Sheridan. Dozens of couples danced around them. Leslie and Peter; the governor and his wife; dozens of her neighbors. She saw Captain Rathwick and ex-Captain Lawson, now working as assistant manager of the Cowdry Mine Company. Each danced with women Samantha knew. Outside, Steve's workmen and their families were dancing beneath hanging lanterns to another musical quartet from Phoenix. Maybe Steve was outside.

Just as she'd given up hope, she saw him in the black devil's suit, dancing with Jennifer Kincaid.

"Who's the devil?" Chane asked, spotting him at the same time and turning her, so she could get a better look at him.

"Devil?" Samantha flushed. So that's what she'd designed. A devil mask. "Oh, it's Steve. You know him."

Chane waltzed her closer to them. "If he keeps dancing with my wife, I expect shortly I'll know him a lot better."

Samantha laughed. "You're not jealous, are you?"

"Have you looked at Jennie lately?" he asked gruffly. "She becomes more beautiful every day."

They danced in silence for a moment. Chane held Sam away from him and looked her over critically to be sure he hadn't hurt her feelings, but her eyes sparkled with merriment. She was holding her own. And she was still one of the most beautiful women he'd ever seen, except for Jennie. Sam looked thinner than he'd remembered. Chane didn't like to think he was too much like his father, but he could hear his father's voice in his own head. *I don't see why the hell a beautiful woman like Samantha can't settle for one of the fifty thousand or so eligible bachelors who'd give their left testicle for a chance to marry her.*

Jennifer thought she liked the man behind the mask, but she couldn't be sure without seeing his eyes. She always judged men by their eyes, and this sturdy young devil was extremely well hidden back there. The light from Samantha's enormous crystal chandelier gleamed off the shiny surface of the ceramic devil's mask, further frustrating her efforts to pierce it.

"Did you attend school in the East, Mr. Sheridan?"

With her mask in place, Steve couldn't tell if she was one of those Eastern snobs who thought a man had to graduate from one of those Episcopalian church schools, room on the Gold Coast, and be accepted by Boston society to be respectable.

Jennifer felt the resistance in him. Nothing overt, just the tensing of muscles in his strong arms. "Forgive me if I sound like a snob, Mr. Sheridan . . . It's just that this is such a magnificent house. I just assumed you did."

"No, ma'am. I served an apprenticeship."

"Well, you certainly learned your trade. The house is grand. I speak from a certain authority, as my husband is also a builder. He said it's first rate. Coming from him, that's quite a compliment."

"Thank you, Mrs. Kincaid."

His voice had a weighty timber she liked—a rich, dark undertone that hinted at depth and masculine savagery. She had no idea how Samantha had resisted him, if she had.

"How long have you been here? Building this house, I mean?"

"Eight months."

"Heavens! That's very fast."

He chuckled. "Mrs. Forrester was in a hurry."

Chane tapped Steve on the shoulder. "May I cut in?"

Samantha's feet ached from dancing. Steve had barely paid any attention to her. He'd danced with almost every woman at least once, Jennifer as many times as he could get her away from Chane, and herself not at all.

She shouldn't care what Steve Sheridan did, but her gaze followed his lithe form everywhere. He danced gracefully, and didn't seem to know she existed.

Finally she could stand it no longer. She intercepted him on his way to the punch bowl. Jennie, Chane, Leslie, and Peter all converged there at the same time.

Steve ignored her and spoke with Jennie. And every time he did, Samantha's heart ached as though there were a cold weight in her chest.

In spite of the imploring look in Samantha's eyes, he nodded his good-bye to her and her friends and strode across the room to leave. At the door he paused to let a couple pass in front of him.

"Dance with me, Steve."

He turned at the sound of Tristera's voice. In a white low-cut gown and with her auburn hair arranged artfully on top of her head, she looked older, more sophisticated, and definitely worth whatever trouble a man had to go to to win her. He looked around for Rathwick.

"I thought you'd be dancing with your *capitán*."

"Humph!"

He wanted to leave, but Tristera looked like she needed a friend. "You sure you can keep up with me?"

"You dance all right, but you have a beeg head, *Señor* Sheridan."

He laughed. When Tristera acted Spanish, she acted very Spanish. "I like generosity in a woman."

Steve danced her past Captain Rathwick, in full military dress, dancing with Samantha, who flashed Steve a brooding glance that started his heart pounding.

"He's too old for her," Tristera grumbled, tossing her head so hard Juana's pins barely held her shiny curls in place. Her eyes followed the captain's tall, military figure.

Steve didn't point out that Samantha was older than Tristera. He'd accepted sometime back that love was truly irrational.

"Seems to me you've already made the conquest," Steve said. "Rathwick hasn't noticed anyone else tonight. He just hasn't surrendered to it yet."

"He never will."

"I wouldn't put money on it."

"Don't try to give me hope, Steve. He would never fall in love with a woman not of his race."

The music stopped. Rathwick tried to concentrate on what Samantha Forrester was saying as he led her toward the punch bowl, but Steve Sheridan led Tristera Rodriguez to within a few feet of where he and Samantha stopped to sample the champagne. Tristera looked like a princess in her white silk gown, cut low in front and lower in back. Her dusky skin gleamed golden in the light of the sparkling chandelier. Her small, perfect breasts swelled above the gathered fabric, which seemed to cup them like two silky white hands. The light picked up the red glints in her hair. He'd never seen hair so shiny or so rich.

"Well," Rathwick said, glancing awkwardly from Tristera to Steve, "I have to say, I admire the job you did on this house."

"Thanks."

Tristera dipped a glass of punch and held it out to Sheridan. Then she dipped another and looked uncertainly at Rathwick. "Would you like . . . ?"

"I'd be delighted," he blurted out, "if he's not going to . . ."

Sheridan's lips twitched in a wry half smile. "Oh, no, thanks. One's plenty for me," he said, lifting his glass.

Rathwick flushed with embarrassment. He'd thought Tristera was asking him to dance.

"Excuse me. I thought . . . would you like to dance?" he asked, feeling like a fool.

"*Sí.* Why not?" Tristera said, shrugging.

The band struck up a waltz. Rathwick held out his arms; Tristera stepped into his embrace. The lights seemed brighter suddenly, the music more melodious. Her black patent slippers barely touched the floor.

"You dance as lightly as a feather," he said.

Tristera leaned her head back and smiled up at him. He seemed taller up close. His uniform smelled new. Her head only reached up to the top of his mouth. If she tilted her head up just so . . .

Matthew Rathwick felt light-headed. Tristera's closeness filled his body with energy. Her slim, wiry back under his hand felt sensuous and alive. Sweat broke out on his forehead; an ache started in his loins. Generally he was proud of his ability to discuss any subject and acquit himself with the best, but suddenly, with this wisp of a girl, he couldn't think of anything to say.

"Slaughtered any wicked Indians lately?" she asked.

Her derision saved him. "You might not think that's so funny if they go back on the warpath. If Wovoka has his way, and his Ghost Dances make them any crazier than they already are . . ."

"Not likely. Starving Indians don't fight very long."

"Our government is far more generous with them than they would have been with us if the tables were turned. They are not starving."

"Not starving? Did the Indian agent who was supposed to steal their allotments get lost in the desert?"

"Arden Chandler's a good man . . . and, from what I've heard, well off. He has no reason to steal anything. Though in all truth I can't say that about Genner Long at the Apache reservation."

"All Indian agents get rich, sooner or later. It is too hot in here," she said, fanning her face with her hand.

Rathwick danced her to the French doors opening onto the veranda. Outside, the air was crisp and cool. Fiddle music wafted from behind the house. Sounds of people dancing, laughing, and shouting attested to the enjoyment of those who preferred to dance outside. Jupiter gleamed brightly. Stars were so bright they looked almost touchable. A new moon hung low in the southern sky, casting its soft light on her slim shoulders.

"*Aiyee*, this was a good idea," said Tristera, twirling into the middle of the veranda, slim and provocative as her skirts billowed out around her shapely calves.

She spun twice around the open balcony and stopped beside Rathwick, whose profile against the starry sky was strong and appealing. He turned slightly and looked into her eyes. A shiver of sensation rippled through her. She ached to touch his face, to feel the roughness of his ruddy skin, the stiff bristle of his mustache. It amazed her that she could feel so much attraction for him when she had felt none for the men of her tribe, except for that jackal Yellow Fox.

"Tristera . . ."

The air between them seemed to shimmer with heat and tension. Then her hand did the unthinkable; it reached up and touched his cheek, warm and slightly damp with perspiration. A quiver shook her. She wanted to draw her hand back, to pretend it hadn't happened, but he lowered his head until his lips were within inches of her own.

"Tris . . . tera . . ."

She lifted her lips slightly, brushed his, and felt the heat of his kiss the length of her body. It wasn't fair . . . if the Great Mystery wanted her to behave herself, He shouldn't make it so hard.

Rathwick's hands closed around her waist and pulled her tight against him. Weakness and strength got confused in her. She surged upward, kissing him, hugging him, forgetting everything except how good he felt in her arms.

He kissed her face, her mask, her hair.

"Take this thing off," he growled. Tristera slipped the mask off and dropped it. The tinkle of it breaking on the adobe porch reminded her it had been ceramic.

"Oh, no!"

"I'll buy you another." Rathwick lowered his head. "The taste of your skin drives me wild."

Beside them, the door opened. A man stepped outside, eased the door shut behind him, and leaned against the banister. Tristera opened her eyes. The man, possibly blinded from the brightness of the lights inside, faced her as if he didn't see her.

Tristera thought how embarrassed he would be when he realized his lack of courtesy. She felt certain no man would purposely walk in on two lovers. Almost before that thought was through her mind, she recognized him.

"Oh, sorry," he muttered. Tristera found herself staring into a face terrifying in its familiarity. A ripple of fear gripped her.

Lawson opened the door to leave. The light from inside spilled out, illuminating the couple he'd accidentally stumbled upon, and he recognized Rathwick. Etiquette demanded he leave without acknowledging his ex-colleague, caught in less than politic circumstances. But something caused him to stop and peer into the face of the woman in Rathwick's arms.

He didn't know her, but unmistakable recognition and fear leapt in her eyes. Lawson tried to break eye contact with the girl, but her expression held him there.

"If you'll excuse us, Lawson," Rathwick said gruffly.

Mortified, Lawson bowed from the waist and turned. "Pardon me, Captain. Carry on."

The door closed behind him. "That was uncalled for," Rathwick whispered, pulling her back into his arms.

Trembling so hard her legs shook, Tristera pushed Rathwick's arms aside and walked to the adobe railing that surrounded the veranda.

"Where are you going?"

"Away," she whispered. Before he could stop her, she slipped over the railing, jumped four feet to the ground below, and ran toward the barn.

"I'll come with you."

"No!" she called over her shoulder.

He thought she would return, but moments passed, and then he heard the clatter of hoofbeats against the hard-packed Earth.

In the moonlight, a horse galloped from the barn, a small, feminine figure clinging to its back.

Curious, he walked to the barn. Near the tack room, he found the beautiful white silk gown lying in the dirt. "I'll be damned."

She was gone.

CHAPTER NINETEEN

Steve Sheridan relinquished his dance partner and headed for the door. Samantha picked up her skirts and ran after him.

"Dance with me, Steve," she said, trying to keep her tone light.

His head turned slowly. The mask she'd made did not hide his anger or his disbelief. "Me?"

"Yes . . . please."

She dazzled him so that nothing mattered suddenly but what she wanted. Reluctantly Steve offered her his arm. On the dance floor, she pressed her slim body against him, puzzling him even more. For weeks she had treated him like poison ivy, except for a few times when she needed something. Now in full view of her friends and family, she tried to seduce him.

They danced in silence for a moment.

"I thought Kincaid would be here tonight."

"So did I."

"So where is he?"

"San Francisco."

"Doing what?"

"He went to testify in his own divorce action. But I don't know if he did or not. I haven't heard from him."

"Are you happy now?" he asked softly.

"Yes, of course," she said, lifting her chin.

"You don't look it."

"Well, of course I'm disappointed he couldn't get here for the party . . ."

"I didn't just walk in the door, you know. I've been here awhile," said Steve, his eyes sparkling with anger.

"I am happy," she insisted, amazed that her eyes would choose that unfortunate moment to mist with tears.

Steve danced her close to the stairway and took her by the arm. "Where are you taking me?" she asked weakly.

"I have to get out of this mask for a while." He guided her forcefully up the stairs, onto the second-floor landing, and into the sun room. Then he closed the door behind her and ripped his mask aside.

She reacted to his angry nearness with pounding heart. His dark hair gleamed in the shaft of light slanting into the room from outside, where strings of brightly colored lanterns hung between the trees. Her hands twitched with the urge to touch his handsome face, to feel the smoothness of his cheek and the small indentation where he'd been cut a long time ago.

He looked into her eyes a moment, then sighed. "I guess this is as good a time as any to say good-bye," he said, his voice gruff.

"Good-bye?"

"The house is finished. The party's over. Unless you want me to just slip away without bothering you."

Anxiety caused pressure in her throat and around her heart. At times she realized she needed Steve, but she could never hold that thought, because needing him didn't fit in her head just right. Her head still had room only for Lance. But her body . . .

Suddenly Samantha felt weak and tired. She never should have had this party. It had been a terrible mistake.

Steve looked past her, out the window, at the people who danced and laughed below. His firm, clenched jaw looked smooth in the pink glow of the lanterns. Samantha knew better than to touch him, but her hands seemed to do what they wanted tonight. With trembling fingers, she reached over, turned his face toward hers. His eyes flashed with anger.

"What now? You want to seduce me, so your family can tell Lando and make him jealous?"

"Do you have such a low opinion of me?" Her throat ached at the picture he painted of her. Bitterness swelled in her, and before she could even think, the hand that had ached to stroke his warm flesh drew back and hit him so hard the palm of her hand tingled.

Steve captured her hands and pressed her back onto the window seat.

"Let me go!"

"Hush! Or you'll have what you wanted, but with a bigger audience."

Samantha brought her knee up and opened her mouth to scream. Blocking her kick, Steve pinned her down and covered her mouth with his own. Samantha struggled, but Steve was heavier and stronger. Then because he couldn't help himself, he kissed her until she stopped struggling.

Finally he relinquished her lips and raised himself off her. In the dim light of the lanterns reflected off the ceiling, her face looked damp. Steve expected her to slap him, scratch him, or scream for help, but her hand slipped up and pulled his head down. Her warm, soft, wet mouth opened, amazing him with the strength and hunger he felt in her.

Still furious, he caught her by the hair and twisted. Samantha's body arched in protest, but her mouth only deepened the kiss. The swell of her breasts beckoned him. He slipped her gown off her shoulders and freed one round breast. Then he lowered his head and took its softness and sweetness into his mouth, groaning at the jolt of sensation that shot through him.

Samantha was beyond sanity. She knew better than to let him make love to her here, but knowing didn't help. In a flash of understanding she realized his pain, confusion, and rage matched hers. Steve didn't want to feel what he felt for her any more than she did. But he couldn't stop any more than she could.

His hands were rough, and his taking her was fierce and heated. With the world spinning around her, she clung to his warm, damp back and prayed that this moment would last forever.

With a party going on, Nicholas missed Young Hawk more than ever. Amy and Chane danced together—and got a lot of attention for that—but Nicholas just sat and watched. Finally he got bored with watching others dance and walked toward the barn to see the horses. Outside, the grounds were lit with red, blue, yellow, and green hanging lanterns. Everywhere people were dancing. On two sides of the house, bands played two different kinds of music—a fast Mexican fandango and a slow waltz.

In the barn, he climbed up into the hayloft. He liked lying in the sweet dried hay, listening to the horses, chickens, and milk cows nearby and the welter of music at a distance.

Clouds covered the stars. Cool wind rattled the tied-down shutters. He and Young Hawk used to sit in the hayloft of the barn at the old house. Nicholas wondered about Young Hawk a lot, but he wished he wouldn't, because thinking about him caused a bad feeling.

He must have dozed off. Sounds below startled him, made him look around to see where he was.

"You going to Waco with Sheridan?" a man below said.

"Naw. I'm not even finishing out the week. The wife's begging me to quit before I catch that kid's consumption. She heard about them Indians dying of it, and she's been driving me crazy ever since. She's the jumpy sport.''

"I thought they died of measles.''

"Hell, I bet you believe in Santa Claus, too, don't ya?''

The sound of a horse stamping was followed by the barn door closing, then silence below. Lightning flashed to the north. Within seconds thunder boomed overhead. Nicholas rubbed his chest, which ached worse than it had in a long time. Steve was leaving—and Young Hawk had died with the coughing and fever.

Nicholas ran to the house to look for his mother.

Steve cradled Samantha on the narrow window seat in silence, listening to the sounds outside. The music was gay. Carefree people were laughing and dancing. He wondered if the world would ever seem that simple to him again. Samantha could take her enjoyment with him. She could tease him, flaunt her beautiful body and her bedazzling, enchanting face before him, but she reserved her love and loyalty for Lando.

He felt half crazed with the pain of knowing that in spite of what they shared, she was going to marry another man. The longer he thought about it, the worse it felt. Finally, without knowing what he was going to do, he stood and adjusted his clothing so that he was properly dressed. Then he pulled her off the window seat and helped her stand. She looked so soft and sweet and disoriented, he pulled her into his arms and kissed her. But too soon, the anger came up in him again; he ended the kiss.

"Nooooo," she moaned. "Kiss me . . .''

"Hush," he whispered, his firm hands giving her a little shake to reinforce the command. While she stood in a daze of interrupted passion, he unfastened the long row of buttons that held her gown together.

Samantha started to protest but couldn't. She wanted to be naked in his arms. It was craziness. Hundreds of her guests danced and laughed downstairs, but she waited blindly and submissively as Steve Sheridan slipped her gown off and let it drop, its wide skirt fanning her legs as it collapsed around her ankle

Steve undid the corsets and stays and eased them down. spite of making love to her only moments ago, his desire for was strong. He had to clamp his jaws to keep from kissing e inch of her beautiful, pale, shimmering body. Even so, his h could not leave her alone. They stroked the smooth curve of her waist, the soft thrust of her breasts. Her flesh, which seemed to gather all incoming light, gleamed pearlescent. Standing perfectly still beneath his hands, naked and beautiful and willing, she was the embodiment of abundant female richness.

Her lover might arrive at any moment, but she was here. And she wasn't asking to leave. Steve sensed so much in the soft raggedness of her breathing, the mindless quality of her submission to his madness. She shivered slightly, as if trying to bring herself back from wherever she had withdrawn, and reached out to fumble with one of his buttons. Steve placed her arms firmly at her sides.

"Be still," he whispered, his voice firm, brooking no opposition. Samantha shuddered at the feel of his warm hands and the chilled air against her bare skin. She knew this was folly. Someone could walk in at any moment. Her reputation would be ruined, but it didn't matter. She had watched Steve dancing with other women all evening. Now nothing mattered except his holding and touching her. She wanted him to kiss her. When he wasn't kissing her or touching her, she felt deprived.

"Steve . . ."

"Hush. This is the last time I'll ever make love to you. The last time I'll ever see you like this."

He positioned her firmly. Trembling, her body humming with soft, muted excitement, she waited as his warm hands stroked her back and hips, then rose again to graze lightly over the sides of her breasts, the curve of her waist, the flare of her hips. His touch cast a spell over her, causing her body to ache sweetly, darkly.

Steve's hands, firm one moment, feather-light the next, hypnotized her, dragged her attention to whatever place he touched, seemed to magnify every sensation.

"Do his hands feel so much better than mine?"

"It isn't like that," she whispered.

"Then how is it?" He sounded so fierce, she shivered.

"I don't know!" she whispered. "Don't talk about him . . ."

"Does he touch you in this way? Does the bastard even know how beautiful you are?"

"Steve . . ."

"Hush," he said softly, his voice heavy with its own darkness. His hands positioned her again. Her heart pounded. Her loins burned.

"Do you know why you obey my commands?" he asked

softly, his hand stroking her thighs and moving very close to the place that ached so sweetly for his touch.

Mute, she shook her head no.

"Because you belong to me," he said fiercely. "That bastard may think he's acquiring title when he marries you, but it'll be as useless to him as your deed to this land."

She trembled, but could not speak. His hands touched every part of her face, head, neck. Finally he lowered his head and kissed her. It was like no other kiss he had ever given her. He kissed her until her knees wobbled, then he yielded her lips and lowered her onto the settee.

She wanted to be kissed again, but he lowered his head to kiss her breasts. His lips were warm and hungry as they burned a trail down her belly.

"Steve, no . . ."

He caught her face in his hands and kissed her urgently. "Let me have you tonight," he whispered. "Don't you understand? I'm leaving. I'll never see you again." His voice was low and desperate, evoking an answering pain in her.

"Oh, God," she moaned, the pain almost insupportable.

From outside the door, a child called out, "Mama! Are you up here, Mama?"

"Nicholas," Samantha whispered, her heart pounding with sudden fright.

Steve groaned softly. Samantha grabbed her gown and rushed to the door and held it shut, waiting to see if he was coming closer or retreating. He didn't call out again.

"Help me get dressed," she said, frantically pulling her gown on and backing up to him. Steve pulled her to the window, where he could see well enough to match the right buttons with the right buttonholes. When she was secured into the gown, he put on his mask and started out the door.

"Wait for me," she whispered.

"Better if we go back separately."

She wanted somehow to hold him, to feel his arms around her one more time, but he was determined to leave. His broad back blocked the doorway for one moment, then it closed between them. He was gone. All she wanted to do was cry, but she had to somehow repair the damage he'd done to her and find her son.

Nicholas couldn't find his mother among the dancers. He called for her a time or two, got a few odd looks from people, then stopped. He went into his room and laid down on his bed to get warm. His lungs ached; he felt cold and scared and jumpy inside.

At the bottom of the steps, Steve paused and leaned against the wall of the ballroom, waiting for his breathing to return to normal. He heard someone approaching and reached up and checked to be sure his mask was in place.

A woman in an old-fashioned bell-shaped skirt and dainty bonnet strode right up to him and stopped in front of him. She was wearing a mask that covered only the top half of her face. She smiled and nudged her companion, who was unmistakably Ham Russell, in spite of the mask covering his eyes. His red beard was braided and tied with clean ribbons. His red hair was tied back from his face by a matching ribbon at his neckline.

"Ah declare, isn't that the devil?" the woman asked, sounding slightly uncomfortable. Steve recognized her now as Chila Dart.

"Sure looks like it to me," Russell growled.

"Why, you are a fine-looking devil, young man," she said, her voice dropping down into coyness.

"Thank you, ma'am."

Chila recognized Denny's voice, and her heart skipped a beat in surprise and consternation.

Steve saw the reaction jolt her; he expected her to walk quickly away from him. Instead, she opened her mouth and let out an ear-shattering scream.

"Ahhhhhhhhhhhhhhhh!"

The music stopped abruptly. People murmured their amazement, searching for the source of that bloodcurdling howl. Then, into that silence, Chila screamed again, louder. Every eye in the room focused on her, Ham, and Steve.

"That's the man I told you about," she yelled at Ham Russell. "That's the man who killed my baby!"

A hush fell over the crowd. Peter Van Vleet left his wife's side and strode toward Steve Sheridan, who looked like he could use a friend. As Peter approached, he saw the screaming woman and recognized her escort. Surprised at the sight of Ham Russell, whom he'd never expected to see again, he stopped short and watched as the woman began to scream again.

"Shoot him! Shoot him! He killed my baby!"

Fortunately Ham Russell was not wearing a gun. From his

vantage point, Peter saw his sister order the musicians to resume playing. Chane and Chantry Two stepped forward and escorted Chila Dart and Ham Russell out of the house, talking to them in low tones, but Chila was not to be shushed. She kept screaming something to the effect that Sheridan was Denny, the devil who had killed her baby and deserted her.

Visibly shaken, Steve Sheridan stalked out the back door.

Peter thought he knew now why Samantha had lost so many cattle. Ham Russell had been one of Dallas Younger's henchmen, privy to the inside workings of his boss's wholesale rustling operation near Phoenix last year.

Peter scowled. It was one thing to know that—and another to prove it, though.

Rathwick shook his head in chagrin and continued his own search. Finally he found Lawson at the punch bowl chatting with the lovely young Leslie Van Vleet. He waited until she finished dipping two glasses of punch and carried them away.

"I need to speak to you, Captain," Rathwick said grimly.

"Ex-captain," Lawson said, following Rathwick to a deserted corner of the ballroom. "Nice greeting. I guess you haven't missed me any more than I've missed you." The musicians changed to a polka. Couples paired off and began a gay romp around the room.

Rathwick stopped and glared at Lawson. "I want to know why the sight of you scared the young lady I was with."

"Must have been my reputation as a womanizer that just overwhelm—" Lawson saw Rathwick's fist coming at him, but he couldn't move away in time. The fist connected . . . and lights flashed in his head.

Enraged, Lawson launched his own punch. Nothing in his life had ever felt as good as hitting Rathwick.

Too soon, men pulled Rathwick off Lawson and tried to drag him outside, but he dragged them back to within three feet of Lawson, bleeding profusely from the mouth. "I want to know why the sight of you scared her!" Rathwick yelled.

"Go to hell!"

"Tell me!" shouted Rathwick.

"Screw you!" Lawson growled, turning away.

Samantha heard screaming, and then what sounded like a brawl, but she could do nothing about it. She walked to the bedroom door and peered out, hoping to figure out what was happening out there, but she could see nothing except an empty hallway.

By the time she finally succeeded in restoring herself and repairing the damage Steve had done to her, the music had resumed and the screaming had stopped. She slipped back downstairs and found the Kincaid family gathered by the musicians.

"Well, sis, you certainly know how to throw a party," Chane said, with a drawl.

"What happened?"

"Oh, nothing much. Your builder was accosted by a woman who called him a child murderer; a captain and a civilian got into a fight; Peter recognized someone from his past; and Steve wisely left."

Chane filled Samantha in on all the details. Chila Dart had been the one screaming. And Peter had recognized Ham Russell. No one knew why Rathwick attacked Lawson.

"Peter," Samantha asked, "you know Ham Russell?"

Peter lifted a tawny eyebrow. The look in his clear blue eyes left no doubt. "Yes. He was one of Dallas Younger's henchmen, highly placed in a wholesale rustling operation. When we disbanded that group, I hoped they would scatter a little farther away."

Samantha had never thought of Peter as a threat before. She'd heard of his reputation, but he had seemed just a handsome young father to her. Now, suddenly, she sensed the steel in him. She wanted to know more about this, but looking for her son took precedence over everything else. She told them he seemed to be missing.

"Have you checked his room?" Jennie asked.

Samantha rushed upstairs and opened his bedroom door. There, on the bed, she saw him. As quietly as possible, she walked across the room and whispered, "Nicholas?"

He didn't answer. She leaned down and pressed her lips to his forehead. It was warm, and probably explained why he had slipped up and put himself to bed. He appeared to be fully clothed. She should undress him and put him into his pajamas, but he considered himself too old to be treated that way, and she might just wake him up. It was better for him if he rested.

She slipped out of his room and back downstairs to report that the lost was found.

Nothing had worked out the way she'd wanted, not for her, not for Steve, and certainly not for Nicholas. She wished she'd never even thought of a party.

* * *

Nicholas waited until his mother left the room, then he put on his jacket and slipped down the back stairway to the outside. He avoided the dancers and took a roundabout way to the barn. Since he couldn't saddle a horse by himself, he chose one in a stall, bridled it, and climbed aboard by standing on the top of the wooden enclosure.

He let himself out of the barn and rode slowly down the hill, not sure himself where he was going.

At last the party inside was breaking up. The one outside sounded like it might go on all night.

Chane and Jennie stopped beside Samantha. "Good night, Samantha. Lovely party," Jennie said, resisting Chane's gentle pressure on her waist as he herded her toward the stairs and their room.

Rathwick hung back until she was alone for a moment. Then he walked over. "I apologize for starting that fight. It was inexcusable."

"What was it about?"

"I had taken Tristera out onto the veranda. Lawson stepped out there, and Tristera took one look at him and ran away. I don't know why, but she took a horse from the barn and left."

"I followed Lawson and tried to get him to tell me why the sight of him should scare her so much, but he wouldn't. I got so furious I just lost control."

Samantha knew then that Lawson must have been the officer in charge of the patrol that killed Tristera's companions. And that she needed to tell Steve. "Thank you, Matthew. Hopefully she'll return soon."

Samantha burned with the desire to find Steve, but people were leaving; she had to be at the door to fulfill her duties as hostess. One by one, Samantha's guests said good night and left to put down bedrolls outside or to climb the stairs to their rooms. In a few cases the people would drive home, but most would spend the night somewhere on the grounds.

Juana and her helpers had cleaned up even before the last guest walked out of the room.

"Excellent job," Samantha said. "Everyone will sleep late. Don't worry about breakfast."

"*Muchas gracias, señora.*"

Samantha switched off the lights, saving for last the chandelier, too beautiful to turn off. The house grew quiet. Lights outside shone into the room. The sparkle of the crystal pendants painted the room with dancing points of light. Steve had chosen well.

Steve . . . His name called up feelings of grief and despair. She sat down at the piano. Steve was leaving soon. She would never see him again.

It suddenly dawned on her that she had changed. Ten years ago, with a party ending, she might have been counting beaus or remembering compliments. Tonight she cared about Tristera's safety and welfare, Nicholas's health, Steve's pain about leaving her, her own pain when she thought about his leaving . . .

She shivered as she remembered his husky whisper, *You belong to me. He may think he's acquiring title when he marries you, but you'll always belong to me.*

She admitted the truth of his words. Even if she married Lance and bore his children, she might never get over her love and longing for Steve.

Despair filled her. As far back as she could remember, she'd longed and cried for the ones she hadn't had, leaving her no energy to appreciate the ones she did have. Maybe the problem was in her.

That seemed like an important realization, but just as quickly as it had come, it was gone, leaving only a bad feeling. She turned off the chandelier and walked to the window, where she could see Steve's cottage. It was dark, and probably surrounded by people sleeping on the ground. There was no way she could go knock on his door tonight. Unless she didn't care a fig for her reputation.

She didn't really, but she realized she was intimidated by a houseful of Kincaids. She walked slowly up to her room. Alone again.

Steve spent the night up on the mountain. When the sky started to lighten in the east, he tramped down the hill to his cottage. It was dark inside. He walked into the lamp table, and pain exploded in his shin. Cursing, he grabbed the kerosene lamp before it could fall and break.

"Dammit!" Fumbling in the dark, he located his matches and lit the lamp. In the bedroom, he lit another lamp, strode to the closet, and pulled out two large satchels. He opened them on the bed and hurled shirts, pants, underwear, and shoes at them until the closet was empty. He walked to his shaving dresser for his razor and soap.

His reflection in the mirror startled him. The face he saw there was almost unrecognizable. He turned away. The room was a shambles. Clothes he had thrown at the bed lay all over the floor and hung from the tops of paintings. Few articles of clothing had actually hit the satchels.

Steve looked back at the mirror. His face looked different. Thinner, more intense, as if every muscle and nerve in his face were alert, aware, intensely interested in something or someone . . .

"Oh, no!" He staggered to the comfortable chair Samantha Forrester had placed beside his window and sank onto it. It was the face of a man in love. He had seen that look once before, when his partner had fallen in love with the woman he finally married.

Until Frank met Julianna, he was a careless man with women and everything else in his life. Suddenly, upon falling in love, everything mattered. Frank went from a man who could laugh if he accidentally sent the wrong building materials to a house site, to a man who inspected every rose in a bouquet to be sure it was flawless enough for his woman.

The biggest change, though, had been in Frank's face, which took on a look of intense alertness and awareness. He agonized over every nuance of every thought or word affecting his beloved.

"God!" Steve sank deeper into the chair. He would hang himself before he turned into Frank. But the thought of leaving made him feel sick.

Dammit! He never should have waited to pack. He should have just gotten on his horse and ridden away. Then he might have had the courage to do it. Now he realized that to ride away might seem like an admission of guilt. Two hundred people had heard him labeled a child murderer. He couldn't ride away with that stigma hanging over his head. And he couldn't stay now that he knew he was in love with Samantha Forrester—a woman in love with another man. He didn't know whether to shoot himself or cry.

Samantha slept sporadically and woke early. Birds sang in the trees, but no humans stirred. It was only six o'clock, but she slipped out of bed, dressed hurriedly, and rushed downstairs. Juana and Steve sat in the kitchen, drinking coffee. At the sight of her, they stopped talking. Steve's face looked pale, his mouth tight. Her heart began to pound, her hands to feel cold.

"I need to speak with you," she said.

Steve gestured at the chair across from him.

"In private, please."

Juana picked up a basket. "I go peek those berries I saw last week before them hungry bears find 'em."

Samantha waited until Juana closed the door behind her.

"Tristera ran away last night."

"Maybe she enjoyed your party as much as I did."

"What set Chila off?"

"I don't know. She said I looked like a handsome devil, and when I thanked her, she started to scream."

"Well, I guess we know who sent the notes—and probably who tried to kill you."

"Yeah, I guess we should send word into town and let Daley know."

Samantha sighed. "Last night you said you were leaving," she whispered around the lump in her throat. "You don't have to leave just yet, do you?"

"The house is almost finished anyway," he said gruffly. "What difference will a week or two make?" He'd already tried to leave and failed, but her asking, the sweet despair he saw in her face, were like balm to his injured pride.

"I don't know, but I don't want you to leave."

"What's the point?"

Steve's bleak eyes wrenched her heart and soul. "Don't go, at least until we find out what's happened to Tristera."

Steve knew as long as he was within sight of Samantha Forrester, he would be in torment. Her cheeks were pale, her eyes soft and luminous. She was so lovely, so wistful and spirited in spite of everything. He had a powerful urge to tell her he'd already tried to leave and hadn't been able to, but she already gave him enough trouble without knowing that.

"No," he said, "I can't stay." Samantha's eyes filled with such misery his heart gave a little leap of happiness. "Well, maybe long enough to find Tristera," he said gruffly.

Samantha felt weak with relief. She sat in silence for a moment while the trembling within slowly eased.

Steve picked up his hat and walked to the outside door. In silence, Samantha watched him walk up the slight incline to ground level. His shoulders seemed more bowed, as if he carried a heavier load.

* * *

As the grandfather clock in the hall chimed ten, Samantha stood up and walked to the window for the hundredth time, hoping for the sight of Steve coming back with Tristera. The sky was covered with clouds. The wind appeared to be blowing in a storm. Samantha wanted to pray for rain, but Tristera and Steve would be caught in it, so she didn't.

Juana trudged up the steps from the kitchen and stopped at the top to catch her breath. "Thees house may be cooler, *señora*, but thees steps weel be death of thees old woman."

"Is Nicholas up yet?"

"No, *señora*. No one is up."

"He stayed up too late last night," she said, smiling at the memory of how tired he'd looked.

Samantha went to his bedroom and found his bed empty. Alarmed, she searched the house. Outside, wind whipped the trees. Lightning flashed north of them.

She found Ian Macready in the unfinished bunkhouse. "Have you seen Nicholas?"

"No, lass. Not since last night."

"Did Steve come back?"

"No. Still out looking for Tristera, me thinks." Ian spread the word, and soon laborers were combing the grounds around the house, yelling Nicholas's name. Samantha climbed the hill behind the house and used a spyglass to search the desert for the sight of Nicholas or Steve.

She saw Steve riding up the slope toward the house and ran to meet him near the front gate. Steve had been riding along deep in thought. Tired and unshaven, he looked up, saw her, and his eyes narrowed.

"Have you seen Nicholas?" she asked, panting, leaning against a tree trunk to catch her breath.

"No."

"I'm worried. We can't find him anywhere."

Steve roused himself. Samantha's lovely eyes looked bright with unshed tears. "You think he ran away?"

Tears spilled over. She blinked them aside. "I . . . don't know what to think. Did you find Tristera?"

"No. This wind made it hard to do any tracking. And even with the heavy traffic, I didn't find anyone who'd seen her. I'll go have a look for Nicholas, though."

"I'm going with you!"

He started to argue with her, but lightning lit the sky and thunder rolled. "A storm's coming up. Nicholas can't be out in this," Samantha said, turning to run toward the barn. Steve's horse trotted alongside. Ian Macready followed them into the nearly dark barn. Wind slammed the door behind him.

"One o' me men thinks he saw the boy on a horse, headed down the hill," Ian said.

"When?"

"Last night sometime."

Steve and Ian saddled horses. Samantha ran to the house, ripped her gown off, changed into a divided riding skirt and blouse, grabbed a coat for herself, and went into Nicholas's room. His jacket was gone. More proof that he'd run away. But she couldn't think why. She ran downstairs, grabbed a blanket, and packed food for Nicholas.

She knocked on Chane and Jennie's door. Chane yelled for her to come in. She opened the door and stuck her head in.

"I'm sorry to bother you, but I think Nicholas has run away."

"Oh, no," Jennie said, gasping.

Chane started to throw off his covers and thought better of it. "Be right there."

Rathwick intercepted Samantha on the way to the barn. "Did Tristera come back?" he asked.

"No. And I think Nicholas has run away, too."

"I can muster a dozen or so men to help look for him."

"I'd appreciate that, Matthew."

Rathwick left on the run. Steve and Samantha led Ramon, Ian, and the Kincaid family of men down the hill in a rising windstorm. Rathwick followed at a distance with a dozen hungover soldiers in dirty uniforms. At the graves of Silver Fish's family, a few wind-battered yellow cactus blossoms lay on the mound, their stems held down by rocks.

"Nicholas did that. He's been wanting me to bring him, so he could put flowers on their graves. I kept putting him off. I was scared . . . I didn't want him to . . ." Her voice failed.

Steve dismounted and checked for footprints around the grave. Prints showed that a set of small shoes had walked to the grave. Two indentations, half filled by blowing sand, showed where he'd knelt for a while, then stood and walked the horse to a rock, where he'd mounted. The tracks appeared to head north, but were soon erased by sifting sand.

"What do we do now?" Samantha asked, shivering from fear and cold.

"The wind has covered his trail, so we split up. Ramon, you and Ian go northwest." Steve turned to Rathwick. "Can you go west into the desert? There are enough of you to fan out and cover an area.'' Then he sent the Kincaids southeast. ''I'll head north.''

''Nicholas knows better than to ride into the desert,'' Samantha said, protesting.

''Nicholas is a smart boy, but we can't count on his doing the smart thing. You go back to the house. We'll bring him back,'' Steve said firmly.

''I'm going with you.'' Her jaw was set.

''All right,'' Steve said, relenting. ''But this storm looks ugly.''

Nicholas's chest ached, and the wind occasionally whipped sand into his face, stinging his eyes and making him cough. He knew his mother would be upset, but he couldn't seem to turn back. Part of him wanted to be home with her, warm and safe in the house. But the other part just wanted to stay on the horse and keep riding, even though it wasn't clear to him where he was going or why.

He untied his cravat, retied it into a bandanna, and pulled it up over his mouth and nose the way his mother had taught him. That helped a little.

He skirted the Dart ranch and headed toward the mountain that sheltered the hidden valley Steve had taken him to in the summer. Riding was harder here. He had to help the horse more. The desert bushes had given way to trees that made loud whining sounds in the rising wind.

He rode on and on, until he was tired and cold. Finally he stopped his horse and looked for shelter, but the thickets were so impenetrable he couldn't find his way through to the cave he was looking for. Part of him wanted to go home, but he knew he wouldn't.

Tristera sat in the mouth of the cave where Steve had hidden Ramon when he was wounded. The wind howled overhead, but it was warm enough inside. She was tired and hungry, but she could not bring herself to search for food. She had eaten all the berries she had picked today and drank most of the water she had carried up the hill in the pail she and Steve had left here for Ramon.

She would have to find more food or die of hunger. Usually that knowledge would motivate her enough to get her up, but it didn't. She couldn't go back to the *señora's* house. Rathwick knew she was the one he searched for.

Of all her problems, Tuvi's death continued to hurt her the most. When she had lived with Samantha's family, she had not been so aware of the sense of loss, but here, surrounded only by the rocks and the scrubby growth of plants, she felt Tuvi's loss in every fiber of her being. It ached through her like hunger.

For uncounted hours she sat so still her body became part of the Earth. Part of the wind blowing through the bushes and tall grasses. Part of everything moving and eternal. Almost effortlessly she pressed her consciousness against the essence of the Great Mystery, the light that glowed like the sun and sounded like distant bells in her head.

There, in the still place, pain and hunger left her. She watched the play of light within, like violet shadows dancing on a dark wall.

She thought of Tuvi, of his dying and suffering, of all the things she'd wished she'd done. Love for him was so strong her whole body ached with it. Her mind formed silent words: *Please let me die. I want to be with thee. I don't belong here.*

The glowing light came closer and the internal sights and sounds receded. Tristera's consciousness moved into a place of perfect stillness. She'd been here before, but this time she remained aware and alert. A great rushing feeling, as if she were being whirled by a dust devil, started at her feet and carried her upward. As her consciousness separated from her body, there was one sharp moment of dizzying sweetness. Then the stillness came again.

She was aware of a light coming on, or of an eye opening. She saw a narrow white tunnel leading upward and found herself following it. As she rose through the tunnel toward an opening, she recognized the top of a dear, familiar head, then thin, square shoulders. Her soul rose up joyously to where Tuvi sat cross-legged.

Tuvi stood up and reached out his hand to greet her. She could see him as clearly as she had ever seen him. His dark eyes were very beautiful. He was the embodiment of divine perfection.

She was so startled she opened her eyes. The rock in front of her was gray in the dim light. The wind still howled.

"No!" She closed her eyes. "Tuvi, come back!" she whispered. She concentrated hard, but she could not bring him back. Tears streamed down her cheeks, part despair, part joy, that even though he had died and left the body, he was still somehow connected to her.

Without being aware that another vision had come, she realized she was watching Nicholas riding toward the thickets that separated him from the mountain's entry. She saw lightning strike the tree directly over his head, saw it falling, and knew that when it hit him it would crush him.

She recognized the tree as one she had ridden past on her way into the hidden valley. It was only a few yards from the cave's entrance.

The vision ended in darkness, and she leapt up, staggered forward on numb legs, and ran awkwardly toward the pivot rock and the tunnel, praying she could get to that tree before he did.

She raced out of the cave and stopped to get her bearings. Through the thickets, she saw Nicholas rein his horse beneath the tree she'd seen in her vision. She yelled, "Nicholas! Ride away! Get away!" But he didn't hear her over the wind. He sat his horse tiredly, probably looking for a way through the thickets. She ran forward, not even stopping for the thickets, charging through them like one maddened, screaming as she fought her way against fiery thorns that tore at her skin.

"Nicholas! Get away!" she screamed again and again, but he still didn't appear to hear her. When her strength was almost gone she broke through the thickets to freedom and ran at him, waving her arms and screaming. At last Nicholas heard her over the howl of the wind and turned to look at her.

"Get away!" she screamed.

"What?" Nicholas yelled, alarmed by the sight of a bloody, screaming Tristera running toward him, mouthing words he couldn't understand. Icy wind tore at his jacket and scarf. Lightning flashed, and fire leapt out of the tree where it branched directly over his head. As he watched, the tree split in half where lightning had struck; the branch dangled for a moment and fell. Nicholas tried to rein the horse out of the way, but it reared; he lost control of it. Then light filled his head, shone brightly for a moment, and went dark.

"Where could he be?" Samantha yelled over the howling wind. Nicholas needed to be inside. He needed to be warm and safe. She was so scared she felt paralyzed. She tried to push her fear into a corner of her mind, so she could still think and function, but it was bigger than her mind.

Steve didn't bother to answer. He had no trail to follow, but he had assumed the boy was making a beeline toward the mountains north of the ranch. Nothing else made sense.

"Nicholas is a smart boy. He went with me to the hidden valley. He loved it and wanted to stay there. I think he's going there now."

"Then why did you send the soldiers the other way?"

"In case I'm wrong."

Arden Chandler heard about the tragedy of Silver Fish's family from his housekeeper. Woman Who Makes Song Magic—Chandler called her simply Song Magic—was a slim, wiry, sharp-faced woman with white hair braided into two thin braids.

"All dead when they got there," she said.

"When did this happen?"

"Several moons ago. Silver Fish not sure. The Man With Bad Eyebrow told Silver Fish they died of a disease, but I don't think so."

"The Man With Bad Eyebrow?"

Song Magic nodded vehemently. "Silver Fish said one eyebrow goes up in the middle."

Chandler put down his pen. "Maybe I'll call on Silver Fish."

"That good. Silver Fish need all good wishes now. He grieve deeply."

Chandler walked from his house to the village. He could have ridden, but he enjoyed walking. He had served as an Indian agent in many parts of the country; this time of year he liked the desert best. It was cooler and smelled of sage, which Chandler found invigorating.

He found Silver Fish sitting in the shade of his *ramada*, a flat roof that jutted out from the house and sheltered the rude table and benches around which the family ate. The mother of one of Silver Fish's dead wives knelt beside the table, grinding dried corn into meal on her stone *metate*. Chandler liked to watch the women at their *metates*. He liked the smell of chili cooking on the slow fire. Indian life suited him. He had long ago tired of cities.

"Afternoon, Silver Fish."

Silver Fish looked up and grunted.

"I've come to pay my respects in your time of grief."

Silver Fish nodded. Chandler pulled out one of the benches and sat down across from Silver Fish. The old woman appeared not to notice. She moved back and forth rhythmically, grinding, brushing the ground corn aside, grinding again.

"What happened to your family?"

"White man disease. I know not the name."

"Where did this happen?"

"Boston House Creek."

Chandler had heard of the place. A white woman from the East had built a tall wooden house at the foot of a mountain.

"This Man With Bad Eyebrow . . . he still works for Mrs. Forrester?"

Silver Fish realized the Indian agent had another reason for coming to see him. "Silver Fish gone from there long time now. He may be gone or not," he said, hedging.

"Crows Walking has a foster son . . . this wouldn't happen to be the same man, would it?"

"Silver Fish not know."

Chandler stood up. The Man With Bad Eyebrow sounded like Crows Walking's white son, Steve Sheridan. It would be worth the ride to find out. He would have to think of something to tell Selena. She didn't want him poking around in things. *Leave it lie, Arden, please* . . . Chandler could hear his wife's sweet voice in his head, but it didn't stop him. Nothing mattered except finding Sheridan and settling this once and for all.

CHAPTER TWENTY

Wind whipped the sand so thickly in the cold air that Ramon knew he was lost.

Ian pulled his coat collar up around his ears. "I hate to think of that bairn out in this storm!" he said, his concern for the boy mounting by the minute.

As if in answer to Ramon's prayer, the wind died down. He squinted into the red sky. For a second he thought he saw . . .

"Come, *señor*," he said, nudging his horse.

They rode for a while, and what he'd seen was clearer now. The square outline of a house appeared before them. Ramon didn't recognize it, but it looked familiar. He quickened his pace. In another lull, he recognized it as the Dart place. He felt trepidation about riding in there, especially if Ham Russell was around, but he could see no way around it.

At the house, Joe Dart and his mother stepped out onto the porch. "Get down and come in out of this wind!" Joe yelled.

"No time," said Ian. "We're looking for Nicholas Forrester. You haven't seen the lad, have you?"

"No. The boy's missing?" Joe Dart asked, cupping his hands to be heard over the whine of the wind.

"The *señora* thinks he ran away," Ramon yelled.

"How long ago?" Joe asked.

"Last night sometime."

"Ought to come in and warm up," Joe said.

"Thank you, *señor*, but we must keep looking."

They turned their horses west. Joe shivered as he watched them ride into the wind. He opened the door and motioned his mother inside. She shook her head. The skin around her mouth was white with strain.

"You go ahead," she said, filled with sudden grief about Nicholas. "I gotta get something from the barn."

"I'll get it for you."

"No! I want to get it myself!"

"You're not doing anything crazy out there, are you?"

"You better keep a civil tongue in your head, you hear!" And

387

before Joe could stop her, she ran down the steps and toward the barn.

Chila knew they'd find Nicholas dead. There was no saving him now. She'd known that right off. They'd find him in a creek if there was one with any water in it. Samantha should have listened to her. She should have listened!

"That rotten bastard!" she yelled, kicking a saddle left on the ground. Thinking about what Denny had done to that sweet child filled her with such fury that she kicked everything within reach. Horses sensed her mood and snorted their fear.

Worn out suddenly, she stopped and sagged against the rough wood of a stall. Her heart ached so badly she wanted to fall down onto the ground and cry, but there was no time.

In the tack room she pawed through the boxes stacked in the corner. Furious when anything resisted her, she threw it across the small room. Finally she located the right box and lifted out the basket of plants she'd hidden from Joe.

Her hand accidentally touched one. "Ow! Ow! Dammit!" The shock reverberated through her system, but she was glad to know they were still potent.

Ever since she'd found her grandmother's diary, Chila had been braiding nettles and puncture vines into long chains, the way it had told her to.

Now it was all coming to a head. And a good thing, too. These wouldn't last forever. Apparently God was on her side. Even the timing was right. Except she didn't know how she would ever find Denny in this storm.

Steve saw the fire first. "See that?"

Samantha urged her tired horse into a run and beat Steve to it. A tree that had fallen onto sandy ground had almost burned itself out. Samantha stopped her horse and dismounted to warm her hands. It was lucky it had fallen this way and not the other. A few feet away, a solid wall of thickets could have started a wildfire that might have burned for a week.

Near the blackened stump of a limb, a shoe caught her attention. With mounting dread, she recognized it as one of Nicholas's.

"Help me!" Samantha screamed, kneeling to drag the blackened limb off her son. It was still smoldering and too hot to touch.

Steve leaped off Calico and kicked the heaviest part of the limb. It broke off and flew in all directions. Samantha kicked smaller limbs aside, looking for her son. Steve kicked the stump clear but there was nothing under it.

"He has to be here," she said, moaning.

Steve walked to where Samantha stared at the blackened, brittle branches. "He isn't here."

"He has to be here!" she insisted.

Lightning struck a nearby tree with a loud crack. Thunder rolled and crashed overhead.

Steve glanced around the blackened, smoldering remains of the tree. He saw a few drops of blood, but didn't point them out to Samantha. "We'd better get out of this," he yelled over the heavy whine of the wind. "It's almost dark. And it might rain."

"He's around here somewhere," she said, resisting his attempt to pull her up.

"The cave is near here. Come on!" he yelled.

"No!"

"He might be in there!" Steve suggested.

Samantha started to cry. He lifted her into his arms, mounted, and urged Calico around the thickets and toward the cave where he'd taken Ramon when he was wounded. Fortunately they weren't far from it. Steve grabbed the reins of Samantha's horse and led it behind them.

Once inside, they were shielded from the roaring wind. Steve dismounted and carried Samantha into the cavern, where the air was still. The wind was a low howl around the mountain. The cave walls shone silver when the lightning flashed. Steve steadied her on the floor of the cave.

Samantha took a few steps. "Nicholas!"

"Nicholas!" echoed back to her.

"He isn't here."

"You wait here. I'm going to look for him."

"I'm going with you."

"It won't do any good for us to look in the same places. You stay here in case he comes this way."

What he said made sense. And once Steve was gone, she could do as she pleased. "Okay."

"Gather wood and build a fire in the front of the cave, so he can see it. Here," he said, handing her his revolver, butt first.

"Why?" she asked, taking it.

"In case you run into a critter."

Steve left; Samantha gathered dried, broken limbs from the thickets surrounding the cave. She built a fire with Steve's matches. Hours passed slowly. The sky darkened and night fell.

Everytime the wind died down, she went outside and yelled for Nicholas.

Finally exhausted, she lay down beside the fire and closed her eyes. A loud noise startled her. She sat up shaking. Looking all around in the dim light of the dying fire she saw nothing. Then it came again—a vibration under her back, as if the floor of the cave was trembling.

Lightning illuminated the front half of the cave. Thunder crashed. Fire shadows leaped in the dim light. An earthquake? She'd lived in Arizona over three years and had never felt the Earth move. A grating sound started in the mountain somewhere; the Earth shook beneath her, harder this time. Then, as if the other tremors had only been preliminary, the Earth beneath her bucked once and began a terrifying rolling motion. It *was* an earthquake. Fear sent a chill down her spine.

The roar grew louder. Alarmed, Samantha struggled to her feet and started to run outside. Before she could make it, the floor beneath her heaved up and sent her flying toward the far wall of the cave. She struggled to her feet again, but the floor of the cave was undulating under her feet. Samantha staggered back against the wall, unable to recover her balance. A loud grating sound over her head made her look upward. The ceiling of the cave also seemed to be in motion.

Before she could pry herself away from the wall, tilted at an angle now, the ground beneath her feet quivered and seemed to go soft for a second. Then it began to collapse under her. Screaming and clawing at the dirt, she tried to pull herself up out of the hole opening under her, but the ground was falling away too fast. There was nothing to hang on to. She fell through the widening hole . . . and blackness closed in around her. She tasted dirt and knew that her mouth and eyes were full of it, but her hands were no use to her now. She didn't even know where they were.

Steve searched the ground for signs, but the wind had scoured them away. He did find random hoofprints going off in a southerly direction, toward the Dart ranch.

If Nicholas had been injured by that falling tree he might have headed for the Dart ranch. Steve decided to go in that direction. He had no idea how long he'd been riding. Thunder still rolled and crashed around him. Darkness was falling fast. He followed the horse's tracks and prayed that Nicholas didn't miss the ranch house in the dimming light.

Calico shied at something. Steve tightened his grip on the
reins, but Calico grabbed the bit in his teeth, reared, turned all
the way around, and leapt into a hard gallop. Steve fought to
regain control. It had happened so fast, he didn't even know
what had spooked the horse.

Calico pounded through the near darkness over sand and
rocks.

"Whoa, boy! Whoa!" Steve called into his ear. Just as he
thought Calico was going to respond, the big horse tripped.
Steve lost his seat and flew through the air, cursing. He hit the
ground and rolled. With Calico's scream in his ears, he sensed
his consciousness narrow down to a point and disappear.

He woke to the soft sound of Calico's whinnying. He sat up
and for a moment couldn't remember how he'd gotten here. He
found Calico ten paces back, lying on his side, panting. His
front leg was broken in two places. The bone protruded through
the skin. Steve stroked his nose and hugged his silky neck.
Calico whinnied softly.

Steve had never felt more powerless in his life. Short of trying
to club Calico to death with a rock, he could do nothing to end
his suffering. The thought of it sickened him.

"I'll be back for you, boy. I won't leave you like this."

He cursed himself for leaving his gun with Samantha. And
for losing his bearings in the dark. Then he stood up . . . and
dizziness engulfed him. He felt himself falling; there was no
way to stop it.

Ham Russell walked out onto the desert every morning to
take a leak. This morning he walked toward something he hadn't
seen there before. And he hit pay dirt. Steve Sheridan out cold.
He twiddled his braided beard and smiled.

Chila Dart would be one happy woman.

He hailed the house; Roy Bowles yelled back.

"Bring a horse!" Ham yelled.

Steve woke to find rough hands on his body and the tip of
a scraggly beard in his face. Men cursed as they tried to lift
him high enough to throw him across a saddle. "What the
hell . . . ?" Steve asked.

"Hey! He's awake."

"Good. Then he can climb aboard himself."

"There's no time for this now," Steve said groggily. "Mrs.
Forrester's boy is hurt. He needs help."

Russell patted Steve's sides and stomach, feeling for a gun.

"Where'd you hide your damn pistol? I know you wouldn't be without one, a troublemaker like you."

"I lost it."

"Get Miz Dart," Russell growled at Bowles. "She'll be real surprised to see our visitor."

Samantha woke up with the sensation of being in a strange place and wondering where she was. The lost feeling lasted only a moment. The inky darkness told her nothing. Except that she was alive. Barely. And trapped at the bottom of the hole that had opened up beneath her feet. She had no idea how long she'd been there. At least she could still breathe. The air felt warm and dusty, but it was plentiful, for the moment anyway.

She held her hand up in front of her face and couldn't see it. Then she remembered. She was in the middle of the mountain into which she had gone for shelter. A very dark mountain.

Nicholas! Oh, God, Nicholas . . . She had no idea where he might be or how to get back to him. Grief filled her.

A rumbling started overhead. Samantha closed her eyes and put her hands over her head. The rumbling grew louder. It sounded as if the whole mountain were going to crash down on her.

Please God, don't let Nicholas be in this mountain.

She huddled there, knowing she was going to die. No one could find her. But Nicholas—would Steve find him? Would he live? She had to survive. She had to find Nicholas. She wouldn't give up the way her mother had.

Samantha struggled to her feet and started climbing the pile of dirt that had fallen around her. If she had fallen from above, there must be an opening where she could climb back up.

Clawing her way a few feet up the mound of rocks and dirt, she realized she could do it. It wasn't impossible. She climbed steadily upward in the darkness, straining to see anything at all. She wanted to scream at the darkness, *Let me see something!* But she saved her energy for climbing.

The dirt kept slipping under her feet. Every step upward was accompanied by a half step backward, but she slogged on until she reached what seemed to be the ceiling of the cave. Panting, she groped around for the opening, felt only rock, but she knew that couldn't be. She had fallen through something.

Dirt sifted down on her arm. With trembling hands, she traced the small streams of dirt falling all around her. The dirt was cool and dry on her arms. Apparently a rock bigger than the hole she'd fallen through had plugged the opening, leaving only enough space for a little dirt to sift through.

The mountain rattled again. Dread gripped her. She wanted Nicholas and Steve. Terrified and frustrated, she sagged down onto the dirt. She was trapped. There was no way back to Nicholas. She felt suffocated by so much darkness.

Samantha doubled forward. Sobs racked her body. "Nicholas!" she sobbed. "Please . . ." *Please let me get back to him . . .*

She remembered Aunt Elizabeth holding her and crying, *Reggie couldn't swim! She always feared and hated water. For her to die in that horrible way! It isn't fair!*

A sweet face shimmered in the darkness of her mind. Tears stung her eyelids. It was her mother's face. Samantha felt such longing and remorse, she doubled over again and cried.

Finally her sobs slowed; she realized she felt strong enough to look for another way out. She eased down the pile of rocks and dirt, wondering how she had ever survived the fall.

The wind still howled. It seemed odd that she could hear it, shut off from the outside as she was. Maybe that was a good sign. On hands and knees, she felt along the dirt floor of the cavern. Without light, her search seemed pointless. She might be feeling the same places over and over.

Finally she realized the low roar she heard was coming from below. She crawled slowly forward until she felt what might be an edge of some sort, perhaps a cliff. The air was damper, wetter. It had the earthy smell of a river marsh.

She picked up a rock, threw it, and waited. Finally, far below, it splashed into water. The roar she'd been hearing was water, not wind at all.

It might be a way out, but she needed to know how deep it was. Groping in darkness, she found a nearby boulder and rolled it over the side, listening for the splash and any accompanying sound. When it hit the water she began to count slowly to herself: *One, two, three, four, five . . .* She thought she heard it clank against something. The sound of it hitting bottom, if that's what it had been, was barely audible and made her wonder if she'd imagined it.

She threw another rock as far as she could and slowly counted: *One, two, three, fo*—The rock hit and clattered against other rocks on the floor. She didn't consider herself an expert on distances, but it sounded about fifty feet away.

Samantha rolled a third boulder over the edge and counted

while it dropped, then again when it hit water. She guessed the depth of the chasm at twenty feet and the depth of the water at maybe fifteen or twenty feet. That was a long drop. Still, the water might be deep enough to fall into and survive.

But she had no idea where the stream went. If it were an underground river, it might go down instead of up. It might not be a way out at all. Just a quicker way to die.

CHAPTER TWENTY-ONE

Samantha walked or crawled the entire perimeter of the cavern and confirmed there was no way out. Except down into the water, which would probably be icy cold.

A loud grating sound started again; the earth shook beneath her. Another earthquake. Terror for her son gripped her. *Nicholas! I have to find Nicholas!*

With the ground shaking all around her, Samantha realized the true depths of her helplessness. She couldn't save Nicholas or herself. She was trapped in this mountain cavern; the land she loved was going to bury her.

With death at hand, the real import of Steve's words struck home for her. *We come into this world empty-handed, and we go out the same way.* He was right. She had only thought she owned this land. In reality it had entrapped her, and now it was about to destroy her. The land was vastly more powerful. And more vengeful. The shaking became more violent, and she hated the land suddenly, with a passion she found almost incredible. Hatred welled up in her, and she stood and screamed furiously into the inky darkness. "Stop it! Stop it!"

As suddenly as the shaking had started, it stopped. Samantha sat down abruptly and waited to see if it was going to start again. When it didn't, she crawled to the edge of the chasm and looked down. She still couldn't see anything. But she could sense that the sides of the chasm dropped straight down. The water continued to slip past the rocky walls with its own muted roar.

She picked up a small rock and threw it at the other side of the chasm. It cracked against the rock, sounding ten or twelve feet away. This sheer drop might go straight down for a while and then be interrupted by a hard outcropping of rock, which would mean certain death for her.

She picked up more rocks and kept throwing them until she felt fairly certain the walls were sheer and straight. She might jump into the water and survive. If she stayed here, she was surely going to die.

Sitting in the cold darkness she hugged her knees and wished she were home with Nicholas. *He's probably home by now, eating in the kitchen with Juana. He'll probably do exactly what I did as a child. He'll wake up, and I won't be there, ever again. And he'll never forgive me.*

Samantha didn't know where that thought had come from. It had oozed out of the depths of her. She tried to reject it, but it felt like truth. And then she realized that Aunt Elizabeth might have been right. Her mother and father might have loved her.

And worse yet, if Nicholas lived, he might grow up in that same horrible way, hating her for dying and leaving him.

That thought was too horrible. Samantha struggled into a standing position. She wouldn't give up the way her mother and father had. She would keep trying to get back to her son until she died or found him.

Samantha peered over the cliff and listened to the sound of the water far below. She weighed her sense of urgency to get back to Nicholas against her fear. The need to reach Nicholas was greater. She took off her riding skirt and pantaloons and wrapped them into a ball. She tied the ends of the pants around the ball to hold it tightly together. Shivering at her nakedness, holding the wad of clothing, she took a deep breath and stepped over the side of the cliff.

It helped to scream. Screaming gave her something to do while she waited to see how this was going to come out. But she fell for so long her heart almost stopped.

She hit the water so hard she went all the way to the bottom and stayed there a moment before she gathered her wits and pushed against it to surge to the surface and sputter. Temporarily, the wad of clothing helped keep her afloat. But soon it would become waterlogged and sink.

The water was icy cold. She relaxed and let the current take her downstream. She wouldn't last long in such cold water. She had to find a way out quickly or die.

With the roar of the water filling her ears and its icy chill burning her skin, she rounded a bend in the channel. The roar was louder here, as if she was approaching a waterfall or rapids, but it was still too dark to see.

Samantha tried to make her way to the side. She wanted to stop herself from being pulled over a waterfall, if that's what was coming up, but the water speeded up. The roar grew louder. There was nothing to hang on to, no turning back. The current had her. At least the water didn't feel cold anymore.

One second she was floating level, the next she was falling. She screamed as she was swept over a small waterfall. All the water in the world seemed to fall on her head. Samantha went down and down . . . until her lungs hurt and she vowed that if she got out of this she wouldn't scream next time. It wasted too much breath and energy.

Her feet touched bottom. She pushed herself away from the falling water and up toward air. She surfaced, sucked in air, and tried to remember her promise as the icy water carried her toward another waterfall.

The next drop-off was less steep. She scraped bottom as she fell over the rocks. This time, mouth tightly shut, she went down and used the bottom to launch herself into a dive that took her farther away from the falling water. Her tactic saved her from being pounded under the water and driven to the bottom.

Away from the waterfall, the current slowed. She floated in smooth water. The roar seemed fainter now, and behind her. Samantha strained her ears to hear if that sound hid another roar ahead of her, but she couldn't tell. Maybe it was over . . .

She rounded another bend in the channel and suddenly the darkness thinned. She was thrilled to be able to see, even if only faint outlines. She couldn't tell where the light was coming from, but its first faint rays illuminated a sheer rock wall straight ahead of her. Either the water flowed beneath it or it was a sheer drop-off that didn't reach the wall at all. If the stream went underground would it ever resurface? The water seemed to speed up as it neared whatever it was.

Samantha pushed herself to the side of the channel and grabbed a cold, wet rock protruding over the water. The current pulled at her stronger now, trying to drag her back into the center, but she held on hard.

Panting, she used her skirt like a thick rope. She tossed it at a boulder and pulled herself up onto a narrow ledge next to a wall that soared straight up.

No way out. She scanned the other side of the river canyon. It looked as if the mountain had split in two; the water had taken the only course it could—down into the bowels of the Earth.

The air felt colder than the water. Samantha shivered on the wet rock. At least her shoes were still laced tightly to her ankles.

She peered at the water and the rock until she realized that the water flowed under the sheer face of the rock. It wasn't a waterfall, but it might hold her under water for seconds or minutes. Or the water might go straight down. Fear quickened in her. She rested for a moment, looked around, but found no other way out.

Samantha was terrified of getting back in the icy water. But she realized she had two choices. She could die gloriously, in a valiant attempt to get back to Nicholas. Or she could die miserably, huddled on this rock, alone, cold, hungry, and cowardly.

She dropped her clothing into the water to make its own way and slipped in beside it. The water felt warm to her now. If only that false feeling of warmth would last.

She floated for a moment until she was almost to the rock wall. Then she gulped in a lungful of air and ducked just in time to keep her head from being banged against it. The downward current caught her and pulled her under. *Count*, she told herself. *It'll give you something to do. One. Two. Three.* The water was icy, dark, claustrophobic. Her lungs ached for air, but her mind kept counting. *Four. Five. Six. Seven.*

Eight. Her lungs burned. She looked up, but could see nothing but water above her. She had been pulled into inky darkness. Water everywhere. Light nowhere. *Nine. Ten. Eleven.* The pain in her chest was unbearable. She couldn't remember the next number.

Arden Chandler stopped what he was doing to listen. Sounded like cavalry coming. He stood up and looked out the window, though with the wind blowing it did little good.

Finally he saw a patrol of cavalry headed straight toward him. He walked to the front door, threw it open, and stepped outside, squinting against a blast of sand that hit him. He fought the door closed, so Selena wouldn't yell at him, and waited. Soon the patrol stopped in front of him.

"Captain! Come in out of this wind!"

Rathwick dismounted and followed Chandler inside. "Name's Rathwick," he said, extending his hand. "I've been meaning to stop by and introduce myself."

"Chandler. Arden Chandler. Good to finally meet you, though we haven't been here that long that you need to apologize. What brings you out in miserable weather like this?"

"Mrs. Forrester's son ran away just before the storm let loose. He's a lunger. You haven't seen him, have you?"

"Nope. Not a thing. You don't think he'd come into the desert do you?"

"Sheridan went north. We fanned out in the other direction, just in case."

"Sheridan?"

"He's Mrs. Forrester's builder."

"I thought Sheridan went on to Texas?"

"No, he stayed on to build a house on the south face of Boston House Mountain, south of the Dart ranch."

"Dart?"

"You don't get around much, do you?" Rathwick asked, wiping sand off his face with the back of his arm.

"No," Chandler said, with a sigh. "The problems here are so overwhelming they keep us tied down. When we do get out, we go to Tucson, which is closer. We know a few folks that way. Tell me about this Dart ranch."

"Northeast of here. Run by Chila Dart and her boy, Joe."

Chandler felt dizzy. "Chila Elaine Dart?"

"Could be I've heard it that way. Is something wrong?" he asked, concerned at the way Chandler paled.

"Which direction would that Forrester ranch be, exactly?" Rathwick pointed east. "About ten miles."

"And the Dart ranch is just north of it? You wouldn't happen to be going that way, would you?"

"Yes. We've come far enough in this direction."

"I want to see Sheridan. You mind if I ride along with you?"

"Not at all."

"Thank you, Captain. You need anything before we go?"

"No, thanks. We've probably got more than you."

Arden Chandler grabbed his jacket, his revolver, and a handful of biscuits and bacon for his saddlebag. He saddled a horse. And while the men watered their horses from the trough he ran to his nearest Indian neighbor and asked the woman there to find Selena and tell her he'd gone.

It was a crazy thing to do, riding off into the desert in a windstorm, but he had a bad feeling that was getting worse by the minute. He wasn't a superstitious man, but it was no accident he'd just been told where he could find both Steve Sheridan and Chila Dart.

Samantha staggered out of the water and sagged over a rock with her head and shoulders hanging upside down. Water gushed out of her. She coughed and vomited another gush of water.

Panting, she struggled into a sitting position on the rock and noticed her riding skirt float past. In spite of her exhaustion, she slogged into the water and pulled it out.

"I made it," she whispered.

She laid the skirt over a boulder and sat down until her lungs stopped hurting. Finally able to move again, she wrung the water out of her skirt, put it on, and trudged out into the hidden valley. Yellow tufts of dead grass stretched out ahead of her. The sky was heavy with sand kicked up by the passing storm, but it was lighter now in the east, signaling sunrise.

Samantha sank down on the grass and lay back. Her blouse was torn in a dozen places. One sleeve hung by a few threads. Her skirt was torn, too. An angry red scratch burned her right arm. She was tired, but her sense of urgency was stronger. Nicholas might still be lost.

She climbed uphill through dense brush that cut off her view of the valley floor. Sweat trickled down her face. Panting, Samantha climbed up the last incline and dropped to her knees on the ground. At first nothing registered in her. Then slowly she realized that rocks now covered the back side of the mountain. There was no way to get back into the cave that led to freedom.

The sky was just turning pink as she scanned the rim of the valley, searching for the shortest way out. The earthquake appeared to have lowered the crest to the south. It looked like a possible escape route now. She decided on a route and began to bushwhack toward it.

"Tie his hands," Chila Dart ordered. She had changed into men's pants. Her gray hair was braided down her back.

Ham Russell complied. When Steve was securely trussed, Ham helped him back onto his horse.

"Now tie his legs so he can't kick." When that was done, she walked over and pulled on heavy gloves. Then she reached into a sack she carried and pulled out what looked like weeds. She moved out of Steve's range of vision, then he felt a sharp pain on his right wrist, then his left. It felt as if he was being stung by a dozen bees.

"Ma!" Joe Dart stepped out onto the porch, glanced at Steve, and then at his mother. "That's a hell of a thing to do to a man—"

"You stay out of this, darlin'!"

"Ma, please!" Joe Dart sounded desperate.

"For once in your life, would you just trust me?" Chila tugged at the ropes holding Steve's arms behind his back. "Good," she muttered.

A man led a horse from the barn for her. She mounted like a man, then led the way around the house and toward the mountain behind the Dart ranch.

Roy Bowles took Steve's reins. Steve looked back at Joe and saw Dart's eyes were filled with regret and helplessness—but not enough to do anything about what was happening. Steve tried to see his wrists, to find out where that fiery pain was coming from, but he couldn't see behind him.

They rode around the house and urged the animals up the side of the mountain. Steve lost track of time. Between sweating with the pain, which was growing worse all the time, and leaning forward to help the strange horse on the steep places, he watched for an opportunity to escape.

But Russell and Bowles made no mistakes. Russell carried a shotgun across his saddle, pointed at Steve. Bowles carried a rifle. If the shotgun missed, the rifle might not. Their combined presence discouraged him from taking any uncertain opportunities.

At last they rode into a small clearing. The pasture was surrounded by scrub pines through which the wind howled. In the middle of the pasture a pale wooden structure rose out of the yellow knee-high grass. It was surrounded by a big pile of brush. A cross and a bonfire. Steve realized Chila Dart was crazier than he'd thought.

"Tie him up there," Chila said.

Rough hands jerked Steve down off his horse. The wide barrel of a shotgun in his ribs urged him forward. Steve stopped. The shotgun prodded him.

"Get up there," Russell growled.

"No, thanks." A sharp pain hit the back of his head. Steve could feel his knees buckle. He tried to hold himself up, but nothing worked anymore.

He awoke with his arms aching dully. He tried to move them

to relieve the ache, then he saw that they were tied to the cross beams, his legs to the main support.

Chila Dart pulled a wooden step stool around behind him, near the piled wood, and climbed up it. Steve knew she was moving by the rustling of cloth, but he couldn't tell what she was doing. He could turn his head to try and see, but since he was helpless, he felt content to wait for bad news.

Something dropped over his forehead. A sting—like the ones on his wrists—caused him to jerk. The thing tightened against his forehead and the intense sting was repeated in a dozen places.

"Uhhhhh . . ." Pain jolted through him. His body jerked. With the part of his mind that still worked, he finally recognized the sting of nettles.

"Good," Chila whispered, stroking Denny's forehead with her gloved hand. She stayed behind him, because she didn't want to take any chances on his giving her the evil eye and getting her in his control.

"That feel tight enough?" she asked.

Steve panted to keep from crying out. His forehead was more sensitive than his wrists apparently. The pain came in waves, each more painful and dizzying than the last.

"Why . . . are you . . . doing this?" he asked.

"To stop you." She pressed something cold against his ear; his body jerked again.

"I never saw you . . . before I rode into Picket Post. Why are you doing this?"

"You killed my baby! Now the Forrester boy is missing!"

"Nicholas . . ."

She dropped another crown of stinging nettles over his head and tightened it around his neck.

"Unnnnn . . ." He jerked so hard the jerking hurt almost as much as the nettles. Pain was so intense, its source got lost.

"Nicholas"—he panted—"is lost . . . His . . . mother . . . is looking—" Chila's gloved hand pressed the nettles against his forehead. "Unnnnhh . . ." Steve almost lost consciousness. He fought the blackness, which part of him wanted and part didn't. "She . . . needs . . . help!"

"Shut up!" Chila screamed into his ear, causing that to hurt, too. "You're trying to trick me." She grabbed his sleeve and tore it loose from his shirt. Taking another strand of the stinging nettles and puncture vines she had sewn around strands of cotton, she wrapped it around his arm to weaken his power, so he would not be able to trick her or anyone else.

"Unnn!" Steve jerked. "Nicholas needs your help. Instead of wasting . . . your time here—" She pressed them hard against his arm. "Ahhhh!" Steve gritted his teeth against the waves of fire and ice burning along his nerves.

"Give me your skinning knife," Chila yelled. Steve refused to think what she was going to do next. He knew he needed to convince her she had the wrong man, but she didn't seem interested in whether he was or not.

She moved the steps around to the front of him. He turned his head slightly; the needle-shaped hairs of the nettles bored into his flesh, renewing the viciousness of their sting. His whole body felt like an open wound.

Chila used the knife to cut off the legs of his pants. Cold wind further confused his senses. He shivered.

Then she wrapped a strand of nettles around his left thigh. He hadn't thought his legs would be so sensitive, but his whole body jerked wildly for a moment, then got control of itself.

She next wrapped another strand of nettles around his right thigh. He clenched his jaws, but his body could not be controlled. It jerked and twitched.

Chila surveyed her handiwork and shook her head. Denny was still too strong. She added another strand lower down on his thigh. According to her grandmother's notes, the nettles would drain off his power, so he could be killed. She hoped she'd made enough of the strands.

She pressed them against him, to be sure the poison got next to his skin. "Uhhhhh . . ." The sound groaned out of him. His body jerked less than usual, and he didn't appear to be feeling it much anymore. Chila saw that as a bad sign. Maybe his devil powers were overcoming her grandmother's remedy. She got off her step stool and moved it over to where she could reach his left wrist.

"Get me my nails and hammer!" she yelled at the men on the ground.

Steve opened his eyes, but he was careful not to move. Every movement, no matter how slight, renewed the attention he got from the nettles.

Ham Russell walked over to the place where the extra lumber lay on the yellowed grass. He poked around for a minute.

"Don't see the hammer or the nails."

Chila got down and stalked over there. Steve had never seen

such a determined woman. She shoved Ham Russell out of her way and lifted every piece of lumber until she had assured herself that what she looked for wasn't there.

"Did you take my hammer and nails?"

Roy Bowles scowled. "I thought you was through with 'em."

"Dammit! Go get 'em! And you better be quick about it."

CHAPTER TWENTY-TWO

Samantha climbed steadily upward. At the crest, she saw the desert, covered by the red fog of sand that was only now settling down on the ground.

She picked what looked like the best route down the side of the mountain and struck off. Downhill was easier and faster. She stopped to catch her breath and wonder if perhaps Nicholas had turned back and was waiting for her at home. She prayed for him to be asleep in Juana's arms.

Buoyed by hope, Samantha resumed her descent. Shortly she came out of the thickets and saw two men riding toward the rocks at the entry of the cave.

"Up here!" she yelled.

They stopped their horses before the rocks piled in front of the cave's entry. Samantha ran down the hill as fast as she could without losing control. Finally she stumbled out onto the level ground and ran forward, yelling.

"Ramon! Ian!"

Ramon looked up and motioned to Ian. Samantha stumbled to a stop before them.

"We thought you were in there, lass," Ian said, pointing to the cave.

"I was," she panted. "Did you find Nicholas? Have you seen Steve? We got separated."

"No, *señora*."

"Did you stop at the Dart ranch?" she asked. Steve had been headed in that direction the last time she'd seen him.

"*Sí, señora*."

"Did you tell Chila?"

"*Sí*."

Chila's knowing seemed ominous. Samantha knew she had to find Steve, and fast. "Ian, will you lend me your horse?"

"Aye, lass. I say anytime a horse's owner wants to borrow him back, she has this Scot's blessing."

"Stay here and look for Nicholas. I'm going to the Dart ranch."

* * *

The ride took less than an hour, but it was the longest hour of her life. At the Dart house, Samantha dismounted and started up the steps. "Hello!" she called out.

At the top of the steps, she yelled again; "Chila?"

Joe Dart opened the door. "Ma's not here."

"Have you seen Steve Sheridan?"

Joe hesitated. He'd never felt more confused. He didn't know, as his mother's child, whether his job was to help his ma do what she seemed to need to do so damned bad, or whether he was supposed to just keep doing what was right, no matter what effect it might have on her.

"Joe, I need help! Steve may be in danger."

Joe felt like his head was gonna bust right open. Samantha Forrester had been a friend to his ma all these years. And before she got involved in this thing with Sheridan, Ma had always taught him to do right. "I don't know what got into her. She's been acting crazy since the minute she saw him ride into town."

"Joe, you know where they are! Take me there."

"Roy Bowles just left here with a hammer and nails." The picture Joe's mind made was an ugly one. He'd thought and thought about all this—and he couldn't even think of a good ending to it all. He ran to the barn and dragged a horse out of one of the stalls. Bareback, he led Samantha up the side of the mountain.

The rising sun showed a clear sky. With the sun would come warmth to ease the chill. Even so, Arden Chandler thought it a hell of a thing for a boy with lung problems to be lost in the desert.

Arden rode with the cavalry patrol until they saw a house half buried in the side of the mountain. "That's the Dart ranch you were looking for," Rathwick said from beside him. "We're going to keep searching for the boy."

"Thank you, Captain. I'll keep an eye out for him, too."

Chandler turned east toward the house. The cavalry patrol continued northwest.

Arden Chandler sat his horse a moment, looking at the house. He might get a cup of hot coffee there, but then again he might not. If this Chila Dart was the one he knew, he might take on a quick load of buckshot. He patted his horse and dismounted stiffly. He was getting too old for long horse rides. His arthritic hip was giving him a fit. He should have remembered that before he set off on this wild-goose chase.

He fumbled in his saddlebags for the biscuits and bacon he'd packed. With them in hand, he limped to the nearest rock and leaned against it.

Idly he chewed his biscuit and gazed at the mountain behind the house. On the side of the hill, he saw riders climbing. One alone, and then a little lower down two others. That was odd. Then he noticed a clearing and what looked like a cross. Frowning, Arden rubbed his eyes. If they weren't deceiving him, and they never had before, there was a man on that cross.

"I'll be double damned," he growled, putting his biscuit in his pocket and heading for his horse.

Tristera saw the soldiers, and her legs went so weak she almost couldn't pull herself up onto them.

"A cavalry patrol," she said. Her heart pounded with sudden fear, but she knew that would not stop her. She knew what she had to do, and she would do it in spite of the fear.

Blue uniforms were only a hundred yards from her. They might pass her hiding place by if she remained quiet, but she could not do that. The boy needed to be taken home.

As she walked closer, she recognized the man at the front of the band as Rathwick. Shakily she stepped into the clearing and waited for him to see her.

Rathwick glanced up and raised his hand; men behind him halted. He said something she couldn't hear to the men, dismounted, and walked toward her alone.

Rathwick was surprised and glad to see Tristera, but something about the way she watched him caused him to stop a few feet in front of her. She looked thinner and older than the girl who'd run away from the dance only a few hours before. Disappointed and chagrined at himself, he took off his hat. He had wanted her to run into his arms.

"Why did you run away, Tristera?"

That seemed an odd question to her. There were so many other things he could have asked her. "Because I am the Indian woman you look for."

Rathwick blinked as if trying to ward off hearing what he'd already heard. His next question caused her to wonder if he had somehow accomplished it.

"Where's Mrs. Forrester?" he asked softly.

"Did you hear what I said? I am the Indian woman you are looking for. I am Elunami."

Joe led Samantha up the hill. Trees on either side of the narrow path obstructed her view. The birds were strangely silent. Even the squirrels didn't show themselves.

Joe turned his horse; Samantha followed. The terrain leveled off. Samantha straightened in the saddle and tried to see around Joe, who appeared to have stopped.

"Hold it right there!"

Samantha recognized Ham Russell's voice.

"I gotta see Ma."

"Not now you don't!"

Samantha rode up beside Joe. "I have to see Chila."

"Sorry, ma'am, but I've got my orders."

Samantha leaned to the right of Russell and saw Steve tied to a cross, with Chila on a short ladder behind him.

"Oh, my God!" Samantha kicked her horse hard. The tired animal lurched forward, spooking Russell's horse so that it reared and let her flash past. At full gallop, Samantha's horse raced into the clearing. Too late, Roy Bowles kicked his horse in the sides and angled to intercept her. But she had not come this far to be stopped. She whipped her mount forward. At the last second, Bowles lost his nerve and let his horse veer away.

Jubilant, Samantha leaned close over her horse's neck to clear the remaining distance between herself and Steve. A rope dropped over her and her horse's heads. Samantha looked back to see that Ham Russell had not given up. Her horse, tired anyway, gave in to the heavy pressure against his throat and stopped.

Grinning, Ham Russell rode up beside her. Over Russell's shoulder, Samantha could see Steve bleeding from a dozen places.

"Stop!" she yelled, lifting Steve's revolver out of her pocket and pointing it at Ham Russell. He halted at the sight of the gun. Behind her, she heard a horse's hooves on the spongy mat of pine needles. Bowles, Russell, and Joe were all in sight. Puzzled, Samantha turned her head slightly, trying to see who was coming. Russell knocked the gun out of her hand and dragged her off the horse.

Samantha fought him, but he was too strong for her. Over his head she saw Joe Dart watching, but he was too dispirited to do anything to help her. She struggled for a moment, but Russell's weight was too much for her. She went limp.

"You give up?" Russell asked.

"Yes," Samantha said, lying.

Ham Russell grabbed Samantha and pulled her to her feet. Keeping a hard grip on her left wrist, he jerked the rope down and wound it around her arms, pinning them to her sides.

"Chila!" Samantha shouted. "Chila, make him let me go! I have to talk to you!"

"So you can defend the man who killed your boy?" Chila yelled back at her.

"I got the hammer and nails," Bowles yelled.

"Chila! Steve didn't hurt Nicholas!"

"Keep her back!" Chila yelled. "Your boy's dead! I seen him!"

"Oh, no," Samantha moaned, praying that she was lying. "Joe! Make them let me go!"

Joe hung his head. Satisfied that Roy and Ham had Samantha under control and that Joe wouldn't be any more trouble than he usually was, Chila took the hammer and nails from Roy Bowles and turned back to attend to Denny. Though Chila hated having to do this herself, she was determined to see it through. Her grandmother's remedy for dealing with devils was specific. You had to do certain things in a certain order, and Chila wasn't about to turn yellow at this point and let him come back at her, madder and more vengeful than ever.

She positioned the step stool under his left hand and climbed up on it. She could hear Samantha Forrester screaming in the background. Usually that much racket would stop her from just about anything, but not this. She positioned the nail over the vein in the palm of Denny's left hand.

Her stomach lurched a little, but she knew that was just the devil trying to stop her. She didn't want to look at him. Grandma's remedy advised against looking at a devil once you'd started, but she couldn't help herself. His head was bloody; his eyes were swelled almost shut.

"Why are you doing this?" he whispered.

Chila turned away from his eyes, which did manage to look hurt and confused. Her stomach lurched with compassion. She would hurry and put him out of his misery. Even a devil had some feelings, apparently.

Chila hit the nail with the hammer. Devil's blood spattered Chila's face. She hit the nail again. Once started, the worst thing you could do was stop.

Samantha felt Steve's pain echo all over her body. Ham Russell lifted the shotgun to menace her with it. Ignoring the threat, Samantha ran at Chila, screaming.

Chila ignored her and pounded on the nail until it seemed deep enough into the wood, then she sank down onto the step stool, shaking so hard her chest hurt.

"Shut her up!" she yelled at Ham Russell, who was just letting Samantha scream. In spite of the rope around her, she managed to get a few feet from the cross, her eyes filled with horror and tears streaming down her cheeks. It was apparent Samantha didn't understand the nature of this beast on the cross. Chila wanted to comfort her friend, but the job had to be finished.

Drive the first nail into the vein, Chila remembered from her grandmother's diary, *in the left hand that goes directly to the heart.* Done. *Drive four nails into the heart.*

"How could you?" Samantha screamed, and launched herself on top of Chila. Though bound, Samantha hit Chila hard enough to knock her off the ladder. Then she fell on top of her, biting and kicking. They fought wildly. Only the knowledge that the job had to be finished gave Chila the strength to lift the hammer and bring it down on Samantha's head. It was only a glancing blow but enough to stun her. Chila hit her again. Samantha fell limply to the ground; Chila struggled up and positioned the step stool, so she could finish the job.

"Now keep her there," she yelled at Ham Russell.

Before Russell could reach her, Samantha staggered up and bumped Chila from behind. Chila kicked her and screamed at Ham Russell, who had apparently decided to just watch.

"Get her off me!" Chila screamed.

Ham ram forward, grabbed Samantha, and started pulling her away. It took both Roy and Ham to make any headway at all with her. She kicked and screamed and bit them.

Panting, Chila climbed up the step stool and positioned the nail over Denny's heart. A hand grabbed her hammer arm and held on tight.

"Get her away from me!" Chila screamed.

"We'd a had more privacy in the town square!" Ham yelled.

Startled, Chila looked around—into the face of the old man holding her with such a strong grip. She had the feeling she should know him, but she couldn't quite place him.

He forced the hammer out of her hand and stepped up onto the step stool. Chila couldn't figure out why Roy or Ham hadn't stopped him from coming forward. Unless he'd walked by as they wrestled with Samantha.

The man dragged her off the step stool.

"You stay put," he growled, glaring at her. She was so stunned by his sudden appearance—and the feeling she should know him—that she just stood there and watched. He stepped up onto the stool, felt Denny's wrist, and looked sadly down at her.

"I'm the one you want up here," he said.

Samantha stopped struggling. She, Ham Russell, and Roy Bowles turned as one to look at the man who spoke. Even Joe Dart seemed to have come out of his stupor.

"What?" Chila asked.

"Don't you recognize me?"

Chila shook her head. Then his resemblance to the man on the cross struck her.

"Denny?"

"Yes. It's me," he said heavily. "And you've killed your boy."

"Denny?" Chila asked, her voice incredulous.

"Who the hell else would come out on a day like this?"

Dumbfounded, Chila looked at the man on the cross.

"He's the baby you thought I drowned back in Tulsa."

"No . . ." Chila shook her head. "No."

"Yes. I'd wager anything on it."

Chila started to cry. It couldn't be, and yet this old man seemed so sure of himself.

"I been looking for you and him for almost twenty-four years now," the man said.

"For me?" Chila asked dumbly.

"To tell you I didn't think that boy they found in the creek was ours. I wrote to your folks, but they'd rather die than let me know where you were. I gave up looking for you years ago. Then I came here. Didn't even ask around for you like I used to do. Selena told me it was foolishness. I finally believed her . . . more or less."

Weak and confused, Chila leaned against the cross. A jolt of pain shot through her and she jumped. Nettles around the man's legs had stung her neck. It burned like fire.

"We got to get these things off him," she said, looking around for her knife. Even if he was already dead, his poor body shouldn't be tortured any more than it had been.

With everyone watching in silence, Chila climbed up and cut

away the strands of puncture vines and nettles around his head, arms, neck, and legs. His skin was blistered and cut and bloody. Her hands shook so, she almost couldn't do it.

Denny and Joe took the nail out of his hand. They cut the ropes holding him to the cross and lowered him as gently as they could to the ground. They untied Samantha Forrester, and she fell on his body and cried.

Feeling sick, Chila sat down on the step stool and cried for a moment herself, then peered up at Denny, who looked a lot older than she did. Time hadn't been as kind to him. His hair was white and his face seamed.

"I loved that baby!" she said defiantly.

"You used to love me, too, but that didn't stop you from trying to kill me when they found that drowned boy."

"You used to love me, too, but it didn't stop you from giving another woman your baby!"

"I can't believe you thought I'd kill my own son."

It puzzled Chila now, too. "I blacked out and woke up more than a year later . . ."

Ignoring them, Samantha pressed against Steve's chest, consumed by grief. She felt sick and outraged and full of despair at the same time.

"Samantha . . ."

Steve's hoarse whisper startled her. "Steve?" She peered into his swollen eyes. "He's alive!" she yelled. Joy replaced grief. She wanted to shout, to dance, to run. "He's alive!"

"I might not stay that way if this hand keeps bleeding," he rasped in a barely audible voice.

Rathwick had orders to kill Elunami on sight. Tristera, who was looking up at him with her jaws clenched in stubborn determination, could not be Elunami. His mind refused to consider it. He had held this girl in his arms and kissed her. Even now he could feel her warm, soft body pressed against his. He had never disobeyed a direct order . . .

The wind whipped around them, pressing her tunic against her slim body. Rathwick stepped forward and gripped her arm so hard she winced. "Speak of this to no one. Do you understand me?"

Confused, Elunami nodded.

"Come along. We have to find Mrs. Forrester and Sheridan."

"Wait, I have to get something."

She came back a moment later, carrying Nicholas Forrester.

"Where did you find him?"

"Not far from here."

Nicholas nodded sleepily. Rathwick found a blanket for the boy and handed him to one of his men. Then he helped Elunami up onto his horse in front of him.

South of the Dart ranch, Rathwick saw Arden Chandler, Samantha Forrester, and a horse pulling a travois.

"Mama!" Nicholas cried. He wriggled out of the soldier's arms, dropped from the horse, and ran to his mother's side.

"Nicholas!" Samantha flashed a look of gratitude at Tristera and Rathwick, then slid off her horse to envelop her son in her arms. Tears of relief and joy streamed down her cheeks as she embraced her son and thanked God for his safe return.

"What happened to Steve?" Nicholas asked, frowning at the man lying so pale and still on the travois.

"He's been hurt."

Nicholas slipped out of her arms and walked to the travois. He touched Steve's face. Swollen eyes opened. Steve tried to smile. "Hey, partner. Good to see you."

"What happened to you?"

"It's a long story, but I'm fine." Steve's voice was hoarse.

"I want to walk beside Steve," Nicholas said.

"No. We have to get Steve to the house. He needs medicine." Samantha took Nicholas onto her horse in front of her. There was more urgency involved than she had let on to Nicholas. The nettle poisoning was making Steve sick, slowing his heart and threatening to stop it.

An hour later they rode into sight of her Boston House cottage and stopped in amazement. The house had been crushed beneath an enormous boulder. Stunned, Samantha stopped her horse. Everyone stopped in unison and sat their horses, looking at the boulder that had turned the old house into a flattened pile of rubble.

"If Steve hadn't stayed, we might have been in there," she whispered, leaning forward to kiss her son's warm forehead. Nicholas didn't respond; he was asleep.

Steve was unconscious on the travois. Arden Chandler, who said he was fairly knowledgeable in the ways of medicine, had wrapped Steve's hand and packed wet clay over his sting wounds. Steve's only concern had been that someone go back and put Calico out of his misery. Joe Dart had promised to do it. Rathwick had sent Chila, Ham, and Roy into town under guard of six soldiers. He'd also sent a rider to the fort to bring back the surgeon to treat Steve's hand.

Chandler had said that if he had the ingredients he could mix a purgative to rid Steve's body of the poison that might otherwise stop his heart. Samantha felt driven by that need.

Arden Chandler rode up next to her. "This was the worst earthquake I've ever seen. It was as bad as a Texas tornado for doing damage."

"I hope the new house is all right," Nicholas said.

An hour later, the sight of the new house framed between the two stone gate posts brought up a multitude of emotions. They had made it. Steve was still alive. And the house had withstood its first test.

Juana and the Kincaid women ran out to meet them. "Take Mr. Chandler to the kitchen and show him all of our remedies," Samantha said to Juana.

Elizabeth, Jennie, and Leslie took charge of Nicholas, still asleep in her arms. "We'll take him upstairs," Elizabeth said, wiping tears from her cheeks.

Ian Macready yelled for men to carry Steve. Samantha ran up the stairs ahead of them. "In here, please," she said, directing them to her bedroom.

She turned back the counterpane. Ian stopped. "Aye, lass, ye've a generous heart, but it would be a shame to put this lad into that nice clean bed, the mess he is now."

"I don't care about bedclothes," she said, amazed Ian would worry about such a thing at a time like this.

"Well, lass, if yourself would be leaving the room, we could lay him on a tarp and clean him up before we ruined a passel of fine linens."

"Very well." Samantha stepped outside and closed the door.

Rathwick carried Nicholas, surrounded by the Kincaid women, into his bedroom and laid him on his bed. "Thank you, Matthew, for everything."

"My pleasure to be of service, however small."

"Tristera told me she confessed to being Elunami."

Chagrin twisted and tightened Rathwick's mouth.

"We're a family," Samantha reminded him. "We share our problems. I need to ask . . . What's going to happen to her?"

"I don't know. And if I did I might not be at liberty to discuss it."

* * *

Rathwick walked downstairs to find Elunami. It felt odd to call her that. He could not reconcile the crazy Indian woman he had envisioned with the girl he had known as Tristera.

He found her in the kitchen with Chandler, who looked up at his entry. Elunami did, too, but quickly down again.

"None of this will do. Do you have any olive oil?" Chandler asked.

"*Sí*, the *señora* gets it from the catalog."

"And chalk?"

"Nicholas has. I will get it."

Elunami ran from the room.

Chandler nodded to Rathwick. "A good paste of chalk and olive oil will take a lot of that poison out of him."

"I didn't know that." Rathwick knew he was speaking automatically.

Elunami returned with the chalk. Chandler took out his knife and began to scrape off a thin dust onto a saucer.

Rathwick took Elunami's arm and pulled her aside. "I'm going to the fort. Will you stay here until I return?"

"I don't know."

His eyes reflected his misery. She shouldn't promise, but she had already been a great deal of trouble to him.

"For a time."

"Thank you. I'll be back as soon as I can."

She watched him ride away at the head of his ragged cavalry patrol, his strong, handsome back bowed in the slanting sunlight. She was Elunami now. Even if they killed her for it she would not change her name again.

She had expected Matthew to take her with him, but he hadn't. He would be back, though. He would recover and realize he had failed to do his duty.

Before her experience in the hidden valley, despair might have filled her. All her life she had waited to be in love, and now she was—with the man whose job it was to kill her.

But now, she saw things differently. Matthew had an interesting decision to make. It would be good to see how the Great Mystery used this to educate them both.

At Fort Thomas, Rathwick rode directly to his commanding officer's building. Ashland looked up from a letter he was reading, glared at the interruption, sighed, and leaned back in his chair. "Captain."

"I need to know the real reason why you ordered me to kill the Indian woman."

General Ashland scowled and put down his letter. "So, you've finally found her. Have a seat, Captain."

Rathwick settled his weary body into the chair. He had been riding for two days now without any real sleep, except what he got in snatches in the saddle.

"Where is she?" the general demanded.

"I need to know why you ordered me to kill her, sir."

Rathwick was being insubordinate, but he had been a good officer. Ashland considered the request a moment and decided to tell him.

Samantha sat by Steve's bed as if his recovery depended upon her full attention. White with bands of Arden Chandler's paste around forehead, neck, arms, chest, and legs, he had drunk Chandler's vile concoction, gagging it down until Chandler said he'd swallowed enough. Then Steve had fallen into a deep sleep.

Dr. Aaron Thomas finally came and checked the damaged vein in Steve's hand. He sent Samantha out of the room, treated the wound, wrapped it, and called her and Chandler back into the room.

"I've taken out the blood clot, tied off the ends of the veins, and cleaned the wound. If he develops a fever, and he's likely to, mix a dram of powdered niter, two drams of carbonate of potash, two teaspoonfuls of antimonial wine, and a tablespoon of sweet spirits of niter in a half a pint of water. If it starts to bleed again, raise the arm and apply cold compresses to the hand to stop the bleeding. But I don't think it will. If he gets hungry give him beef tea. Do you have everything you need for the fever water?"

"I think so. I've made that for Nicholas."

Dr. Thomas left.

"I'll be going, too," Chandler said, picking up his hat.

"Thank you for your help."

He nodded at her. "He's in good hands now. I'm satisfied on that score."

Chandler clumped down the stairs. Samantha checked on Nicholas and then sat down beside Steve's bed. She reached out to touch his face, where it wasn't covered by the thick white paste, and her hand shook.

"Have you eaten anything at all today, *señora*?" Juana asked, startling Samantha, who hadn't heard her come in.

"No. I don't think so."

"I'll bring up a tray." Fortunately Juana knew her well enough not to ask her to leave his side.

At four o'clock in the morning, by the clock on the mantel, Peter Van Vleet slipped out of bed without waking his wife. He dressed noiselessly and buckled on the guns he had laid aside when he married.

Nicholas was home safe. Steve was injured but recovering. And Ham Russell was in custody. There was a good possibility that the rest of the rustlers might be careless enough to give away their hiding place.

Peter rode down the hill before dawn and asked directions from Eagle Thornton, who had just gotten up and was standing on the front porch of the old bunkhouse, appreciating the sunrise.

"Which way to the Dart ranch?"

"North," he growled, pointing with his right hand.

Peter thanked him and kicked his horse into a gallop. At the ranch house, he climbed the hill behind the house and concealed himself and his horse, then settled down to watch and wait.

Finally, at seven o'clock six unshaven men rode in, conferred with a man on the bunkhouse porch, and then all seven of them rode out.

Peter followed them into the hills and through a carefully hidden canyon corridor. There he saw a large herd of cattle, bellowing and milling in a second box canyon, pinned in by less than a dozen men and three strands of barbed wire. As he watched, cowboys roped a steer, brought it down, and branded it with a running iron. Peter recognized three of the men as former members of Dallas Younger's wholesale rustling operation.

Satisfied that he'd seen enough, Peter rode back to Samantha's old house and sent Eagle Thornton into town with a message for the marshal. Within two hours Thornton, Daley, and a posse appeared on the horizon.

Peter led them to the herd. The posse surrounded the men, disarmed them, and then prepared to hang them on the spot. Peter singled out the youngest man there, barely seventeen by the looks of his tender stubble, and put a rope around his neck. The boy's face turned white; he looked like he was going to vomit.

The rest of the posse looked uncomfortable, but Peter ignored them. He adjusted the rope around the boy's neck and said, "I guess you can say a few words if you like."

"Tell my mama . . ." His voice gave out; he started again. "Tell her that I'm sorry," he croaked.

Peter scowled at him. "How old are you, boy?"

"Sixteen, sir."

"What the hell are you doing rustling cattle? Don't you know that's a hanging offense in this territory?"

The boy licked his lips. "I . . . my pa died, and Ma's broke and sick. I . . . didn't know what else to do, and the pay was good."

"I sure hate to hang a boy, though," Peter said, shaking his head sorrowfully. "I don't suppose you'd be willing to say who you worked for, would you, in exchange for a lighter sentence?"

The boy swallowed and looked at the others. Their stony faces told him nothing. Shame flushed up, darkening his face. "I was hired by Ham Russell," he mumbled. "As far as I know, he was the leader of the gang."

"How long have you been doing this?" Peter asked.

"Not long. About two months."

"How about Joe Dart? Did he have anything to do with this operation?"

"No, sir. Not as far as I know."

Daley nodded. He was satisfied. "Well, thanks, son," he said to Peter. "I'll wager that Russell and his entire band will be sweating blood in prison in Yuma by this time next month."

Elizabeth and Chantry Two were the first to announce their departure. Now that Nicholas and Samantha and Steve were home, they decided to leave so Samantha could put her energies into nursing Steve. And they were expected in San Francisco by friends.

When their baggage was loaded, everyone followed Chantry Two and Elizabeth outside to where their darkly polished carriage waited. The beautiful, big-footed black Shires, their white manes braided into jaunty upright pom-poms, stamped impatiently in their trace chains.

Chantry Two patted his Shires, rattled a few of the chains, and spoke to his uniformed driver, but his attention was on his wife. Elizabeth had a determined look about her that boded ill for someone. She saw him watching her and walked over to stand beside him while the others gathered around the carriage, chatting. Finally, when the others were laughing about something Jennie had said, Elizabeth eased him aside.

"Just what does that look mean?" she demanded.

"I have no idea what you're up to, Lizzy, but . . ."

"Me?"

"You, madam, are about as subtle as a traincock."

"Samantha is going to nurse that young man back to health and then destroy him . . ."

"Let it be, Lizzy. If she doesn't destroy him one way, she'll figure out another way."

"Mind your manners, Chantry Kincaid," Elizabeth said, brushing a piece of lint off his sleeve. She was well acquainted with her husband's view that a woman's job in life was to destroy a man.

"Any man who can be brought down by a woman doesn't deserve to live anyway," Chantry growled.

"You wouldn't agree if he were your son."

"Hell I wouldn't!"

Nicholas came over and put his small, warm hand into hers. Elizabeth gave her husband a warning look and knelt down to say good-bye to Nicholas. His thin arms clasped tightly around her neck. He hugged her for a long time, then finally stepped back.

"I wish you wouldn't go."

"We'll be back, sooner than you'll know," Elizabeth said, wiping sudden tears that had come up at the memory of how close they'd come to losing him. It was a miracle Nicholas had survived, thanks to Elunami . . . or Tristera . . . or whatever her name really was. Elizabeth patted Nicholas's head and stood up to hug Samantha, standing at her son's side.

"You take care of my grandson," Elizabeth said.

"You know I will."

"He's too skinny."

"We feed him five times a day," Samantha said, protesting.

"I like your young man."

Samantha flushed. "He's my builder, Aunt Elizabeth."

"And a very good one." Elizabeth took Samantha by the elbow and steered her away from the others. "I'm an old woman now, eccentric, some say, so I can say anything I please. Have you given up your hopes of getting Lance away from Angie?"

Samantha's eyes filled with consternation and her mouth tightened. Elizabeth could see that she hadn't. She also knew Chantry would give her hell for this.

Chantry glowered at her. Elizabeth continued before he could walk over and stop her. "I know they're getting a divorce, and I know you'll probably get him, if you still want him. And maybe there won't be anything so awful about that, if it happens.

"But I remember that every time I looked at Angie I saw how much she loved my son—and how badly she wanted and needed his baby—and how aware she was of his need for one." She paused for a breath. "I know there must have been many nights when she lay beside my son and tried to decide if she could send him to you—a woman who *could* give him a son."

Stricken, Samantha cupped her hands over her mouth as if to stop the flow of words that shouldn't have been uttered.

"But I can see you're as stubborn now as you've ever been. Which brings me to one other thing. I don't appreciate the fact that all your life you've held yourself apart from me. Instead you went to Lance or Mrs. Lillian. You could have let me help you, but you never did. It's almost as if you blame me *and* your parents for their dying and leaving you."

"I don't know what you're talking about," Samantha whispered, horrified.

"Yes, you do. I was right. There isn't a portrait of your mother or your father in this house," Elizabeth said angrily. "Not one! And they loved you so much."

Samantha trembled with pent-up emotion. "I—"

"I shouldn't say this, but I've said everything else. You remember the other day when you walked in and caught Jennie and Leslie talking about me?"

"How did you know that?"

"I was right behind you, dear. They were talking about me with affectionate condescension—the way we talk about people we love. But it upset you. Do you know why?"

"No."

"Well, I didn't either at first. But a few seconds ago I saw a look on your face, and I realized why it upset me that you scolded them for that. It was because you feel so guilty about never having loved me that you have to treat me like some goddess who must always be admired, never corrected or spoken about with anything less than perfect respect."

Samantha shook her head in denial.

"No, dear, it's true. I don't hold it against you. I'm mentioning it merely so you will see the difference. If you truly loved me the way the others do, you would have smiled gently and condescendingly—and been one of them, one of the women who truly love me. But you've held yourself away from me just as you have from everyone except Lance. I don't blame you for it, but I think I know why you've always been so daft for Lance. You transferred all your love and need onto him. I have no idea when or how it happened, but it won't bring you happiness. And it may ruin your life—not to mention his and Angie's.''

Elizabeth pulled Samantha into her arms and hugged the stiff, stunned young woman. ''You think about what I've said. And you take care of my grandson!''

Samantha struggled to speak around the lump in her throat. ''I thought . . .''

''What dear?''

''I thought you had enough girls to love you.''

Elizabeth shook her head. ''God love your little heart. How we torture ourselves . . .''

Tears streamed down Samantha's cheeks. ''I do love you, Aunt Elizabeth, I do.'' And for the first time in her life, she felt that love welling up in her for the woman who'd raised her.

Elizabeth recognized it in the girl's eyes. Gently she pulled Samantha into her arms. ''Yes, you do, child. And it's about time.''

Chane and Jennie were the last to go. Chane helped the children into the carriage. Nicholas climbed in with them to bounce on the heavily upholstered seats a moment.

''Nicholas!'' At her reprimand, he sat down properly.

Samantha hugged Jennie. Chane put his hands in his pockets, rocked back on his heels, and looked at the house. ''Well, you'll be glad to know I've decided to forgive you for building a house without my advice or help.''

''Chane!'' Jennie said, halfway shocked.

''Oh, Chane, I'm sorry,'' Samantha said.

''You should be. Fortunately, Sheridan did an excellent job. Otherwise I would have taken him to task. Any chance this thing with Sheridan could turn into something useful?''

''No,'' Samantha said, feeling heat come up into her face. ''Steve's a tumbleweed.''

''Every tumbleweed finds a fence sooner or later.''

''Well, he won't,'' she said.

Chane noted the regret in her voice and was glad for it. ''For a boy to grow into a man,'' he said, ''it helps to have a model to follow. Sheridan looks like he'd make a pretty fair model, if he survives,'' he said, watching Samantha to see if Sheridan had a chance with her. She turned a little pink, but he couldn't tell if it was worry over his condition, which remained serious, or unadmitted love. Unfortunately he'd never found a woman's color to be a reliable barometer of anything.

Jennie hugged Samantha again. Then Chane helped his wife into the brougham. Nicholas stood beside Samantha, waving until the carriage rolled out of sight behind the trees and abutting rocks on the curving mountain road.

With her company gone, Samantha turned all her energies to nursing Steve. His fever seemed to come in waves, each cresting higher than the last. He was a stoic patient. The only way she knew his fever was rising again was that his teeth would start to chatter, and she would pile on blankets. When he kicked them off finally, she knew the fever had broken—for the moment.

Samantha stayed at his side, praying Arden Chandler's vile concoction and his paste were working. For the moment, Steve was between crises, his skin felt hot and dry. His face was unshaven, his eyes closed. He looked so weak and so dear that she felt tears welling up in her.

Avoiding the paste caked on his throat, she leaned over, put her arms around him, pressed her face to his chest, and let the tears flow. She had no idea why she was crying. But the emotional events of the past few days had left her feeling like an exposed nerve.

Steve woke slowly to the feel of her. He wanted to pat her soft hair, but his arms didn't respond to his willed command. At first that frightened him, but there was something sweet and dark about being helpless in the arms of the woman he loved. She had fought like a tigress to save him from Chila Dart. Her struggles on his behalf had delayed Chila long enough for that stranger to intervene.

So, he owed his life to this warm, sweet, trembling woman. He had realized on the long, miserable ride home, when he was so sick even his skin felt like vomiting, that he loved her the way he would love no other. Before, he had loved her a little and lusted after her a lot. In lust there was great excitement and sometimes great satisfaction, but it was only when he had truly surrendered to his love for her, as he had done on that ride, that he had felt a sense of joy and realized that love was a rare privilege. Every moment he had been conscious, his only desire had been to look at her, any angle of her.

He had stored memories of her holding her sleeping son's

head against her breast. He remembered her profile as she gazed at the rock crushing her old house, and of her looking back over her shoulder at him time and again during that interminable ride, her lovely face expressing fear for his safety and frustration that they were moving so slowly.

Those were sweet memories. But now he could tell the paralysis was deepening, soon to take his life. He needed to purge himself of his guilt and shame.

"Samantha?" He licked dry, swollen lips. His voice was a hoarse croak. Samantha straightened.

"Steve! How do you feel?"

"Okay," he said, lying.

"You need to take a drink." She reached for the water glass by the bedside.

"No more of that stuff."

"Sissy. This is just water." She held him and the glass. Steve took a swallow to please her and sank back on the pillow.

"I need to tell you . . . that I was lower than a worm the other night." He couldn't remember how much time had passed since the party, but it didn't matter. "You're sweet and beautiful and perfect. I never should have touched you. I was furious, and I said things I shouldn't have. You don't belong to me. Or anyone, for that matter. You're an angel, and I want you to know that it has been a privilege to know you and to love you. I'll always love you. If there's any way you can forgive me for what I almost did to you . . . I don't deserve it . . ."

"Hush!" Tears streamed down her cheeks. "Save your strength for getting well," she whispered. "I forgive you."

"You're too easy on me . . ."

"I take it back then, Steve Sheridan. I will forgive you only if you promise to get well."

Steve grinned weakly. "Bargain."

His eyes closed; he appeared to sleep. Samantha sat beside him for a long time, watching the slow rise and fall of his chest and the colors in the room fading as the sun left the sky. She checked his heart; the beat seemed more muted. Terror filled her, and she put her head down and cried softly and quietly. His hand twitched, as if he wanted to soothe her but lacked the strength.

She cried bitter tears and realized that she would always love him, too. She didn't know how this had happened to her, but she loved two men with equal desperation. And she realized that, even if Steve lived, she might never find happiness with either one of them, because her head didn't seem to work right. She slept in the chair beside him. Every time she woke, she gave him the fever remedy.

By the third night she began to have hope. Each time she checked his temperature it was lower than the last.

The fourth morning his head was cool. Steve opened his eyes, and they were clear for the first time in days. "How's Nicholas?"

Samantha was so giddy to see him lucid, she laughed. "What about me? I've been the one running between the two of you."

"I can see how you are . . . mouthy."

"Nicholas is better. Rathwick knows Elunami is the Indian woman he's been looking for. I have no idea what he will do about it, though. He looked like a man in shock. But if I know Matthew, he will come to his senses and be back, probably with an official warrant for her arrest, maybe even mine . . ."

"I want to see Nicholas."

"You're in no shape to be walking around."

But Steve would not be stopped. Samantha followed him into Nicholas's room. The boy made such a small dent in the big feather mattress, Steve had to look twice to be sure he was there.

"Sleeping," Samantha whispered.

Steve leaned down, kissed Nicholas's forehead, and swayed. She grabbed him. "You have no business leaning over as weak as you are," she protested, guiding him back to bed.

Samantha spent that night in one of the spare rooms, but she couldn't sleep. Finally she lit a candle and walked down the stairs and into the pantry. She stood staring at the box Elizabeth had brought with her. She had meant to open it sooner, but with all the excitement, she'd forgotten.

Samantha put the candle down on a shelf and pulled the box out of the corner. The lid was nailed shut. Samantha found a crowbar and pried it free. Frames were separated by a heavy quilt. With difficulty Samantha lifted one of the heavy gilt-edged frames out of the box. She peered at it, but the candle did not give off enough light. She carried it into the kitchen and turned on the overhead light. From another part of the basement, she heard the generator kick on and hum quietly. Within a second the light flickered on and grew steady.

The photograph was of a family. A young woman who looked a great deal like herself held a little girl on her lap. A handsome young man stood behind them in a traditional pose. Samantha looked at it for a moment and then walked back into the pantry. She pulled out another heavy frame and carried it into the light.

This one was of a woman, smiling down at an infant cradled in her arms. It looked like herself and Nicholas, but she couldn't remember posing for it. The gilt-edged frame was a neo-rococo, which had gone out of fashion in the seventies. With a start, Samantha realized it wasn't herself in the picture but her mother, looking down at her as a baby. The look on her mother's face was one of such love and tenderness and joy that tears filled her eyes. Her hands started to tremble, she had to put down the frame. Completely overwhelmed, she leaned forward and sobbed into her hands.

When that spasm of emotion passed, she wiped her face, walked into the pantry, and pulled out another picture. In this one, her mother stood beside her father, smiling, holding a tiny bundle in her arms.

"She was just a child herself," Samantha whispered. Fresh tears, hot and flooding, blurred her eyes; she sagged against the wall, holding the frame and crying. But she couldn't stop unpacking the box. Each picture caused her to tremble and cry. But she realized that something new and important was happening to her as she pored over each image. At last the box was empty.

Exhausted, she sat down, surrounded by the portraits of her family, and let the tears come.

Forgive me, Mother. Father. I didn't mean to hate you, but I woke up all alone. I thought you had abandoned me. Then I needed you, and you didn't come. I cried and cried, and you still didn't come.

The older I got, the more I blamed you. I didn't realize how easy it is to get caught up in something that gets out of control. I blamed you for leaving me to grow up in the midst of a loving family—where I never once felt like I belonged.

I always felt like an outsider, an imposter. I always knew I was just minutes away from overstaying my welcome, from being thrown out. It didn't matter how wonderful Aunt Elizabeth and Uncle Chantry were to me, how mean or how loving the Kincaid children were to me. And they were both. I had no birthright there, and I never once forgot it.

As she sobbed, a terrible tightness around her heart eased. It felt as if a clenched fist had finally opened gently.

Samantha dried her tears and carried the pictures, one at a time, up the stairs and laid them along the entry hallway, where she would have the workmen hang them. It took an hour to decide where they would go. When she felt fully satisfied, she turned out the lights and carried her candle back upstairs.

In bed she cried again, but the tears didn't hurt so much. They felt cleansing and necessary. Her parents *had* loved her. They had loved her every bit as much as she loved Nicholas.

Rathwick knew he should go back to the Forrester house, but the truth he had learned from Ashland was barbarous. Knowing it had debilitated him to such a degree that he felt too sick at heart to face Elunami. It was a terrible thing to feel such shame for an organization he had devoted his life to.

He sat for days, too dispirited to do more than eat an occasional meal. High government officials had tricked the Hopi. They had negotiated a new treaty with them, then substituted different wording in the document the Hopi elders had signed.

Why kill her? Rathwick had asked.

Because they don't want her going back to her tribe and telling them they were tricked. The Hopi won't sit still for it if she does that.

They might not anyway.

We have five hundred troops in Arizona Territory now. One hint of trouble and we'll have five thousand. Ashland had looked as if he'd just realized something important. *The Secretary might welcome an uprising . . .* He had smiled suddenly. *That would give him an opportunity to send in enough troops to finish off the Indians once and for all.*

You asshole!

The words had just slipped out. Rathwick had been a military man for twenty years. With two words, he had destroyed himself. The icy gleam in Ashland's eyes had told him that quite clearly. There was no turning back then. He had stood up, ripped off his captain's bars, and dropped them on the desk.

So he was a civilian now. He would tell Elunami the truth. He rented a horse at the livery stable.

Steve slept all that day and night. The next morning he looked different. Samantha tried to decide what it was. With his left hand resting in the white cotton sling she had made, his shoulders propped against two pillows, and with a real breakfast inside him for the first time in days, he looked handsome and pale above nearly a week's growth of black beard. His skin seemed to glow with an inner fire. His eyes followed her everywhere.

"What happened to Chila Dart?" Steve asked, as if he had just remembered.

"Rathwick's men took her to jail. Daley sent a messenger out just this morning to say that they'd had to take her to the insane asylum at Prescott. She's no threat to you anymore, I'm sure of that."

"How's Nicholas doing now?"

"I don't know . . ." She felt so frustrated. "He doesn't seem sick exactly, but he's listless. He sleeps too much. It isn't like him to sleep so much."

Steve got out of bed and walked into Nicholas's room. Inside the door, he sniffed the air. Usually a sickroom had an odd smell, no matter how careful the nurse. Nicholas's room smelled fine.

Steve walked to the bed and leaned close to the boy, who appeared to be feigning sleep. He waited until the dizziness passed. "I know you can hear me, Nicholas," he said quietly. "I also know you're a smart boy and that you blame yourself for what happened to Young Hawk—"

"Steve!" Samantha hissed from behind him.

Steve glanced back at her. She looked scared.

"You think Nicholas doesn't know or suspect? I was seven years old when my adopted brother died. I knew damned good and well I'd had something to do with that. Adults think kids don't know what's going on. But generally it's the other way around. The kids know, and the adults don't."

"Nicholas is just a baby . . ."

"He's six years old. At some point in a boy's life he has to decide if he's going to be a man or not. At seven my foster father saved my life, literally pulled me from the jaws of death. A shaman isn't supposed to show off his mystic powers in that fashion. The next day, his own son was killed in an accident. He knew he'd done something wrong, but he chose to blame me. Being a kid, I took the blame on myself for a long time, but at some point I had to decide if I was going to be crushed under it or throw it off. Nicholas is making that decision now, whether we pretend to notice or not."

"But what if he . . ."

". . . isn't?" Steve finished for her. "Then he's stupid, which I know damned good and well he's not."

Steve sat down on the bed and took Nicholas's hand in his. "Your mother doesn't want me to, but I'm going to tell you what your choices are as I see 'em." To Samantha's surprise, Nicholas opened his eyes and looked at Steve, who nodded his satisfaction and continued.

"A man by the name of Pasteur discovered what he called germs a while back. And ever since he did that, people have been thinking that everything that happens to them comes from germs. Some folks are even saying that people spread the germs. Maybe you've heard some of that talk, I don't know."

"I've heard it," Nicholas said solemnly.

"Most of us have. The Indian woman who taught me most of what I know about life says germs, if they exist at all, are like buzzards. They go where the dead or dying tissue is."

Steve paused. Samantha breathed for the first time since he'd started speaking. Perhaps he wouldn't say what she'd feared he was going to say.

"You may see other options, but as I see it, you can either stop punishing yourself and get well, or you can die."

"Steve!"

"Or you can come out of this sicker than you went into it. If I were you, I'd get well."

"You don't think I killed Young Hawk and his family?"

Nicholas's voice was thin.

"No, I don't."

"But I heard that Indians catch white people's diseases easier because they don't have any—any . . ."

"Immunity against them? I've heard that, too, but I think they got the cart before the horse again. According to my theory germs are like a flock of hungry buzzards who recognize the Indians as a breeding ground."

"But the newspaper said that scientists have proven that germs kill people," Nicholas whispered.

"Those are the same men who would come to Arizona and conclude that buzzards and maggots are the cause of death of all the livestock or wild animals that die. I know that what I told you isn't the accepted theory, but it's not original with me. There are some brilliant scientists who believe the same way."

"But how come?"

"Because Indians don't fit in, don't even want to fit in. America's like a river. People who aren't willing or able to swim in the mainstream of life get pushed into stagnant places. Eventually they die, the way Young Hawk and his family did when they caught the measles.''

''Steve!'' Samantha looked stunned, as if she could not believe he had gone so far.

''Nicholas knows how they died. Why do you think he's sick?''

Icy with rage, Samantha stood up, took Steve by the arm, and led him outside the door. So furious she could barely speak, she slammed the door and faced him. ''I'll decide what to tell my son,'' she whispered. ''I'll decide how to heal him.''

Steve forgot everything except the fury he felt at her for denying the truth. ''You can't even heal yourself. How the hell do you expect to heal your son?''

''What?''

''You're so hooked on Lando, you can't do anything else.''

''I thought you said I was perfect!'' Samantha whispered.

''I didn't say you were perfectly behaved.''

''Get back into bed!''

''All right, I'm going. But that doesn't relieve you of your responsibility to the boy.''

''What responsibility?'' she said, running after him. At the door to his room, angrier than she'd ever seen him, Steve stopped and faced her.

''Your responsibility to heal yourself. The Indians may not fit in this world, but they know better than to keep a shaman who can't even heal himself. An Indian shaman gets sick, they pick another.''

''What are you trying to say?''

''Kids learn by example. You want your son to get well, you have to show him how to let go of grief and live, dammit.''

''What if all you did was put a lot of terrible ideas into his head?''

''Then he'll die, and it'll be my fault. Is that what you want to hear?''

Sudden tears flushed hotly into Samantha's eyes. ''No.''

''Little boys are people. He knows he probably gave the measles to Young Hawk. Why the hell do you think he ran right to their graves?''

''I ho—hoped he didn't know.''

''Hopes don't make it so.'' She looked tense, miserable, and scared. He wanted to shake her or take her into his arms.

''I know what he's going through, Samantha. I went through it when I was a boy. It just made it worse that no one would put words to what was eating at me. A boy that young doesn't know the words. He just feels the pain and gets sick. He isn't doing this on purpose. But if I tell him what he's doing, maybe he can stop.''

''But maybe he can't.''

''I guess we'll see.''

CHAPTER TWENTY-THREE

Halfway up the hill to the Forrester house, Rathwick stopped his horse. Coming down the hill, Elunami rode bareback on a small pinto. A bundle, probably of her clothes, protruded on either side of her saddle. Her face was still scratched from tearing through the thickets to save the boy.

"Where are you going?"

"To turn myself in."

"You don't care to live any longer?"

"I don't care to hide any longer."

"Tristera, dammit!"

"My name is Elunami," she said, her voice steely. "If you won't take me there, then kill me yourself."

He dismounted and pulled her down beside him. The agony in his eyes as he faced her made the thought of her death bearable to her. He *had* loved her a little. He might never have the courage to tell her, but he had cared for her.

Elunami slipped a knife out of its sheath on her belt. Her hand pressed the cool handle into his hand and squeezed his fingers around it. "Do it quickly."

In that second, Rathwick realized what it was to be Indian in a world dominated by white men. How it must feel to live without hope. To be treated no better than dogs.

"You must think me an animal. No," he said, repulsed.

Elunami shook her head. "It might be harder later, if you have to watch someone else do it."

His heart felt crushed. He took her by the shoulders and shook her. Touching her robbed him of control. Before he could stop himself, he pulled her into his arms and kissed her soft, sweet skin, her lips, her eyes. Once started, he could not stop himself.

Elunami accepted his hungry kisses. A knot that had burned in her chest for weeks seemed to dissolve, but something still did not feel right. While meditating in the hidden valley she had had a number of visions that she had not understood. Now, as if they had germinated in darkness for the last week, she realized their meaning.

The Ghost Dances were wrong. They would only lead her people into greater trouble and discord with the whites. The Great Mystery wanted all his people, even the Hopi, to realize that this life is transitory and that to lose touch with that and become attached to any part of this creation, be it land or customs, is to lose touch with the eternal.

Life is a flow, a river, and it cannot be stopped. To survive in any fashion, the Hopi needed to adjust to changes, to flow with the rest of society, to let go of the old ways, and to find new ways to live that honored the essence of the old and the new.

And that was why she had to live. She was the only one who knew this. The others wanted to dance the Ghost Dances and bring back the old days when the land was theirs—empty and beautiful and free. But those days were gone, and they could never come back. The increasing numbers of white people flooding into the West could not be stopped.

For the first time in her life, she knew what she was supposed to do.

Elunami pushed against Rathwick; he slowly relinquished her lips and raised his head.

"I love you. Marry me. Come away with me."

"I cannot."

"I thought you loved me, too, at least a little . . ."

"I do love you. But my people need me. This is a hard time for them."

"What can you do?"

"I don't know, but I cannot abandon them now. They are about to lose the only way of life they have ever known." It was becoming clearer as she spoke. Losing their right to live in the pueblos would throw them into chaos. They would need the help and guidance of one who had lived in chaos all her life.

"You won't make a difference. You're just one woman. But you would make a difference to me."

His words healed something in her. "Thank you."

"I resigned my commission. I'm a free man. We can make a life together. Please stay with me. Marry me."

"I cannot."

Rathwick groaned. The look in her shining eyes appeared unchangeable. She would sacrifice herself, trying to help them adjust to the travesty the government had visited on them.

"Elunami, I need you."

"Not as badly as they're going to."

"What makes you think they'll accept your help?

"If they don't, then I'm free, but I think they will. When they had to negotiate with the Great White Father, they came to me."

"Then let me come with you. I'll live among your people . . ."

"No," she said softly. "If I marry a white man, they will never trust me. I'll never be accepted as one of them. It is hard enough for me already as a half-breed."

Seeing her determination, he felt torn between admiration at her idealism, and hopelessness at her belief that she could actually make a difference. What she planned would doom their chance for a life together, possibly doom her as well. She was too young for such a terrible, killing burden.

"You're too fine to spend your life for them."

"I'm not good enough. And I must."

"God . . . Elunami . . ."

The look in his eyes told her all she needed to know about him. He loved her. Wonder and joy filled her. She smiled at him through tears, but it changed nothing. She had to go to her people. She had to do what she could to help them through this catastrophe that was about to befall them.

A fat raindrop—warm and wet and startling—splattered on her upturned face. At first she didn't realize the significance of it. Then she did. "It's raining," she whispered.

Rathwick tilted his face to the sky. A half-dozen fat raindrops splattered on it. Lightning flashed. Thunder boomed. The few raindrops turned into a steady downpour, the kind that looked as if it would last a week.

Joy filled Elunami. Tuvi had been right. When your heart is pure, the rain will come.

Samantha looked out the window at water running in small rivulets around the house. Ten days had passed since they'd returned from the hidden valley. It had rained for the last five. Ian reported the reservoir above the house was half full; for the first time, they had water in the storage tank behind the house. That was a relief. The lack of water had been the one thorn in her side.

Steve healed quickly. He discarded the sling and seemed almost well. Nicholas gained strength every day, but he still ran a fever every night.

"Is Tristera back yet?" Nicholas asked, as if reading her mind.

"No."

"Maybe she's dead."

Samantha started to deny it to spare him worry, but she looked at his solemn face and nodded. "I'm worried, too."

"But maybe she's okay," Nicholas said. "I think I'd feel different if she were dead."

Quick tears of pride filled her eyes. "I think you're right. I think we'd all feel differently if she were dead."

That night the fever didn't come.

On Thursday Samantha received a letter from her attorney.

We won in court. I have to tell you, though, we shouldn't have. Crows Walking had papers to prove his ownership of your land. Apparently your husband bought the property from a man who had no right to sell it.

The way the award was granted to us, Crows Walking might be able to take the land if he reimbursed you for the full cost of your improvements. As you can imagine, that is patently impossible, so you have nothing to fear. Crows Walking has little more than the shirt on his back . . .

The court was very unhappy with Crows Walking for waiting so long to come forward with his claims. Fortunately this particular judge refused to honor the old land grant. I was right to keep this from going to court as long as I did, though. We had a newly appointed judge who disdained just about everything to do with Indian rights. So, the land is yours, Mrs. Forrester. Forever, if you should live so long.

The letter went on, but tears of happiness blinded her. Nicholas was getting better—and she would keep her land. Gratitude and joy were so strong in her they were almost insupportable.

"Rider coming!" Juana called out.

Samantha wiped her eyes and hurried down the stairs. At the front door, she saw Elunami riding toward the house. With a glad cry, she picked up her skirts and stepped outside.

Elunami rode up to the porch and dismounted. Samantha skipped down the steps to embrace the girl.

"Elunami, I was so worried about you!"

"I should have come back sooner, but I went on the train to visit my people." Elunami looked freer. There was no anger in her soft brown eyes.

Steve joined them in the parlor, and Elunami told them that Rathwick had resigned his commission. Four days ago he and

Lawson had testified before a special grand jury in Phoenix. They told of the plot to kill Elunami's entire party to prevent them from telling the Hopi that high government officials had substituted different wording in the treaty that was signed.

"This official must have been new," she ended. "Otherwise he would have known better. For years they've broken their treaties with us. When we complain, they just ignore us."

"So your name has been cleared. Where will you go?" Samantha asked. "What about Rathwick?"

"He asked me to marry him. I told him no. I have to stay with my people. And that they would never accept me if I were married to a white man."

Steve settled back in his chair. If he knew anything about men, Rathwick would not give up that easily.

"Where will you go?"

"Back to Third Mesa."

"Surely not right away?"

Elunami looked from Steve to Samantha. It was apparent they had not settled their differences. "Perhaps I could stay a week or so."

That afternoon Arden Chandler rode up to the front door and hailed the house. Samantha immediately sent for Steve. She hadn't really had a chance to look at Chandler the day Steve had been hurt. Now she realized that he was an older, grayer, rougher version of Steve's dark smoothness.

He dismounted at her urging.

Steve walked around the side of the house. Seeing the two of them together was a revelation. It was apparent that Steve was Chandler's son.

"Oh," she said softly.

"What?" Steve asked, frowning at her, then at Chandler.

"You look so much like him."

"So, you're the reason she tried to kill me all those times," Steve said.

Chandler cleared his throat. "I leave a deep impression on womenfolk," he said dryly. "I guess I'd better explain some of the background. I'm ashamed to tell you this, Mr. Sheridan, but it was my fault as much as Chila's, maybe more so."

Samantha realized they needed to be alone. "If you'll excuse me, I have to check on Nicholas."

Steve watched her leave, then turned back to Chandler, who

looked uncomfortable. "Please, call me Steve. Would you like to sit down, sir?"

Chandler walked toward a shady knoll and eased himself down onto the grass. "Ah, that's better. Riding in the sun at my age isn't real smart. Well, I've stalled long enough." He looked down at the grass and picked a blade of it.

"When I was a young man, Chila, who was my wife then, contracted scarlet fever, which left her fragile for quite a long spell. During that time I—I'm ashamed to say . . . I took a mistress who died in childbirth." He expelled a heavy breath. "I frankly didn't know what else to do, so I took the baby—you—home and gave you to my Chila, who, at that time anyway, hadn't been able to have a child. At first I thought I would tell her the truth, but it didn't seem to be necessary. She loved you and took good care of you. Then one day when you were about four years old—"

"Four and a half," Steve interjected.

"Four and a half years old . . . someone told her that you were mine, not hers. That day she changed toward both of us, and I didn't know what to do about it. Chila was basically a good woman, Mr. Sheri—uh, Steve. Oh, she had her flaws, but she always had a good heart.

"After she found out that you were my son, she pitched a fit and stayed about as mad as a woman could stay for a lot longer than I expected. She was pretty hard on us both. I guess, being young and all, and not understanding what was wrong, you just got tired of being mistreated and ran away. I searched everywhere. But it was as though you'd disappeared off the face of the Earth.

"Then about two weeks later, the sheriff came and told us they'd found the body of a little boy. Chila insisted on going with me to see it. We couldn't tell exactly, because neither one of us remembered what you'd been wearing, but it looked like it could have been you. The body had been in the water so long the skin had swelled up. We figured since no one else was missing a boy, it had to be you."

Chandler expelled a heavy breath. "Chila was so grief-stricken she went wild and tried to kill me."

"She hasn't changed much," Steve said dryly.

"No, I'm afraid not."

"What was my real mother like?"

Chandler squinted at the sun a moment. "She was dark like you. Part Italian. Her name was Flamenia, Anna Flamenia Gaspari. Her father was Italian, her mother French. Blackest hair I ever seen. And the prettiest eyes. Like yours, only brown. You've got some green in your eyes. Didn't get it from her. She was too young to die, though. I've never stopped missing her.''

Steve sensed that Chandler wanted to ask his forgiveness, but he didn't know how. And, even if he did, Steve wasn't sure he could give it. Somehow his crime seemed worse than Chila's. And even though Chandler did resemble him, Steve felt no emotional connection with the man.

''Well, thanks for coming. I'd better get back to work,'' Steve said, standing up.

Chandler looked crestfallen. But he only nodded, struggled to his feet, and walked toward his horse.

Steve suddenly felt bad, but he couldn't seem to stop himself from walking away. He strode behind the barn and stopped, feeling foolish. He supposed he should go back to work—if sitting in a chair watching men work could be called that—but he felt disoriented. He walked away from the barn before Samantha could come out and ask him what had happened. He felt odd enough without having to explain.

He climbed up the mountainside until he reached a small plateau far away from the activity down at the house. He lay back, panting. It was his first climb since his recuperation.

Below, he saw Chandler riding slowly down the hill.

Birds called out overhead. The wind ruffled the trees and bushes, sounding like rain. The pine mat beneath him was spongy and soft. He felt shattered inside.

A wound had opened in him—an ancient raw oozing wound that had been hidden from him all these years. It didn't make any sense to his mind. But his heart realized he'd known his mother was dead. He'd known she'd died giving birth to him. He closed his eyes and let this knowledge seep into all his parts. Awash in grief, he finally turned over and wept.

Arden Chandler probably was his father. It was good to get that out and to realize his father had not deliberately abandoned him to Chila Dart's wrath. He had just been overwhelmed by it. That wouldn't have been good enough for a little boy, but it was enough for the man he was now. Steve had been overwhelmed by his share of women. A woman's anger was a formidable thing.

Perhaps his own fear of a woman's anger explained why he'd just walked away from Caroline, breaking off what had been a good relationship. He had a history of not giving two chances to any woman. Looking back, he realized the breaks had always come after some show of anger by the woman. Only Samantha Forrester had ever been able to show her anger and not drive him away.

Oh, he'd wanted to go at first, but the house had held him. Then he'd stopped wanting to leave. Samantha was different. Her anger lacked the bite and venom of a Chila Dart. Samantha never got so angry she forgot what was important. And her anger was based on fear, usually for her son or someone she cared about.

At least now he realized what had held him here in spite of his proclivity to run away from any angry female. Samantha was the woman of his dreams, but unfortunately he wasn't the man of hers. He had done everything he could to win her, but she was still in love with Kincaid.

Steve ached from that knowledge. But even aching, he knew that when the house was truly finished, he'd leave. She had cared enough to try to keep Chila Dart from killing him, but not enough to ask him to stay. She wasn't about to do anything that would tie her up in case her beloved broke free of his wife. And now, loving her the way he did, Steve understood even that. If he had even a tiny hope she might someday love him, he'd do whatever he had to do to stay free for her.

But that was an empty hope. He would finish her adobe palace and ride away to pursue a career that now felt like an albatross around his neck. He would spend the rest of his life loving her from a distance. Samantha Forrester was the woman he could never forget and never have.

Knowing what he knew now, he could truly forgive his father. Probably loving Chila, feeling all the guilt of his betrayal, and knowing Chila had once loved his son, he'd held on, hoping she would come to her senses.

Steve may have dozed off. He opened his eyes feeling slightly startled. Some sound had jolted him. He waited, but heard only bird calls and the sounds of men working below. A few hammers smacking into wood, a few lusty cries, a child's piping voice. Probably Nicholas.

Poor Nicholas.

Suddenly Steve knew what was wrong with Nicholas. Samantha had gotten her release after the Indians fell ill. She had wallowed chin deep in their pain and misery. She had held them while they died, felt their deaths all the way to her soul, and cried over their graves. But Nicholas hadn't. He'd suffered all that guilt and pain alone. Nicholas needed what Samantha had had. He needed to be part of it, suffer it, and let it go.

But how? His mind stayed blank a long time. Then he knew. He would send a messenger to Uncheedah. She'd help him.

He should have done this a long time ago, but he realized he'd lacked the courage to push Samantha as hard as he'd have had to. But now, knowing what he did about his own past—and that he had absolutely nothing to lose anyway—he could do what needed to be done.

Steve woke at four o'clock in the morning. He dressed quickly and walked to the barn to saddle one of Samantha's horses. He wrote a note for Ian and gave it to the head cook, so no one would worry about him, then slipped away before dawn.

The desert was still gray by the time he reached the foot of the mountain. He pointed his horse southeast. The sun came up and rose steadily in the sky behind him. He rode past flowering turpentine bushes and the soaring saguaro cacti that were the hallmark of the Papago Indian Reservation. By noon he entered the small settlement at North Komelik and spotted the Indian agent's house. It was better built than the others. Steve had been gone before this one was built.

Steve dismounted at the door. A woman inside looked up and walked to the door. "Yes?" she asked.

"I—is—" Steve couldn't find the words.

The woman peered at him a moment. "You're here to see your father, aren't you?"

Steve nodded, too stricken to do more.

The woman turned away. "Arden, your son is here."

Those words jolted Steve all the way to his heels. He had ridden all this way without figuring out what he was going to say or how.

Chandler grunted and strode to the door. He looked as startled as Steve felt. For a moment Steve just looked at the man who had fathered him.

"Sir . . . you didn't ask—and I don't even know that it's necessary—but I wanted to tell you—" Steve swallowed. What had seemed so necessary in the middle of the night that it had gotten him out of bed now seemed ludicrous. But the look on Chandler's face was of a man dying inside. The woman, slightly to the left of him, seemed to wait without breathing.

"Yes . . . Go on, boy."

Feeling like a fool, Steve took a breath and wished he'd gotten lost in the desert instead. He'd probably imagined that Chandler had wanted his forgiveness. But it was too late now. "I wanted to tell you . . . in case you might feel like you need it . . . that I . . . I forgive you."

Tears welled up in the woman's eyes and spilled down her cheeks. Chandler cleared his throat. "Thank you," he said, his voice husky with emotion. "I can't believe we just left you standing in the sun. Come in. Come in out of the heat and have some of Selena's lemonade. She makes the best lemonade this side of the Mississippi."

Next, Steve rode to Uncheedah's house. Seeing Crows Walking sitting in the shade of the *ramada*, smoking his pipe, upset Steve. He knew Samantha had won her court case against Crows Walking. And that only made him feel more love for his foster father. He realized he still wanted Crows Walking's approval and love, though it might never be forthcoming in any recognizable way. Uncheedah saw him and stepped outside to greet him.

"It's good to see you again," he said, smiling at the woman who'd raised him. Uncheedah was not demonstrative by white standards, but her smile—shy and hopeful and filled with the same love he had seen beaming down at him when he was a boy—caused his heart to swell with happiness.

"It is good to see you again, too, my son."

"I think you gone to Comanche country long time ago," Crows Walking said, his voice gruff.

"I intended to, but I took a job here instead."

After a dinner of corn cakes and government beef, Steve told them what he needed. That night he slept on the ground—near where he had slept as a boy. He thought he might lie awake most of the night, but he barely remembered lying down.

The next morning he rode back to Samantha's house. He arrived in time to eat lunch and fall exhausted into his bed, where he stayed until the next morning. The next day he had two men load a wagon with staples, then drove it down the hill to the old house crushed under the rock.

Uncheedah and Crows Walking were already there, camping beside the creek.

"You build this smashed house?" Crows Walking asked.

"No. A different one, up on the mountain."

Crows Walking grunted his acknowledgment. Steve turned to Uncheedah. "Did you ask for the ceremony?" He'd asked a lot of her. To request a ceremony obligated her to feed all the dancers who participated.

She smiled. "Everything, just as you asked."

Others arrived all that day and evening—some singly, some in pairs, some in groups of a dozen or more. Two dozen tepees sprang up. Uncheedah's family and friends helped her prepare the food Steve had brought in the wagon.

The Indian leaders, Hopi and Papago, formed a group near one of the tepees and began the negotiations. They smoked, sang, prayed, and built an altar. It was decided that since it was November, *Kamiyaw*, the month of the Dangerous Moon, they would combine a Hopi Soyal ceremony with *masawi*, a ritual to beseech the god of death. Several men erected a standard. The old men, the leaders, argued over the wording of the announcement, directed primarily to the clouds.

Uncheedah and the women ground corn, cooked meat, and made crisp, rolled blue corn *piki* wafers to give to the dancers. At the council, Uncheedah did a good job of seeing to it that Steve's concerns were dealt with. Steve sat off to one side, watching and listening. When everything was ready, he rode back to the new house to get Nicholas. He had no idea if Samantha would let him bring the boy, but he was going to try.

"You want me to *what*?" she demanded.

"I want you to let Nicholas go to an Indian funeral for Young Hawk and his family."

"No! Absolutely not! I don't want him to have anything to do with it. I've kept him away from all that. He's getting better."

"Nicholas is still sick and feeling guilty about their deaths. It helped me to learn the truth about my folks. It might help him to bury Young Hawk and his family."

"I don't believe in your Indian superstitions."

Steve realized he'd handled the situation all wrong. Samantha looked like a woman cornered by a reality too awful to confront.

Nicholas trudged into the room like a boy carrying a heavy load. He looked from Samantha to Steve and tensed slightly. "What's wrong?" he asked.

Samantha glared at Steve. Her look clearly said, *If you tell him, I will never forgive you*. Steve had wrestled with the effect his defiance would have on her. He had faced the fact that even though he loved her, his duty was to a boy struggling with a life-and-death decision. This would be his going-away present to Nicholas.

"The Indians are having a funeral celebration for Young Hawk and his family. I came to invite you and your mother."

Samantha's eyes flamed with outrage. Nicholas brightened instantly. "Can I, Mama? Please!"

"No!"

"Mother, I have to! Young Hawk was my friend! He was my friend! I have to!" Tears streamed down his cheeks.

Samantha turned to Steve with hell and damnation in her eyes. "Now see what you've done!" Her voice was tight with frustration and fury.

"Let him go," Steve urged.

"Please, Mama, please!"

Samantha flashed Steve a look, then said, "No, Nicholas. And that's final."

Steve knew he had failed—and had only made things worse for the boy. Feeling so low he could have slipped under the door, he turned and left the two of them alone.

Samantha put Nicholas down for a nap. she heard him crying two rooms away. Her jaws ached from gritting her teeth; her whole body shook with rage. She wanted to strangle Steve Sheridan.

Finally Nicholas cried himself to sleep. But nothing helped to calm Samantha. Juana tried to tempt her with food, but just the thought sickened her.

That night Nicholas's temperature soared to a hundred and four. Samantha did everything—garlic compresses and alcohol rubs—but his fever defied her and stayed high.

Elunami came in at two-thirty to relieve her. "Get some sleep. I will sit with the boy."

Samantha raised agonized eyes to Elunami. "Did I do the wrong thing?"

"About the funeral?"

Samantha nodded.

"Indians believe it is better to let go of the dead."

"Then why wallow in a stupid funeral ceremony?"

Elunami chose her words carefully. "Tuvi, the wisest elder in our tribe, said it is better to embrace the dead than to try and hide from them. To withdraw from pain and death is to die. If we embrace the pain and suffering of others, we live fully. It is more painful for a moment, but it quickly subsides. When my father killed my mother, my older brother just ran around a tree and screamed. But my sister went to my mother's body and lay with her, crying. My brother still seems crippled by what he saw—my sister does not.''

"Oh, God . . ." Samantha was stricken by the images and by her own fear for Nicholas. "But if I let him embrace Young Hawk's death, Nicholas might die."

Elunami shook her head. "No. One does not die by acknowledging death. One dies by denying it."

"I'm so scared for him."

"Then trust Nicholas. Perhaps he knows best for himself."

"He's just a boy . . ."

Elunami shrugged. It seemed self-evident to her. Samantha had imposed her will on Nicholas—and he had moved closer to death.

Samantha saw Elunami look at her son; she followed her gaze. "You think he's sick now because I won't let him participate in the funeral?"

Elunami shrugged.

"You do, don't you?"

"*Si.*"

They sat in silence, waiting for dawn.

Samantha was glad of Elunami's presence. Except for the weeks right after Jared had died, she'd never felt so alone. She had never trusted anyone where Nicholas was concerned. He was her responsibility. She'd even thought Jared too easygoing, too daredevil to be trusted with her son. Nicholas was hers really. Jared had only fathered the boy. True, Nicholas had belonged emotionally to Jared, and the boy had never recovered from the loss of his father. In that he was like her.

Now Steve was trying to take Nicholas away from her. And Steve was as reckless in his own way as Jared had been. She hated this in men. They got ideas in their heads and acted on them, no matter what the cost. A man would start a war, join the fight, and die without once realizing it was all nonsense. Wars solved nothing. After all the men were dead, the survivors would negotiate a settlement they could have negotiated before the war and life would go on. But not for the grieving widows and orphans. Steve could decide Nicholas needed something and give it to him . . . and then just watch him struggle with it or die. He didn't care. Nicholas wasn't his son.

A small voice within objected. Her mind flashed on a picture of Steve holding Nicholas while he cried. Steve loved Nicholas, and Nicholas loved Steve. Did every mother of a young boy resent the headstrong masculinity in her husband because she could see her son admiring it, copying it, preparing to make it his own? Perhaps, but the paradox was that a woman could not truly admire a man who didn't have those qualities. And they had to be acquired sometime.

Maybe Steve was right. Maybe she was the problem— standing between her son and his life as if she could stop the flow of it long enough to keep him safe.

But what if she was the only thing keeping Nicholas alive? What if she let go and he died?

Hot tears filled her mouth and eyes. Panting, she fought down the sobs that ached to burst out of her.

"Mama . . ."

Nicholas's voice startled her. Samantha wiped her eyes with her skirt.

"Yes, dear?"

"What's wrong?"

She started to lie to him. "I'm scared."

"Wolfess?"

"No."

"Wolfess go away if you're nice to them," he said.

"How do you know that?"

"You told me. Don't you remember?"

"Yes . . . Yes, I forgot."

Samantha felt Nicholas's forehead; it was cooler now.

"Mama, I want to go to Young Hawk's funeral."

"We'll see tomorrow morning. If you're well enough.

An hour after dawn, a messenger came from Samantha, summoning Steve to the new house.

"Is Nicholas all right?"

"The missus didn't say."

Steve saddled his horse and rushed up the mountain. The house looked dark. Expecting to be met by gunfire, he opened the front door and stepped into the dim entryway.

Samantha's voice floated down to him from the top of the stairs. Then she appeared, gliding down to greet or kill him.

She saw him halfway down and stopped. Her gaze met his and held for several heartbeats. Pale and slim, poised above him, she was so beautiful Steve felt her in every cell in his body. His blood beat hard against his temples. At least this woman was worth dying for.

She looked away first, glanced down at her hand on the banister, and then proceeded down the stairs. She hadn't forgiven him, that was clear, but she seemed different.

She stopped at the bottom of the stairs. Looking at Steve Sheridan, seeing how solid and sure and masculine he was, she wanted to double her fists and beat on him.

Her thoughts were bitter as quinine. *You've been pulling me toward this moment since the day I met you.* She'd seen herself being pulled toward her destiny, a lone woman against a team of strong horses, and she'd been right. Except what had been pulling her was him, this one man, and no matter how she had struggled and fought, he'd drawn her forward relentlessly.

If she'd ever once guessed Steve would force her to the point where she would have to risk her son's life in the hopes of saving him . . . But it was too late for that. She and Nicholas were here, and there was no turning back without loss. She was helpless to stop the events unfolding without precipitating what she'd tried so hard to avoid.

"If I let Nicholas go to this funeral, will you take care of him?" She couldn't say what worried her. "See that he doesn't overexert himself?"

Steve nodded.

"Then take him," she said bitterly, grimly.

Steve searched her eyes, hoping for a clue as to why she'd changed her mind so quickly, but her eyes revealed only her fear and resentment. His heart sank.

"It starts tonight after sunset," he said, forcing his voice to be brisk and sure. "It'll be cool after dark. Bring a wrap for you and a coat and some blankets for Nicholas. It will probably last three or four days. We have food."

They reached the creek at sunset. It was a shock to see the old house again. To remember that if not for Steve Sheridan, she and Nicholas might have been inside when the boulder crushed it.

The area around the creek was crowded with tepees and campfires and horses. The air was filled with sounds of women chattering, men chanting, and children playing. The Indians were busy with many tasks. It was such an ordinary scene, Samantha was slightly relieved. Maybe Nicholas wouldn't feel the presence she and Elunami had felt that day.

It was odd, though. The Indians couldn't have known where the dead family's tepee had been—Steve had cleared away the burned remnants of the fire—but they had avoided that area. Not one camp had been placed there, even though the rest of the area was crowded with campsites.

"What now?"

"I'll introduce you to the chiefs."

"Is this absolutely necessary?"

"Yes."

Steve offered her a hand down, but she wouldn't touch him. He helped Nicholas down. The boy was pale and cautious. Maybe he had picked up his mother's fears.

Steve led them to the campfire where the old men sat, wrapped in their blankets, smoking their pipes and nodding their heads. As they approached, all grew silent.

Steve looked back for Nicholas. The boy had stopped by the horses and sat down. Steve walked back and squatted beside him. Samantha followed in silence.

"What's wrong?" Steve asked.

"I can't go over there."

"How come?"

Nicholas shook his head. He wouldn't look at Steve.

Steve decided to take a shot in the dark. "Because you're afraid you might give it to them, too?"

Samantha sucked in an outraged breath and held it. Nicholas nodded.

"That's a fair concern," Steve said, nodding as well. "I'll ask them what they think."

He turned to Samantha. "Is he running a fever now?"

"No."

Steve walked to the main tepee, where Uncheedah stood with Crows Walking. Steve led Crows Walking back to where Nicholas waited. Steve introduced each in turn. Samantha's eyes widened at the mention of Crows Walking's name. Crows Walking grunted at the mention of hers. Steve realized they had other business between them, but it would have to wait.

"The boy is worried. He has consumption, which some white doctors think may be contagious. Nicholas is afraid now to mingle with the Indians for fear he will give them his disease." Steve knew the answer as soon as he'd stated the question. Nicholas was right. He didn't belong anywhere near the Indians, who were more susceptible to consumption than whites. He also realized that such an answer might plunge Nicholas into despair.

Crows Walking seemed to swell with pride and indignation. "The boy thinks he is the Great Spirit that he decides when even Indians sicken and die?"

"The boy fears so, yes." Once started, Steve couldn't seem to control what came out his mouth. The words came from some deep place in him, some place that needed answers for its own reasons.

Crows Walking nodded as if he could believe this of a white person. "The Great Spirit of the Papago is called First Born," he said to the boy. "First Born brings whatever He brings. You have to struggle with that, as we all do."

The old man's words opened something in Steve. It was as if a dam had suddenly given way, bathing his insides with warm, healing water. Crows Walking looked at him as if he knew that what he'd said had more than one meaning, and that he'd intended it to be that way.

Steve realized that somehow, sometime, Crows Walking had forgiven him for whatever part he'd had in his young son's death. Steve glanced at Nicholas and saw the same strong release on the boy's face, wet with sudden tears.

Steve nodded at the boy and motioned him forward. Nicholas wiped his sleeve across his eyes and followed.

Now Steve knew why, in spite of the underlying conflict between himself and Crows Walking, he had always loved the old man. Crows Walking was fair and honest. He would probably tell his version of the truth even if doing so would result in his own death.

Uncheedah introduced Nicholas to the chiefs seated around the ceremonial fire. Nicholas kept a respectful distance between himself and the others. Uncheedah explained in the Papago tongue that the boy needed to take part in the ceremony, as he had been a good friend to Young Hawk. The old men in their blankets remained silent.

After a moment one of the Indians grunted. Others nodded. Finally one of the chiefs invited the boy to attend. Steve nodded at Nicholas.

Silver Fish arrived with his brothers-in-law. Samantha softened when she saw them. In her opinion, Silver Fish was entitled to whatever it took to put his heart at rest.

As dusk fell, Crows Walking emerged from one of the tepees, and the ceremonies began. They consisted of singing, dancing, praying, feasting, and drinking the specially fermented wine made from the saguaro fruit.

Steve watched from beside Samantha. "The Papago are sort of Catholics," he explained.

"Sort of?" she asked stiffly.

"True Catholics probably wouldn't think so, because the Papago have reinvented Catholicism, based on their own ancient religious ceremonies."

Crows Walking carried rattles in one hand and walked to the place where Silver Fish's tepee had been. Crows Walking shook the rattles in each direction. When he had moved around the entire site, he motioned some men forward; they put down bundles of wood and lit a fire. As the wood flamed up, men stood and began to dance. A few women stood, then the children. Everyone except the drummers danced and chanted: *"Aiyee, hiiii, aiyee."*

Samantha looked questioningly at Steve. He leaned near her to whisper, "Big medicine."

Nicholas looked at his mother. "Please, Mama?"

"You aren't going to insist that he dance, are you?" Samantha asked anxiously. "He was sick last night."

Steve knew he couldn't get into any more trouble than he already was. And dancing was one of the best ways he knew for Nicholas to learn what he needed to learn—in his body—where it would do him the most good.

"I'll leave that up to Nicholas. Do you feel well enough to dance?"

"Yes, but I don't know how."

Steve showed him a few basic male steps. When the boy had mastered high-knee stepping and ritual bending and bowing, Steve pointed him toward the circle.

Steve glanced at Samantha. She looked so miserable and scared he wanted to take her into his arms. "I know how you must feel about this, and I know I'm finished with you, not that I ever had a chance."

"I didn't know you every really wanted one."

Steve narrowed his eyes. "It's a good thing those eyes are beautiful. Otherwise, they wouldn't be worth a damn." He turned back to watching the dancers.

Nicholas danced for an hour, then walked over to where Samantha had sat down to watch. He dropped onto the yellowed grass beside her. "Water," he said, panting.

Steve passed the canteen to Nicholas.

"Can we go now?" Samantha asked.

"No, Mama. I want to stay till the end."

She looked at Steve, who shrugged. "It could be days until they feel they've freed the spirits."

"Freed the spirits? I . . ." Her voice lost power as she remembered the icy chill she'd felt here earlier.

"Crows Walking is a powerful shaman. He said the spirits of the dead family got trapped here and haven't left. I wouldn't say one way or the other, but he's not wrong about many things."

"I want to speak to him again," Samantha said.

Steve waited until Crows Walking dropped out of the dance, then he led Samantha over to the old man's side. "Crows Walking, this is Samantha Forrester, who owns this land now."

With his mask off, dressed in buckskins and moccasins the same color as his skin, Crows Walking looked as dry and brittle as old parchment. With his skeletal head, wide face, and large features, he looked odd, even for an Indian. He nodded to Samantha, but he spoke to Steve.

"This is one who bought my land from white man who spoke from both sides of his mouth?"

"The man who bought the land is long dead. This woman is his widow."

"A woman holds all this land? Does she have need of it all?" Crows Walking's voice rang with incredulousness. Clearly the old man could not see what one person could do with so much property. A small patch of ground would feed a whole family.

Elunami rode up and bowed her head in a deep bow. Crows Walking grunted his acknowledgment. Then she walked her horse back to the brush corral, where horses nipped at patches of grass. For the first time, she wore traditional Hopi clothing—a straight black wool dress sashed at the waist and covering only one shoulder. She'd put up her hair in maiden whorls on each side of her head. It changed her, made her seem more serious.

Crows Walking nodded. "I think I will win this land back," he said abruptly.

Steve explained that only days ago Samantha had received word that she had won the court case.

Bitterness sparkled in Crows Walking's eyes. "So, the courts are a fraud, too," he said. "All white man paper is a fraud. Anytime the white man gets two chances to negotiate with Indians, we have two chances to lose more of our land. It was a mistake to trust the white man's court. I was a fool."

Steve felt Crows Walking's disappointment keenly, but he didn't know any way to lessen it. A sudden cooling breeze pulled at the old man's feathered costume and whipped his long white single braid. Crows Walking looked tiny and frail. Steve felt like a betrayer, siding with the white men who had stolen his land.

* * *

The dancing went on for four days, short for a Papago cere-mony. Every day, Uncheedah and her helpers fed everyone, and Steve passed out generous gifts of food and blankets. Samantha gave up fighting it. Every night she watched, and in the daytime, when the ceremonies were more inexplicable, she and Elunami rode up to the new house to sleep and to freshen up.

Steve stayed with Nicholas, who could not be pulled away. Each night he danced until he dropped. The boy was like one possessed. Finally, on the fourth day, something changed. Steve saw it in the boy's face, in all their faces. They stopped dancing. Nicholas walked over to where Steve leaned against a tree, as if for protection.

"Ready for a rest?" Steve asked.

Nicholas looked past Steve as if transfixed. Steve glanced in that direction but saw nothing. The other dancers appeared to be looking in the same direction.

An east wind came up suddenly and blew through the camp. Nicholas opened his mouth to speak and then closed it. Tears spilled down his cheeks. A murmur rose among the dancers and fell quickly into silence. Only the sound of the wind was audi-ble. Not even a horse whinnied. Birds did not sing. The wind in the trees grew louder, sounded almost like music, rising to a crescendo.

Nicholas smiled at something off in the distance. The wind stopped. Silence stretched out for a long moment, then the In-dians cheered.

"They're gone," Nicholas said.

It was apparent to Steve that the Indians, too, believed the spirits of Young Hawk and his family were gone, that they had been danced free to take their proper place, wherever that might be.

The dancers went to their blankets. Steve covered Nicholas and lay down beside him. The boy smiled at Steve, snuggled close to him, and dropped instantly into sleep.

Hours later Steve struggled awake and gave out the last gifts of food. The Indians departed.

"Ready?" Steve said to Nicholas, who looked amazingly bright-eyed.

"Is Mama still mad?"

"Yes."

Nicholas's eyes were clear and frank. "Too bad for you."

"Yeah."

"Look!" Nicholas pointed behind Steve.

Samantha and Elunami galloped toward them. Samantha reined her horse, dismounted, and stepped close to Nicholas. Avoiding Steve's eyes, she touched Nicholas's head.

Elunami walked over to the place where Silver Fish's tepee had been. She walked through the center of the site and turned, smiling. "They're gone!"

Samantha, too, walked through the center of the campsite, stood over the spot where the tepee had been, and felt none of the earlier icy chill of foreboding. Something lifted in her, lightened.

"We can go back to the house now," Steve said.

Samantha looked at her son. Nicholas looked different to her. She hated to admit Steve might have been right, but the difference in her son was too shining. He should have been exhausted, but he looked energized, filled with a lightness and confidence she hadn't seen since before Jared died. It seemed to beam out of him with such force and certainty. "Nicholas?"

"Young Hawk is gone now, Mama. He forgave me."

"Nicholas . . ."

"He did, Mama. Mr. Crows Walking was right. The Great Spirit decides who lives and dies. Young Hawk doesn't blame me. None of them do."

Stricken, she looked at Steve, who smiled and picked up Nicholas. An odd little ache quivered within her. Seeing how gentle Steve was with her son—and knowing how much trouble he had gone to in order to give Nicholas that experience . . .

Fighting tears, she looked at Steve. "I want to apologize. And to thank you for doing all this."

"Apology accepted."

"I used to think I was smart, but the longer I live, the clearer it becomes that I don't seem to know anything."

"I've heard that's a sign of oncoming wisdom."

"Mama, I forgot to tell you"—Samantha stepped close to her son, cradled like a baby in Steve's arms—"I forgot to tell you," he repeated, his eyes shining with joy. "Daddy was one of the angels who came for Young Hawk."

CHAPTER TWENTY-FOUR

At the house, Steve carried Nicholas in, put him on his bed, and left Samantha alone with him. Nicholas looked up at her, his blue eyes sleepy and smiling, and Samantha realized Nicholas *could* heal himself. He couldn't have before, but now he could. She had no idea how she knew that or where that thought had come from, but realizing it startled her.

She wanted to go to Steve, to thank him for everything he had done for her and for Nicholas. She had learned a valuable lesson. There really couldn't be two levels of honesty, one for adults and one for children. Nicholas had needed to know the truth. Steve had been right.

Samantha went to her bedroom and took the half-finished reata off the topmost shelf of her armoire. She carried it into Nicholas's room and laid it on his bed.

"You might want to finish this."

A glad light filled her son's eyes. "Can I tie it around my bedpost?"

"*May* I tie it around my bedpost," she said, correcting him. "When you're in the house, but I think it would be more fun outside." She smiled, liking the idea of him outside, surrounded by plants and trees.

Lance Kincaid stopped his horse in sight of the house. Chane had been right and wrong. He'd been right that the house was big, solid, and imposing, that it had presence.

Lance grinned. Chane must have been green with envy, because this house had more than presence. It blended into the surrounding mountainside with such artistry it affected Lance the way seeing a masterpiece did. He had no idea of the skill it took to place a house in that fashion, but admiration filled him.

Lance had heard Jennie's ecstatic description of Steve Sheridan. Now he understood. The Chinese claimed a man could not build a better house than he was a person. If that were the case, Steve Sheridan must be one hell of a man.

Its adobe brick walls looked two feet thick. He would be glad for its coolness. *If* Sam let him inside.

Samantha looked out the window, saw Lance riding through the open gates, and dropped the vase she'd been dusting.

"At least eet weel be clean, when I peek up the pieces," Juana grumbled.

Samantha ran from the room and stepped out onto the porch. For a moment she was too stunned to say anything. Lance looked more tired and much thinner than the last time she'd seen him. Beneath the brim of his tan hard-brimmed hat, his blue eyes smiled at her with a mixture of amusement and curiosity. With the harsh sunlight hitting his face from the side, she saw the dim shadows filling in wrinkles she hadn't noticed before.

"Lance, you came!"

"Told you I would."

Lance stopped on the top step and held out his arms to her. Surprised, she stepped into them for a warm hug.

"You've been busy," he said, glancing around at the house and yard, cluttered with workmen carrying tools.

"How have you been?"

"It's been hell actually," he said, his raspy voice firm in spite of the bleak look that came into his eyes.

"Did you go to San Francisco?" she asked softly.

"Yes."

"How is Angie?"

Something flashed in Lance's eyes. He had something to tell her; her heart pounded.

Just then, Steve Sheridan and Ian Macready walked around the side of the house. At the sight of Lance, Steve and Ian stopped talking. Samantha motioned them over.

"Steve, Ian . . . you remember Lance Kincaid, don't you?"

Lance offered his hand, and Steve shook it.

"Magnificent house," Lance said.

"Thanks," Steve said, surprised.

"And this is Ian Macready, Steve's superintendent." Ian shook hands with Kincaid.

Steve's heart sank. Dressed in white shirt, black trousers, and black frock coat, Kincaid was one of those men who looked good in clothes. Steve became aware of how he must look in comparison—scabbed over on his forehead, neck, and arms, the bandage on his left hand dirty. And it was apparent that Kincaid had come for Samantha. The flush on her lovely cheeks confirmed it.

"Would you like to see the house?" Samantha asked hopefully.

Kincaid nodded. "Sure."

"Nice meeting you, Kincaid. I'm sure I'll see you again before you leave," Steve said, preparing to make his escape.

"No, Steve." Samantha said. "You come with us. He might have questions I can't answer."

Steve wanted only to escape, but Samantha's eyes pleaded with him—and curiosity prevailed. He followed Samantha and her lover into the house.

Kincaid looked like a potentially decent man, but Samantha's fawning over him set Steve's teeth on edge.

After a while, Steve's heart ached with the need to save Samantha from making a fool of herself in front of Kincaid, but there was nothing he could do. She was like a puppy, wanting Kincaid's approval so badly she couldn't help herself. She fairly skipped from prized possession to prized possession, hauling them out for Kincaid to admire and comment on. To Steve's surprise and relief, Kincaid seemed to genuinely enjoy Samantha and her enthusiasm for her new home. He said all the right things to placate her and keep her happy. Steve was grateful for that.

They reached the master bedroom on the second floor. Kincaid looked at the room, then walked out onto the veranda. "You should have put the house on the other side of this mountain, then at night you'd be able to see the North Star and the Big Dipper."

Samantha flashed a look at Steve that begged him to convince Kincaid she'd done the right thing. Steve shrugged.

"We chose this side of the mountain because it's cooler in the summertime," she said weakly.

"You've got a point, but I wouldn't be comfortable looking at a night sky with no North Star or Big Dipper." Kincaid grinned apologetically at Steve. "I've spent too many nights on the desert, I guess."

"Doing what?" Steve asked.

"Chasing horse thieves mostly."

"Lance was an Arizona Ranger," Samantha interjected.

"I was an Arizona Ranger for . . . two weeks," Steve said.

Kincaid grinned. "That indicates a higher level of intelligence than me, then. I stuck it out for three years."

"Where did you serve?"

"Southeast quadrant. There were only four of us then. One for each quarter of the territory. How about you?"

"It was an accident really. A man by the name of McNamara shanghaied me."

"That's the man!" Kincaid slapped his thigh. "I lost at poker to him—and ended up serving more time than if I'd robbed a bank."

They laughed together. At first Samantha was relieved that Lance was no longer picking on where they had sited the house, but once started, he and Steve went on and on about McNamara and his Ranger unit.

After a while, when the McNamara stories didn't subside, she showed Lance to his room and then led Steve downstairs.

"Why didn't you say something to help me?"

"When?"

"When he said we should have built on the other side of the mountain."

"Oh, he didn't mean anything by it."

"He did, too!"

"Naw. He was just reminiscing."

"You certainly did enough of that."

"I like him. He's quite a man."

"You laughed enough."

"Well, I guess it had to go one way or the other. And it's stupid for me to argue with the man you love."

"So, you're just going to smile and hand me over to him?"

"Love is like faith, Samantha. You either have it or you don't. And if you do, no one can talk you out of it. I already know how you feel about him."

"We're not even going to discuss it?"

"Arguments only make the faithful mad." With that sage reply, Steve nodded to her and headed for the door, humming under his breath what sounded like a marching tune. Probably an Arizona Ranger marching tune, she thought sourly.

Steve kept up the jaunty tune until he reached his cottage. Inside, he walked to the sofa and sank down onto it. He closed his eyes and tried not to think, but his mind would not be still.

Grief filled him. The man Samantha loved had finally come for her. Steve had sensed Kincaid's vulnerability to her instantly. He loved her as much as she loved him. Except for the awful feeling in his gut, Steve was grateful, because he didn't want her hurt. But he hadn't guessed how Kincaid's coming to claim her would affect him until now.

He felt as though all his loved ones had died at once. He felt sick and weary and filled with despair.

Working on the house with her day after day, even knowing Kincaid would someday come, it had been easy to forget about the future. Her lovely presence had lulled him into complacency. He hadn't realized it could end so suddenly and irrevocably, or that he could feel so sick in his soul.

He got up abruptly and walked to the window. As he watched, Samantha and Kincaid walked out of the front door hand in hand. They strolled across the backyard and began to climb the mountain behind the house. They made a striking couple. Kincaid was tall and well proportioned; Samantha was incredibly beautiful and vibrant in a red-and-white gown that hugged her slender waist.

"Steve." Nicholas's voice called through the open doorway. "Can I come in?"

Steve struggled to hide his bleeding insides. "Sure, partner. Come on in."

"Are you okay?" Nicholas asked, watching him closely.

"Sure, why not?" he lied.

"I heard Juana talking about—about—She said you might leave because Uncle Lance—That he might stay and marry my mom."

"Well," Steve said, stalling, trying to think of a suitable response. "Well . . ."

"I don't want you to leave."

"Thanks."

"I want *you* to marry my mom. If you'd just ask her, I'm sure I could talk her into it," he said earnestly.

Steve shook his head. "It isn't that easy."

"She'll do just about anything for me," Nicholas said quickly.

"I know," Steve admitted ruefully. "And, I appreciate the recommendation. I'd marry her in a minute, if I got the opportunity, but she . . . ummm . . . prefers your uncle Lance."

Nicholas frowned. "You don't think there's any hope, do you?"

"Not much."

Nicholas stared glumly out the window. "I think women should just have to do what they're told."

In spite of himself, Steve laughed.

Nicholas frowned in frustration. "Well, then," he said, "if you leave, I'm going with you."

Steve was deeply touched. "I wish you could, but you can't leave your mother. She needs you."

"She'll have him. Besides, all men leave home sooner or later. I'm almost seven, and I work full time. I'm earning enough to live on, so . . ."

Steve laughed and sent the boy off to bed.

"*Señor*," Juana called through the open doorway.

"Come in, Juana," Steve said, standing up with some effort.

"Sit, sit," she urged him, waving her hand. "Me, I just come to see how you are doing, *señor*."

"I'm . . . okay."

"The *señora* should be spanked, letting that—that interloper come here," she said, scowling at the new house.

"She's entitled. It's her house."

"*Humph!* If not for you, we would all be crushed under a rock like so many bugs. If she belong to me, I would turn her over my lap so fast."

Steve smiled at the idea of Juana spanking Samantha.

"*Señor* Steve, this is a secret between me and you, okay?"

"Okay."

"I have this *veneno* that I got a long time ago . . ."

"*Veneno?*" Steve questioned, not recognizing the word.

"Shhhh!" Juana hissed, looking from side to side. "*Poison,*" she mouthed, "and I wanted to know if you would like me to feex heem?"

Steve laughed. "Poison him? Are you serious?"

"Shhhh! *Sí!* Me, I wouldn't keel him, but I could make heem so seek."

Steve suppressed the urge to laugh hysterically. "I appreciate your help, Juana, but I think we'd better hold off on that."

Juana scowled fiercely. "Eef you change your mind, *señor*, just let Juana know. Me, I weel fix him such a dinner you would never believe."

"No, thank you, Juana." She left and Steve sank back on the sofa.

Knock, knock. Steve opened his eyes to see Elunami standing in the doorway.

"Come in," he said, sighing, rising to his feet.

Elunami walked close to him and peered into his eyes. "You are in great pain," she whispered.

Steve started to deny it. "Yeah, I guess so."

"What will you do?"

"Nothing. She's in love with him. He's come to claim her. There's nothing I can do."

"She loves you."

"No, you're wrong about that. At the most she has perhaps enjoyed being with me at times, but she loves him."

"So, you will just give up? Without a fight?"

"Yes."

"That is not good."

"What would you do?"

"I would tell her how I feel."

"She knows how I feel."

"You have told her?"

"Enough. She knows."

"Women never know. Men are like brick walls to women."

"I'm not. I'm like a pickle in a glass jar to her. She knows everything about me worth knowing."

Elunami shook her head sadly. "You are making a mistake."

"Well, thanks anyway for your concern."

Elunami pressed his hand and slipped out the door. Steve sank down on the sofa again.

Lance helped Samantha up the last incline, and they settled on a spongy mat of pine needles. The tree sheltered them from the sun, slanting in at a late-afternoon angle.

Lance picked up a pine needle and began breaking it into small pieces with his thumbnail. "Well, it's done," he said. "Getting a divorce is a hellish, ticklish thing, but we did it."

He tossed away a couple of pine needles that were too flexible to break. "Did you know there's a law against collusion? If two people want a divorce badly enough to make up a story, they can't get one? We finally settled on desertion, because I could prove Angie deserted me."

"How did Angie take it?"

"Cool as ice. Didn't even take her coat off. But that was probably because she had the good grace to be embarrassed by the fact that she was pregnant."

"Pregnant?"

"Yes." Lance covered his face with his hands and Samantha realized with horror that he was crying. *My God*, she thought. *He's only a man.* That disloyal thought was accompanied by a seemingly contradictory feeling of great warmth and love for him. Confused, she leaned close and hugged him.

Lance wiped his eyes and got control of himself.

"So," Samantha asked gently, "how long have you been home?"

"Three weeks."

"You could have come to my party," she said, chiding him.

Lance grimaced. "I came home feeling sick and weary—and as full of poison as a rattler. You and the party were better off without me."

"So, when will you be free?"

"I'm free now." Lance glanced over at her. "So, I was wondering if you would consider coming to Durango now?"

Samantha's mind went blank. "What for?"

"Well, if we're going to marry, it makes good sense for us to live in the same town."

Samantha frowned down at the pine needles, glistening pink in the sunlight. "This reminds me of when we were children," she said softly.

"In what way?"

"All this negotiating."

Lance shrugged. Then Samantha sighed. "It isn't going to work, is it?"

"We can make it work."

"No, we can't. You're still in love with Angie. Maybe we love each other enough to make a marriage work anyway, but if I marry you the way things are, and it doesn't work, we might lose our friendship. And that friendship is one of the most important things in the world to me. I don't think I could stand that."

"That's a hell of a thought," Lance growled.

"But it's true."

"Damn," Lance said heavily. "You know I just divorced her at great emotional and financial expense. And she's expecting another man's baby. She wouldn't come back to me no matter what you and I do, but you're right. I value your friendship. I guess I need that even more than I need a wife. Hell, I don't think I'm fit company for a wife anyway. Maybe I won't be for years," he admitted ruefully.

They talked for hours, until the sun was setting. Then Samantha said, "I think I hear Nicholas calling me."

Lance stood up and gave her his hand. They smiled at each other, then he pulled her into his arms. He was warm and strong and brotherly. "Thank you, Sam," he whispered against her hair.

"Thank you," she said. "You'll always be my best friend in the whole world. I wouldn't trade that for anything."

Hours later, near sunset, Steve saw Kincaid and Samantha returning from their walk. They looked close and happy. Steve was glad for her, for both of them actually, but the sight of her smiling up into Kincaid's face caused his heart to ache with such intensity he wished he hadn't seen it.

Hand in hand they skirted his cottage and walked toward the gate. Then Steve saw why. An arriving carriage crunched through gravel toward the front door of the house. The carriage stopped; Kincaid helped a blond woman in a heavy tan coat to step down. In spite of the bulky coat, Steve could tell she was expecting. They talked for a moment, then Samantha went inside; Kincaid followed the woman.

Curious, Steve sought out Juana to inquire who the visitor was.

Juana rolled her eyes. "*Señora* Kincaid."

"His wife?"

"*Sí.*"

"What's she doing here?"

Juana grinned gleefully. "He could be in beeg trouble, huh?"

Samantha left them together. Angie angled away from the workmen swarming over one of the outbuildings and headed toward the front of the mountain, where she could look out over the desert to the south. Lance walked beside her, waiting and watchful, his old self, apparently. His stance reminded her of his Ranger days.

"Being in love with Samantha seems to be good for you," she said finally.

"It does?" he asked, frowning. "In what way?"

"You look whole again."

Lance decided to let that pass. "I never expected to see you again," he said softly.

"Well, your luck can't *always* be good," she replied.

Lance quirked an eyebrow at her. "Still presumptuous, I see."

"My spirit wasn't entirely broken by the courts."

"I think it was pretty close, though," he said, grimacing at the memory. "It was for me anyway."

"The worst part was learning that a woman cannot get a divorce if her husband commits adultery, unless she has other, more serious grounds. But of course, any man in the country can get a divorce if his wife commits adultery. No other grounds needed for that," she said, her lovely brown eyes flashing with inner fire.

Lance grinned. "I knew that rankled."

"How on Earth can men get away with these things?" she asked, astonished anew.

"We wrote those laws carefully," he admitted, smiling with unabashed happiness. It felt so good to see her, in spite of everything, that he couldn't stop smiling. Fortunately she wasn't looking at him.

"That was obvious," she said, surveying the setting sun, which was casting provocative shadows and golden lights on everything in sight. "What a beautiful view."

"Yeah. I can tell you're deciding on camera angles."

Angie smiled in spite of herself and looked at him fully for the first time. His finely chiseled features looked so dear that her throat started to ache. "So," she asked abruptly, "are you curious as to why I've come?"

"Yes."

"Well, I hate to tell you this, and I know it's too late, but . . . I realize I've been wrong about a lot of things, and I'd like to . . . tell you something that you need to know. You don't have to do anything about it or change any of your plans. I'm not asking you to reconsider anything . . ."

"Tell me what?"

"I lied to you. About Hal Stockton. I never slept with Hal or anyone else. I did that to get rid of you, because I saw how badly you still wanted a baby, and I knew I could never give you one."

"That was a lie?"

"Yes."

Lance turned her and looked into her eyes. They were clear and lovely as ever. Angie had frustrated and irritated and discombobulated him any number of times, but he believed her about Stockton.

"So, why are you . . . telling me this now?" he asked, his voice breaking with emotion.

"Because . . . I learned some things while I was away."

"What?" he asked cautiously.

"I figured out why I've not been able to conceive or carry a baby to full term."

"Why not?"

"This probably won't make sense to you. You've never understood what you call female voodoo, but I think it was because

I was afraid to.'' He scowled, then she told him about her little brother who had died during the fire.

Her face crumpled; she couldn't continue for a moment. "Anyway," she said, wiping tears aside impatiently, "I guess it hurt me so badly that I never wanted to take a chance on feeling that way again."

Lance reached into his jacket pocket and handed her his handkerchief.

"So," he asked, looking uncomfortable, "how do you know that had anything to do with . . . this?" he asked, pointing at her stomach.

"Because, after I remembered everything I stopped being sick every day."

That made sense, even to him. "You mean we actually made a baby together?" he asked, grinning suddenly.

"Yes, and my doctor in San Francisco says that he sees no reason why I can't carry this baby to term. He says the baby seems perfectly healthy, and so do I."

"I can't believe it," he whispered, still stunned. She smiled up at him; an answering smile tugged his face out of shape. He felt hope and love swelling within, replacing the grief and loneliness he'd carried like a rock in his stomach ever since she'd left him.

"I know that after all we've been through, I shouldn't ask this, especially after promising not to, but can I come back?" she whispered.

Lance pulled her into his arms and held her. His heart ached with the sudden inflow of love and warmth and hope. For the first time since she'd left him, he felt alive again.

"Well," he said, groping for the right words, "only if you promise to be your old cantankerous self again. You have to take a lot of pictures, and smell up the entire house with developing fluid, and forget to give Yoshio money for groceries . . ."

Angie laughed. "You're still a lunatic, aren't you?"

"Yes. I guess I'll always be crazy over you."

Angie hugged him hard, and then at last he kissed her. His kiss was tender—and filled with all the love she could ever want. Her heart felt as if it was overflowing with love for him. He finally, reluctantly, ended the kiss and held her close.

"If you don't stop crying," he said, his voice barely more than a raspy whisper, "you're going to turn this into a sloppy mess."

"What about Samantha?"

"She can get her own handkerchief."

"I mean—I thought you and she . . ."

"Well, with your usual wisdom, you gave us all the rope we needed to discover that we have what we've always wanted. Samantha is my best friend. And that's the way we want it."

"Then you didn't . . . ? I'd forgive you if you did . . ."

"We did a lot of things together," he said, smiling at the memory of how close they had come to spoiling the wine, "but we didn't do that."

"Oh, that is such a relief to me. You have no idea."

"To me, too," he admitted, grinning.

"I don't think I've heard the whole story yet," Angie said, smiling up at him.

"Good. Let's keep it that way."

Samantha wanted to tell Steve immediately, but she had three crises to deal with before she could get away. Finally, with everything done, she freshened herself with a sponge bath, changed into a clean gown, and sent Juana to ask him if he could please come up to the house for a few moments.

Juana came back shortly.

"Well, what did he say?"

Juana shrugged. "I knock on hees door. Then I hear heem groan, finally hees footprints cross the parlor, and he opens the door. I tell heem what you say, and he groans again." She spread her hands and shrugged again.

"So, we still don't know if he will come," Samantha said.

"No, señora."

"Thank you, Juana."

Samantha wanted to put his mind and heart at peace, but she realized that it might not be as easy as she had thought. While she waited, an idea came to her, and she felt excitement growing in her. She could hardly wait to tell Steve, or better yet, to show him.

Finally Steve appeared at her door, freshly shaved and dressed in pressed trousers and a clean white shirt. His face was paler than usual, his eyes darker. His hand was still bandaged, and his tanned skin contrasted darkly against the whiteness of the fabric.

"You wanted to see me?" he asked gruffly.

Samantha stepped back and motioned him inside. "Yes. I need to go away for a few days—and I wanted to be sure that you are not intending to leave while I'm gone."

A stubborn light came into his eyes. "Why should you care what I do?"

"Because I do. Many things have happened in my life lately, and I am struggling to assimilate them and . . . do the things I need to do as a result. But I don't want you to disappear before I'm ready to talk to you."

"Well, it's nice to know that I'm on the list of chores to be taken care of, however low my status."

"Well, I didn't handle this very well, did I? Maybe I should begin again." She inhaled deeply and lifted her chin. "I need to go into town and then take a short trip. Would you be so kind as to escort me?"

"Where to?"

"To . . . the Papago Indian Reservation."

"What for?"

"A surprise."

"What happened to your guests?"

"They needed to be alone for a while. They're leaving tomorrow morning. Going home."

"Together?"

"Yes."

"And you're okay with that?"

"Yes."

"Can I ask what happened?"

"We decided to share him," she said, stepping close to Steve and slipping her arms around his waist. He felt warm and solid and resistant, and her heart started to pound.

Steve felt like a fool, letting her hug him. He wanted to tell her that he wasn't one of her toys, but words didn't come. The sweetness of her nearness robbed him of even his good sense.

"Lance is so lucky," she said, sighing and pressing her cheek against Steve's heart. It sounded powerful and fast beneath his warm chest. She could tell just by touching him that he loved her. She felt it in his skin, and in her own. She ached with love for him and wanted to prolong this sweet moment—and relieve his anxiety. But she knew that the tasks she had in mind were some of the most important of her life.

"I know this sounds crazy to you, Steve," she said, reaching up to kiss his warm neck, loving the way it smelled after he'd shaved. "But I think if I want you to take me seriously, then I have to show you something before you and I talk about our future, if you want a future with me."

He wasn't sure he wanted a future with a woman who maintained a married lover. But with her arms around him, he couldn't say no. "Okay," he said reluctantly.

"If it is all right with you then, we will leave early in the morning."

Steve agreed, and she walked him to the door. She hated letting him go, but it seemed necessary, for now. He and Elunami had taught her the importance of timing and ritual.

The next morning at seven o'clock, just as the sun was rising, she kissed her sleeping son and entrusted him to Elunami and Juana. Then she went downstairs to say good-bye to Lance and Angie. They couldn't stop looking at or touching each other. Samantha was so happy for them that she cried. Angie knew and pulled her into her arms.

"Thank you, Samantha."

"Thank you," Samantha said, sniffing back tears. "Take care of yourself and my friend."

"I will."

Lance hugged her hard, and they climbed into the carriage. Samantha waved until it passed through her gates and rounded the first bend.

She and Steve mounted their horses and headed for Camp Picket Post. The horses were fresh, and the desert was cool and beautiful. Mesquite, acacia, and ironwood trees dotted the desert floor. The acacias' abundant fruit pods had turned reddish, making a colorful display against the pale sand and the evergreen cacti.

Steve was remote and careful with her. He appeared strong, though. Strong and handsome—and determined not to give up any more of his dignity than he had already. She accepted that condition and didn't try to break through his reserve.

They reached Picket Post early, just as the town was opening for work. She stopped her horse at Owen's hotel and turned to Steve. "I have some business to take care of. Can we meet back here at Mary Francis's for lunch?"

"Sure."

He turned his horse toward the barber shop; she turned hers toward the only attorney in town.

When she finished there, she went to the general store to purchase supplies. She got out the list Elunami had helped her with last night and bought every item on it. Then she rented a buckboard and hired a driver. She finished just in time for lunch. Steve was already inside, drinking coffee.

"Well," she asked, slipping into the chair opposite his, "did you have a nice morning?"

"Nice enough."

She ordered and ate in silence, glad Steve allowed her the space to keep her secret.

As they rode south toward the *papagueria*, the desert became more thickly populated by the giant saguaro cacti. The sky was filled with big white cumulus clouds, shadowing the desert below. It was a cool, crisp, beautiful day for a ride, and she wished she and Steve had resolved every issue that stood between them, so they could enjoy this completely.

They reached the *papagueria* at sunset. She was tired and achy, but Steve appeared to be holding up well. For all that he had been through, he seemed strong and resilient.

"One more favor, then I'll stop bothering you for a while," she said, as they stopped before Chandler's house.

"What?"

"Would you find Silver Fish for me? Tell him I need his services."

Steve rode away. Samantha dismounted and knocked on the Indian agent's door. Chandler opened it and stepped back, surprised to see her.

"Come in, come in," he said, looking out to see Steve riding away.

"He'll be back." Samantha assured him, and then told him what she wanted to do. She asked the questions Elunami couldn't answer for her, because of possible differences between Hopi and Papago tradition.

Steve returned with Silver Fish. "Thank you," she said.

"Anything else?" Steve asked, watching her carefully.

"No," she said sweetly. "That will be all for now. But I hope you will wait to escort me home."

"Of course."

Selena Chandler stepped outside and invited Steve in for something to drink and eat. Samantha waved good-bye to him and rode away with Silver Fish.

Steve enjoyed the visit with his father and stepmother, but he kept looking out the window for the sight of Samantha. Finally he saw her, Crows Walking, Silver Fish, and a few of the elders come outside and sit down in a circle.

Selena kept talking to him, but he was so engrossed in trying to figure out what Samantha was up to that he lost track of what Selena was saying. Finally she gave up talking, and he gave up pretending to listen and just watched through the window.

Samantha distributed packages from the wagon to all the men, then the old men sat and talked for a long time, and the ceremonial pipe came out. Steve couldn't believe his eyes. When the pipe came around to Samantha, she took a puff of it and coughed. He grinned despite his mood.

An hour later Samantha walked from the meeting toward the agent's house. Steve stepped outside to greet her.

"I sure hope you're going to tell me what's going on soon," he said, squinting at her.

"I will."

" 'Soon' was the important word," he said.

"I know." She seemed different to him. Stronger and more determined and even more womanly. Her lovely eyes seemed to sparkle like diamonds in the little bit of light that came through the window of his father's house. He wondered if he would ever be able to see her clearly. He doubted it.

The next morning they said good-bye to the Chandlers and headed home, arriving near sunset. At the house Steve took the horses and started to walk toward the barn with them.

"Steve, would you have dinner with me tonight?"

"What time?"

"Seven."

At seven sharp he appeared at the door. Samantha greeted him and led him into the dining room. Juana served fried chicken and mashed potatoes and gravy. Steve ate lightly and then pushed his plate aside.

"Would you like desert?" she asked.

"No, thank you."

"You'd like answers," she said.

"If you don't mind."

"I guess it's time," she said softly.

"Past time," he said grimly.

"Well, I . . . uh . . . traded Crows Walking thirty thousand acres of land . . . for you."

"What?"

"We traded."

Steve stared at her in stunned silence. "Well, it's finally happened. An Indian has gotten the best of a white person in a trade. Unfortunately, I don't belong to Crows Walking, so you just got cheated.''

"Well, according to him, you do. He saved your life. He said when he was forty moons old he was given a vision in which he was told to walk toward the northeast until he received another vision. He walked for fifty days, and then he saw you squatting in the snow, scratching for nuts to eat. That night he had the second vision, and he traded a blanket to the band of Indians you had been following in exchange for you. To me that seemed good enough. And we smoked on it.''

"But why?" he asked, knowing she could have had him for nothing.

"I realized I didn't feel comfortable taking the land the way my attorney said I could. So I had the attorney in town split the land almost in half, and I gave the western half to Crows Walking. We discussed it thoroughly with the elders; they allowed me to keep the parcel with my house and most of my improvements on it if I promised to stay away from any sacred burial grounds or other sites of religious importance to the Papago.''

"You actually gave him part of your land?" he asked, incredulous. "In exchange for me?"

"Yes. I did. He now owns everything west of the creek. I haven't improved those sections. Actually I didn't say that correctly. He accepted stewardship for the land, and I for you. We traded responsibility, not ownership.''

Steve was stunned. She had not only learned an important lesson, she had given Crows Walking land and water. That was more than any man would do. Most men, faced with having to split their land, would find a way to do it without giving away access to the river.

"Were you sure you wanted to do it that way?"

"Yes. He can't do anything without water. And we'll have plenty. When I was trapped inside the mountain, I found an enormous underground river. We'll have all the water we'll ever need.''

A weight Steve hadn't been aware of lifted off him. He felt lighter, more forgiving of Samantha. She couldn't seem to give up Kincaid, even though he was married and had gone back to his wife. But at least he could climb out of hell on the knowledge that he'd fallen in love with one of the finest women in the world. She was generous, fair, and beautiful, if somewhat deluded.

"Thank you for doing that." He almost couldn't speak around the lump in his throat.

"Well, I'm glad that's settled. Now to the next. I know you've never understood about Lance, and how I felt about him."

Steve nodded.

"But you need to understand."

"I don't care to."

"You have to listen, even if you don't want to. At first, when he married Angie, my loss was like the sun—always before me, so bright and close and intense I was blind to everything else for years, even to you. I know you never understood, but Lance was like a god to me, standing between me and the awful loneliness and misery of childhood."

"I know it was hard for you."

"But now I've changed, Steve."

"Changed?"

"Don't be alarmed. I think it's for the better."

Her voice was so incredibly sweet, almost as sweet and beguiling as the look on her lovely face, which seemed to shimmer with inner light. He felt like a man being played with by a tiger. "I'm glad for you, then."

Samantha stood up and walked around to his side of the table. She tugged on his hand; he stood up. She slipped into his arms and felt a quiver go through his lean body. He tried to step away from her, but she wouldn't let him.

"I love you, Steve." Silence stretched out between them. She pressed her face against his warm, strong chest, listened to the powerful beat of his heart.

"But you need him more," he said finally.

"No."

"What are you saying?"

"When I saw Lance this time, I realized he wasn't a god. He was just a man. And that it wasn't a choice between him or you. Now that I know who I am, I realize that you are the only man who can complete me."

"I saw him hug you—"

"Yes," she interrupted, sighing contentedly. "It was our first hug as brother and sister. I used to believe that because I loved Lance I had to marry him. Now I know that I don't have to. I can love him as my brother and my best friend."

"I thought you had decided to share him."

"We did. But perhaps not the way you think." She hugged Steve hard and felt some of the tension leave his body. "Lance was my inspiration. He started me on this house-building adventure with you. But somehow in the process, I changed. I'm not who I was.''

Steve took her by the shoulders and turned her, so the light shone on her tear-wet cheeks. He searched her face, loving the incredible radiance and clarity of her skin, the shine of her silky hair, the way her lovely eyes sparkled with confusing warmth and humor. She bedazzled his helpless brain and probably always would, but somehow he could read her better, or thought he could. Her eyes shone with joy, love, and incredible sweetness. She *was* free. He pulled her into his arms and held her close.

''Samantha Forrester, you scared the hell out of me.''

''Me, too!''

Steve lifted her chin, stared into her lovely eyes for a long, heart-pounding moment. ''Say it,'' he said.

''I love you.''

He kissed her, gently at first, then with all the hunger and need she could ever ask for. He ended the kiss and held her for a long time. Then he whispered, ''Will you marry me?''

''We have to discuss something first. I realized, when I was trapped in that underground cavern and the Earth was shaking overhead and ready to come down and crush me, that you were right. People really don't own land. It *is* powerful enough to do anything it wants. I still love the land, but I can love it anywhere we go.''

She hugged him hard for a moment, then continued. ''In the last few days I've been thinking about all the things I've learned to love since coming here. I loved putting together the house and furnishings, making pottery, and sculpting and painting the masks. I think I'd like to study art and sculpting, maybe even interior architecture. I think I could help people furnish the houses you build for them. Most people do a terrible job of that. We could team up. You build the houses. I could furnish them.'' She shrugged. ''we can figure it out.''

''Do you mean that?''

''Yes, I do.''

''But what about this house?''

''I'll always love this house. It was the beginning of a new life for Nicholas, for me, and for you. We can always come back here to restore ourselves. It can be our vacation home. Our special hideaway, whenever we have time for it. Juana can raise Eliptio here. She can close off most of the rooms until we get back. When we get old, it can be our retirement home.''

"I can't believe you're saying these things."

"It's true," she said solemnly. "As much as I love this house, I don't *need* it the way I used to. I was trying to own something so solid I wouldn't have to be scared anymore. But you were right. Ownership is an illusion. And so is safety. I'll always love Lance, and I'll probably always feel safe with him. But I realized that the safe way is not always the right way."

"I never expected to hear you say that," he marvelled.

Samantha laughed. "I never expected to say it, either. How is it you had a worse childhood than I did and yet you didn't grow up odd the way I did?" she said, leaning back against the circle of his arms to look at him, loving the strength and masculinity she felt in him.

"Different expectations maybe. Uncheedah told me that First Born doesn't make mistakes, that he had wanted her to have me and me to have her, so he arranged it. I believed her and lived a good life. And"—Steve hesitated to tell Samantha about Caroline and the other women he'd loved and left—"and . . . I *was* twisted by it. But somehow I got over it in time to make the right decisions about you. But what happened to Kincaid? I thought . . ."

"A long time ago Elunami told me that a miracle would happen in Lance's life. Well, today his wife came to tell him that she is expecting *his* baby."

"I saw she was expecting. When did that happen?"

"Six months ago. The first time he went to San Francisco."

"I'll be damned."

"You should be. I've been through hell since the day I met you, Steve Sheridan!"

Steve chuckled, then sobered. "If you want to talk about hell, let's talk about Denver."

Samantha sighed, then giggled. "I was afraid you'd bring that up."

"I can imagine—"

"Though not for the reasons you think," she interrupted.

"Oh?" He lifted the unruly eyebrow and scowled.

"We got sick. Both of us. The worst case of flu I've ever had in my life. I thought Elunami had put a hex on us. They wouldn't let us stay at the hotel, and we were too sick to take care of ourselves anyway."

"Are you serious?" Steve asked, beginning to grin.

Samantha grimaced. "Or maybe you put the hex on us."

Steve laughed. "If I'd thought of it, I would have. But *now* I think it's time for dessert,'' he said, picking her up and carrying her up the stairs toward the bedroom.

''You aren't strong enough for this,'' she protested.

''Want to wager any serious money on that?''

Steve carried her into her bedroom, laid her gently on the bed. ''I love you, Samantha Forrester.''

As if he had all the time in the world, he undressed her and held her close to his heart, kissing her and making love to her slowly and sensuously. Merging into her and letting her merge into him. One skin, one heart, one love.

Sometime during the night, while he was still holding her, she realized that she had finally found the home she'd been looking for all her life. It was in her own heart.

Log cabins,
 Wood-burning stoves,
  Hill Country

JAMES ALEXANDER THOM

Available at your bookstore or use this coupon.

____**FOLLOW THE RIVER**   33854 **$5.95**
A best-seller based on the story of Mary Ingles' daring escape from Indian captivity.

____**FROM SEA TO SHINING SEA**   33451 **$5.95**
Based on the lives of the Clarke family of Virginia, the novel of America's westward expansion.

____**STAYING OUT OF HELL**   30665 **$4.95**
A gripping semi-autobiographical novel that deals with assassination and moral crisis.

____**PANTHER IN THE SKY**   36638 **$5.95**
The magnificent story of the life and times of Tecumseh, the Shawnee warrior.

BB BALLANTINE MAIL SALES
400 Hahn Road, Westminster, MD 21157

Please send me the BALLANTINE or DEL REY BOOKS I have checked above. I am enclosing $ . . . . (Add $2.00 to cover postage and handling for the first book and 50¢ each additional book. Please include appropriate state sales tax.) Send check or money order—no cash or C.O.D.'s please. To order by phone, call 1-800-733-3000. Prices are subject to change without notice. Valid in U.S. only. All orders are subject to availability of books.

Name_____

Address_____

City_____ State_____ Zip_____

20   Allow at least 4 weeks for delivery.   8/92   TA-264